From the Pages of
Fairy Tales

"You see, ladies and gentlemen, Your Royal Majesty! You can never know what to expect from the real nightingale, but everything is determined in the artificial bird. It will be so-and-so, and no different! You can explain it; you can open it up and show the human thought—how the cylinders are placed, how they work, and how one follows the other!" (from "The Nightingale," page 10)

It's an old innate law and privilege that when the moon is in the precise position it was last night, and the wind blows as it blew yesterday, then all will-o'-the-wisps born at that hour and minute can become human beings. (from "The Will-o'-the-Wisps Are in Town," page 37)

"This is certainly an interesting tinderbox if it will give me what I want like this!" (from "The Tinderbox," page 90)

"I almost didn't close my eyes the whole night! God knows what could have been in the bed? I was lying on something hard, so I am completely black and blue all over my body. It's quite dreadful!" (from "The Princess on the Pea," page 107)

Way out at sea the water is as blue as the petals on the loveliest cornflower, and as clear as the purest glass, but it's very deep, deeper than any anchor rope can reach. Many church steeples would have to be placed end to end to reach from the bottom up to the surface and beyond. Down there the sea people live. (from "The Little Mermaid," page 188)

The emperor came to them with his most distinguished cavaliers. Both swindlers lifted one arm in the air as if they were holding something and said, "See, here are the pants. Here's the jacket, and here's the cape!" They continued on and on. "They are as light as cobwebs. You might think you weren't wearing anything, but that's the beauty of this fabric." (from "The Emperor's New Clothes," page 215)

In the middle of a garden there was a rose tree that was completely full of roses, and in one of these, the most beautiful of them all, lived an elf. He was so tiny that no human eye could see him. He had a bedroom behind every rose petal. He was as well formed and lovely as any child could be and had wings from his shoulders all the way down to his feet. What a lovely fragrance there was in his rooms, and how clear and lovely the walls were! Of course they were the fine, pink rose petals.   (from "The Rose Elf," page 289)

Dance she did and dance she must, dance in the dark night. The shoes carried her away over thorns and stubble that scratched her until she bled. She danced over the heath until she came to a lonely little cottage. She knew that the executioner lived there. . . .
                    (from "The Red Shoes," page 395)

The poor duckling who had been last out of the egg and who looked so dreadful was bitten, pushed, and made fun of, both by the ducks and the chickens. "He's too big," they all said, and the turkey rooster, who was born with spurs and thought he was an emperor, blew himself up like a clipper ship under full sail, went right up to him, gobbled at him, and turned red in the face. The poor duckling didn't know whether he was coming or going, and was very sad because he was so ugly. Indeed, he was the laughing stock of the entire hen yard.
                    (from "The Ugly Duckling," pages 485–486)

Once upon a time there was a darning needle that was so refined and stuck-up that she was under the illusion that she was a sewing needle.
                    (from "The Darning Needle," page 555)

Everything was once again where it was before except for the two old portraits of the peddler and the goose girl. They had been blown up to the wall in the great hall, and when someone who was an art expert said that they were painted by a master, they were repaired and remained hanging there. No one knew before that they were any good, and how would you know that? Now they hung in a place of honor. "Everything in its proper place" and eventually that's where everything ends up. Eternity is long—longer than this story.
                    (from "Everything in Its Proper Place," page 597)

Fairy Tales

Hans Christian Andersen

Translated by Marte Hvam Hult

Illustrations by Harry Clarke

*With an Introduction and Commentaries on the
Tales by Jack Zipes and Textual Annotations
by Marte Hvam Hult*

George Stade
Consulting Editorial Director

BARNES & NOBLE CLASSICS
NEW YORK

BARNES & NOBLE CLASSICS

NEW YORK

Published by Barnes & Noble Books
122 Fifth Avenue
New York, NY 10011

www.barnesandnoble.com/classics

Hans Christian Andersen published his first collection of fairy tales in 1835 and continued to issue subsequent volumes until 1872, three years before his death. Marte Hvam Hult's new translation is based on the first five volumes of *H. C. Andersens Eventyr* (1963–67).

Published in 2006 by Barnes & Noble Classics with new Translation, Introduction, Notes, Biography, Chronology, Commentaries, Inspired By, Comments & Questions, and For Further Reading.

Introduction, Commentaries on the Tales, and For Further Reading Copyright © 2007 by Jack Zipes.

Note on Hans Christian Andersen, The World of Hans Christian Andersen and His *Fairy Tales*, textual annotations, Inspired by Andersen's *Fairy Tales*, Comments & Questions, and Marte Hvam Hult's original translation of Andersen's *Fairy Tales* Copyright © 2007 by Barnes & Noble, Inc.

Fairy Tales
ISBN 978-1-59308-260-4
LC Control Number 2006925199

Produced and published in conjunction with:
Fine Creative Media, Inc.
325 West 38th Street, Room 605
New York, NY 10018

Michael J. Fine, President and Publisher

Printed in the United States of America

LB

13   15   17   16   14   12

Hans Christian Andersen

❧

The future author of the classic stories "The Ugly Duckling,"
"The Little Mermaid," and "The Red Shoes," Hans Christian
Andersen was born on April 2, 1805, into humble circumstances in the Danish city of Odense. His father, Hans Andersen, was an impoverished cobbler who had taught himself to
read and write; his mother, illiterate and superstitious, worked
as a washerwoman and died an alcoholic. From an early age,
Hans shared his father's love of the theater. When Hans was a
boy, he and his father built a puppet theater, where Hans
would enact dramas of his own invention. Desperate for
money, in 1812 Hans Andersen Sr. was paid to take another
man's place in the army of Denmark, allied with the French in
the Napoleonic Wars. When he returned home, he was sick
and suffering from an illness that would prove fatal in 1816.
Before his mother remarried, young Hans worked in a factory,
but the family's economic woes continued.

In 1819 Hans—fourteen years old and with little education,
but endowed with a remarkable singing voice and a gift for
performance—left Odense to seek his fortune in Copenhagen
as a singer, dancer, or actor. Through his talents and ambition,
as well as a certain audacity, he attracted wealthy patrons who
arranged singing lessons and a small stipend for him. In 1820
he joined the choir of the Royal Theater, one of whose directors, Jonas Collin, had Hans sent to a private school in Slagelse,
50 miles from Copenhagen. When he returned to the city in
1827, he maintained his relationship with Collin, became a frequent dinner guest at the homes of the city's elite, and blos-
somed as a writer. His first poem, "The Dying Child," appeared
in 1827, and two years later he published a travel sketch in the
style of German Romantic writer E. T. A. Hoffmann, who had
a great influence on him.

In 1833 and 1834 Andersen visited France, Switzerland, and

Italy, where he set his first successful novel, *The Improvisatore* (1835). He began writing fairy tales in the folk tradition and published them as *Fairy Tales Told for Children* (1835), a volume that included "The Princess on the Pea" and "Little Claus and Big Claus." The same year he produced a second installment of stories including "Thumbelina." Thereafter, for the rest of his life he published a new volume of tales every year or two. Among the best known are "The Emperor's New Clothes," "The Steadfast Tin Soldier," "The Nightingale," and "The Little Match Girl." He also published several travelogues, dozens of plays, six novels, and three autobiographies.

For inspiration, Andersen drew on the people he knew as well as on traditional folk tales. His unique style—his inventive, entertaining stories appeal to children and adults alike—attracted many admirers, including the Danish king, who, when Andersen was a young man, granted him a royal annuity. Andersen was an international celebrity, and the royalties from his books made him wealthy. An avid traveler, he made frequent sojourns throughout Europe, most frequently to the cultured city of Weimar, Germany. Hans Christian Andersen died on August 4, 1875, in Copenhagen.

Contents

ANDERSEN'S FAIRY TALES

THE ARTIST AND SOCIETY

FOLK TALES

Contents

THE HUMANIZATION OF TOYS AND OBJECTS

LEGENDS

List of Illustrations

❧❧❧

The World of Hans Christian Andersen and His Fairy Tales

1805 Hans Christian Andersen is born on April 2, in the Danish city of Odense. His father, Hans Andersen, is a cobbler; his mother, Anne Marie Andersdatter, works as a washerwoman.

1812 Hans Andersen Sr. leaves his family to serve in the Danish army at a time when Denmark is an ally of Napoleon. Jacob and Wilhelm Grimm publish the first volume of *Children's and Household Tales.*

1813 Danish philosopher and theologian Søren Kierkegaard is born.

1814 Hans Andersen Sr. returns to Odense, suffering from an illness contracted while he was in the army. Denmark cedes control of Norway to Sweden.

1815 The Grimm brothers publish the second volume of *Children's and Household Tales.*

1816 Hans Andersen Sr. dies. Young Hans takes a factory job to help support the household.

1818 Anne Marie remarries, but the family's financial situation does not improve. Endowed with an exceptional singing voice, Hans earns money singing in the salons of the town's educated middle class.

1819 Young Hans leaves Odense and travels to Denmark's capital, Copenhagen, where he pursues a career as a singer, dancer, and actor. He solicits leading figures in the city's arts establishment before winning the patronage of composer C. E. F. Weyse, among others; he is provided with singing lessons and a small stipend.

1820 His stipend depleted, a desperate Andersen joins Copenhagen's Royal Theater choir and lands several minor roles with the company.

1822   A play written by Andersen is rejected by the theater. With the help of one of the theater's directors, Jonas Collin, Andersen obtains a scholarship that allows him to attend a private school in Slagelse, 50 miles from Copenhagen. The Grimms publish a third volume of *Children's and Household Tales.* German Romantic author E. T. A. Hoffmann dies.

1827   Returning to Copenhagen and still under the patronage of Jonas Collin, Andersen begins dining with the cultured families of the cosmopolitan city and develops a lifelong friendship with his patron's son, Edvard Collin. He publishes his first work, a poem called "The Dying Child."

1829   Andersen passes entrance exams for the University of Copenhagen but does not enroll. He publishes his first book, *A Walking Tour from the Holmen Canal to the Eastern Point of Amager.* His first play, *Love at St. Nicholas Tower,* is performed at the Royal Theater.

1831   He makes his first major trip to Germany and meets many important authors and writers, including Ludwig Tieck, a German writer of fairy tales.

1832   Andersen writes *The Book of My Life,* the first of three autobiographies he will produce; it will not be published until 1926. The second part of Johann Wolfgang von Goethe's *Faust* is published posthumously.

1833   Andersen's mother, overcome by alcoholism, dies. During this year and the next, Andersen travels to Germany, Paris, Switzerland, and Italy. Slavery is abolished in the British Empire.

1835   *The Improvisatore,* an autobiographical novel set in Italy, is so successful that it is immediately published in German. Andersen's first booklet of fairy tales, *Fairy Tales Told for Children,* is published in May; the volume includes "The Tinderbox," "Little Claus and Big Claus," and "The Princess on the Pea." In December he publishes a second booklet of *Fairy Tales* that includes "Thumbelina" and "The Naughty Boy." American novelist Mark Twain is born. German scholar and philosopher Wilhelm von Humboldt dies.

1836 Andersen's second autobiographical novel, *O.T.: Life in Denmark*, is published. Charles Dickens's *The Pickwick Papers* begins to be published in monthly installments.

1837 A third booklet of Andersen's *Fairy Tales* is published, this one containing "The Little Mermaid" and "The Emperor's New Clothes." A third autobiographical novel, *Only a Fiddler*, is published.

1838 The King of Denmark awards Andersen an annual grant that allows him to concentrate on writing. He publishes the first booklet of a new collection of *Fairy Tales Told for Children* that includes "The Steadfast Tin Soldier" and "The Wild Swans." Dickens's *Oliver Twist* is a best-seller in England. Naturalist and artist John James Audubon completes publication of the four volumes of *The Birds of America*.

1839 The second booklet of the new *Fairy Tales* collection, including "The Flying Trunk" and "The Storks," is published.

1840 Andersen's plays *The Mulatto*, which dramatizes the evils of slavery, and *The Moorish Maiden* debut at the Royal Theater. During this year and the next, he travels to Italy, Greece, and Turkey.

1842 Andersen publishes the third booklet of the new collection of *Fairy Tales*; it includes "The Rose Elf" and "The Swineherd." He publishes the travel book *A Poet's Bazaar*.

1843 Dickens publishes *A Christmas Carol*. German poet Friedrich Hölderlin dies. English critic John Ruskin publishes the first volume of his critical work *Modern Painters*. The Tivoli Gardens open in Copenhagen.

1844 *New Fairy Tales*, a collection of tales containing "The Ugly Duckling" and "The Nightingale," is published. Andersen makes his first visit to Weimar, Germany, a cultured city to which he will return repeatedly in the years that follow.

1845 He publishes a second collection of *New Fairy Tales*, which includes "The Snow Queen" and "The Spruce

Tree," and a third collection, which includes "The Red Shoes" and "The Shepherdess and the Chimney Sweep."

1847   He produces a third volume of *New Fairy Tales*; it includes "The Shadow." Andersen's second autobiography, *The True Story of My Life*, is published in German and is shortly translated into English. Andersen visits England and meets Dickens.

1848   He publishes a fourth volume of *New Fairy Tales*, which includes "The Little Match Girl," and a patriotic novel, *The Two Baronesses*. Frederick VII becomes the Danish king. Denmark goes to war with Germany and Prussia over control of the region Schleswig-Holstein. German political theorist and revolutionary Karl Marx produces his *Communist Manifesto*.

1851   *In Sweden*, a travel narrative of Andersen's visit to that country, is published. German-French poet Heinrich Heine publishes *Romanzero*. American writer Herman Melville publishes *Moby-Dick*.

1852   Andersen publishes *Stories*, which includes "It's Perfectly True!" Dickens begins monthly serialization of *Bleak House*. German playwright Christian Friedrich Hebbel's *Agnes Bernauer* debuts.

1853   Andersen publishes a second collection of *Stories* that includes "Everything in Its Proper Place."

1855   *The Fairy Tale of My Life*, Andersen's third and final autobiography, is published. Kierkegaard dies. American poet Walt Whitman publishes *Leaves of Grass*.

1857   Andersen publishes the novel *To Be or Not to Be*.

1858   Andersen publishes the first two volumes of the series *New Fairy Tales and Stories*; included are " 'Something' " and "The Bog King's Daughter."

1859   A third volume of *New Fairy Tales and Stories*, including "The Girl Who Stepped on Bread," is published.

1860   English playwright J. M. Barrie, author of *Peter Pan*, is born.

1861   Andersen publishes the first volume in a second series of *New Fairy Tales and Stories*; included are "The Snowman" and "What Father Does Is Always Right."

1862 He publishes a second volume in the second series of *New Fairy Tales and Stories*; included are "The Ice Maiden" and "The Butterfly."

1863 Andersen publishes the travel book *In Spain*.

1864 Denmark goes to war with Prussia and Austria over Schleswig-Holstein, which Denmark is forced to relinquish. French scientist Louis Pasteur demonstrates that treatment with heat protects certain foods from damaging microorganisms.

1865 Andersen publishes a third volume in the second series of *New Fairy Tales and Stories*, including "The Will-o'-the-Wisps Are in Town." Russian writer Leo Tolstoy begins publishing *War and Peace*. English author Lewis Carroll publishes *Alice's Adventures in Wonderland*. English author Rudyard Kipling is born.

1866 Andersen publishes a fourth volume in the second series of *New Fairy Tales and Stories*, including "The Snowdrop."

1870 *Lucky Peter*, Andersen's last novel, appears.

1872 Andersen publishes two volumes in the third series of *New Fairy Tales and Stories*, including "The Gardener and the Gentry," "Auntie Toothache," and "The Story Old Johanna Told"; he begins to experience the first symptoms of liver cancer.

1875 Hans Christian Andersen dies on August 4 in Copenhagen. His funeral is attended by hundreds of admirers, including the Danish king.

The Hans Christian Andersen
We Never Knew

Long before publishers knew how to market their authors with
dexterity, long before Walt Disney made his name into an international logo, Hans Christian Andersen knew how to create
himself as a celebrity and glorify his name, despite the fact that
he was a writer with limited talents. As a young country boy—
perhaps, one could even say, a country bumpkin—who was
poor as a church mouse, Andersen tried to take Copenhagen
by storm in 1819, when he was only fourteen years old, and
very few people would have wagered at that time that he would
become the most famous fairy-tale writer of the nineteenth
century, even more famous than the Brothers Grimm. But his
fame was also tainted. Andersen was a nuisance, a pest, a de-
manding intruder, and a clumsy actor, whose greatest desire
was to write plays and star in them. He never fully realized this
ambition, but he did become an inventive and innovative
writer of fairy tales, and he used his tales therapeutically to
come to terms with the traumas and tensions in his life. All this
led to the formation of an extraordinary personality, for Andersen was one of the greatest mythomaniacs, hypochondri-
acs, and narcissists of the nineteenth century. He custom-made
his life into a fairy tale that he sold successfully from the moment he arrived in Copenhagen, and it is impossible to grasp
him or any of his tales without knowing something about the
reality of his life and his strategies for survival.

But how is it possible to know the reality of Andersen's life
when he consciously concealed many vital facts and incidents
in the three autobiographies he wrote? How is it possible to re-
late his unusual, autobiographical tales to his life when they
are so fantastic and can be interpreted in many different ways
and on many levels? Andersen appears to defy definition and

categorization, and it may not even be necessary to know something about his life to appreciate his tales. Yet because he wove himself so imaginatively into his narratives and because there are so many misunderstandings about his life and the meanings of his tales, it is crucial to attempt to sort through the myths about him and investigate how his tales came into existence so that we can have a fuller and clearer appreciation of the difficulties he overcame to achieve the success he did. Moreover, it is important to realize how diverse his stories are, for they were not all fairy tales about his life. Nor were they written for children. Nor did they always end happily. There is something uncanny and often chilling about Andersen's tales, a bitter irony that makes us wonder whether the pursuit of happiness and success is worth all the effort.

Andersen was born on April 2, 1805, into a dirt-poor family in Odense, in a squalid section of the provincial town of about 15,000 people. His father, Hans, was a shoemaker, several years younger than his wife, Anne Marie Andersdatter, a washerwoman and domestic. His parents suffered from poverty all their lives; his father became so desperate at one point that he took money from another man for replacing him as a soldier in a draft recruitment and serving for two years in the Danish army during the Napoleonic Wars. Overly sensitive about his family's poverty and his homely appearance, Andersen kept to himself as a young boy. When he was seven, his parents took him to the theater, and a new, fantastic world exploded before his eyes: From this point on theater life came to represent a glorious realm of freedom, and he hoped to become a great writer involved with the stage. But there was a lot of misery to overcome: His father, a sick and broken man, died in 1816, two years after he returned from the wars; his mother was afflicted by alcoholism; the teenager Andersen was often humiliated at work by older boys and men; he was haunted by the insanity that ran in the family and felt shame about an aunt who ran a brothel in Copenhagen. The traumas of his youth cast him into the role of outsider, and they undoubtedly led him to imagine how he might abandon Odense and create a different life for himself as an actor or writer. Indeed, he showed an early proclivity for reading and writing, even though his schooling was modest, and he believed deeply that he belonged elsewhere—perhaps he was the son of a royal couple, he imagined. Clearly, his imagination was fertile, but his drive and ambition were just as important.

Andersen's immense desire to become a famous writer or actor drove him to transcend his poor start in life and his social status. In 1819, when he was only fourteen, he convinced his mother to allow him to travel to Copenhagen to pursue his dreams. But once he arrived, he again faced one trial after the next. At that time Copenhagen was a relatively small port city of 120,000 inhabitants, and Danish society, dominated by the aristocracy and upper-middle class, was highly stratified. Armed with a letter of introduction from Mr. Iversen, an Odense printer, to Madame Schall, a renowned solo dancer at the Royal Theater, Andersen made numerous attempts to impress people with his talent, but he was too raw and uncouth to be accepted into the art world. To rectify the situation he took singing and acting lessons and even had a bit part as a troll in a play performed at the Royal Theater in Copenhagen. In addition he tried to write plays that he continually submitted to the theater management, which always rejected them. Then a wealthy legal administrator, Jonas Collin, took him under his wing and sent him to a private boarding school to fine-tune him for polite society. From 1822 to 1827, Andersen was indeed trained and re-tooled, largely by a neurotic taskmaster named Simon Meisling, first in Slagelse, a provincial town 50 miles from Copenhagen, and later in Helsingør. Andersen, who was several years older and much taller than his classmates, was instructed to forget all ideas of becoming a writer or poet; Meisling, a notable scholar but a notoriously mean and petty man, who delighted in humiliating Andersen, tried to drill him according to the strict regulations of a classical education and often humiliated Andersen in and outside the classroom. Though he did learn a great deal and managed to keep writing poems and sketches, Andersen suffered greatly from Meisling's constant persecution. Only the support of

Collin and friendships with elderly men—such as the great Danish poet B. S. Ingermann, the physicist H. C. Ørsted, and the commodore Peter Frederick Wulff—and their families enabled him to tolerate the five years with Meisling. By 1827 Collin allowed Andersen to return to the city and prepare himself for admission to the University of Copenhagen. When he passed the matriculation examination in 1829, however, Andersen took the bold step of embarking on a career as a free-lance writer. That same year he had a modest success with a fantasy sketchbook, *A Walking Tour from the Holmen Canal to the Eastern Point of Amager*, influenced by German Romantic writer E. T. A. Hoffmann, and a sentimental comedy, *Love at St. Nicholas Tower*, which was performed at the Royal Theater in Copenhagen. These works enabled Andersen to convince Collin that he was "destined" to become a writer, and it was Collin, who assisted him time and again to obtain royal stipends and to make connections that were to be beneficial for Andersen throughout his life. At that time in Denmark and in Europe as a whole, it was very difficult to earn a living as a free-lance writer unless one was born into money, was supported by an aristocratic patron, or received a royal grant.

Although Collin's help was significant, it was Andersen's perseverance, audacity, and cunning that enabled him to climb to fame starting in the early 1830s. It is difficult to say whether Andersen consciously conceived plans for his success or whether he intuitively knew what he had to do to survive in Danish and European high society. In his scrupulously researched biography, *Hans Christian Andersen: A New Life* (Woodstock, NY: Overlook Press, 2005), Jens Andersen notes that the young writer early on concocted a story about himself that gained him admission into the upper classes. It was truly a kind of fairy tale, in which Andersen, the poor ugly duckling, triumphs against the odds and becomes a gifted writer because God has ordained it so. Sometimes he blended it with the motif of Aladdin and the magic lamp, which he introduced in his first fairy tale, "The Tinderbox" (1835). Andersen had to prove that he was a soldier of fortitude who had the makings of a king, or that he was an oppressed and awkward fowl who would develop into an elegant swan. This was the story that he repeated to himself, and it formed the basis of his three autobiographies. At the same time, Andersen learned how to market himself as the Lord's chosen writer whenever he traveled abroad—he made more than thirty trips throughout Europe and the Middle East during his lifetime. Beginning with his first major trip to Germany in 1831, he would send his books to famous authors and wealthy people in advance of his arrival, implying that he was a kind of poetic genius who was stunning the world and was thus worth meeting and befriending. Indeed, Andersen did have a peculiar charm that made him an odd and delightful performer for court societies and upper-middle-class salons, which were always on the lookout for "sensational" entertainment.

Andersen knew exactly what he had to do and wanted to do to maintain his early success: forge a name for himself, influence and cater to the public, and become a respectable member of the upper classes through marriage. From 1831 to 1840, he worked hard in both the artistic and social domains, succeeding in art and failing only in his plan to wed a proper wife. After his trip to Germany, where he met two of the great romantic writers, Ludwig Tieck and Adelbert Chamisso, Andersen published *Shadow Pictures* (1831), which describes his journey, and the long dramatic poem *Agnete and the Merman* (1833), which would serve as the basis for his fairy tale "The Little Mermaid" (1837). At the same time, he wrote a short autobiography that circulated only among his closest friends and was not published until 1926. He did publish an autobiographical novel, *The Improvisatore,* in 1835; it was so successful that it was immediately translated into German. The year 1835 also marked the publication of his first two pamphlets of fairy tales, which included "The Tinderbox," "Little Claus and Big Claus," "The Princess on the Pea," "Little Ida's Flowers," "Thumbelina," and "The Naughty Boy." In 1836 he produced his second autobiographical novel, *O. T.: Life in Denmark* and in 1837 his third, *Only a Fiddler;* in 1837 he added "The Little Mermaid" and "The Emperor's New Clothes" to his collection of fairy tales. These works led to Andersen's receiving an annual grant from the King of Denmark in 1838; this grant, the amount of which was raised from time to time, enabled Andersen to live as a free-lance writer for the rest of his life. Finally, two of his plays, *The Mulatto: A Comedy in Green* and *The Moorish Maiden*, were performed at the Royal Theater in Copenhagen in 1840.

While the 1830s were highly productive and successful years for Andersen's artistic career, there were some personal setbacks. He proposed to Riborg Voigt, the sister of a schoolmate, in 1830, and courted Louise Collin, daughter of his patron, in 1832. Both young women rejected his advances, as did Jenny Lind, the famous Swedish singer, in 1843. Andersen was never able to achieve the happy married life he ostensibly sought because he was never fully acceptable in upper-class society and because he felt strong attractions toward men. For most of his life, he was in love with Edvard Collin, the son of his patron Jonas Collin, and his diaries and papers reveal that he often used women to draw closer to men or that he favored the company of young men. Some critics have argued that Andersen was a homosexual who had an occasional relationship and veiled his sexual preferences his entire life. Others maintain that Andersen may have been gay or bisexual but never had any sexual affairs because he was painfully afraid of sex, often thought he would contract a venereal disease, and repressed his urges. Whatever the case may be, his diaries and letters reveal just how confused and frustrated, if not tortured, Andersen was because he could not fulfill his sexual desires. Throughout his life he suffered from migraine headaches, paranoia, hypochondria, and other neuroses that might be attributed to the repression of his sex drive. Ironically, all this suffering also played a significant role in his producing some of the greatest fairy tales and stories in Western literature.

By 1840 Andersen had become famous throughout Europe, his fame resting more on his fairy tales and stories than on any of the other works he produced. Though the title of his first collection was *Eventyr, fortalte for Børn* (*Fairy Tales Told for Children*), Andersen had not had much contact with children and did not tell tales to children at that point. He basically intended to capture the tone and style of a storyteller as if he were telling tales to children. Indeed, he thrived on the short narrative form. Although his novels and plays were sometimes well received, his writing was clearly not suited for these forms; the novels, plays, and even his poetry are flaccid, conventional, sentimental, and imitative—barely readable today, if they are read at all. On the other hand, he had an extraordinary gift for writing short narratives. During the 1840s he produced some of his best tales, including "The Ugly Duckling" (1844), "The Nightingale" (1844), "The Snow Queen" (1845), and "The Shadow" (1847). By this time Andersen no longer made the pretense that his tales were addressed to children. He eliminated the phrase "for children" in the title of his collections, and many of the tales became more complex. For instance, "The Shadow" was purposely written to address the hurt and humiliation that Andersen felt because his beloved Edvard Collin refused throughout his life to address him as "you" with the familiar *du* in Danish; instead, Collin kept Andersen at a distance by using the formal *de*. "The Shadow," in which Andersen reveals the feelings of obliteration caused by this relationship, is also a brilliant reflection of the master/slave relationship and the condition of paranoia.

It was clearly due to the appreciation of adults that Andersen became immensely successful by the 1840s. Not only were his tales well received; he also published an official autobiography, *The True Story of My Life*, in 1846, the same year his stories were first translated into English. The next year he planned and organized his first trip to England, where he was treated as a celebrity. He published a patriotic novel, *The Two Baronesses*, in 1848, and though he felt drawn to the Germans, he defended Denmark in its conflict with Germany and Prussia from 1848 to 1851 over control of the Schleswig-Holstein region. In fact, Andersen's loyalties were split because he felt more comfortable in foreign countries, especially when he was hosted by rich aristocratic families and sorely mistreated and unrecognized in Denmark. In 1846 he wrote the following letter from Berlin to his patron Jonas Collin:

You know, of course, that my greatest vanity, or call it rather joy, resides in the knowledge that you consider me worthy of you. I think of you as I receive all this recognition. Yet I am truly loved and appreciated abroad; I am—famous. Yes, you may well smile. But the foremost men fly to meet me, I see myself welcomed into all their families. Princes, and the most talented of men pay me the greatest courtesies. You should see how they flock around me in the so-called important circles. Oh, that's not something any of all those people back home think about, they overlook me completely and no doubt they would be happy with a droplet of the tribute I receive. Yet my writings must have greater merit than the Danes give them (Jens Andersen, *Hans Christian Andersen: A New Life*, p. 114).

Andersen could never reconcile himself to the fact that he was not praised unconditionally by the Danish critics and public. He had an enormous ego and insatiable need for compliments and special treatment. From 1850 until his death in 1875, the more he wrote the more he tended to repeat the plots and styles of his earlier tales, and though some like "Clod Hans" (1855), "What Father Does Is Always Right" (1861), and "The Gardener and the Gentry" (1872) were masterful works of art, most waxed pale in comparison to those that had preceded them. His last two novels, *To Be or Not to Be* (1857) and *Lucky Peter* (1870), were poorly conceived and boring to read. His plays were performed but were not very successful. If anything, it was not Andersen's unusual talents as a storyteller that grew in the latter part of his life, but rather his vanity, and he was often a burden on others. For instance, when he returned to England in 1857 and spent five weeks with Charles Dickens and his family, they could not wait to see him leave because he was too nitpicky and overbearing. Andersen continued to make annual excursions to other countries and cities, and wherever he went he insisted on being coddled and pampered, and he sought close male friendships that were often amorous but never fulfilled in the way he desired. The older he became, the more lonely he felt, and the more he needed some kind of warm family life to replace the Collins, who continued to assist him and manage his affairs but kept their distance. In 1865 Andersen began close friendships with two wealthy Jewish families, the Melchiors and the Henriques, who became his dedicated supporters; though he maintained a residence in Copenhagen, when he visited the World Exposition in Paris in 1867 and such countries as Spain, Germany, and Switzerland, Andersen often stayed at their estates. By 1873 it was clear that he was suffering from cancer of the liver, and though he courageously fought the disease and even made a few trips and attended social functions during the next two years, he finally succumbed to the cancer on August 4, 1875.

Most anthologies of Andersen's fairy tales and stories tend to present them chronologically, according to the dates they first appeared in Danish. This type of organization enables readers to follow Andersen's development as a writer and to draw parallels with the events in his life, but that can be a disadvantage if critics and readers go too far in interpreting the tales autobiographically and tracing biographical details in his tales. For example, "The Ugly Duckling" is generally regarded as a representation of the trials and tribulations of the outsider Andersen, who had to overcome obstacles to reveal his aristocratic nature as a swan. "The Little Mermaid" has frequently been interpreted as a reflection of the unrequited love Andersen felt for Edvard Collin. "The Nightingale" mirrors the tenuous relationship between Andersen the artist and his patron the King of Denmark. There is undoubtedly some truth to these interpretations. All writing has psychological and biographical dimensions. But to relentlessly view most of Andersen's tales as symbolic stories about his own life and experiences can diminish our appreciation of the depth and originality of many of his narratives.

At his best, Andersen was an unusually creative and sensitive writer whose imagination enabled him to transform ordinary occurrences and appearances into extraordinary stories that open new perspectives on life. He was not a profound philosophical thinker, but he had a knack of responding spontaneously and naively to the world around him, and he possessed a talent for conveying his wonder about the miracles of life through short narrative prose that could be awe-inspiring. Moreover, because he always felt oppressed, dominated, and misunderstood, he sought to assess and grasp the causes of suffering, and offered hope to his readers—a hope that he himself needed to pursue his dreams.

It thus makes sense to try to "categorize" Andersen's tales in a non-traditional—that is, non-chronological—manner in order to try to appreciate some of the common themes that he tried to weave into his narratives time and again from 1835 to 1875. Though it is difficult to typify all his tales, a consideration of their common themes will allow for a broader and more critical appreciation of his works and might make some of his intentions clearer. I have divided the tales into the following categories: the artist and society; folk tales (the adaptation of folklore); original fairy tales; evangelical and religious tales; the anthropomorphizing of animals and nature; the humanization of toys and objects; and legends. There are, of course, overlapping themes and motifs, and a tale that appears in one category might have been included in another. Yet from the vantage point of these categories, Andersen's tales may assume more relevance in a socio-cultural context. (See "Commentaries on the Tales" for more on each tale in this collection.)

THE ARTIST AND SOCIETY

One of Andersen's most insightful and profound fairy tales, one that fully addresses his philosophy of art and the artist, is "The Nightingale"; it deserves to be placed first in any anthology of Andersen's tales, followed by "The Gardener and the Gentry." The first is clearly a fairy-tale allegory about the relationship of the artist to his patron; the second is a bitter, ironic story, also about patronage, but more specifically about folklore and the artist's role in Denmark. While it is difficult to state which category of Andersen's tales is most important, it is clear that there was an overriding concern in all his tales with the virtue of art and with the genuine storyteller as a cultivator of the social good. Andersen was writing at a time when the status of the professional and independent writer was in the process of being formed; before Andersen's time, in Denmark and most of Europe it was virtually impossible to earn a living as a professional writer. Therefore, a writer had to have an independent income, trade, and profession, or a wealthy patron to support his work, and as there was no copyright law, a writer's works were not fully protected. If a writer was dependent on a patron, he would be obliged to respect and pay attention to the expectations of his benefactor.

In "The Nightingale" and "The Gardener and the Gentry," Andersen depicts the quandary of the artist who must suffer the indignities of serving upper-class patrons who do not appreciate his great accomplishments; in each case, the artist is a commoner or is common-looking but capable of producing uncommon art. For Andersen, uncommon art was "authentic" and "true" and stemmed from nature—that is, the natural talents of the artist. It is also essential and therapeutic, for humankind cannot do without it. In "The Nightingale," the artist/bird heals the emperor, who realizes that mechanical art is artificial. In "The Gardener and the Gentry," a more cynical Andersen depicts an arrogant, rich man and his wife who are unable to appreciate the originality of their innovative artist/gardener. Despite their ignorance and closed minds, true art succeeds, an indication of Andersen's strong belief that the artist who is naturally endowed with talent will somehow shine forth.

One can always distinguish the true art from the false, and all the other tales in this category reflect Andersen's constant re-examination of the nature of storytelling and the salvation it offered all people. In one of his last tales, "The Cripple" (1872), it is the fairy tale that enables a sick boy to regain his health; the story is a personal wish-fulfillment that transcends the conditions in Andersen's life to become a universal narrative about art's wondrous powers.

FOLK TALES (THE ADAPTATION OF FOLKLORE)

Many famous writers of fairy tales have made and continue to make extraordinary use of folk tales that were spread by word of mouth, and Andersen was no exception. In fact, most of Andersen's early tales—including "The Tinderbox," "Little Claus and Big Claus (1835)," "The Princess on the Pea," and "The Traveling Companion" (1835)—are based on Danish folk tales that he had heard or read. He may have also used German and European tales collected by the Brothers Grimm as his sources; for instance, "The Tinderbox" and "Little Claus and Big Claus" are closely related to the Grimms' "The Blue Light" and "The Little Farmer," and other of Andersen's tales show the influence of the Grimms. Knowing the sources enables us to study how Andersen appropriated and enriched these tales to reflect upon conditions in Danish society and upon the trajectory of his life. A good example is "The Traveling Companion," an oral tale widespread in the Scandinavian countries and most of Europe. Folklorists refer to it as a tale type about the "grateful dead," in which a dead man whose corpse is maltreated helps a young man who kindly protects the corpse from abuse. In Andersen's version, the young man is devout and trusts the Lord and his dead father in Heaven to guide him through life. Andersen combines pagan and Christian motifs to illustrate the rise of a poor, naive man whose goodness enables him to marry a princess.

Andersen colored his tales based on folklore with his personal experience while using the folk perspective to expose the contradictions of the aristocratic class. In "The Swineherd" (1842) he remained close to the folk perspective, which he also developed in some of his original fairy tales, such as "The Emperor's New Clothes."

In Andersen's early adaptations of folklore we see him in an "apprentice" phase as a writer of short prose. Taking the structure and contents of these tales as a basis, he developed his own style and tone, which was characterized by the simple folk mode of storytelling. Andersen's style overall is really not so much "childlike" as it is "folksy," and it was this blend of intimate, down-to-earth storytelling with folk motifs and literary themes that gave rise to some of his most significant fairy tales.

ORIGINAL FAIRY TALES

It is perhaps an exaggeration to assert that Andersen's fairy tales are "original" because all his narratives reveal how much he borrowed from literature and from the folklore tradition. Nevertheless, he endowed them with his own original touch and personal experiences, and that makes them somewhat unique narratives. The major feature of Andersen's original literary fairy tales is that he turned known literary motifs into provocative and uncanny stories that challenge conventional expectations and explore modes of magic realism he learned from the German Romantics, especially E. T. A. Hoffmann. Two of his greatest fairy tales—"The Shadow" and "The Little Mermaid"—demonstrate his talent for transforming known folk and literary motifs into highly complex narratives about identity formation. "The Shadow," clearly based on German writer Adelbert Chamisso's novella *Peter Schlemihl* (1813), in which a man sells his shadow to the devil, can also be traced to E. T. A. Hoffman's tale "The New Year's Adventure" (1819), in which a man gives up his reflection for love. For Andersen, this loss of a shadow or reflection is transformed into a psychological conflict in which unconscious forces debilitate and eventually destroy a strong ego. The learned man's identity is literally effaced by his shadow. In "The Little Mermaid," based on his poem *Agnete and the Merman* and Friedrich de la Motte Fouqué's fairy-tale novella *Undine* (1811), Andersen depicts the quest for identity in a more positive light. There are strong religious overtones in this narrative, in which a young girl learns that becoming human involves self-sacrifice, humility, and devotion. Christian redemption is promised if the mermaid will fulfill her destiny. Other tales, including "The Bronze Pig" (1842) and "Ib and Little Christine" (1855), feature this motif. Many others reflect Andersen's desire to uncover social contradictions.

What often makes Andersen's original tales original is their irony—a key element in "The Shadow" but one that is even more pronounced in "The Emperor's New Clothes" (1837) and "The Naughty Boy" (1835). Andersen used the metaphorical mode of the fairy tale to expose social hypocrisy, and in the best of his original fairy tales, he left his readers not with happy endings, but with startling ones aimed at making them reflect upon ethical and moral behavior.

EVANGELICAL AND RELIGIOUS TALES

Andersen is not commonly thought of a religious writer; yet religious motifs and themes run through a majority of his tales. This religious dimension is one reason Andersen became so popular in the nineteenth century: He "tamed" the pagan or secular aspects of the folk-tale and fairy-tale traditions and made them acceptable to the nineteenth-century European and American reading publics. To a certain extent, some of his tales fit the standards of evangelical literature, which was very strong and popular throughout Europe and North America. "The Snow Queen" (1845) and "The Red Shoes" (1845) are good examples; both depict young girls who place their lives in the hands of God and are saved because they trust in the Lord's powers of redemption. The beginning of "The Snow Queen" establishes the connection between the devil and the snow queen, and the narrative develops into a Christian conflict between good and evil; it becomes clear by the end of the tale that Gerda will need the assistance of angels and the Lord to save Kai. In "The Red Shoes," the unfortunate Karen is mercilessly punished for her pride, and she must have her feet cut off and learn Christian humility before she can be accepted into heaven.

Andersen tended to chastise girls or use them as examples in Christian allegorical fairy tales that celebrate the intelligent design of God. Whether the girl is reprimanded, as in "The Girl Who Stepped on Bread" (1859), or elevated to the level of a saint, as in "The Little Match Girl" (1845), Andersen insisted that she become self-sacrificial and pious. It was not much different for the male characters in Andersen's tales, but interestingly, he did not treat males as harshly as he did females. Overall, almost all of Andersen's religious tales and many others indicate that the only way to fulfill one's destiny is to place one's trust in the Lord.

The Anthropomorphizing of Animals and Nature

In his traditional tales in which animals, insects, and plants speak and come to life, Andersen often didactically conveys moral values. Placing one's faith in God is an undercurrent in his most famous fairy tale, "The Ugly Duckling." There are no Christian references in this narrative; instead Andersen uses the tradition of animal tales to demonstrate that there is such a thing as "intelligent design." The duckling must have faith in order to overcome all the obstacles in his life and triumph in the end.

Andersen's anthropomorphizing tales are not always religious. In many, he pokes fun at human foibles—for example, pomposity is his target in "The Spruce Tree" (1845) and "The Dung Beetle" (1861). His short tales, pungent and often bitterly ironic, stand in the tradition of Aesop's fables and reflect Andersen's notions of "survival of the fittest." Though in fact he rejected Darwin's ideas, many of Andersen's tales that deal with anthropomorphized animals and plants are concerned with intense social and natural conflict. He understood the fierce battles waged in the European societies of his day, such as the revolutions of 1848 and the uprisings of peasants and workers, but instead of recounting these conflicts in realistic stories, Andersen anthropomorphized animals and nature to comment critically on more than one of the delicate issues and taboo subjects of his time.

The Humanization of Toys and Objects

Much in the same way that he used animals and nature, Andersen "humanized" toys and inanimate objects to comment on social issues and human weaknesses. Here his model was E. T. A. Hoffmann, who had experimented with this narrative mode in such tales as "The Nutcracker and the Mouse King" (1816). Another obvious example is "The Steadfast Tin Soldier" (1838). Perhaps more important is "The Shepherdess and the Chimney Sweep" (1845), in which he uses porcelain figures to meditate philosophically on the fear of freedom. What is intriguing in Andersen's tales about toys and objects is the way he realistically describes them; he had a great eye for detail and depicted toys, objects, and their settings so carefully and precisely that it almost seems natural they would come to life. Andersen often took tiny incidental or neglected objects, such as a darning needle or rags, as the subject matter for a consideration of serious philosophical and social concerns or even survival and immortality.

LEGENDS

Andersen was also concerned about traditions, and though he became very cosmopolitan and developed a hate-love relationship with Denmark, he sought to mine the Danish soil, so to speak, to celebrate its richness. Throughout his tales he relied on references to Danish legends and proverbs to add local color to his narratives. Often on his trips in Denmark, he would hear a local legend or see something legendary that would inspire his imagination; two good examples are "Holger the Dane" (1845) and "Everything in Its Proper Place" (1853). While the legend about a king who rises from the dead to save his country can be found in many cultures, Andersen bases "Holger the Dane" on Danish lore; he wrote at a time when Denmark was engaged in a conflict with Prussia, and the story is clearly patriotic in spirit, something unusual for Andersen, who was a loyal Danish citizen but never really patriotic.

More typical of Andersen is "Everything in Its Proper Place," in which he invents his own local legend about a family's history and its house to comment on class conflict. Houses and mansions abound in Andersen's stories, and though he knew some of their legendary histories, he was at his best when he invented legends; his inventions were always bound up with his real experiences and his realistic appraisal of Danish society.

Andersen's range as a short-story writer was great. Not only did he experiment with a variety of genres; he also dealt with diverse social and psychological problems in unusual narrative modes. A master of self-irony, he often employed the first-person narrative to poke fun simultaneously at himself and at conceited people who tell stories that reveal their pretentiousness. Some of his more imaginative fairy tales are told in a vivacious, colloquial style that appears to be flippant, until he suddenly introduces serious issues that transform the tale into a complex narrative of survival and salvation. Though he could over-emphasize sentimentality, religiosity, and pathos, Andersen was deeply invested in the issues he raised in his tales. It was almost as if life and death were at risk in his short prose, and he needed to capture the intensity of the moment. This is perhaps why he kept trying to write from different vantage points, used different genres, experimented with forms and ideas borrowed from other writers, and inserted his own life experiences into the narratives.

Little is known in the English-speaking world about the tireless creative experiments of the tormented writer called Hans Christian Andersen. He tried to make a fairy tale out of his life to save himself from his sufferings. Whether he succeeded in saving himself is open to question, but he did leave us fantastic tales that still stun us and compel us to reflect on the human will to survive.

Jack Zipes is professor of German and comparative literature at the University of Minnesota and is a specialist in folklore and fairy tales. Some of his major publications include *Breaking the Magic Spell: Radical Theories of Folk and Fairy Tales* (1979), *Fairy Tales and the Art of Subversion* (1983), *Don't Bet on the Prince: Contemporary Feminist Fairy Tales in North America and England* (1986), *The Brothers Grimm: From Enchanted Forests to the Modern World* (1988), and *Sticks and Stones: The Troublesome Success of Children's Literature from Slovenly Peter to Harry Potter* (2001). He has also translated *The Complete Fairy Tales of the Brothers Grimm* (1987) and edited *The Oxford Companion to Fairy Tales* (2000) and *The Great Fairy Tale Tradition* (2001). Most recently he has served as the general editor of the *Norton Anthology of Children's Literature* (2005).

Translator's Preface

"There are so many delightful stories in this book," said Hans. "So many that you haven't heard." "Well, I don't care about them," said Garden-Ole. "I want to hear the one I know."

The sentiment expressed by Garden-Ole in Andersen's story "The Cripple" is one that might be familiar to many English readers of Hans Christian Andersen's stories. It is tempting in reading a new translation to want to hear again the stories that we know. And most of the old favorites are here: "The Tinderbox," "The Princess on the Pea," "The Little Mermaid," "The Emperor's New Clothes," "The Steadfast Tin Soldier," "The Ugly Ducking," and others. But here too are "many that you haven't heard"—or, at least, have not heard as often. It is my hope that reading some of the less often translated tales will help the modern English reader understand why Andersen is considered by Danes to be at the center of the Danish literary canon, not primarily a children's author, as he continues to be thought of in the English-speaking world.

When I told a friend that I was working on a translation of Andersen's stories she looked at me with a puzzled expression and said, "But hasn't that been done?" I replied that of course it had, but while Andersen's nineteenth-century Danish words remain forever unchanged upon the page, our splendid English language continues on its merry way, evolving and adapting and challenging us to renew the old stories in the idioms of our time. Many of the early English translations were quite deplorable, and while there have been good recent translations of "the ones you know," the most complete edition of recent years, Erik Christian Haugaard's comprehensive *Hans Christian Andersen: The Complete Fairy Tales and Stories* (Garden City, NY: Doubleday, 1974) can really best be described as an excellent adaptation rather than a translation. So the fact remains that many of Andersen's less-often translated stories remain unknown to English readers in anything approximating their original forms.

The translations in this book were made directly from the first five volumes of the critical edition of *H. C. Andersens Eventyr* (Copenhagen: 1963–1967), edited by Erik Dal and Erling Nielsen. For the textual annotations to this collection, I made extensive use of the notes and commentaries by Erik Dal, Erling Nielsen, and Flemming Hovmann from volume 7 of this work, which appears on the Arkiv for Dansk Litteratur (Archive of Danish literature) website: *http://www.adl.dk.*

Andersen often made references to or citations from other texts in his work, and whenever a standard English translation was available, I have used that. These borrowings are recorded in the annotations, which immediately follow each story. Andersen's own footnotes are indicated in the annotations by "[Andersen's note]." Since this text is intended for a broad range of readers, no efforts have been made to censor Andersen's expressions or adapt them to a younger audience.

It is a popular practice to lament the difficulty in translating Andersen's style, and it is true that his fondness for puns and word play, alliteration, and stylistic originality can be challenging for the translator. In fact, as Viggo Hjørnager Pedersen writes in his excellent 2004 study *Ugly Ducklings? Studies in the English Translations of Hans Christian Andersen's Tales and Stories* (see "For Further Reading"), "Andersen's style is not easy to imitate in English and few have done so with success." Despite this daunting observation by a native Danish scholar, I have made no conscious effort to convey a comprehensive stylistic whole, because I believe that Andersen actually used diverse techniques, depending on the demands of the story and at different times in his life. I have rather seen my task as one of capturing the mood and tenor of each individual story. My goal throughout has been to attempt to give the modern English reader a reading experience as similar as possible to that of a Danish reader of the original, one story at a time. This has sometimes necessitated taking a few liberties with Andersen's text when conveying jokes and puns, adding alliteration when possible, and sometimes changing pronouns for the sake of consistency. The most notorious example of the latter (and one for which I expect to be severely criticized) is changing the single gender-specific pronoun referring to the nightingale from "her" to "it." I did this because it is the male nightingale that sings, and because Andersen uses "it" except in this one instance. In a few rare instances, I have actually changed or even added a few words in order to keep a rhyme, a joke, or the sense of the original. For example, in "The Flea and the Professor," when the professor ascends skyward in his balloon, the original has "'Slip Snorer og Toug!' sagde han. 'Nu gaaer Ballonen!' De troede han sagde: 'Kanonen!'" [The final sentence translates as: "They thought he said: 'the cannon!'"] I have changed this exchange to: "'Let go of the ropes and cords,' he said. 'Up goes the balloon!' They thought he said, 'Let's make a boom!'" The exchange makes sense only if the expressions rhyme. Such liberties with the original are rare and always deliberate.

If I have not been consciously concerned with a stylistic whole, I have been extremely conscious of Andersen's use of poetic language in many of the later stories, and with his delightful sense of play and fun in his use of Danish. To this end I found Fritse Jacobsen's *H. C. Andersens ordspil* (*H. C. Andersen's Puns*; Copenhagen: University of Copenhagen Center for Translation, DAO 9, 2000) very useful. Unfortunately, it has not always been possible to convey Andersen's jokes and puns, with specific Danish cultural references, successfully through English. In some cases I have compensated for this loss by adding a joke of my own or slightly twisting Andersen's original (my favorites include giving the darning needle "the bends," and the deliberate misspelling of "do" in the story "In the Duckyard"). In some cases I have found that the best English solutions for jokes and puns have already been discovered. Those familiar with earlier translations will hear echoes of Leyssac, Hersholt, Spink, Haugaard, and Keigwin in my work. Scholars of all disciplines build on the work of others, and there is no reason why translators should not appropriate best solutions. The goal, after all, is the most perfect possible rendering of Danish to English, and despite Viggo Pedersen's

attempts to find influence between translators by comparing
short sentences or paragraphs, there really are a finite number
of possible ways to translate a set Danish sentence to a corre-
sponding English one.

Many people helped in one way or another with my work. I
would like to acknowledge and thank Gracia Grindal, Dennis
Omoe, Ole Stig Andersen, Kathie Crawford, Erik Horak-Hult,
Michael Hult, Jeffrey Broesche at Fine Creative Media, and my
entire email address book for responding to my English language usage survey. I am deeply grateful to Anne Hvam for her
countless hours of work on the poetic sections of "The Galoshes of Fortune." I am confident that "Mormors briller" has
never been rendered as well in English. Finally, I am enormously indebted to Jack Zipes for his careful corrections, en-
lightening commentary, and valuable suggestions throughout
the project, and not least for his observations on the art of
translating. All remaining errors in the "many delightful stories in this book" are my own.

Minneapolis, Minnesota
September 28, 2005

Marte Hvam Hult holds a Ph.D. in Scandinavian languages
and literatures from the University of Minnesota. She is the au-
thor of *Framing a National Narrative: The Legend Collections of
Peter Christen Asbjørnsen,* published by Wayne State University
Press in 2003. She is working on a translation of Asbjørnsen's
Huldreeventyr.

Andersen's Fairy Tales

THE ARTIST AND SOCIETY

THE NIGHTINGALE

OF COURSE YOU KNOW that in China the emperor is Chinese, and all the people around him are Chinese. It was many years ago, but just because of that, it's worth while hearing the story before it's forgotten! The emperor's palace was the most splendid in the world, completely made of fine porcelain—so expensive, but so brittle, so fragile to touch that you had to be really careful. There were the most remarkable flowers in the garden, and to the most beautiful were tied silver bells so that you couldn't walk by without noticing the flower. Everything was so artful in the emperor's garden, and it was so big that even the gardener didn't know where it ended. If you kept walking, you would enter the loveliest forest with high trees and deep lakes. The forest went right down to the deep, blue sea. Big ships sailed right under the branches, and in the branches lived a nightingale that sang so sweetly that even the poor fisherman, who had so much else to do while pulling up his nets, lay still and listened when he was out at night and heard the nightingale. "Dear God, how beautifully it sings," he said, but then he had to pay attention to his task and forget the bird. But when it sang again the next night, and the fisherman was out again, he said the same: "Dear God, how beautifully it sings!"

Travelers came to the emperor's city from all the countries of the world, and they were astounded by it all: the palace and the garden, but when they heard the nightingale, they all said, "this is the best of all!"

And the travelers talked about the bird when they got home, and scholars wrote many books about the city, the palace, and the garden. But they didn't forget the nightingale. It was placed at the very top of the wonders, and those who could write poetry wrote the most beautiful poems, all about the nightingale in the forest by the deep sea.

The books circulated around the world, and in the course of time one reached the emperor. He sat on his golden throne and read and read. He nodded his head constantly because he

5

was pleased to hear the magnificent descriptions of the city, palace, and garden. "But the nightingale is the best of all!" it said in the book.

"What?!" said the emperor. "The nightingale! I don't know anything about that bird at all! Is there such a bird in my kingdom, even here in my own garden? And I've never heard about it? I have to read about this?!"

And he called his chamberlain, who was so distinguished that when someone who was inferior to him dared to speak to him, or asked about something, he didn't say anything but "P!" and it didn't mean anything.

"There's supposed to be a highly remarkable bird called a nightingale here," said the emperor. "They say it's the best thing in my entire kingdom! Why hasn't anyone told me about it?"

"I've never before heard it mentioned," said the chamberlain. "It's never been presented at court."

"I want it to come here this evening and sing for me," said the emperor. "The whole world knows what I have, and I don't know it myself!"

"I've never heard anything about it before," said the chamberlain, "I'll go find it."

But where to find it? The chamberlain ran up and down all the steps, through the rooms and hallways. None of those he met had heard anything about the nightingale, and the chamberlain ran back to the emperor and said that it must have been a fable made up by those who wrote books. "Your royal majesty should not believe what is written! They are mostly made up, and something called black magic."

"But the book I read it in," said the emperor, "was sent to me by the powerful emperor of Japan, and so it can't be untrue. I want to hear the nightingale! It shall be here this evening! It's my greatest pleasure, and if it doesn't come, the entire court will be thumped on the stomach after they've had dinner."

"Tsing-pe!" said the chamberlain, who ran up and down all the steps again, through the rooms and hallways, and half the people at court ran along too because they didn't want to be thumped on the stomach. They went asking about the remarkable nightingale which the whole world knew, but no one at court had heard of.

Finally, they met a poor little girl in the kitchen, and she said, "Oh God, the nightingale! I know it well. Oh my, how it can sing! Every evening I'm allowed to bring some of the scraps from the table home to my poor sick mother who lives down by the shore. When I walk back, I get tired, and rest in the woods. Then I hear the nightingale singing, and it brings tears to my eyes. It's like being kissed by my mother."

"Little kitchen maid," said the chamberlain, "I'll get you a permanent job in the kitchen and permission to watch the emperor eat if you can lead us to the nightingale. The emperor has ordered him to perform this evening!"

And then they all went into the woods where the nightingale used to sing. Half the court went along. As they were starting out, they heard a cow mooing.

"Oh," said the young court nobles, "Here we have it! What remarkable power in such a little animal! We have most assuredly heard it before."

"No, those are cows mooing," said the little kitchen maid. "We're still far from the place."

Then the frogs croaked in the pond.

"Lovely!" said the Chinese palace chaplain. "Now I hear it— like little church bells."

"No, those are the frogs," said the little kitchen maid. "But I think we'll hear it pretty soon."

And then the nightingale started singing.

"That's it," said the little girl. "Listen! listen! And there it is!" and she pointed at a little grey bird up in the branches.

"Is this possible?" asked the chamberlain. "I wouldn't have imagined it to look like that. How plain it looks! It must have lost its colors from seeing so many distinguished people looking at it!"

"Little nightingale," called the little kitchen maid quite loudly, "our Most Gracious Emperor so dearly wants you to sing for him!"

"With the greatest pleasure!" said the nightingale and sang so beautifully that it was a pleasure to hear.

"It sounds like glass bells," said the chamberlain. "And look at its little throat, how it's throbbing! It's remarkable that we haven't heard it before. It'll be a big success at court!"

"Shall I sing one more time for the emperor?" asked the nightingale, who thought the emperor was with them.

"My splendid little nightingale," said the chamberlain. "I have the great honor of summoning you to a court party this evening, where you will enchant his great Royal Highness the Emperor with your charming song!"

"It really sounds better out in the open air," said the nightingale, but it gladly followed along when it heard that it was the emperor's wish.

At the palace everything had been polished. The walls and floors of porcelain were shining with the light of many thousand golden lamps. The most beautiful flowers with their bells were lined up in the hallways. There was a running back and forth and a draft so that all the bells rang, and you couldn't hear what anyone said.

In the middle of the big chamber where the emperor sat, a golden perch had been set up, and the nightingale was to sit on that. The entire court was there, and the little kitchen maid had been allowed to stand back by the door since she now had the official title of *Real Kitchen Maid.* They were all dressed up in their finest, and all looked at the little grey bird as the emperor nodded for it to begin.

And the nightingale sang so beautifully that it brought tears to the emperor's eyes. They rolled down over his cheeks, and then the nightingale sang even more beautifully so it touched everyone's heart. The emperor was very happy, and he said that the nightingale should have his golden slipper to wear around its neck. But the nightingale thanked him and said it had already had payment enough.

"I've seen tears in the emperor's eyes, and that is the greatest treasure for me. An emperor's tears have a remarkable power. God knows I have payment enough!" and then it sang again with its blessed, sweet voice.

"That's the most delightful coquetry and flirtation we've ever seen," said all the ladies, and they kept water in their mouths so they could cluck when someone talked to them. They thought they were nightingales too. Well, the footmen and chambermaids also let it be known that they were satisfied, and that says a lot since they are the most difficult to please. Yes, the nightingale was a great success!

It was going to remain at court and have its own cage, but freedom to walk out twice a day and once at night. Twelve servants were to go along with silk ribbons tied to the nightingale's leg, and they were to hold on tightly. There was no pleasure to be had from walks like this!

The whole town talked about the remarkable bird, and if two people met each other, then the first said only "Night" and the other said "gale," and then they sighed and understood each other. Eleven grocers named their children after the nightingale, but none of them could sing a note.

One day a big package came for the emperor, on the outside was written *Nightingale.*

"Here's a new book about our famous bird," said the emperor, but it wasn't a book. It was a little work of art lying in a box: an artificial nightingale that was supposed to resemble the real one, but it was studded with diamonds, rubies and sapphires. As soon as you wound the artificial bird up, it would sing one of the songs the real bird could sing, and the tail bobbed up and down and sparkled silver and gold. Around its neck was a little ribbon, and on the ribbon was written: "The emperor of Japan's nightingale is a trifling compared to the emperor of China's."

"It's lovely," they all said, and the one who had brought the artificial bird was immediately given the title of *Most Imperial Nightingale Bringer.*

"They have to sing together. A duet!"

And so they had to sing together, but it didn't really work since the real nightingale sang in his way, and the artificial bird sang on cylinders. "It's not its fault," said the court conductor. "It keeps perfect time and fits quite into my school of music theory." Then the artificial bird was to sing alone and was just as well received as the real bird. Moreover it was so much more beautiful to look at, for it glittered like bracelets and brooches.

Thirty three times it sang the same song, and it never got tired. People would gladly have listened to it again, but the emperor thought that now the live nightingale should also sing a little—but where was it? No one had noticed that it had flown out of the open window, away to its green forest.

"What's the meaning of this?" cried the emperor, and all the members of the court scolded the bird, and thought that the nightingale was a most ungrateful creature. "We still have the best bird," they said, and then the artificial bird had to sing again, and that was the thirty-fourth time they heard the same piece, but they didn't quite know it yet for it was so long, and the conductor praised the bird so extravagantly. He insisted that it was better than the real nightingale, not just in appearance with its many lovely diamonds, but also on the inside.

"You see, ladies and gentlemen, Your Royal Majesty! You can never know what to expect from the real nightingale, but everything is determined in the artificial bird. It will be so-and-so, and no different! You can explain it; you can open it up and show the human thought—how the cylinders are placed, how they work, and how one follows the other!"

"My thoughts exactly," everyone said, and on the following Sunday the conductor was allowed to exhibit the bird for the public. The emperor also said that they were to hear it sing, and they were so pleased by it as if they had drunk themselves merry on tea (for that is so thoroughly Chinese), and they all said "Oh" and stuck their index fingers in the air and nodded. But the poor fisherman, who had heard the real nightingale, said, "It sounds good enough, and sounds similar too, but there's something missing. I don't know what."

The real nightingale was banished from the country and the empire.

The artificial bird had its place on a silk pillow right by the emperor's bed. All the gifts it had received, gold and gems, were lying around it, and it had been given the title of *Most Imperial Nightstand Singer of the First Rank to the Left* because the emperor considered the side towards the heart to be the most distinguished. The heart is on the left side also in emperors. The Royal Conductor wrote twenty-five volumes about the ar-

*The artificial bird had its place on a silk pillow
right by the emperor's bed.*

tificial bird that were very learned and very long and included all the longest Chinese words. All the people said that they had read and understood the books. Otherwise they would have been stupid, of course, and would have been thumped on the stomach.

It continued this way for a whole year. The emperor, the court, and all the other Chinamen knew every little cluck in the artificial bird's song, but they were therefore all the more happy with it—they could sing along, and they did. The street urchins sang "zizizi, klukklukkluk," and the emperor sang it, too. Yes, it was certainly lovely.

But one evening, as the artificial bird was singing beautifully, and the emperor was lying in bed listening, there was suddenly a "svupp" sound inside the bird, and something snapped: "Surrrrrr." All the wheels went around, and the music stopped.

The emperor leaped out of bed at once and had his court physician summoned, but what good could he do? So they called for the watchmaker and after a lot of talk and a lot of tinkering, he managed to more or less fix the bird, but he said it had to be used sparingly because the threads were so worn, and it wasn't possible to install new ones without the music becoming uneven. This was a great tragedy! The artificial bird could only sing once a year, if that. But then the Court Conductor would give a little speech with big words and say that it was as good as before, and so it was as good as before.

Five years went by and the whole country was greatly saddened because it was said that the emperor was sick and wouldn't live much longer. The people had been very fond of him, but a new emperor had already been selected. His subjects stood out on the street and asked the chamberlain how the old emperor was doing.

"P!" he said and shook his head.

Cold and pale, the emperor lay in his big magnificent bed. The whole court thought he was dead, and all of them ran to greet the new emperor. The chamber attendants ran about to talk about it, and the palace maids had their usual gossip. There were cloth runners spread in all the rooms and hallways so that you couldn't hear anyone walk, and therefore it was very quiet—so quiet. But the emperor wasn't dead yet. Stiff and pale, he lay in the magnificent bed with the long velvet curtains and the heavy gold tassels. High on the wall a window was open, and the moonlight shone on the emperor and the artificial bird.

The poor emperor was barely able to draw a breath; it was as if something was sitting on his chest. He opened his eyes, and then he saw that it was Death sitting there. He had put on the emperor's golden crown and held in one hand his golden sword, and in the other his magnificent banner. Round about in the folds of the velvet bed curtains strange heads were peeping out, some quite terrible and others blessedly mild. They were the emperor's good and evil deeds looking at him, now that Death was sitting on his heart.

"Do you remember that?" whispered one after the other. "Do you remember that?" and then they spoke to him of so many things that the sweat sprang out on his forehead.

"I knew nothing about that!" said the emperor. "Music, music, the big Chinese drum!" he called, "so that I won't hear everything that they're saying."

But they continued, and Death nodded like a Chinaman along with everything that was said.

"Music, music!" cried the emperor. "You little blessed golden bird. Sing, just sing! I have given you gold and precious things. I have myself hung my golden slipper around your neck. Sing, oh sing!"

But the bird stood still. There was no one to wind it up, and otherwise it didn't sing, but Death with his big empty eye sockets continued to look at the emperor, and it was quiet, so terribly quiet.

Suddenly outside the window came a beautiful song. It was the little, live nightingale, sitting on the branch outside. It had heard about the emperor's sorrows and had come to sing with comfort and hope for him, and as it sang, the figures became paler and paler, the blood flowed quicker and quicker in the emperor's weak limbs, and Death itself listened and said: "Sing on, little nightingale, sing on."

"Music, music!" cried the emperor.
"You little blessed golden bird. Sing, just sing!"

"Will you give me the magnificent golden sword? Will you give me the precious banner? Will you give me the emperor's crown?"

And Death gave each treasure for a song, and the nightingale continued to sing. It sang about the quiet churchyard, where the white roses grow, where the elder trees emit their scent, and where the fresh grass is watered by tears of the survivors. Then Death felt a longing for his garden and glided, like a cold, white fog, out the window.

"Thank you, thank you," said the emperor. "You heavenly little bird, I know you well. I chased you away from my country and my empire, and yet your song has cast away the evil sights from my bed and taken Death from my heart! How shall I reward you?"

"You have rewarded me," said the nightingale. "I received tears from your eyes the first time I sang for you, and I'll never forget that. Those are the jewels that enrich a singer's heart. But rest now and become healthy and strong. I'll sing for you."

It sang—and the emperor fell into a sweet sleep, a gentle restoring sleep.

The sun shone through the windows on him when he awoke, stronger and healthy. None of his servants had come back because they thought he was dead, but the nightingale was still sitting there singing.

"You must stay with me always," said the emperor. "You'll only sing when you want to, and I'll crush the artificial bird into a thousand pieces."

"Don't do that!" said the nightingale. "It has done what good it could. Keep it as always. I can't live here at the palace, but let me come when I want to, and in the evenings I'll sit on the branch by the window and sing for you so you can be happy and thoughtful too. I'll sing about the happy and about those who suffer. I'll sing about the good and evil that is hidden from you! Your little songbird flies far and wide to the poor fishermen, to the farmer's roof, to everywhere that's far from you and your palace. I love your heart more than your crown, and yet your crown has a scent of something sacred

about it!—I'll come, I'll sing for you.—But you must promise
me one thing."

"Everything!" said the emperor, standing there in his royal
clothing that he'd put on himself. He was holding the sword,
heavy with gold, up to his heart.

"I ask you this one thing. Don't tell anyone that you have a
little bird that tells you everything. Then things will go even
better."

And the nightingale flew away.

Soon after the servants entered the room to see to their
dead emperor—there they stood, and the emperor said,
"Good morning."

THE GARDENER AND THE GENTRY

ABOUT FIVE MILES FROM the capital there was an old manor
house with thick walls, towers, and corbie gables.

A rich, noble family lived there, but only in the summer.
This manor was the best and most beautiful of all the proper-
ties they owned. It looked like new outside and was full of comfort and coziness inside. The family coat of arms was engraved
in stone above the estate gate, and beautiful roses were entwined around the crest and bay windows. A carpet of grass was
spread out in front of the manor house. There were red and
white hawthorn and rare flowers, even outside the greenhouse.

The family also had a very capable gardener. It was a delight
to see the flower garden, and the fruit orchard and vegetable
garden. Next to this there was still a remnant of the original
old garden—some box hedges—clipped to form crowns and
pyramids. Behind these stood two huge old trees. They were always almost leafless, and you could easily have believed that a
stormy wind or a waterspout had spread big clumps of manure
over them, but every clump was a bird nest.

A huge flock of shrieking rooks and crows had built nests
here from times immemorial. It was an entire city of birds,
and the birds were the masters, the occupiers of the property,

the oldest family on the estate, and the real masters of the manor. None of the people down there concerned them, but they tolerated these crawling creatures, except that sometimes they banged with their guns, so it tickled the birds' backbones and caused every bird to fly up in fear and cry, "scum, scum!"

The gardener often talked to the master and mistress about having the old trees cut down. They didn't look good, and if they were gone, they would most likely be rid of the screaming birds, who would go elsewhere. But the master and mistress didn't want to be rid of either the trees or the birds because they were from old times. Anything from old times was something the estate could and should not lose.

"Those trees are the birds' inheritance, my good Larsen. Let them keep them." The gardener's name was Larsen, but that's neither here nor there.

"Larsen, don't you have enough room to work? The whole flower garden, the greenhouses, fruit and vegetables gardens?"

He did have those, and he cared for, watched over, and cultivated them with zeal and skill, and the master and mistress acknowledged that, but they didn't conceal from him that they often ate fruits and saw flowers when visiting that surpassed what they had in their own gardens. That saddened the gardener because he always strived to do the best he could. He was good-hearted and good at his job.

One day the master and mistress called him in and told him in a gentle and lordly manner that the day before they had eaten some apples and pears at distinguished friends that were so juicy and so delicious that they and all the other guests had expressed their greatest admiration. The fruits were certainly not domestic, but they should be imported, and should be grown here if the climate would allow it. They knew that the fruits had been bought in town at the best greengrocer's. The gardener was to ride into town and find out where the apples and pears had come from and then write for grafts.

The gardener knew the greengrocer well because he was the

very one to whom, on the master's behalf, he sold the surplus fruit that grew in the estate gardens.

And the gardener went to town and asked the greengrocer where he had gotten those highly acclaimed apples and pears.

"They're from your own garden!" said the greengrocer and showed him both the apples and pears that he immediately recognized.

Well, how happy this made the gardener! He hurried back to the master and mistress and told them that both the apples and pears were from their own garden.

But the master and mistress simply couldn't believe it. "It's not possible, Larsen! Can you get this confirmed in writing from the greengrocer?"

And he could and did do that. He brought the written certification.

"This is really strange!" said the master and mistress.

Every day big platters of the magnificent apples and pears from their own garden appeared on the table. Bushels and barrels full of these fruits were sent to friends in town and out of town, even to foreign countries! What a pleasure! But of course they had to add that it had been two amazingly good summers for the fruit trees. Good fruit was being produced all over the country.

Some time passed. The master and mistress were invited to dinner at court. The day after this they called in the gardener. They had gotten melons at the table from the royal greenhouses that were so juicy and tasty.

"You must go to the royal gardener, dear Larsen, and get us some of the seeds of those priceless melons!"

"But the royal gardener got the seeds from us!" said the gardener, quite pleased.

"Well, then that man has the knowledge to bring fruit to a higher level of development!" said the master. "Each melon was remarkable."

"Well, I can be proud then," said the gardener. "I must tell your lordship that the royal gardener didn't have luck with his melons this year, and when he saw how splendid ours were and tasted them, he ordered three of them for the castle."

"Larsen! You're not telling me those were melons from our garden?!"

"I think so!" said the gardener, who went to the royal gardener and got written confirmation that the melons on the kingly table came from the manor.

It really was a surprise for the master and his lady, and they didn't keep quiet about the story. They showed the certificate, and melon seeds were sent around widely, just as the pear and apple grafts had been earlier.

And word was received that they grew and produced exceptional fruit, and these melon seeds were named after the noble estate, so that that name could now be read in English, German, and French.

No one could have imagined this!

"Just so the gardener doesn't get a swollen head about this," said the master and mistress.

But the gardener took it all in a different way. He just wanted to establish his name as one of the country's best gardeners, to try each year to bring forth something superior in all the types of garden plants, and he did that. But often he was told that the very first fruits he had produced, the apples and pears, were really the best. All later types were inferior to them. The melons had certainly been very good, but that was something completely different. The strawberries could be called exceptional, but yet not better than those other noble families had, and when the radishes didn't turn out one year, only those unfortunate radishes were discussed, none of the other good things that were produced.

It was almost as if the master and mistress felt a relief in saying, "Things didn't work out this year, Larsen!" They were quite happy to be able to say, "It didn't work out this year."

A couple of times a week the gardener brought fresh flowers up to the living room, and they were always so beautifully arranged. The colors seemed to be more vibrant through the arrangement.

"You have taste, Larsen," said the master and mistress. "It's a gift, given by the Lord, not of your own doing."

One day the gardener brought a large crystal saucer in which a lily pad was floating. On top of this was placed a shining blue flower, as big as a sunflower with its long thick stem trailing down in the water.

"The lotus of the Hindus!" exclaimed the master and mistress.

They had never seen such a flower, and during the day it was placed in the sunshine and in the evening under reflected light. Everyone who saw it thought it was remarkably lovely and rare. Even the most distinguished of the country's young ladies said so, and she was a princess. She was both wise and good.

The master and mistress were honored to give her the flower, and it went with the princess to the palace. Then they went down into the garden to pick such a flower themselves, if one was still there, but they couldn't find one. So they called the gardener and asked where he had gotten the blue Lotus.

"We've searched in vain," they said. "We've been in the greenhouses and round about in the flower gardens."

"No, it's not to be found there," said the gardener. "It's just a simple flower from the vegetable garden! But isn't it true that it's beautiful? It looks like a blue cactus, but it's only the blossom on the artichoke!"

"You should have told us that straight off!" said the master and mistress. "We thought it was a rare, foreign flower. You have disgraced us with the young princess! She saw the flower here, and thought it was beautiful and didn't know what it was. She is very knowledgeable about botany, but her knowledge doesn't have anything to do with vegetables! How could it occur to you, Larsen, to bring such a flower up to the house? It makes a laughing stock of us!"

And the beautiful, gorgeous blue flower, which had been picked in the vegetable garden, was taken out of the living room, where it didn't belong.[1] Then the master and mistress apologized to the princess and told her that the flower was just a kitchen herb that the gardener had wanted to display, but he had been sternly admonished about placing it on display.

"That's a shame and not fair," said the princess. "He has opened our eyes to a magnificent flower that we had not paid any attention to. He has shown us beauty where we did not think to seek it. As long as the artichokes are blooming, the royal gardener will bring one to my parlor every day." And that's what happened.

So then the master and mistress told the gardener that he could bring them a fresh artichoke flower again. "It is pretty after all," they said, "quite remarkable!" And the gardener was praised. "Larsen likes that," they said. "He's a spoiled child!"

In the autumn there was a terrible storm. It started at night, and became so powerful that many big trees at the edge of the forest were torn up by the roots, much to the distress of the master and mistress. A great distress for them, but to the joy of the gardener, the two big trees with all the bird nests blew over. You could hear rooks and crows screaming at the height of the storm. People at the manor said that they flapped their wings against the windows.

"Well, now you're happy, Larsen," said the master and mistress. "The storm has knocked down the trees, and the birds have fled to the forest. Now nothing's left from the old days here. Every sign and every allusion are gone! It's very sad for us."

The gardener didn't say anything, but he thought about what he had long thought about—how to utilize the splendid sunny spot he didn't have access to before. It would become the ornament of the garden, and the joy of his master and mistress.

The big fallen trees had crushed and completely destroyed the ancient box hedges, with their topiary. Here the gardener planted a thicket of growth—native plants from the meadows and forest. He planted with rich abundance what no other gardeners had thought belonged in a gentry's garden, into the type of soil the plants needed and with the amount of shade and sun required by each type. He took care of them with love, and they grew splendidly.

The juniper bushes from the heaths of Jutland grew in form and color like the cypress of Italy. The shiny prickly holly, evergreen in winter cold or summer sun, was a delight to see. In front of them grew ferns of many different kinds. Some looked like they were children of the palm tree, and others as if they were parents of the delicate lovely vegetation we call maidenhair. Here too was the despised burdock that is so lovely in its freshness that it can appear in bouquets. The dock stood on high ground, but lower, where it was damper, grew the common dock, also a despised plant, but with its height and huge leaves still so artistically lovely. Transplanted from the meadow grew the waist-high mullein like a magnificent many-armed candelabra with flower next to flower. There were woodruff, primroses, and forest lily of the valley, the white Calla, and the delicate three-leafed wood sorrel. It was beautiful to see.

In the front small pear trees from France grew in rows tied to wire cord. They received sun and good care and soon produced big, juicy fruit as in the land they came from.

Instead of the old leafless trees, a tall flagpole was installed, where the Danish flag flew and close to that another pole where in the summer and autumn the hop vines twisted with their fragrant cones of flowers, but where in winter an oat sheaf was hung, according to an old custom, so that the birds of the sky should have food in the merry time of Christmas.

"Larsen is getting sentimental in his old age," said the master and mistress, "but he is loyal and attached to us."

At the New Year there was a picture of the old estate in one of the capital's illustrated magazines. You could see the flagpole and the oat-sheaf for the birds at Christmas time, and it was stressed what a good idea it was that an old custom was upheld and honored. So appropriate for the old estate!

"Everything that that Larsen does," said the master and mistress, "is heralded by drums! He's a lucky man! We almost have to be proud that we have him!"

But they were not at all proud of that. They felt that they were the master and mistress, and they could let Larsen go anytime, but they didn't do that. They were good people, and there are many good people of their type, and that's good for many a Larsen.

Well, that's the story of the gardener and the gentry, and now you can think about it.

NOTE

1. Andersen evidently forgot that the flower has been given to the princess and is no longer in the living room.

THE FLYING TRUNK

ONCE UPON A TIME there was a merchant who was so rich that he could pave the entire street and almost another little alley with silver coins. But he didn't do that. He knew of other ways to use his money, and if he paid out a penny, he got a dollar back. That's the kind of merchant he was—and then he died.

His son got all this money, and he lived merrily, went to parties every night, made kites from his dollar bills, and skipped stones on the water with gold coins instead of pebbles. That makes money go, and go it did. Finally he only had four coins left and no other clothes than a pair of slippers and an old robe. Now none of his friends cared about him anymore since they couldn't walk down the street together, but one of them, who was kind, sent him an old trunk and advised, "pack it in!" That was all well and good, but he had nothing to pack so he sat in the trunk himself.

It was a strange trunk. As soon as you pressed on the lock, the trunk could fly. And that's what it did. Whee! It flew with him up the chimney and high up over the clouds, further and further away. The bottom kept groaning, and he was afraid that it would fall to pieces, and then he would have done a nice somersault, heaven knows! Soon he came to the land of the Turks. He hid the trunk in the forest under some wilted leaves and walked into town. He could do that safely because all the Turks walked around like him in robes and slippers. Then he met a wet nurse with a little child. "Listen here, you Turkananny," he said, "what kind of castle is that here close to town? The windows are so high up."

"The king's daughter lives there," she said. "It's been prophesied that she will be unlucky in love, and therefore no one can visit her unless the king and queen are there."

"Thanks," said the merchant's son, and then he went back into the forest, sat in his trunk, flew up on the roof, and crept through the window to the princess.

She was lying on the sofa sleeping. She was so beautiful that the merchant's son had to kiss her. She woke up and was quite alarmed, but he said he was the Turkish God, who had come down through the sky to her, and she liked that.

Then they sat side by side, and he told stories about her eyes: they were the most lovely, dark oceans, and thoughts were swimming there like mermaids. Then he talked about her forehead: it was a snow-topped mountain with the most magnificent rooms and pictures, and he told her about the stork that brings the sweet little babies.

They were certainly some wonderful stories! Then he proposed to the princess, and she said yes at once!

"But you have to come on Saturday," she said. "The king and queen are coming here for tea then. They'll be very proud that I'm going to marry the Turkish God, but listen, be sure you can tell a really lovely fairy tale because they particularly like them. My mother likes them to be elegant and moralistic, and my father likes funny ones so he can laugh."

"I'll bring no other wedding gift than a fairy tale," he said, and then they parted, but the princess gave him a sword that was studded with gold coins, something he could really use.

Then he flew away, bought himself a new robe, and sat in the forest composing a fairy tale to be finished by Saturday. That's not so easy either.

But he finished it, and then it was Saturday.

The king and queen and all the court were waiting with tea at the princess's tower, where he was very well received!

"Won't you tell a fairy tale?" asked the queen. "One that is profound and educational."

"One that can make you laugh, too," added the king.

"Yes certainly," he said and told this story. Listen carefully.

"Once upon a time there was a package of matches that were extremely stuck-up because they were of such high origin. Their family tree, that is to say, the big pine tree that each of them was a little stick of, had been a tall old tree in the forest. The matches were now lying on a shelf between a tinder-box and an old iron kettle, and they told them stories about their youth. 'Yes, when we were riding high,' they said, 'we really *were* riding high! Every morning and evening we had diamond tea, that was the dew. We had the sunshine all day when the sun was shining, and all the little birds had to tell us stories. We could easily tell that we were rich because the ordinary trees only wore clothes in the summer, but our family could afford nice green clothes both summer and winter. But then the foresters came. It was the big revolution, and our family tree was split up. The head of the family got a place as the topmast on a magnificent ship that could sail around the world if it wanted to. The other branches went to other places, and we now have the task of bringing light to the common crowd. That's how we who are so noble came to be here in this kitchen.'

" 'Yes, it's quite different for me,' said the iron kettle, standing next to the matches. 'From the time I came into the world, I have been in hot water many times. I have the responsibility for the most substantial work and am strictly speaking the most important one in the house. My only joy is to sit here clean and tidy after dinner and have pleasant conversations with my companions. But with the exception of the water pail, who gets out in the yard once in a while, we all live a secluded indoor life. Our only news comes from the marketing basket, but he talks very critically of the government and the people. Just the other day an old jug over there fell over in alarm at what he said and smashed to pieces. He's markedly liberal, I'll tell you.' 'You spout off too much,' the tinderbox said, and the flint struck the stone so the sparks flew. 'Let's have a cheerful, merry evening.'

" 'Yes, let's talk about who is most distinguished,' the matches said.

" 'No, I don't like talking about myself,' said the clay pot. 'Let's have an evening of entertainment. I'll start. I'll tell about something that we've all experienced. Everyone can follow along then, and it's so amusing: On the Baltic where the Danish beech trees . . .'

" 'That's a great beginning,' all the plates said, 'this'll definitely be a story we'll like.'

" 'Yes, I spent my youth there with a quiet family. The furniture was polished, the floors washed, and there were clean curtains every other week.'

" 'How interestingly you tell that!" said the broom. 'You can hear at once that it's a woman telling the story—there's no dirt in it at all.'

" 'Yes, one can tell that," the water pail said, and it made a little hop of joy so that there was a splash on the floor.

"And the pot continued the story, and the ending was as good as the beginning.

"All the plates were rattling with pleasure, and the broom took some green parsley out of the parsley pot and crowned the pot with a wreath because he knew it would irritate the others, and 'if I crown her today,' he thought, 'she'll crown me tomorrow.'

" 'Now I'll dance,' said the fire tongs and danced. Oh, God bless us, how she could kick a leg in the air! The old seat cover in the corner split from watching it! 'May I also be crowned?' asked the fire tongs, and so she was.

" 'These are just riffraff,' thought the matches.

"Then the tea urn was supposed to sing, but she had a cold, she said. She couldn't sing unless she was warmed up. Actually it was due to conceit because she didn't want to sing except for the master and mistress in the dining room.

"On the windowsill sat an old quill pen that the maid used for writing. There was nothing remarkable about him, except that he had been dipped too deeply in the inkwell, but he was proud of that. 'If the tea urn doesn't want to sing,' he said, 'then she doesn't have to. There is a nightingale hanging outside in a cage. It can sing. Granted it hasn't had lessons, but we won't criticize it this evening.'

" 'I find it highly inappropriate,' said the tea kettle, who usually sang in the kitchen and was a half sister of the tea urn, 'that a foreign bird like that should sing. Is that patriotic? I'll let the marketing basket judge!'

" 'I'm just so annoyed,' the marketing basket said. 'I'm so thoroughly annoyed, you can't imagine! Is this an appropriate way to spend the evening? Wouldn't it be better to rearrange things and set the house in order? Then everyone would be in his correct place, and I would control the whole shebang. That would be something else!'

" 'Yes, let's cause a riot!' they all said. At that moment the door opened. It was the maid, and so everyone stopped talking. No one said a word. But there wasn't a pot who didn't know what it could do and how dignified it was. 'Well, if I had wanted it,' they all thought, 'it really would have been a merry evening!'

"The maid took the matches and made a fire with them— God bless us, how they sizzled and burned in flames!

" 'Now everyone can see,' they thought, 'that we are the best! What radiance we have! What light!'—and then they were burned out."

"That was a lovely fairy tale," the queen said. "I felt just like I was in the kitchen with the matches. You may certainly marry our daughter."

"Of course," the king agreed, "you'll marry our daughter on Monday!" Now they said "du" to him, since he was going to be part of the family.[1]

So the wedding day was decided, and the evening before the whole town was lit up. Rolls and pastries were thrown to the crowds. Street urchins stood on their toes, shouted hurrah, and whistled through their fingers. It was extremely splendid.

"Well, I'd better also do something," the merchant's son thought, and so he bought some rockets, caps, and all the fireworks you could think of, put them in his trunk, and flew up in the air with it.

Whoosh, how it went! And how it popped and puffed!

All the Turks jumped in the air at this so that their slippers flew around their ears. They had never seen such a sight in the sky before. Now they understood that it really was the Turkish God himself who was going to marry the princess.

As soon as the merchant's son landed in the forest with his trunk, he thought, "I'll just go into town to find out how that looked to everyone." And it was understandable that he wanted to do that.

Well, how the people were talking! Every single one he asked about it had seen it in his own way, but it had been beautiful for all of them.

"I saw the Turkish God himself," one said. "He had eyes like shining stars and a beard like foaming water."

"He flew in a coat of fire," another one said, "and the most gorgeous little angels peeked out from the folds."

Yes, he heard lovely things, and the next day he was getting married.

Then he went back to the forest to put himself in his trunk—but where was it? The trunk had burned up. A spark from the fireworks had remained, had started a fire, and the trunk was in ashes. He couldn't fly any longer and couldn't get to his bride.

She stood all day on the roof waiting. She's still waiting, but he's wandering the world telling fairy tales. But they aren't any longer so lighthearted as the one he told about the matches.

NOTE

1. Danish shares with many European languages formal and informal forms of direct address. "Du" is informal.

THE WILL-O'-THE-WISPS ARE IN TOWN

THERE WAS A MAN who at one time had known so many new fairy tales, but now they had come to an end, he said. The tale used to come by its own accord, but now it didn't knock at his door anymore. And why didn't it come? Well, it's true enough that the man hadn't thought about it for a whole year, had not expected it to come knocking, and it evidently hadn't been around there either, since there was war without, and within the sorrow and distress that war carries with it.

The stork and the swallow returned from their long voyages. They didn't think of any danger, but when they arrived their nests had been burned. People's houses were burned, gates broken, or just entirely gone. The enemy's horses trampled on the old graves. They were hard, dark times, but even those have an end.

And now it was over, they said, but the fairy tale still hadn't come knocking, nor was it heard from.

"I guess it's dead and gone along with many others," said the man. But the fairy tale never dies!

And over a year passed, and he longed sorely for it.

"I wonder if the fairy tale will ever come knocking again?" And he remembered so vividly all the many shapes in which it had come to him. Sometimes young and beautiful, like spring itself, a lovely little girl with a wreath of woodruff in her hair and beech branches in her hand. Her eyes shone like deep forest lakes in the clear sunshine. Sometimes it had also come as a peddler, opened its pack of wares and let silk ribbons wave with verses and inscriptions from old memories. But still, it was most beautiful when it came as a little old woman with silvery white hair and with eyes so big and wise. She had told about the oldest times, long before princesses spun gold while dragons and serpents lay outside keeping watch. She told stories so vividly that the eyes of everyone who listened would go dim, and the floor would become black with human blood. Awful to see and to hear, and yet so delightful because it all happened so very long ago.

"I wonder if she'll never come again!" the man said, and stared towards the door until he saw black spots in front of his eyes and black spots on the floor. He didn't know if it was blood or mourning crepe from the heavy, dark days.

And as he sat, it occurred to him that maybe the fairy tale had gone into hiding, like the princesses in the old folk tales, and now had to be sought out. If she were found, she would shine with a new splendor, more beautiful than ever before.

"Who knows? Maybe she lies hidden in the littered straw that's tilted at the edge of the well. Careful! Careful! Maybe she has hidden in a withered flower that's lying in one of the big books on the shelf."

And the man went to the shelf and opened one of the newest instructive books, but there was no flower there. It was about Holger the Dane, and the man read that the entire story had been invented and put together by a monk in France. That it was just a novel that had been "translated and published in the Danish language." And that Holger the Dane had not existed at all and so would certainly never come again, as the Danes had sung about and so wanted to believe. Holger the Dane was just like William Tell, idle talk, not to be relied upon, and all this was written in this most scholarly book.

"Well, I believe what I believe," said the man. "There's no smoke without fire."

And he shut the book, put it back on the shelf, and went over to the fresh flowers on the windowsill. Maybe the fairy tale had hidden there in the red tulip with the golden yellow edges, in the fresh rose, or the vibrantly colored camellia. Sunshine lay amongst the leaves, but no fairy tale.

"The flowers that were here during the sad times were all much more beautiful, but every one of them was cut off, bound into wreaths, and laid into coffins and over the folded flag. Maybe the fairy tale is buried with those flowers! But the flowers would have known about that, and the coffin would have sensed it. The earth would have sensed it too, and every little blade of grass that shoots forth would have told about it. The fairy tale never dies!"

"Maybe it was even here and knocked, but who at that time would have had an ear for it, or even a thought about it? We looked dark and heavily, almost angrily, at the sunshine of the spring, the twittering of birds, and all the pleasant greenery. Our tongues couldn't sing the favorite old folk songs. They were put away with so many other things that had been dear to our hearts. The fairy tale could very well have knocked, but not have been heard, not welcomed, and so it just went away."

"I will go out and find it. Into the country, out in the forest, along the sweeping seashore!"

An old manor house can be found out there with red brick walls, corbiestep gables, and a fluttering flag on the tower. The nightingale sings under the finely fringed beech leaves while it looks at the garden's blooming apple blossoms and thinks they are roses. The bees are busy here in the summertime, and they swarm around their queen in buzzing song. The storms of autumn can tell about the wild hunt, about mankind, and the leaves of the forest that blow away. At Christmas time the wild swans sing from the open sea, while inside the old manor, by the side of the stove, people are in the mood for hearing songs and old stories.

Down in the old part of the garden, where the big avenue of wild chestnut trees lures you into the shade, the man who was seeking the fairy tale was walking. The wind had once whispered to him here of *Valdemar Daa and His Daughters.* The dryad in the tree, none other than Mother fairy tale herself, had told him *The Old Oak Tree's Dream* here. In grandmother's time trimmed hedges stood here, but now only ferns and nettles grew there. They spread over the abandoned remains of old statuary. Moss grew from their stony eyes, although they could see just as well as before, but the man looking for the fairy tale couldn't. He couldn't see the fairy tale. Where was it? Above him and over the old trees hundreds of crows flew crying, "Fly from here, from here!"

And he walked from the garden over the manor's moat, and into the grove of alders. There was a little six-sided house here and a hen and duck yard. In the middle of the room sat the old woman who ruled all of this. She knew about every egg that was laid, and every chick that came from the egg, but she was not the fairy tale the man was looking for. She could prove that with a Christian baptism certificate and a vaccination certificate, both lying in the chest of drawers.

Outside, not far from the house, was a hill filled with red hawthorn and laburnum. There's an old tombstone there that

had come from the churchyard in the market town. It was
carved to honor one of the town's councilmen. His wife and
his five daughters, all with folded hands and ruffed collars,
were standing around him, chiseled from stone. If you looked
at it long enough, it somehow affected your thoughts, and
those thoughts in turn affected the stone so that it told about
the old times. Anyway, that's how it happened for the man
searching for the fairy tale. As he arrived here now, he saw a living butterfly sitting on the forehead of the carved councilman.
It fluttered its wings, flew a short distance, and then landed
again right by the tombstone as if to show him what was growing there. It was a four-leaf clover, and there were seven of
them, side by side. When luck comes, it comes in earnest! He
picked the clovers and put them in his pocket. Good luck is
just as good as ready money, although a new lovely fairy tale
would have been even better, thought the man. But he didn't
find it there.

The sun set, red and huge. Fog rose from the meadow. The
bog witch was brewing.

———————

It was late in the evening. He stood alone in his room, looking
out over the garden and meadow, the moor and the seashore.
The moon was shining clearly and there was a mist hanging
over the meadow as if it were a big lake. There had been one
there once, according to legend, and in the moonlight you
could see for yourself. Then the man thought about what he
had read in town, how William Tell and Holger the Dane had
not existed, but in folklore they became, like the sea out there,
living visions for legend. Yes, Holger the Dane would return!

As he was standing there and thinking, something hit the
window quite strongly. Was it a bird? A bat or an owl? Well, you
don't let them in if they knock! The window sprang open by itself, and an old woman looked in at the man.

"What's this?" he said. "Who is she? She's looking right into
the second story. Is she standing on a ladder?"

"You have a four-leaf clover in your pocket," she said. "You
actually have seven, one of which is a six-leaf clover!"

"Who are you?" asked the man.

"The bog witch!" she said. "The bog witch, and I'm brewing. I was in the process of doing that, and the tap was in the barrel, but one of the frisky little bog children drew the tap out in fun and flung it up here against the house where it hit the window. Now the beer's running out of the barrel, and that's not a good thing for anyone!"

"Well, but tell me—" said the man.

"Wait a moment," said the bog witch. "I have other things to attend to," and then she was gone.

The man was about to close the window, and then she reappeared.

"Now that's done," she said, "but half of the beer I'll have to brew again tomorrow if the weather holds. Now what did you want to ask about? I came back because I always keep my word, and you have seven four-leaf clovers in your pocket, one of which has six-leaves and that earns respect. They're badges that grow by the road, but aren't found by everyone. What did you want to ask about? Don't just stand there like a silly sap. I have to get back to my barrel and tap."

And the man asked about the fairy tale, asked if the bog witch had seen it on her way.

"Oh, for brewing sassafras!" said the witch. "Haven't you had enough of fairy tales yet? I do believe that most people have. There are other things to take care of and be concerned about. Even the children have outgrown them. Give the little boys a cigar and the little girls a new petticoat—they care more about that! Listen to fairy tales? No, there are other things to attend to, more important things to do!"

"What do you mean by that?" the man said. "And what do you know of the world? You only see frogs and will-o'-the-wisps!"

"Well, watch out for the will-o'-the-wisps!" said the witch. "They're out! They're on the loose. We should talk about them. Come to me in the bog, where I need to be now. I'll tell you all about it, but hurry while your seven four-leaf clovers with the one sixer are fresh, and the moon is still up!"

And the bog witch was gone.

The clock struck twelve on the tower clock, and before it struck
the quarter hour the man was out of the yard, out of the garden and standing in the meadow. The fog had lifted, and the
bog witch had stopped brewing.

"It took a long time for you to get here," said the bog witch.
"Trolls get around faster than people, and I'm glad I was born
of troll folk."

"What do you have to tell me?" asked the man. "Is it something about the fairy tale?"

"Can't you think of anything but that?" said the witch.

"Well, can you tell me about the poetry of the future then?"
asked the man.

"Don't be so hifalutin," said the witch, "and I'll answer you.
You only think about poetry, and ask about the fairy tale, as if
she's the one who gets everything going. But she's just the oldest, although she is always taken for the youngest. I certainly
know her. I have been young too, and that's not a childhood
illness. I was once quite a pretty elf maiden, and danced with
the others in the moonlight, listened to the nightingale,
walked in the forests and met the fairy tale maiden, who was always out gadding about. Sometimes she spent the night in a
partly opened tulip or in a globe flower. Sometimes she slipped
into the church and wrapped herself in the mourning crepe
that hung from the altar candles."

"You have a lot of lovely information," said the man.

"Well, I should hope I know as much as you do anyway!" said
the bog witch. "Fairy tales and poetry—Well, they're two of a
kind. They can go lie down wherever they want. All their work
and talk can be brewed both better and cheaper than they do
it. You can get them from me for nothing. I have a whole cupboard full of poetry in bottles. It's the essence of it, the best,
the actual herb, both the sweet and the bitter. I have bottles of
all the poetry people need, so they can put some on their
handkerchiefs to smell on Sundays and holidays."

"You're saying some really strange things," said the man.
"You have bottled poetry?"

"More than you can stand!" said the witch. "You must know

the story about the girl who stepped on bread to avoid dirtying her new shoes? It's been both written and printed."

"I wrote that story myself," said the man.

"Well, then you know it." said the witch, "And you know that the girl sank right down into the ground to the bog witch just as the devil's great-grandmother was visiting to see the brewery. She saw the girl who sank and requested her for a pedestal, a souvenir of her visit. She got her, and I got a gift that I have no use for: a portable apothecary, a whole cupboard of poetry in bottles. Great-grandmother decided where it was to stand, and it's still standing there. Just look! You have your seven four-leaf clovers, one of which is a six-leaf clover, in your pocket so I'm sure you'll be able to see it."

And truly, right in the middle of the bog there was a sort of big hollow alder stump, and that was great-grandmother's cupboard. It was open to her and to everyone in all countries and in all times, the bog witch said, as long as they knew where the cupboard was. It could be opened in the front and the back, and on all sides and corners. It was a real work of art, but just looked like an old alder stump. The poets of all countries, especially our own, were copied there. Their essence was figured out, reviewed, cleaned up, concentrated and bottled. With sure instinct (as it's called when one doesn't want to say "genius") great-grandmother had taken the taste of this and that poet from nature, added a little witchcraft, and then she had his poetry bottled for eternity.

"Let me look!" said the man.

"But there are more important things to hear," said the bog witch.

"But we're right here by the cupboard," said the man and looked inside. "There are bottles of all sizes here. What's in that one? And that one there?"

"Here is what they call *Essence of May*," said the bog witch. "I haven't tried it, but I know that if you splash just a little on the floor, you'll immediately get a lovely forest lake with water lilies, rushes, and curled mint. Only two drops on an old notebook, even from the elementary grades, and the book turns into a fragrant fantasy play that can be produced with a scent

strong enough to put you to sleep. I'm sure it's meant as a
courtesy to me that it's labeled 'Bog Witch's Brewery.'"

"Here is the *Scandal Flagon*. It looks like it only has dirty
water in it, and it is dirty water, but with fizz powder of city-
chatter added: three portions of lies to two grains of truth. It
was stirred with a birch branch, but not from one soaked in salt
and used on a criminal's bloody back, or from one used by a
schoolmaster for spanking, but taken directly from the broom
that sweeps the gutters."

"And here is the bottle with pious poetry, to be used for
hymns. Every drop has the sound of hell's gates slamming shut
and is made of the blood and sweat of punishment. Some say
it's just bile of dove, but doves are the best and gentlest of creatures and have no bile. That's what people who know nothing
of zoology say."

There stood the mother of all bottles! It took over half the
cupboard—the bottle of *Everyday Stories*.[1] It was wrapped in
both pigskin and bladder so it wouldn't lose its strength. Each
nation could make its own soup here, depending on how you
turned and tipped the bottle. There was old German blood
stew with robber dumplings, and also thin crofter's soup with
real courtiers at the bottom, and a pat of philosophy floating
in the middle. There was English governess gruel and the
French *potage à la Kock*,[2] made from cock bones and sparrow
eggs. In Danish it's called cancan soup. But the best soup was
the Copenhagian, that's what the family said.

Tragedy was bottled in champagne bottles that start out with
a bang, as tragedy should. Comedy looked like fine sand that
could be thrown in people's eyes. That is to say, the finer comedy. The coarse kind was also in bottles, but these were made
up only of future playbills, where the name of the piece was the
most powerful. There were excellent comedy titles, such as
"Do you Dare to Spit in the Mechanism?" "One on the Jaw,"
"The Sweet Ass," and "She's Dead Drunk."

The man became lost in thought from all this, but the bog
witch was thinking ahead, and she wanted an end to it.

"You've looked long enough at that junk box," she said.
"Now you know what's here, but you still don't know the most

important thing you should know! The will-o'-the-wisps are in town! That's more important than poetry or fairy tales. I shouldn't say anything about it, but there must be some guidance, a fate, something that has overtaken me. Something has stuck in my throat the wrong way and must come out! The will-o'-the-wisps are in town! They are on the loose! Just watch out, people!"

"I don't understand a word you're saying," said the man.

"Please sit down there on the cupboard," she said. "But don't fall in and break the bottles. You know what's in them. I'll tell you about the great event; it just happened yesterday, and it's happened before. There are still three hundred and sixty four days to go. Well, I guess you know how many days are in a year?"

And the bog witch told the following:

"There was great excitement in the swamp yesterday! A big celebration! A little will-o'-the-wisp was born. Actually twelve of them were born, by that brood of will-o'-the-wisps who have the ability, if they wish, to appear as people, and act and rule among them as if they were born human beings. That's a big event in the swamp, and that's why all the will-o'-the-wisp males and females danced as little lights over the bog and meadows. There are female ones you see, but we're not talking about them. I sat on the cupboard there and had all twelve little newborns on my lap. They were shining like glowworms and had already begun to hop around. They grew bigger by the minute, so that before a quarter hour had passed, they were as big as their father or uncle. It's an old innate law and privilege that when the moon is in the precise position it was last night, and the wind blows as it blew yesterday, then all will-o'-the-wisps born at that hour and minute can become human beings. And each of them flits around for a whole year exercising their power. A will-o'-the-wisp can travel around the country and the world too, if he's not afraid to fall in the sea, or to be blown out in a great storm. He can get right inside a person, speak for him, and make all the movements he wants to. The will-o'-the-wisp can take any form, male or female, act in their minds, but with all his own nature, so he can get what he wants. In one year he must show that he can lead three hundred and sixty five people astray, and in grand fashion. He must lead them away from what's true and right. Then he'll obtain the highest a will-o'-the-wisp can aspire to: becoming a runner in front of the Devil's finest coach. He'll receive a glowing orange uniform and breathe fire from his throat. That's something a common will-o'-the-wisp can really lick his lips over. But there's also danger and a lot of worry for an ambitious will-o'-the-wisp who intends to play a part. If a person becomes aware of who he is, he can blow him away, and the will-o'-the-wisp is put out and must return to the swamp. And if the will-o'-the-wisp is moved by longing for his family before the year is over and betrays himself, then he's also out of it. He no longer burns clearly and soon goes out and can't be relit. And if the year ends without him leading three hundred and sixty five people away from truth, and what's good and beautiful, then he's sentenced to lie in a rotten tree and shine without moving, and that's the worst possible punishment for a lively will-o'-the-wisp. I knew all of this, and I told all of it to the twelve little will-o'-the-wisps, who were sitting on my lap. They were wild with joy. I told them that it was surest and most comfortable to give up glory and not do anything. But the young licks didn't want that. They already saw themselves in glowing orange with flames coming out of their mouths.

"'Stay with us!' said some of the elders.

"'Trick the humans!' said others. 'People are drying out our meadows, draining them. What will become of our descendants?'

"'We want to go blow blazes!' said the newborn will-o'-the-wisps, and so it was decided.

"They immediately had a minute-long dance. It couldn't have been shorter. The elf maidens swung around three times with all the others because they didn't want to appear haughty. They actually preferred to dance by themselves. Then it was time for the godparents' gifts. 'Skipping stones' as it's called. The presents flew like small stones across the bog water. Each of the elf maidens gave a piece of her veil. 'Take it!' they said, 'and then you will right away at a pinch know the higher forms of dance with the most difficult swings and turns. You'll have the proper carriage and can appear at the most elegant parties.' The nightjar[3] taught each of the young will-o'-the-wisps to say, 'Braaa, braaa, braaa' and to say it at the right times, and that's a big gift that pays off. The owl and the stork also gave something, but they said it wasn't worth mentioning so we won't talk about it.

"Just then King Valdemar on his wild hunt[4] came thundering over the bog, and when that company heard about the celebration, they sent a couple of fine dogs as gifts, dogs who could hunt with the wind and could surely carry a will-o'-the-wisp or three. Two old nightmares, who make a living by riding, were at the party. They taught the young will-o'-the-wisps the art of slipping through keyholes, which would open every door to them. They offered to convey the young will-o'-the-wisps to town, where they knew their way around. Usually they ride through the air on their own long manes, that they tie into knots to sit firmly on, but this time each of them straddled the back of a wild hunt dog and took the young Wills who were to trick and bewilder people on their laps. Swoosh! They were gone.

"That was all last night. Now the will-o'-the-wisps are in town. They have set to work. But how and what they are doing, you tell me! I have a pain in my big toe because of a weather wire that always tells me something is up!"

"But this is a whole fairy tale!" said the man.

"Well, it's really just the beginning of one," said the bog witch. "Can *you* tell me how the will-o'-the-wisps are romping about and carrying on, and in what shape they are appearing in order to lead people astray?"

"I do think," said the man, "that a whole novel could be written about the will-o'-the-wisps with twelve chapters, one for each will-o'-the-wisp; or maybe even better, an entire folk comedy!"

"You should write that!" said the bog witch, "or maybe it's best to let it go."

"Yes, that's more comfortable and pleasant," said the man. "Then you avoid being staked in the newspapers which is just as hard as it is for a will-o'-the-wisp to lie in a rotten tree, shining but unable to say a word!"

"It's all the same to me," said the bog witch. "But just let the others write, those who are able and those who are not. I'll give an old tap from my barrel that will open up the cupboard with poetry in bottles, and from there they can get what they're lacking. As for you, my good man, it seems to me that you have gotten enough ink on your fingers and have reached the age and maturity not to run after fairy tales every year, when there are much more important things to do here now. You must have understood what is going on, haven't you?"

"The will-o'-the-wisps are in town!" said the man. "I have heard it, and I understand it! But what do you want me to do about it? I'll just be raked over the coals if I see one and tell people: Look! There goes a will-o'-the-wisp in the guise of an honest man."

"They also wear skirts!" said the bog witch. "The will-o'-the-wisp can assume all shapes and appear in all places. He goes to church, not for the Lord's sake, but maybe he's gone into the minister! He speaks on election day, not for the country's sake, but just for his own. He's an artist, both in the painter's paint jar and the theater's make-up jar, but when he gets complete power, then there's the end of it: the jar's empty. I talk and talk, but I must get out of my throat what's stuck there, even though it harms my own family. I'm going to be the savior of humanity. It's truly not something I can help, and I'm not doing it for the sake of a medal. But I'm doing the craziest thing I could—I'm telling a poet, so then the whole town will soon know about it!"

"The town won't pay any attention," said the man. "It won't affect a single person. They'll all think I'm telling a fairy tale when I tell them in complete seriousness 'The will-o'-the-wisps are in town,' said the bog witch. 'Beware!'"

NOTES

1. Reference to *En Hverdagshistorie* (1828; *A Story of Everyday Life*) by Thomasine Gyllembourg; the novella gave its name to a whole genre

of stories about contemporary Copenhagen. Andersen did not like the genre.
2. Reference to Paul de Kock (1793–1871), French author of popular novels of Parisian life.
3. In Danish the word the nightjar teaches the will-o'-the-wisps to say is *bra*, which means "fine" or "good."
4. According to legend, fourteenth-century King Valdemar mocked God by preferring hunting to heaven. Hence he was condemned to ride and hunt the Danish countryside every night.

THE PIXIE AND THE GARDENER'S WIFE

YOU KNOW THE PIXIE, but do you know *Madame*, the gardener's wife? She was well-read, knew verses by heart, and could even write them easily herself. Only the rhyming, the "riveting together" as she put it, sometimes gave her a little trouble. She had the gift of writing well, and the gift of gab. She could certainly have been a minister, or at least a minister's wife.

"The earth is beautiful in its Sunday dress," she said, and she had put that thought in a composition, including "riveting." She had written it into a ballad that was both beautiful and long.

Her cousin, the seminarian, Mr. Kisserup—his name is really not relevant—was visiting the gardener's, and heard her poem. He said that it really did him good. "You have soul, *Madame!*" he told her.

"What nonsense!" said the gardener. "Don't go putting *that* idea into her head. A wife should be a body, a decent body, and watch her kettles so the porridge doesn't get crusty."

"What gets crusty I remove with a wooden spoon," said *Madame*, "and I take the crusty from you with a little kiss! One would think that you only thought about cabbages and potatoes, but you love the flowers!" And then she kissed him. "Flowers are the soul," she said.

"Watch your kettle!" he said and went out into the garden. That was his "kettle," and he took care of it.

But the seminarian sat and talked to *Madame*. In his own way he held almost a little sermon over her lovely words, "The earth is beautiful."

"The earth is beautiful. We were told to subdue it and be its masters. One person does so by his spirit, another with his body. One person comes into the world as astonishment's exclamation mark, another like a dash, so you really can ask what he's doing here. One becomes a bishop, another just a poor seminarian, but it's all done wisely. The earth is beautiful and always in its Sunday best! That was a thought-provoking poem of yours, *Madame*, full of feeling and geography."

"You have soul, Mr. Kisserup!" said *Madame*, "a deep soul, I assure you. One feels so much clarity after talking with you."

And they continued talking, just as nicely and well as before. But in the kitchen there was also someone talking, and that was the pixie, the little grey-clothed pixie with the red stocking cap. You know him! The pixie sat in the kitchen and was watching the kettle. He talked, but nobody heard him except the big black pussycat, "Creamsneaker," as he was called by *Madame*.

The pixie was furious at her because he knew she didn't believe that he was real. Granted, she had never seen him, but with all her reading she must have known that he existed and should therefore have given him a little attention. It never occurred to her to put out so much as a spoonful of porridge for him at Christmas. All his ancestors had gotten that, and from *madames* who didn't read at all. The porridge had been swimming in butter and cream. The cat got wet whiskers just hearing about it.

"She calls me a concept!" said the pixie. "It's beyond my conception that she can say that. She completely repudiates me! I overheard that, and now I've been listening again. She is sitting in there gossiping with that boy-beating seminarian. I'm with father: 'Watch your kettle!' She's not doing that, so now I'll make it boil over."

And the pixie blew on the fire. It flamed up and burned. "Surri-rurri-rupp!" There the kettle boiled over!

"Now I'm going in to pick holes in father's socks," said the pixie. "I'll unravel a big hole in the toe and the heel, so there'll be something to darn, if she doesn't start sprouting poetry then. Darn poet lady—darn father's socks!"

The cat sneezed at that. He had a cold, even though he always wore a fur coat.

"I've opened the pantry door," said the pixie. "There's some boiled cream there, as thick as flour porridge. If you don't want to lick it up, I will!"

"Since I will get the blame and the beating, I may as well lick the cream," said the cat.

"First eating, then beating," said the pixie. "But now I'm going to the seminarian's room to hang his suspenders on the mirror and put his socks in the water basin. He'll think the punch was too strong, and that his head's swimming. Last night I sat on the wood pile by the doghouse. I really enjoy teasing the watchdog. I let my legs hang over and dangle. The dog couldn't reach them, no matter how high he jumped. It made him mad. He barked and barked. My legs dangled and dangled. It was a riot, and woke the seminarian up. He peered out three times, but he didn't see me, even though he was wearing glasses. He always wears them when he sleeps."

"Miaow when the mistress comes," said the cat. "I can't hear so well. I'm sick today."

"You're lick-sick!" said the pixie. "Lick away! Lick the sickness away! But dry your whiskers so the cream doesn't stick to them. Now I'll go eavesdrop."

And the pixie stood by the door, and the door was ajar. There was no one in the living room except *Madame* and the seminarian. They were talking about "gifts of the spirit." Gifts that should be set above the pots and pans of every household, as the seminarian so beautifully put it.

"Mr. Kisserup," said *Madame*. "In this connection I will show you something that I have never shown another human soul, least of all a man: my little poems, although some of them are quite long. I have called them *Poems of a Danneqvinde*.[1] I am so very fond of old Danish words."

"And they should be kept and used!" agreed the seminarian. "The language must be cleansed of all German."

"I do that," said *Madame.* "You'll never hear me say *Kleiner* or *Butterteig.* I say *donuts* and *butter pastry.*"

And she took a notebook out of a drawer. It had a light-green cover with two ink spots on it.

"There's a great deal of seriousness in this book," she said. "I have the strongest sense for tragedy. Here's 'The Sigh in the Night,' 'My Sunset,' and 'When I married Klemmensen.' Of course, that's my husband. You can skip that one. But it's deeply felt and thought-out. The best one is called 'The Housewife's Duties.' They're all very sad. That's where my talent lies. Only one poem is humorous. There are some cheerful thoughts. It's possible to have those too, of course. Thoughts about—you mustn't laugh at me! Thoughts about being a poetess! This is only known to myself, my drawer, and now you too, Mr. Kisserup. I love poetry. It comes over me. It teases me, rules, and has me in its power. I have expressed it with the poem titled 'Little Pixie.' I'm sure you know the old folk belief about the house pixie, who's always up to tricks around the house. I have imagined that I am the house and that poetry, the feelings in me, is the pixie, the spirit that controls me. I have sung about his power and greatness in 'Little Pixie,' but you must give me your hand and swear that you'll never breathe a word of this to my husband or anyone. Read it aloud, so I can tell if you understand my handwriting."

And the seminarian read, and *Madame* listened, and the little pixie listened. He was eavesdropping, you know, and had just come in time to hear the title: "Little Pixie."

"Why, it's about me!" he said. "What could she have written about me? Well, I'll pinch her, pinch her eggs, pinch her chickens, and chase the fat off the fatted calf! You'd better look out, *Madame!*"

And he eavesdropped with pursed lips, but everything he heard about the pixie's splendor and strength, and his power over the gardener's wife made him smile more and more. She meant poetry, you know, but he took it literally, from the title. His eyes glistened with happiness. Quite a noble expression appeared around the corners of his mouth. He lifted his heels and stood on his toes and became a whole inch taller than before. He was delighted with what was said about "Little Pixie."

"*Madame* has soul, and she is very cultured. How I have misjudged that woman! She has put me in her rhyme. It will be printed and read! I won't let the cat drink her cream anymore. I'll do it myself! One drinks less than two, and that's a savings I'll introduce to respect and honor *Madame.*"

"He's sure like a human being, that pixie!" said the old cat. "Just one sweet miaow from the mistress, a miaow about himself, and he immediately changes his mind. She is clever, *Madame.*"

But she wasn't clever. It was the pixie who was human.

If you can't understand this story, ask about it, but don't ask the pixie or the *Madame.*

NOTE

1. *Danneqvinde* is an old spelling of the word for "Danish woman."

THE PUPPETEER

THERE WAS AN ELDERLY man on the steamship with such a contented face. If it wasn't lying, he must have been the happiest man on earth. He was too, he said. I heard it from his own mouth. He was Danish, a countryman of mine, and a traveling theater manager. He was a puppeteer, and had his whole personnel with him in a big box. His innate cheerfulness had been strengthened by a technology student, and from that experiment he had become completely happy. I didn't understand him right away, but then he told me the whole story, and here it is.

"It happened in Slagelse," he said. "I gave a performance at the coach inn and had an excellent audience, all young except for a couple of old ladies. Then a fellow who looked like a student, dressed in black, comes and sits down. He laughs in all the right places and claps when he should. He was an exceptional spectator! I had to know who he was, and then I hear that he's a graduate candidate from the Polytechnic Institute, sent out to instruct the people in the provinces. My show was over at eight o'clock because children have to go to bed early of course, and you have to be considerate of the public. At nine o'clock the candidate started his lecture and experiments, and then I was his spectator. It was remarkable to hear and see. Most of it was Greek to me, as the saying goes, but I did think this: If we humans can find out all this, we must also be able to exist longer than till we're put in the ground. He just did small miracles, but all of it went slick as a whistle, and straight from nature. In the time of Moses and the Prophets such a technological student would have become a wise man of the land, and in the Middle Ages he would have been burned at the stake. I didn't sleep all night, and when I gave another performance the next night and saw that the student was there again, I was really in a good mood. An actor once told me that when he played a lover he thought about just one person in the audience. He played to her and forgot the rest of the spectators. The technology candidate was my 'her'—the only one I performed for.

"When the performance was over, all the puppets took their curtain call, and the technology student invited me to have a glass of wine with him in his room. He talked about my play, and I talked about his science, and I think we both enjoyed them equally, but I got the best of it because there was so much in his presentation that he couldn't himself explain; for example, the fact that a piece of iron that goes through a coil becomes magnetic. What is this? The spirit comes over it, but where does it come from? It seems to me it's like human beings here on earth. God lets them fall through the coil of time, and the spirit comes over them, and you have a Napoleon, a Luther, or another person like that. 'The whole world is a series of miracles,' said the candidate, 'but we are so used to them that we take them for granted.' And he talked and explained, and at last it was as if he lifted my skull, and I confessed truly that if I weren't already an old fellow, I would at once go to the Polytechnic Institute and learn to see the world with a fine-toothed comb, and I'd do that even though I was one of the happiest of men."

"'One of the happiest!' he said, and it was as if he tasted the words. 'Are you happy?' he asked. 'Yes,' I answered, 'I'm happy and I'm welcomed in all the towns where I come with my company. It's true that there's one wish that sometimes comes over me like a nightmare and disrupts my good mood, and that's to become a theater manager for a real live troupe of human beings.' 'You wish that your puppets would come to life. You wish they would become real actors,' he said, 'and you yourself the director. You think you would be completely happy then?' He didn't believe it, but I did, and we talked back and forth, and we both kept our own opinion, but we toasted each other, and the wine was very good. But there had to be something magical in it because otherwise the whole story would simply be that I got drunk. It wasn't that because I saw quite clearly. There was a kind of sunshine in the room, shining out of the technological candidate's face, and it made me think about the old gods with their eternal youth, when they walked the earth. I told him that, and he smiled, and I would have sworn that he was a disguised god, or one of their family. And that's what he was! My highest wish would be granted, the puppets become real, and I would be a director of people. We drank to it. He packed all my puppets in the wooden case, tied it to my back, and then he had me fall through a coil. I can still hear how I fell. I was lying on the floor—this is all true—and the entire company jumped out of the case. The spirit had come over all of them, and every puppet had become a remarkable artist— they said so themselves—and I was the director."

"Everything was ready for the first performance. All the actors wanted to talk to me, and the audience too. The dancer said that if she didn't get to pirouette, the performance would be a flop. She was the star of the show and wanted to be treated that way. The puppet who played the empress wanted to be treated like the empress off the stage as well because otherwise she would be out of practice. He who had the part of coming in with a letter was just as self-important as the star lover, since he said that there were no small actors, only small parts. Then the hero demanded that all his lines should be exit lines, since they always got the applause. The primadonna would only perform under red lights—not blue ones—because they were the most becoming to her. It was like flies in a bottle, and as the director, I was in the middle of the bottle. I lost my breath, I lost my wits, and I was as miserable as a person can be. These were new types of people I was among, and I wished that I had them all back in the box, and that I had never become a director. I told them straight out that they really were all just puppets, and then they beat me to death. Then I was lying on the bed in my room. How I got there from the technological student's room he must know, because I don't. The moon was shining in on the floor where the puppet case had tipped over, and all the puppets were spread around, big and little ones, all of them. But I didn't waste any time. I jumped out of bed and got them all in the box, some on their heads and some on their feet. I slammed down the lid and then sat down on the box. It was quite a sight, can you see it? I can. 'Now you can stay in there,' I said, 'and never again will I wish that you were flesh and blood!' I was in such a good mood, and the happiest person. The technological candidate had purified me. I sat there in pure bliss and fell asleep on the case, and in the morning—it was actually in the afternoon, but I slept so strangely long in the morning—I was still sitting there, happy, because I had learned that the only thing I'd ever wished for had been stupid. I asked about the technological candidate, but he was gone, like the Greek or Roman gods. And from that time on, I have been the happiest of men. I am a happy manager for my personnel doesn't argue with me, nor does the public. They enjoy themselves thoroughly. I freely put together the pieces myself, and take the best parts of the plays I want, and nobody bothers about it. I produce pieces that are now despised on the stage, but that the audience flocked to and cried over thirty years ago. I give them to the young ones, and they cry like father and mother did. I do *Johanna von Montfaucon*[1] and *Dyveke*,[2] but I shorten them because the young ones don't care for a lot of love nonsense. They want it sad but quick. I have traveled up and down Denmark, back and forth, and I know everyone, and they all know me. Now I'm going to Sweden, and if I do well there and earn good money, then I'll become a Pan-Scandinavian.³ Otherwise, I won't. I can tell you this since you're my countryman."

And I, as his countryman, am repeating it immediately, of course, just for the fun of telling it.

NOTES

1. Five-act tragedy by German playwright August von Kotzebue (1761–1819), translated and adapted by N. T. Bruun, with music by Claus Schall; it was performed for the first time at Copenhagen's Royal Theater on April 29, 1804.
2. Tragedy by Ole Johan Samsøe; it was performed for the first time at Copenhagen's Royal Theater on January 30, 1796.
3. Reference to the movement called Scandinavianism, which called for a closer union between Norway, Sweden, and Denmark; the movement was particularly active in the 1840s and 1850s.

"SOMETHING"

"I WANT TO BE something!" said the eldest of five brothers. "I want to be of some use in the world, be it ever so humble a position. As long as I am doing something good, it will be something. I will make bricks. You can't do without them! Then I will have done something anyway!"

"But an all-too-little something!" said the second brother. "What you're doing is as good as nothing. It's just a helping job, something that can be done by a machine. No, become a mason instead. That's something I want to be. That's a trade! With that I'll get into a guild and become a middle-class citizen. I'll have my own banner and my own public house. If I do well, I'll be able to have journeymen, become a master, and my wife will become a Mrs. Master Mason! That is something!"

"That's absolutely nothing!" said the third. "That's completely outside of the middle-class structure, and there are many classes in town that are above the master Masons. You can be a worthy man, but as a master you are only what is called a 'common' worker. No! I know something better. I want to be a builder, and get into the artistic area, the theoretical, and rise up to the highest in the realm of the mind. Of course I have to start at the bottom. I might as well admit it straight out. I have to begin as a carpenter's apprentice and wear a cap, even though I'm used to a silk hat, and run to get beer and spirits for the lowly journeymen. They'll be familiar and say "du" to me, and that's bad, but I'll just imagine that it's all a masquerade, and the masks will come off tomorrow—that is to say when I become a journeyman and go off on my own, it'll be no business of theirs. I'll go to the academy and learn to draw. I'll become an architect! That's something! That's something big! I can become both high-born and well-born with a little something more in front and back of my name, and I'll build and build like those who came before me. That's something you can always rely on, and all of it is *something*!"

"But that's something I don't care about!" said the fourth. "I don't want to ride in the wake, or be a copy of something. I want to be a genius, and more skillful than all of you! I'll shape a new style, create the idea for a building that fits the country's climate, materials, the national spirit, the developments of our age, and then another story for my own genius!"

"But if the climate and the materials aren't any good," said the fifth, "that would be too bad, and it would have an impact. National spirit can also easily develop into something affected, and the developments of the age can often cause you to run riot, just as adolescents often do. I can see that none of you will actually become something, no matter how much you may think so yourselves. But do as you want. I won't copy you. I'll place myself outside and criticize what you do. There is always something wrong with everything. I will point it out and discuss it. That is something!"

And that's what he did, and people said about the fifth brother: "He's really something! He's got a good head, but he doesn't do anything!"—Yet because of that he *was* something.

See that's just a little story, and there's no end to it as long as the world goes on.

Well, what happened to the five brothers? What we've heard

wasn't anything, was it? Listen further. It's really a complete fairy tale.

The oldest brother, who made bricks, noticed that a little penny rolled out of each brick when it was finished. Only a copper penny, but many small copper pennies piled on top of each other become a shiny dollar, and wherever you knock on the door with that, whether it's at the baker, the butcher, or the tailor—yes, at all of them—the doors fly open, and you get what you need. See, that's what came from the bricks. Even though some fell to pieces or broke in the middle, they could be used too.

Up on the embankment a poor woman, old mother Margrethe, so badly wanted to slap up a little house. She got all the brick pieces and a couple of unbroken ones because the oldest brother had a good heart, even if he was only a brick maker. The poor woman built the house herself. It was narrow, and the one window was crooked. The door was much too low, and the straw roof could have been better laid, but it gave shelter against wind and weather, and you could see way out to sea, which broke against the dike in its might. The salty drops of water sprayed over the whole house, which was still standing when he who had made the bricks was dead and gone.

The second brother really knew the art of building. Well, he was trained for it. When he finished his apprenticeship, he packed his knapsack and sang the song of the craftsman:

> *While young I can the world traverse,*
> *And houses build out there.*
> *My craftsmanship becomes my purse,*
> *My youthfulness my flair.*
> *And if, again, I see home's soil*
> *My sweetheart's told "I'm able"*
> *For an active craftsman it's no toil*
> *To populate the table!*

And he did. When he came back and became a Master mason, he built house after house—a whole street full. When they were finished and looked good, they gave the city esteem, and then the houses built a little house for him that was to be his own. But how could houses build, you ask? Well, just ask them. They won't answer, but people will answer, and they'll say, "Yes indeed, that street built him his house!" It was small and had a dirt floor, but when he danced on it with his bride, the floor became shiny and polished. And a flower grew from every brick in the wall. That was just as good as expensive wallpaper. It was a lovely house and a happy couple. The banner of the guild waved outside and the journeymen and apprentices shouted "Hurrah!" Well, that was something! And then he died, and that was also something!

Then there was the architect, the third brother, who had been an apprentice first, worn a cap and run errands in the town, but from the academy he had worked his way up to a master builder "high-born" and "well-born." If the houses in the street had built a house for his brother who was the mason, now the street itself was named after the architect and the most beautiful house in the street was his. That was something, and he was something—and with a long title in front of and back of his name. His children were called aristocratic, and when he died, his wife was a widow of distinguished social status. That is something! And his name was up on the street sign and always on everyone's lips as the street name—Well, that is something!

And then there was the genius, the fourth brother, who wanted to build something new, something different with a top story for himself. Well, it collapsed, and he fell and broke his neck—but he had a beautiful funeral, with guild banners and music, flowers on the street over the pavement, and flowery notices in the paper. There were three sermons for him, each longer than the one before, and that would have pleased him, because he liked being talked about. He got a monument on his grave, only one story, but even that's something!

Now he was dead, like the other three, but the last one, the critic, outlived them all and that was only right, because then he got the final word, and it was of great importance to him to have the last word. He's the one who had the good head, as everyone said! Then his time came too, and he died and went to the Pearly Gates. People always arrive there two by two, and there he was standing with another soul who also really wanted to get in. It was no one other than old mother Margrethe from the house by the dike.

"It must be for the sake of contrast that I and this miserable soul should arrive here at the same time," said the critic. "So who are you, Granny? Do you want to get in here too?"

And the old woman curtsied as best she could. She thought it was St. Peter himself who was speaking to her. "I'm just a poor old woman without any family. Old Margrethe from the house by the dike."

"What have you done, and what have you accomplished down there?"

"I haven't accomplished anything at all in this world that can open up the door for me here! It would be a true act of grace if I were to be allowed inside the gate."

"How did you come to leave the world?" he asked her to make conversation about something, since he was bored standing there and waiting.

"Well, how I left it, I don't know! I've been sick and ailing for the last few years, so I guess I wasn't able to tolerate crawling out of bed to go out in the cold and frost outdoors. It's a hard winter, you know, but now I have escaped it. There were a few days when there was no wind, but bitterly cold, as Your Reverence probably knows. The ice had formed as far out from the beach as one could see. All the people from town went out on the ice and were skating and dancing too, I think. There was music and food and drink out there. I could hear it from where I was lying in my simple room. Evening was approaching, the moon was up, but it was a new moon. From my bed through the window I could see way out over the shore, and right there between sky and sea a strange white cloud appeared. I lay and looked at it, looked at the black dot in the middle of it that got bigger and bigger, and then I knew what it meant. I am old and experienced, but that sign you don't see often. I recognized it and felt a horror! I had seen that thing coming twice before in my life and knew that there would be a terrible storm with a spring tide that would rush over the poor people out there who were drinking and running and frolicking.

Young and old, the whole town was out there. Who would warn
them if no one there saw and recognized what I now knew? I
became so afraid, and I felt more life in me than I had felt for
a long time! I got out of the bed and went to the window, but
I couldn't manage to get any further. I did get the window
open. I could see the people running and jumping out there
on the ice, see the neat flags and hear how the boys shouted
"hurrah," and girls and boys sang. They were having a good
time, but the white cloud with the black bag inside rose higher
and higher! I shouted as loudly as I could, but no one heard
me. I was too far away. Soon the storm would break out, the ice
would break, and everyone out there would sink through without hope of rescue. They couldn't hear me. I wasn't able to
reach them. If only I could get them to come on land! Then
God gave me the idea of lighting fire to my bed, letting the
whole house burn up, rather than that all those people should
die so wretchedly. I lit the candle, saw the red flame—I was
able to get out the door, but there I lay—I couldn't get any further. The flames shot out behind me and out the window and
across the roof. They saw me from out there, and they all ran
as fast as they could to help me—poor old me—whom they
thought was trapped inside. Every one of them came running.
I heard them coming, but I also heard the sudden roaring in
the air. I heard the rumbling that sounded like cannon fire.
The spring tide lifted the ice, and it broke in pieces, but they
reached the dike where the sparks were flying over me. They
were all safe and sound, although I must not have been able to
stand the cold and the fright, and so here I am at the Pearly
Gates. They say they can be opened even for a poor person like
me. Now I don't have a house anymore there on the dike, although that doesn't gain me entrance here."

Then the Pearly Gates opened, and the angel let the old
woman in. A straw from her bed fell outside the gates. It was
one of those that had laid in her bed and that she had lit to
save the many people, and it turned to the purest gold, but a
gold that grew and that twined itself into the most beautiful
decorations.

"See, that's what the poor woman brought," said the angel.

"What are you bringing? Well, I know already that you didn't accomplish anything. You didn't even make a brick! If you could just go back and bring at least a brick that you had made, it would count for something. It wouldn't be any good, since you made it, but if you made it with good will it would at least be something. But you can't go back, and I can't do anything for you!"

Then the poor soul, the woman from the embankment, pleaded for him. "His brother made and gave me all the bricks and broken bits that I slapped up my miserable little house with. That was a lot for a poor wretch like me. Can't all those bits and broken bricks count as one brick's worth for him? That would be an act of mercy, and he needs it, and this is the home of mercy, after all."

"Your brother, the one you called the poorest, whose honest work you considered lowest, gives you his heavenly mite. You will not be turned away. You will be allowed to stand out here and think things over, try to promote your life down there, but you won't get in before your good deeds have accomplished— *something!*"

"I could have said that better," thought the critic, but he didn't say it out loud, and that was already really *something*.

WHAT ONE CAN THINK UP

THERE WAS A YOUNG man who was studying to be a writer. He wanted to become one by Easter, get married, and live by his writing. He knew it was just a question of hitting on something. But he couldn't think of anything. He was born too late. Everything had been examined before he was born. Everything had been written about.

"Those lucky people who were born a thousand years ago!" he said. "They could become immortal! Even those born a hundred years ago were lucky. There was still something to write about then. Now there's nothing in the world left to write about, so what can I write about?"

He mulled and stewed over it to the point that he became

ill, the miserable fellow. No doctor could help him, but maybe the wise woman could. She lived in a little house by the gate that she opened up for those driving or riding on the road. But she was able to open much more than the gate. She was wiser than the doctor, who drove in his own coach and paid a tax because of his rank.

"I must go out and see her," said the young man.

The house she lived in was small and neat, but drab to look at. There wasn't a tree or a flower. There was a beehive outside the door—very useful! There was a little potato patch—very useful! There was also a ditch with blackthorn bushes that had flowered and set berries—bitter berries that purse the lips if they're tasted before frost.

"It's like an image of our prosaic times, I see here," thought the young man, and that was a thought. A pearl he found by the wise woman's door.

"Write it up!" she said. "Half a loaf is better than no bread. I know why you're here. You can't think of anything, but you want to be a writer by Easter."

"Everything's been written!" he said. "Our times aren't like the old days."

"No!" said the woman. "In the old days wise women were burned at the stake, and poets walked around with shrunken bellies and holes in their sleeves. Our times are good times—they're the very best! But you aren't looking at it the right way, nor have you sharpened your hearing. I'm sure you never say the Lord's prayer in the evening either. There are all sorts of things to write and tell about here for those who are able. You can take stories from the earth's plants and crops, scoop them up from the running and standing water, but you have to understand, understand how to catch a sunbeam! Now try on my glasses, put my hearing trumpet in your ear, pray to God, and stop thinking about yourself."

The last part was very hard, and more than a wise woman could ask for.

He got the glasses and the ear trumpet and was positioned in the middle of the potato patch. She put a big potato in his hand. It was ringing. It rang out a song with words—the potato's history—interesting. An everyday story in ten parts. Ten lines would have been enough.

And what did the potato sing about?

It sang about itself and its family—the potato's arrival in Europe, and the lack of appreciation they had experienced and suffered before they, like now, were recognized as a bigger blessing than a nugget of gold.

"We were distributed at the city hall in all cities by order of the King. Our great importance was proclaimed, but people didn't believe it and didn't even understand how to plant us. One man dug a hole and threw a whole half bushel of potatoes into it. Another stuck a potato into the ground here and there and waited for them to shoot up like a tree that he could shake potatoes from. And there was growth, flowers, and watery fruit, but everything withered away. No one thought that the blessing lay under the ground—the potatoes. Well, we have had our trials and sufferings, that is to say, our ancestors—they and us, it makes no difference. What stories!"

"Well, that's enough," said the woman. "Look at the blackthorn!"

"We also have close relatives in the potato's homeland," said the blackthorn bushes, "further north than they grew. Norwegians from Norway sailed west through fogs and storms to an unknown land where under the ice and snow, they found herbs and greenery and bushes with wine's dark blue berries—sloeberries. They froze to ripe grapes, and so do we. And that country was called Vineland, Greenland, Sloethornland."

"That's a very romantic story," said the young man.

"Come along," said the wise woman and led him over to the beehive. He looked into it. What a hustle and bustle! There were bees in all the hallways beating their wings to bring a healthy breeze into the entire big factory. That was their job. From outside bees born with baskets on their legs came bringing flower pollen. It was shaken off, sorted, and made into honey and wax. They came and went. The Queen bee wanted to fly too, but then they would all have to fly along, and it wasn't time for that yet. But since she wanted to fly, they bit the wings from her majesty, and then she had to stay put.

"Climb up on the embankment," said the wise woman. "Take a look at the road, and all the folks there!"

"What a swarming throng!" said the young man, "Story upon story! Humming and buzzing! It's too much for me! I'm going back!"

"No, go straight ahead!" said the woman. "Go right into the teeming crowd. Have an eye for them, and an ear—and yes—a heart too. Then you'll soon think of something. But before you go, I must have my glasses and ear trumpet back." And she took both of them.

"Now I can't see anything," said the young man, "and I can't hear any longer."

"Well, then you can't be a writer by Easter," said the wise woman.

"But when then?" he asked.

"Neither by Easter nor Pentecost! You can't learn imagination."

"But what shall I do to make my living by writing?"

"Oh, you can manage that by Shrove Tuesday! Become a critic! Knock down the poets. Knock down their writings—that's just like knocking them. Just don't be over-awed. Hit at them without ceremony. You'll get enough dough to support both yourself and a wife!"

"You've hit upon the very thing!" said the young man, and he knocked down all the poets because he couldn't become one himself.

We heard this from the wise woman. She knows what people can think up.

THE MOST INCREDIBLE THING

HE WHO COULD DO the most incredible thing was to have the King's daughter and half the kingdom.

The young people—well, the old ones too—strained all their thoughts, tendons, and muscles over this. Two died from over-eating, and one drank himself to death. All trying to do the most incredible thing according to their taste, but that wasn't how it was supposed to be done. The little street urchins practiced spitting on their own backs. They thought that was the most incredible thing.

On a pre-assigned day everyone was to produce what they had to show as the most incredible thing. The judges were children from the age of three all the way up to folks in their nineties. There was a whole exhibition of incredible things, but everyone soon agreed that the most incredible was a huge clock in a case, remarkably artistic both inside and out. At the striking of the hour, lifelike images appeared to show what time had struck. There were twelve performances in all with moving figures and song and speech.

"This is the most incredible thing!" people said.

The clock struck one, and *Moses* was standing on a mountain writing the first commandment on a tablet: "You shall have no other gods before me."

The clock struck two and the *Garden of Eden* appeared, where Adam and Eve met. They were both happy despite not owning so much as a clothes closet. They didn't need it either.

At the stroke of three the *three wise men* appeared. One was as black as coal, but he couldn't help it. The sun had blackened him. They carried incense and precious objects.

At four o'clock, the seasons of the year came out. *Spring* with a cuckoo on a leafed-out beech branch. *Summer* with a grasshopper on a ripe ear of corn. The *autumn* with an empty stork's nest for the bird had flown away. And *winter* with an old crow that could tell stories in the stove corner, old memories.

When the clock struck five the five senses were there. *Sight* came as a maker of eye glasses. *Hearing* was a coppersmith. *Smell* was selling violets and woodruff. *Taste* was a cook, and *Feeling* was a funeral director with mourning crepe hanging down to his heels.

The clock struck six. A gambler was sitting there throwing dice. The die landed with the highest number up—it was six.

Then came the seven *days of the week* or the seven *deadly sins*. People couldn't agree which they were, but of course they belong together and aren't easy to tell apart.

Then a choir of monks sang eight o'clock matins.

The *nine muses* followed at the stroke of nine. One worked at the observatory, one at the historical archives, and the rest belonged to the theater.

At ten *Moses* came back again with the tablet of laws. Now all God's commandments were there, ten of them.

The clock struck again and little boys and girls hopped and ran around. They were playing a game and singing along: "Four plus seven, the clock strikes eleven," and that's what it was.

Then twelve struck and the night watchman came out wearing his hat with ear-flaps and carrying his spiked mace. He sang the old song of the watchman: "It was at midnight that our savior was born," and as he sang roses grew and turned into heads of angels, borne by rainbow colored wings.

It was lovely to hear and beautiful to see. The whole thing was an exceptional work of art. Everybody said it was the most incredible thing.

The artist was a young man, good-hearted and as happy as a child. He was a faithful friend and helpful to his impoverished parents. He deserved the princess and half the kingdom.

The day of decision had arrived. The whole town was decorated, and the princess sat on the throne of the land. A new curled horsehair stuffing had been added, but that didn't make it any more comfy or classy. The judges looked around slyly at the one who was going to win. He stood there confident and happy. His happiness was assured, for he had made the most incredible thing.

Just then a tall, strong strapping fellow yelled, "No, I'm going to do that now! I'm the man to do the most incredible thing!" And then he swung a big axe at the work of art.

"Crunch, crash, smash!" There the whole thing lay. Wheels and springs were flying all over. It was completely destroyed!

"*I* was able to do that!" said the man. "*My* strikes have struck down his, and struck down all of you. I have done the most incredible thing!"

"Destroying such a work of art!" said the judges. "Yes, that really was the most incredible thing."

All the people agreed, and so then he was to have the

princess and half the kingdom, because the law's the law, even an incredible one.

From the embankments and all the town's towers it was proclaimed that the wedding was to take place. The princess was not at all happy about it, but she looked beautiful and was magnificently dressed. The church was ablaze with candles, late in the evening when it looks best. Young noble maidens of the town sang and attended the bride. Knights sang and attended the groom. He strutted as if he could never snap.

Then the singing stopped, and it was so quiet that you could have heard a pin drop. In the middle of that silence the big church doors flew open with a rumbling and tumbling—"boom!" The entire clock mechanism came marching right up the church aisle and stood between the bride and the bridegroom. People who are dead can't walk again, we know that very well, but works of art can haunt. The body was broken, but not the spirit. The spirit of art was spooking, and that was no spoofing matter.

The work of art looked just like it had when it was whole and untouched. The hours started to strike, one after the other, all the way to twelve, and the figures swarmed forth. First came *Moses*, and it was as if flames shone from his forehead. He threw the heavy stone laws tablets on the bridegroom's feet which pinned them to the church floor.

"I can't pick them up again!" *Moses* said. "You chopped my arms off! Stay as you are!"

Then came *Adam and Eve, the three wise men from the East*, and *the four seasons*. All of them hurled unpleasant truths at him. "Shame on you!"

But he wasn't ashamed.

All of the figures that every hour had at its disposal stepped out of the clock, and all grew to a tremendous size. There almost wasn't room for the real people. And when at the stroke of twelve, the watchman stepped out with his hat and spiked mace, there was a singular commotion. The watchman went right up to the bridegroom and struck him on the head with the spiked mace.

"Lie there!" he said. "Tit for tat! We are avenged, and so is our master! We're leaving!"

And the whole great work of art disappeared. But the candles changed into big flowers of light throughout the church, and the gilded stars on the ceiling sent out long, clear rays. The organ played by itself. Everybody said that it was the most incredible thing they had ever experienced.

"Will you summon the right one?" said the princess. "The one who made the artwork—he shall be my husband and master."

And he stood in the church with all the people as his attendants. Everyone rejoiced, and everyone blessed him. There wasn't a person who was jealous. And that was really the most incredible thing!

AUNTIE TOOTHACHE

WHERE DID WE GET this story?

—Would you like to know?

We got it from the waste barrel in the store with all the old papers in it. Many good and rare books have ended up at the grocer's and the greengrocer's—not for reading, but as useful articles. They need paper to make paper cones for starch and coffee, and paper to wrap salt herring, butter, and cheese in. Handwritten materials can be used too.

Often things go into the barrel that shouldn't go there.

I know a greengrocer's apprentice, son of a grocer. He has advanced from the basement to the first floor store. He's well-read, well-read in wrapping paper, both printed and handwritten. He has an interesting collection, including several important documents from the wastepaper baskets of one or another much too busy and absent-minded official, several confidential letters from girlfriend to girlfriend: scandalous stories which must not be revealed—not spoken of by anyone. He is a living salvage operation for a considerable amount of literature, and he has a large working area. He has both his parents' and employer's stores and has saved many a book or page of a book that probably deserve to be read twice.

He has shown me his collection of printed and written materials from the barrel, most of it from the grocer's. There were a couple of pages of a good-sized notebook, and the especially beautiful clear handwriting drew my attention immediately.

"The student wrote this," he said. "The student who lived across the street and died a month ago. They say he suffered a lot from toothaches. It's quite amusing to read, but there's only a little of it left now. There was a whole book plus some. My parents gave the student's landlady half a pound of green soap for it. Here is what I've saved of it."

I borrowed it, and read it, and now I'll tell it. The title was:

AUNTIE TOOTHACHE

I.

—My aunt gave me candies when I was little. My teeth withstood it and weren't ruined. Now I'm older and have become a college student, and she still spoils me with sweets. She says that I'm a poet.

I have something of the poet in me, but not enough. Often when I'm walking the city streets, it seems to me like I'm in a big library. The houses are bookcases and each story a shelf with books. *There* stands an everyday story. *There* a good old fashioned comedy. There are scientific works about all kinds of subjects. *Here* smut and good literature. I can fantasize and philosophize about all that literature.

There's something of the poet in me, but not enough. Many people have just as much of it as I have and yet don't carry a sign or a collar with *poet* written on it.

They and I have been given a gift from God, a blessing big enough for oneself, but much too small to be parceled out to others. It comes like a sunbeam and fills your soul and mind. It comes like a waft of flowers, like a melody you know but can't remember from where.

The other evening I was sitting in my room and felt like reading. I had no magazine or book to leaf through. Suddenly a leaf fell fresh and green from the linden tree, and the breeze blew it in the window to me.

I looked at all the many branching veins. A little bug was moving across them, as if it were making a thorough inspection of the leaf. That made me think of human wisdom. We crawl around on the leaf too and know only that. But then we deliver lectures about the entire big tree, the root, trunk, and crown. The big tree—God, the world, and immortality, and of the whole we only know a little leaf!

Just then Aunt Mille came for a visit.

I showed her the leaf with the bug and told her my thoughts about it, and her eyes lit up.

"You're a poet!" she said. "Maybe the greatest we have! I will gladly go to my grave if I can live to see that. You've always amazed me by your powerful imagination, ever since brewer Rasmussen's funeral."

That's what Aunt Mille said, and she kissed me.

Who was Aunt Mille, and who was brewer Rasmussen?

II.

We children always called mother's aunt "auntie." We had no other name for her.

She gave us jam and sugar, even though it was bad for our teeth. She said she had a soft spot for the sweet children. It was cruel to deny them a little of the sweets that they loved so much.

And so we loved Auntie very much too.

She was an old maid, and as far back as I can remember she was always old. Her age never changed.

In earlier years she had suffered a lot from toothaches and was always talking about it. That's why her friend, brewer Rasmussen, jokingly started calling her Auntie Toothache.

In his last years he no longer did brewing, but lived off the interest of his money. He often visited Auntie and was older than she was. He had no teeth at all, just some black stumps. He told us children that he had eaten too much sugar as a child, and that's what one looks like from doing that.

Auntie must not have eaten any sugar in her childhood because she had the most beautiful white teeth.

Brewer Rasmussen said that she saved on using them—she didn't sleep with them at night! We children knew it was mean to say that, but Auntie said he hadn't meant anything by it.

One morning at breakfast she told us a bad dream she had had that night. One of her teeth had fallen out. "That means I am going to lose a true friend," she said.

"If it was a false tooth," the brewer chuckled, "then it only means you'll lose a false friend."

"You're a rude old man!" Auntie said as angrily as I have ever seen her, before or since. Later she said that he had only been teasing her. He was the noblest person on earth, and when he died some day, he would become a little angel of God in heaven.

I thought a lot about that transformation and wondered if I would be able to recognize him in his new form.

When Auntie was young, and he was young too, he had proposed to her. But she deliberated over it too long and didn't make up her mind. Didn't make up her mind for *too* long, and so became an old maid, but she was always a loyal friend to him.

And then brewer Rasmussen died.

He was driven to his grave in the most expensive hearse, and a big procession followed, many people with medals and wearing uniforms.

Auntie stood by the window in her black mourning together with all us children, except for my little brother, whom the stork had brought a week ago.

When the hearse and procession had passed and the street was empty, Auntie wanted to go, but I didn't want to. I was waiting for the angel, brewer Rasmussen. He had become a little winged child of God and had to appear.

"Auntie," I said, "Don't you think he'll be coming now? Or when the stork brings us another little brother, will he bring angel Rasmussen?"

Auntie was completely overwhelmed by my imagination and said, "That child will become a great poet!" She repeated that all through my school years, after my confirmation, and now into my years as a college student.

She was and is the most sympathetic friend to me, both in my pains with my poetry and pains in my teeth. I have bouts of both.

"Just write down all your thoughts," she said, "and put them in the drawer. That's what *Jean Paul*[1] did, and he became a great poet, although I don't really like him. He isn't exciting. You must be exciting! And you will be exciting!"

The night after this conversation I lay awake in longing and distress, with the want and need to become the great poet that Auntie saw and sensed in me. I was in "poet pain," but there's a worse pain, and that's a toothache. It crushed and squashed me. I became a writhing worm with an herbal hot pad on my cheek and Spanish fly.

"I know all about that," said Auntie. She had a sad smile on her lips, and her teeth shone so white.

I must start a new section of my story and Auntie's.

III.

I had moved into my new apartment and had lived there a month. I talked with Auntie about it.

"I live with a quiet family. They don't pay any attention to me, even if I ring three times. Actually it's a real madhouse with racket and noises of wind and weather and people. I live right over the entrance portal, and every coach that drives in or out makes the pictures on the wall shake. The gate slams and shakes the house as if it were an earthquake. If I'm lying in bed, the jolts go through all my limbs, but that is supposed to be good for the nerves. If the wind's blowing, and it's always windy here in this country, then the long casement window hooks dangle back and forth and slam against the brick wall. The neighbor's portal bell rings with every gust of wind.

The residents of the building come home in batches from late in the evening until far into the night. The lodger right above me, who gives trombone lessons during the day, comes home last, and he doesn't go to bed until he has had a little midnight walk around his room with heavy tromping in iron-clad boots.

There are no double windows, but there's a broken pane that the landlady has pasted paper over. The wind blows through the crack anyway and makes a sound like a humming horsefly. It's music to put you to sleep. When I finally do fall asleep, I'm soon awakened by the crow of the rooster. The rooster and hens announce from the chicken coop of the man in the cellar that it'll soon be morning. The little ponies, who don't have a stable, are tethered in the sandpit below the stairs. They kick at the door and the walls for exercise.

At daybreak, the janitor, who lives in the attic with his family, comes lumbering down the stairs. Wooden shoes clack, the gate slams, the house shakes, and when that's over, the lodger upstairs begins his exercises. He lifts a heavy iron ball in each hand, but he can't keep a hold of them. They fall again and again, while at the same time all the children in the building run screaming on their way to school. I go to the window and open it to get some fresh air—it's refreshing when I can get it—if the lady in the back building isn't washing gloves in stain remover. That's how she makes her living. All in all, it's a nice building, and I live with a quiet family."

That was the account I gave my aunt about my apartment. It was more lively though, because an oral presentation is more vivid than the written word.

"You're a poet!" shouted Auntie. "Just write up what you said, and you'll be just as good as Dickens. Actually you interest me much more. You paint when you speak! You describe your building so that one can see it. It makes one shudder! Keep writing, make it come alive. Put people in, beautiful people and preferably unhappy ones!"

I really did write it down, as it stands with the noises and sounds, but just with myself in it, no action. That came later!

IV.

It was in the winter, late in the evening after the theater. There was a terrible snowstorm, so it was almost impossible to make any headway walking.

Auntie had been to the theater, and I was there to see her home, but it was hard to walk oneself, much less help someone else. All the cabs were taken. Auntie lived far over in town, but my room was close to the theater. If that hadn't been the case, we would have had to stand in the sentry box for who knows how long.

We struggled along in the deep snow, surrounded by the whirling snowflakes. I lifted her, held her, and pushed her along. We only fell twice, but we fell softly.

We reached my gate where we shook ourselves off. We shook ourselves on the stairs too, and we still had enough snow on us to fill up the floor in the entry.

We took off our coats and other clothing that could be taken off. The landlady lent Auntie dry stockings and a robe. She said it was a necessity, and added that Auntie could not possibly get home that night, which was true. She asked her to make do with the sofa in her living room, where she would make up a bed in front of the always locked door to my room. And that was done.

A fire burned in my stove. The teapot was brought to the table, and the little room became cozy, if not as cozy as at Auntie's, where there are thick curtains in front of the door in the winter, thick curtains over the windows, and two-ply carpets with three layers of heavy paper underneath. You sit there as if in a tightly corked bottle of warm air. But, as I said, it was cozy there in my place too. Outside the wind howled.

Auntie talked and told stories. Back came the days of her youth and back came the brewer, old memories.

She remembered when I got my first tooth, and the pleasure the family took in it. The first tooth! The tooth of innocence, shining like a little white drop of milk—the milk tooth.

First came one, then others, a whole line. Side by side, upper and lower—the most lovely baby teeth, but yet just the vanguards, not the real ones that have to last for a lifetime.

They came too, and the wisdom teeth also. Flankers of the rank, born in pain and with great difficulty.

And they leave again, every one of them! They go before

their service is up. Even the last tooth goes, and that's not a day of celebration. It's a melancholy day.

And then you're old, even if your spirit is young.

Such thoughts and talk aren't pleasant, and yet we talked about all this. We went back to childhood years. We talked and talked. It was midnight before Auntie went to bed in the room next door.

"Good night, my sweet child," she called. "Now I'll sleep as if I'm lying in my own bed."

And she slept peacefully, but there was no peace either in the house or outside. The storm shook the windows, slammed the long dangling iron hooks, and rang the neighbor's portal bell in the back building. The lodger upstairs had come home. He was still taking his little walk up and down. He took off his boots and went to bed and to rest, but he snores so loudly that good ears can hear it through the ceiling.

I couldn't sleep, and couldn't calm down. The weather didn't calm down either. It was immensely lively. The wind whistled and sang in its fashion and my teeth also began to get lively. They whistled and sang in their fashion, and struck up a terrific toothache.

There was a draft from the window. The moonlight shone onto the floor. The lighting changed as the clouds came and went in the stormy weather. There was a shifting of shadow and light, but at last the shadow on the floor took shape and looked like something. I looked at the moving shape and sensed an icy cold blast.

A figure was sitting on the floor, thin and long, as when a child tries to draw a person on a blackboard with chalk. The body is a single long line. A line and one more are the arms, and the legs are also each just a line, with the head a polygon.

The figure soon became more distinct. It seemed to have some kind of dress on—very thin and fine, but that showed the figure was a female.

I heard a humming sound. Was it her, or the wind that was buzzing like a horsefly in the window crack?

No, it was Mrs. Toothache herself! Her Awfulness *Satania infernalis*.[2] God deliver and preserve us from her visits!

"It's nice to be here," she hummed. "These are good lodgings. Swampy ground, boggy ground. The mosquitoes have been buzzing around here with poison in their sting, and now I have the stinger. It has to be sharpened on human teeth, and they're shining so whitely on him in the bed. They have held their own against sweet and sour, hot and cold, shells of nuts and stones of plums! But I am going to rock them and shock them, nourish their roots with a drafty wind, and give them cold feet!"

It was a horrible speech from a horrible guest.

"So you're a poet!" she said. "Well, I'll teach you all the meters of agony. I'll give you iron and steel in your body, and put wires in all your nerves."

It was as if a glowing awl plunged into my cheekbone. I twisted and turned.

"An excellent set of teeth!" she said. "An organ to play upon—a mouth-organ concert, splendid, with kettledrums and trumpets, a piccolo, and a trombone in the wisdom tooth! Great music for a great poet!"

She struck up her music, and she looked horrible, even though I saw no more of her than her hand—a shadow grey, ice-cold hand with long thin awl-like fingers. Each of them was a tool of torture. The thumb and index finger were pliers and a thumbscrew. The middle finger ended in a sharp awl. The ring finger was a drill, and the little finger a needle injecting mosquito poison.

"I'll teach you to write poetry!" she shouted. "A great poet shall have a great toothache. A small poet, a small toothache."

"Oh, let me be a small one!" I begged. "Or not be at all! And I'm not a poet. I only have bouts of writing, like I have bouts of toothache. Go away! Go away!"

"Then do you acknowledge that I am more powerful than poetry, philosophy, mathematics, and all music?!" she asked. "More powerful than all the feelings and sensations painted and carved in marble? I am older than all of them. I was born right beside the Garden of Eden, outside where the wind blew, and the soggy toadstools grew. I got Eve to put on clothing in cold weather, and Adam too. You'd better believe there was power in that first toothache!"

"I believe all of it!" I said. "Go away! Go away!"

"Well, if you'll give up being a poet, never set verse on paper, blackboard or any other writing material again, then I'll let you go. But I'll come back if you start writing."

"I swear!" I said. "Just never let me see or sense you ever again!"

"You will see me, but in a plumper figure, more dear to you than I am now! You will see me as Aunt Mille, and I'll say 'Write, my sweet boy! You are a great poet, perhaps the greatest we have!' But if you believe me and start writing, then I'll set your verses to music and play them on your mouth organ! You sweet child!—Remember me when you see Aunt Mille!"

And then she disappeared.

As she left, I felt a glowing stab of the awl in my cheekbone, but it soon subsided. I felt like I was gliding on soft water, saw white water lilies with their wide green leaves bending, sinking down under me, then withering, dissolving—and I sank with them, dissolving in peace and rest.

"Die, melt away like snow" sang and clang in the water. "Dissolve into the clouds, drift away like the clouds!"

Great lighted names shone down to me through the water, inscriptions on waving victory banners—Immortality's patent applications—written on Mayfly wings.

My sleep was deep, sleep without dreams. I didn't hear the whistling wind, the slamming gate, the neighbor's ringing portal bell, or the lodger's heavy exercising.

Such bliss!

Then a gust of wind blew open the locked door to where Auntie was sleeping. She leapt up, put on her shoes and clothes, and came in to me.

I was sleeping like an angel of God, she said, and she didn't have the heart to wake me.

I awoke on my own, opened my eyes and had completely forgotten that Auntie was in the house. But I soon remembered it, and remembered my toothache vision. Dream and reality merged together.

"I don't suppose you wrote anything last night, after we said good night to each other?" she asked. "I wish you had! You're my poet, now and always."

It seemed to me that she smiled so cunningly. I wasn't sure if it was the good Auntie Mille, who loved me, or the terrible figure I had sworn to in the night.

"Did you write anything, dear child?"

"No, no!" I cried. "You are Aunt Mille, aren't you?"

"Who else?" she said. And it *was* Aunt Mille.

She kissed me, got a cab, and went home.

I wrote down what's written here. It's not in verse, and it will never be printed—.

———

Here the manuscript ended.

My young friend, the future greengrocer apprentice, couldn't procure the missing pages. They had gone into the world as wrapping paper around salt herring, butter and green soap. They had fulfilled their destiny.

The brewer is dead. Auntie is dead. And the student is dead, he whose sparks of poetry went into the waste barrel.

Everything goes to waste.

And that's the end of the story, the story about Auntie Toothache.

NOTES

1. Pen name of German writer Johann Paul Friedrich Richter (1763–1825).
2. Equating the toothache with the devil, Andersen adds the Latin *infernalis* (of hell) to create his title for the personified toothache.

THE CRIPPLE

THERE WAS AN OLD estate with an excellent young master and mistress. They had blessings and riches. They enjoyed themselves, and they also did a lot of good. They wanted everyone to be as happy as they themselves were.

On Christmas Eve a beautiful, decorated Christmas tree stood in the old great hall. Fires were burning in the fireplaces, and the old portraits were decorated with spruce branches. The master and mistress and their guests gathered here, and there was singing and dancing.

There had already been Christmas joy in the servants' hall earlier in the evening. Here too was a big spruce tree with lighted red and white candles, small Danish flags, cut-out paper swans, and paper hearts woven of colorful paper filled with goodies. The poor children of the district were invited, and each had its mother along. They didn't look at the tree much, but at the tables with gifts. There was wool and linen cloth for sewing dresses and trousers. That's what the mothers and older children looked at. Only the very little ones stretched out their hands towards the candles, gold tinsel, and flags.

The gathering took place early in the afternoon. Everyone ate Christmas pudding and roast goose with red cabbage. And when the tree had been looked at, and the gifts distributed, everyone got a little cup of punch and apple fritters filled with apples.

Then they went home to their poor rooms and talked about "the good way of life," that is to say, the good food, and the gifts were once again carefully inspected.

Garden-Kirsten and Garden-Ole were a married couple who kept their home and made their living by weeding and tending the garden on the estate. At each Christmas celebration they always got their share of presents. They had five children, and all five were clothed by the master and mistress.

"They are generous people, our master and mistress," they said. "But they can afford it, and they take pleasure in it."

"There's good clothing for four of the children," said Garden-Ole. "But why isn't there anything here for the cripple? They usually remember him too, even though he can't go to the party."

It was their oldest child they called "the cripple." His name was actually Hans.

When he was little he was the quickest and most lively of

children, but he had suddenly became "limp legged" as they called it. He could not stand or walk, and he had been bedridden for five years.

"Well, I did get something for him too," said his mother. "But it's nothing much, just a book for him to read."

"He won't get much out of that," said his father.

But Hans was happy to get it. He was a really bright boy who liked to read, but he also spent his time working. He did as much as someone who's always in bed could to make himself useful. He had busy hands and used them to knit wool stockings, even whole bedspreads. The mistress on the estate had praised them and bought them.

The book that Hans had received was a book of fairy tales. There was much to read and much to think about in it.

"That's of no use in this house!" said his parents. "But let him read. It will pass the time, and he can't always be knitting stockings."

Spring came, and flowers and greenery began to sprout. Weeds too, as you can certainly call the nettles, even if they are so nicely talked about in the hymn:

> *"Tho' all the kings on earth did show*
> *Their upmost strength and power,*
> *They could not make a nettle grow*
> *Nor mend a broken flower."* [1]

There was a lot to do in the manor garden, not just for the gardener and his apprentices, but also for Garden-Kirsten and Garden-Ole.

"It's total drudgery," they said, "and when we have raked the paths and gotten them really nice, they immediately are walked on again and messed up. There's a constant stream of strangers here on the estate. What a lot it must cost! But the master and mistress are rich."

"Things are oddly distributed," said Ole. "The pastor says we're all the Lord's children. Why is there such a difference between us then?"

"It's because of the fall from grace," said Kirsten.

They talked about it again in the evening, where cripple Hans was lying with his fairy tale book.

Straitened circumstances, drudgery, and toil had hardened the parents' hands and also hardened their judgment and opinions. They couldn't manage, couldn't deal with things, and the more they talked, the more disgruntled and angry they became.

"Some people have wealth and good fortune, others only poverty! Why should we have to suffer for our first parents' disobedience and curiosity. We wouldn't have behaved the way those two did!"

"Yes, we would have!" cripple Hans said at once. "It's all here in this book."

"What's in the book?" asked his parents.

And Hans read them the old fairy tale about *The Woodcutter and His Wife*.[2] They also complained about Adam and Eve's curiosity, the cause of their misfortune. Then the king of the country came by. "Come home with me," he said, "And you'll live as well as I do. Seven course meals and a dish for show. That one's in a closed tureen and you mustn't touch it, or your life of luxury will be over." "What can be in the tureen?" asked the wife. "It isn't our business," said the husband. "Well, I'm not curious," said his wife. "I would just like to know why we can't lift the lid. It must be some delicacy." "Just so there's no booby trap about it," said the man, "like a pistol shot that would go off and wake the whole house." "Uff!" said the wife and didn't touch the tureen. But during the night she dreamed that the lid lifted by itself, and there was the fragrance of the most lovely punch like you get at weddings and funerals. There was a big silver shilling lying there with the inscription: "If you drink of this punch you'll become the richest in the world and everyone else will become beggars." And she woke up right away and told her husband her dream. "You're thinking too much about that thing!" he said. "We could just lift it slightly and gently," said the wife. "Very gently," her husband answered. And the wife lifted the lid very slowly. Two nimble little mice jumped out and ran away into a mouse hole. "Good bye!" said the king. "Now you can go home to your own bed. Don't berate Adam and Eve any longer. You yourselves have been just as curious and ungrateful!"

"Where did that story come from and how did it get into the book?" asked Garden-Ole. "It's just as if it pertains to us. It gives you a lot to think about."

They went to work again the next day. They were scorched by the sun and soaked to the skin by rain. They were filled with grumpy thoughts and chewed them over in their minds.

It was still daylight that evening when they had eaten their milk porridge, and Garden-Ole said, "Read that story about the woodcutter for us again."

"There are so many delightful stories in this book," said Hans. "So many that you haven't heard."

"Well, I don't care about them," said Garden-Ole. "I want to hear the one I know."

And he and his wife listened to it again, and more than one evening they came back to the same story.

"But I don't really understand the whole thing," said Garden-Ole. "People are like milk that curdles. Some become fine cottage cheese and others thin, watered whey. Some people are lucky in everything, always given the place of honor, and never knowing sorrow or want."

Cripple Hans was listening to this. His legs were weak, but his mind was sharp. He read a story for them from the book of fairy tales. He read about *The Man without Sorrow or Want.*[3] Well, where could he be found? Because he had to be found.

The King lay ill and could not be cured except by wearing a shirt that had been worn and worn out by a person who could truthfully say that he had never known sorrow or want.

Messengers went out to all the countries of the world, to all palaces and estates, to all wealthy and happy people, but when it came right down to it, they had all known sorrow and want.

"I haven't!" said the swineherd, sitting by the ditch, laughing and singing. "I am the happiest person."

"Then give us your shirt," said the messengers. "You'll be paid half a kingdom for it."

He didn't have a shirt, and yet he called himself the happiest person.

"That was a fine fellow!" exclaimed Garden-Ole, and he and his wife laughed like they hadn't laughed for years.

Just then the schoolteacher came by.

"How merry you all are," he said. "That's rare in this house. Did you pick a lucky number in the lottery?"

"No, nothing like that," said Garden-Ole. "It's Hans. He read a story for us from his fairy tale book. He read about *The Man without Sorrow or Want,* and the fellow had no shirt. You laugh till you cry hearing something like that, and from a printed book, too. Everyone has his burdens to bear. We're not alone in it, and there's a comfort in that."

"Where did you get that book?" asked the schoolteacher.

"Hans got it at Christmas over a year ago from the master and mistress. You know he loves to read, and he's a cripple, of course. At that time we would rather he'd gotten a couple of everyday shirts, but the book is remarkable. It answers your questions somehow."

The schoolteacher took the book and opened it.

"Let's hear the same story again," said Garden-Ole. "I don't quite have a grasp of it yet. And then he will have to read the other one about the woodcutter."

Those two stories were enough for Ole. They were like two sunbeams that shone into the simple cottage and into the downtrodden thoughts that had made them grumpy and cross.

Hans had read the whole book, read it many times. The fairy tales carried him out into the world, there where he couldn't go since his legs couldn't carry him.

The schoolteacher sat by his bed. They talked together, and it was pleasant for both of them.

From that day on the schoolteacher came more often to see Hans when his parents were working. It was like a celebration for the boy every time he came. How he listened to what the old man told him! About the earth's size and about many other countries, and that the sun was almost a half million times the size of the earth and so far away that a cannonball would take twenty five years to travel from the sun to earth, while light rays could reach the earth in eight minutes.

Every capable schoolboy knows all this now, but for Hans it

was new and even more marvelous than everything written in the book of fairy tales.

A couple of times a year the schoolteacher was invited to dinner at the manor house, and on one such occasion he told them how important the fairy tale book had been in the poor cottage, where just two stories had resulted in revival and blessings. The weak, clever little boy had brought reflection and joy to the house through his reading.

When the schoolteacher went home from the manor, the mistress pressed a couple of shiny silver dollars in his hand for little Hans.

"Father and mother must have those!" said the boy when the schoolteacher brought him the money.

And Garden-Ole and Garden-Kirsten said, "Cripple Hans is, after all, a benefit and a blessing."

A few days later when the parents were at work on the estate, its family coach stopped outside. It was the tender-hearted mistress who came, happy that her Christmas present had been such comfort and brought such pleasure to the boy and his parents.

She brought along some fine bread, fruit, and a bottle of sweet syrup, but what was even better, she brought him a little black bird in a gilded cage. It could whistle so beautifully. The cage with the bird was placed on the old chest of drawers, not far from the boy's bed. He could see the bird and hear it, and even people way out on the road could hear the bird singing.

Garden-Ole and Garden-Kirsten didn't come home until the mistress had left. They saw how happy Hans was, but thought that such a gift could only bring inconvenience.

"Rich people don't consider things!" they said. "Now we'll have that to take care of too. Cripple Hans can't do it, and the cat will end up taking it."

A week went by, and then another. During that time the cat had been in the room many times without scaring the bird, let alone harming it. Then something great occurred. It was in the afternoon. His parents and the other children were working, and Hans was quite alone. He had the fairy tale book in his hands and was reading about the fisherman's wife, who had all her wishes fulfilled.[4] She wanted to be King, and she became it. She wanted to be emperor, and she became it. But then she wanted to be God and so ended up in the muddy ditch, where she had come from. This story has nothing to do with the bird and the cat, but it happened to be the story he was reading when the event happened. He always remembered that.

The cage was standing on the bureau. The cat was standing on the floor staring hard with its yellow-green eyes at the bird. There was something in the cat's face—as if it wanted to tell the bird, "How beautiful you are! I would really like to eat you!"

Hans understood this. He could read it in the cat's face.

"Scram, cat!" he shouted. "Get out of here!"

It was as if the cat was readying itself to spring.

Hans couldn't reach it. He had nothing to throw at it except his dearest treasure, the fairy tale book. He threw it, but the cover was loose and flew to one side, and the book itself with all the pages flew to the other side. The cat slowly retreated a little bit and looked at Hans, as if it wanted to say: "Don't involve yourself in this matter, little Hans. I can walk, and I can spring, and you can do neither."

Hans kept his eye on the cat and was very uneasy. The bird became uneasy too. There was no person to call upon, and it was as if the cat knew this. It once again readied itself to spring. Hans could use his hands, and he waved his bedspread, but the cat didn't care about the bedspread and when this too was thrown at it, to no avail, it leaped up on the chair and then into the windowsill, where it was closer to the bird.

Hans sensed the warm blood flowing in his veins, but he didn't think about that. He only thought about the cat and the bird. He couldn't get out of bed, couldn't stand on his legs, much less walk. It was as if his heart turned over in his chest when he saw the cat jump from the window right onto the bureau and push the cage so it tipped over. The bird was fluttering around confusedly in there.

Hans gave a cry. His body jerked, and without thinking, he sprang from the bed, towards the chest of drawers. He threw

the cat down and grasped the cage firmly. The bird was scared
to death. With the cage in his hand he ran out the door and
onto the road.

The tears were streaming down his face. He shouted for joy
and screamed loudly, "I can walk! I can walk!"

He had regained the use of his limbs. Such things can happen, and it happened to him.

The schoolteacher lived close by, and the boy came running
in to him in his bare feet, wearing only his shirt and bed jacket
and carrying the bird in the cage.

"I can walk!" he shouted. "Lord, my God!" and he sobbed
tearfully from pure joy.

And there was joy in the home of Garden-Ole and Garden-
Kirsten. "We'll never see a happier day!" they both said.

Hans was summoned to the manor house. He hadn't walked
that way for many years. It was as if the trees and hazelnut
bushes that he knew so well nodded to him and said, "Hello,
Hans. Welcome back out here." The sun shone into his face
and right into his heart.

At the manor the young, kind master and mistress had him
sit by them, and looked as happy as if he were one of their own
family.

Happiest of all was the mistress, who had given him the
book of fairy tales, and the little songbird. It was, true enough,
dead now. It had died of fright, but in a way it had been the
means to his recovery, and the book had been an awakening
for him and his parents. He still had it, and he would keep it
and read it, no matter how old he became. And now he could
also be useful to them at home. He would learn a trade, preferably become a bookbinder, "because," he said, "then I can read
all the new books."

In the afternoon the mistress summoned Hans' parents.
She and her husband had talked about Hans. He was a good
and clever boy, had a love of reading and good aptitude. Our
Lord always approves a worthy cause.

That evening the parents came home happy from the
manor, especially Kirsten, but the next week she cried because
little Hans was going away. He had new clothes and was a good

boy, but now he was going over the sea, far away, to go to school, a classical education. It would be many years before they would see him again.

He didn't take the book of fairy tales along with him. His parents wanted it as a keepsake. And father often read it, but only the two stories that he knew.

And they received letters from Hans, one happier than the next. He lived with nice people in good circumstances, but the very best thing was going to school. There was so much to learn and know. He wanted only to live to be a hundred and become a schoolteacher sometime.

"If we could live to see that!" said his parents, and they held each other's hands, as if they were at communion.

"Think what's happened to Hans," said Ole. "It shows that our Lord also thinks of poor people's children. And that it happened to a cripple! It's just like something Hans could read to us from his book of fairy tales!"

NOTES

1. The second stanza of H. A. Brorson's hymn "Arise All Things That God Has Made" (*Op! al den ting, som Gud har gjort*). This translation is by Anton M. Andersen from the *Hymnal for Church and Home* (fourth edition), published in 1849 by the Lutheran Publishing House in Blair, Nebraska. Here the word Andersen translated as "leaflet" appears as "nettle."

2. A fairy tale by Madame Leprince de Beaumont that Andersen could have known from Christian Molbech's *Udvalgte Eventyr og Folkedigtninger* from 1843, published under the title "Den nysgierrige Kone" ("The Curious Wife").

3. Andersen may have known this motif from A. F. E. Langbein's poem *Das Hemd des Glücklichen* (*The Shirt of the Happy [One]*); 1805), which appeared in *Neue Gedichte* (1812), according to Poul Høybye.

4. This refers to the common fairy tale *The Fisherman and His Wife*, found in the collections made by the Brothers Grimm.

FOLK TALES

THE TINDERBOX

A SOLDIER CAME MARCHING along the road: One, two! One, two! He had his knapsack on his back and a sword by his side, for he had been to war, and now he was on his way home. As he was striding along the road, he met an old hag. She was so disgusting that her lower lip hung down on her chest. "Good evening, soldier," she said. "What a handsome sword and big knapsack you have! You're a real soldier! And now you're going to get as much money as you could ever want."

"Thanks very much, old hag," the soldier replied.

"Do you see that big tree?" asked the hag, and pointed at a tree beside them. "It's completely hollow inside. Climb up to the top, and you'll see a hole that you can slide through. I want you to go deep down inside the tree, and I'll tie a rope around your waist so that I can pull you up when you call me."

"And what should I do down in the tree?" asked the soldier.

"Get money!" said the hag, "Listen, when you reach the bottom of the tree, you'll be in a big passage. It will be quite bright there because there are over a hundred burning lamps. You'll see three doors, and you can open them because the keys are in the locks. When you go into the first room, you'll see a large chest in the middle of the floor with a dog sitting on top of it. He has eyes as big as a pair of teacups, but don't worry about that. I'll give you my blue-checkered apron that you can spread out on the floor, but move quickly, take the dog, and set him on the apron. Then open the chest and take as many coins as you want. They're all made of copper, but if you would rather have silver, go into the next room where you'll see a dog with eyes as big as a mill wheel, but don't worry about that. Set him on my apron and take the money! On the other hand, if you want gold, you can have that too, and as much as you can carry, if you go into the third room. But the dog that is sitting on the money chest in there has two eyes, each as big as the Round Tower,[1] and that's quite a dog, I can tell you, but don't worry about it! Just set him on my apron, and he won't do anything

"And what should I do down in the tree?" asked the soldier.

to you, so you can take as much gold as you want from the chest."

"That doesn't sound too bad," said the soldier, "but what am I to give you, you old hag? For you want something, I imagine."

"No," said the hag, "I don't want a single penny. Just bring me an old tinderbox that my grandmother forgot the last time she was down there."

"Very well! Let's wrap that rope around my waist," said the soldier.

"Here it is," said the hag, "and here's my blue-checkered apron."

Then the soldier climbed into the tree, slid down the hole, and found himself, as the hag had said, in the big passageway, where hundreds of lamps were burning.

He opened the first door. Oh! There sat the dog with eyes as big as teacups, glaring at him.

"You're a fine fellow!" said the soldier, and he set him on the hag's apron and took as many copper coins as he could pack into his pockets. Then he closed the chest, put the dog back, and went into the second room. Yikes! There sat the dog with eyes as big as mill wheels.

"Stop staring at me so much!" said the soldier. "You might hurt your eyes!" and he set the dog on the hag's apron. When he saw so many silver coins in the chest, he threw away the copper money and filled his pockets and his knapsack with the silver coins. Then he went into the third room!—Oh, the dog was so repulsive! It really did have two eyes as big as the Round Tower that rolled around in its head like wheels!

"Good evening," said the soldier and tipped his cap, for he had never seen such a dog before. But after he had looked at him a little, he thought, enough of that! He lifted him down to the floor and opened up the chest. Oh, bless me! How much gold there was! He could buy all of Copenhagen and all the pastry-women's candied pigs, all the tin soldiers, riding crops and rocking horses there were in the world! Now *there* was money!—Then the soldier threw away all the silver coins he had poured into his pockets and knapsack and took gold instead. All his pockets, the knapsack, his cap and boots were so

There sat the dog with eyes as big as teacups, glaring at him.

full that he could barely walk! Now he had money! He put the dog on the chest, locked the door and called up through the tree, "Hoist me up now, old hag!"

"Do you have the tinderbox with you?" asked the hag.

"Oh, that's right," said the soldier, "I'd completely forgotten it," and he went and got it. The hag hoisted him up, and there he was once again standing on the road with his pockets, boots, knapsack and cap full of money.

"What do you want that tinderbox for?" asked the soldier.

"That doesn't concern you," said the hag, "Now that you've got your money, just give me the tinderbox!"

"Nothing doing!" said the soldier. "Tell me right now what you want it for, or I'll pull out my sword and chop off your head!"

"No," said the hag.

So the soldier chopped her head off, and there she lay. But he wrapped all his money up in her apron, stuck it into his knapsack on his back, put the tinderbox in his pocket, and walked into town.

It was a lovely town, and he went to the very best inn, asked for the very best rooms, and ordered his most favorite foods because now he was rich.

The servant who polished his boots thought that they were rather funny old boots for such a rich man to have, but the soldier hadn't bought new ones yet. The next day he did indeed buy boots and beautiful clothes! Now the soldier was a distinguished gentleman, and the people told him all about the fine things to be found in their town, and about their king, and what a lovely princess his daughter was.

"Where can I see her?" asked the soldier.

"You can't see her at all," they all answered. "She lives in a big copper castle, surrounded by walls and towers. No one but the king is allowed to go in and out of there, because he was told by a fortuneteller that the princess is going to marry a common soldier, and the king can't bear the thought that this might happen."

"I would like to see her though!" thought the soldier, but of course he wouldn't be allowed to do that.

Now he lived merrily, went to the theater, took drives in the king's garden, and gave away lots of money to the poor, which was kind of him. He knew from the old days how bad it was not to have a cent to one's name.—Now he was rich, had fine clothes, and made many friends. Every one said that he was a nice fellow, a proper cavalier, and the soldier liked this very much. But since he gave away money every day, and did not have any coming in, he finally had only two coins left and had to move away from the handsome rooms where he had lived, into a tiny little chamber, right beneath the roof, and had to brush his boots himself and sew them up with a darning needle, and none of his friends came to see him because there were too many steps to climb.

One evening it became very dark, and he couldn't even buy himself a candle. But then he remembered there was a little stump of one in the tinderbox that the hag had asked him to take from the hollow tree. So he took out the tinderbox and the candle stump, and just as he struck the flint, causing sparks to fly from the stone, the door sprang open, and the dog that had eyes as big as teacups and whom he had seen beneath the tree, stood in front of him and said, "What does my master command?"

"What's this!" cried the soldier. "This is certainly an interesting tinderbox if it will give me what I want like this! Get me some money," he said to the dog, and presto it was gone! Then presto it returned and held a big bag full of coins in its mouth.

Now the soldier understood what a wonderful tinderbox it was. If he struck once, the dog who sat on the chest with copper coins came. If he struck twice, the dog who had silver money appeared, and if he struck three times, the one with the gold coins came.—The soldier moved back into his handsome rooms and wore beautiful clothes once again. Suddenly all his friends recognized him, and once more they were so terribly fond of him.

Then one day he thought: it's really odd that no one gets to see the princess. She's supposed to be so beautiful, they all say, but what good is that when she always sits inside the big copper castle with all the towers?—Can't I get to see her somehow?—Where's my tinderbox! And then he struck the flint, and presto the dog with eyes as big as teacups came.

"Even though it's the middle of the night," the soldier remarked, "I very much want to see the princess, just for a little moment!"

The dog was out the door at once, and before the soldier could think about it, the dog was back again with the princess. She sat sleeping on the dog's back and was so lovely that it was clear for all to see that she was a real princess. The soldier couldn't help himself. He had to kiss her, for he was a true soldier.

Then the dog ran back with the princess, but when morning came, and the king and queen were having tea, the princess said that she was disturbed by a strange dream that she had in the night about a dog and a soldier. She had ridden on the dog, and the soldier had kissed her.

"That's quite some story!" said the queen.

So one of the old ladies-in-waiting was ordered to keep watch over the princess the next night to see if it was a real dream, or what it could be.

The soldier longed so frightfully to see the lovely princess again and had the dog go to her in the night. The dog took her and ran as fast as he could, but the old lady-in-waiting put on high boots and ran just as fast after them. When she saw that they disappeared into a big house, she thought, "Now I know where it is," and she marked a large cross on the door with a piece of chalk. Then she hurried home and went to bed, and the dog also came back with the princess. When he saw the cross on the door where the soldier lived, however, he took a piece of chalk and marked crosses on all the doors in the whole town, and that was smart of him because now the lady-in-waiting could not find the right door. Indeed, there were crosses on all of them.

Early in the morning the king and queen, the old lady-in-waiting, and all the officers came to see where the princess had been.

"There it is!" said the king, when he saw the first door with a cross on it.

"No, there it is, my dear," said the queen, who saw another door with a cross on it.

"But there's one, and there's one!" they all cried out. Wherever they looked, there were crosses on the doors. So then they realized that there was no use in searching further.

However, the queen was a very wise woman, who could do more than just ride in a coach. She took her big golden scissors, cut a large piece of silk into pieces, and sewed a lovely little bag. She filled it with fine little grains of buckwheat, tied it to the back of the princess, and when that was done, she cut a little hole in the bag, so the grains could sprinkle out wherever the princess would go.

During the night the dog came again, took the princess on his back, and ran with her to the soldier, who was so very fond of her, and dearly wished he were a prince so that he might marry her.

When the dog ran back to the castle with the princess, he failed to notice that the grain had spilled out all the way from the castle to the soldier's window. In the morning the king and queen could easily see where their daughter had been, and they ordered the soldier to be arrested and put into prison.

There he sat. Oh, how dark and boring it was! And then they told him: "Tomorrow you'll be hanged." That wasn't pleasant to hear. Moreover, he had forgotten his tinderbox which he had left at the inn. In the morning, through the bars of the little window, he could see people hurrying from all parts of the town to see him hanged. He heard the drums and saw the soldiers marching. All the people were running along, and among them was also a shoemaker's boy wearing a leather apron and slippers. He was running so fast that one of his slippers flew off and landed right by the wall where the soldier was peering through the iron bars.

"Hey, boy! Don't be in such a hurry," the soldier told him. "Nothing will happen until I get there! So, if you'll run to where I live and bring me my tinderbox, I'll give you four silver coins. But don't let the grass grow under your feet."

The shoemaker's boy was eager to get the four silver coins

and rushed off to fetch the tinderbox. He gave it to the soldier, and—Well, listen to what happened!

Outside the town a big gallows had been built, and all around stood the soldiers and thousands of people. The king and queen sat on a beautiful throne right opposite the judge and the entire council.

The soldier was already standing up on the ladder, but when they wanted to place the noose around his neck, he said that a condemned man was always granted a last wish before his punishment. He wanted so very much to smoke his pipe—it would be the last smoke he would get in this world.

The king didn't want to deny him this wish, and so the soldier took his tinderbox and struck the flint, one, two, three! And there stood all three dogs: the one with eyes like teacups, the one with eyes like mill wheels, and the one who had eyes as big as the Round Tower!

"Help me!" the soldier cried out. "Don't let them hang me!"

Immediately the dogs tore into the judges and all the councilors. They grabbed some by their legs and some by their noses and threw them high up into the air so that they fell down and were dashed to pieces.

"Not me!" screamed the king, but the largest dog took both him and the queen and threw them after all the others. Now the soldiers became frightened, and all the people shouted, "Little soldier, you will be our king and marry the beautiful princess!"

Then they placed the soldier in the king's coach, and all three dogs danced in front and roared "hurrah!" and boys whistled through their fingers, and the soldiers presented arms. The princess came out of the copper castle and became the queen and was very pleased with that! The wedding lasted for eight days, and the dogs sat at the table in wide-eyed wonder.

NOTE

1. Astronomical observatory, 118 feet tall, in the heart of Copenhagen. King Christian IV laid the first stone in 1637; the observatory was completed in 1642.

LITTLE CLAUS AND BIG CLAUS

In this one town there were two men who both had the same name. Both were called Claus, but one of the men owned four horses, and the other had only one horse. In order to distinguish between them, they called the one who had four horses Big Claus, and the one who had only one horse, Little Claus. Now listen to what happened, for it's quite a story!

All week long Little Claus had to plow for Big Claus and lend him his only horse. Then Big Claus paid him back with all his horses, but only one day a week, and that was on Sunday. Whew! How Little Claus cracked the whip over all five horses! After all, they were as good as his on that one day. The sun shone so brightly, and the church bells chimed for services. People were all dressed up and walked with their psalm books under their arms to hear the pastor preach. They all looked at Little Claus, plowing with his five horses, and he was so pleased with himself that he cracked the whip again and called out, "Giddy-up, all my horses!"

"You mustn't say that," said Big Claus. "Only one horse is yours, you know."

But when some more people went by on their way to church, Little Claus forgot he wasn't supposed to say that and yelled, "Giddy-up, all my horses!"

"Now cut that out!" said Big Claus. "If you say that one more time, I'll hit your horse on the head so it drops dead on the spot! It'll be all over for him."

"I certainly won't say it again," promised Little Claus, but then when people walked by again and nodded to him, he thought having five horses to plow his field was so impressive that he cracked the whip and called out, "Giddy-up, all my horses!"

"I'll giddy-up your horse!" said Big Claus, and took his tethering mallet and whacked Little Claus' only horse on the head so it fell down quite dead.

"Oh! Now I don't have a horse anymore," said Little Claus and started to cry. Afterwards he skinned the horse, dried the skin in the wind, put it in a bag on his shoulder, and headed into town to sell his horse-skin.

It was a long way to walk. He had to go through a big dark forest, and a dreadful storm arose. He became completely lost, and before he found the right road, evening came, and it was too far to get to town or home again before nightfall.

There was a big farm right by the road. The windows were shuttered, but light could and did shine out the top. "I imagine they will let me stay here overnight," thought Little Claus, and went up and knocked on the door.

The farmer's wife opened the door, but when she heard what he wanted, she told him to leave because her husband wasn't home, and she wouldn't let a stranger in.

"Well then, I'll have to sleep outside," Little Claus said, and the farmer's wife shut the door on him.

Close by was a big haystack, and between that and the house was a little shed with a flat thatched roof.

"That's where I'll sleep!" said Little Claus when he saw the roof. "That's a lovely bed indeed. I'm sure the stork won't fly down and bite my legs." You see, there was a live stork up on the roof, where he had his nest.

So Little Claus climbed up onto the shed, where he lay and twisted about to get comfortable. The wooden shutters on the windows didn't close completely at the top, and so he could look right into the room. There was a big table set with wine, a roast, and such a lovely fish. Only the farmer's wife and the sexton were at the table, and she poured wine for him, and he stuffed himself with fish because that was something he really liked.

"Oh, if only I could have a bite of that!" Little Claus said and stretched his head way over by the window. God, what a beautiful cake he could see there! Here was luxury for sure!

Then he heard someone riding towards the house on the road. It was the woman's husband, who was coming home. He was a kind man, but he had the most remarkable malady— he could not tolerate the sight of sextons. If a sexton came into view, he became absolutely furious. And that was why the sexton had come to visit the woman when he knew the farmer was not at home, and why the good woman treated him to all the best food she had in the house. When they heard the husband coming, they became very frightened, and the woman told the sexton to get into a big empty chest in the corner. He did that at once because he knew, of course, that the poor man couldn't tolerate the sight of sextons. The farmer's wife hurried to hide the scrumptious food and wine in the oven, because if the husband saw it, he would certainly have asked what the meaning of this was.

Up on the shed, Little Claus sighed, "Oh well," when he saw all the good food disappear.

"Is there somebody up there?" asked the farmer and peered up at Little Claus. "What are you doing up there? Come down into the house instead."

So then Little Claus explained how he had gotten lost and asked if he could spend the night.

"Sure!" the farmer said. "But first we'll have a bite to eat!"

The woman welcomed them both warmly, set the long table, and gave them a big bowl of porridge. The farmer was hungry and ate with a good appetite, but Little Claus couldn't help but think about the lovely roast, fish, and cake that he knew was in the oven.

He had put the bag with his horse-skin under the table by his feet, because we know, of course, that's why he left home—to sell it in town. The porridge didn't taste very good to him, and so he stepped on the bag, and the dry skin in the sack creaked pretty loudly.

"Hush!" Little Claus said to the bag, but at the same time he stepped on it again, so it creaked much louder than before.

"Say, what do you have in your bag?" asked the farmer.

"Oh, it's a wizard," answered Little Claus. "He says that we shouldn't eat porridge because he has conjured up the whole oven full of roast and fish and cake."

"What's that!" the farmer cried, and he quickly opened the oven where he saw all the lovely food his wife had hidden, but which he now thought the wizard had conjured up for them. The woman didn't dare say a thing, but put the food on the table right away, and they ate fish and roast and cake. Then Little Claus stepped on the bag again, so the skin creaked.

"What's he saying now?" asked the farmer.

"He says," Little Claus said, "that he has also conjured up three bottles of wine for us. They are over in the corner by the oven." So then the woman had to bring out the wine she had hidden, and the farmer drank, became very merry, and said that he would really like to own a wizard like the one Little Claus had in the bag.

"Could he conjure up the devil, too?" asked the farmer. "I would really like to see him because I'm in such a good mood."

"Yes," Little Claus answered. "My wizard can do anything I want. Isn't that right?" he said and stepped on the bag so it creaked. "Can you hear him answer, 'yes?' But the devil is so disgusting, it's not worth seeing him."

"Oh, I'm not a bit afraid no matter what he looks like."

"Well, he looks just like a real live sexton!"

"Whew!" the farmer said, "that's bad. You see I can't tolerate the sight of sextons. But never mind. As long as I know it's the devil, maybe I can stand it better. I'm brave now, but he mustn't come too close to me."

"Well, I'll ask my wizard," Little Claus said, stepped on the bag, and held his ear close.

"What does he say?"

"He says you can go over and open that chest in the corner. You'll see the devil sitting there pondering, but you have to hold on to the lid so he doesn't slip out."

"Will you help me hold it?" asked the farmer, who went over to the chest where the woman had hidden the real sexton, who was sitting in there terrified.

The farmer lifted the lid a little bit and peeked in: "Ugh—!" he screamed and sprang backwards. "I saw him there all right. He looked just like our sexton! Oh, it was terrible!"

They had to drink to that, and they kept drinking way into the night.

"You have to sell me that wizard," the farmer said. "Just name your price. I'll give you a whole bushel of money right now!"

"No, I can't do that," answered Little Claus. "Just think of all the uses I have for this wizard."

"Oh, I really really want it," said the farmer and continued to beg.

"Well," Little Claus finally said, "Since you've been kind enough to put me up tonight, then never mind. I'll give you the wizard for a whole bushel of money, but I want a heaping bushel."

"You'll have it," the farmer said. "But you have to take the chest with you. I don't want it in the house a minute longer. He might still be sitting in there."

Little Claus gave the farmer the bag with the dried skin inside and received a heaping bushel full of money for it. The farmer also gave him a big wheelbarrow to carry the money and chest.

"Good bye!" said Little Claus, and he took off with his money and the big chest, with the sexton still inside.

On the other side of the forest there was a big deep river. The water ran so swiftly that it was almost impossible to swim against the current. A big new bridge had been built across it, and Little Claus stopped right in the middle of it and said so loudly that the sexton could hear every word: "Well, what am I going to do with this dumb old chest? It's as heavy as if it had stones in it. I'm tired of hauling it further so I'll just throw it into the river. If it sails home to me, fine, and, if not, that's all right too."

So he grabbed the chest with one hand and lifted it a little, as though he were going to throw it into the water.

"No! Stop!" yelled the sexton inside the chest. "Just let me out of here!"

"Yikes!" Little Claus shouted, and acted afraid. "He's still in there! I'll have to throw it into the river right away so that he'll drown."

"Oh no, oh no!" the sexton screamed. "I'll give you a whole bushel of money if you don't."

"Well, that's another matter," Little Claus said, and he opened the chest. The sexton climbed out right away, pushed the empty chest into the water, went home, and gave Little

"Where have you gotten all that money from?"

Claus a whole bushel full of money. Since he already had one from before from the farmer, remember, his wheelbarrow was now completely full of money!

"Well, I was pretty well paid for that horse," Little Claus said to himself when he got back to his own house and dumped all the money in a big pile on the floor. "Big Claus will be annoyed when he finds out how rich I've become from my one horse, but I'll be darned if I tell him about it right away."

Then he sent a boy over to Big Claus' place to borrow a bushel scale.

"I wonder what he wants that for?" Big Claus thought and spread some tar under the bottom so something would remain of whatever was measured. And it did too because when he got the scale back, there were three new silver coins stuck on it.

"What's this?" said Big Claus and ran right over to Little Claus' house. "Where have you gotten all that money from?"

"Oh, it's from my horse-hide. I sold it last night."

"That was really a good deal!" Big Claus said, ran right home, took an axe, struck all four of his horses in the head, skinned them, and drove off with them to town.

"Hides! Hides! Who wants hides?!" he shouted through the streets.

All the shoemakers and tanners came running and asked what he wanted for them.

"A bushel full of money each," Big Claus said.

"Are you nuts?" they all asked him, "Do you think we have bushels of money?"

"Hides! Hides! Who wants hides?!" he shouted again, but to everyone who asked how much they cost, he answered, "A bushel full of money."

"He's making fun of us," they all agreed. Then the shoemakers took their straps, and the tanners took their leather aprons, and they started to beat Big Claus.

"Hides! Hides!" they mimicked him. "We'll give you a hide that'll be both black and blue! Out of town with you!" they shouted, and Big Claus had to ski-daddle out of there as fast as he could, for he had never been thrashed so much in his life.

"Little Claus is going to get it!" he said when he got home. "I'm going to kill him for this."

But back at Little Claus' house, his old grandmother was dead. Even though she had been cross and mean to him, he was pretty sad anyway, and he took the dead woman and laid her in his warm bed to see if she would come back to life. She could lie there the whole night, and he himself would sit on a stool in the corner and sleep. He had done that before.

As he sat there during the night, the door opened, and Big Claus came in with his axe. He must have known exactly where Little Claus' bed was because he went right over to it and hit the dead grandmother on the head, thinking it was Little Claus.

"So there!" he said. "You won't fool me again!" and then he went home.

"That is really a bad and mean man," said Little Claus, "He wanted to kill me. It's a good thing for the old lady that she was already dead, or he would have killed her."

Then he dressed the old grandmother in her best Sunday clothes, borrowed a horse from his neighbor, hitched it to the carriage, and set the grandmother up in the backseat, so that she couldn't fall out while he was driving, and away they went through the forest. When the sun came up, they were outside a large inn. Little Claus stopped there and went inside to get something to eat.

The innkeeper had lots of money and was also a very kind man, but he was quick-tempered, as if he were full of pepper and tobacco.

"Good morning," he said to Little Claus, "You're out early in your fancy clothes today."

"Yes," Little Claus said, "I'm on my way to town with my old grandmother. She's sitting out there in the carriage, and I can't get her into the inn. Would you please take her a glass of mulled wine? But you have to speak loudly because she's very hard of hearing."

"Yes, I'll do that," said the innkeeper and poured a large glass of wine that he took out to the dead grandmother, who was propped up in the carriage.

"That is really a bad and mean man."

"Here's a glass of wine from your son," said the innkeeper, but the dead woman didn't say a word, just sat completely still. "Can't you hear?" shouted the innkeeper as loudly as he could. "Here's a glass of wine from your son."

He shouted it again and again, but when she didn't budge an inch, he got mad and threw the glass right into her face so the wine ran down over her nose, and she fell over backwards in the carriage since she was just propped up, not tied.

"What's this!" yelled Little Claus. He ran out of the door and grabbed the innkeeper, "You've killed my grandmother! Look here—she has a big hole in her forehead!"

"Oh, it was an accident!" cried the innkeeper and clasped his hands together. "It's all because of my quick temper. Oh, sweet Little Claus, I'll give you a whole bushel of money and have your grandmother buried as if she were my own, but just don't say anything about it, or they'll chop my head off, and that's so unpleasant."

Then Little Claus got a whole bushel of money, and the innkeeper buried the old grandmother as if she had been his own.

When Little Claus got home with all the money, he immediately sent his boy over to Big Claus to ask whether he could borrow his scale.

"What?!" said Big Claus. "Didn't I kill him? This I have to see for myself," and so he took the scale over to Little Claus in person.

"Now where did you get all that money from?" he asked, his eyes open wide at the sight of all the additional money.

"You killed my grandmother, not me," said Little Claus. "Now I have sold her and got a bushel of money for her."

"That was really a good deal," Big Claus said and hurried home. He took an axe and immediately killed his old grandmother, laid her in his wagon, and drove into town to the drug store, and asked the druggist if he wanted to buy a dead body.

"Who is it, and where have you gotten it?" asked the druggist.

"It's my grandmother," said Big Claus. "I've killed her for a bushel of money!"

"God save us!" said the druggist. "You're out of your mind! Don't say something like that, or you'll lose your head!"

Then the druggist told him sternly what a terrible thing he had done, and what a dreadful person he was, and that he should be punished. Big Claus became so frightened that he ran out and sprang into his wagon, whipped the horses, and hurried home, but the druggist and all the other people thought he was crazy, and therefore let him go wherever he wanted.

"You're going to pay for this!" said Big Claus when he was out on the road. "Yes, you're going to pay for this, Little Claus!" And when he got home he took the biggest sack he could find and went over to Little Claus and said, "You've fooled me again. First I killed my horses, then my old grandmother! It's all your fault, but you'll never fool me again." Then he took Little Claus by the waist and put him into the sack, threw the sack on his back, and yelled, "Now I'm going to drown you!"

It was a long walk to the river, and Little Claus was not so easy to carry. The road went right by the church. The organ was playing, and people were singing so beautifully inside. Big Claus set the sack holding Little Claus right beside the church door. He thought that it might be a good idea to go in and hear a hymn before he went any further. After all, Little Claus would not be able to get out, and all the people were inside the church. So he went in.

"Oh no! Oh no!" sighed Little Claus inside the sack. He turned and twisted but it was impossible for him to loosen the rope. Just then an old, old shepherd with grey hair and a big walking stick came by. He was driving a herd of cattle in front of him, and they ran into the sack Little Claus was in and tipped it over.

"Oh poor me!" Little Claus sighed, "I'm so young, and I'm already going to heaven!"

"And poor me," said the shepherd, "who's so old and can't get there yet."

"Open the sack," shouted Little Claus, "take my place, and you'll soon be in heaven!"

"Yes, I would really like that," said the shepherd and untied the sack for Little Claus, who jumped out at once.

"Will you take care of the animals?" asked the old man, and climbed into the sack. Little Claus tied it up and went on his way with the cows and oxen.

A little later Big Claus came out of the church, took the sack on his back again, and thought it had become lighter because the old shepherd wasn't more than half as heavy as Little Claus. "How light he's become! It must be because I listened to a hymn." He went to the river, which was wide and deep, threw the sack with the old shepherd into the water, and shouted after him, "So there! You won't fool me again!" because he thought it was Little Claus, of course.

Then he went home, but when he got to the crossroads, he met Little Claus, who was herding his cattle.

"What's this!" said Big Claus, "Didn't I drown you?"

"Sure," said Little Claus. "You threw me in the river about half an hour ago, you know."

"But where did you get all those nice cattle?" asked Big Claus.

"They're sea cattle," Little Claus said. "I'll tell you the whole story, and thank you for drowning me. Now I'm on top of things, and I'm really rich, I can tell you. I was so afraid when I was inside the sack, and the wind was blowing around my ears when you threw me off the bridge into the cold water. I sank right to the bottom, but I didn't even get bumped because the most lovely, softest grass grows down there. I fell on that, and right away the sack opened, and the loveliest girl, wearing white clothes and a green wreath on her wet hair, took my hand. She said, 'Are you Little Claus? Here are a few cattle for you to start with, and a mile up the road is a whole herd that I want to give you!' Then I saw that the river was a big highway for the people of the sea. They walked and drove down there on the bottom, all the way from the ocean up the countryside to where the river ends. It was so beautiful with flowers and the freshest grass, and the fish that swam in the water slipped by my ears just like the birds do in the air here. What splendid

people they were and what fine cattle were grazing in the fields
and ditches there!"

"But then why did you come back up here again right away?"
asked Big Claus, "I wouldn't have done that if it was so lovely
there."

"Well," said Little Claus, "it was clever of me, you see. You
heard that the mermaid told me that a mile up the road there
was a whole herd of cattle for me. And by road she meant the
river, of course, because there's nothing else she can walk on.
But I know how the river winds around, first this way, then that,
a really roundabout way, you know. So it's much shorter to
come up here on land and go straight across to the river again.
I save almost a half mile by doing that and will get to my herd
quicker."

"Oh, you're a lucky man!" said Big Claus, "Do you think I
would get a herd of sea cattle too if I went down to the bottom
of the river?"

"Well, I would think so," said Little Claus, "but I can't carry
you in the sack all the way to the river because you're too heavy
for me. If you'll go there yourself and climb into the sack, I will
throw you in with the greatest pleasure."

"Oh, thank you!" Big Claus said, "but if I don't get a herd of
sea cattle when I get down there, I will beat you up for sure,
you know."

"Oh no! Don't be so mean to me!" And they went to the
river. When the cattle, who were thirsty, saw the water, they ran
as fast as they could to get down to drink.

"Look how they are hurrying," said Little Claus, "They are
yearning to get down to the bottom again."

"Well, help me first," said Big Claus, "otherwise I'll beat you
up!" and he crawled into the big sack, which had been lying
across the back of one of the oxen. "Put a stone in," Big Claus
said, "otherwise I'm afraid I won't sink."

"It'll work out," said Little Claus, but he put a large rock in the
sack, tied the rope tightly, and pushed it over. Plop! Big Claus was
thrown into the river and sank to the bottom right away.

"I'm afraid he won't find the cattle," said Little Claus, and
then he drove home with the ones he had.

THE PRINCESS ON THE PEA

ONCE UPON A TIME there was a prince. He wanted a princess, but she had to be a *real* princess. He traveled all around the world to find one, but there was always something wrong. There were enough princesses, but he couldn't quite find out if they were real—there was always something that wasn't quite right. So he came home again and was very sad because he wanted a real princess so very much.

One evening there was a terrible storm. There was lightning and thunder. Rain was pouring down, and it was quite frightening. Then someone knocked at the town gates, and the old king went to open them.

There was a princess standing out there. But what a sight she was in the rain and terrible weather! Water was streaming from her hair and clothes, and it ran in at the toe of her shoes and out at the heel. She *said* she was a real princess.

"Well, we will find out about that!" thought the old queen, but she didn't say anything. She went into the bedroom, took off all the sheets and blankets, and placed a pea on the bedspring. Then she laid twenty mattresses on top of the pea, and on the mattresses she placed twenty down comforters.

The princess was to sleep there for the night.

In the morning they asked her how she had slept.

"Oh, just terribly!" said the princess. "I almost didn't close my eyes the whole night! God knows what could have been in the bed? I was lying on something hard, so I am completely black and blue all over my body. It's quite dreadful!"

So they knew that she was a real princess since she had felt the pea through twenty mattresses and twenty down comforters. Only a real princess could have such sensitive skin.

The prince married her because he knew that now he had a real princess, and the pea was displayed in the art museum, where it can still be seen if no one has taken it.

See, that was a *real* story!

THE TRAVELING COMPANION

POOR JOHANNES WAS TERRIBLY sad, because his father was very sick and would not live much longer. Only the two of them were in the little room. The lamp on the table was about to burn out, and it was very late at night.

"You've been a good son, Johannes," said his sick father. "The Lord will surely help you further in this life," and he looked at him with serious gentle eyes, drew a deep breath, and died. It was as if he were sleeping. But Johannes wept. Now he had no one in the world, neither mother nor father, sister nor brother. Poor Johannes! He lay on his knees beside his father's bed, kissed his hand, and cried a great many salty tears, but finally his eyes closed, and he fell asleep with his head on the hard edge of the bed.

Then he had a strange dream. He saw the sun and moon bow down to him, and he saw his father hale and hearty again, and he heard him laugh, the way he always laughed whenever he was really pleased. A lovely girl with a gold crown on her long beautiful hair reached out her hand to Johannes, and his father said, "Look at the bride you have! She is the most wonderful in the world." Then he woke up, and all the splendor was gone. His father lay dead and cold in the bed, and there was no one else there. Poor Johannes!

The burial was the next week, and Johannes followed the coffin closely. He could no longer see his kind father, who had loved him so much. He heard the earth falling on the coffin, and saw the last corner of it, but then the next shovelful covered it, and the coffin was gone. He was so sad that he thought his heart would break to pieces from grief. Those around him were singing a beautiful hymn, and tears came to his eyes. He cried, and it felt good to cry in his sorrow. The sun shone brightly on the green trees, as if it wanted to say, "You mustn't be so sad, Johannes! Can't you see how blue the sky is? Your father is up there now and is asking the good Lord to watch out for you."

"I'll always be good," Johannes said, "then I'll also go to

heaven and be with my father, and what a joy it'll be when we see each other again! There's so much I have to tell him, and he'll show me many things again, and teach me about the splendors of heaven, just as he taught me here on the earth. Oh, what a joy that will be!"

Johannes imagined this so clearly that he smiled, although the tears were still streaming down his face. Little birds sat in the chestnut trees and chirped, "tweet, tweet." They were happy even though they were at a burial, but they probably knew that the dead man was in heaven now and had wings much more beautiful and larger than theirs. They knew he was happy because he had been good on earth, and that pleased them. Johannes saw how they flew from the green trees, way out into the world, and he felt a great desire to fly away with them. But first he cut a big wooden cross to place on his father's grave, and when he brought it there in the evening, the grave was decorated with sand and flowers. Other people had done that, because they were all very fond of his dear departed father, who now was dead.

Early the next morning Johannes packed a little bundle. He put his inheritance in his belt—fifty dollars[1] and a couple of silver coins. He was ready to wander out into the world. But first he went to the cemetery to his father's grave, said the Lord's Prayer, and then, "Good bye, dear father! I will always be a good person so you can ask God to take care of me."

In the meadow where Johannes walked, all the flowers looked so beautiful in the warm sunshine, and they nodded in the wind as if they were saying, "Welcome into the green fields, isn't it nice here?" But Johannes looked back one more time, to see the old church where he had been baptized as a little child, and where he and his old father had gone every Sunday to sing hymns. Way up in one of the little windows in the tower he saw the church pixie with his little pointed red cap. He was shielding his face with his bent arm, so the sun wouldn't shine in his eyes. Johannes nodded good bye to him, and the little pixie waved his red cap, laid his hand on his heart, and blew kisses again and again to show that he wished him luck and a happy journey.

Johannes thought about all the wonders he would now see in the big marvelous world and walked further and further, further than he had ever been before. He didn't know the towns he passed through, or the people he met. He was far away among strangers.

The first night he had to sleep in a haystack in a field; he had no other bed. But he thought it was just lovely. The king couldn't have it any better. The whole field with the river, the haystack, and the blue sky above was a beautiful bedroom. The green grass with the small red and white flowers was the carpet, and the elderberry bushes and the wild rose hedges were flower bouquets. For a wash basin he had the whole river with the clear, fresh water where the rushes curtsied with both evening and morning greetings. The moon was a really big nightlight, high up under the blue roof, and it wouldn't set the curtains on fire. Johannes could sleep peacefully, and that's what he did. He didn't wake up until the sun rose, and all the little birds were chirping, "Good morning! Good morning! Aren't you up yet?"

The bells rang for church. It was Sunday, and people were going to hear the minister. Johannes went with them, sang a hymn, and heard the word of God. It was as if he were in his own church, where he had been baptized and where he had sung hymns with his father.

There were many graves in the churchyard, and tall grass was growing on some of them. Johannes thought of his father's grave and that it would look like these too, now that he wasn't there to weed and tend it. So he sat down and pulled the grass, set up wooden crosses that had fallen over, and laid the wreaths, which the wind had torn from the graves, back in place again. He thought that perhaps someone else would do the same for his father's grave, now that he couldn't.

Outside the cemetery gate an old beggar was standing supported by his crutch. Johannes gave him the silver coins he had and went happily on his way into the wide world.

Towards evening a terrible storm came up, and Johannes hurried to find a place of shelter, but soon it was completely dark. He finally reached a small church, standing quite apart on a hill. Fortunately the door was ajar, and he slipped inside. He would stay there until the storm passed.

"I'll sit down here in a corner," he said. "I'm pretty tired and need to rest a little." He sat down, folded his hands, and said his evening prayers, and before he knew it, he slept and dreamed, while thunder and lightning raged outside.

When he awoke, it was the middle of the night, but the storm had passed, and the moonlight came shining through the windows. There was an open casket standing in the middle of the church floor with a dead man in it, soon to be buried. Since he had a clear conscience, Johannes wasn't afraid at all, and he knew that the dead hurt no one; it's evil living people who cause harm. Two such living, wicked people were standing by the casket, which had been placed in the church before the burial. They wanted to cause harm by throwing the poor dead man out of his casket and out the church doors.

"Why would you do that?!" asked Johannes. "That's evil and wicked. Let him sleep in Jesus' name."

"Oh, rubbish!" said the two wicked men. "He fooled us and owes us money that he couldn't repay. Now he's dead as a doornail, and we won't get a penny. We want revenge, and so he'll lie like a dog outside the church doors!"

"I only have 50 dollars," Johannes said. "That's my whole inheritance, but I'll gladly give it to you if you'll promise me to leave the poor dead man in peace. I'll manage without the money. I'm healthy and strong, and the Lord will surely help me."

"Well," the nasty men said, "If you'll pay his debt, then we won't do anything to him, you can be sure of that." They took the money that Johannes gave them, laughed loudly at his kindness, and went on their way, but Johannes arranged the corpse again in the casket, folded its hands, said good bye, and went quite contentedly further into the big forest.

All around, where the moon shone in through the trees, he could see the lovely little elves playing happily. They weren't bothered by him because they knew well enough that he was an innocent good person, and only wicked people aren't allowed to see the elves. Some of them were no bigger than a finger, and their long yellow hair was fastened with golden combs. They seesawed two by two on the large dewdrops that lay on the leaves and high grass. Sometimes the dewdrops rolled so that they fell down between the long blades of grass, and then there was hilarious laughter from the other little ones. It was great fun! They sang, and Johannes recognized very well all the beautiful melodies he had learned as a small boy. Big motley spiders with silver crowns on their heads spun long suspension bridges from one hedge to another, and palaces that looked like glistening glass when the moonshine struck the dew. All this continued until sunrise. Then the little elves crept into the flower buds, and the wind took the bridges and castles, which flew up as great cobwebs into the air.

Johannes had just come out of the forest when he heard a man's loud voice behind him. "Hello, comrade! Where are you headed?"

"Into the wide world!" Johannes said. "I have neither father nor mother and am a poor lad, but the Lord will surely help me."

"I'm going into the wide world too," the stranger said. "Shall we join forces?"

"Yes, let's do that," said Johannes, and so they did. They soon came to think very highly of each other since they were both good people. Johannes couldn't help but notice that the stranger was much more clever than he was. He had been almost everywhere and could tell about all sorts of things that existed in the world.

The sun was already high in the sky when they sat down under a large tree to eat breakfast. All at once an old woman came by. She was very old and quite bent over, supporting herself with a crutch, and on her back she had a bundle of firewood that she had gathered in the forest. Her apron was folded up, and Johannes saw that three big bunches of ferns and willow branches stuck out from it. When she was quite close to them, her foot slipped, and she fell and uttered a loud cry, for she had broken her leg, the poor old thing.

Johannes immediately wanted to carry the old woman to her home. But the stranger opened his knapsack, took out a

"I'm going into the wide world too," the stranger said.

jar, and said that he had a salve that would heal her leg right away, so that she could walk home herself as though the leg had never been broken. But he wanted her to give him the three bundles she had in her apron.

"That's a stiff fee," said the old woman and nodded her head oddly. She didn't want to part with her bundles, but it wasn't pleasant lying there with a broken leg either. So she gave him the bundles, and as soon as he smeared the salve on her leg, the old woman got up and walked better than before. That's how well the salve worked, but you couldn't get it at the drugstore either.

"What are you going to do with those bundles?" Johannes asked his traveling companion.

"These are three nice bouquets!" he said, "I like them because I'm an odd fellow."

Then they walked quite a distance.

"There's a storm brewing," Johannes said and pointed straight ahead, "Those are some awfully thick clouds!"

"No," the traveling companion said. "Those aren't clouds, they're mountains. Big beautiful mountains, where we'll come way up over the clouds into the fresh air! You can imagine how marvelous that is! Tomorrow we'll be that far up in the world!"

They were not as close as they looked. It took them a whole day of walking before they came to the mountains, where the dark forests grew right up towards the sky, and there were rocks as big as whole towns. It would be a long and hard journey over the mountains, so Johannes and his traveling companion went into an inn to rest and gather their strength for the next day's march.

A whole group of people were gathered down in the big bar in the inn because there was a man there who was going to put on a puppet show. He had just set up his little theater, and people were sitting around waiting to see the play, but an old fat butcher had taken the best place right in front. His big bulldog—Oh, he looked so ferocious!—sat by his side wide-eyed like everyone else.

Then the play started, and it was a fine piece with a king and a queen. They sat on beautiful thrones and had gold crowns on their heads and long trains on their robes because they could afford it. The most gorgeous wooden puppets with glass eyes and big handlebar moustaches stood by all the doors and opened and closed them to let in fresh air. It was a lovely play, and not at all sad, but just as the queen stood up and walked across the floor, then—God knows what the bulldog was thinking, but since the big butcher didn't keep a hold of him—he leaped right into the scene, and took the queen by her thin waist so it went "crack, crunch!" It was just terrible!

The poor man who directed the play was very frightened and upset about his queen, since it was the most beautiful puppet he had, and now the nasty bulldog had bitten her head off. But when all the people had left, Johannes's traveling companion said that he could repair her, and he took out his jar and smeared the puppet with the salve he had used on the old woman with the broken leg. As soon as the salve was applied, the puppet was good as new. In fact, it could move its own arms and legs, and it wasn't necessary to pull the strings any longer. The puppet was like a living person, except that it couldn't talk. The man who owned the puppet show was very pleased that he didn't have to hold that puppet any more; it could dance by itself. None of the others could do that.

Later during the night, when all the people in the inn had gone to bed, there was someone who was sighing so loudly and who kept it up for so long that everybody got up to see who it could be. The man who had produced the play went to his little theater because the sighing was coming from there. All the puppets were lying there piled together, the king and all the henchmen, and they were the ones who were sighing so pitifully and starring with their big glass eyes because they desperately wanted to be smeared with the salve like the queen so that they could move by themselves. The queen got down on her knees and held her gold crown into the air, while she begged, "Just take this, but treat my consort and the courtiers!" The poor man who owned the puppet theater and all the puppets could not help crying because he felt so badly for them. He promised to give the traveling companion all the money from the next night's performance if he would just smear the salve on four or five of the prettiest puppets, but the traveling companion said that he didn't want anything except the big sword the man had at his side. After he had received it, he smeared the salve on six of the puppets, who right away began dancing, and so beautifully that all the girls, the living human girls, who were watching, started to dance along. The coachman danced with the cook, the waiter and the parlor maid danced, all the guests danced, and the fire shovel danced with the fire tongs, but those two fell over when they made their first leap—Oh, it was a merry night!

The next morning Johannes and his traveling companion left them all and climbed up the high mountains and through the deep spruce forests. They climbed so high up that at last the church steeples down below looked like small red berries, down among the greenery, and they could see far, far away, many, many miles, to where they had never been! Johannes had never seen so much of the beauty of the world at one time, and the sun shone warm in the fresh blue air, and he heard the hunters blowing on their horns in the hills, so gloriously that his eyes filled with tears of joy, and he could not help exclaiming: "Oh my dear God! I could kiss you because you are so good to us all and have given us all the beauties of the earth!"

The traveling companion also stood with his hands folded, looking out over the forests and towns, lying in the warm sunshine. Just then a delightful sound rang out right above their heads, and they looked up to see a big white swan hovering in the air. It was beautiful and sang like they had never heard a bird sing before. But the song became softer and softer as the swan bowed its head and sank quite slowly down by their feet, where the beautiful bird then lay quite dead.

"Two such beautiful wings as white and big as those the bird has are worth a lot," said the traveling companion. "I'll take them with me. See, it's a good thing I have a sword!" Then with one stroke he cut both wings from the dead swan, for he wanted to keep them.

Then they traveled for many, many miles over the mountains until they finally saw a big city with over a hundred towers shining like silver in the sunshine. In the middle of the city was a magnificent marble castle with a roof of red gold, and that's where the king lived.

Johannes and the traveling companion didn't enter the city right away. Instead they stayed at an inn on the outskirts because they wanted to get dressed up before appearing in the streets. The innkeeper told them that the king was a very good man, who never did harm to anyone at all. However, his daughter, God help us, was a very wicked princess. She was marvelously beautiful. Indeed, no one was as beautiful and lovely as she was, but what good did that do when she was an evil, wicked witch, who was responsible for the deaths of so many fine princes? She had allowed all sorts of men to court her. Anyone could come, whether he was a prince or a tramp; it didn't make any difference. He only had to guess three things she was thinking about. If he could do that, she would marry him, and he would become king of the whole country when her father died. But if he couldn't guess the three things, then she would have him hanged or beheaded. That's how wicked and evil the beautiful princess was.

Her father, the old king, was very sad about all this, but he couldn't forbid her from being so bad because he had once said that he didn't want to have anything to do with her suitors. So, she could do as she pleased. Every time a prince came to claim the princess and make a guess to win her, he would lose, and so he was hanged or beheaded. He had been warned in time, after all. He didn't have to court her! The old king was so upset about all the sorrow and misery that he kneeled with all his soldiers one whole day every year and prayed that the princess would become good and kind, but this she absolutely refused to do. Old women who drank strong spirits dyed their drinks quite black before they drank them. That's how grieved they were, and more than that they couldn't do.

"What a hideous princess!" Johannes said. "She really should have a spanking. That would be good for her. If I were the old king, I'd beat her till she bled!"

Just then they heard the people outside shouting "hurrah!" The princess was riding by, and truly she was so beautiful that everyone forgot how evil she was. That's why they shouted "hurrah." Riding beside her on coal-black horses were twelve lovely maidens, all in white silk dresses and holding a gold tulip. The princess herself was riding a chalk-white horse, decorated with diamonds and rubies, her riding outfit was made of pure gold, and the whip she had in her hand looked like a sunbeam. The gold crown on her head was like little stars from the sky, and her coat was sewn from thousands of lovely butterfly wings, but she was even more beautiful than all her clothes.

When Johannes saw her, his face turned as red as dripping blood, and he couldn't say a word because the princess looked just like the lovely girl with the golden crown that he had seen in his dream the night his father died. He thought she was so beautiful that he couldn't help falling in love with her. It couldn't be true, he said, that she was an evil witch who had men hanged or beheaded if they couldn't guess what she asked of them. "Everyone has the right to propose to her, after all, even the poorest tramp. I'm going up to the castle. I just can't help myself!"

They all told him not to do it; he would meet the same fate as all the others. The traveling companion also advised him against it, but Johannes was sure it would turn out well. He polished his shoes and brushed his clothes, washed his face and hands, combed his lovely yellow hair, and went quite alone into the city and to the castle.

"Come in!" said the old king when Johannes knocked on the door. He opened the door and saw the old king come towards him, wearing a robe and embroidered slippers. He had a gold crown on his head, a scepter in one hand, and a golden apple in the other. "Just a minute," he said and put the apple under his arm, so he could shake hands with Johannes. But as soon as he heard that Johannes was a suitor, he began to cry so violently that the scepter and apple fell on the floor, and he had to dry his eyes on his robe. The poor old king!

"Don't do it!" he said. "It will go badly for you like it has for all the others. Just look at this," and he led Johannes into the princess' flower garden, which was frightful! From every tree four or five princes, who had proposed to the princess but were unable to guess her thoughts, were hanging. Whenever it was windy, the bones rattled and scared the little birds so much that they didn't dare fly into that garden. All the flowers were tied up with human bones, and skulls sat grinning in the herb pots. That was some garden for a princess!

"Just look," said the king. "You'll have the same fate as all these others you see here. Please give it up! You're really making me unhappy because I take it all to heart."

Johannes kissed the good, old king on the hand and assured him that it would surely go well, since he was so fond of the lovely princess.

Just then the princess came riding into the castle grounds with all her attendants, and they went out to greet her. She was so lovely and gave Johannes her hand, and now he thought even more of her than before. She certainly couldn't be the evil, wicked witch that everyone said she was! They went up to the hall, and the little pages brought peppernut cookies and jam for them, but the old king was so sad that he couldn't eat anything, and the peppernut cookies were too hard for him anyway.

It was decided that Johannes would come back to the castle the next morning, when the judges and the entire council would be gathered, and they would hear how he'd fare at guessing. If it went well, he would come again two more times, but so far no one had guessed the first time, and so they had all lost their lives.

Johannes was not at all worried about how it would go. He was happy thinking only about the lovely princess and believed firmly that the good Lord would help him. He didn't have the slightest idea how, but he didn't want to think about it either. He danced along the country road on his way back to the inn, where the traveling companion was waiting for him.

Johannes couldn't say enough about how nicely the princess had greeted him, and how beautiful she was. He was already longing for the next day when he would return to the castle and try his luck at guessing.

But the traveling companion shook his head and was pretty sad. "I'm really fond of you," he said, "and we could have been together for a long time yet, but now I'm already going to lose you. Poor, dear Johannes! I could cry, but I don't want to disrupt your joy on what might be the last evening we're together. We'll be merry, really merry. Tomorrow when you're gone, I'll allow myself to cry."

All the people in the city soon found out that a new suitor for the princess had arrived, so there was great sadness. The theater was closed, and all the bakery women put black ribbons on their candied pigs. The king and queen prayed on their knees in church, and there was great misery because it couldn't turn out any different for Johannes than it had for all the other suitors.

In the evening the traveling companion made a big bowl of punch and told Johannes that they were going to be very merry and drink a toast to the princess. But when Johannes had drunk two glasses, he became so sleepy that he couldn't hold his eyes open. He had to sleep. The traveling companion lifted him slowly from the chair and put him to bed, and when it was dark, he took the two big wings he had cut from the swan and fastened them to his shoulders. In his pocket he put the largest bundle he had gotten from the old woman who had broken her leg, opened the window, and flew over the city, right to the castle, where he sat in a corner under the window that led to the princess' bedroom.

It was very quiet throughout the city. When the clock struck 11:15, the window opened, and the princess, dressed in a big white coat and with long black wings, flew out over the city to a large mountain. The traveling companion made himself invisible so she couldn't see him, flew after her, and whipped the princess with his switch so that blood ran where he struck. They rushed through the air. The wind caught her coat and spread it out on all sides, like a big sail, and the moon shone through it.

"What a hailstorm! What a hailstorm!" the princess cried with every stroke from the whip, and it served her right. Finally she got to the mountain and knocked. It sounded like thunder as the mountain opened, and the princess went inside. The traveling companion followed, for no one could see him; he was quite invisible. They walked through a large, long hallway whose walls sparkled strangely; over a thousand glowing spiders ran up and down the wall, lighting like fire. Then they went into a large chamber, built of silver and gold where red and blue flowers as big as sunflowers shone from the walls, but no one could pick those flowers because the stems were awful, poisonous snakes, and the flowers themselves were fire coming from their mouths. The whole ceiling was bedecked with shining glow worms and sky-blue bats that flapped their thin wings—it looked very strange. There was a throne in the middle of the floor, carried by four horse skeletons that had harnesses of red fire spiders. The throne itself was made of milk-white glass, and the pillows to sit on were small black mice, that bit each other in the tails. There was a canopy over it of rose-colored spider-webs, decorated with the most beautiful little green flies that shone like gemstones. In the middle of the throne sat an old troll with a crown on his ugly head, and a scepter in his hand. He kissed the princess on the forehead, let her sit beside him on the precious throne, and then the music started. Big black grasshoppers played the harmonica, and the owl struck himself on the stomach because he didn't have a drum. It was a weird concert. Small black pixies with fireflies on their caps danced around the hall. No one could see the traveling companion for he had positioned himself right behind the throne and heard and saw everything. The courtiers, who entered at that point, were so stately and elegant, but anyone with eyes in his head could notice what they were. They were nothing other than broomsticks with cabbage heads that the troll had conjured into life and given embroidered clothes. But it didn't matter, for they were only for decoration.

When the dancing had gone on for a while, the princess told the troll that a new suitor had arrived, and so she asked what question she should put to him the next morning when he came to the castle.

"Listen," said the troll, "I'll tell you something. Think of something really easy, then he won't come up with it. Think about one of your shoes. He won't guess that. Then have his

"Then have his head chopped off."

head chopped off, but don't forget to bring me his eyes when you come out here tomorrow night because I want to eat them."

The princess curtsied deeply and said that she wouldn't forget the eyes. Then the troll opened the mountain, and she flew home again, but the traveling companion followed after her and whipped her strongly with the whisk so that she sighed deeply about the terrible hail, and hurried as fast as she could to get through the window into her bedroom. Then the traveling companion flew back to the inn, where Johannes was still sleeping, took off his wings, and lay down on the bed, for he had reason to be tired.

Johannes woke up very early in the morning. The traveling companion got up too and said that he'd had a very strange dream about the princess and her shoes, and told Johannes to be sure to ask if the princess was thinking about her shoe. Of course that was what he had heard the troll say in the mountain, but he didn't want to tell Johannes anything about that. So he just told him to ask if she was thinking about her shoe.

"I can just as well ask about that as about something else," Johannes said. "Maybe what you dreamed is right because I've always believed that the Lord will help me. But I'll say good bye anyway because, if I guess wrong, I'll never see you again."

They kissed each other, and Johannes went into the city and to the castle. The whole chamber was quite full of people. The judges were sitting in their easy chairs and had goose-down pillows under their heads because they had so much to think about. The old king stood up and dried his eyes with a white handkerchief. Then the princess walked in. She was even more beautiful than the day before and greeted everyone very warmly. However, to Johannes she gave her hand and said, "Good morning to you!"

Then Johannes had to guess what she had thought about. God, how friendly she looked at him. But when she heard him say the one word "shoe," her face turned chalk-white, and she trembled all over. Of course, it didn't do her any good because he had guessed correctly!

Hallelujah! How happy the old king was! He turned a

somersault with a vengeance, and all the people clapped their hands for him and for Johannes, who had guessed right the first time.

The traveling companion was also very happy when he heard how well it had gone, but Johannes folded his hands and thanked God, whom he was sure would help him again the next two times. Indeed, he had to go back the very next day to guess again.

The evening went by the same as the one before. While Johannes slept, the traveling companion followed the princess out to the mountain, beating her even harder than the last time, because he had taken two of the switches along. No one saw him, and he heard everything. The princess was going to think about her glove, and he told Johannes all about this as if it had been a dream. So Johannes was able to guess correctly, and there was great joy at the castle. All the courtiers turned somersaults, as they had seen the king do the first time, but the princess just lay on the sofa and would not say a single word. Now it would all depend on whether or not Johannes could guess the third time. If all went well, he would marry the lovely princess and inherit the kingdom when the old king died. If he guessed incorrectly, he would lose his life, and the troll would eat his beautiful blue eyes.

That night, Johannes went to bed early, said his prayers, and slept quite peacefully. Meanwhile the traveling companion strapped the wings to his back, tied the sword to his side, took all three switch bundles with him, and flew away to the castle.

It was a dark and stormy night. It was so stormy that the roof tiles flew off the houses, and the trees in the garden where the skeletons were hanging swayed like rushes in the wind. Lightning struck every minute, and thunder was rolling as though it were a single thunderclap that lasted all night. Then the window flew open, and the princess soared into the air. She was pale as death, but laughed at the terrible weather; she didn't think it was bad enough. Her white coat swirled around in the air like a huge ship-sail, and the traveling companion beat her with the three switches until blood was dripping on the ground, and until she could barely fly. But at last she came to the mountain.

"It's hailing and stormy," she said. "Never have I been out in such weather."

"Yes, it's possible to get too much of a good thing," the troll said. Then she told him that Johannes had guessed correctly the second time too. If he did the same tomorrow, he would win, and she could never come to the mountain again or do witchcraft as before. She was very saddened by this.

"He won't be able to guess!" the troll said. "I'll come up with something that he has never imagined, or he's a better magician than I am. But now we'll be merry!" He took the princess in both hands and they danced around with all the little pixies and will-o-wisps that were in the hall. The red spiders ran merrily up and down the walls, and the fire flowers were sparkling. The owl played the drum; the crickets chirped; and the black grasshoppers played the harmonica. It was a very merry ball!

When they had danced long enough, the princess had to go home because she could be missed at the castle. The troll said that he would accompany her so they could be together for a while yet.

They flew away in terrible weather, and the traveling companion wore out his three switches on their backs. The troll had never been out in such a hailstorm. Outside the castle the troll said good bye to the princess and whispered to her, "Think about my head," but the traveling companion heard it all right, and the moment the princess slipped through the window into her bedroom, and the troll turned to go, he grasped him by his long black beard and chopped his nasty troll head off at the shoulders with the sword, so quickly that the troll didn't even see it. He threw the body out into the ocean for the fish, but he dipped the head in the water. Then he wrapped it up in his silk handkerchief, took it back to the inn, and went to bed.

The next morning he gave Johannes the handkerchief, but told him not to open it until the princess asked what she had thought about.

There were so many people in the big chamber at the castle

that they were standing on top of each other like radishes tied in a bunch. The councilors sat in their chairs with their soft pillows, and the old king was wearing new clothes. His gold crown and scepter were polished and looked beautiful, but the princess was quite pale and was wearing a coal-black dress, as though she were going to a funeral.

"What have I been thinking about?" she asked Johannes, and he immediately opened the handkerchief and became frightened himself when he saw the terrible troll head. Everyone shivered because it was dreadful to see, but the princess sat like a statue and could not utter a single word. Finally, she stood up and gave Johannes her hand because he had guessed correctly. She didn't look at anyone, but sighed deeply and said, "Now you are my master! We'll have the wedding this evening."

"I like that!" said the old king, "That's what we'll do." All the people shouted "hurrah," the guard played music in the streets, bells rang, and the bakery women took the black ribbons off the candied pigs, for now there was joy! Three whole grilled oxen stuffed with ducks and hens were set up in the marketplace; everyone could cut off a piece. The fountains flowed with the most delectable wine, and if you bought a little pastry at the bakery, you got six big buns thrown in, and with raisins in them at that.

In the evening the entire city was lit up, and soldiers fired cannons and boys fired caps, and there was eating and drinking, toasting and dancing at the castle, where all the elegant men and lovely women danced with each other; you could hear their song from far away:

"Here's many a lovely girl
Who wants to take a swirl,
Shoo shoo—shoo fly shoo.
They prefer a lively tune,
Pretty girls, swing and swoon
Shoo shoo—shoo fly shoo.
Dance and carouse
Until your soles wear out!"
Shoo fly shoo—and **shoe** *fly——!"*

But the princess was still a witch, of course, and didn't care about Johannes at all. The traveling companion knew this, and so he gave Johannes three of the swan feathers and a little flask filled with some liquid and told him that he should have a large tub set by the bridal bed. When the princess was ready to climb into bed, he was to give her a little push so she fell into the water, where he was to dunk her three times after throwing in the feathers and the drops. Then she would be free of her spell and would fall in love with him.

Johannes did everything the traveling companion told him to do. The princess shrieked loudly when he dunked her under the water and squirmed under his hands in the shape of a big black swan with flashing eyes. When she came up the second time, the swan was white except for a black ring around its neck. Johannes prayed piously to the Lord, and let the water for the third time slip over the bird, and in that instant it changed into the most beautiful princess. She was even lovelier than before and thanked him with tears in her marvelous eyes because he had broken the spell.

The next morning the king came with all the court, and the receiving line went on until late in the day. At the very end came the traveling companion. He had his walking stick in his hand and his knapsack on his back. Johannes kissed him over and over and asked him not to go away—he wanted him to stay with them since he was responsible for all his happiness. But the traveling companion shook his head and said mildly and gently, "No, my time is up. I have only repaid my debt. Do you remember the dead man plagued by those wicked men? You gave everything you had so that he could have peace in his grave. That dead man is me!"

He disappeared at once.

The wedding feast lasted for an entire month. Johannes and the princess were very much in love, and the old king lived many happy days. He bounced their little children on his knee and let them play with his scepter. But Johannes was the king of the whole country.

NOTE

1. In 1820 a typical wage for a tradesman would be about ten dollars (Danish *rigsdaler*) for three weeks' work; in 1850 wages were about a dollar a day.

THE WILD SWANS

FAR AWAY FROM HERE, where the swallows fly during the winter, there lived a king who had eleven sons and one daughter, Elisa. The eleven brothers, who were princes, went to school with stars on their breasts and swords by their sides. They wrote on gold slates with diamond pencils and knew their lessons by heart, and you could tell right away that they were princes. Their sister Elisa sat on a little footstool of plate glass and had a picture book that had cost half the kingdom.

Oh, those children had a good life, but it wasn't going to stay that way!

Their father, who was the king of the entire country, married an evil queen, who was not good to the poor children; they noticed it already on the first day. There was a big celebration at the castle, and the children were playing house, but instead of the cookies and baked apples they usually got plenty of, she gave them sand in a teacup and told them to pretend it was something else.

The next week she farmed little sister Elisa out to some peasants in the country, and it wasn't long before she was able to get the king to imagine all sorts of wicked things about the princes so that finally he didn't care about them anymore.

"Fly out in the world and take care of yourselves!" said the evil queen. "Fly as great voiceless birds!" but she wasn't able to make it quite as bad as she wanted—they became eleven lovely wild swans. With a strange cry they flew out of the castle windows and over the park and the forest.

It was still early morning when they flew over the peasant's cottage where their sister Elisa was sleeping. They hovered over the roof, twisted their long necks, and flapped their wings, but no one saw or heard them. They flew away again, high up towards the clouds and far away into the wide world and into a big dark forest that stretched all the way to the sea.

Poor little Elisa stood in the peasant's cottage playing with a green leaf because she didn't have any other toys. She pierced a hole in the leaf and peeked up at the sun through it, and it was as if she saw her brothers' clear eyes, and each time the sunshine hit her cheek, she thought about their many kisses.

One day passed like another. When the wind blew through the big rose hedges outside the house, it whispered to the roses, "Who can be more beautiful than you?" but the roses shook their heads and answered, "Elisa." And when the old woman sat by the door reading her hymnal on Sundays, the wind turned the pages and said to the book, "Who can be more pious than you?" "Elisa," said the hymnal, and what the roses and the hymnal said was the solemn truth.

When she was fifteen years old, she was to return home, and as soon as the queen saw how beautiful she was, she became angry and hateful to her. She would have liked to turn Elisa into a wild swan, like she did to her brothers, but she didn't dare do it right away since the king wanted to see his daughter.

Early in the morning the queen went into her bathroom, which was built of marble and was decorated with soft cushions and the loveliest carpets. She took three toads, kissed them, and said to the first, "Sit on Elisa's head when she gets into the bath, so that she will become sluggish, like you."

"Sit on her forehead," she said to the second one, "so she will become ugly like you, and her father won't recognize her."

"Sit on her heart," she whispered to the third. "Give her a bad disposition, so she'll suffer from it."

Then she put the toads into the clear water, which immediately took on a greenish hue, called Elisa, undressed her, and had her step into the bath, and as she went under the water, the first toad sat on her hair, the second on her forehead, and the third on her breast, but Elisa didn't seem to notice. As soon as she rose up, there were three red poppies floating on the water. If the animals hadn't been poisonous and kissed by the witch, they would have been changed to red roses, but they became flowers anyway by resting on her head and on her heart. She was too pious and innocent for the black magic to have any power over her.

When the evil queen saw this, she rubbed walnut oil on Elisa so she became dark brown. Then she spread a stinking salve over the beautiful face and left her lovely hair tangled and matted. It was no longer possible to recognize the lovely Elisa at all.

When her father saw her, he became quite alarmed and claimed that she wasn't his daughter. No one else would acknowledge her either, except the watchdog and the swallows, but they were just poor animals and didn't count.

Poor Elisa wept and thought about her eleven brothers, all of whom were gone. She crept sadly out of the castle and wandered the whole day over moor and meadow and into the big forest. She didn't know where she wanted to go, but she felt so sad and longed for her brothers, who had been chased out into the world like her. Now she would search them out and find them.

She had only been in the woods for a short time before night fell. She had wandered clear away from the path, so she lay down on the soft moss, said her prayers, and rested her head on a stump. It was so quiet, the air was so mild, and around about her in the grass and on the moss there were hundreds of glowworms shining like green fire. When she gently touched one of the branches with her hand, the shining insects fell down to her like falling stars.

All night she dreamed about her brothers. They were children playing again, writing with the diamond pencil on golden slates, and looking at the lovely picture book that had cost half the kingdom. But they didn't draw only circles and lines on the slates, like before, rather they wrote about the most daring deeds that they had done, everything they had experienced and seen. Everything in the picture book was alive. Birds sang and the people came out of the book and talked to Elisa and her brothers, but when she turned the page, they leaped back in again, so that the pictures wouldn't get mixed up.

When she awoke, the sun was already high in the sky. She couldn't see it because the branches of the tall trees were spread across the sky, but the rays danced up there in the tree-tops like a fluttering veil of gold. All the green plants gave off a fragrance, and the birds almost perched on her shoulders. She heard water splashing from a great many large springs that all pooled into a pond with a lovely sand bottom. All around the pond bushes were growing densely, but in one spot the deer had cleared a big opening, and Elisa was able to get to the water, which was so clear that if the wind hadn't stirred the branches and bushes so they moved, you would have thought that they were painted on the bottom, so vividly was every leaf reflected there, both in sunshine and in shade.

When she saw her own face, she was frightened because it was so brown and ugly, but when she took water in her little hand and rubbed her eyes and forehead, the white skin shone through again. Then she took off all her clothes and went into the refreshing water, and there was no more beautiful princess anywhere.

When she was dressed and had braided her long hair, she went to the bubbling spring, drank from the hollow of her hand, and wandered further into the forest, not knowing where she was going. She thought about her brothers and about the good Lord, who wouldn't desert her. He let the wild crab apples grow, to feed the hungry, and He showed her such a tree with branches heavy with fruit. She had her dinner here, propped up the branches of the tree, and then walked into the darkest part of the forest. It was so quiet that she could hear her own footsteps, hear every little shriveled leaf that crunched under her feet. Not a bird could be seen, and not a ray of sun-shine could shine through the big thick tree branches. The tall trunks stood so close together that when she looked straight ahead, it was as if she had a fence of thick posts all around her. Oh, here was a loneliness such as she'd never known!

The night became pitch dark, and there was not a single lit-tle glowworm shining on the moss. Sadly she lay down to sleep. Then she thought that the tree branches above her parted, and the Lord with gentle eyes looked down on her, and small angels peered out over his head and under his arms.

When she awoke in the morning she didn't know if it had

been a dream or if it had really happened. After walking a short way, she met an old woman who had some berries in her basket. The old woman gave her some of these, and Elisa asked if she had seen eleven princes riding through the forest.

"No," said the old woman, "but yesterday I saw eleven swans with gold crowns on their heads swimming in the river not far from here."

And she led Elisa a little further to a steep slope with a river winding below it. The trees on each bank stretched out their long leafy branches towards each other, and wherever they couldn't reach with natural growth, they had torn their roots out from the soil and were leaning out over the water with branches woven together. Elisa said goodbye to the old woman and walked alongside the river until it flowed out onto a wide open shore.

The whole beautiful ocean lay there in front of the young girl, but neither a sail nor a boat could be seen out there. How was she to get any further? She looked at all the innumerable little stones on the shore; the water had polished them smooth. Glass, iron, stone—everything that was washed up on the beach had been shaped by water, water that was softer still than her white hand. "They roll tirelessly, and so they smooth out the roughness; I'll be just as tireless! Thank you for your wisdom, you clear rolling waves. My heart tells me that some day you'll carry me to my dear brothers."

Lying in the washed-up seaweed there were eleven white swan feathers that she gathered in a bouquet. There were water drops on them, but no one could tell if it was dew or tears. It was lonely there on the beach, but she didn't feel it since the ocean changed constantly—more in a few hours than a lake would change in a whole year. If a big black cloud came over, it was as if the ocean said, "I can also look dark," and then the wind blew, and the waves showed their white caps. If the clouds were glowing red and the wind was sleeping, then the sea was like a rose petal. First it was green, then white, but no matter how quietly it rested, there was always a slight move-ment by the shore; the water swelled softly, like the chest of a sleeping child.

Just before the sun went down, Elisa saw eleven white swans with gold crowns on their heads flying towards land. They were gliding across the sky one after the other like a long white ribbon. Elisa climbed up on the slope and hid behind a bush while the swans landed close by her and flapped with their great white wings.

After the sun had set, the swan skins suddenly slipped off, and there stood eleven handsome princes, Elisa's brothers. She gave a loud cry, because even though they had changed a lot, she knew that it was them. Indeed, she felt that it must be them and ran into their arms, calling them by name, and they became so happy when they saw and recognized their little sister, who had grown so big and beautiful. They laughed and they cried, and soon told each other how badly their stepmother had treated them all.

The eldest brother said, "We brothers fly as wild swans so long as the sun is up, but when it sets, our human shapes are returned to us. That's why we always have to be careful to be on land at sunset because, if we were to be flying up in the clouds, then we would fall to the ground. We don't live here, but in a land just as beautiful as this one on the other side of the sea. It's far far away, and we have to cross the ocean. There is no island on our route where we can spend the night except a lonely little rock that sticks up way out in the middle of the sea. It's so small that we have to rest there side by side. In high seas the waves spray over us, but still we thank God for it. We spend the night there in our human shape, and without it we could never visit our dear fatherland because it takes two of the longest days of the year to make the flight. We can only visit our homeland once a year, and we don't dare stay more than eleven days. We fly over this huge forest, from where we can see the castle where we were born, and where father lives. We can see the high tower of the church, where mother is buried.—We feel related to the trees and bushes here. The wild horses run over the plains here, as we saw them in our childhood. The coal-burners still sing the same old songs here that we danced to as children. Our fatherland is here. We're drawn here, and here we have found you, dear little sister! We can only stay two more days, and then we have to fly over the sea to that lovely country that isn't our native land. How can we bring you with us? We have neither ship nor boat."

"How can I save you?" their sister responded.

They spoke together almost the whole night and slept only a few hours.

Elisa awoke to the sound of swans' wings whistling over her. Her brothers were once again transformed, and they flew in a big circle and finally far away, but one of them, the youngest, stayed behind and laid his head in her lap. She patted his white wings, and they spent the whole day together. Towards evening, the others came back, and when the sun went down, they stood there in their natural form.

"We have to fly away tomorrow and don't dare come back for a whole year, but we can't leave you! Do you have the courage to come with us? My arm is strong enough to carry you through the forest. Together we should have strong enough wings to fly with you across the sea."

"Yes! Take me along!" said Elisa.

They spent the whole night braiding a net of the supple willow bark and thick rushes, and it was of great size and strength. Elisa laid down on this, and after the sun came up, and the brothers were changed to swans, they took hold of the net with their beaks and flew high up towards the clouds with their dear sister, who was still sleeping. When the rays of the sun shone on her face, one of the swans flew over her head so that his wide wings shaded her.

They were far from land when Elisa woke up. She thought she was still dreaming because it was so strange for her to be carried high in the air above the ocean. By her side lay a branch with delicious ripe berries and a bunch of tasty roots. Her youngest brother had gathered them and placed them there for her, and she smiled her thanks at him. She knew that it was he who was flying right above her head, shading her with his wings.

They were so high up that the first ship they saw under them looked like a white seagull floating on the water. There was a huge cloud behind them like a mountain, and on it Elisa could

All day they flew, like a rushing arrow through the air.

see the enormous shadows of herself and the eleven swans as they flew. It was a picture more magnificent than anything she had seen before, but as the sun rose higher and the cloud receded behind them, the floating shadow picture disappeared.

All day they flew, like a rushing arrow through the air, but it was slower than usual since they had to carry their sister. A storm was gathering, and evening was coming. Anxiously, Elisa saw the sun sink, and the lonely rock in the sea was not in sight. It seemed to her that the swans were strengthening their wing strokes. Alas! It was her fault that they weren't moving faster! When the sun set, they would change into men, fall into the sea, and drown. Deep in her heart she said a prayer to the Lord, but she still couldn't see the rock. The black cloud came closer, and strong gusts of wind told of the storm's approach. The clouds came rolling towards them like a single big threatening wave of lead, and lightning bolt followed lightning bolt.

The sun was just at the rim of the sea, and Elisa's heart trembled. The swans shot downward so quickly that she thought she was falling—then they glided again. The sun was halfway down in the sea when she first saw the little rock below her. It didn't look any bigger than a seal sticking its head up from the water. The sun sank quickly and was now no bigger than a star. Then her foot felt the hard rock as the sun went out like the last spark in a piece of burning paper. She saw her brothers standing around her, arm in arm, but there wasn't room for anyone else. The sea crashed against the rock and splashed over them like a cloudburst of rain. The sky was shining like never-ending fire, and clap after clap of thunder rolled by, but the sister and her brothers held hands and sang a hymn, which gave them comfort and courage.

At dawn the air was clear and still, and as soon as the sun came up, the swans flew away from the rock with Elisa. There was still a high sea, and when they were high in the air, the white foam on the dark green sea looked like millions of swans floating on the water.

When the sun climbed higher, Elisa saw ahead of her, half floating in the air, a mountainous land with shining glaciers on the mountains, and in the middle was a mile-long castle with one bold colonnade on top of the other. Below there were waving palm forests and gorgeous flowers big as mill wheels. She asked if that was their destination, but the swans shook their heads. What she saw was a mirage, *Fata Morgana's*[1] lovely sky castle that was constantly changing, and they didn't dare bring humans there. As Elisa stared at it, the mountain, forests, and castle collapsed and twenty splendid churches stood there, all alike, with high steeples and arched windows. She thought she heard the organ playing, but it was the ocean she heard. When she was quite close to the churches, they changed to an entire fleet of ships that sailed below her. She looked down, and it was only sea-fog chasing across the water. She was watching an ever-changing scene, and then she saw the real country that was their destination. There were lovely blue mountains with cedar forests, towns and castles. Long before sunset, she was sitting on a mountain in front of a big cave, overgrown with fine green twining plants, which looked like embroidered carpets.

"Now we'll see what you dream about here tonight," said the youngest brother and showed her to her bedroom.

"I wish I would dream about how I could rescue you all!" she said, and this thought occupied her so vividly that she prayed fervently to God for help. Even in sleep she continued her prayer; and it seemed to her that she flew high up in the air to *Fata Morgana's* sky castle, and a fairy came towards her, lovely and glittering, but she looked exactly like the old woman who had given her berries in the forest and told her about the swans wearing the gold crowns.

"Your brothers can be rescued," she said, "if you have the courage and perseverance. It's true that the sea is softer than your fine hands and can shape the hard stones, but it doesn't feel the pain your fingers will feel. It has no heart and doesn't suffer the dread and terror you must tolerate. Do you see this stinging nettle I'm holding in my hand? Many of these grow around the cave where you're sleeping. Only those and those that grow on the graves in the churchyard can be used—take note of that. You have to pick them, although they will burn your skin to blisters. Then you must tramp the nettles with your feet to get flax, and with that you must spin and knit eleven thick shirts with long sleeves. Throw these over the eleven wild swans, and the spell will be broken. But remember this: from the moment you begin this work and until the day it is finished you cannot speak, even if your work takes years. The first word you speak would be like a dagger in your brothers' hearts, and it would kill them. Their lives hang upon your tongue. Pay attention to all that I've told you!"

And she touched Elisa's hand with the nettle, which like a burning fire, woke her up. It was bright day, and right next to where she had been sleeping, lay a nettle like the one she had seen in her dream. Then she fell on her knees and thanked God, and went out of the cave to begin her work.

With her fine hands, she reached down into the nasty nettles, which were like scorching fire. They burned big blisters on her hands and arms, but she bore it gladly, to rescue her dear brothers. And so she broke each nettle with her bare feet and spun the green flax.

When the sun went down, her brothers came, and they were frightened to find her so silent. They thought their evil stepmother had cast a new spell, but when they saw her hands, they realized what she was doing for their sakes, and the youngest brother burst into tears. Wherever his tears fell, the pain left her, and the burning blisters disappeared.

She worked all night because she could have no rest until she had saved her beloved brothers. All the next day, while the swans were away, she sat there alone, but time had never flown so quickly. One shirt was already finished, and she started on the next one.

Then she heard a hunting horn echo through the hills, and it scared her. The sound came closer, and she heard dogs barking. Frightened, she ran into the cave and wound the nettles and her knitting into a bundle and sat down on it.

Just then a big dog sprang from the thicket, and then another and another; they barked loudly and ran back and forth. Within a few minutes all the hunters were standing outside the cave, and the most handsome of them all was the king of the country. He went into the cave, and never had he seen a more beautiful girl than Elisa.

"How did you get here, you beautiful child?" he asked.

Elisa shook her head. She didn't dare speak, of course, since her brothers' lives and safety were at stake, and she hid her hands under her apron, so the king would not see what she was suffering.

"Come with me!" he said, "You can't stay here! If you're as good as you are beautiful, I'll dress you in silk and velvet and set a gold crown on your head, and you'll live in my richest castle."

He lifted her up onto his horse, and she cried and wrung her hands, but the king said, "I only want your happiness. Some day you'll thank me for this." Then he galloped away through the hills with her in front of him on the horse, and the hunters followed after them. As the sun was setting, the magnificent royal city with its churches and domes was lying before them, and the king led her into the castle, where enormous fountains splashed under the high ceilings in rooms of marble. The walls and ceilings were decorated with paintings, but she had no eye for them. She cried and grieved, and passively let the women dress her in royal clothing, braid pearls in her hair, and draw fine gloves over her burned fingers.

When she stood there in all her glory, she was so dazzlingly beautiful that the court bowed down deeply to her, and the king chose her for his queen, even though the arch-bishop shook his head and whispered that the beautiful forest maiden must be a witch, who had bedazzled their eyes and bewitched the king's heart.

But the king didn't listen to him. Instead he had the musicians play and had the most splendid dishes served. The most beautiful girls danced around Elisa, and she was led through fragrant gardens into magnificent chambers, but not a smile crossed her lips, or appeared in her eyes, where sorrow seemed to have taken up eternal residence. Then the king opened a door to a tiny room, close by her bedroom; it was decorated with expensive green carpets and resembled the cave where she had been. The bundles of flax she had spun from the nettles were lying on the floor, and hanging up by the ceiling was the shirt she had finished. One of the hunters had brought all this along as a curiosity.

"You can dream about your former home here," said the king. "Here's the work that you used to do. It'll amuse you to think back to that time now that you're surrounded with luxury."

When Elisa saw these things that were so close to her heart, a smile came to her lips, and the blood returned to her cheeks. She thought about her brothers' salvation and kissed the king's hand. In return he pulled her to his heart and had all the church bells proclaim the wedding feast. The beautiful silent girl from the forest was to be queen of the land.

The arch-bishop whispered evil words into the king's ear, but they did not reach his heart. The wedding was set, and the arch-bishop himself had to place the crown on her head. Although he pressed the narrow band down on her forehead with evil resentment so that it hurt, there was a heavier band pressing on her heart—the sorrow she felt about her brothers, and she did not feel the bodily pain. Since a single word would kill her brothers, her mouth was silent, but in her eyes lay a deep love for the good, handsome king, who did everything he could to please her. Day by day she grew to love him more and more. Oh, if only she dared to confide in him, to tell him of her suffering! But she had to remain silent, and in silence she had to finish her work. Night after night she stole away from his side and went into her little closet that resembled the cave. She knit one thick shirt after the other, but when she started on the seventh one, she ran out of flax.

She knew that the nettles that she should use grew in the churchyard, but she had to pick them herself. How was she going to get there?

"Oh, what is the pain in my fingers compared to the agony in my heart!" she thought. "I must risk it. God won't desert me!" With terror in her heart, as if she were on her way to do an evil deed, she stole down to the garden in the moonlit night. She went through the long avenues of trees and out on the empty streets, to the churchyard. On one of the widest tombstones she saw a ring of vampires—hideous witches, who took off their rags as if they were going to bathe and then dug down into the fresh graves with their long, thin fingers, pulled the corpses out, and ate their flesh. Elisa had to pass right by them, and they cast their evil eyes on her; but she said her prayers, gathered the burning nettles, and carried them home to the castle.

Only a single person saw her—the arch-bishop. He was awake when others slept. Now he felt vindicated, for the queen was not what she seemed. She was a witch, who had bewitched the king and all the people.

In the confessional he told the king what he had seen, and what he feared, and when the harsh words came from his tongue, the images of the carved saints shook their heads as if they wanted to say, "It isn't so. Elisa is innocent!" But the arch-bishop explained it differently. He said they were witnessing against her and shaking their heads over her sin. Two heavy tears rolled down the king's cheeks, and he went home with doubt in his heart. He pretended to sleep that night, but remained wide awake. He noticed how Elisa got up, and how she repeated this every night, and every night he followed her quietly and saw her disappear into her little chamber.

Day by day his face grew more troubled. Elisa saw this and didn't know why, but it worried her, and she was still suffering in her heart for her brothers. Her salty tears streamed down and fell upon her royal velvet and purple clothing. They lay there like glimmering diamonds, and everyone who saw the rich magnificence wished to be the queen. In the meantime she had finished her work. Only one shirt was left, but she was again out of flax and didn't have a single nettle. One last time she would have to go to the churchyard and pick a few handfuls. She thought about the lonely trip and about the terrible vampires with dread, but her will was firm, as was her faith in God.

Elisa went, but the king and arch-bishop followed her. They saw her disappear at the wrought iron gate of the cemetery, and when they came closer to the gravestones, they saw the vampires, as Elisa had seen them. The king turned away because he thought she was among them—his wife whose head had rested against his breast this very night!

"The people must judge her," he said, and the people judged that she should be burned in the red flames.

From the splendid royal chambers she was led into a dark, damp hole, where the wind whistled through the barred windows. Instead of velvet and silk they gave her the bundle of nettles she had gathered; she could rest her head on those. The hard, burning shirts she had knit were to be her bedding, but they couldn't have given her anything dearer to her. She started her work again and prayed to God while outside the street urchins sang mocking ditties about her, and not a soul consoled her with a friendly word.

Toward evening a swan wing whistled right by the window grate. It was the youngest brother who had found his sister, and she sobbed aloud in joy, even though she knew that the approaching night could be the last she would live. But now the work was almost done, and her brothers were here.

The arch-bishop came to spend the last hours with her, as he had promised the king he would do, but she shook her head and asked him to leave with expressions and gestures. She had to finish her work this night, or everything would be to no avail—everything: pain, tears and the sleepless nights. The arch-bishop went away with harsh words for her, but poor Elisa knew that she was innocent and continued her work.

Little mice ran around on the floor, and pulled the nettles over to her feet, to help a little. By the barred window the thrush sat and sang all night long, as merrily as he could, so she wouldn't lose her courage.

It was an hour before dawn when the eleven brothers stood by the gate to the castle and asked to see the king, but they were told that they couldn't because it was still night. The king was sleeping, and they didn't dare wake him. They begged, and they threatened. The guards came, and even the king himself appeared and asked what this meant. At that moment the sun came up, and there were no brothers to be seen, but over the castle flew eleven wild swans.

All the people in the town streamed out of the gates. They

wanted to see the witch burn. A miserable horse pulled the cart she was sitting in. They had given her a smock of coarse sackcloth, and her lovely long hair hung loosely around her beautiful head. Her cheeks were deathly pale, and her lips moved slowly while her fingers twined the green flax. Even on her way to her death she did not stop the work she had started. Ten shirts lay by her feet, and she was knitting the eleventh. The mob insulted her.

"Look at the witch! See how she's mumbling. And she doesn't have her hymnal in her hands! She is sitting with her magic things. Let's tear them into a thousand pieces!"

And the crowd approached her and wanted to tear her things apart, but then eleven white swans flew down and sat around her on the cart and flapped with their huge wings. The mob fell back terrified.

"It's a sign from heaven! She must be innocent!" many whispered, but they didn't dare say it aloud.

As the executioner grabbed her hand, she hastily threw the eleven shirts over the swans. There stood eleven handsome princes, but the youngest one had a swan's wing instead of one arm, since there was a sleeve missing in the shirt. She hadn't been able to finish it.

"Now I dare speak!" she said, "I am innocent!"

And the people who saw what had happened bowed down before her as if for a saint, but she sank lifeless into the arms of her brothers. The tension, terror, and pain had affected her this way.

"Yes, she's innocent!" said the eldest brother, and he told them everything that had happened. While he was speaking, the people could smell the scent as of a million roses because all of the logs in the bonfire had sprouted roots and branches. There was a fragrant hedge standing there, big and tall with red roses. At the top was a flower, white and shining that lit up like a star. The king picked it and set it on Elisa's breast, and she awoke with peace and happiness in her heart.

Then all the church bells rang by themselves, birds came flying in big flocks, and the bridal procession that led back to the castle was like no other seen before by any king.

NOTE

1. A mirage (an optical phenomenon, often characterized by distortion) that appears near an object, often at sea; named after the sorceress Morgan le Fay, sister to King Arthur, who was said to be able to change her shape.

THE SWINEHERD

ONCE UPON A TIME there was a poor prince. He had a kingdom that was quite small, but it was big enough so he could afford to get married, and that's what he wanted to do.

Now it was pretty fresh of him to ask the emperor's daughter, "Do you want to marry me?" But he dared it because his name was known far and wide, and there were hundreds of princesses who would have accepted him, but we'll see if she does.

Now listen to what happened.

On the grave of the prince's father there grew a rose tree, and a lovely rose tree it was! It only flowered every five years and then only with a single rose, but it was a rose that smelled so sweet that when you smelled it, you forgot all your sorrows and worries. The prince also had a nightingale that could sing as if all the most beautiful melodies sat in its little throat. That rose and that nightingale were to be given to the princess, and so they were both placed in big silver cases and were sent to her.

The emperor had the cases brought into the big room where the princess was playing house with her chambermaids, and when she saw the big cases with the gifts inside, she clapped her hands in joy.

"If only it's a little pussycat!" she said, but then the rose tree with the lovely rose was unveiled.

"Oh, how beautifully it's made," said all the chambermaids.

"It's more than beautiful," the emperor said. "It's neat!"

But the princess felt it and then was ready to cry.

"Oh yuck, pappa!" she said. "It's not artificial, it's *real*!"

"Yuck!" all the chambermaids said. "It's real!"

On the grave of the prince's father there grew a rose tree,
and a lovely rose tree it was!

"Let's see what's in the other case before we get angry," said the emperor, and then the nightingale was brought forth. It sang so beautifully that it would be impossible to say anything against it.

"*Superbe! Charmant!*" said the chambermaids for they all spoke French, one more badly than the next.

"How that bird reminds me of the saintly old empress's music box," said an old gentleman-in-waiting. "Oh yes, it's just the same tone, the same delivery!"

"Yes indeed!" said the emperor, and he cried like a little child.

"But I don't believe it's real," said the princess.

"Yes, it's a real bird," said those who had brought it.

"So let the bird fly away with the ideas of that prince," said the princess, and she would not allow him to come under any circumstances.

But he kept his spirits up and smeared his face brown and black, pulled a peaked cap low on his head, and knocked at the door.

"Hello, emperor," he said. "Do you have a job for me here at the castle?"

"Sure," said the emperor. "I need someone to take care of the pigs because we have a lot of them."

So the prince was hired as the royal swineherd. He was given a humble little room down by the pig sty, and that's where he had to stay, but all day he sat and worked, and when it was evening, he had made a lovely little pot. There were bells all around it, and as soon as the pot boiled, they rang beautifully and played the old melody:

> *Ach, Du lieber Augustine,*
> *Alles ist weg, weg, weg.*[1]

But the most wonderful thing of all was that when you held your finger in the steam from the pot, you could immediately smell what food was being cooked at each chimney in town. See, this was really something different than that rose!

The princess came walking by with all her chambermaids,

and when she heard the melody she stopped and looked so contented because she could also play "Ach, Du lieber Augustine." It was the only thing she could play, and she played it with one finger.

"That's the one I know!" she said. "That swineherd must be a cultivated man! Listen, go down and ask him what that instrument costs."

So one of the chambermaids had to go into the pigpen, but she put on clods first.

"What do you want for that pot?" asked the attendant.

"I want ten kisses from the princess," said the swineherd.

"God save us!" said the attendant.

"Well, I won't take less," answered the swineherd.

"Well, he is certainly rude," said the princess, and she walked away, but when she had walked a little distance, the bells rang so lovely:

> *Ach, Du lieber Augustine,*
> *Alles ist weg, weg, weg.*

"Listen," said the princess, "ask him if he'll take ten kisses from my chambermaids."

"No thanks!" said the swineherd. "Ten kisses from the princess, or I keep the pot."

"How unpleasant this is!" said the princess to the chambermaids, "but you'll have to stand in front of me so no one sees it!"

And the chambermaids lined up and spread out their skirts, and the swineherd got his ten kisses, and she got the pot.

Well, what an amusing thing that was! All evening and all day the pot had to cook, and there wasn't a chimney in the whole town where they didn't know what was cooking, both at the mayor's and the shoemaker's. The chambermaids danced and clapped their hands.

"We know who's having soup and spam! We know who's having leg of lamb! How interesting this is!"

"Yes, but watch your mouths. I'm the emperor's daughter!"

"God save us!" they all said.

The swineherd, that is to say, the prince—but they didn't know he wasn't a real swineherd—didn't let the day go by without doing something, and so now he made a rattle. When you swung it around, it played all the waltzes and lively dances known since the start of time.

"But that's superb," said the princess when she went by. "I have never heard a more delightful composition. Listen! Go in and ask him what that instrument costs, but I won't kiss for it!"

"He wants a hundred kisses from the princess," said the chambermaid who had been sent to ask.

"I believe he's crazy," said the princess, and she walked away, but when she had walked a short distance, she stopped. "One has to support art!" she said. "I am the emperor's daughter! Tell him that he can have ten kisses like yesterday, the rest he can take from my chambermaids."

"Well, but we don't want to do that," the chambermaids said.

"Oh, fudge!" said the princess. "If I can kiss him, so can you. Remember I give you room and board and a salary," and then the chambermaid had to go back into the pig sty again.

"A hundred kisses from the princess," he said, "or no deal."

"Stand around!" said she, and so all the chambermaids stood in front of her and he started kissing.

"What is that crowd doing down there by the pig sty?" asked the emperor, who had stepped out on the balcony. He rubbed his eyes and put on his glasses. "Why it's the chambermaids at it again! I'd better go down and see." And he pulled his slippers up in back because they were just shoes that he had worn down.

My heavens how he hurried!

As soon as he came into the yard, he slowed way down, and the chambermaids were so busy counting the kisses to be sure it was accurate that they didn't notice the emperor, who stood up on his tiptoes.

"What's this!?" he said when he saw them kissing, and then he hit them on their heads with his slipper, just as the swineherd got the eighty-sixth kiss. "Get out of here!" said the emperor, for he was very angry, and both the princess and the swineherd were banished from the kingdom.

She stood there crying, while the swineherd scolded, and the rain came pouring down.

"Alas, I'm a miserable person," said the princess. "If only I'd accepted that lovely prince! Oh, how unhappy I am!"

The swineherd went behind a tree, wiped the black and brown colors from his face, threw away the dirty clothes, and stepped out in his prince outfit, so handsome that the princess had to curtsy before him.

"I have come to despise you, you see," he said. "You didn't want an honorable prince! You didn't appreciate the rose or the nightingale, but you kissed a swineherd for the sake of a plaything! Now it serves you right."

Then he went back to his kingdom and locked her out so she truly could sing:

> *Ach, Du lieber Augustine,*
> *Alles ist weg, weg, weg.*

NOTE

1. From an eighteenth-century German folksong; the lines translate as: "Oh, my dearest Augustine / Everything is gone, gone, gone."

MOTHER ELDERBERRY

ONCE UPON A TIME there was a little boy who had a cold. He had been out and gotten wet feet. No one could understand how he had done that because the weather was quite dry. So his mother undressed him and put him to bed, and she brought in the tea urn to make him a good cup of elderberry tea because that warms you up! Just then the old amusing gentleman who lived on the top floor of the house came through the door. He lived quite alone because he had neither a wife nor children, but he was very fond of children and knew so many good fairy tales and stories that it was a delight.

"Now drink your tea," said the mother, "and maybe you'll get a fairy tale."

"If I just knew a new one," said the old man and nodded gently. "But where did the little guy get his feet wet?" he asked.

"Where indeed?" said his mother. "No one knows."

"Are you going to tell me a story?" asked the boy.

"Well, first you have to tell me exactly how deep the gutter is in that little street where you go to school. I must know that."

"Exactly to the middle of my boots," said the boy, "but that's when I walk in the deepest hole."

"See, that's where the wet feet came from," said the old man. "Now I should really tell a fairy tale, but I don't know any new ones."

"You can make one up," said the little boy. "Mother says that everything you look at can become a fairy tale, and that you can get a story from everything you touch."

"But those fairy tales and stories are no good! No, the real ones come by themselves. They knock at my forehead and say, 'Here I am!'"

"Won't one knock soon?" asked the little boy, and his mother laughed as she put the tea in the pot and poured boiling water over it.

"A story! a story!"

"Well, if one would just come by itself, but they are so uppity that they only come when they want to—stop!" he said suddenly. "There it is! Look now, there's one in the teapot."

The little boy looked at the teapot. The lid raised itself higher and higher, and elderberry blooms came out so fresh and white. They shot out big, long branches, even out of the spout. They spread to all sides and became bigger and bigger. It was the most beautiful elderberry bush—a whole tree. It protruded onto the bed and shoved the curtains to the side. Oh, how it flowered and smelled! And in the middle of the tree sat a friendly old woman wearing an odd dress. It was quite green like the leaves of the elderberry tree and covered with white elderberry blossoms. You couldn't tell right away whether it was cloth or real greenery and flowers.

"What's that woman's name?" asked the little boy.

"Well, the Romans and Greeks called her a dryad,"[1] said the old man, "but we don't understand that. Over in Nyboder[2] they have a better name for her. They call her *Mother Elderberry*. Now keep your eye on her and on the beautiful elderberry tree while you listen:

"A tree just like this one stands blooming over there in Nyboder in the corner of a poor little garden. One afternoon two old people sat under that tree in the beautiful sunshine. They were a very old seaman and his very old wife. They were great-grandparents, and they were soon going to celebrate their fiftieth wedding anniversary, but they couldn't quite remember the date. *Mother Elderberry* sat in the tree and looked self-satisfied, like she does here. 'I certainly know when your anniversary is,' she said, but they didn't hear her. They were talking about the old days.

"'Can you remember the time when we were small children?' said the old seaman, 'And we ran around in this same garden where we're now sitting. We stuck sticks in the ground to make a garden.'

"'Yes,' said the old woman. 'I remember it well. And we watered the sticks, and one of them was an elderberry branch which took root and shot out shoots. Now it's the big tree we're sitting under as old people.'

"'Yes indeed,' he said, 'And over there in the corner was a water tub where my little boat sailed. I had carved it myself, and how it sailed! But soon I had sailing of a different kind!'

"'But first we went to school and learned a few things,' she said, 'and then we were confirmed. We both cried, but in the afternoon we walked hand in hand up to the top of the Round Tower and looked out over Copenhagen and the water.[3] Then we went to Fredericksberg where the king and queen were sailing on the canals in their splendid boat.'

"'But my sailing for many years was of a different kind. Far away on big trips!'

"'And I often cried for you,' she said. 'I thought you were dead and gone and lying down there in the deep waters. Many a night I got up to see if the weather vane had shown a wind change. And it did turn, but you didn't come! I remember so clearly how the rain was pouring down one day when the garbage man came where I was working. I came down with the garbage pail and was standing by the door. What terrible weather! And as I stood there, the mailman was by my side and gave me a letter. It was from you! And how it had been around! I tore right into it and read—laughed and cried. I was so happy! You wrote that you were in the warm countries where the coffee beans grow. What a wonderful land that must be! You described so much, and I saw it all, while the rain was pouring down and I was standing with the garbage pail. Just then someone put his arm around my waist—'

" 'And you gave him such a box on the ears that his head spun around!'

" 'I didn't know it was you! You came home as fast as your letter, and you were so handsome—as you still are, and you had a long yellow silk handkerchief in your pocket, and you were wearing a shiny hat. You were dressed up so fine. But dear God, what weather there was, and how the street looked!'

" 'Then we got married.' he said, 'Do you remember? And we had our first little boy, and then Marie, and Niels, and Peter, and Hans Christian.'

" 'And they all grew up to be decent people that everyone likes.'

" 'And their children have children!' said the old sailor, 'And those great grand-children have some spirit in them!— But it seems to me it was this time of year that we got married.'

" 'Yes, today is your Golden Anniversary,' said *Mother Elderberry* and stuck her head right down between the two old people. They thought it was their neighbor who had popped in. They looked at each other and held hands. A little later their children and grandchildren came. They knew very well that it was the Golden Anniversary day. They had, in fact, been around with congratulations in the morning, but the old couple had forgotten that, although they remembered very well everything that had happened many years before. The elderberry tree gave off such a lovely fragrance and the sun, that was about to set, shone right into the old ones' faces. They both looked so red-cheeked, and the smallest of the grandchildren danced around them and yelled happily that tonight there would be a feast—they were going to have roasted potatoes! And *Mother Elderberry* sat in her tree nodding and cheering 'hurray' along with everyone else."

"But that wasn't a fairy tale," said the little boy who had listened to it.

"Well, that's what you think, but let's ask *Mother Elderberry*," said the story-teller.

"That wasn't a fairy tale," said *Mother Elderberry*, "but here it comes! The most wonderful fairy tales grow right out of reality, otherwise my lovely elderberry tree couldn't have sprouted from the teapot!" And then she took the little boy out of the bed, held him by her breast, and the elderberry branches, full of flowers, closed around them. They sat as if in a completely enclosed garden pavilion, and it flew away with them through the air. Oh, it was marvelous! *Mother Elderberry* had at once become a beautiful young girl, but her dress was still the same green, white-flowered one that *Mother Elderberry* had worn. On her breast was a real elderberry flower, and on her curly yellow hair was a wreath of elderberry blossoms. Her eyes were so big and so blue. Oh, how beautiful she was! She and the boy kissed, and then they were the same age and felt the same.

They walked hand in hand out of the arbor of leaves and into the lovely garden of the boy's home. His father's walking cane was tethered to a stick on the lawn. There was life in that cane for the little ones. As soon as they put a leg over it, the shiny button changed to a magnificent neighing head with a long black flowing mane, and four slender, strong legs pushed out. The animal was strong and lively. They rushed around the lawn at a gallop. Giddy-up! "Now we'll ride for many miles," said the boy, "we'll ride to the big manor house where we were last year," and they rode and rode around on the grass. The little girl, whom we know was no one other than *Mother Elderberry*, called out, "Now we're in the country. Do you see the farmer's house? There's a big baking oven—it was a big lump like an egg in the wall out towards the road. The elderberry tree is holding its branches out above it, and the rooster is scratching about in front of the hens. See, how he's swaggering! Now we're at the church! It stands high on a hill between the big oak trees. One of them is partly dead. Now we're at the smithy's, where the fire is burning, and half-naked men are hammering so sparks are flying. Away! Away to the magnificent manor house!" Everything the little girl mentioned went flying by. She was sitting behind him on the cane. The boy saw it all, but still they were just riding on the lawn. Then they played in the side yard and scratched out a little garden in the soil. She took the elderberry flower from her hair and planted it, and it grew just as it had for the old people in Nyboder when they were little, like the story we heard earlier. They walked hand in hand like the old couple had done as children, but they didn't go up to the top of the Round Tower or out to Fredericksberg. No, the little girl put her arm around the boy's waist, and they flew around all over Denmark. Spring turned to summer, then autumn, followed by winter. A thousand pictures were mirrored in the little boy's eyes and heart, and the entire time the little girl sang for him, "you'll never forget this," and the whole time the sweet and lovely scent of the elderberry blossoms was with them. He noticed the roses and the fresh beech trees, but the elderberries' perfume was even more wonderful because the blossoms were fastened by the little girl's heart, and his head often rested there during the flight.

"How lovely it is here in the spring!" said the young girl, and they stood in the newly green sprouted beech woods where the green sweet woodruff wafted under their feet, and the pale pink anemones looked so lovely in the open air. "Oh, if it could always be spring in the fragrant Danish beech forests!"

"How lovely it is here in the summer!" she said, and they sped past old manor houses from the age of chivalry where the red walls and notched gables were reflected in the canals where the swans were swimming and looking up at the old cool avenues of trees. In the fields the grain was billowing as if it were a sea. There were red and yellow flowers in the ditches, and the fences were covered with wild hops and flowering bindweed. And in the evening the moon rose round and huge, and the scent of cut hay in the meadows filled the air. "This will never be forgotten!"

"How lovely it is here in the fall!" said the little girl, and the sky seemed doubly high and blue. The forest had the most lovely colors of red, yellow, and green. The hunting hounds bounded away, and big flocks of screeching wild birds flew over the burial mound where blackberry vines hung on the old stones. The sea was dark blue with white sails, and old women, girls, and children sat on the threshing floor picking hops into a big vat. The young sang songs, but the old told fairy tales about gnomes and trolls. It couldn't get better than this!

"How lovely it is here in the winter!" said the little girl. And all the trees were heavy with frost. They looked like white coral. The snow crunched under your feet as if you were always wearing new boots, and from the sky fell one falling star after another. The Christmas tree was lit in the living room, and there were presents and good cheer. In the country the fiddle was played in the farmer's living room. Little apple cakes were everywhere, and even the poorest child said, "it really is lovely in winter!"

It was lovely! And the little girl showed the boy everything, and the smell of elderberry flowers was always with them. The red flag with the white cross, under which the old sailor in Nyboder had sailed, waved everywhere. And the boy became a young man and was going out into the wide world, away to the warm countries where coffee beans grow. At parting the little girl took an elderberry flower from her bosom and gave it to him to keep. It was placed in his hymnal, and in foreign lands, whenever he opened the book, it always opened to the place where the keepsake flower was lying. The more he looked at it, the fresher it became, and it was as if he smelled the fragrance of the Danish forests, and he saw clearly the little girl with her clear blue eyes peer out from between the petals. And she whispered, "how lovely it is here in spring, in summer, in fall and in winter!" and hundreds of pictures passed through his mind.

Many years passed, and then he was an old man and sat with his old wife under a flowering tree. They were holding hands, like great-grandfather and great-grandmother in Nyboder did, and they talked like they had about the old days and about their Golden Anniversary. The little girl with the blue eyes and the elderberry flowers in her hair sat up in the tree, nodded at them both and said, "today is your Golden Anniversary," and then she took two flowers from her wreath and kissed them. First they shone like silver, then like gold, and when she placed them on the old folks' heads, each flower became a golden crown. There they sat like a king and a queen under the fragrant tree that looked absolutely just like an elderberry tree. And he told his old wife the story about *Mother Elderberry* as it had been told to him when he was a little boy. They both thought there was much in it that reminded them of their own story, and those were the parts they liked best.

"That's the way it is!" said the little girl in the tree. "Some call me *Mother Elderberry*, others call me a dryad, but my real name is *Memory*. I'm the one who sits in the tree that grows and grows. I can remember, and I can tell stories! Let me see if you still have your flower."

And the old man opened his hymnal. The elderberry flower was lying there as fresh as if it were just placed there, and *Memory* nodded, and the two old people with the gold crowns sat in the rosy evening sunshine. They closed their eyes—and—and then the fairy tale was over!

The little boy lay in his bed. He didn't know if he had been dreaming, or if he had heard a story. The teapot stood on the table, but there was no elderberry tree growing from it, and the old man who had told the story was just going out the door, and that's what he did.

"How beautiful it was," said the little boy. "Mother, I've been in the warm countries!"

"That I can well believe," said his mother. "When you drink two brimming cups of elderberry tea you surely do come to warm countries!" And she tucked him in so he wouldn't get cold. "You must have been sleeping while we sat and argued about whether it was a story or a real fairy tale."

"And where is *Mother Elderberry*?" asked the boy.

"She's in the teapot," his mother said, "and there she can stay!"

NOTES

1. In Greek and Roman mythology, dryads are wood nymphs that live in trees.
2. Section of Copenhagen founded by Christian IV as a neighborhood for seamen; it is characterized by small gardens with elderberry trees.
3. It was a custom for confirmands to climb to the top of the Round Tower the day after their confirmation.

THE HILL OF THE ELVES

SOME FIDGETY LIZARDS WERE running around in the cracks of an old tree. They could understand each other very well because they spoke lizard language.

"My, how it's rumbling and humming in the old elf hill!" said one lizard. "I haven't been able to close my eyes for two nights because of the noise. I could just as well be lying there with a toothache because then I don't sleep either!"

"There's something going on in there," said the second lizard. "They had the hill standing on four red pillars up until cockcrow. They're really airing it out, and the elf maidens have learned some new dances that have stamping in them. Something is going on."

"I've talked to an earthworm of my acquaintance," said the third lizard. "He was right up at the top of the hill, where he digs around night and day. He heard quite a bit. Of course he can't see, the miserable creature, but he can feel around and understands how to listen. They are expecting guests in the elf hill, distinguished guests, but who they are he wouldn't say, or he probably didn't know. All the will-o'-the-wisps have been reserved to make a torchlight procession, as it's called, and the silver and gold—and there's enough of that in the hill—is being polished and set out in the moonlight."

"But who in the world can the guests be?" all the lizards asked. "I wonder what is going on? Listen to how it's humming! Listen to the rumbling!"

Just then the hill of the elves opened up, and an old elf lady came toddling out. She had a hollow back, but was otherwise

very decently dressed. She was the old elf king's housekeeper
and a distant relative. She had an amber heart on her forehead. Her legs moved very quickly: trip, trip. Oh, how she
could get around, and she went straight down in the bog to the
nightjar!

"You're invited to the elf hill tonight," she said, "but first will
you do us a tremendous favor and see to the invitations? You
must make yourself useful since you don't have a house yourself. We're having some highly distinguished guests—very important trolls—and the old elf king himself will be there."

"Who's to be invited?" asked the nightjar.

"Well, everyone can come to the big ball, even people, so
long as they can talk in their sleep or do one or another little
bit in our line. But for the main banquet the guests are very se-
lect. We are only inviting the absolutely most distinguished. I
have argued with the elf king about this because I'm of the
opinion that we can't even let ghosts attend. The merman and
his daughters have to be invited first. They aren't crazy about
coming onto dry land, but each of them will have a wet rock or
better to sit on, so I don't think they'll refuse this time. We
must have all the old trolls of the highest rank with tails, the
river sprite, and the pixies. And I don't think we can exclude
the grave-hog, the hell-horse, or the church-shadow. Strictly
speaking they belong to the clergy, not our people, but it's just
their jobs after all, and they are close relatives and visit us
often."

"Suuuper!" croaked the nightjar and flew away to issue invitations.

The elf maidens were already dancing on the elf hill, and
they danced in long shawls woven from mist and moonlight,
which is lovely for those who enjoy this type of thing. Way inside the middle of the elf hill the big hall had been fixed up.
The floor had been washed with moonlight, and the walls were
polished with witches' wax, so they shone like tulip petals in
the light. The kitchen was full of frogs on the spit, little children's fingers rolled in grass snake skins, and salads of mush-
room seeds, wet snouts of mouse, and hemlock. There was
beer from the bog woman's brewery, and saltpeter wine from

They danced in long shawls woven from mist and moonlight.

the tomb cellar. It was hearty fare. Desert was rusted-nail hard candy, and church window glass tidbits.

The old elf king had his golden crown polished in slate pencil powder. It was deluxe powder, from the smartest boy's pencil, and it's very hard for the elf king to get hold of that. They hung up curtains in the bedroom and fastened them up with snake spit. Yes, there was quite a hustle and bustle!

"Now we'll fumigate with curled horsehair and pig bristles, and then I think my share of the work will be done," said the old elf maid.

"Dear daddy," said the smallest daughter, "Won't you tell who the distinguished guests are?"

"Well," he said, "I guess I must tell you. Two of you daughters must prepare to get married—because two of you are going to get married. The troll king from Norway—the one who lives in the Dovre mountain and has many granite mountain castles and a gold mine that's worth more than people think[1]—is coming with his two boys. Each of them is looking for a wife. The troll king is one of those down-to-earth, honest old Norwegian fellows, cheerful and straightforward. I know him from the old days when we were on familiar terms with each other. He had come down here for a wife. She is dead now. She was the daughter of the chalk cliff king from Moen.[2] You could say she was chalked up to be his wife. Oh, how I'm looking forward to seeing him! They say that his boys are a couple of bratty conceited fellows, but that may not be true, and the acorn doesn't fall far from the tree. They'll straighten out when they get older. You girls will whip them into shape!"

"When are they coming?" one daughter asked.

"It depends on the wind and weather," the elf king said. "They are traveling by the cheapest method and will come when they can obtain passage on a ship. I wanted them to come by way of Sweden, but the old fellow wouldn't think of it! He doesn't keep up with the times, and I don't like that!"[3]

Just then two will-o'-the-wisps came hopping, one faster than the other, and so one came first.

"They're coming! They're coming!" they shouted.

"Give me my crown, and I'll go stand in the moonlight!" said the elf king.

His daughters lifted their long shawls and curtsied right down to the ground.

There was the troll king from Dovre with a crown of stiff icicles and polished pinecones. In addition he was wearing a bearskin coat and sleigh boots. In contrast his sons were bare-necked and weren't wearing suspenders because they were strapping fellows.

"Is that a hill?" the smallest of the boys asked and pointed at the elf hill. "We'd call it a hole up in Norway."

"Boys!" said their father. "Holes go inward, hills go upward. Don't you have eyes in your heads?"

The only thing that surprised them here, they said, was that they could understand the language right away!

"Don't carry on now!" said the old king, "one would think you're still wet behind the ears."

Then they went into the elf hill, where there really was a fine company assembled. They had been gathered in such haste that you would think they had been blown together. It was just lovely and neatly arranged for everyone. The sea folks sat at the table in big vats of water and said that they felt right at home. All of them had good table manners except the two young Norwegian trolls. They put their feet up on the table, but then they thought that everything they did was becoming.

"Feet out of the food!" said the old troll, and they obeyed him but not right away. They tickled the elf maidens next to them with pinecones that they had in their pockets, and then they took their boots off to be comfortable and gave them to the elf maidens to hold. But their father, the old Dovre troll, was completely different. He told lovely stories about the glorious Norwegian mountains, and about the waterfalls that rushed down in white foam with a roar like thunder and organ music. He told about the salmon that jumped up the rushing waters when the water sprite played its gold harp. He told about the glistening winter nights when the sleigh bells rang out, and the lads ran with burning torches over the shiny ice that was so transparent that they could see the fish swim away

"Don't carry on now!" said the old king.

in fright underneath their feet. He could tell stories so that you could see and hear what he talked about: it was as if the sawmills were going, as if the boys and girls sang folksongs and danced the halling. Suddenly the old troll gave the old elf maiden a hearty familial smack—it was a real kiss—and they weren't even related!

Then the elf maidens had to dance, and they danced both slowly and the tramping dance, and it suited them very well. Then they did the hardest dance, the one that's called "stepping out of the dance." Oh my! How they kicked up their legs. You couldn't tell what was the beginning or what was the end. You couldn't tell arms from legs. They swirled around each other like sawdust, and then they twirled around so that the hell-horse got sick and had to leave the table.

"Prrrr . . . they can surely shake a leg," said the troll king, "but what else can they do besides dance, do high kicks, and make whirlwinds?"

"You'll see," said the elf king, and he called his youngest daughter forward. She was very slender and as clear as moonlight. She was the most delicate of all the sisters. She put a white twig in her mouth, and then she disappeared. That was her skill.

But the old troll said that he wouldn't tolerate such a skill in his wife, and he didn't think his boys would like it either.

The second one could walk beside herself as if she had a shadow, and trolls don't have those.

The third was quite different from the others. She had been in training at the bog woman's brewery, and she knew how to garnish elder stumps with glowworms too.

"She'll be a good housewife!" said the old troll, and he drank to her with his eyes because he didn't want to drink too much.

Then the fourth elf maiden came to play a big golden harp. When she played the first string, they all lifted their left legs because trolls are left-legged, and when she played the second string, they all had to do what she wanted.

"That's a dangerous woman," said the old troll, but both of his sons left the hill because they were bored.

"What can the next daughter do?" asked the troll king.

"I have become so fond of Norwegians," she said, "and I'll never marry unless I can come to Norway."

But the smallest daughter whispered to the old troll, "It's just because in a Norwegian song she heard that when the world comes to an end, the Norwegian mountains will stand like a monument, and she wants to get up there because she's afraid of dying."[4]

"Ho, ho," laughed the troll king. "So that's the scoop. But what can the seventh and last daughter do?"

"The sixth comes before the seventh," said the elf king because he could count, but the sixth didn't want to come out.

"All I can do is tell people the truth," she said. "Nobody cares about me, and I have enough to do sewing my burial shroud."

Now came the seventh and last, and what could she do? Well, she could tell fairy tales, and as many as she wanted to.

"Here are my five fingers," said the old troll. "Tell me one about each of them."

And the elf maiden took him by the wrist, and he laughed so hard he gurgled, and when she came to the ring finger that had a golden ring around its middle as if it knew there was going to be an engagement, the troll king said, "Hold on to what you have! My hand is yours! I want to marry you myself."

And the elf maiden said there were still stories to hear about the ring finger and a short one about little Per Pinkie.

"We'll hear those in the winter," said the old troll, "and we'll hear about the spruce trees and the birch and about the gifts of the hulder people and the tinkling frost. You will be telling stories for sure because nobody up there can do that very well yet. And we'll sit in the stone hall by the light of the blazing pine chips and drink mead from the golden horns of the old Norwegian kings. The water sprite has given me a couple of them. And as we're sitting there, the farm pixie will come by for a visit. He'll sing you all the songs of the mountain dairy girls. That'll be fun. The salmon will leap in the waterfalls and hit the stone wall, but they won't get in! Oh, you can be sure it's wonderful in dear old Norway. But where are the boys?"

Well, where were the boys indeed? They were running

around in the fields blowing out the will-o'-the-wisps, who had come so good-naturedly to make the torchlight parade.

"What's all this gadding about?" said the troll king. "I've taken a mother for you, now you can take wives among your aunts."

But the boys said that they would rather give a speech and drink toasts. They had no desire to get married. And then they gave speeches, drank toasts, and turned the glasses over to show that there wasn't a drop left. Then they took off their coats and lay down on the table to sleep because they weren't a bit self-conscious. But the troll king danced all around the hall with his young bride, and he exchanged boots with her because that's more fashionable than exchanging rings.

"The rooster's crowing!" said the old elf who was the housekeeper. "Now we have to shut the shutters so the sun doesn't burn us to death."

And the elf hill closed.

But outside the lizards ran up and down the cracked tree, and one said to the other:

"Oh, I really liked that old Norwegian troll king!"

"I liked the boys better," said the earthworm, but of course he couldn't see, the miserable creature.

NOTES

1. Andersen likely took this motif from Peter Christen Asbjørnsen and Jørgen Moe's famous Norwegian folktale collection *Norske folkeeventyr*, the first volume of which appeared in 1841. Dovrefjell is a mountain range south of Trondheim.
2. According to folklore, a supernatural creature was thought to live inside the chalk cliffs on Moen, an island in the Baltic Sea off the Danish coast.
3. Reference to Norwegian opposition to the 1814 union with Sweden.
4. Reference to the first line of the poem "Til mit födeland" ("To My Native Land"), by S. O. Wolff (1796–1859), which appeared in *Samlede poetiske forsög lst. volume*, published in Christiania in 1833. The first line is "Hvor herligt er mit Fødeland" ("How splendid is my native land").

CLOD-HANS
AN OLD STORY RETOLD

IN AN OLD MANOR house in the country, there lived an old squire who had two sons, who were too clever by half. They wanted to propose to the king's daughter, and they dared to do so because she had announced that she would marry the man who could speak up the best for himself.

The two prepared themselves for a week, which was all the time they had for it, but it was enough too because they had previous knowledge, and that's useful. One of them knew the entire Latin dictionary by heart and three years' worth of the town's newspaper, both forward and backwards. The other one had learned all the articles of the guilds, and what every alderman had to know. He thought he could discuss state affairs. In addition he knew how to embroider suspenders because he was quick fingered and deft.

"I'll get the princess," they both said, and their father gave each of them a lovely horse. The one who knew the dictionary and newspapers got a coal-black one, and he who was up on the alderman's rules and who embroidered got a milk-white one. They smeared cod liver oil on the corners of their mouths so they could speak more smoothly. All the servants were in the courtyard to watch them depart. Just then the third brother came down, for there were three of them, but nobody counted him since he didn't have the knowledge of the other two. They just called him Clod-Hans.

"Where are you going all dressed up?" he asked.

"To Court to win the princess with our wit. Haven't you heard what's been announced all over the country?" And they told him about it.

"Gee, I'd better go along too!" said Clod-Hans, and his brothers laughed at him and rode away.

"Father, let me have a horse!" shouted Clod-Hans. "I've got a fancy to get married! If she'll take me, she'll take me. And if she won't take me, I'll take her anyway."

"What nonsense!" said his father. "I won't give you a horse.

166

You have nothing to talk about! But your brothers are splendid fellows!"

"If I can't have a horse," said Clod-Hans, "then I'll take the goat. He's mine, and can easily carry me." Then he straddled the goat, stuck his heels in its sides, and took off down the road. Wow, what speed! "Here I come," said Clod-Hans, and he sang shrilly.

The brothers rode silently in front. They didn't say a word. They had to think over all the good ideas they would talk about because they had to be clever.

"Hey, hallo," shouted Clod-Hans. "Here I come! Look what I found on the road!" and he showed them a dead crow he'd found.

"Clod!" they said, "What do you want that for?"

"I'm going to give it to the princess!"

"Yes, you do that!" they said, as they laughed and rode on.

"Hey, hallo! Here I come! Look what I found now—You don't find something like this on the road every day!"

And the brothers turned back again to see what it was. "Clod!" they said, "It's just an old wooden shoe with the top missing. Is that for the princess too?"

"Yes, it is," said Clod-Hans, and the brothers laughed and rode far ahead of him.

"Hey, hallo. Here I am!" shouted Clod-Hans. "Oh no, it's getting worse and worse! Hey, hallo! This is marvelous!"

"What did you find now?" asked the brothers.

"Oh!" said Clod-Hans. "It's unbelievable! How happy the princess will be!"

"Ugh!" said the brothers. "It's just mud thrown up from the ditch!"

"Yes, that's what it is!" said Clod-Hans, "and it's the finest kind. It's so fine you can't keep a hold of it," and he filled his pocket.

But the brothers rode away as fast as they could, and they came an hour early to the city gates. There the suitors received a number as they arrived, and were lined up in a row, six in each rank and so close together that they couldn't even move their arms. That was a good thing though; otherwise they would have stabbed each other in the back just because one was ahead of the other.

All the inhabitants stood around the castle, right up to the windows, in order to see the princess receive the suitors, and as soon as one came into the room, his powers of speech failed him.

"Won't do!" said the princess. "Scoot!"

Now the brother who knew the dictionary came, but he had completely forgotten it while waiting in line, and the floor creaked, and the ceiling was a mirror so that he saw himself upside down. And at each window stood three reporters and a guild master, who wrote up everything that was said, so that it could be printed in the papers right away and be sold for two shillings on the corner. It was horrible, and they had fired up the stove so that it was red hot!

"It's awfully hot in here!" said the suitor.

"That's because my father is roasting roosters today," said the princess.

"Duh!" There he stood—he hadn't expected that. He couldn't think of a word to say because he wanted to say something amusing. Duh!

"Won't do!" said the princess. "Scoot!" And so he had to leave. Then came the second brother.

"It's terribly hot in here," he said.

"Well, we're roasting roosters today," said the princess.

"Excuse—what?" he said, and all the reporters wrote "Excuse—what?"

"Won't do," said the princess. "Scoot!"

Then Clod-Hans came. He rode his goat right into the room. "What a terrific heat!" he said.

"That's because I'm roasting roosters!" said the princess.

"That's lucky," said Clod-Hans. "I should be able to get a crow roasted then, shouldn't I?"

"Yes, you certainly may," said the princess, "but do you have something to roast it in? Because I have neither a pot nor a pan."

"But I have!" said Clod-Hans. "Here's a cooker with a handle." And he took out the old wooden shoe and set the crow in the middle of it.

"That's an entire meal," said the princess, "but where will we get the sauce?"

"I have it in my pocket!" said Clod-Hans. "I have a lot of it so I can waste some," and he poured a little mud out of his pocket.

"I like this!" said the princess. "You sure can answer! And you can talk, and I want you for my husband. But do you know that every word we say and have said is being written up and will appear in the papers tomorrow? There are three reporters and a guild master by each window, and the guild master is the worst because he can't understand anything!" She said this to scare him. And all the reporters giggled and spilled ink on the floor.

"That must be the gentry," said Clod-Hans, "and I must give the guild master the best," and he turned his pocket inside out and threw mud in his face.

"That was well done!" said the princess, "I couldn't have done that, but I'll learn."

And then Clod-Hans became king. Indeed, he got a wife of his own, a crown, and a throne. And we have it right from the guild master's newspaper—but you can't rely on that!

WHAT FATHER DOES IS ALWAYS RIGHT

NOW I'M GOING TO tell you a story that I heard when I was little, and every time I've thought about it since, I think it becomes more lovely. Stories are like many people—they get more and more lovely with age, and that's a good thing!

Of course you've been out in the country? Then you've seen a really old farmhouse with a straw roof where moss and herbs grow by themselves. There's a stork nest on the ridge of the roof—you've got to have a stork. The walls are crooked, the windows are low, and there's only one that can be opened. The oven sticks out like a little chubby stomach, and the elder bush leans over the fence where there's a tiny pond of water with a duck or ducklings right under the gnarled willow tree. And there's always a tied watchdog that barks at each and all.

In just such a farmhouse in the country there lived a couple, a farmer and his wife. Even with as little as they had, they could have gotten along without one thing, and that was a horse that grazed in the road ditch. The farmer rode it to town, and the neighbors borrowed it, and gave a favor in return, but they thought it would be more worthwhile to sell the horse or trade it for something even more useful. But what could that be?

"You'll understand what's best, father," said his wife. "There's a fair in town. Go ahead and ride in there and sell the horse, or make a good trade. Whatever you do is always right. Ride to the fair."

And she tied his neckerchief because she could do that better than he could. She tied a double knot—it looked elegant— and she brushed his hat with the flat of her hand, and kissed his warm mouth. And then he rode away on the horse that was to be sold or traded. Oh yes, father knew what to do.

The sun was burning hot, and there were no clouds. The road was dusty because there were so many going to the fair, in wagons, on horses, or on foot. It was hot, and there was no shade on the road.

There was one man leading a cow that was as lovely as a cow can be. "It must give delicious milk," thought the farmer. "That would make a pretty good trade."

"Say, you there with the cow," said the farmer. "Let's have a chat. You know a horse costs more than a cow, I believe, but that doesn't matter. I have more use for the cow. Shall we trade?"

"Sure," said the man with the cow, and so they traded.

That was done, and now the farmer could have turned around. After all, he had accomplished what he wanted to do, but since he had decided to go to the fair he wanted to go to the fair, just to look, and so he continued with his cow. He walked fast, and the cow walked fast, and soon they were walking side by side with a man leading a sheep. It was a good sheep, in good shape and with lots of wool.

"I wouldn't mind owning that," though the farmer. "It

would have plenty to eat grazing in the ditch, and in the winter we could bring it into the house with us. It really makes more sense for us to have a sheep than a cow."

"Shall we trade?"

Yes, the man who had the sheep wanted to do that. The exchange was made, and the farmer walked along the road with his sheep. By a stile he saw a man with a big goose under his arm.

"That's a big one you've got there," said the farmer. "It's got both feathers and fat. It would look good tied up by our pond. That would be something for mother to gather peelings for. She has often said, 'If only we had a goose!' Now she can have one, and she shall have one! Will you trade? I'll give you the sheep for the goose and throw in a thank-you."

Well, the other man certainly wanted to trade, and so they did. The farmer got the goose. He was close to town, and the road got more crowded. What a throng of man and beast! They walked on the road and in the ditch right up to the tollkeeper's potato field, where his hen was tied up so she wouldn't get scared and run away. It was a short-tailed hen that blinked with one eye and looked like a good one. "Cluck, cluck," it said. What it meant by that I can't say, but the farmer thought when he saw her: "She's the prettiest hen I have ever seen. She is prettier than the minister's brood hen. I'd love to own her! A hen can always find grain, and can almost take care of itself. I think it would be a good trade if I get her for the goose. Shall we trade?" he asked. "Trade?" said the other man, "Well, that wouldn't be too bad," and so they traded. The tollkeeper got the goose, and the farmer got the hen.

He had accomplished a lot on his trip to town, but it was warm, and he was tired. He needed a drink and a bite to eat. He was near an inn and was about to go in, but the innkeeper's servant was just coming out the door. The man had a big bag full of something.

"What have you got there?" asked the farmer.

"Rotten apples," said the fellow, "a whole bag full for the pigs."

"That's an awful lot! I wish mother could see that. Last year we only had one apple on the old tree by the peat shed. That apple had to be saved, and it stood on the chest until it burst. 'There's always something,' said mother. Here she could see something! Yes, I wish she could see this."

"Well, what will you give me for them?" asked the fellow.

"Give? I'll trade my hen for them," and so he gave the hen in exchange, got the apples, and went into the inn, right to the counter. He put his bag with apples up against the stove and didn't think about the fire burning in it. There were many strangers in the room—horse and cattle dealers, and two Englishmen. They are so rich that their pockets are bursting with gold coins, and they like to gamble. Now listen to this!

"Sizz, sizz!" What was that noise by the stove? The apples were starting to bake.

"What's that?" Well, they soon heard the whole story about the horse that was traded for a cow, and right down to the rotten apples.

"Well, you'll get knocked about by your wife when you get home!" said the Englishmen. "She'll raise the roof!"

"I'll get kisses, not knocks," said the farmer. "My wife will say, 'What father does is always right.'"

"Shall we bet on that?" they asked. "Pounds of gold coins. A barrel full."

"A bushel will be enough," said the farmer, "I can only bet my bushel of apples, and I'll throw in my wife and me, but that'll be more than even—a heaping measure."

"Done! Done!" they said, and the bet was made.

The innkeeper's wagon was brought out. The Englishmen got in, the farmer got in, the rotten apples were gotten in, and then they got to the farmer's house.

"Good evening, mother!"

"Welcome home, father!"

"I've been trading!"

"Well, you know how to do it," said his wife and put her arms around his waist. She forgot both the sack and the strangers.

"I traded the horse for a cow!"

"Thank God for the milk!" said his wife. "Now we can have

"I like that," said the Englishmen.

dairy products—butter and cheese on the table. That was a lovely trade!"

"Yes, but then I traded the cow for a sheep."

"That's even better!" said his wife. "You're always thinking. We have enough grazing for a sheep. Now we can have sheep's milk and cheese and woolen stockings. Even woolen night-shirts! A cow can't give that. She loses her hair. How you think things through!"

"But I traded the sheep for a goose."

"Will we really have a Martinmas goose this year, dear father? You always think of pleasing me! What a delightful thought. The goose can be tethered and fattened up for Martinmas."

"But I traded the goose for a hen," said the husband.

"Hen! That was a good trade," said his wife. "A hen will lay eggs, and they'll hatch. We'll have chicks, a henyard! That's something I've really wished for."

"Well, I traded the hen for a sack of rotten apples."

"I must kiss you!" said his wife. "Thank you, my own dear husband! Now I'll tell you something. While you were gone, I thought about making you a really good meal—an omelet with chives. I had the eggs, but not the chives. So I went over to the school master's. I know they have chives, but that woman is stingy, the troll. I asked to borrow—'borrow?' she said. Nothing grows in our garden, not even a rotten apple! I can't even loan her that. Now I can lend her ten, yes, a whole bag full! Isn't that fun, father!" And then she kissed him right on the lips.

"I like that," said the Englishmen. "From bad to worse, but always just as happy. That's worth the money!" And then they paid a bushel of gold coins to the farmer, who got kisses, not knocks.

Yes, it always pays off for a wife to realize and admit that father is the wisest and what he does is always right.

See, there's the story! I heard it as a child, and now you have heard it too, and know that what father does is always right.

Original Fairy Tales

THE SHADOW

THE SUN REALLY BURNS in the warm countries! People become quite mahogany brown there, and actually in the warmest countries they burn completely black. Now it was to one of these warm countries that a scholar had come from a cold one. He thought that he could run around there like he did at home, but that habit soon changed. He and all other sensible people had to remain indoors. The window shutters and doors had to be closed the entire day. It seemed as if everyone was sleeping, or no one was at home. The small street with the high houses where he lived was built so that the sun shone on it from morning till night. It was really intolerable! The scholar from the cold country—he was a young man, a smart man—felt like he was sitting in a red-hot oven. The heat really took a lot out of him. He became quite thin, and even his shadow shrank. It became much smaller than it was at home. The sun was hard on it as well. The man and his shadow didn't perk up until evening, after the sun had set.

It was really a pleasure to watch: as soon as the light was brought into the living room, the shadow stretched way up the wall, even onto the ceiling. It had to stretch way out like that to regain its strength. The scholar went out onto the balcony to stretch there, and as the stars came out in the beautiful clear sky, it was as if he came to life again. People came out on all the balconies on the street—and in the warm countries every window has a balcony—because they had to have air even if they were used to being mahogany brown! What life there was up and down the street! Shoemakers and tailors, all the people flowed out into the street. They set up tables and chairs and lit candles, over a thousand candles, and one person talked and another one sang, and people walked about. Coaches went by, the donkeys walked: cling-a-ling-a-ling because they wore bells. Hymns were sung for funerals, the street urchins shot fire crackers, and the church bells rang. Oh yes, there was plenty of life down in the street. Only one house, straight across from where the scholar lived, was completely quiet. But someone

177

did live there because there were flowers on the balcony. They
grew so beautifully in the hot sun and couldn't have done that
unless they had been watered, and someone had to do that.
There had to be people there. The balcony door was partly
open during the evening, but it was dark in there, at least in
the first room. From further inside you could hear music. The
foreign scholar thought it was quite incredible, but perhaps he
was imagining things because he found everything incredible
there in the warm countries. If only it hadn't been for that sun!
The foreigner's landlord said that he didn't know who had
rented the neighbor's house. You never saw anyone, and as far
as the music was concerned, he thought it was terribly boring.
"It's as if someone is practicing a piece he can't master, and all
the time it's the same one. 'I'll get it,' he is probably saying, but
he won't get it no matter how long he plays!"

One night the foreigner woke up. He was sleeping by the
open balcony door, and the curtain in front of it was fluttering
in the wind. It seemed to him that a remarkable radiance was
coming from the neighbor's balcony. All the flowers were shining like flames in the most beautiful colors, and in the middle
of the flowers stood a slender, lovely young woman. It was as if
she was shining too. It actually hurt his eyes, and then he
opened them wide and woke up. He leaped to the floor and
slowly moved behind the curtain, but the maiden was gone—
the radiance was gone. The flowers weren't shining at all but
stood as they always had. The door was ajar and from deep inside the music played so softly and beautifully that it could
really sweep you into sweet dreams. It was almost like magic—
but who lived there? Where was the entrance? The entire
ground floor was just shops, and people couldn't constantly be
running through them.

One evening the foreigner was sitting on his balcony. In the
room behind him the light was burning, so naturally his
shadow fell on the neighbor's wall. It was sitting right in between the flowers on the balcony. And when the foreigner
moved, the shadow moved too, because that's what shadows
do.

"I believe my shadow is the only living thing over there," said the scholar. "See how nicely it's sitting amongst the flowers. The door is ajar—now my shadow should be kind enough to go inside, look around, and then come tell me what it's seen. You should make yourself useful!" he said jokingly. "Please step inside! Well, are you going?" and he nodded at the shadow, and the shadow nodded back. "Ok, go but don't get lost." The foreigner got up, and his shadow that was cast on the neighbor's balcony got up too. The foreigner turned around and the shadow turned around too. And if someone had paid close attention to it, he would clearly have seen that the shadow went into the partly opened balcony door at the neighbor's, just as the foreigner went into his room and let the long curtain fall down behind him.

The next morning the scholar went out to drink coffee and read the papers. "What's this?" he asked when he got out into the sunshine. "I don't have a shadow! So it really went over there last night and hasn't come back. This is really awkward!"

It annoyed him, but not so much because the shadow was gone, but because he knew that there was another story about a man without a shadow.[1] Everyone at home in the cold countries knew the story, and if he were now to show up and tell his, then everyone would say that he was just a copy-cat, and he didn't need that. He just wouldn't talk about it, and that was sensible of him.

In the evening he went out on his balcony again. He had quite rightly set the light behind him because he knew that the shadow always wants his master for a screen, but he couldn't coax it out. He made himself short, he made himself tall, but there was no shadow. No shadow at all! "Hm, hm!" he said, but that didn't help.

It was irritating, but in the warm countries everything grows so quickly, and after a week went by he noticed to his great pleasure that a new shadow was growing out from his legs when he was in the sunshine. The root must have remained behind. After three weeks he had a quite passable shadow that, when he traveled home to the cold countries, grew more and more on the trip so that at last it was too tall and too big by half.

So the scholar went home, and he wrote books about what was true in the world, and about what was good and what was beautiful. And days and years went by. Many years passed.

One evening he was sitting in his study when he heard a soft knock at the door.

"Come in," he called, but no one came. He opened the door, and there in front of him stood an extraordinarily skinny person. It made him feel quite odd. For that matter the person was very well dressed, evidently a distinguished man.

"Whom do I have the honor of addressing?" asked the scholar.

"Just as I thought!" said the elegant gentleman. "You don't recognize me! I have become so solid. I really have flesh—and clothes too. You probably never expected to see me so well off. Don't you recognize your old shadow? Well, you probably didn't think that I would come back. Things have gone very well for me since I was last with you. I have in all respects become very well-off. If I'm to buy my freedom, I can do so!" And he shook a whole bundle of valuable seals that were hanging by his pocket watch, and he thrust his hand into the thick golden chain that hung around his neck. My, how all his fingers were dazzling with diamond rings! And everything was real.

"I can't fathom any of this," said the scholar, "What's going on here?"

"Well, it is extraordinary," said the shadow, "but you yourself aren't ordinary either, and you know perfectly well that I have followed in your footsteps ever since childhood. As soon as you felt I was mature enough to be alone in the world, I went my own way. I am in the most brilliant of circumstances now, but a kind of longing came over me to see you once again before you die. You will die of course! I also wanted to see these parts again because one always cares about one's fatherland. I know you have another shadow now. Do I owe him something or owe you something? Please just tell me if I do."

"Is it really you?" said the scholar. "This is most remarkable! I never thought that one's old shadow could return as a human being!"

"Tell me what I owe," said the shadow, "because I don't want to be in debt to anyone."

"How can you talk like that?" asked the scholar. "What debt is there to talk about? You are as free as anyone, and I'm very happy about your success. Sit down, my old friend, and tell me a little about how things have happened, and what you saw over at the neighbor's place in that warm country."

"Yes, I'll tell you about it," said the shadow and sat down, "but you must promise me that you won't tell anyone here in town, if you meet me, that I used to be your shadow! I have a mind to get engaged. I can support more than one family."

"Don't worry," the scholar said, "I won't tell anyone who you really are. Here's my hand on it. I promise, and a man is as good as his word."

"And a word's as good as its shadow," said the shadow. He had to talk like that.

Otherwise, it was really very remarkable how human the shadow was. He was dressed all in black made of the very best black cloth with patent leather boots and a hat that could be collapsed to only the crown and the shadowing brim, not to mention the seals, gold necklace, and diamond rings mentioned before. The shadow was indeed very well dressed, and it was just this that made him so very human.

"Now I'll tell you all about it," said the shadow, and he put his legs with the patent leather boots down as hard as he could on the sleeve of the scholar's new shadow that was lying like a poodle by its master's feet. Maybe it was from arrogance, or maybe he wanted him to stick, and the lying shadow stayed so quiet and calm, in order to listen. It undoubtedly wanted to know how it could get free and earn its way to independence.

"Do you know who lived in the neighbor's house across the street?" asked the shadow. "It was the most beautiful of all things. It was *Poetry*! I was there for three weeks, and that had the same effect as living for three thousand years and reading everything that has been written. This I say, and it's true. I've seen everything, and I know everything!"

"*Poetry*!" exclaimed the scholar. "Well, well—she is often a recluse in big cities! *Poetry*! Well, I saw her for just a short moment, but sleep was in my eyes. She stood on the balcony shining like the northern lights do. Tell me more! Go on! You were on the balcony, you went through the door, and then—"

"I was in the vestibule," said the shadow. "You were always sitting and looking over at the vestibule. There wasn't any light there, just a kind of twilight, but one door after another stood open in a long row of rooms and halls. And in those there was lots of light. I would have been killed by the radiance if I had gone all the way to her room. But I was cool-headed. I took my time, as one should do."

"And what did you see then?" asked the scholar.

"I saw everything, and I'm going to tell you about it, but—it isn't a matter of pride for me, but—as a free man and with the knowledge I have, not to mention my good position and my excellent circumstances—I really wish you would address me formally!"[2]

"Oh, excuse me!" said the scholar, "it's just an old habit, and I can't get rid of it all that easily. But you're completely right. And I'll remember it! But now tell me everything that you saw."

"Everything!" said the shadow, "because I saw everything, and I know everything!"

"What did it look like in the innermost room?" asked the scholar. "Was it like being in the fresh forest? Was it like a holy church? Were the halls like the clear starry sky when one stands on a mountain?"

"Everything was there," the shadow said. "I didn't go completely in, you know. I stayed in the vestibule in the twilight, but I had a good position there. I saw everything, and I know everything! I have been to the vestibule of *Poetry's* court."

"But what did you see? Did all the ancient gods walk through the great halls? Did the old heroes do battle there? Were sweet children playing and telling their dreams?"

"I tell you, I was there and believe me, I saw everything that there was to see! If you had gone over there, you would not have become human, but I did! And I got to know my inner nature as well, my innate qualities, the relationship I had to *Poetry*. I didn't think about it when I was with you, but you know, whenever the sun came up or the sun set, I always became so strangely large. In moonlight I was almost easier to see than you. I didn't understand my nature at that time, but in the vestibule it became clear to me, and I became human! I came out of there fully developed, but you weren't in the warm country any longer. I was ashamed as a human being to walk around like I was. I needed boots, clothes, all the human veneer that makes a person recognizable. I found a way, well I can tell you—you won't write it in any book—I hid under the baker woman's skirts. The woman had no idea what she was hiding, and I didn't come out until evening. I ran around on the street in the moonlight and stretched myself tall against a wall that tickled my back so beautifully. I ran up and down, peeked into the highest windows, into rooms and on the roof. I peeked where no one else could, and I saw what no others saw, what no one should see! All things considered, it's a mean world. I wouldn't want to be human, if it weren't considered the thing to be! I saw the most unbelievable things in the wives and husbands, in parents and in the sweet exceptional children. I saw," said the shadow, "what people shouldn't know, but what all people want to know: their neighbor's dirty laundry. If I had published everything I saw in a newspaper, it would have been read, let me tell you! But I wrote to the people themselves, and that caused consternation in all the towns I visited. They were so afraid of me! And they were so fond of me! The professors made me a professor. The tailors gave me new threads, so that I'm well turned out. The master of the mint made money for me, and the women said I was so handsome! And so I became the man I am! And now I'll say farewell. Here's my card. I live on the sunny side of the street, and I'm always home when it rains." And then the shadow went away.

"How very odd," said the scholar.

A long time passed, and then the shadow came again.

"How's it going?" he asked.

"Alas!" said the scholar. "I write about truth and about the good and about the beautiful, but no one wants to hear about that. I'm really in despair because I take it too much to heart."

"But I don't!" said the shadow. "I'm getting fat, and that's what one ought to do. You don't understand the world, and it's making you sick. You should take a trip! I'm taking a trip this summer. Do you want to come with me? I'd like to have a traveling companion. Would you like to come along as my shadow? It would really be a great pleasure for me to have you along, and I'll pay for the trip!"

"That's going too far!" said the scholar.

"It depends on how you look at it," said the shadow. "It would be really good for you to take a trip. If you'll be my shadow, you'll get everything on the trip for free!"

"That's really too much!" said the scholar.

"But that's how the world is," said the shadow, "and how it will remain." And then the shadow went away.

Things went badly for the scholar. He was plagued by sorrow and troubles, and what he said about truth, goodness, and the beautiful was for most people like giving roses to a cow. Finally he was really ill.

"You look like a shadow," people told him, and it made the scholar shudder when he thought about it.

"You should go to a spa," said the shadow, who had come to visit him. "That's the clear ticket. I'll take you along for old time's sake. I'll pay for the trip, and you can write and talk about it, and amuse me on the trip. I want to get to a spa because my beard isn't growing the way it should, and that's an illness. You have to have a beard, you know! Be sensible now and accept my offer. We'll travel as friends, of course."

And so they went. The shadow was the master now, and the master was the shadow. They drove together, they rode and walked together, side by side, in front or back of each other, depending on the sun. The shadow was always careful to be on the controlling side, and the scholar didn't think much about it at all. He had a very kind heart, was gentle and friendly, and one day he said to the shadow, "Now that we've become traveling companions as we are, and since we've grown up together from childhood, shouldn't we say 'du' to each other? It's more intimate."

"There's something in what you say," said the shadow, who was now really the master. "What you say is very frank and well meant, and I will be just as straight-forward and well meaning. You know, as an educated man, how strange nature is. Some people can't tolerate touching grey paper; they get sick from it. Others get a shiver up their spine from hearing a nail scratch glass. I get the same feeling when you say 'du' to me. I feel as if I'm pressed flat to the ground as in my first position with you. It's a feeling, you see, it's not pride. I can't let you say 'du' to me, but I'll gladly say 'du' to you. I'll meet you halfway."

And then the shadow started addressing his former master with "du."

"This really is the limit," thought the scholar, "that I have to say 'De' and he says 'du,'" but he couldn't do anything about it.

Then they came to the spa where there were many foreigners and among them a lovely princess, who was afflicted by a sickness that caused her to see too sharply, and it was very worrying to her.

Right away she noticed that the man who had just arrived was a quite different kind of person than anyone else. "They say he's here to get his beard to grow, but I see the real reason: He can't cast a shadow."

She had become curious, and so she immediately engaged him in conversation while on her walk. As a princess, she didn't need to stand on ceremony, so she said, "Your illness is that you can't cast a shadow."

"Your royal majesty must be much improved," said the shadow. "I know that your failing is that you see too well, but you're improving. You must be cured. I just happen to have a very unusual shadow. Do you see that person who is always with me? Other people have an ordinary shadow, but I don't go in for ordinary things. Often you give your servants better clothes for uniforms than you wear yourself, and I have had my shadow dressed up like a human being. You can see that I have even given *him* a shadow. It's very expensive, but I like having something unique."

"What?" the princess thought. "Have I really gotten better? This spa is the best in the world! The waters certainly have quite remarkable powers these days. But I won't leave, because now it's going to be amusing here. I think a lot of this stranger, and I just hope his beard doesn't grow because then he'll leave."

That evening the princess and the shadow danced in the big ballroom. She was light on her feet, but he was even lighter. She had never had such a dancing partner. She told him what country she was from, and he was familiar with that land. He had been there, but she hadn't been at home then. He had peeked through the windows above and below and had seen both this and that so he could answer the princess and throw out hints so that she was quite surprised. He must be the world's wisest man! She gained such a respect for his knowledge, and when they danced again, she fell in love with him. The shadow noticed this because she almost looked through him with her gaze. Then they danced once again, and she almost told him, but she was cautious. She thought about her country and kingdom and about the many people she would rule over. "He's a wise man," she said to herself, "and that's good. And he's a wonderful dancer, and that's also good, but I wonder if he's truly very knowledgeable. That's just as important! He must be tested." And so she started ever so gradually to ask him about some of the most difficult things she couldn't have answered herself, and an odd expression came to his face.

"You can't answer that!" said the princess.

"I learned that as a child," said the shadow. "I think even my shadow over there by the door could answer that!"

"Your shadow!" exclaimed the princess. "That would really be extraordinary!"

"Well, I'm not saying that he can for sure," said the shadow, "but I should think so. He has followed me and listened for so many years—I would think so. But your royal highness must allow me to remind you that since he is so proud of passing as a human, he must be in a good mood in order to answer well for himself. He has to be treated as a human being."

"That's fine," said the princess.

She went over to the scholar by the door and talked to him

about the sun and the moon, and about people, both their insides and out, and he answered everything so cleverly and well.

"What a man he must be to have a shadow like that!" she thought. "It would be a true blessing for my people and kingdom if I were to choose him as my husband—I'll do it!"

And they soon agreed upon it, both the princess and the shadow, but no one was to know about it before she was back in her own kingdom.

"No one, not even my shadow," said the shadow, and he had his own reason for that!

And then they arrived in the country where the princess reigned when she was home.

"Listen to this, my good friend," said the shadow to the scholar. "Now I have become as happy and as powerful as anyone can be, and I want to do something special for you. You'll always live with me at the castle, drive in my royal coach with me, and have a hundred thousand dollars a year. But you must allow yourself to be called shadow by each and all. You mustn't tell anyone that you were ever a human being, and once a year when I sit on the balcony in the sunshine to be admired, you must lie by my feet as a shadow does. I'll tell you: I am going to marry the princess. The wedding will be this evening."

"No, this is really over the top!" said the scholar. "I don't want to do that, and I won't do that. It would be deceiving the whole kingdom, as well as the princess. I'll reveal everything! That I'm the human being and that you are the shadow. You're only dressed up as a man."

"No one will believe that," said the shadow. "Be sensible, or I'll call the guard."

"I'm going right to the princess," the scholar said. "But I'm going first," said the shadow, "and you'll be arrested." And so he was because the sentries obeyed the man the princess was going to marry.

"You're shaking," said the princess when the shadow came to her room. "Has something happened? You mustn't get sick tonight, when we're having the wedding."

"I've been through the most terrible experience possible!" said the shadow. "Just think! The poor mind of a shadow can't bear much! Imagine! My shadow has gone insane. He thinks he's a human being and that I'm—imagine this—that I'm his shadow!"

"That's dreadful!" said the princess. "He's locked up, right?"

"Yes, he is. I'm afraid he'll never recover."

"Poor shadow," said the princess. "He's very unfortunate. It would truly be a good deed to free him from the little life that he still has, and when I really think it over, I believe it'll be necessary to dispose of him quietly."

"But it's very hard," said the shadow, "because he's been a faithful servant," and he gave what sounded like a sigh.

"You have such a noble nature," said the princess.

That night the whole town was illuminated, the cannons were fired—boom!—and the soldiers presented arms. It was quite a wedding! The princess and the shadow went out on the balcony to be seen by the people and to receive yet another "hurrah!"

But the scholar heard nothing of it, for his life had been taken.

NOTES

1. Reference to *Peter Schlemihls wundersame Geschichte* (1814; *The Wonderful History of Peter Schlemihl*), by Adelbert von Chamisso.
2. *"I really wish you would address me formally!"* Here the shadow is asking his former master to use the Danish formal form of address.

THE LITTLE MERMAID

WAY OUT AT SEA the water is as blue as the petals on the loveliest corn-flower, and as clear as the purest glass, but it's very deep, deeper than any anchor rope can reach. Many church steeples would have to be placed end to end to reach from the bottom up to the surface and beyond. Down there the sea people live.

You mustn't think that it's just a bare white sand bottom. No, the most wonderful trees and plants grow there, and they have such supple stems and leaves that they move as if they were alive with the slightest motion of the water. All the big and little fish slip between the branches like the birds do in the air up here. The sea king's castle is at the very deepest point. The walls are made of coral, and the long sharp windows of the clearest amber, but the roof is made of sea shells that open and close with the water currents. It looks lovely because there are glittering pearls in each shell; just one of them would be a fine ornament for a queen's crown.

The sea king had been a widower for many years, but his old mother kept house for him. She was a wise woman, but proud of her nobility, and so she wore twelve oysters on her tail; the other aristocracy could only carry six. Apart from that she deserved a lot of praise, especially since she was so fond of the little sea princesses, her grandchildren. There were six beautiful children, all lovely, but the youngest was the most beautiful. Her skin was as clear and delicate as a rose petal, and her eyes were as blue as the deepest sea, but just like all the others, she had no feet. Her body ended in a fish tail.

All day long they could play in the castle, in the big hall where living flowers grew out of the walls. Whenever the big amber windows were opened up, the fish swam in, like swallows fly into our windows when we open them, but the fish swam right up to the little princesses and ate from their hands and allowed themselves to be petted.

Outside the castle was a big garden with fire-red and dark blue trees where the fruit shone like gold, and the flowers like a flaming fire, because the stems and petals were always moving. The ground itself was the finest sand, but blue, like a flame of sulphur, and there was a strange blue cast over everything down there. Rather than being on the bottom of the ocean, you could imagine yourself high up in the air, with sky both above and below you, and if it was very still, you could glimpse the sun for it appeared as a scarlet flower with all light streaming from its center.

Each of the little princesses had a plot in the garden, where she could dig and plant as she wished. One gave her flower garden the shape of a whale, another thought that hers should resemble a mermaid, but the youngest princess made hers quite round, like the sun, and only had flowers that shone just as red as it did. She was an odd child, quiet and thoughtful, and while her sisters decorated their gardens with all sorts of strange things they had found in sunken ships, she only wanted, except for the red flowers that resembled the sun, a beautiful marble statue of a lovely boy, carved from white, clear stone that had sunk to the sea bottom from a shipwreck. Beside the statue she planted a rose red weeping willow, which grew beautifully and whose branches hung over the statue and down towards the blue sand bottom, where its shadow was violet and moved like the branches. It looked as if the tree and the roots were playing at kissing each other.

Nothing gave her greater pleasure than hearing about the human world above them. The old grandmother had to tell all she knew about ships and towns, people and animals. She especially thought it was strange and splendid that up on the earth the flowers gave off a fragrance that they didn't do on the bottom of the ocean; and that the forests were green; and that the fish that one saw among the branches could sing so loudly and delightfully that it was a joy. The grandmother called the little birds fish because otherwise they couldn't understand her since they had never seen a bird.

"When you turn fifteen," grandmother said, "you'll be allowed to swim up from the ocean, sit in the moonlight on the rocks, and see the big ships sail by, and forests and towns you'll see, too!" The following year, one of the sisters would turn fifteen, but the others—well, they were all one year younger than the next, so the youngest had five whole years left before she could rise up from the bottom of the sea to see how we have it up here. But each promised to tell the others what she had seen, and what she had found the most beautiful on the first day, for their grandmother hadn't told them enough—there was so much they wanted to know!

None of them yearned as much as the youngest, the very one who had the longest time to wait, and who was so quiet and thoughtful. Many a night she stood by the open windows and looked up through the dark blue water, where the fish flapped their fins and tails. She could see the moon and stars, although they shone dimly, but through the water they looked much bigger than to our eyes; and if it seemed like a dark cloud slipped under them, she knew that either a whale was swimming above her, or it was a ship with many people onboard. Little did they know that there was a lovely little mermaid standing below them, reaching her white hands up towards the ship.

Then the eldest princess turned fifteen and was permitted to go above the surface.

When she came back, she had hundreds of things to tell, but the most lovely thing, she said, was to lie in the moonlight on a sand bank in the calm sea, and see the big city right by the coast, where lights were twinkling like hundreds of stars; to hear the music, and the noise and commotion of carts and people; to see the many church towers and spires, and hear how the bells rang. Just because she couldn't get there, she longed the most for all these things.

Oh, how intently the youngest sister listened to all this, and afterwards, when she stood by the open window in the evenings and looked up through the dark blue water, she thought about the big city with its noise, and then she thought she could hear the church bells ringing all the way down to where she was.

The next year the second sister was allowed to rise to the surface of the water and swim wherever she wanted. She broke the surface just as the sun set, and that was the sight she found the most beautiful. The whole sky had looked like gold, she said, and she couldn't describe how wonderful the clouds were. They had sailed over her, red and violet, but even more quickly than the clouds, a flock of wild swans had flown like a long white ribbon over the water towards the setting sun, and she swam towards it, but it sank, and the rosy hue faded from the sea and the clouds.

The following year the third sister ascended. She was the boldest of them all, so she swam up a wide river that ran out to sea. She saw splendid green hills with grapevines; castles and farms peeked out from magnificent forests. She heard how all the birds were singing, and the sun was so warm that she often had to dive under the water to cool her burning face. In a little inlet she met a group of small human children who were quite naked, and they were running and playing in the water. She wanted to play with them, but they ran away frightened, and a little black animal came and barked terribly at her. It was a dog, but since she had never seen a dog before she became frightened and swam out to the open sea, but she never forgot the magnificent forests, the green hills, and the beautiful children who could swim in the water, even though they didn't have a fish tail.

The fourth sister was not so bold. She stayed out in the wild sea and explained how that was the most beautiful sight. You could see around for many miles, and the sky above was like a huge glass bell jar. She saw ships, but they were so far away that they looked like seagulls. The amusing dolphins had turned somersaults, and the big whales had sprayed water from their blow holes so that it looked like a hundred fountains all around.

Then it was the fifth sister's turn. Her birthday was during the winter, and so she saw what the others had not seen the first time. The sea appeared quite green, and there were big icebergs floating around. Each one looked like a pearl, she said, and they were even bigger than the church steeples that people built. They had the most fantastic shapes and glittered like diamonds. She had sat on one of the biggest ones, and all the sailing ships gave her a wide berth where she sat with the wind blowing her long hair, but later in the evening it became overcast, and there was lightning and thunder while the black sea lifted the icebergs so high up that they shone red in the strong flashes of lightning. All the ships took in sail, and there was fear and dread, but she sat calmly on her floating iceberg and watched the blue bolts of lightning zigzag into the shining sea.

The first time each of the sisters came up to the surface, she was enthusiastic about all the new and lovely things she saw, but when they now were grown up and could go up there whenever they wanted, they became indifferent to it. They longed for home, and at the end of a month they said that it was, after all, most beautiful down there, and that's where you felt at home.

On many evenings the five sisters took each other's arms and rose up over the water in a row. They had lovely voices, more beautiful than any person, and when a storm was brewing so that they thought ships could be lost, they swam in front of the ships and sang so soulfully about how lovely it was on the floor of the ocean and told the sailors not to be afraid to come down there. Of course, the sailors could not understand their words. They thought it was the storm, and they also did not see the wonders of the sea, because when the ship sank, the people drowned and only came as dead men to the sea king's castle.

When the sisters rose up in the evenings, arm in arm, to the surface of the sea, the little sister stood quite alone and looked after them, and she felt that she was going to cry, but mermaids have no tears, and so she suffered even more.

"Oh, if only I were fifteen!" she said. "I know that I'll love that world up there and the people who live in it."

Finally she turned fifteen.

"Now we're getting you off our hands," said her grand-mother, the old widowed queen. "Come and let me dress you up, like your sisters," and she placed a wreath of white lilies on her head, but every petal of the flower was half a pearl, and the old queen let eight big oysters clamp onto the princess' tail to indicate her high rank.

"That really hurts!" said the little mermaid.

"No pain, no gain," her grandmother said.

Oh, how she wanted to throw off all the finery and take off the heavy wreath! The red flowers in her garden suited her much better, but she didn't dare change anything. "Good bye," she said, and floated so easily and lightly, like a bubble, up through the water.

The sun had just gone down as she lifted her head over the sea, but all the clouds were still shining red and gold, and in the middle of the pale pink sky the evening star shone clearly and beautifully. The air was mild and fresh, and the sea was dead calm. There was a large ship with three masts on the sea, but only one sail was up because there wasn't a breath of wind, and sailors were sitting in the rigging and on the yardarms. There was music and singing, and as the evening grew darker, hundreds of multi-colored lanterns were lit. It looked as if the flags of all nations were waving in the air. The little mermaid swam right up to the cabin porthole, and every time the waves lifted her up, she could see in through the clear panes where she saw many people in evening dress, but the most beautiful was a young prince with big black eyes. He could not have been much over sixteen years old. It was his birthday, and that was the reason for all the festivities. The sailors danced on the deck, and when the young prince appeared, over a hundred rockets were fired into the air and lit up the sky like daylight, so the little mermaid became frightened and dove down into the water. But she soon stuck her head up again, and it seemed as if all the stars in the sky fell down to her. She had never seen such fireworks. Big suns swirled around; magnificent fire-fish were swaying in the blue air; and everything was reflected in the clear, calm sea. It was so light on the ship itself that you could see each little rope, let alone the people. Oh, how gorgeous the little prince was! And he shook hands with people and laughed and smiled, while the music played through the lovely night.

It grew late, but the little mermaid couldn't take her eyes from the ship and the wonderful prince. The colorful lanterns were extinguished. There were no more rockets shooting into the air, and the cannons were silent, but deep in the sea there was humming and buzzing. She floated on the water and rocked up and down, so she could look into the cabin, but the ship increased its speed; one sail after another filled; and the waves became bigger. Great clouds gathered, and far away there was lightning. A terrible storm was coming! The sailors pulled in the sails. The big ship rocked ahead at a furious pace on the wild sea; the water rose like big black mountains, wanting to break over the masts, but the ship dove like a swan down between the huge waves and let itself be lifted high up again on the towering waters. The little mermaid thought it was a pleasing ride, but the sailors didn't think so. The ship creaked and groaned as the thick planks bulged from the strong thrusts as the sea pushed against it. The mast cracked in the middle, as though it were a reed, and the ship listed on its side, while water came rushing into the hold. Now the little mermaid realized that they were in danger. She herself had to watch out for beams and pieces of the ship that were drifting on the water. One moment it was so coal black that she couldn't see a thing, but in a flash of lightning, it became so clear that she could see all of them on the ship; each was doing the best he could for himself. She was especially looking for the young prince, and as the ship fell apart, she saw him sink down into the deep sea. At first, she was very happy because now he would come down to her, but then she remembered that people could not live in the sea, and the only way he could come to her father's castle was as a dead man. No, he must not die! So she swam between beams and planks, drifting on the sea, forgetting entirely that they could crush her. She dove deep into the water and rose again high between the waves and came at last to the young prince, who could hardly swim any longer in the surging sea. His arms and legs were beginning to go limp, the beautiful eyes closed; he would surely have died if the little mermaid had not come. She held his head above the water and let the waves drive them where they would.

In the morning the storm was over; there was not a sliver to be seen of the ship. The sun rose red and shining from the water, and it was as if the prince's cheeks took life from it, but his eyes remained closed. The mermaid kissed his lovely high forehead and stroked his wet hair. She thought he looked like the marble statue down in her little garden. She kissed him again, and wished that he would live.

Then she saw land ahead, high blue mountains with white snow shining on top like a flock of swans. Down by the seashore there were lovely green forests, and in front of the woods was a church or a convent. She wasn't exactly sure which, but it was a building. There were lemon and orange trees growing there in the garden, and in front of the gate there were tall palm trees. There was a little bay in the sea, where it was completely calm, but very deep, all the way to the rocks, where the fine white sand washed up. She swam there with the handsome prince, laid him on the sand, and made sure that his head was up in the warm sunshine.

Then the bells rang out from the big white building, and many young girls came through the grounds. The little mermaid swam out behind some high rocks that protruded from the water, covered her hair and breast with sea foam so no one could see her little face, and watched to see who would come and find the poor prince.

It wasn't long before a young girl came. She seemed quite frightened, but only for a moment. Then she hurried to bring other people, and the mermaid saw that the prince was alive, and that he smiled at all those around him, but he didn't smile at her. Of course he didn't know that she had saved him. She felt very sad, and when he was carried into the big building, she dove sorrowfully down into the water and found her way home to her father's castle.

She had always been quiet and thoughtful, but now she became even more so. Her sisters asked her what she had seen on her first trip to the surface, but she didn't tell them anything.

Many evenings and mornings she swam up to the place where she had left the prince. She saw how the fruits in the garden ripened and were picked. She saw how the snow melted on the high mountains, but she didn't see the prince, and so she always returned home sadder than before. Her only consolation was to sit in her little garden with her arms around the marble stature who looked like the prince, but she neglected her flowers. They grew as in a wilderness, over the pathways, and braided their long stems and petals into the tree branches so it became quite dark there.

Finally she couldn't stand it any longer and told one of her sisters. So, immediately the other sisters knew about it, but no one else, except a couple other mermaids, who didn't tell anyone but their closest friends. One of them knew who the prince was. She had also seen the festivities on the ship and knew where he was from and where his kingdom was.

"Come, little sister," the other princesses said, and with their arms around each other's shoulders, they swam in a long row up in the water in front of the prince's castle, which was built of a pale yellow shiny type of rock with big marble staircases; one went way down into the water. There were magnificent gilded domes rising from the roof, and between the pillars that went all around the building there were life-like marble carvings. Through the clear glass in the tall windows, you could see into the most marvelous rooms, where expensive silk curtains and tapestries were hanging, and all the walls were decorated with large paintings that were a pleasure to look at. In the middle of the main chamber, a large fountain was spraying; the jets of water rose high up to the glass cupola in the roof, through which the sun shone on the water and on all the lovely plants that were growing in the big basin.

Now that she knew where he lived, she swam in the water there many nights and evenings, and swam much closer than any of the others had dared to do. She even went way into the narrow channel under the magnificent marble balcony that cast a long shadow over the water. She sat there and watched the young prince, who thought he was all alone in the clear moonlight.

Many evenings she saw him sailing in his fine boat with music playing and flags waving. She peeked out from between the green rushes, and if the wind caught her long silvery veil, anyone seeing it would think it was a swan stretching its wings.

Many a night when the fishermen were at sea in the torchlight, she heard them tell so many good things about the young prince that it made her happy she had saved his life when he was tossed half-dead in the waves, and she thought about how firmly his head had rested against her breast, and how fervently she had kissed him. But he knew nothing about it and couldn't even dream about her.

She became more and more fond of human beings, and more and more she wished she could live among them. She thought their world was much bigger than her own because they could sail on the oceans in ships and climb on the high mountains over the clouds, and the lands they owned with forests and fields stretched farther than her eyes could see. There was so much she wanted to know, but her sisters couldn't answer everything she asked, so she asked her old grandmother, who was well acquainted with the higher world, which is what she quite correctly called the lands above the sea.

"If people don't drown," asked the little mermaid, "do they live forever? Don't they die like us down here in the sea?"

"Oh yes," said the old woman, "they must also die, and their lifetime is shorter than ours too. We can live for three hundred years, but when we cease to exist, we become only foam on the water and don't even have a grave amongst our dear ones down here. We have no immortal soul, and can never live again. We are like the green rushes that can't become green again once they are cut down. Human beings, on the other hand, have a soul that lives forever. It lives after the body has become dust and rises up through the clear air, up to the shining stars! Just as we surface from the sea and see the human's land, so they surface to unknown lovely places that we can never see."

"Why didn't we get an immortal soul?" asked the little mermaid sadly, "I would give all the three hundred years I have to live for just one day as a human and then to share in the world of heaven!"

"You mustn't think about that!" said her old grandmother. "We are much happier and much better off than the people up there."

"So I shall die and float as foam on the sea, not hear the music of the waves, nor see the lovely flowers or the red sun! Isn't there anything at all I can do to win an immortal soul?"

"No!" said the old queen. "Only if you became so dear to a human that you meant more to him than his father and mother, if he clung to you with all his mind and heart, and if you let the minister lay his right hand in yours with promises of faithfulness here and for all eternity, then his soul would flow into your body and you would share in the happiness of humanity. He would give you a soul and yet keep his own. But that can never happen! What is so lovely here in the sea—your fish tail—they find ugly up there on earth. They don't know any better because there you must have two clumsy props that they call legs to be considered beautiful!"

The little mermaid sighed and looked sadly at her tail.

"Let's be satisfied with what we have," said the old grandmother. "We'll spring and skip about during the three hundred years we have to live. It's a good long time. Later we can so much the better rest in our graves.[1] This evening we are going to have a court ball!"

That was also a splendor you never see on the earth. The walls and ceiling of the big dance hall were made of thick clear glass. Several hundred colossal sea shells, rosy red and grass green, stood in rows on each side with burning blue fire that lit up the whole hall and shone out through the walls so that the sea outside was quite illuminated. You could see all the countless fish, big and small, swim towards the glass walls. On some of them the scales glistened a purplish red, on others silver and gold. Straight through the hall a wide stream flowed, and mermen and mermaids were dancing on it to their own lovely song. People on the earth do not have such beautiful voices. The little mermaid sang more beautifully than all the others, and they clapped for her so that she felt joy in her heart for a moment because she knew she had the prettiest voice on earth or in the sea! But soon she began thinking of the world above once again, and she couldn't forget the charming prince and her sadness over not having an immortal soul like he did. So she sneaked out of her father's castle, and while there was nothing but joy and song inside there, she sat sad and alone in her little garden. She heard a horn sound down through the water, and she thought, "Now I guess he's sailing up there, *he* whom I love more than my father and mother, he who holds all my thoughts, and in whose hands I would place my happiness in life. I would risk everything to win him and an immortal soul! While my sisters are dancing there in father's castle, I'll go to the sea witch. I've always been so afraid of her, but maybe she can advise and help me."

Then the little mermaid went out from her garden to the roaring whirlpools; the sea witch lived behind them. She had never gone this way before. There were no flowers growing there, no sea grass, only the bare gray sand bottom that stretched towards the whirlpools, where the water swirled around like roaring mill wheels and pulled everything they grasped down into the deep. She had to walk right between these crushing eddies to enter the sea witch's property, and for most of the way there was no other approach than over a warm bubbling mud that the witch called her bog moss. Her house lay behind it in a strange forest. All the trees and bushes were polyps, half animal and half plant. They looked like snakes with hundreds of heads growing out of the ground. The branches were long slimy arms with fingers like supple worms, and from joint to joint they moved from the root to the outermost tip. They wrapped themselves around everything they could grasp in the sea and never released them. The little mermaid was terrified as she stood outside. Her heart beat fast from fear, and she would have turned around, but then she thought about the prince and about the human soul, and these thoughts gave her courage. She tied her long streaming hair tightly to her head so the polyps couldn't grasp it, folded her arms across her chest, and darted ahead. She moved as fish swim through the water, in between the awful polyps, who stretched out their elastic arms and fingers after her. She saw how they all had something they had caught with their hundreds of small arms holding on like strong bands of iron. People who had died at sea and sunk deep down to the sea bottom peered as white skeletons from the polyps' arms. They were holding fast to ship rudders and chests, skeletons of land animals, and a little mermaid, whom they had caught and strangled. That was almost the most frightful for her.

Then she came to a big slimy clearing in the forest, where large, fat water grass snakes slithered around and showed their ugly whitish-yellow bellies. In the middle of the clearing there was a house built from the white bones of shipwrecked people. The sea witch was sitting there, letting a toad eat from her mouth, much like people let little canaries eat sugar. She called the hideous fat grass snakes her little chicklets and let them squirm around on her large, swampy breast.

"I know what you want," said the sea witch. "It's stupid of you! Nevertheless, you'll get your way because it will just lead to catastrophe for you, my lovely princess. You want to be rid of your fish tail, and instead have two stumps to walk upon just

"I know what you want," said the sea witch.

like people do so that the young prince will fall in love with you, and so that you can win him and gain an immortal soul!" Then the sea witch laughed so loudly and dreadfully that the toad and the snakes fell down writhing on the ground. "You came just in time," said the witch. "After sunrise tomorrow, I wouldn't have been able to help you for a year. I'm going to fix you a drink, and before the sun rises, you are to swim to land with it, sit on the bank there, and drink it. Then your tail will separate and turn into what people call lovely legs, but it will hurt. It will be as if a sharp sword were cutting through you. All who see you will say that you're the most beautiful child of man they've ever seen. You'll keep your floating gait; no dancer will float like you, but every step you take will be like stepping on a sharp knife so the blood flows. If you'll suffer all this, I'll help you."

"Yes!" said the little mermaid with a trembling voice as she thought about the prince and about winning an immortal soul.

"But remember," said the witch, "when you have taken a human shape, you can never again become a mermaid. You can never sink down through the water to your sisters and to your father's castle, and if you don't win the prince's love, so that he forgets his father and mother for your sake, thinks of you constantly, and has the minister place your hands in each other's as man and wife, you won't gain an immortal soul! The first morning after he marries someone else, your heart will break, and you'll become foam on the water."

"I want to do it!" said the little mermaid, pale as death.

"But you'll have to pay me too," the witch said, "and it's not a small thing I demand. You have the most beautiful voice here on the ocean floor, and you think you're going to bewitch him with it, but you must give that voice to me. I want the most precious thing you have for my priceless drink. After all, I have to add my own blood so the drink will be as sharp as a double-edged sword!"

"But if you take my voice," said the little mermaid, "what will I have left?"

"Your beautiful appearance," said the witch, "your graceful

gait, and your expressive eyes. You should be able to capture a human heart with those. Well, have you lost your courage? Stick out your little tongue so I can cut it off in payment, and then you'll get the potent drink."

"Let it happen," the little mermaid said, and the witch prepared the kettle to cook the potion. "Cleanliness is next to Godliness," she said and scrubbed the kettle with the snakes, which she tied into a knot. Then she slashed her breast and let her black blood drip into the kettle. The steam made the most remarkable figures so that you had to be anxious and afraid. The witch kept putting ingredients into the kettle, and when it was boiling rapidly, it sounded like a crocodile crying. Finally the drink was done, and it looked like the clearest water!

"There you are," said the witch as she cut out the tongue of the little mermaid, who now was mute and could neither sing nor speak.

"If the polyps should grab you when you go back through my forest," the witch said, "just throw a single drop of this drink at them, and their arms and fingers will crack into a thousand pieces." But the little mermaid didn't have to do that because the polyps pulled back in fear when they saw the drink shining in her hand like a sparkling star. So she quickly made it through the forest, the moss, and the roaring whirlpools.

She could see her father's castle. The lights were out in the big dance hall, and they were probably all sleeping in there, but she didn't dare seek them out since she was mute now and was leaving them forever. She felt as if her heart would break in two from grief. She crept into the garden, and took one flower from each of her sister's flowerbeds, blew a thousand kisses towards the castle, and then rose up through the dark blue sea.

The sun wasn't up yet when she saw the prince's castle and crept up the marvelous marble steps. The moon was shining beautifully clear. The little mermaid drank the sharply burning drink, and it was as if a sharp double-edged sword cut through her fine body so that she fainted from it and lay as if dead. When the sun shone over the sea, she woke up and felt a stinging pain, but there in front of her was the wonderful young prince. He fastened his coal black eyes on her, and she cast hers downward and saw that her fish tail was gone, and that she had the finest little white legs any girl could have, but she was quite naked, so she wrapped herself in her thick, long hair. The prince asked who she was and how she had gotten there, but she just looked mildly and sadly at him with her dark blue eyes. After all, she couldn't speak. Then he took her by the hand and led her into the castle. As the witch had warned, she felt like she was stepping on sharp awls and knives with each step, but she gladly tolerated it. Holding the prince's hand, she moved as lightly as a bubble, and he and everyone else marveled at her charming, floating gait.

She was dressed in precious clothes of silk and muslin, and she was the most beautiful one in the castle, but she was mute, could neither sing nor speak. Beautiful slave girls dressed in silk and gold came out and sang for the prince and his royal parents. One sang more sweetly than the others, and the prince clapped his hands and smiled at her. This made the little mermaid sad because she knew that she herself had sung much better! She thought, "Oh, if he only knew that I gave my voice away for all eternity to be with him!"

The slave girls danced in a lovely floating dance to the most marvelous music, and then the little mermaid raised her beautiful white arms, stood on tiptoe, and floated across the floor, and danced as no one else had danced. Her loveliness became more evident with every movement, and her eyes spoke deeper to the heart than the songs of the slave girls.

Everyone was delighted with it, especially the prince, who called her his little foundling, and she danced more and more, even though every time her feet touched the floor, it was like stepping on sharp knives. The prince said that she must always be with him, and she was allowed to sleep outside his door on a velvet pillow.

He had a man's outfit sewed for her so she could go horseback riding with him. They rode through the fragrant forests, where the green branches hit her shoulders and the small birds sang behind the new leaves. She climbed up the high mountains with the prince, and even though her fine feet bled

She floated across the floor, and danced as no one else had danced.

so all could see, she laughed at it and followed him until they saw the clouds sailing below them, as if they were a flock of birds flying to distant lands.

At home at the prince's castle, when the others slept at night, she went down the wide marble steps, and cooled her burning feet in the cold sea water, and then she thought about those down in the depths of the sea.

One night her sisters came arm in arm and sang so sadly, as they swam across the water, and she waved at them, and they recognized her and told her how she had made all of them so sad. They visited her every night after that, and one night far out at sea she could see her old grandmother, who hadn't been to the surface for many years, and the sea king, with his crown on his head. They stretched their arms out to her, but didn't dare come so close to land as her sisters did.

Every day she became dearer to the prince, who loved her as one would a good, dear child, but it certainly didn't occur to him to make her his queen, and his queen she had to become, or she wouldn't gain an immortal soul, but would turn to sea foam the morning after his wedding.

"Don't you love me most of all?" the little mermaid's eyes seemed to ask, when he took her in his arms and kissed her lovely forehead.

"Yes, I love you best," said the prince, "because you have the kindest heart of all of them. You're the most devoted to me, and you look like a young girl I once saw, but will never find again. I was on a ship that sank. The waves drove me ashore to a holy temple, where several young girls were serving. The youngest found me on the shore and saved my life. I only saw her twice, but she's the only one I could love in this life. You look like her and have almost replaced her memory in my heart. She belongs to the holy temple, and so good fortune has sent you to me. We'll never part!"

"Oh, he doesn't know that I saved his life," thought the little mermaid. "I carried him through the sea to the temple by the forest, and I hid behind the foam and watched for someone to come. I saw the beautiful girl whom he loves more than me," and the mermaid sighed deeply, since she couldn't cry.

"He said that the girl belongs to the holy temple, and she'll never leave there so they won't meet again. I'm with him and see him every day. I'll take care of him, love him, and offer him my life."

Then rumor had it that the prince was to be married to the beautiful daughter of the neighboring king, and because of that he was preparing a splendid ship for a voyage. He was supposedly traveling to see the neighboring king's country, but people knew that he really was going to see the daughter. A large party was to accompany him, but the little mermaid just shook her head and laughed because she knew the prince's thoughts much better than anyone else. "I have to go," he had told her. "I have to go see the lovely princess, my parents insist, but they can't force me to bring her back here for my wife. I can't love her! She doesn't look like the beautiful girl in the temple, like you do. If I ever do choose a bride, it would sooner be you, my silent foundling with the speaking eyes!" He kissed her red mouth, played with her long hair, and laid his head against her heart, so she dreamed of human happiness and an immortal soul.

"You aren't afraid of the sea, my silent child?" he asked, when they climbed aboard the magnificent ship that was to take them to the neighboring kingdom. And he told her about storms and calm seas, about strange fish in the depths and what divers had seen, and she smiled at his stories since she knew better than anyone what the ocean floor was like.

In the moonlit night when everyone was sleeping, the little mermaid sat close to the helmsman, who was at the wheel, and stared down into the clear water, and thought she saw her father's castle. On the highest tower stood her old grandmother with her silver crown on her head, starring up at the keel of the ship through the currents. Then her sisters came up to the surface, stared sadly at her, and wrung their white hands. She waved to them and smiled, and wanted to tell them that she was well and happy, but then the ship's boy approached, and the sisters dove down, and he thought that the white that he had seen was foam on the sea.

The next morning the ship sailed into the magnificent port

in the neighboring kingdom. All the church bells rang, and trombones were played from the high towers while soldiers marched with waving banners and dazzling bayonets. There was a party every day. One festivity followed another, but the princess wasn't there yet. She was being educated far away in a holy temple, they said, where she was learning all the royal virtues. But at last she came.

The little mermaid waited eagerly to see her beauty, and she could not deny it. She had never seen a more lovely creature. Her skin was so clear and fine, and behind the long dark eyelashes smiled a pair of faithful dark-blue eyes!

"It's you!" exclaimed the prince, "you, who saved me, when I lay like a corpse on the beach!" And he gathered his blushing bride in his arms. "Oh, I'm so incredibly happy!" he said to the little mermaid. "The best thing I could wish for has come true. You'll share my joy since you love me better than any of the others." And the little mermaid kissed his hand, and thought she felt her heart breaking already, for his wedding night would bring her death and change her to foam upon the sea.

All the church bells rang, and heralds rode through the streets, proclaiming the engagement. Fragrant oils burned in precious silver lamps on all the altars. The priests waved their censers, and the bride and groom grasped hands and received the blessing of the bishop. The little mermaid was dressed in silk and gold and was holding the bride's train, but her ears did not hear the festive music; her eyes didn't see the sacred ceremony. She was thinking about her last night of life and about everything she had lost in this world.

That same evening the bride and groom went aboard the ship. The cannons boomed, all the flags were waving, and in the center of the ship a precious tent of gold and purple with the loveliest cushions had been raised. The bridal couple were going to sleep there in the cool, quiet night.

The sails swelled in the wind, and the ship glided smoothly and almost motionlessly across the clear sea.

When it became dark, colorful lamps were lit, and the sailors danced merrily on the deck. The little mermaid had to think about the first time she peered above the waves and saw the same splendor and joy, and she whirled in the dance, swaying as a swallow when it's being chased. Everyone cheered her, and never had she danced so well before. It was as if sharp knives cut into her fine little feet, but she didn't feel it; the pain was sharper in her heart. She knew it was the last evening she would see the man for whom she had left her home and family, and for whom she had given her beautiful voice and suffered unending agony without him having the least idea. It was the last night she would breathe the same air as him, would see the deep sea, and the starry blue sky. An eternal night without thought or dreams awaited her, she who had no soul and could not win one. And there was joy and merriment on the ship until long past midnight; she laughed and danced with the thought of death in her heart. The prince kissed his lovely bride, and she played with his black hair, and arm in arm they went to bed in the magnificent tent.

It became hushed and still on the ship, only the helmsman was on deck. The little mermaid laid her white arm on the railing and looked to the east towards dawn. She knew that the first sunbeam would kill her. Then she saw her sisters rise up from the sea, and they were as pale as she was, their long beautiful hair no longer streaming in the wind. It had all been cut off.

"We have given it to the sea witch so she would help you, so that you won't die tonight! She has given us a knife. Here it is! Do you see how sharp it is? Before the sun rises, you must stab the prince in the heart, and when his warm blood drips on your feet, they will grow together into a fish tail, and you'll become a mermaid again, and come back into the sea with us and live your three hundred years before you become dead, salty sea foam. Hurry! Either you or he must die before the sun rises. Our old grandmother is grieving so much that all her white hair has fallen out, as ours fell to the witch's scissors. Kill the prince and come back! Hurry, don't you see the red streak in the sky? In a few minutes the sun will rise, and then you must die!" and they heaved a strange, deep sigh and sank in the waves.

The little mermaid drew the purple curtain away from the tent and saw the beautiful bride sleeping with her head on the prince's chest. Then she bent down and kissed him on his handsome forehead, looked at the sky, where the morning glow was increasing, looked at the sharp knife, and cast her eyes again upon the prince, who in his dreams said his bride's name. Only she was in his thoughts, and the knife quivered in her hand, but then she threw it far out into the waves that turned red where it fell, like drops of blood trickling up from the water. One last time she looked at the prince with her partly glazed eyes, dove from the ship into the sea, and felt her body dissolving into foam.

The sun rose from the sea. The rays fell warmly and gently upon the deadly cold sea foam, and the little mermaid did not feel death. She saw the clear sun, and above her swirled hundreds of beautiful, transparent creatures. Through them she could see the ship's white sails and the red clouds in the sky. Their voices were melodies, but so unearthly that no human ear could hear them, just as no earthly eye could see them. They swayed though the air on their own lightness without wings. The little mermaid saw that she had a shape like them that rose up more and more from the foam.

"To whom am I going?" she said, and her voice sounded like the others and so heavenly that no earthly music could express it.

"To the daughters of the air!" the others answered. "The mermaid has no immortal soul and can never win one unless she wins the love of a human. Her eternal existence depends on an outside power. Daughters of the air don't have an eternal soul either, but they can shape one through their good deeds. We fly to the warm countries, where pestilence kills people, and we bring cool breezes. We spread the scent of flowers through the air and send peaceful rest and healing knowledge. After we have struggled to do all the good we can for three hundred years, we can earn an immortal soul and share in the human's eternal joy. You, poor little mermaid, have striven with all your heart for the same thing we have. You have suffered and endured and raised yourself to the world of the air spirits. Through good deeds you can earn yourself an immortal soul in three hundred years."

The little mermaid lifted her clear arms up towards God's sun, and for the first time she felt tears. There was noise and life on the ship again, and she saw the prince with his beautiful bride searching for her. They stared mournfully at the bubbling foam, as if they knew she had thrown herself on the waves. Invisibly she kissed the bride's forehead, smiled at the prince and rose with the other children of the air up into the rosy cloud sailing in the sky.

"In three hundred years we'll sail into God's kingdom like this."

"We can get there even faster," whispered one. "We swirl unseen into a human home, where there are children, and every day we find a good child who brings joy to his parents and deserves their love, God reduces our time of testing. A child doesn't know when we fly through the room, and if we smile with joy at him, a year is subtracted from the three hundred years, but if we see a naughty child, then we must cry in sorrow, and every tear adds a day to our time of trial."

NOTE

1. Andersen evidently forgot that the grandmother has just explained that mermaids do not have graves.

THE EMPEROR'S NEW CLOTHES

MANY YEARS AGO THERE lived an emperor who was so tremendously fond of stylish new clothes that he used all his money for dressing himself. He didn't care about his soldiers, didn't care about the theater, or driving in the park, except to show off his new clothes. He had an outfit for each hour of the day, and as they say about a king that he's "in council," here they always said, "The emperor's in the dressing room!"

There were lots of amusements going on in the big city where he lived. Many strangers came every day, and one day two swindlers arrived. They said they were weavers, and that they could weave the most beautiful material one could imagine. Not only were the colors and patterns unusually lovely, but

"The emperor's in the dressing room!"

the clothes sewn from the fabric had a remarkable characteristic: they were invisible to any person who was incompetent in his job, or who was simply grossly stupid.

"Those would be some wonderful clothes," the emperor thought, "by wearing them I could find out which men in my kingdom aren't fit for their jobs, and I'd be able to tell the wise from the stupid! That fabric must be woven into some clothing for me at once!" and he gave the two swindlers a big deposit so that they could start their work.

They set up two looms and pretended to work, but they had absolutely nothing on the loom. Right away they demanded the finest silk and the most splendid gold. And they put these things into their bags, and worked on the empty looms long into the night.

"I would really like to know how far they've come with the material," thought the emperor, but he was a little uneasy with the thought that those who were dumb, or not at all fit for their jobs, couldn't see it. Of course, he knew very well that he didn't have to worry about himself, but he decided to send someone else first to see how it was going. All the people in town knew about the power of the fabric, and everyone was eager to see how incompetent or stupid his neighbor was.

"I'll send my honest old envoy over to the weavers," the emperor thought, "He can best determine how the fabric is turning out because he's smart, and no one is better suited to his job than he is."

So the dependable old envoy went to the hall where the two swindlers were working on the empty looms. "Good God!" thought the old envoy as his eyes flew wide open, "I can't see anything!" But he didn't say that.

Both swindlers asked him to come closer and asked him if it wasn't a beautiful pattern and lovely colors. They pointed at the empty loom, and the poor old envoy continued to stare, but he couldn't see anything because nothing was there. "Dear God!" he thought. "Could it be that I'm stupid? I never thought that, and no one must find out! Is it possible I'm not fit for my job? It's just totally impossible to admit that I can't see the fabric!"

"Well now, you're not saying anything about it," said one who was pretending to weave.

"Oh, it's beautiful! Absolutely too awesome for words!" the old envoy said and peered through his glasses. "What a pattern and what colors! Yes, I'll tell the emperor that I like it very much!"

"We're pleased to hear that," both weavers said, and then they pointed out the strange pattern and colors by name. The old envoy paid close attention so he could repeat the information when he came back to the emperor, and that's what he did.

Then the swindlers demanded more money and more silk and gold, needed for the weaving. They put it all in their own pockets, and not a shred appeared on the loom, but they continued as before to weave on the empty loom.

Soon the emperor sent another competent official to see how the weaving was progressing, and if the fabric would soon be finished. The same thing happened to him: he peered and stared, but since there wasn't anything on the empty loom, he couldn't see a thing.

"Well, isn't this a beautiful piece of material?" both swindlers asked him, and pointed out and explained the lovely pattern, which wasn't there.

"I'm not stupid!" the man thought. "So then I'm not fit for my excellent job? That's odd enough, but no one must find out about it." So he praised the fabric he didn't see and assured them that he was delighted with the beautiful colors and the lovely pattern. "It's just marvelous," he told the emperor.

Everyone in town was talking about the beautiful fabric.

So then the emperor wanted to see the fabric while it was still on the loom. With a large group of selected advisers, among them the two who had already been there, he went off to see the clever crooks, who were weaving with every fiber of their being, but without a thread on the loom.

"Isn't it *magnifique*?" asked both of the wise, old officials. "Look at the pattern, your majesty, and the colors!" and they pointed at the empty loom, because they thought the others could see the fabric.

"What!" thought the emperor. "I don't see a thing! This is dreadful! Am I stupid? Am I not fit to be emperor? This is the most terrible thing that could happen to me!"

"Oh, it's just splendid!" said the emperor. "It has my highest approval," and he nodded contentedly as he observed the empty loom for he didn't want to say that he couldn't see anything. The whole group that accompanied him looked and looked but didn't get anything more out of it than any of the others. So they echoed the emperor, "Oh, it's very lovely," and they advised the emperor to wear the splendid new clothes from the fabric for the first time at the big parade that was soon to occur. "It's magnificent! Delightful! Excellent!" was on everyone's lips, and they were all thoroughly pleased with the fabric. The emperor gave each of the swindlers a knight's cross to hang on his chest, and the title of Knight of the Loom.

The entire night before the parade the swindlers sat illuminated by a flood of light from more than sixteen candles. People could see that they were busy getting the emperor's new clothes ready. They pretended to take the fabric from the loom and cut into thin air with huge scissors. They sewed with thread-less needles, and at last they said, "There, now the clothes are finished!"

The emperor came to them with his most distinguished cavaliers. Both swindlers lifted one arm in the air as if they were holding something and said, "See, here are the pants. Here's the jacket, and here's the cape!" They continued on and on. "They are as light as cobwebs. You might think you weren't wearing anything, but that's the beauty of this fabric."

"Yes!" said all the cavaliers, but they couldn't see a thing, for there wasn't anything to see.

"Now, if your royal majesty would be so kind as to remove your clothes," said the swindlers, "we'll put the new ones on, right here in front of this big mirror."

The emperor laid aside his clothes, and the swindlers acted as if they gave him each piece of the new outfit they had sewed, and the emperor turned and twisted in front of the mirror.

"Lord, how good that looks on you! How beautifully it fits!"

"Lord, how good that looks on you! How beautifully it fits!"

they all said. "What a pattern! What lovely colors! What a precious outfit it is!"

"They're waiting outside with the canopy that will be carried over the throne in the parade," said the Master of Ceremonies.

"Well, I'm ready," said the emperor. "Doesn't it fit beautifully?" and he pirouetted in front of the mirror one more time. He was pretending to admire his splendid outfit.

The chamberlains who were to carry the train of the cape, fumbled around on the floor, as if they were lifting up the train. They walked carrying their arms in the air and didn't dare act as if they saw nothing.

So the emperor paraded under the lovely canopy, and all the people on the streets and in the windows said, "Good God, how awesome the emperor's new clothes are! What a splendid train he has on his cape! How beautifully it fits!" None of the people would admit that they didn't see anything because then they wouldn't be fit for their jobs, or they'd be called terribly stupid. None of the emperor's clothes had been so admired before.

"But he isn't wearing anything at all," said a little child.

"Dear God, listen to the voice of innocence," his father said, and each person whispered to the other what the child had said.

"But he isn't wearing anything at all!" everyone shouted at last.

The emperor shuddered because he was afraid they were right, but he thought, "I have to finish the parade." And the chamberlains walked on, carrying the train that wasn't there.

THUMBELINA

ONCE UPON A TIME there was a woman who desperately wanted a little child, but she didn't know where to get one. She went to an old witch and said to her, "I really want so badly to have a little child! Can you tell me where I can get one?"

"Yes, I'm sure we can manage that!" the witch said. "Here's a barley seed, but it's not the kind that grows in a farmer's field, or the kind that the chickens eat. Plant it in a flower pot, and you'll really see something!"

"Thanks so much!" the woman said and gave the witch twelve coins, went home, and planted the barley seed, and right away a beautiful big flower sprouted. It looked just like a tulip, but the petals were closed tightly together like a bud.

"That's a beautiful flower!" said the woman and kissed it on the pretty red and yellow petals, but just as she kissed it, the flower gave a huge bang and opened up. It was clear that it was a real tulip, but right in the middle of the flower, sitting on the green perch, was a tiny little girl, graceful and lovely. She was no bigger than your thumb, and so she was called Thumbelina.

She had a splendid lacquered walnut shell for a cradle with a mattress of blue violet petals, and her blanket was a rose petal. She slept there at night, but during the day she played on the table where the woman had filled a saucer with water and put flowers all around the edge with their stems in the water. A large tulip petal floated on the water, and Thumbelina would sit on the petal and sail back and forth from one side of the saucer to the other. She had two white horse hairs for oars. It looked like fun. She could sing too, more beautifully than anyone had heard before.

One night when she was lying in her pretty little bed, a nasty toad hopped in through the window, for one of the panes was broken. The toad was big, ugly, and wet, and it hopped right down on the table where Thumbelina was sleeping under the red rose petal.

"That'll be a lovely wife for my son," said the toad, and then she grabbed the walnut shell where Thumbelina was sleeping and hopped away with her through the window and down into the garden.

There was a big wide river there, but right by the bank it was muddy and boggy, and that is where the toad lived with her son. Ugh! He was ugly and nasty too and looked just like his mother. "Croak, croak, brekka krekka" was all he could say when he saw the lovely little girl in the walnut shell.

"Don't talk so loudly, or she'll wake up," said the old toad. "She could still run away from us because she's as light as a feather. We'll put her out on the river on one of the lily pads. It will be like an island for her since she's so small, and she won't be able to escape from there while we prepare the parlor down under the mud where you'll live."

Many lily pads with wide green leaves were growing in the river. They looked like they were floating on top of the water, and the pad that was furthest out was also the biggest. The old toad swam out there and left the walnut shell with Thumbelina inside.

The poor little thing woke up quite early in the morning, and when she saw where she was, she began crying bitterly. There was water on all sides of the big green leaf, and she could not get to land.

The old toad was down in the mud decorating the parlor with rushes and yellow cowslips so it would be truly nice for her new daughter-in-law. Then she and her ugly son swam out to the lily pad where Thumbelina was standing because they wanted to get her pretty bed to set it up in the bridal chamber before the wedding. The old toad curtsied deeply in the water and said to her, "This is my son. He's going to be your husband, and you'll live so nicely together down in the mud!"

"Croak, croak, brekka krekka" was all her son could say.

Then they took the lovely little bed and swam away with it, but Thumbelina sat alone on the green lily pad and cried because she didn't want to live with the nasty old toad, or have her ugly son for a husband. The little fish who were swimming in the water must have seen the toad and heard what she had said, and they wanted to see the little girl. They stuck their heads out of the water, and as soon as they saw her and saw how lovely she was, they thought it was terrible that she was going to be married to that nasty toad. No, that should never happen! They swarmed in the water around the green stalk that held the lily pad she was standing on and gnawed through the stalk with their teeth. Then the lily pad floated away down the river—away with Thumbelina, far away where the toad could not follow.

Thumbelina sailed past many places, and the little birds sitting in the bushes saw her and sang, "What a lovely little girl!"

Thumbelina on her leaf floated further and further away, and that is how she traveled out of the country.

A beautiful little white butterfly flew around and around Thumbelina and finally sat down on the lily pad because it liked her. Thumbelina was so happy because the toad could not get her, and because they were sailing through such lovely country. The sun shone on the water like the finest gold. Then she took a sash she had around her waist and tied one end around the butterfly, and the other she connected to the lily pad. It started floating more quickly and Thumbelina too, of course, since she was on the leaf.

Just then a big June bug came flying by. It saw her and immediately grabbed her around her slim waist and flew up in a tree with her. But the green lily pad floated away down the river and the butterfly too, since it was tied to the leaf and couldn't get loose.

Oh, dear God, how frightened poor Thumbelina was when the June bug flew up in the tree with her! But most of all she was sad about the beautiful white butterfly that she had tied to the lily pad. Since it couldn't get loose, it would starve to death. But the June bug didn't care about that. He sat with her on the largest, greenest leaf in the tree and gave her the sweetest flowers to eat and said that she was so beautiful, even though she didn't look like a June bug in the least. Later all the June bugs who lived in the tree came to visit. They looked at Thumbelina, and the lady June bugs pulled on their antennas and said, "She doesn't have more than two legs—that looks pitiful." "She has no antennas!" said another. "She is so slim-waisted, yuck! She looks like a human. How ugly she is!" said all the female June bugs, yet Thumbelina really was so lovely. The June bug who had taken her thought she was, but when all the others said she was ugly, he finally thought so too and didn't want her any longer. She could go where she pleased, and they flew down from the tree with her and set her on a daisy. She sat there crying because she was so ugly that the June bugs didn't want her, even though she really was the loveliest thing you could imagine—so fine and clear as the most beautiful rose petal.

All through the summer poor Thumbelina lived alone in

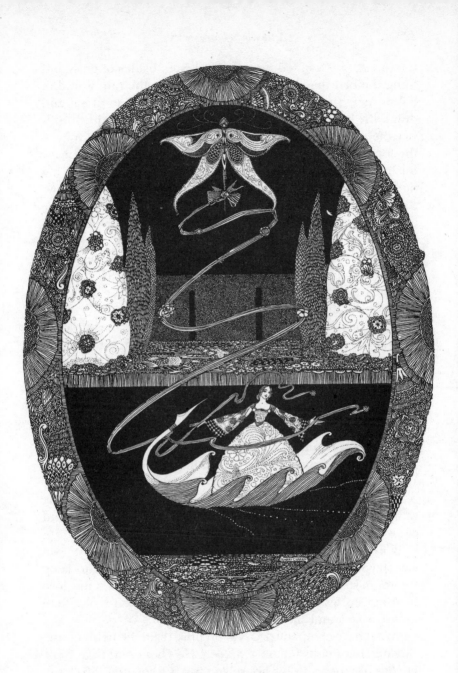

Then she took a sash she had around her waist
and tied one end around the butterfly.

the forest. She braided herself a bed from blades of grass and hung the bed under a big dock leaf so that the rain wouldn't fall on her. She plucked the nectar out of flowers to eat and drank the dew that gathered on the leaves each night. In this way the summer and autumn passed, but then winter came— the long, cold winter, and all the birds that had sung so nicely for her flew away. The trees and flowers withered, and the big dock leaf she had lived under rolled up and became a yellow, dried-up stalk. She froze terribly because her clothes were torn, and she herself was so little and thin. Poor Thumbelina! She would freeze to death. It started to snow, and every snowflake that fell on her would have felt like a whole shovel-ful on us since we are big and she was only an inch tall. She wrapped herself in a withered leaf, but that didn't help, and she shook with the cold.

Right outside the forest was a big corn field, but the corn was long since gone. Only a little dry stubble stood there on the frozen ground, but for her it was like walking through a whole forest. And oh, how she shivered! Then she came to the door of the field mouse—it was a little hole under the stubble of corn. The field mouse lived there warm and cozy. She had the whole living room full of corn and a nice kitchen and pantry. Poor Thumbelina stood right inside the door like any other poor beggar and asked for a little grain of barley because she hadn't had anything to eat for two days.

"You poor little thing!" said the field mouse, because she was actually a kind old mouse. "Come into my warm house and eat with me!"

Because she liked Thumbelina the field mouse said, "you can stay here with me for the winter, but you'll have to keep the room spick and span and tell me stories because I just love hearing stories." Thumbelina did what the kind old field mouse asked, and she had it very nice there.

"We'll have company pretty soon now!" said the field mouse. "My neighbor visits me once a week. He's better off than I am. He has big rooms in his house and wears a splendid black vel-vet coat! If you could get him for a husband, you'd be well taken care of, but he can't see. You'll have to tell him the very best stories you know!"

But Thumbelina didn't care for that. She didn't want the neighbor for a husband because he was a mole, who came visiting in his big velvet coat. He was very rich and very well educated, the field mouse told her. His home was twenty times larger than the field mouse's house, and he certainly knew a lot, but he couldn't stand the sun or flowers. He spoke ill of them because he'd never seen them. Thumbelina had to sing for him, and she sang both "Three Blind Mice" and "The Farmer in the Dell," and the mole fell in love with her because of her beautiful voice, but he didn't say anything because he was such a slow and steady man.

He had recently dug a long hallway through the ground between his house and theirs. Thumbelina and the field mouse were allowed to walk there whenever they wanted to, but he told them not to be afraid of the dead bird that lay in the hallway. It was a whole bird with feathers and a beak that had evidently died quite recently, just at the beginning of winter, and was buried exactly where the mole had dug his hallway.

The mole took a piece of dry rotted wood in his mouth since it shines like fire in the dark and walked ahead of them lighting the long dark corridor. When they came to the place where the dead bird was lying, the mole pushed his broad nose up to the roof and shoved up the earth so a big hole appeared, and light could enter. A dead swallow lay in the middle of the floor with its lovely wings pulled tightly to its body, and the legs and head drawn in under the feathers. The poor bird had clearly frozen to death, and Thumbelina felt so sorry for it because she was very fond of all the small birds that had chirped and sung for her the whole summer. But the mole pushed at it with his small feet and said, "now it's not chirping anymore! It must be miserable to be born as a little bird! Thank God that none of my children will be birds, for a bird has nothing but its twitter and starves to death in the winter."

"You're a sensible man to say that," said the field mouse. "What do the birds gain for their songs when winter comes? They starve and freeze as if there's any value in that."

Thumbelina didn't say anything, but when the other two turned their backs, she knelt down, brushed aside the feathers that covered its head, and kissed the closed eyes. "Maybe it was this one who sang so beautifully for me this summer," she thought. "How much joy it gave me—the dear lovely bird!"

The mole filled in the hole that allowed the light to shine through and escorted the ladies home, but that night Thumbelina couldn't sleep. She got up from her bed, braided a little blanket from the hay, and carried it down to cover the dead bird. She put some soft cotton she had found in the field mouse's living room around the bird so that it could be warm in the cold ground.

"Good bye, lovely little bird," she said. "Good bye and thank you for your beautiful song this summer when all the trees were green, and the sun shone so warmly on us." Then she lay her head on the bird's breast, but was immediately alarmed because there seemed to be something beating in there—it was the bird's heart. The swallow was not dead, but had been outcold, and now the heat had warmed it up and brought it back to life.

In the fall all the swallows fly away to warmer countries, but if there's one who is delayed, it freezes and falls as if dead and remains lying where it falls, covered by the cold snow.

Thumbelina trembled. She was very frightened because the bird was big, so much bigger than she, who was only an inch tall. But she summoned her courage, pushed the cotton closer around the poor swallow, fetched a curled mint leaf that she had used as a comforter, and laid it over the bird's head.

The next night she sneaked down there again and saw that it was clearly alive, but still very weak. It only had the strength to open its eyes for a moment and look at Thumbelina, who held a piece of dried, rotted wood in her hand because she didn't have any other light.

"Thank you so much, you lovely little child," the sick swallow said to her. "I've warmed up very nicely. Soon I'll regain my strength and be able to fly again—out into the warm sunshine."

"Oh," she said, "it's so cold out. It's snowing and freezing. Stay in your warm bed, and I'll take care of you."

Then she brought the swallow water in a flower petal, and it drank and told her how it had torn its wing on a wild rose bush and couldn't fly as well as the other swallows. They flew away, far away to warmer countries while it finally fell to the ground. It couldn't remember anything else, or how it had gotten there.

So it stayed there the whole winter, and Thumbelina treated it with affection and kindness, but neither the mole nor the field mouse knew anything about it because they didn't like the poor little swallow.

As soon as spring came, and the sun warmed the ground, the swallow said good bye to Thumbelina, who opened the hole that the mole had made. The sun shone in on them so delightfully, and the swallow asked if she would like to come along with him. She could sit on his back, and they would fly far, far away into the green forest. But Thumbelina knew that the old field mouse would be saddened if she were to leave her.

"No! I can't!" said Thumbelina.

"Good bye, good bye! You lovely, good girl," said the swallow and flew out into the sunshine. Thumbelina looked after it, and tears came to her eyes because she was so fond of the poor swallow.

"Tweet, tweet" sang the bird and flew into the green forest.

Thumbelina was very sad. She wasn't allowed to go out into the warm sunshine. The corn sown in the field over the field mouse's house grew so high up in the air that it was like a huge forest for the poor little girl, who was only an inch tall, of course.

"This summer you will sew your trousseau," the field mouse told her because the neighbor, the boring mole in the black velvet coat, had proposed. "You're going to have all the comforts—both wool and linen to sit and lie upon—when you become the mole's wife."

Thumbelina had to spin on the spindle, and the field mouse hired four spiders to spin and weave day and night. The mole visited every evening and always talked about the end of summer when the sun would not shine so warmly—it was actually burning the ground hard as a rock. When summer was over, the wedding with Thumbelina would take place, but she was not looking forward to that because she didn't like the boring mole. Every morning when the sun came up and every evening when it set, she slipped out the door, and when the wind separated the tops of the corn tassels so that she could see the blue sky, she thought about how light and beautiful it was outside, and she wished so very much that she could see the dear swallow again, but it never came back. It must have been flying far away in the beautiful green forest.

When fall came, Thumbelina had her trousseau ready.

"The wedding will take place in four weeks," the field mouse told her, but Thumbelina cried and said that she didn't want the dull old mole.

"Nonsense!" the field mouse said. "Don't be obstinate, or I'll bite you with my white tooth! After all, this is a fine husband you're getting! Even the queen doesn't have a velvet coat like his. He's well off and has both kitchen and cellar, and you can thank God that you're getting him!"

The wedding day came, and the mole had already come to get Thumbelina. She was to live with him, deep down under the ground, never to come out into the warm sunshine because he couldn't tolerate that. The poor child was very sad because she had to say good bye to the lovely sun, which she had at least been able to see in the field mouse's doorway.

"Good bye, bright sun!" she said and raised her arms high up in the air. She also took a few steps out of the field mouse's house because the corn had been harvested, and only the dry stubble remained. "Farewell, farewell," she said and threw her thin arms around a little red flower standing there. "Greet the little swallow from me if you see it."

"Tweet, tweet," she heard right above her head. She looked up, and there was the little swallow just flying by, and as soon as it saw Thumbelina, it was very happy. She told the swallow that she didn't want to marry the ugly mole, and that she would have to live deep under the ground where the sun didn't shine. She couldn't help but cry at the thought.

"Now the cold winter's coming," the swallow said. "I'm going to fly away to the warm countries. Would you like to come with me? You can sit on my back. Tie yourself on with your belt, and we'll fly away from the ugly mole and his dark home. We'll fly far away over the mountains to the warm countries, where the sun shines brighter than here, and where there's always summer and lovely flowers. Just come with me, sweet little Thumbelina, who saved my life when I was lying frozen in the dark earth."

"Yes, I'll come with you," Thumbelina said and climbed up on the bird's back with her feet on its outspread wings. She tied her belt to one of the strongest feathers, and then the swallow flew high up in the air over the forest and over the water and high up over the big mountains where there's always snow. Thumbelina was shivering from the cold air, but then she crept in under the bird's warm feathers, and only stuck her little head out so she could see all the delights below.

They came to the warm countries. The sun shone a lot brighter there than here; the sky was twice as high, and the most marvelous green and blue grapes grew in the ditches and fields. Lemons and oranges hung in the woods. They were surrounded by the smells of myrtle and mint, and beautiful children ran on the lanes playing with huge gay butterflies. But the swallow flew even further, and everything became more and more beautiful. Under lovely green trees beside the blue ocean there was a shining white marble castle that was from the old days, and which had grapevines climbing up the high pillars. At the very top there were many swallow nests, and one was the home of the swallow who carried Thumbelina.

"Here's my home," the swallow said. "But if you'll pick one of those splendid flowers growing down there, I'll set you there, and it'll be as nice as you could wish."

"Wonderful!" she said and clapped her small hands.

One of the big white marble pillars had fallen and was lying on the ground broken in three pieces, and around these grew the most lovely big, white flowers. The swallow flew down and set Thumbelina on one of the wide leaves, but what a surprise she had! There was a little man sitting in the middle of the flower—

He asked her to marry him and become the queen of all the flowers.

so white and transparent as if he were made of glass. He had the most beautiful gold crown on his head, and the loveliest clear wings on his shoulders, and altogether he was no bigger than Thumbelina. He was the angel of the flowers. Such a little man or woman lives in all the flowers, but he was the king of them all.

"God, how adorable he is," Thumbelina whispered to the swallow. The little prince was frightened of the swallow since it was a monstrous bird while he was so little and delicate, but when he saw Thumbelina, he became very happy because she was the most beautiful girl he'd ever seen. So he took the gold crown from his head and placed it on hers, asked her name, and asked her to marry him and become the queen of all the flowers. This would be a different husband than the toad's son or the mole with his black velvet coat! So she accepted the charming prince at once, and out of every flower came a lovely young man or woman—a joy to see. Each of them brought Thumbelina a gift, but the best of all was a pair of beautiful wings from a large white fly. They were fastened to Thumbelina's back so she could fly from flower to flower. Everyone was very happy, and the little swallow sat and sang for them as best he could up in his nest, but in his heart he was sad because he was so fond of Thumbelina and never wanted to be parted from her.

"Your name won't be Thumbelina any more," the flowers' angel told her. "That's an ugly name, and you're so beautiful. We'll call you Maja!"

"Good bye, good bye," called the little swallow and flew away from the warm countries again, far away back to Denmark. There he had a little nest over the window of a man who can tell fairy tales, and for him he sang, "tweet, tweet." That's how we know the whole story.

THE NAUGHTY BOY

ONCE UPON A TIME there was an old poet—a really kind old poet. One evening when he was sitting at home, a terrible storm arose. The rain poured down, but the old poet sat cozy

and warm by his wood burning stove, where the fire was crack-
ling, and the apples cooking on the stove were sizzling.

"There won't be a dry thread on the poor people who are
out in this weather," he said because he was such a kind poet.

"Oh, let me in! I'm freezing, and I'm so wet," called a little
child standing outside. The child cried and knocked on the
door, while the rain poured down and the wind rattled all the
windows.

"Oh, poor little thing!" said the old poet and went over to
open the door. There was a little boy standing there. He was
completely naked, and the water was dripping off his long, yellow hair. He was shivering from the cold, and if he couldn't
come inside, he would surely die in that terrible weather.

"Oh, you poor thing," said the old poet and took his hand.
"Come in here, and I'll get you warmed up! You shall have
wine and an apple, for you're a sweet little fellow."

And he was, too. His eyes looked like two clear stars, and
even if water was running from his yellow hair, it curled beautifully. He looked like a little angel, but was pale from the cold,
and his body was trembling all over. In his hand he held a
lovely bow, but the rain had ruined it, and all the colors on the
fine arrows were running into each other from the wet
weather.

The old poet sat down by the stove and took the little boy in
his lap, wrung the water out of his hair, warmed the little hands
in his, heated wine for him, and then the little boy felt better.
His cheeks turned pink, and he hopped down on the floor and
danced around the old poet.

"You're a cheerful fellow," said the old man. "What's your
name?"

"I'm Cupid," he said. "Don't you recognize me? There's my
bow, and I can shoot with it, let me tell you! Look, it's nice out
now. The moon is shining."

"But your bow is ruined," said the old poet.

"That's too bad," said the little boy, and picked up the bow
and looked at it. "But it's dry already, and it's not ruined! The
string is completely taut. Now I'll try it!" So he drew the bow,
inserted an arrow, aimed, and shot the kindly old poet right in

the heart. "You can see that my bow isn't ruined," he said and laughed loudly and ran off. That naughty boy—to think that he shot the old poet who had let him into the warm room, been kind to him, and had given him good wine and the best apple!

The old poet lay on the floor crying. He really had been shot right in the heart. Then he said, "Oh, what a bad boy that Cupid is! I'm going to tell all the children this so they can watch out and never play with him, for he'll only hurt them."

And all the good children he told about Cupid, both girls and boys, watched out for him, but Cupid fooled them anyway because he's so cunning. When the students leave their lectures, he runs along side them with a book under his arm and dressed in a black cloak. They don't recognize him then, and take him by the arm, and think that he's also a student, but then he shoots the arrow into their chests. When the girls have been studying with the minister, and when they go for Confirmation, he's after them there, too. He's always after people! He sits in the big chandelier in the theater among the flames so people think it's a lamp, but afterwards they notice something else! He runs around in the king's garden and on the embankment. Indeed, at one time he shot your father and mother right in their hearts! Just ask them, and you'll hear what they say. Yes, that Cupid is a naughty boy, and you must never have anything to do with him! He's out to get all people! Just think, once he even shot an arrow at old grandmother, but that was long ago, so it's worn off. But something like that she'll never forget. Oh, how naughty Cupid is! But now you know him. You know what a bad boy he is.

THE GALOSHES OF FORTUNE

1. A BEGINNING

ON EAST STREET IN Copenhagen in one of the houses not far from King's New Market, there was a big party. Sometimes you have to throw a big party, and then it's done, and you're invited in return. Half of the guests were already at the card tables, and the other half were waiting to see what would come from the hostess's "now we'll have to think of something!" That's as far as they had gotten, and the conversation went here and there. Among other things, they talked about the Middle Ages. Some declared it a better time than our own. In fact, Justice Councilman Knap defended this view so eagerly that the hostess soon agreed with him. Then they both started in on Ørsted's words in the almanac[1] about former and present eras, in which our own time is in most respects considered superior. The councilman considered the age of King Hans[2] to be the best and happiest time.

There was a great deal of talk pro and con, and it was only interrupted for a moment when the newspaper came, but there was nothing worth reading in that, so let's go out to the foyer where the coats and walking sticks, umbrellas, and galoshes have their place. Two maids were sitting there: one young and one old. You might think they had come to escort their mistresses home, one or another old maid or widow. But if you looked a little closer at them, you soon noticed that these were not ordinary servants—their hands were too fine, and their bearing and movements too regal for that. Their clothing also had a quite distinctly daring cut. They were two fairies. The youngest surely wasn't Good Fortune herself, but rather one of her attendant's chambermaids, who pass around the lesser of Fortune's gifts. The elder looked extremely grave. This was Sorrow, who always does her errands in her own distinguished person so that she knows that they are properly carried out.

They talked about their day. The one who was Good Fortune's attendant's chambermaid had just taken care of a few minor errands. She said she had saved a new hat from a rain-shower, obtained a greeting for a decent man from a distinguished nonentity, and things like that. But what she had left to do was something quite extraordinary.

"I have to tell you," she said, "that today is my birthday, and in honor of this I have been entrusted with a pair of galoshes that I am going to give human beings. These galoshes have the characteristic that whoever puts them on is immediately carried to the place or time where he most wants to be. Any wish with respect to time or place is fulfilled at once, and now people will finally find happiness down here!"

"Don't you believe it," said Sorrow. "People will be dreadfully unhappy and bless the moment they get rid of those galoshes!"

"How can you say that?" said the other. "I'll set them here by the door. Someone will mistake them for his own and become the lucky one!"

That was their conversation.

2. WHAT HAPPENED TO THE COUNCILMAN

It was late, and Councilman Knap, absorbed in the time of King Hans, wanted to go home. It so happened that he put on Good Fortune's galoshes instead of his own and walked out onto East Street, but the power of the galoshes' magic had taken him back to the time of King Hans, and so he stepped straight out into ooze and mud since at that time there was no sidewalk.

"It's dreadful how muddy it is here!" the judge said. "The sidewalk is gone, and all the street lights are out."

The moon hadn't risen high enough yet, and the air was quite foggy so everything disappeared in the dark. At the closest corner a lantern was shining in front of a picture of a Madonna, but it gave off almost no light. He first noticed it when he was standing right under it, and his eyes fell on the painting of the mother and child.

"This must be an art gallery," he thought, "and they've forgotten to take in the sign."

A couple of people dressed in the clothes of the time walked by him. "What weird outfits! They must have come from a costume party."

Then he heard drums and flutes, and big torches flared in the dark. The councilman watched an odd procession pass by. A whole troop of drummers marched first, skillfully handling their instruments. They were followed by henchmen with bows

"This must be an art gallery," he thought,
"and they've forgotten to take in the sign."

and crossbows. The most distinguished person in the parade was a clergyman. The councilman was surprised and asked what this meant and who the man was.

"It's the Bishop of Zealand,"[3] he was told.

"My God, what's the matter with him?" the judge sighed and shook his head. It certainly couldn't be the Bishop. Brooding over this and without looking to left or right he walked along East Street and over High Bridge Place. He couldn't find the bridge to the Palace Plaza, but he glimpsed an expanse of the river, and he finally came across two fellows there in a boat.

"Do you want to be rowed over to Holmen?" they asked him.

"Over to Holmen?" asked the judge, who didn't know what age he was wandering in. "I want to get over to Christian's Harbor, to Little Market Street."

The men just looked at him.

"Just tell me where the bridge is," he said. "It's a disgrace that there aren't any streetlamps lit here, and it's as muddy as if you're walking in a bog."

The longer he spoke with the boatmen, the more incomprehensible they became to him.

"I don't understand your Bornholm dialect,"[4] he finally said angrily and turned his back on them. He absolutely couldn't find the bridge, and there were no guard rails either. "It's a scandal, the way things look here!" he said. He had never thought his own age was as miserable as on this evening. "I think I'll take a cab," he thought, but where were the cabs? There were none in sight. "I'd better walk back to King's New Market; there will be some there. Otherwise I'll never get out to Christian's Harbor!"

So he walked back to East Street and had nearly walked the length of it when the moon came out.

"Dear God, what kind of scaffolding have they put up here?" he said when he saw the East Gate, which at that time was at the end of East Street.

He finally found a gate and by going through it, he came out on our New Market, but at that time it was just a big meadow. There was a bush here and there and through the middle of the meadow was a wide channel or creek. On the opposite bank there were some wretched wooden shacks where the Dutch seamen lived, and so the place was called Holland Meadow.

"Either I am seeing *fata morgana*, a mirage, as it's called, or I'm drunk," groaned the councilman. "What is this? What's going on?"

He turned around again in the firm belief that he was sick. As he came back to the street, he looked a little closer at the houses: most of them were of half-timbered construction, and many had only straw roofs.

"No, I am not at all well," he sighed. "I only drank one glass of punch, but I can't tolerate it. It was also very wrong of them to serve punch with poached salmon! I am going to tell the representative's wife that, too. Should I go back and tell them I'm sick? But it's so embarrassing. And maybe they've already gone to bed."

He looked for the house, but couldn't find it.

"This is terrible! I can't even recognize East Street. Where are the shops? I only see old, miserable hovels as if I were in Roskilde or Ringsted! Oh, I'm sick. There's no sense in being shy. But where in the world is the Representative's house? It doesn't look right, but there are clearly people up in there. Oh, I'm really awfully sick."

Then he came across a half-opened door with light coming through the crack. It was an inn of that time, a kind of pub, quite country-like. The good folks inside were seamen, citizens of the town, and a few scholars who were in deep conversation over their cups and didn't pay much attention to him when he came in.

"Excuse me," the councilman said to the hostess who approached him. "I'm in bad shape. Can you get me a cab out to Christian's Harbor?"

The woman looked at him, shook her head, and then spoke to him in German. The councilman thought that maybe she couldn't speak Danish so he repeated his request in German. This, along with his clothing, confirmed for the woman that he was a foreigner. She soon realized that he was ill and gave him a glass of water, admittedly a little brackish since it came from the creek.

The councilman rested his head on his hand, took a deep breath, and pondered his strange surroundings.

"Is that this evening's *Daily*?" he asked just to say something when he saw the woman move a big paper.

She didn't understand what he meant, but handed him the paper. It was a woodcut that showed a vision in the sky above the city of Cologne.

"It's very old," the judge said. He was quite excited to run across such an old item. "Where in the world have you gotten this rare print? It's very interesting, although it's all a myth. These sky visions are explained by northern lights that people have seen. Most likely they come from electricity."

Those who were sitting close by and heard him speak looked at him in wonder. One of them got up, took off his hat respectfully, and said, "You are evidently a very highly educated man, *Monsieur*!"

"Oh no!" The councilman answered. "I can discuss this and that, as one is expected to be able to do."

"Modesty is a lovely virtue," the man said, "for that matter, I'll say that your remarks seem different to me, but I'll suspend my *judicium* here!" He spoke mostly in Latin.

"May I ask with whom I have the pleasure of speaking?" asked the councilman.

"I have a Bachelor's in Theology," the man continued.

This answer was enough for the councilman. The title matched the outfit: "Must be an old country school teacher," he thought, "an eccentric fellow, such as those you can still meet up in Jutland."

"I guess it's not the place for a lecture," the man began in Latin, "but I would ask you to continue speaking since it's clear that you have read a lot of the classics."

"Yes, I certainly have," said the judge. "I really like reading useful old writings, but I also enjoy the newer ones. Not *Everyday Stories*[5] though. There are enough of those in reality."

"*Everyday Stories*?" asked our scholar.

"Yes, I mean those new fangled novels."

"Oh," smiled the man, "but they are very entertaining, and they read them at court. The King is especially fond of the one about Sir Yvain and Sir Gawain. It's about King Arthur and the Knights of the Round Table. He was joking about it with his courtiers."[6]

"I haven't read that one yet," said the councilman. "It must be a pretty new one put out by Heiberg."[7]

"No," the man answered. "It was not published by Heiberg, but by Godfred von Gehmen."[8]

"So that's the author," the judge said. "That's a very old name. The first printer in Denmark had that name."

"Yes, he's first among our book publishers," the man said. So the conversation went pretty well. One of the citizens talked about the terrible pestilence that had raged a couple of years before, meaning the one in 1484. The councilman thought he was talking about the cholera epidemic[9] so the discussion went swimmingly. The Freebooters War of 1490 was so recent that it had to be mentioned. The English buccaneers had taken ships right in the harbor, they said, and the councilman, who was well versed on the events of 1801, blasted the English with relish. But the rest of the conversation didn't go as well. There was very often a mutual incomprehensibility. The good scholar was much too ignorant, and the councilman's most simple utterances struck him as being too audacious and fantastic. They looked at each other, and if it got too bad, the scholar spoke Latin because he thought he would be better understood, but it didn't help at all.

"How are you doing?" asked the hostess, who pulled at the councilman's arm. Then he came to his senses because, when he was talking, he had forgotten everything that had happened before.

"Dear God, where am I?" he said and felt dizzy at the thought.

"We're going to drink claret! Mead and German beer!" yelled one of the men, "and you'll drink with us!"

Two maids came in. One had two colors in her cap,[10] and they poured and curtsied. The judge felt a shiver go down his spine.

"What is this? What is happening?!" he said, but he had to drink with them. They set to work on the poor man, and he was quite disconsolate. When one of them said that he was drunk, he didn't doubt the man at all. He just asked them to call him a cab, a *drosche*, and then they thought that he was speaking Russian.

He had never been in such raw and simple company. You would think the country had fallen back into paganism. "This is the worst moment in my life!" he thought, but at the same time he got the idea that he could slip down under the table, crawl over to the door, and slip out. But when he reached the entrance, the others noticed what he was doing and grabbed him by the legs. Then, luckily for him, the galoshes slipped off, and with them, all the magic.

The councilman saw quite distinctly a clear light burning in front of him, and behind it was a large property. He recognized it and the property next to it. They were on East Street, such as we all know it. He headed for a gate, and next to it the watchman sat sleeping.

"Good God! Have I been lying here on the street dreaming?" he asked. "Of course, this is East Street, with its blessed light and color. It's simply dreadful how that glass of punch affected me!"

Two minutes later he was sitting in a cab on his way to Christian's Harbor. He thought about the fear and distress he had overcome and praised with all his heart the reality of our own time with all its defects, still so much better than where he had just been. And that was sensible of the councilman, of course.

3. THE WATCHMAN'S ADVENTURE

"Hm, there's actually a pair of galoshes lying there!" said the watchman. "They must belong to the lieutenant who lives up above there. They're lying right by the gate."

The honest fellow would have rung the bell right away and delivered them since the lights were still on, but since he didn't want to waken the others in the house he didn't do it.

"It must be pretty comfortable to walk around with those things on," he thought. "They are such soft leather." They fit beautifully. "How strange the world is! The lieutenant could go to his warm bed, but he doesn't do that; he's pacing about. He's a happy fellow, has neither a wife nor children, and goes to parties every night. I wish I were him, I'd be a happy man then!"

As he said that, the galoshes worked their magic. The watchman passed into the lieutenant's person and thoughts. There he stood, up in the lieutenant's room, holding between his fingers a little pink piece of paper with a poem on it, written by the lieutenant himself, for who has not at one time or another been inspired to write poetry? And if you write down the thoughts, then the poem is there. On the paper was written:

"I wish I were rich!"

"I wish I were rich!" That was my song
When I was barely a meter long.
"I wish I were rich." I joined the army,
Had a uniform, cap and saber on me.
With time a lieutenant I came to be.
But sorry to say nothing could I afford—
Help me Lord!

One eve as I sat young and gay,
A young girl kissed my lips to repay.
Rich in stories and tales I was willing,
Although in money I hadn't a shilling.
But the child thought the stories were thrilling.
Rich I was then, but not in gold's hoard—
Knows the Lord!

"I wish I were rich," still to God I pray.
That young girl is all grown up today.
So lovely, so clever and so good,
If she my heart's story understood,
If she to me now would be as good—
Too poor to speak, silence I hoard—
So wills the Lord!

Oh were I rich in faith, my soul at rest,
My sorrow wouldn't herein be expressed.
You whom I love, if me you understand,
Read this as a missive from a youthful hand.
It would be best you do not understand.
For I am poor, my future dark, abhorred—
But bless you will the Lord!

Yes, you write these kinds of lines when you're in love, but a sensible man wouldn't have them printed. A lieutenant, love and poverty: that's a triangle, or just as good, you can say it's the broken half of the square of happiness. The lieutenant felt that way, and that's why he leaned his head against the windowsill and sighed deeply:

"That poor watchman out on the street is far happier than I am! He doesn't want for anything. He has a home, a wife, and children, who cry with him in sorrow and are happy with his joys. If I were more fortunate than I am, I could trade places with him, because he is happier than I am."

At that moment the watchman became the watchman again since it was through the magic galoshes that he had become the lieutenant. As we have seen, he felt much less satisfied, and wanted to be what he really was. So the watchman was the watchman again.

"That was a bad dream," he said, "but diverting too. I thought I was the lieutenant up there, and it wasn't fun at all. I missed my wife and the kids, who are always ready to smother me with kisses."

He sat down again and nodded off. The dream wasn't completely out of his mind. He was still wearing the galoshes. A falling star flew across the sky.

"There one fell!" he said, "but there are enough of them anyway. I would like to see those things closer up, especially the moon because then it wouldn't disappear between two hands. The student that my wife washes for says that when we die, we fly from star to star. That's a lie, but it would be rather fun anyway. I wish I could just make a little jump up there, and my body could just stay here on the steps."

Yes, you write these kinds of lines when you're in love.

You see, there are certain things in the world you have to be very careful in saying, but you should be even more careful when you are wearing the magic galoshes on your feet. Just listen to what happened to the watchman!

So far as we people are concerned, almost all of us know the speed of steam travel. We've tried it either on the railroad, or on a ship at sea. But even this pace is like the creeping of the sloth or the march of the snail compared to the speed of light. It flies nineteen million times faster than the best racer, but electricity is even faster. Death is an electric shock to the heart, and our released souls fly to heaven on the wings of electricity. Sunlight takes eight minutes and some seconds to travel a distance of over ninety-three million miles. With the speed of electricity, the soul needs fewer minutes to cover the same distance. For the soul the distance between worlds is no more than that between our friends' houses in the same town is for us, even if these are pretty close to each other. But this electric shock to the heart costs us our bodies, unless we are, like the watchman, wearing the magic galoshes.

Within a few seconds, the watchman had traveled the nearly 240,000 miles to the moon, which is, as you know, made of a material much lighter than our soil and as soft as newly fallen snow. He found himself on one of the innumerable craters that we know from Dr. Mädler's big moon map.[11] You're familiar with that, of course? On the interior the crater sides went steeply down like a pot for a whole Danish mile, and down there on the bottom was a town that looked like an egg white in a glass of water—just as soft and with the same kind of towers, domes and sail-shaped balconies, transparent and swaying in the thin air. Our world was hovering like a big fire-red ball above his head.

There were a lot of creatures, and all of them, I guess, what we would call human, but they looked a lot different than us. They also had a language, and no one could expect that the watchman's soul could understand that, but nevertheless he could.

The watchman's soul understood the residents of the moon very well. They were arguing about our world and doubted that it was inhabited. The air would have to be too thick for any reasonable moonie to live in. They thought that only the moon had living creatures, and that the moon was the original world where life originated.

But let's go back down to East Street and see how the watchman's body is getting along.

It was sitting lifeless on the steps. The night stick had fallen out of its hand, and the eyes were looking up at the moon towards the soul that was wandering around up there.

"What's the time, watchman?" someone asked as he walked by. But the watchman didn't answer. Then the man snapped his fingers slowly at the watchman's nose, and the body lost its balance and lay there stretched out—the watchman was dead, after all. The fellow who had snapped his fingers was very upset, but the watchman was dead and stayed dead. The death was reported and discussed, and during the morning the body was carried to the hospital.

Now it would have been a nice kettle of fish for the soul if it had come back and most likely had looked for its body on East Street, but couldn't find it. It would probably first run up to the police department, then to the Census Bureau so it could be looked for in lost-and-found, then finally to the hospital. But we can take comfort that the soul is most clever when it's on its own. The body only dumbs it down.

As mentioned, the watchman's body came to the hospital where it was brought into the morgue. Of course, the first thing they did was take off the galoshes so then the soul had to get back right away. It made a beeline for the body, and suddenly the man was alive again. He insisted that it had been the worst night of his life. He wouldn't experience such sensations again for neither love nor money, but now it was over.

He was released the same day, but the galoshes remained at the hospital.

4. A HEADY MOMENT. A RECITAL. A MOST UNUSUAL TRIP.

Every resident of Copenhagen knows what the entrance to Frederiks Hospital in Copenhagen looks like, but since it's likely that some non-residents also are reading this story, we must give a brief description.

The hospital is separated from the street by quite a tall grate, but the thick iron bars are far enough apart so that it's said that very thin interns were able to squeeze through and in that way make little excursions outside. The part of the body that was most difficult to press through was the head. Here, as often in the world, those with the smallest heads were often the most fortunate. That's enough of an introduction.

One of the young residents, who was pretty thick-headed in the purely physical sense, was on duty this particular evening. There was pouring rain, but despite these two obstacles, he had to get out for only fifteen minutes. He didn't think it was anything worth mentioning to the gatekeeper since he could just squeeze through the bars. The galoshes that the watchman had forgotten were lying there, and it didn't occur to him that they could be Good Fortune's galoshes; he just thought they would be nice to have in this terrible weather. He put them on—now to see if he could squeeze himself through. He had never tried it before. He stood in front of the bars.

"I wish to God I had my head through," he said, and right away, although it was very big and thick, it slid through easily, thanks to the galoshes. The body had to follow, but there he stood.

"Ugh, I'm too fat!" he said. "I would have thought my head would have been the hardest, but I can't get through."

He quickly tried to pull his head back, but it wouldn't go. He could only manage to move his neck, but that was all. First he got angry, and then his spirits sank to below zero. The magic galoshes had brought him to this most dreadful position, but unfortunately it didn't occur to him to wish himself free. No, he struggled but couldn't budge from the spot. The rain was pouring down, and there wasn't a soul to be seen on the street. He couldn't reach the bell so how was he going to get loose? He foresaw that he might have to stay there until morning, and then they would have to get a smithy to saw through the bars. That would take a while. All the boys from the elementary school across the street would come to watch, and all the residents of the neighborhood would see him standing there in pillory. There would be large crowds, more than saw the giant agave[12] last year. "Oh, the blood is rushing to my head, I'm going crazy!—Yes, I'm going crazy! Oh, I wish I were free again, then it would be all right."

See, he should have said that a little sooner. As soon as he thought it, his head was free, and he rushed inside, very confused about the fright he had gotten from the magic galoshes.

We mustn't think that it's all over. Oh no, it gets worse.

The night passed, and also the following day, but no one called for the galoshes.

There was going to be a performance at the little theater in Canon Street that evening. The place was packed, and between the recital numbers a new poem was recited. We should hear it. The title was:

GRANDMA'S GLASSES

My Grandmother's wisdom is popular lore,
She'd be burned at the stake in times of yore.
She knows all that occurs and even more,
Can see future events, that is for sure.
The following decades she can see
But she wouldn't reveal her secrets to me.
What'll happen next year? What wonders great?
Yes, I would gladly see my own fate!
My fate, the arts, the country and empire,
But Grandmother wouldn't let me inquire.
I pestered then and it went very well,
First silence, and then she gave me hell.
Lectured me up and down, and yet
There is no doubt that I am her pet!

"For once, your wishes I'll grant," she said
And she gave me the glasses from her head.
"Now hurry out and choose a place
Where flocks of people sit or pace,
Stand where you can see what passes
And look at the masses through my glasses.

Trust my word on this, you'll at once be able
To see the crowd like cards on a table.
And from these cards you can foresee
The future that is meant to be."

"Thanks," I said and ran to see,
But then, where would most people be?
On Long Line? There one catches cold.
On East Street? Bah! Dirt, filth and mold!
But in the theater? Ah, that'd be dandy,
Tonight's entertainment was so handy-
Here I am, then! Myself I'll introduce,
Permit me Grandma's glasses to produce,
So I can see—No, don't go away!
To see, if a playing card display
Truly can predict what Time will make.
Your silence for a "Yes" I'll take;
For thanks, you'll be confirmed into the group,
All together here within the troupe.
I'll predict for you, for me, for country and more,
And we'll see what the cards can have in store.

(And then he put the glasses on.)

Yes, that's right! Now I laugh! Hee hee,
Oh, if you could just come up and see!
Where here are many manly cards,
And a whole row of Queens of Hearts.
The black ones there—clubs, spades too,
Now soon I'll have a perfect view.
The Queen of Spades with intense attack
Has turned her thoughts to Diamond Jack.
Oh yes, this view's making me quite drunk
There's lots of money in here sunk,
And strangers from afar return—
But that's not what we want to learn.
Politicians? Let's see! Yes, The Times!
We'll read it later, save our dimes.

Slander now would harm the paper's fate,
Let's not take the best bone from the plate.
The theater then? What news? tone and taste?
The good graces of the director I can't waste.
My own future? Yes, you know, one's fate,
Lays on our hearts a heavy weight.
I see!—I cannot say just what I see,
But you will hear it immediately.
Who is the happiest in our sphere?
The happiest? Easily I'll find him here.
It is, of course,—No, that will disconcert,
And many surely will be hurt!
Who'll live the longest? The lady there? That man?
No, revealing that is a worser plan!
About—? Yes, in the end, I myself don't know; when,
Being shy and so embarrassed, it's easy to offend.
Now I would know what you believe and think
I should with seer's power offer you to drink?
You think? No, beg pardon, what?
You think it will end up in naught?
You surely know it's merely ring-a-ding.
I'll not say more, dear honored gathering.
And let you have your own view of this thing.

The poem was superbly delivered and was very well received. Among the audience was the intern from the hospital, who seemed to have forgotten his adventure of the night before. He was wearing the galoshes since no one had claimed them, and since the street was muddy, they were useful to him.

He liked the poem.

He was very taken with the notion and would really have liked to have such glasses. Maybe if they were used correctly, you could look right into people's hearts. That was really more interesting, he thought, than to find out what would happen next year. After all, you'll find that out, but never the other. "Imagine if one could look into the hearts of that row of ladies and gentlemen there in the first row. There would have to be some kind of opening, a kind of shop; how my eyes would go shopping then! In that lady over there I would most likely find a dress shop. At that one over there—the store is empty, but it needs to be cleaned out. But there are some well established shops too! Well, well," he sighed. "I know one in which everything is of the best, but there is already a clerk there, and he is the only thing wrong with the whole store! Some of them would call out, 'Please come in.' Oh, I wish I could go in, like a lovely little thought right through their hearts."

See, that was enough for the galoshes. The intern shrunk together and began a most unusual trip right through the hearts of the audience in the front row. The first heart he passed through was a woman's, but he thought at once that he was at the Orthopedic Institute, which is what you call those places where doctors take off growths to help people straighten their backs. He was in the room where the plaster casts of the deformed limbs were hanging on the walls. The difference was that at the Institute they were cast when the patients come in, but here in this heart they were preserved as the healed patients went out. The casts of the physical and mental flaws of friends were preserved here.

Then he quickly passed into another woman's heart, but this one seemed to him like a big, holy church. The white dove of innocence was fluttering over the high altar, and he would have sunk to his knees here, but he had to hurry into the next heart. He could still hear the organ music, and he felt that he had become a new and better person. He did not feel unworthy to set foot in the next shrine which was a poor garret with a sick mother, but God's warm sun was shining through the open window. Lovely roses were nodding from the little wooden crate by the roof, and two sky-blue birds were singing about childhood's joy, while the sick mother prayed for blessings for her daughter.

Then he crept on his hands and feet through an overfilled butcher shop. All he saw was meat and more meat. This was the heart of a rich, respectable man, whose name you would know from the newspaper.

Next he was in the heart of the rich man's wife. It was an old, run-down pigeon coop. The husband's picture was the weather

Then he quickly passed into another woman's heart,
but this one seemed to him like a big, holy church.

vane and was connected to the doors, and these opened and closed as the man moved.

Then he came into a room of mirrors like the one in Rosenborg Castle, but here the mirrors enlarged objects to a great extent. In the middle of the floor sat, like the Dali Lama, the person's insignificant self, amazed to see its own greatness.

After that he thought he was in a cramped needle case full of sharp needles. This must be the "heart of an old maid," he thought, but that was not the case. It was a quite young military man with several medals. A man of both spirit and heart, it was said.

The poor intern came out of the last heart in the row terribly dizzy. He wasn't able to gather his thoughts, and thought that his overactive imagination had run away with him.

"Dear God," he sighed. "I definitely have a touch of madness! It's also incredibly hot in here! The blood is rushing to my head." Then he remembered the big adventure of the night before when his head had been stuck between the iron bars at the hospital. "That's where I must have caught it," he thought. "I have to nip this in the bud. A steam bath would be good. I wish I were already lying on the top bench."

And then he was lying on the top bench in the steam bath, but he had all his clothes on including his boots and galoshes. The hot water from the roof dripped on his face.

"Yikes!" he cried and hurried down to get a shower. The attendant also gave a loud cry when he saw a fully dressed man in there.

The intern was quick minded enough to whisper to him, "It's a bet." But the first thing he did when he got to his own room was to apply a big Spanish-fly plaster to the back of his neck and one down his back, to draw out the craziness.

The next morning he had a bloody back, and that's all he got from Good Fortune's galoshes.

5. The Clerk's Transformation

In the meantime the watchman, whom we haven't forgotten, remembered the galoshes that he had found and brought along to the hospital. He picked them up there, but when neither the lieutenant nor anyone else in the street claimed them, they were delivered to the police department.

"They look just like my own galoshes," said one of the clerks, as he observed the lost property and set them side by side with his own. "Not even a shoemaker's eye could tell them apart!"

"Look here!" said an employee who came in with some papers.

The clerk turned around and talked to the man, but when he was finished and looked at the galoshes again, he was completely bewildered about whether his were the ones on the left or those on the right. "Mine must be the wet ones," he thought, but that was wrong because they were Good Fortune's. But why can't the police also make mistakes? He put them on and put some papers in his pocket and others under his arm. He was going to read through and sign them at home, but it was Sunday morning, and the weather was nice. He thought it would do him good to take a little walk to Frederiksberg, and so he went out there.

No one could be more unassuming and diligent than this young man, and we won't begrudge him his little walk. It will undoubtedly be good for him because he sits so much. In the beginning he just walked without thinking about anything so the galoshes did not have a chance to show their magic power.

On the street he met an acquaintance, a young poet, who told him that he was going on a summer trip the next day.

"So, you're off again!" said the clerk. "You're a lucky, free spirit! You can go wherever you want. The rest of us have chains on our feet."

"But they're attached to a breadfruit tree," answered the poet. "You don't have to worry about tomorrow, and when you're old, you'll get a pension."

"But you're better off!" said the clerk. "It's a pleasure to sit and write poetry. The whole world pays you compliments, and you're your own boss. You should try sitting in court with trivial cases!"

The poet shook his head. The clerk shook his head, too. Each retained his own opinion, and so they separated.

"Those poets are a race apart," the clerk said. "I should try becoming such a nature, become a poet myself. I'm sure I wouldn't write such wimpy verse as the others do! This really is a spring day for a poet! The air is so unusually clear, the clouds so pretty, and there is such fragrance in all the greenery! I haven't felt like I do at this moment for many years."

We notice that he has become a poet already. It wasn't exactly glaring, since it's a foolish conceit to think that a poet is different from other people. These can have much more poetic natures among them than many a great and famous poet. The difference is just that the poet has a better spiritual memory. He can maintain ideas and feelings until they clearly flow over into words. Others can't do that. But to change from an everyday nature to a gifted one is always a transition, and the clerk had now done that.

"Oh what a lovely smell," he said. "How it reminds me of the violets at Aunt Lona's house. That was when I was a little boy. Dear God, I haven't thought about that for a very long time! Dear old auntie. She lived there behind the stock exchange. She always had a twig or a couple of green shoots standing in water, no matter how cold the winter was. I smelled the violets as I laid warmed-up copper pennies on the frozen windowpane and made peepholes—what a strange perspective! Out in the canal the boats lay frozen in ice, deserted by all hands. The only crew was a shrieking crow. But things got busy when the spring breezes came. They cut the ice apart, singing and shouting "hurrah." The ships were tarred and rigged and then departed for foreign lands. I remained behind here and must always remain. Sit always at the police station and see others get passports to travel abroad. That's my fate! Alas." He sighed deeply, but then stopped suddenly. "Dear God, what's become of me? I have never thought or felt like this before! It must be the spring air. It's both worrying and pleasant." He grasped the papers in his pocket. "This will give me something else to think about," he said and skimmed through the first page. "*Mrs. Sigbrith, original tragedy in five acts*," he read. "What's this? But it's my own handwriting! Have I written this play? *Intrigue on the Ramparts* or *Big Holiday. Comedy.*—But where have I gotten this? Someone must have put it in my pocket. Here's a letter." It was from the theater director. Both pieces were rejected, and the letter itself was not at all polite. "Hm, hm," the clerk said and sat down on a bench. His thoughts were so agitated, his heart so moved. Spontaneously he picked one of the closest flowers. It was a simple little daisy, and it proclaimed in a minute what the botanists tell us in many lectures. It told the myth of its birth and of the power of the sunshine that develops the fine petals and forces their scent. Then he thought about life's struggles that awaken feelings in our breasts in the same way. The air and light were the flower's lovers, but light was the favorite. It turned to the light, and if that disappeared, it rolled its petals together and slept in the embrace of the air. "It's light that adorns me," said the flower. "But the air lets you breathe," whispered the poet's voice.

A boy was standing nearby hitting a muddy ditch with a stick. Drops of water flew up into the green branches, and the clerk thought about the millions of invisible little animals in the drops that were hurled so high that, for their size, it would be as if we were flung high over the clouds. As the clerk was thinking about this and about the change that had happened to him, he smiled. "I'm sleeping and dreaming! But it's remarkable anyway, that you can dream so naturally and still know that it's a dream. I wish I could remember it tomorrow when I wake up! I seem to be in an unusually good mood right now. I have an open eye for everything and feel so fit, but I'm sure that when I remember parts of it tomorrow, it'll all be nonsense. I've experienced that before. All the wisdom and magnificence you hear and see in dreams is like the gold of the mound people. When you get it, it's splendid and glorious, but seen in the light of day, it's just rocks and shriveled leaves, alas." He sighed quite sadly and looked at the chirping birds hopping from branch to branch quite happily. "They are better off than I am. To be able to fly is a wonderful skill. How lucky they are who are born with that ability! If I were to be anything other than what I am, I'd be a little lark like that!"

At once his sleeves and arms changed into wings. His clothes became feathers, and the galoshes turned to claws. He noticed it all and laughed to himself. "Well, now I can see that

I'm dreaming, but I've never dreamed anything so silly before." Then he flew up into the branches and sang, but there was no poetry in the song because the poetic nature was gone. As is the case with anything done thoroughly, the galoshes could only do one thing at a time. He wanted to be a poet, and he became one. Then he wanted to be a little bird, but in becoming that, he gave up the former characteristic feature.

"This is good though," he said. "During the day I sit at the police station in piles of prosaic papers, and at night I dream of flying like a lark in Frederiksberg Garden. You could actually write a whole play about it."

Then he flew down into the grass and turned his head from side to side and pecked with his beak at the soft blades of grass that, in comparison to his size now, were as big as palm trees in North Africa.

Within a second everything was as black as midnight around him. Some monstrous object was thrown over him. It was a big cap that a boy from Nyboder had thrown over the bird. A hand came in and grabbed the clerk around his body and wings, so he peeped. In his first fright he called aloud, "You impertinent pup! I'm a clerk at the police department," but to the boy it sounded just like chirping. He slapped the bird's beak and wandered off.

On the street he met two upper-class schoolboys. Upper class as people, that is to say. From a spiritual point of view, they were among the school's lowest. They bought the bird for 25 cents, and in this way the clerk came to Copenhagen, home to a family in Gothers Street.

"It's a good thing I'm dreaming," said the clerk, "otherwise I'd be really angry. First I was a poet, now a lark. It was my poetic nature that transported me into the little animal. But it's a pitiful thing, especially when you fall into the hands of boys like these. I would like to know how this will end."

The boys brought him into an extremely elegant living room where they were greeted by a fat, laughing woman. She was not at all happy that a simple field bird, as she called the lark, was brought in. She'd let it pass today, however, and told them to put the bird in the empty cage by the window. "Maybe it will amuse Poppy-boy," she added and laughed at a big green parrot that was swinging proudly on his ring in a magnificent brass cage. "It's Poppy-boy's birthday," she said childishly, "and the little field bird is here to congratulate him."

Poppy-boy didn't say a single word in reply, but just kept rocking in a dignified way back and forth. But, in contrast, a beautiful canary, which had been brought there the past summer from its warm, luxuriant native land, began to sing loudly.

"Loudmouth!" the woman said and threw a white handkerchief over its cage.

"Pip, pip," it sighed, "What a terrible snowstorm," and then it fell silent.

The clerk, or the field bird, as the woman called him, was placed in a little cage close to the canary and not far from the parrot. The only human sentence the parrot could prattle was, "Come, let's now be human," which was often quite comical. Everything else he said was as unintelligible as the song of the canary except to the clerk, who was now himself a bird and could understand his companions very well.

"I flew under the green palms and the flowering almond trees," sang the canary. "I flew with my brothers and sisters above the splendid flowers and over the crystal clear sea with plants waving on the bottom. I also saw many lovely parrots who told the most amusing stories—long ones and so many of them!"

"Those were wild birds," said the parrot. "They had no education. Come, let's now be human! Why aren't you laughing? If the woman and all the strangers can laugh, so can you. It's a great flaw not to be able to appreciate the comical. Come, let's now be human."

"Oh, do you remember the beautiful girls who danced under the tents stretched from the flowering trees? Do you remember the soft fruit and the soothing juices of the wild herbs?"

"Yes, yes," answered the parrot. "But I'm much better off here! I get good food and am treated very well. I know that I'm clever, and I don't need anything more. Come, let's now be human. You are a poetic soul, as they call it, but I have deep knowledge and wit. You have your genius but no moderation. You fly into these high natural raptures, and that's why they cover you up. They don't do that to me because I have cost them a lot more. I tell jokes by the beaker-full and impress them with that. Come, let's now be human!"

"Oh, my warm, flowering native land!" the canary sang. "I'll sing about your dark green trees, about your quiet coves, where the branches kiss the clear surface of the water. I'll sing about all my brilliant brothers' and sisters' joy, where the desert's plant source[13] grows."

"Lay off those whining notes," said the parrot. "Say something we can laugh at. Laughter is a sign of the highest spiritual stage. See if a dog or a horse can laugh. No, they can cry, but laughter only belongs to people. Ho, ho, ho," laughed Poppy-boy and added his joke, "Come, let's now be human."

"You little grey Danish bird," said the canary. "You have also been captured. It must be cold in your forests, but at least there's freedom there. Fly away! They have forgotten to close the cage, and the upper window is open. Fly, fly!"

And that's what the clerk did. In a second he was out of the cage. At the same moment the half-opened door to the next room creaked, and the housecat with green shining eyes snuck lithely in and started hunting him. The canary fluttered around in its cage. The parrot flapped his wings and shrieked, "Come, let's now be human!" The clerk felt a deadly fear and flew away through the window over houses and streets. Finally he had to rest for a while.

The house across the street had something familiar about it, and a window was open. He flew in there and found that it was his own room! He sat down on the table.

"Come, let's now be human," he said without thinking about what he said. He was copying the parrot, but in the same instance he became the clerk again, but he was sitting on the table.

"God save us!" he said, "How did I get up here and then fall asleep? That was really a troubling dream I had. The whole thing was a lot of stupid nonsense."

6. The best thing the Galoshes brought

Early the next morning when the clerk was still in bed, someone knocked on his door. It was his neighbor on the same
floor, a student who was studying to become a minister. He
walked in.

"Let me borrow your galoshes," he said. "It's so wet in the
yard, but the sun is shining so beautifully, and I want to go
smoke a pipe down there."

He put on the galoshes and was soon down in the garden
where there was a plum tree and a pear tree. Even a little
garden like this is considered wonderful in central Copenhagen.

The student walked up and down the path. It was only six
o'clock, and out on the street he heard a coach horn.

"Oh, travel, travel!" he exclaimed. "That's the most splendid thing in the world. That's my heart's fondest desire and
would quiet this restlessness I feel. But it has to be far away!
I want to see the wonders of Switzerland, travel in Italy,
and—"

Well it's a good thing that the galoshes work so quickly, or
he would have gotten around way too much for both himself
and for us. He traveled. He was in the middle of Switzerland,
but was packed with eight others into a stagecoach. His head
hurt, his neck was tired, and the blood had settled into his
legs, which were swollen and pinched by his boots. He swayed
between a dozing and waking state. In his right hand pocket
he had his letter of credit, in his left he had his passport, and
in a little leather pouch on his chest he had sewn some gold
coins. Every dream proclaimed that one or another of these
treasures was lost, and therefore he leapt up feverishly, and
the first movement his hand made was a triangle from right
to left and up to his chest to feel if he had them or not. There
were umbrellas, canes, and hats rocking in the net above
him, and they obstructed much of the view, which he saw was
really impressive when he glimpsed it. Meanwhile his heart
was singing with thoughts that at least one poet, whom we

know, has written in *Switzerland* (but which have not yet appeared in print):

Here's beauty and more, sublime to tout
I'm eyeing Mt. Blanc, my dear.
If only my money will hold out
Oh, it would be good to stay here.

All of nature around was grand, severe and dark. The fir forests looked like a carpet of heather on the high mountains whose tops were hidden in the clouds. Then it started to snow, and the cold wind blew.

"Oh," he sighed. "I wish we were on the other side of the Alps, then it would be summer, and I would have gotten money on my letter of credit. I can't enjoy Switzerland because of the anxiety I have about this. Oh I wish I were on the other side!"

And so he was on the other side, deep within Italy, between Florence and Rome. Lake Trasimeno lay bathed in evening sun, like flaming gold, between the dark blue mountains. Here, where Hannibal defeated Flaminius, the grapevines now stood peacefully with green fingers intertwined. Delightful half-naked children were shepherding a litter of coal-black pigs under a grove of fragrant laurel trees by the side of the road. If we showed this as a painting, everyone would shout, "Lovely Italy," but the young theologian and his traveling companions in the hired coach surely didn't say that.

Thousands of poisonous flies and mosquitoes flew into the coach. In vain they swatted at them with a myrtle branch, but the flies bit anyway. There wasn't a person in the coach whose face wasn't bloated and bloody from bites. The poor horses looked like carrion. The flies were sitting on them like big crusts, and it only helped momentarily when the driver got down and scraped them off. Then the sun went down, and a short but icy chill went through all of nature. It was not at all pleasant, but the mountains and clouds had the most beautiful green color, so clear and shining. Go and see for yourself—that's better than reading this description! It was unparalled! The travelers thought so too, but their stomachs were empty, their bodies tired. With all their hearts they yearned for a place to spend the night, but where would this be? They were looking more for that than at the beautiful view of nature.

The road went through an olive grove. It was like driving through a gnarled forest of willows at home. There lay a lone inn there. Ten to twelve crippled beggars were camped outside. The best of them looked like "Famine's eldest son just arriving to years of discretion."[14] The others were either blind, had withered legs and crept on their hands, or shriveled arms with fingerless hands. It was pure misery wrung from the rags. "*Eccellenza, miserabili!*" they sighed and reached out their withered limbs. The innkeeper's wife met the travelers herself. She was barefoot, had uncombed hair, and was wearing a dirty blouse. The doors were tied together with twine, and the floor tiles in the rooms were partly dug up. Bats were flying around under the roof and the smell in there—

"Well, she should set up our table down in the stable," said one of the travelers. "At least there we'd know what we're breathing."

The windows were opened so that a little fresh air could get in, but, quicker than that, came the withered arms and the perpetual whimpering: *miserabili, Eccellenza!* There were a lot of inscriptions on the walls, and at least half of them were critical of *bella Italia.*

The food was brought out. There was a soup of water, spiced with pepper and rancid oil and then the same oil on the salad. The main course was tainted eggs and roasted rooster combs. Even the wine had a sour taste. It was a real mish-mash.

At night the suitcases were piled up against the door, and one of the travelers stood watch while the others slept. The student had the watch. Oh, how stuffy it was in there! The heat was oppressive, the mosquitoes swarmed and stung, and outside the *miserabili* whimpered in their sleep.

"Yes, traveling is very well," sighed the student, "if one just didn't have a body! If only the body could rest and the spirit could travel. Wherever I am, there are miseries that press on my heart. I want something better than the present. Yes, something better, the best. But where and what is it? After all, I do know what I want—to go to a happy place, the happiest place of all!"

And when the word was spoken, he was in his home. The long white curtains hung in front of the windows, and in the middle of the floor stood the black coffin. He lay there in the quiet sleep of death. His wish was granted—his body rested, his spirit traveled. "Call him till he dies, not happy but fortunate," said Solon.[15] These words were reaffirmed once again.

Every corpse is the Sphinx of Immortality. And the sphinx here in the black coffin couldn't say what the student had written only two days earlier:

> *Oh strong death, dread is your silent token,*
> *Your only footprint does the churchyard save.*
> *Shall the Jacob's ladder of thought be broken—*
> *Shall I arise as grass upon death's grave?*
>
> *Our greatest sufferings here we don't impart,*
> *You who were alone at last, and often;*
> *Know that in life much presses harder on the heart*
> *Than all the soil that's cast upon your coffin.*

Two figures moved in the room, and we know both of them. It was the Fairy of Sorrow and Good Fortune's messenger. They leaned over the dead man.

"Do you see what Good Fortune your galoshes brought to humankind?" asked Sorrow.

"At least they brought the man who's resting here a lasting good!" answered Good Fortune's messenger.

"Oh no," said Sorrow. "He went away on his own; he was not called. His spiritual power here was not strong enough to gain the treasures that he was destined for. I will do him a favor."

And she took the galoshes from his feet. The sleep of death ended, and the resurrected arose. Sorrow disappeared, but also the galoshes. She must have considered them her property.

NOTES

1. A professor at the University of Copenhagen, H. C. Ørsted (1777–1851) wrote an essay entitled "Gamle og nye Tider" ("Old and New Times"). Andersen admired Ørsted, who discovered electromagnetism.

2. King Hans was born in 1455 and ruled Denmark and Norway from 1481 to 1513.

3. Zealand is the largest island of Denmark, separated from Funen by the Great Belt and from Scania in Sweden by the Øresund. Copenhagen is partly located on the eastern shore of Zealand and partly on Amager.

4. The medieval dialect of Copenhagen was similar to that of the present-day island of Bornholm, in the Baltic Sea, and could be somewhat comical to those who live in Copenhagen.

5. After Thomasine Gyllembourg, a popular author of the time, published *En Hverdagshistorie* (*A Story of Everyday Life*) in 1828, the term *hverdagshistorie* came into use as a genre definition for stories of contemporaneous Copenhagen. Andersen was not an admirer of the genre.

6. In his *Danmarks Riges Historie*, Holberg tells how one day King Hans was joking with the famous Otto Rud, of whom he was very fond. The King had been reading about King Arthur and said, "Yvain and Gawain, whom I read about in this book, were remarkable knights. You don't find knights like that anymore." To which Otto Rud replied, "If there were Kings like King Arthur, you would find knights like Yvain and Gawain." [Andersen's note] Andersen cites Holberg's "The History of the Kingdom of Denmark." Ludwig Holberg (1684–1754) was the most important writer in eighteenth-century Denmark/Norway. [translator's note]

7. Writer and critic Johan Ludvig Heiberg (1791–1860); he published writings of his mother, Thomasine Gyllembourg, among others.

8. Godfred von Gehmen was the first publisher in Copenhagen; in 1493 he published Latin grammars for the new university.

9. Cholera was a serious problem in most of Europe from 1830 to 1837, but except for Holstein, Denmark was not much affected.

10. A statute of 1496 prescribed that prostitutes wear caps that were half red and half black, to distinguish them from other women.

11. Johann Heinrich von Mädler was a German astronomer who (with Wilhelm Beer) issued *Mappa Selenographica* (1834–1836) in four volumes; it presented the most complete map of the moon at that time.

12. The agave is a tropical plant that in Denmark flowers only in green-

houses after a period of forty to sixty years; in 1836 a sixty-year-old plant that bloomed in Copenhagen was nearly 20 feet tall.
13. Cactus. [Andersen's note]
14. Snarleyyow. [Andersen's note] The citation, given in the original English, is from *Snarleyyow; or, The Dog Fiend* (1837), a historical novel by Captain Frederick Marryat, a naval officer and writer of adventure novels. [translator's note]
15. Statesman and poet (c.630–560 B.C.), known as one of the Seven Wise Men of Greece.

THE GARDEN OF EDEN

ONCE THERE WAS A prince, and no one had so many or such beautiful books as he had. He could read about and see splendid pictures of everything that had happened in the world. He could find out about all nationalities and every country, but there was not a word about where the Garden of Eden was, and that was what he thought most about.

When he was still quite little, just beginning his education, his grandmother had told him that every flower in the Garden of Eden was the sweetest cake, and each stamen the finest wine. History was on one flower, geography or math tables on another. All you had to do was eat the cakes to know your lessons. The more you ate, the more history, geography, and math you would take in.

He believed that as a boy, but as he grew older, learned more, and became wiser, he understood, of course, that there must be a far different kind of beauty in the Garden of Eden.

"Oh, why did Eve pick from the tree of knowledge? Why did Adam eat the forbidden fruit? It should have been me, and then it wouldn't have happened! Sin would never have come into the world!"

He said it then, and he said it now that he was seventeen years old. All he thought about was the Garden of Eden.

One day he was walking in the forest. He walked by himself because that was his favorite pastime.

Evening came. Clouds gathered, a rainstorm came up, and rain fell as if the whole sky was a floodgate with water gushing from it. It was as dark as it usually is at night in the deepest well. Sometimes he slipped in the wet grass, and sometimes he tripped over the bare rocks that stuck up from the rocky ground. Water poured off everything, and there wasn't a dry thread on the poor prince. He had to climb up and over big boulders where the water was seeping out of the thick moss. He was ready to drop, but then he heard a strange whistling sound and saw in front of him a big cave, all illuminated. Right in the middle was a fire so big you could cook a stag on it, and that is exactly what was happening. A magnificent stag with huge antlers was on a spit and was slowly rotating between two felled spruce trees. There was an elderly woman, tall and strong, like a man in disguise, sitting by the fire, and throwing on one log after the other.

"Just come a little closer," she said. "Sit down by the fire so you can dry your clothes."

"There's a bad draft in here," the prince said and sat down on the floor.

"It'll get even worse when my sons get home," the woman answered. "You're in the Cave of the Winds now, and my sons are the four winds. Do you understand that?"

"Where are your sons?" asked the prince.

"Well, it's not so easy to answer a stupid question," the woman said. "My sons are out on their own. They're playing ball with the clouds up there in the sky," and she pointed up into the air.

"I see," said the prince. "You talk a little tougher and are not as mild as the women I'm used to."

"Well, they must not have anything else to do then. I have to be tough to keep my boys in check. But I can do it too, even though they are pretty stiff-necked. Do you see those four sacks hanging on the wall over there? They are just as afraid of them as you were of the belt in the woodshed. I can fold the boys up, let me tell you, and put them in the sacks without further ado. They sit there and can't get out to gad about until I say so. But here's one of them!"

It was the North Wind who breezed in with freezing cold surrounding him. Big hail stones hopped around on the floor, and snowflakes swirled all around. He was dressed in pants and a jacket of bearskin, and a hood of sealskin covered his ears. He had long icicles hanging from his beard, and one hailstone after another rolled down the collar of his jacket.

"Don't go right over to the fire," the prince shouted. "You can easily get frostbite on your face and hands!"

"Frostbite!" The North Wind laughed out loud. "I love frost! What kind of a whippersnapper are you, by the way? How did you get to the Cave of the Winds?"

"He's my guest," said the old woman, "and if you're not satisfied with that explanation, you'll go into the sack. You know what to expect!"

That helped, and the North Wind told where he'd come from and where he'd been for almost a whole month.

"I've come from the Arctic Ocean," he said. "I've been to Bear Island with the Russian whalers. I sat and slept by the tiller when they sailed out from the North Cape. Once in a while I woke up to find the storm petrels flying around my legs. It's an odd bird. It flaps its wings once quickly and then holds them out unmoving and coasts."

"Don't be so long-winded," said the wind's mother. "And then you came to Bear Island?"

"It's lovely there. What a floor to dance on, flat as a plate! Half melted snow with a little moss, sharp rocks, and skeletons of walruses and polar bears were lying there. They looked like the arms and legs of giants, green with mold. You'd think that the sun had never shone on them. I blew a little of the fog away so a shack became visible. It was a house made of a wrecked ship and covered with walrus skins. The flesh side was turned outward—it was red and green, and there was a live polar bear growling on the roof. I went to the beach and looked at the bird nests, looked at the little featherless chicks who were shrieking and gaping, and then I blew down into the thousand throats, and that taught them to close their mouths. Furthest down the walruses were wallowing like living entrails, or giant worms with pig heads and teeth two feet long!"

"You tell a good story, my boy," said his mother. "It makes my mouth water to listen to you."

"Then the hunt started. The harpoon went into the walrus' breast so steaming blood was like a fountain on the ice. Then I thought about my own game and blew up the wind, and let my sailing ships, the peaked mountainous icebergs, squeeze the boats inside. Oh, how people whimpered and how they wailed, but I whistled louder! They had to lay the dead walruses, chests, and ropes out on the ice. I sprinkled snow flakes on them and let them drift south with their catch on the encapsulated boats, there to taste salt water. They'll never return to Bear Island!"

"So you've done bad things then," the wind's mother said.

"Others can talk about the good I've done," he said, "but here comes my brother from the west. I like him better than any of them because he smells of the sea and brings a blessed coldness with him."

"Is it little Zephyr?"[1] the prince asked. "Yes, certainly it's Zephyr," the old woman answered, "but he's not so little any more. In the old days he was a lovely boy, but that's past now."

He looked like a wild man, but he had a crash helmet on so he wouldn't get hurt. He was holding a mahogany club, felled in an American mahogany forest. Nothing less would do!

"Where did you come from?" his mother asked.

"From the primeval forests," he answered, "where thorny vines make fences between each tree, where water snakes lie in the wet grass, and where people seem unnecessary!"

"What did you do there?"

"I looked at a deep river and saw how it came rushing from the mountains, became spray, and flew towards the clouds where it carried the rainbow. I saw a wild buffalo swimming in the river, carried away by the current. He rushed past a flock of wild ducks that flew into the air where the water was tumbling down. The buffalo had to go over the rapids. I liked that and blew up a storm so the ancient trees went flying and became crushed to splinters."

"And you didn't do anything else?" asked his old mother.

"I turned somersaults on the savannas, petted wild horses, and shook coconuts! Oh yes, I have stories to tell! But, as you know, you can't tell everything you know, old mother!" And

then he kissed his mother so she almost fell over backwards.
He really was a wild boy.

Then the South Wind came wearing a turban and a flying
Bedouin cape.

"It's really cold in here," he said, and threw wood on the
fire. "You can tell that North Wind was here first!"

"It's hot enough in here to roast a polar bear," the North
Wind said.

"You're a polar bear yourself," the South Wind answered.

"Do you two want to be put into the bag?" the old woman
asked. "Sit down on that rock and tell where you've been."

"In Africa, mother," he answered. "I've been on a lion safari
with the Hottentots in the land of the Kaffirs.² Such grass
grows on those plains, green as an olive! The gnus dance
there, and the ostrich ran a race with me, but I'm faster. I came
to the desert, to the yellow sands. It looks like the bottom of
the ocean. I met a caravan! They butchered their last camel to
get water to drink, but they didn't get much. The sun burned
above them, the sand burned below them, and there was no
end to the boundless desert. Then I romped about in the fine,
loose sand and whirled it up into big pillars. What a dance! You
should have seen how dispirited the camels were, and the merchant pulled his caftan over his head. He threw himself down
in front of me as if I were Allah, his God. They're buried now.
A pyramid of sand is standing over all of them. When I blow it
away one day, the sun will bleach the white bones so travelers
can see that people have been there before. Otherwise, you
would never believe people had been in the desert."

"So you have only done evil!" his mother said. "Into the bag
with you!" and before he knew what had happened, she had
him around the waist and put him into the sack. He rolled
around on the floor, but she sat down on the bag, and he had
to lie still.

"Those are some lively boys you have!" said the prince.

"Yes, no kidding," she answered, "but I can manage them.
Here comes the fourth!"

It was the East Wind, and he was dressed like a Chinaman.

"So you're coming from that quarter," his mother said. "I thought you had been to the Garden of Eden?"

"I'm flying there tomorrow," the East Wind said. "Tomorrow it'll be a hundred years since I've been there. I'm coming from China now where I was dancing around porcelain towers so all the bells were ringing. Down on the street, the officials, from the first to the ninth rank, got a beating. Bamboo rods were broken on their shoulders, and they cried out: 'many thanks, my fatherly benefactor,' but they didn't mean it, and I rang the bells and sang tsing, tsang, tsu!"

"You're a blow-hard about it," said the old woman. "It's a good thing that you're going to the Garden of Eden tomorrow since that always helps your manners. Drink deeply from the spring of wisdom and bring a little bottle full home to me!"

"I'll do that," the East Wind said. "But why have you put my brother from the south into the bag? Let him out! He's going to tell me about the bird phoenix—the bird that the princess in the Garden of Eden always wants to hear about every hundred years when I visit. Open the bag, dearest mother, and I'll give you two pockets full of fresh green tea that I picked on the spot."

"Well, for the sake of the tea and because you're my pet child, I'll open the sack." She did, and the South Wind crept out, but the wind was out of his sails since the foreign prince had witnessed it.

"Here is a palm leaf for the princess," the South Wind said. "That leaf was given to me by the old bird phoenix, the only one who existed in the world. With his beak he inscribed his whole life story there, the hundred years he lived. Now she can read it for herself. I saw how the phoenix set his nest on fire himself and burned up like a Hindu widow. Oh, how the dry branches crackled, what smoke and smells! At last it all went up in flames. The old phoenix lay in ashes, but his egg lay glowing red in the fire. It cracked with a big bang, and the young bird flew out. Now he is the ruler of all the birds, and the only phoenix in the world. He bit a hole in the palm leaf I gave you as a greeting to the princess."

"Now we have to have something to eat," the Winds' mother

said, and they all sat down to eat roasted venison. The prince sat beside the East Wind, and they soon became fast friends.

"Tell me something," said the prince, "who is this princess you all talked so much about, and where is the Garden of Eden?"

"Ho, ho," the East Wind said. "If you want to go there, fly with me tomorrow. But I must tell you, no human has been there since Adam and Eve's time. You surely know about them from your Bible history?"

"Of course!" the prince said.

"At the time they were banished, the Garden of Eden sank down into the earth, but it kept its warm sunshine, its mild air, and all its splendor. The Queen of the Fairies lives there, and there too lies the Island of Bliss, where death never comes. It's a lovely place to be! Climb on my back in the morning, and I'll take you along. I think it can be done. But now you have to be quiet because I want to sleep."

And then they all slept.

Early in the morning the prince woke up and was not just a little puzzled at already being high up over the clouds. He was sitting on the back of the East Wind, who was faithfully holding on to him. They were so high in the air that fields and forests, rivers and lakes looked like they would on a big illuminated map.

"Good morning," the East Wind said. "You might as well sleep a bit more because there's not much to see here on the flat lands below us. Unless you want to count churches! They're standing like chalk marks on the green board." The green board was what he called the fields and meadows.

"It's too bad I didn't get to say good bye to your mother and brothers," the prince said.

"When you're asleep, you're excused," said the East Wind, and then they flew even faster—you could hear it by the branches and leaves rustling through the tops of the forests when they flew over them. You could hear it by the sea and lakes—wherever they flew the waves broke higher, and the big ships bowed deeply down in the water like swimming swans.

Towards evening when it got dark, it was fun to see the big

cities. Lights were burning down there in different places. It was just like when you burn a piece of paper and see all the little sparks of fire blinking and disappearing like children coming out from school and running in all directions. And the prince clapped his hands, but the East Wind told him to stop that and hold on; otherwise, he could easily fall down and find himself hanging on a church steeple.

The eagles in the dark forest flew quickly, but the East Wind flew more quickly. The Cossack on his little horse rushed across the plains, but the prince rushed faster.

"Now you can see the Himalayas," said the East Wind. "The highest mountain in Asia is there. We'll be at the Garden of Eden soon." They veered to the south, and soon there was a smell of spices and flowers. Figs and pomegranates were growing wild, and the wild grapevines were full of blue and red grapes. They landed there and stretched on the soft grass where the flowers nodded to the wind as if they wanted to say, "welcome back."

"Are we in the Garden of Eden now?" the prince asked.

"Certainly not," said the East Wind, "but we'll soon be there. See that wall of rock over there and that big cave where the grapevines are hanging like big green curtains? We're going through there. Wrap your coat around you. The sun is shining warmly here, but just a step away it's freezing cold. That bird that's flying past the cave has one wing out here in the warm summer and the other in there in the cold winter."

"So that's the way to the Garden of Eden?" the prince asked.

They went into the cave. Oh, it was freezing cold, but it didn't last long. The East Wind spread out his wings, and they shone like the clearest fire. But what caves! Big boulders hung over them in the most fantastic configurations, and water was dripping from them. Sometimes it was so narrow that they had to creep on their hands and knees, sometimes so wide and open as if they were out in the open air. It was like a funeral chapel in there with silent organ pipes and petrified banners.

"I guess we're taking death's path to the Garden of Eden," said the prince, but the East Wind didn't say a word, just pointed ahead where a beautiful blue light was beaming towards them. The boulders above became more and more a mist and finally were as clear as a white cloud in moonlight. Then they entered the loveliest mild atmosphere, as fresh as in the mountains, as fragrant as in a valley of roses.

There was a river running there as clear as the air itself, and the fish were like silver and gold. Crimson eels that shot off blue sparks with every movement were sparkling in the water, and the wide water lily leaves were the colors of the rainbow. The flower itself was a burning red-yellow flame fed by the water, just like oil always gets the lamp to burn. A solid bridge of marble, so artistically and finely carved as if it were made of lace and glass beads, led over the water to the Island of Bliss where the Garden of Eden was blooming.

The East Wind took the prince in his arms and carried him over. Flowers and leaves were singing the most beautiful songs of his childhood there, but far more lovely than any human voice can sing.

Were they palm trees or gigantic water plants growing there? The prince had never before seen such succulent large trees. Creeping plants were slung in big garlands through the trees like you only see them pictured with colors and gold in the margins or entwined in the initial letters of medieval manuscripts. They were a strange combination of birds, flowers, and twisting vines. Close by in the grass was a flock of peacocks with their radiant widespread tails. Or so they seemed, but when the prince touched them, he discovered that they weren't animals but plants. They were big burdock leaves that were shining like beautiful peacock tails. Tame lions and tigers ran like lithe cats through the green hedges that smelled like apple blossoms, and the wild wood pigeon, shining like the most perfect pearl, flapped its wings on the lion's mane. The antelope, usually so shy, stood nodding its head as if it wanted to play too.

Then the fairy of paradise came. Her clothes were shining like the sun, and her face was gentle as a happy mother's when she is pleased with her child. She was very young and beautiful, and the loveliest girls, each with a shining star in her hair, were following her.

She took the prince by the hand and led him into her castle.

The East Wind gave her the leaf from the phoenix, and her eyes sparkled with joy. She took the prince by the hand and led him into her castle where the walls were the colors of the most radiant tulips held up to the sun. The ceiling itself was a big brilliant flower, and the more you stared up at it, the deeper the calyx appeared. The prince went to the window and looked through one of the panes, and he saw the tree of knowledge with the snake and Adam and Eve standing close by. "Weren't they banished?" he asked, and the fairy smiled and explained to him that time had burned an image in each pane of the window, but not as you usually see pictures. These had life in them. The leaves of the trees moved, people came and went, as in a reflection. And he looked through a different pane, and there was Jacob's dream where the ladder went clear up into heaven, and angels with huge wings were floating up and down. Everything that had happened in this world lived and moved in the glass panes. Only time could create such inspired paintings.

The fairy smiled and led him into a chamber with a big high ceiling. The walls appeared as transparent paintings, each face on them more lovely than the next. There were millions of these happy ones who smiled and sang together with one melody. Those high on top were so small that they appeared smaller than the tiniest rosebud when drawn as a dot on a piece of paper. In the middle of the chamber stood a big tree with superb hanging branches. Big and small gilded apples hung like oranges between the green leaves. It was the Tree of Knowledge, from which Adam and Eve had eaten. There was a red drop of dew dripping from each leaf; it was as if the tree were crying tears of blood.

"Let's get into the boat," said the fairy. "We'll enjoy refreshments out on the water. The boat pitches back and forth although it doesn't leave the spot, and all the countries of the world will pass before our eyes." And it was marvelous to see how the entire coast moved. First came the high snow-covered Alps, with clouds and black evergreens. The horn sounded deep and mournfully, and the shepherd yodeled sweetly in the valley. Then the banana trees bent their long, hanging branches down over the boat. Coal black swans swam on the water, and the strangest animals were seen on the beaches—this was Australia, the fifth continent of the world, gliding by with a view of the blue mountains. You could hear the singing of medicine men and see the wild men dancing to the sound of drums and bone flutes. The pyramids of Egypt sailed by with their tops in the clouds, along with overturned pillars and sphinxes half buried in sand. The northern lights burned over the glaciers of the north. It was a fire works display that no one could match. The prince was ecstatic. Of course he saw a hundred times more than we can describe here.

"Can I stay here forever?" he asked.

"That depends on you," the fairy answered. "As long as you don't act like Adam, and let yourself be tempted to do what's forbidden, you can stay here forever."

"I won't touch the apples on the Tree of Knowledge," the prince said. "There are thousands of fruits here just as lovely as they are."

"Test yourself, and if you aren't strong enough, then return with the East Wind, who brought you here. He's flying back now and won't return for a hundred years. For you that time will pass as if it were only a hundred hours, but it's a long time for temptation and sin. Every evening when I leave you, I must call you to 'follow me.' I'll wave you to follow, but you must stay behind. Don't come with me because then every step will increase your longing. You'll come into the chamber where the Tree of Knowledge grows. I sleep under its fragrant hanging branches. You'll bend over me, and I'll smile, but if you kiss my lips, paradise will sink deep into the earth, and it will be lost to you. The sharp winds of the desert will whirl around you, and cold rain will drip from your hair. Sorrow and troubles will be your fate."

"I'll stay here!" the prince said, and the East Wind kissed him on the forehead and said, "Be strong, and we'll meet here again in a hundred years. Farewell! farewell!" The East Wind spread out his enormous wings. They shone like the flash of heat lightning at harvest time, or the northern lights on cold winter nights. "Farewell! farewell!" sounded from the flowers

"Now our dances will begin," said the fairy.

and trees. Storks and pelicans flew along in rows, like a waving ribbon, and followed to the border of the garden.

"Now our dances will begin," said the fairy. "At the end of our dance, you'll see me waving at you as the sun sinks, and you'll hear me call to you: 'follow along!' But don't do it! Every evening for a hundred years I'll repeat this, and every time it's over you'll gain more strength. Finally, you'll never think about it. Tonight is the first time, and now I have warned you!"

And the fairy led him into a big chamber with white transparent lilies. The yellow stamen in each one was a little gold harp that played like a stringed instrument and with tones of flutes. The most beautiful slender girls floated about, dressed in waving gauze so you could see their lovely limbs. They swayed in the dance and sang about how splendid it was to live—that they would never die, and that the Garden of Eden would blossom forever.

The sun went down. The whole sky turned to gold and gave the lilies the cast of the most beautiful rose, and the prince drank of the frothing wine that the girls gave him. He felt happiness like never before, and then he saw how the back of the chamber opened up, and the Tree of Knowledge was standing in a glow that burned his eyes. The song from there was soft and lovely, like his mother's voice, and it was as if she sang, "My child! My beloved child!"

Then the fairy waved and called so fondly, "Follow me, follow me!" and he rushed towards her, forgot his promise, forgot it already on the first evening, and she waved and smiled. The fragrant spicy perfume of the air grew stronger; the tones of the harps more beautiful; and it was as if the millions of smiling faces in the chamber where the tree grew nodded and sang, "You should know everything! Man is the master of the earth." And he thought there was no longer blood dripping from the leaves of the Tree of Knowledge, but red sparkling stars. "Follow me, follow me," sang the trembling tones, and with every step the prince's cheeks burned hotter, and his blood pounded harder. "I must," he said, "it's not a sin, it can't be! Why not follow beauty and joy? I want to see her sleeping.

Nothing is lost as long as I don't kiss her, and I won't do that. I'm strong, and have a firm will."

And the fairy threw aside her shining fancy dress, bent the branches back, and a second later she was hidden within.

"I haven't sinned yet," said the prince, "and I won't do it either." He pulled the branches aside. She was already sleeping, lovely as only the fairy in the Garden of Eden can be, and she smiled in her sleep. He leaned down over her and saw tears tremble among her eyelashes.

"Are you crying over me?" he whispered. "Don't cry, you beautiful woman. Now I finally understand the happiness of paradise. It's rushing through my blood, through my thoughts. I feel in my earthly body the cherub's power and eternal life. Let me suffer eternal night—a minute like this is richness enough." And he kissed the tears on her eyes, and his mouth moved to hers—

Then there was a clap of thunder so deep and terrible as had never been heard before, and everything collapsed. The beautiful fairy and the blooming paradise sank, sank so deeply, so deeply. The prince saw it sink in the black night; it shone like a little shining star far in the distance. A deathly cold shot through his limbs. He closed his eyes and lay a long time as if dead.

Cold rain fell on his face, the sharp wind blew around his head, and he came to himself again. "What have I done?" he sighed. "I've sinned like Adam! Sinned so that the Garden of Eden has sunk way down there." And he opened his eyes. He could still see the star, far away, the star that sparkled like the sunken paradise—It was the morning star in the sky.

He stood up and saw that he was in the big forest close to the Cave of the Winds, and the Winds' mother sat by his side. She looked angry and lifted her arm in the air.

"Already on the first evening!" she said, "I might have known. If you were my son, I'd put you into the bag right now!"

"He'll go there," said Death, who was a strong, old man with a scythe in his hand and with big black wings. "He'll come to his coffin, but not yet. I'll just make a note of him, and let him wander around in the world for a while yet. He can atone for his sin, become good and better!—I'll come one day. When he least expects it, I'll put him into a black coffin, set it on my head, and fly up towards the star. The Garden of Eden blossoms there too, and if he is good and pious, then he'll enter there. But if his thoughts are evil and his heart is still full of sin, he'll sink deeper in his coffin than the Garden of Eden sank, and I'll only fetch him again every thousand years, either to sink deeper yet or to be taken to the star—that sparkling star up there!"

NOTES

1. The west wind of Greek mythology. Zephyr (or Zephyrus) is the brother of Boreas (the North Wind) and the father of Achilles' horses Xanthus and Balius.
2. Present-day Zimbabwe and South Africa. The name "Kaffir" (from the Arabic for "non-believer") was given by the Arabs to the native races of the east coast of Africa.

THE BRONZE PIG

IN THE CITY OF Florence not far from the Piazza del Granduca there is a little cross street. I think it's called Porta Rossa. In this street in front of a vegetable market, there's an artful and well cast metal pig. The fresh clear water trickles out of the animal's mouth. It is quite dark green from age, only the snout is shiny as if it were polished, and so it is by the many hundreds of children and poor people who take hold of it and set their mouths to the fountain to drink. It is quite a picture to see the well-formed animal caressed by a lovely, half-naked boy who sets his cheerful mouth to its snout.

Anyone who comes to Florence can find the place. He only has to ask the first beggar he sees about the bronze pig, and he'll find it.

It was late one winter evening. There was snow on the mountains, but there was moonlight, and moonlight in Italy gives a light that is just as good as a dark winter day in the North. Well, actually even better because the air has a shine to

it; it lifts you up, while in the North the cold lead-grey sky
presses us to the ground—the cold wet ground that one day
will press on our coffins.

Over in the Duke's Palace garden under a roof of pines,
where thousands of roses bloom in the wintertime, a little
ragged boy had been sitting all day, a boy who might be the
picture of Italy, so lovely and smiling, but yet so full of suffering. He was hungry and thirsty. No one had given him a penny,
and when it became dark and the garden was to be locked up
for the night, the porter chased him away. For a long time he
stood dreaming on the bridge over the Arno River and looked
at the stars that twinkled in the water between him and the
magnificent marble bridge.

He took the road to the bronze pig, knelt half down, threw
his arms around its neck, and set his little mouth to the shining snout and drank deep draughts of the fresh water. Close by
lay some lettuce leaves and a couple of chestnuts that became
his evening meal. There wasn't a soul on the street—he was
quite alone. He sat down on the bronze pig's back and leaned
forward so his little curly head rested on the pig's, and before
he was aware of it, he fell asleep.

It was midnight. The bronze pig moved, and he heard it say
quite distinctly, "Little boy, hold on tight. I'm going to run!"
and away it ran with him. It was an odd ride—First they came
to the Piazza del Granduca, and the bronze horse who bore
the Duke's statue neighed loudly. The colored coat-of-arms on
the old court house shone like transparent pictures, and
Michelangelo's David swung his sling. There was a strange life
everywhere. The bronze group with Perseus and the Rape of
the Sabines was a bit too life-like: a deathly scream flew from
them across the magnificent empty plaza.

At the Uffizi Palace, in the arcade where the aristocracy
gathers for Carnival, the bronze pig stopped.

"Hold on tight!" the animal said. "Hold on tight because
now we're going up the steps!" The little boy didn't say anything. He was half trembling, half happy.

They entered a long gallery that he knew well. He'd been
there before. The walls were covered with paintings. There

were statues and busts, all seen in the most beautiful light as
though it were daytime. But the most magnificent was when
the door to a side gallery was opened. The little boy remembered this splendid sight, although in this night everything
looked its most beautiful.

Here stood a lovely, naked woman, as beautiful as only nature and marble's greatest master could form her. She moved
her lovely limbs while dolphins leaped at her feet, and immortality shone from her eyes. The world calls her the Venus de
Medici. On each side of her were resplendent marble statues,
handsome men; one of them was sharpening a sword. He is
called the Knife Grinder. The Wrestlers composed the other
group. The sword was sharpened, and the warriors fought for
the Goddess of Beauty.

The boy was as if blinded by the magnificence. The walls
were shining with colors, and everything was alive and moving
there. The earthly Venus appeared as Titian had seen her, so
buxom and ardent, but as if doubled. There were two paintings of lovely women. The beautiful bare arms stretched out
on the soft cushions, the breasts heaved and the heads moved
so that the rich locks fell down on the round shoulders while
the dark eyes expressed fiery thoughts, but none of the pictures dared to step completely out of their frames. The Goddess of Beauty herself, the Wrestlers, and the Knife Grinder
remained in their places because the glory that streamed from
the Madonna, Jesus, and John bound them. The holy pictures
were no longer just pictures; they were the holy ones themselves.

What brilliance and what beauty from gallery to gallery!
And the little boy saw it all. The bronze pig went step by step
through all the splendor and magnificence. One sight super-
seded the next, but just one picture engraved itself in his
thoughts, and that was because of the happy, joyful children in
it. He had once nodded to them in daylight.

Many pass quickly by this picture, and yet it holds a treasure
of poetry. It shows Christ descending to the underworld, but it
isn't the damned you see around him, but rather the heathen.
Angolo Bronzino[1] from Florence painted this picture. The

most splendid thing is the expression of the children's certainty that they are going to heaven. Two little ones are caressing each other. One reaches his hand to another below and points to himself as if he is saying, "I am going to heaven!" All the adults stand doubtfully, hopefully, or bowed humbly before the Lord Jesus.

The little boy looked at this picture longer than at any of the others. The bronze pig rested quietly in front of it, and a slow sigh was heard. Did it come from the painting or from the animal's breast? The boy lifted his hand towards the smiling children, and then the animal tore away with him again, away through the open vestibule.

"Thanks and blessings, you wonderful animal!" the little boy said, and patted the bronze pig, who thump! thump!—ran down the steps with him.

"Thanks and blessings yourself," said the bronze pig. "I've helped you, and you've helped me because only with an innocent child on my back do I have enough energy to run. You see, I even dare go into the light of the lamp in front of the Madonna. I can carry you anywhere except into the church, but when you are with me, I can see through the open door. Don't climb off my back because if you do that, I will lie dead like you see me during the day on Porta Rossa street."

"I'll stay with you, my dear animal," said the little boy, and they flew with great speed through Florence's streets to the plaza in front of the Church of Santa Croce. The great double doors flew open, and light streamed from the altar through the church and out onto the empty plaza.

A strange beam of light shone from a sarcophagus in the left aisle, and thousands of moving stars seemed to form a halo around it. There was a coat-of-arms on the grave, a red ladder on a blue field, and it seemed to glow like fire. This was the grave of Galileo. It is a simple monument, but the red ladder on the blue field is a meaningful symbol. It could be Art's own because its road always goes up a glowing ladder, but to heaven. All the prophets of the spirit go to heaven like the prophet Elijah.

All the statues on the rich tombs in the right aisle of the

church seemed to be alive. Here stood Michelangelo; there Dante with a laural wreath on his head. Alfieri,[2] Machiavelli, side by side these great men rest, the pride of Italy.[3] It is a magnificent church and much more beautiful, if not as large as Florence's marble Cathedral.

It was as if the marble clothing moved, as if the big figures lifted their heads and gazed in the night, amid singing and music, towards the colorful, gleaming altar where white-clad boys swung golden censers. The strong scent streamed from the church onto the open plaza.

The boy stretched his hand out towards the radiance of light, and at the same instant the bronze pig took off again. The boy had to hang on tightly. The wind whistled around his ears, and he heard the church doors creak on their hinges as they closed, but then he lost consciousness. He felt an icy chill—and opened his eyes.

It was morning. He had slid part way off the bronze pig which was standing where it always stood in Porta Rossa street.[4]

Fear and dread filled the boy as he thought of the person he called mother. She had sent him out yesterday and told him to get money. He didn't have any, and he was hungry and thirsty. Once again he grabbed the bronze pig by the neck, kissed its snout, nodded to it, and wandered away to one of the narrowest streets, only wide enough for a pack donkey. He came to a big, iron-clad door that stood ajar. He went in and up a stone stairway between dirty walls that had an oily rope as a banister and came to an open balcony where rags were hanging. A staircase led from here to the courtyard where there was a well. From there big iron wires led to all stories of the building, and one water pail swayed next to another while the pulley squeaked. The pails danced in the air so that water splashed down in the courtyard. He went further up yet another dilapidated stone staircase. Two sailors, Russians, came lurching down cheerfully and almost knocked the poor boy down. They were coming from their nightly merriment. A strongly built woman, not young, with thick, dark hair came behind them. "What have you brought?" she asked the boy.

"Don't be angry," he begged. "I got nothing, nothing at all!"

And he grabbed his mother's dress as if he wanted to kiss it. They went into their room. I won't describe it, only to say that there was a jar with handles with charcoal burning in there—it's called a *marito*. She picked it up, warmed her fingers and thrust at the boy with her elbow. "Of course you've got money!" she said.

The child cried. She kicked at him with her foot, and he moaned aloud. "Shut up, or I'll smash your bawling head to pieces!" she yelled and swung the firepot that she had in her hand. The boy ducked down to the floor with a shriek. Then the neighbor came through the door. She had her *marito* on her arm also. "Felicita! What are you doing to the child?"

"The child is mine," said Felicita. "I can murder him if I want to, and you too Gianina!" and she swung the firepot. The other lifted hers in the air in defense, and both pots crashed into each other so that shards, fire, and ashes flew around the room. The boy was out the door in the same instant, across the courtyard, and out of the house. The poor child ran until he finally couldn't breathe at all. He stopped by the Church of Santa Croce, the church that had opened its wide doors to him the night before. He went inside where radiance shone from everything, and knelt by the first tomb to the right. It was Michelangelo's, and soon he was sobbing aloud. People came and went. Mass was said, but no one paid any attention to the boy. Only an elderly man stopped, looked at him, and then went away like the others.

The little one was suffering from hunger and thirst. He felt quite faint and sick and crawled into the corner between the wall and the marble monument and fell asleep. It was almost evening when he awoke from someone shaking him. He sprung up startled, and the same old man stood in front of him.

"Are you sick? Where do you live? Have you been here all day?" were some of the many questions the old man asked him. After the boy answered them, the old man took him along to a little house close by in one of the side streets. They walked into a glove-making workshop and found the old man's wife sewing busily when they entered. A little white Bolognese dog, clipped so closely that the pink skin showed, was hopping on the table, and jumped to the little boy.

"Innocent souls recognize each other," said the *signora* and petted both dog and boy. These good people gave him food and drink, and they said he could spend the night there. The next day old Giuseppe would talk to his mother. He was given a small, simple bed, but for him it was princely since he often slept on the hard stone floor. He slept very well and dreamed about the precious paintings and about the bronze pig.

The next morning old Giuseppe set out, and the poor child wasn't happy about it because he knew that the old man was going to arrange to take him back to his mother. He cried and kissed the lively little dog, and the woman nodded to them both.

And what news did old Giuseppe bring back? He talked a long time to his wife, and she nodded and petted the boy. "He's a lovely child," she said. "He will be a good glove-maker, like you were! And he has the fingers for it, so fine and flexible. Madonna has determined him to be a glove-maker."

And the boy stayed there, and the *signora* herself taught him to sew. He ate well. He slept well. He grew cheerful, and he started to tease Bellissima. That was the little dog's name. The woman shook her fingers at him, scolded, and was angry, and the little boy took it to heart. He sat thoughtfully in his little chamber that faced the street. Hides were being dried in there, and there were thick iron bars on the windows. He couldn't sleep, and the bronze pig was in his thoughts. Suddenly he heard "clop, clop." Oh, it must be him! He ran to the window, but there was nothing to see. It had already gone by.

"Help the gentleman to carry his paint box!" said the *signora* to the boy in the morning, as the young neighbor, who was a painter, came lugging his box and a big, rolled-up canvas. The child took the box and followed the artist, and they took the road to the gallery. They went up the same steps that he remembered well from the night he rode on the bronze pig. He recognized statues and paintings, the beautiful marble Venus, and the living colorful portraits. He once again saw the Mother of God, Jesus, and John.

Now they stood silently in front of the painting by Bronzino, where Christ descends into hell, and the children around him smile in sweet anticipation of heaven. The poor boy smiled too because he was in his heaven here.

"Well, go home now," the artist told him after he had stood there so long that the painter had raised his easel.

"Can I watch you paint?" asked the boy. "Can I see how you get the picture over to this white sheet?"

"I'm not going to paint now," the man answered and took out his black chalk. Quickly his hand moved, and his eye measured the big painting. Even if it was only a thin line, there stood Christ outlined as on the colorful painting.

"Go away now," said the artist, and the boy wandered quietly home, sat up at the table, and learned to sew gloves.

But the entire day his thoughts were in the gallery, and because of that he stuck himself in the fingers and was clumsy, but he didn't tease Bellissima either. When evening came, and the street door stood ajar, he slipped outside. It was cold, but there was lovely, clear starlight. He wandered through the quiet streets, and soon he was standing in front of the bronze pig. He leaned over it, kissed its shiny snout, and sat on its back. "You dear animal," he said, "how I have longed for you. We must take a ride tonight!"

The bronze pig stood unmoving, and the fresh water spurted from its mouth. The boy sat there like a horseman, and then something tugged at his clothes. He looked over and saw that it was little, closely-clipped Bellissima. The dog had slipped out of the house with him and had followed without the boy noticing. Bellissima barked as if it wanted to say, "See, I came too. Why are you sitting here?" Not even a fire-breathing dragon could have frightened the boy more than that little dog in this place. Bellissima on the street and without being dressed, as the *signora* called it! How would this go? The dog never went outside in the winter without wearing a little sheepskin coat that had been cut out and sewn for it. The coat could be tied tightly around the neck with a red band, and there were bells and ribbons on it. There was a similar band under the belly. The dog almost looked like a little lamb in this outfit when it was allowed to walk out in the winter time with its mistress. Bellissima had come along and wasn't dressed! Oh, what would happen? All his fantasies disappeared. The boy kissed the bronze pig and took Bellissima in his arms. The little dog was trembling with cold, and so the boy ran as fast as he could.

"What's that you're running with?" called two policemen who encountered him, and Bellissima barked. "Where have you stolen that cute little dog?" they asked and took it from him.

"Oh, give it back to me!" pleaded the boy.

"If you haven't stolen it, then you can report at home that the dog can be picked up at the station," and they gave the location and went away with Bellissima.

Now the boy was in a fine fix. He didn't know whether to jump into the Arno, or go home and admit everything. They would probably kill him, he thought. "But I want to be killed. I will die, and then I'll go to Jesus and Madonna!" and he went home, chiefly in order to be killed.

The door was closed, and he couldn't reach the knocker. There was no one on the street, but there was a loose stone, and with that he pounded on the door. "Who is it?" someone called from inside.

"It's me," he said. "Bellissima is gone! Open up and then kill me!"

There was a hue and cry for poor Bellissima, especially from the *signora*. She looked at once at the wall where the dog's outfit should be hanging, and the little sheepskin was there.

"Bellissima at the police station!" she yelled loudly. "You evil child! Why did you take him out? He'll freeze to death! That delicate animal with those coarse officers!"

And the old man had to go at once. The *signora* moaned, and the boy cried. All the people in the house gathered, including the painter. He took the boy on his knee and questioned him, and in bits and pieces he got the whole story about the bronze pig and the gallery. It wasn't easy to understand. The painter consoled the little one and defended him before the woman, but she wasn't satisfied until her husband came back with Bellissima, who had been among the officers. Then there was joy, and the painter patted the poor boy and gave him a handful of pictures.

Oh, what marvelous pictures, and comical heads! But best of all, there was the bronze pig itself, so lifelike! Oh, nothing could have been more splendid! With a few lines, there it was on the paper, and even the house behind it was depicted.

"Oh, to be able to draw and paint! Then you can capture the whole world!"

The next day, as soon as he was alone, the little one grasped a pencil and tried to reproduce the drawing of the bronze pig on the white side of one of the drawings. He was successful! A little crooked, a little up and down, one leg thick, another thin, but you could make it out. He himself was thrilled with it. He noticed that the pencil wouldn't quite go just as straight as it should, but the next day another bronze pig was standing beside the first. It was a hundred times better, and the third was so good that everyone could recognize it.

But things did not work out so well with the glove-making, and he was slow at doing his errands. The bronze pig had taught him that all pictures can be transferred to paper, and the city of Florence is an entire picture book; you only have to turn the pages. There is a slender column on the *piazza della Trinità*, and on the top stands a blind-folded Goddess of Justice holding her scales. Soon she was on paper, and it was the glove-maker's little lad who had put her there. The picture collection grew, but all the pictures were still of inanimate things. Then one day Bellissima jumped in front of him. "Stand still!" he said, "and you will become lovely and be one of my pictures." But Bellissima wouldn't stand still, so he had to be tied up. His head and tail were tied, and he barked and squirmed so the cord had to be tightened. Then the *signora* came!

"You ungodly boy! That poor animal!" was all she could say, and she pushed the boy to the side, kicked him with her foot, and threw him out of the house. He was the most ungrateful wretch, the most ungodly child! And she kissed her little half-strangled Bellissima tearfully.

Just at the same time the painter came up the steps, and that's the turning point in the story.

In 1834 there was an exhibition at the Academy of Art in Florence. Two paintings displayed beside each other attracted a lot of viewers. On the smallest painting a little boy was portrayed. He was drawing, and for a model he had a little white closely-clipped dog, but the animal wouldn't stand still and was therefore tied with string both at the head and the tail. The life and reality in the painting appealed to all who saw it. They said that the painter was a young Florentine who had been found on the streets as a little child. He had been raised by an old glove-maker and had taught himself to draw. An artist who had become famous had discovered the boy's talent when he had been chased away because he had tied up his mistress's favorite, the little dog, to use as a model.

That the glove-maker's little apprentice had become a great painter was clear from this painting, but even more so from the one next to it. Here only one figure was represented: a lovely tattered boy who sat sleeping on the street next to the bronze pig on Porta Rossa street. All of the spectators knew the spot. The child's arm rested on the pig's head, and the little one slept so securely. The lamp by the Madonna painting cast a strong light on the child's marvelous, pale face. It was a magnificent painting, enclosed by a big gilded frame. On the corner of the frame a laurel wreath was hanging, but between the green leaves a black ribbon was entwined—and a long black mourning crepe hung down from it.—

For the young artist had just died.

NOTES

1. Italian artist Agnolo di Cosimo, called Il Bronzino (1503-1572); he painted *Descent of Christ into Hell*, which hangs in the Uffizi Gallery in Florence.
2. Italian dramatist and poet Vittorio Alfieri (1749–1803) was a leading figure in the development of modern Italy.
3. Just opposite Galileo's tomb is Michelangelo's. On his monument are located his bust, as well as three figures: Sculpture, Painting, and Architecture. Close by is Dante's tomb (but the body itself is buried in Ravenna). On the monument you can see *Italia*, pointing at Dante's

enormous statue. *Poesi* is crying over the Lost. A few steps from here is Alfieri's monument. It is adorned with laurels, lyres, and masks. *Italia* is crying over his coffin. This row of famous great men ends with Machiavelli. [Andersen's note]

4. The bronze pig is a cast. The original is antique and of marble and is found by the entrance to *Galleria degli Uffizi*. [Andersen's note]

THE ROSE ELF

IN THE MIDDLE OF a garden there was a rose tree that was completely full of roses, and in one of these, the most beautiful of them all, lived an elf. He was so tiny that no human eye could see him. He had a bedroom behind every rose petal. He was as well formed and lovely as any child could be and had wings from his shoulders all the way down to his feet. What a lovely fragrance there was in his rooms, and how clear and lovely the walls were! Of course they were the fine, pink rose petals.

All day he amused himself in the warm sunshine, flew from flower to flower, danced on the wings of the flying butterfly, and measured how many steps he had to take to run over all the roads and paths on a single linden leaf. What we call veins in the leaves is what he called roads and paths. They were long roads for him and before he was finished, the sun went down. He had also begun pretty late.

It became cold. The dew fell, and the wind blew. It was best to get home. He hurried as fast as he could, but the rose had closed, and he couldn't get in—not a single rose stood open. The poor little elf was so scared. He had never been out at night before, had always slept so cozily behind the snug rose petals. Oh, this would surely be the death of him!

He knew that there was a bower of lovely honeysuckle at the other end of the garden. The flowers looked like big painted horns. He would climb down in one of those and sleep until tomorrow.

He flew over there. Hush! There were two people in there: a handsome young man and the loveliest maiden. They sat beside each other and wished that they never had to part for all eternity. They loved each other so much. Much more than the best child can love his mother and father.

"But we must part," said the young man. "Your brother doesn't like me, and that's why he has sent me on an errand far away over the mountains and seas. Farewell, my sweet bride, for that is what you are to me!"

And then they kissed each other, and the young girl gave him a rose, but before she handed it to him, she pressed a kiss on it—so firm and heartfelt that the flower opened up, and the little elf flew into it and snuggled his head up against the fine fragrant walls. But he could clearly hear them saying good bye, and he felt it when the rose was placed on the young man's chest—Oh, how the heart was pounding in there! The little elf couldn't fall asleep, for it was pounding too hard.

The rose didn't lie still on his chest for long. The man took it off, and while he was walking through the dark forest, he kissed the flower so often and so fervently that the little elf was nearly crushed to death. He could feel through the petals how the man's lips burned, and the rose itself had opened as from the strongest midday sun.

Then another man came, dark and angry. He was the beautiful girl's wicked brother. He took out a knife so sharp and long, and while the other kissed the rose, the wicked man stabbed him to death, cut off his head, and buried it with the body in the soft earth under the linden tree.

"Now he's gone and forgotten," the wicked brother thought. "He'll never come back again. He was going on a long trip, over mountains and seas, where one could easily lose one's life, and that's what happened. He won't be back, and my sister dare not ever ask me about him."

Then he scraped together some wilted leaves with his foot over the disturbed earth and walked home in the dark night, but he didn't walk alone as he thought. The little elf was with him. He sat in a wilted rolled-up linden leaf that had fallen in the evil man's hair when he dug the grave. His hat was placed over it. It was very dark in there, and the elf was shaking with fright and anger over the dreadful deed.

In the early morning the wicked man came home. He took off his hat and went into his sister's bedroom. The lovely, blooming girl was lying there dreaming of him whom she loved so much, and whom she thought was now far away over mountains and forests. The evil brother bent over her and laughed as wickedly as a devil can laugh; then the wilted leaf fell out of his hair down on the bedspread, but he didn't notice it and went off to sleep a few hours himself. But the elf slipped out of the wilted leaf, crept into the ear of the sleeping girl, and told her, as if in a dream, of the terrible murder. He described the place where her brother had killed him and buried his corpse, told about the flowering linden tree close by, and said, "So you won't think it's only a dream I've told you, you'll find a wilted leaf on your bed," and she found it when she woke up.

Oh, what salty tears she shed! And she didn't dare speak to anyone of her grief. The window was open the whole day so the little elf could easily have gone into the garden to the roses and all the other flowers, but he didn't have the heart to leave the bereaved. There was a bush with miniature roses in the window, and he sat in one of the flowers and watched the poor girl. Her brother came into the room many times, and he was so merry and wicked, but she didn't dare say a word about her great sorrow.

As soon as it was dark, she snuck out of the house and into the forest where the linden tree was standing, tore the leaves away from the earth, dug down, and found him, who had been killed, at once. Oh, how she cried and prayed to the Lord that she too might soon die.

She wanted to take the corpse home with her, but she couldn't do that so she took the pale head with the closed eyes, kissed the cold mouth, and shook the soil from his lovely hair. "This I will keep!" she said, and when she had placed dirt and leaves on the dead body, she took the head home with her. She also took a little branch from a jasmine tree that bloomed in the woods where he was killed.

As soon as she was back in her room, she got the largest

flowerpot she could find and placed the dead man's head in it, put soil on top, and planted the jasmine branch in the pot.

"Farewell, farewell," whispered the little elf. He couldn't stand seeing all the sorrow any longer and flew away into the garden to his rose, but it had faded away. Only a few pale petals were hanging on the green rosehip.

"Oh, how quickly the beautiful and good pass away!" sighed the elf. He finally found another rose, and it became his house. Behind its fine fragrant petals he could live and build his home.

Every morning he flew to the poor girl's window, and she always stood crying by the flowerpot. The salty tears fell on the jasmine branch, and every day as she became paler and paler, the branch became fresher and greener. One shoot after another grew forth. Small white buds appeared for flowers and she kissed them, but the wicked brother scolded her and asked if she had become a fool. He couldn't understand or tolerate that she was always crying over the flowerpot. He didn't know, of course, whose eyes were closed there, and whose red lips had become earth there. She leaned her head up against the flowerpot, and the little elf found her slumbering there. He climbed into her ear, told about the evening in the bower, about the smell of roses, and the love of the elves. She dreamed so sweetly and while she dreamed, life faded away. She died a quiet death and was in heaven with him whom she had loved.

And the jasmine flowers opened their beautiful big flowers. They smelled so wonderfully sweet. They had no other way to cry over the dead.

But the wicked brother looked at the beautiful flowering tree and took it, like an inheritance, to his bedroom and placed it next to his bed, because it was beautiful to see, and the fragrance was so sweet and delicious. The little rose elf followed along and flew from flower to flower. A little soul lived in each of them, and he told them about the murdered young man, whose head was now earth under them, and told about the wicked brother and the poor sister.

"We know this," every soul in the flowers said. "We know it.

Didn't we grow forth from the dead man's eyes and lips? We know it, we know it!" and they nodded their heads so strangely.

The rose elf couldn't understand how they could be so calm, and he flew over to the bees, who were gathering honey, told them the story about the wicked brother, and the bees told their Queen, who commanded that the next morning they should all kill the murderer.

But the night before, the first night after the sister's death, when the brother was sleeping in his bed close to the fragrant jasmine tree, each flower opened up. Invisibly, but with poisonous spears, the flower souls climbed out. First they sat by his ears and whispered bad dreams, then flew over his lips and stuck his tongue with the poisonous spears. "Now we have avenged the dead," they said and searched out their white flowers again.

When morning came and the window to the bedroom was opened, the rose elf with the Queen of the bees and the whole swarm flew in to kill him.

But he was already dead. People were standing around the bed saying, "The fragrance of the jasmines has killed him!"

Then the rose elf understood the flowers' revenge, and he told the Queen bee, and she buzzed around the flower pot with her whole swarm. The bees couldn't be chased away so a man took the flower pot away, and one of the bees stuck his hand so that the flowerpot fell and broke in two.

They saw the white skull, and they knew that the dead man in the bed was a murderer.

And the Queen bee buzzed in the air and sang about the flowers' revenge and about the rose elf, and that behind the smallest leaf lives one who can tell about wickedness and avenge it.

THE PIXIE AT THE GROCER'S

ONCE THERE WAS A real student—he lived in the garret and owned nothing. There was also a real grocer—he lived on the ground floor and owned the whole house. And the pixie stuck to him because every Christmas Eve he got a bowl of porridge with a big lump of butter in it. The grocer treated him to that, so the pixie stayed in the store, and it was worthwhile and educational for him.

One evening the student came in the back door to buy himself a candle and some cheese. He had no one to send, so he came himself. He got what he wanted, paid for it, and the grocer and his wife nodded "good evening" to him. There was a woman who could do more than nod! She had the gift of gab. The student nodded back and remained standing reading the paper that the cheese was wrapped in. It was a page torn from an old book that shouldn't have been torn apart—an old book full of poetry.

"There's more of it lying there," said the grocer. "I gave an old woman some coffee beans for it. If you give me eight shillings, you can have the rest."

"Thanks," said the student. "Let me have that instead of the cheese. I can eat plain bread. It would be a shame if that whole book should be torn into bits and pieces. You're a fine man, a practical man, but you don't understand poetry any more than that trash bin does!"

That wasn't very nice to say, especially about the trash bin, but the grocer laughed and the student laughed. It was said as a kind of joke, after all. But it annoyed the pixie that someone dared speak that way to the grocer, who owned the house and sold the very best butter.

At night, when the store was closed and everyone except the student was asleep, the pixie went in and took the *gab-gift* from the mistress. She didn't need it when she was sleeping. And wherever he set it on an object in the room, the object was able to speak, could express its thoughts and feelings as well as the mistress. But only one at a time could have it, and that was a good thing, or they all would have been talking at once.

The pixie set the *gab-gift* on the trash bin. It had old newspapers in it. "Is it really true," he asked, "that you don't know what poetry is?"

"Oh, I know that," said the trash bin. "It's something that appears at the bottom of the newspapers and is clipped out! I think that I have more of it in me than the student does, and I'm just a poor trash bin compared to the grocer."

The pixie placed the *gab-gift* on the coffee mill. My, how it ground on and on! Then he set it on the butter tub and the money till. Everybody was of the same opinion as the trash bin, and what the majority agree upon must be respected.

"Now the student is going to get it!" and the pixie went quietly up the kitchen stairs to the garret where the student lived. There was a light on in there, and the pixie peeked through the keyhole and saw that the student was reading the tattered book from downstairs. But how bright it was in there! From the book came a bright ray of light that turned into the trunk of a magnificent tree that rose up high and widely spread its branches over the student. Every leaf was so fresh, and each flower was the head of a beautiful girl, some with dark and shining eyes, and others with eyes so blue and wonderfully clear. Each fruit was a shining star, and there was sweet and lovely song and sound all around.

The little pixie had never imagined such splendor, much less seen or felt it. So he remained there on his tiptoes, peering and peeking until the light in there went out. The student must have blown out his lamp and gone to bed, but the little pixie continued to stand there because the song was still sounding so softly and sweetly, a delightful lullaby for the student as he lay down to rest.

"It's wonderful here," said the little pixie. "I hadn't expected that. I think I'll stay with the student!" And he thought and thought about it sensibly, and then he sighed: "The student doesn't have any porridge." And then he left and went back down to the grocer. And it's a good thing he returned because the trash bin had almost used up the mistress' *gab-gift* by repeating on one side everything it contained. It was just turning to replay the same thing to the other side when the pixie came and took the *gab-gift* back to the mistress. But everything in the store, from the money till to the firewood, took their opinions from the trash bin from then on. They respected it so much and believed it so thoroughly that when the grocer read the art and theater reviews from the *Times* in the evenings, they thought it came from the bin.

But the little pixie didn't sit still any longer and listen to all the wisdom and knowledge down there. No, as soon the light went on in the garret, it was as if the rays were strong cables pulling him up there, and he had to go peek through the keyhole. Then a feeling of grandeur encompassed him, like how we feel when God moves over the rolling sea in a storm, and the pixie burst into tears. He didn't know himself why he cried, but there was something blessed in the tears. How wonderful it would be to sit under that tree with the student, but that could never happen. He was happy just to look through the keyhole. He even stood there in the cold hallway when the autumn winds blew down from the attic vent, and it was so cold, so terribly cold. But the little fellow didn't feel it until the light went out in the garret, and the strains of music died in the wind. Brrrr—then he froze and crept down to his cozy corner again. It was comfortable and pleasant!—And then when Christmas came with the big lump of butter—well, then the grocer was the tops!

One evening the pixie was awakened in the middle of the night by a dreadful racket at the window shutters. People were pounding on them. The watchman was blowing his whistle. There was a big fire, and the whole street was lit up by flames. Was it here in the house or at the neighbor's? Where? It was horrifying! The grocer's wife became so bewildered that she took her gold earrings out of her ears and put them in her pocket in order to save something. The grocer ran to get his bonds, and the servant the silk cape she had saved for. Everyone wanted to rescue the best they had, and so did the little pixie. He ran up the stairs and into the student's room. The student was standing calmly by the window looking out at the fire. It was at the neighbor's house across the street. The little pixie grabbed the wonderful book from the table, put it inside his red cap, and held on to it with both hands. The greatest treasure in the house was saved! Then he ran off, way out onto the roof and up on the chimney, where he sat illuminated by the burning house across the street, and with both hands he held onto his red cap that held the treasure. Now he knew his own heart and knew to whom he really belonged. But when the fire had been extinguished, and he thought about it; well—"I'll divide myself between them," he said. "I can't completely give up the grocer, because of the porridge."

And that was quite human of him! The rest of us go to the grocer too, for the sake of the porridge.

IB AND LITTLE CHRISTINE

CLOSE TO THE GUDEN River in Silkeborg forest,[1] there is a ridge that rises up like a big bank. It's just called "the ridge," and below it on the west side there lay—and still lies—a little farm house with some poor land. You can see the sand through the thin rye and barley crops. It happened quite a few years ago now. The people who lived there cultivated their little plot, and they also had three sheep, a pig, and two oxen. In short, they were able to make a living on what the farm could produce, if they were careful to take things as they came. They probably could have kept a couple of horses too, but they said, as did the other farmers there, that "a horse eats itself"—it eats as much as it produces. Jeppe-Jens, the farmer, worked his little plot in the summer, and in the winter he was a diligent clog maker. He also had a helper, a fellow who knew how to carve clogs that were both strong, light-weight, and shapely. They also made spoons and ladles, which brought in some money. No one could say that the Jeppe-Jenses were poor people.

Little Ib, seven years old and the only child in the house, watched and whittled a stick. He also cut his fingers, but one day he had carved two pieces of wood that looked like little wooden shoes. He said he was giving them to little Christine, the bargeman's daughter. She was as delicate and lovely as a child of the gentry. If her clothes had been made as well as she was, no one would think she was from the heather thatched cottage on the heath. That's where her father lived. He was a widower who made his living by hauling wood from the forest down to the Silkeborg eel works and often further up to Randers.

He didn't have anyone to take care of little Christine, who was a year younger than Ib, and so she was almost always with him on the barge and among the heather and lingonberries. When he went all the way to Randers, little Christine stayed at the Jeppe-Jenses.

Ib and little Christine got along well together, both at play and at mealtimes. They dug and rummaged, they crawled and they wandered around, and one day they dared to go almost to the top of the ridge and deep into the woods by themselves. They found snipe eggs there one day, and that was a great event.

Ib hadn't been up on the high heath yet, had never gone on the barge between the lakes on the Guden, but now he was going. He had been invited by the bargeman, and the evening before, Ib went home with him.

Early in the morning the two children sat high on the piles of firewood on the barge eating bread and raspberries. The bargeman and his helper poled the barge along with the current, rapidly down the river, through the lakes that always seemed to be closed up with woods and reeds. But there was always a way through, even though the old trees leaned way out, and the oak trees stretched their peeling branches as if they had tucked-up sleeves and wanted to show their lumpy naked arms. Old Alder trees, that the current had torn from the slope, held themselves by their roots on the bottom, and looked like small wooded islands. Water lilies rocked on the water. It was a lovely ride, and then they came to the eel works, where the water roared through the sluices. That was really something for Ib and Christine to watch!

At that time there was neither a factory nor a town there, just the old breeding farm, and there weren't many people. The water rushing through the sluices, and the cry of the wild ducks—those were the most constant sounds at that time. After the wood was unloaded, Christine's father bought himself a big bundle of eels and a little slaughtered pig, which were placed in a basket in the stern of the barge. They sailed against the current on the way home, but the wind was with them, and when they added a sail, it was just as good as having two horses pulling them.

After they reached the point in the woods where the helper only had a short distance to walk home, he and Christine's father went ashore and told the children to remain there quietly and behave themselves, but they didn't do that for long. They had to look in the basket where the eels and pig were hidden. Then they had to pick up the pig and hold it, and since they both wanted to hold it, they dropped it, and it fell into the water and drifted away on the current. Oh, what a terrible thing!

Ib jumped on shore and ran a short distance. Then Christine came too. "Take me with you!" she shouted, and soon they were in the bushes. They couldn't see the barge or the river any longer. They ran a short way further, and then Christine fell down and started crying. Ib helped her up.

"Come with me," he said. "The house is that way!" But it wasn't that way at all. They walked and walked, over withered leaves and dry fallen branches that crackled under their feet. Then they heard a loud cry—they stood still and listened. An eagle screamed. It was an awful sound, and they became frightened, but ahead of them in the woods were growing enormous amounts of the most beautiful blueberries. It was much too inviting not to stay. So they stayed and ate. Their mouths and cheeks turned quite blue. Then they heard a cry again.

"We'll get spanked because of the pig," said Christine.

"Let's go home to our house," said Ib. "It's here in the woods." And away they went. They came to a road, but it didn't lead home. It got dark, and they were afraid. The wonderful silence around them was broken by terrible screams from the big horned owl, or sounds from birds they didn't recognize. Finally they were both tangled up in a bush. Christine cried and Ib cried, and after they had cried for a while, they laid down in the leaves and fell asleep.

The sun was high in the sky when they awoke. They were freezing, but up on the heights close by, the sun shone down through the trees. They could warm themselves there, and from there Ib thought they could see his parents' house. But

they were far away from it in another part of the forest. They
climbed all the way to the top of the heights and stood on a
slope by a clear, transparent lake. There was a school of fish
there shining in the sunlight. What they saw was so unexpected, and close by was a large bush full of nuts, as many as
seven in a bunch. They picked them, cracked them, and ate
the fine kernels that were ripening. Then came yet another
surprise—a terrifying one! A large old woman stepped out
from the bush. Her face was dark brown, and her hair was very
black and shiny. The whites of her eyes flashed like a black person's. She had a bundle on her back and a knotty stick in her
hand. She was a gypsy. The children didn't understand what
she said right away. She took three big nuts out of her pocket
and said that the most beautiful things were hidden in them—
they were wishing nuts.

Ib looked at her, and since she was so friendly, he gathered
his courage and asked if he could have the nuts. The woman
gave them to him and then picked a whole pocket full from
those on the bush.

Ib and Christine gazed wide-eyed at the three wishing nuts.

"Is there a coach with horses in this one?" Ib asked.

"There's a gold carriage with golden horses," said the
woman.

"Give it to me!" said little Christine, and Ib gave it to her.
The woman tied the nut up inside Christine's scarf.

"Is there a beautiful little scarf like the one Christine is wearing in this one?" asked Ib.

"There are ten scarves," said the woman. "There are fine
dresses, stockings, and a hat."

"I want that one too!" said Christine, and little Ib gave her
the second nut too. The third nut was a little black one.

"You can keep that one," said Christine. "It's pretty too."

"What's in that one?" asked Ib.

"The very best thing for you," said the woman.

Ib held the nut tightly. The woman promised to set them on
the right path home, and so they walked, but they went in exactly the opposite direction than they should have gone, but

you can't accuse her of wanting to steal children because of that.

In the pathless forest they met Chrœn, a forest ranger. He knew Ib and led the children home. Everyone was very worried about them, and they were forgiven, although they both deserved a good spanking, first because they let the pig fall into the water, and then because they ran away.

Christine came home to the heath, and Ib remained in the little house in the woods. The first thing he did that night was to take out the nut that hid the *very best*. He laid it between the door and the door jam and shut the door until the nut cracked, but there was no kernel to be seen. It was filled with something like snuff or humus. It was worm-eaten, as it's called.

"Well, I suppose I could have guessed that," thought Ib. "How would there be room inside that little nut for the *very best thing*? Christine won't get fine clothes or a gold carriage from her nuts either."

And winter came and then the New Year.

Several years went by. It was time for Ib to be confirmed, and he lived far from the minister. At that time the bargeman came one day and told Ib's parents that little Christine was now going out to earn her living. It was very fortunate for her that she had come into such good hands. She was going to work for the rich innkeeper further west in Herning. She was going to help the mistress there, and if she did well and was confirmed there, they would keep her on.

Then Ib and Christine said good bye to each other. People called them sweethearts, and she showed him at their parting that she still had the two nuts he had given her when they were lost in the woods, and she told him that in her chest she kept the little wooden shoes he had carved for her as a boy. And so they parted.

Ib was confirmed, but he lived at home with his mother because he was a good clog maker, and he took good care of the little plot of land in the summer. His mother had no one else to help because Ib's father had died.

Only rarely did they hear anything about Christine from a

postal carrier or an itinerant eel-trader. She was doing well at
the rich innkeeper's, and when she was confirmed, she wrote
her father a letter with greetings for Ib and his mother. She
wrote that she had gotten six new shifts and a lovely dress from
the master and mistress. The news was certainly good.

The next spring, on a beautiful day, there was somebody at
Ib and his mother's door. It was the bargeman with Christine.
She had come for a visit for the day. She had been given the
opportunity to catch a ride to Tem and back and took advan-
tage of it. She was beautiful, like a real lady, and was wearing
fine clothes that were well sewn and suited her nicely. There
she stood in all her glory, and Ib was in his old, everyday
clothes. He couldn't think of anything to say, but he took her
hand and held it tightly. He was intensely happy, but couldn't
get his tongue to work. Little Christine didn't have that problem. She could talk and had much to say, and she kissed Ib
right on the lips.

"Don't you know me any more?" she asked, but even when
they were alone and he was still holding her hand, all he could
say was, "You've become a fine lady! And I look so straggly! But
oh, how I have thought about you, Christine! And about old
times!"

And they walked arm in arm up the ridge and looked out
over the Guden river to the heath with the wide slopes of
heather, and Ib didn't say anything. But when they separated,
it was clear to him that Christine had to become his wife. They
had been called sweethearts from their childhood. He thought
of them as an engaged couple, even though neither of them
had said it.

They only had a few hours together before she would go
back to Tem where early the next morning she would catch a
coach back west. Her father and Ib followed her to Tem. There
was clear moonlight, and when they got there, Ib was still holding her hand. He couldn't let go of it, and his eyes were so
clear. He spoke very little, but his heart was in every word. "If
you haven't become too used to finery," he said, "and if you
could put up with living in Mother's house with me as your

husband, then you and I will get married one day—but we can wait a while."

"Let's wait and see, Ib," she said. He squeezed her hand and kissed her lips. "I trust you, Ib," said Christine, "and I think I love you. But let me sleep on it."

And then they parted. Ib told the bargeman that he and Christine were as good as engaged, and the bargeman said that he had always pictured that, and he went home with Ib and spent the night there, but nothing more was said about the engagement.

A year passed. Two letters had been exchanged between Ib and Christine. "Faithful unto death" was written by the signature. One day the bargeman came to Ib with greetings from Christine. It took him a while to finish what he had to say, but it was that things were going well for Christine, more than that. She was a beautiful girl, respected and well regarded. The innkeeper's son had been home for a visit. He was employed at an office in some big firm in Copenhagen. He was very fond of Christine, and she also found him to her liking. His parents weren't unwilling, but it weighed on Christine's heart that Ib was still in love with her. So she had decided to cast aside her chance at good fortune, said the bargeman.

Ib didn't say a word at first, but he turned as white as a sheet. Then he shook his head slightly and said, "Christine mustn't cast her good fortune away!"

"Write her a few words," said the bargeman.

Ib did write, but he couldn't quite put the words together the way he wanted, and he crossed things out and ripped things up—but in the morning there was a letter for little Christine, and here it is:

I have read the letter you sent your father and see that everything is going well for you, and that you can do even better! Ask your heart, Christine. And think about what your future might be if you choose me. I do not have much. Don't think about me or how it affects me, but think about your own good. You are not tied to me by any promise, and if you have given me one in your heart, then I release you from it. I wish you all the joy in the world, little Christine. Our Lord will surely console my heart.

                    Always your sincere friend,
                    Ib

So the letter was sent, and Christine received it.

At Martinmas in November the banns were read in the church on the heath and also in Copenhagen, where the bridegroom was working. Christine traveled there with her mistress since the bridegroom couldn't travel as far as Jutland on account of his many business affairs. Christine had arranged to meet her father in the town of Funder since the road went through there, and it was the closest meeting place. The two said good bye to each other there. A few words were said about it, but Ib didn't say anything. He had become so pensive, said his old mother. He was pensive indeed, and therefore he started thinking about the three nuts that he had gotten from the gypsy woman as a child. He had given two of them to Christine. They were wishing nuts, and there had been a gold carriage with horses in one of them and the most beautiful clothes in the other. It turned out to be true! She would have all that splendor now in Copenhagen. Her wishes were fulfilled. But for Ib there was only black soil in the nut. The *very best* for him, the gypsy had said. Well, that also would come true. The black humus was the best for him. He understood clearly now what the woman had meant: the black earth, shelter in the grave, was the *very best* for him.

Years passed—not many, but long ones for Ib. The old innkeepers died, one shortly after the other. All the wealth, many thousands of dollars, passed to the son. Well, now Christine would have enough gold carriages and fine clothes.

For two long years there was no letter from Christine. When her father did finally get one, it was not about happiness and affluence. Poor Christine! Neither she nor her husband had known how to handle the money. Easy come, easy go. There was no blessing from it because they didn't see the blessing themselves.

The heather bloomed, and the heather dried. The snow had drifted over the heath for many winters, over the lee of the ridge where Ib lived. The spring sun was shining when Ib set his plow in the ground. It hit what he thought was a flint-stone. It came up from the ground like a big black shaving, and when Ib picked it up, he saw that it was metal, and it was shiny where the plow had cut into it. It was a big, heavy bracelet of gold from prehistoric times. A burial mound had been leveled here, and Ib had discovered its precious treasure. He showed it to the pastor who told him how magnificent it was. Then Ib took it to the sheriff who reported it to Copenhagen and advised Ib to deliver the precious find himself.

"You have found the best thing you could possibly find in the earth!" said the sheriff.

"The best!" thought Ib. "The *very best* for me—and in the ground! So then the gypsy woman was right about me too, since *this* was the best!"

Ib took the boat from Aarhus to Copenhagen. It was like a trip across the ocean for him, given that he had only sailed on the Guden. Once he arrived in Copenhagen, Ib was paid the value of the gold he found. It was a large sum: six hundred dollars. And Ib from the woods by the heath walked through the winding streets of great Copenhagen.

The evening before he was to take the ship back to Aarhus, he got lost in the streets and went in an entirely wrong direction than he wanted to go. He crossed the Knippels bridge and ended up in Christian's Harbor instead of down by the rampart at Westport. He was heading westward as he should, but not where he should have gone. There was not a soul on the street. Then a little girl came out from a humble house. Ib asked her about the street he was looking for. She started, looked up at him, and was crying. Now he asked her what was wrong. She said something that he didn't understand, and as they were both under a streetlight, and the light shone right into her face, a funny feeling came over him. She looked just

like little Christine as he remembered her from their childhood.

He went with the little girl into the humble house, up the
narrow worn stairs, high up to a tiny slanting room right under
the roof. The air was heavy and stuffy, and there was no light.
Over in the corner someone sighed and breathed wheezily. Ib
lit a match. The child's mother was lying on the shabby bed.

"Is there anything I can do for you?" asked Ib. "The little
one brought me up, but I'm a stranger in town myself. Is there
a neighbor or someone I can summon?" He lifted her head.

It was Christine from the heath.

For years her name hadn't been mentioned at home in Jutland. It would have disturbed Ib's quiet thoughts. And what
was rumored, and what was true, wasn't good either. All the
money that her husband had inherited from his parents had
made him arrogant and unbalanced. He had quit his job and
traveled abroad for six months, come back and gone into debt,
but still lived opulently. More and more the carriage tilted, and
finally it tipped over. His many cheerful friends who had par-
tied at his table said that he deserved what he got, because he
had lived like a madman! His corpse was found one morning
in the canal in the castle garden.

Christine was dying. Her youngest little child, only a few
weeks old, conceived in prosperity but born in squalor, was already in its grave, and now Christine was deadly ill and for-
saken in this wretched little room. She might have tolerated
the wretchedness in her young years on the heath, but now
used to better, she felt the misery of it. It was her elder little
child, also named Christine, who suffered want and hunger
with her, who had brought Ib up there.

"I'm afraid I'll die and leave my poor child!" she sighed.
"What in the world will become of her!" She couldn't say more.

Ib lit another match and found a candle stump to lighten
the miserable little chamber.

Then Ib looked at the little girl and thought about Christine
when she was young. For her sake he would be good to this
child, whom he didn't know. The dying woman looked at him,

and her eyes grew larger and larger. Did she recognize him? He didn't know. He didn't hear her utter a word.

It was in the woods by the Guden, close to the heath. The air was grey, and the heather out of bloom. The storms from the west drove the yellow leaves from the woods into the river and over the heath where the sod-house stood—Strangers lived there now. Under the lee of the ridge behind high trees stood the little house, white-washed and painted. Inside in the living room a peat fire was burning in the stove. There was sunshine in the room; it shone from two childish eyes. The spring trills of the lark rolled from the red, laughing mouth. There was life and cheerfulness because little Christine was there. She sat on Ib's knee. Ib was father and mother to her since her parents were gone, gone like a dream for the child and the grown-up. Ib sat in his neat and pleasant little house, a well-to-do man. The little girl's mother lay in the pauper's cemetery in Copenhagen.

They said that Ib had provided for a rainy day—gold from mold, they said, and of course, he also had little Christine.

NOTES

1. Forested area in central Jutland (the peninsular continental portion of Denmark); between 1850 and 1880 nearly 200 barges were in service on the Guden River between Randers and Silkeborg.

THE ICE MAIDEN

1. Little Rudy

LET'S VISIT SWITZERLAND. LET'S look around in that magnificent mountainous country where the forests grow upon steep rocky walls. Let's climb upon the dazzling fields of snow, and go down again to the green meadows, where rivers and rivulets roar along as if they're afraid that they won't reach the sea soon enough and will disappear. The sun burns hot in the deep valley, and it also burns on the heavy masses of snow so that through the years they melt together to form bright blocks of ice that become rolling avalanches and towering glaciers.

Two such glaciers lie in the wide ravines under *Schreckhorn* and *Wetterhorn*,[1] close to the little mountain town of Grindelwald. They're extraordinary to see, and therefore many foreigners come here in the summer from all over the world. They come over the high, snow-covered mountains, or they come from down in the deep valleys, after a several hour climb. As they climb, the valley seems to sink deeper. They look down on it as if they were up in a hot-air balloon. At the top the clouds often hang like thick heavy curtains of smoke around the peaks, while down in the valley, where the many brown wooden houses are spread out, a ray of sun captures a patch of shiny green and makes it look transparent. The water roars, rumbles, and rushes down there. The water trickles and tinkles above. It looks like fluttering ribbons of silver falling down the cliffs.

On both sides of the road there are log chalets and each house has a little potato patch. This is a necessity because there are many mouths inside the doors. There are many children who have big appetites. They swarm out from all the houses and press around the tourists, both those on foot and in coaches. All the children are little merchants. The little ones offer and sell lovely little carved wooden houses, like the ones you see built there in the mountains. Rain or shine the swarms of children come out with their wares.

Twenty some years ago there was sometimes a little boy there, standing a little apart from the other children, who also wanted to sell his wares. He had such a serious face and stood with both hands tightly clasping his wooden box, as if he didn't want to drop it. It was just this seriousness, and the fact that he was so little, that caused him to be noticed and called upon. Often he sold the most, but he himself didn't know why. His grandfather, who carved the lovely, delicate houses, lived higher up the mountain. In the living room up there stood an old cabinet, full of all kinds of carvings. There were nut crackers, knives, forks, and boxes with carved leaves and jumping antelopes. There was everything there that could please the eyes of children, but the little boy—whose name was Rudy— looked with greatest pleasure and longing at the old rifle under the rafters. Grandfather had said that it would be his when he was big and strong enough to use it.

As little as he was, the boy was set to tend the goats, and if climbing with them was a sign of a good goatherd, then Rudy was a good goatherd. He climbed even higher than the goats. He liked gathering birds' nests from high in the trees. He was daring and brave, but you only saw him smile when he was standing by a roaring waterfall, or when he heard an avalanche. He never played with the other children, and he was only together with them when his grandfather sent him down to sell carvings. Rudy didn't care much for that, for he would rather clamber alone up in the mountains, or sit by grandfather and listen to him tell about the old days, or about the people close by in Meiringen where he was from. People hadn't lived there from the beginning of the world, Grandfather said, they had migrated. They had come from way up north, and they had relatives there. They were called Swedes. This was real knowledge, and Rudy knew that, but he received even more knowledge from other good companions, and those were the animals in the house. There was a big dog, Ajola, that Rudy had inherited from his father, and there was a tomcat who meant a lot to Rudy because he had taught him how to climb.

"Come out on the roof with me," the cat had said, quite clearly and intelligibly. When you're a child and can't talk yet, you can understand hens and ducks, cats and dogs very well indeed. They are just as easy to understand as father and mother when you are really small. Even grandfather's cane can whinny and become a horse with a head, legs, and tail. Some children lose this understanding later than others, and people say that those children are slow in developing and are children for an exceedingly long time. People say so many funny things!

"Come out on the roof, little Rudy," was one of the first things the cat said, and Rudy understood. "All that about falling is just imagination. You won't fall if you aren't afraid of falling. Come on, set one paw like this, and the other like this! Feel your way with your front paws. Use your eyes, and be flexible in your limbs. If there's a gap, then jump and hold on. That's what I do."

And that's what Rudy did too. He often sat on the ridge of the roof with the cat. He sat with it in the tree tops too, and then he sat high on the edge of the cliffs, where the cat never went.

"Higher! higher!" the trees and bushes said. "Do you see how we climb up? How high we reach and how we hold on, even on the outer narrow cliff tops?"

And Rudy often reached the mountain top before the sun did, and there he'd have his morning drink, the fresh fortifying mountain air. The drink that only God can make, though people can read the recipe. It says: the fresh scent of mountain herbs and the valley's mint and thyme. The hanging clouds absorb everything that's heavy and then the winds card them in the spruce forests. The fragrances' spirits become air, light and fresh, always fresher. This was Rudy's morning drink.

The sunbeams—her daughters bringing blessings—kissed his cheeks and *Vertigo* lurked nearby, but didn't dare approach. The swallows from grandfather's house, where there were never less than seven nests, flew up to him and the goats, singing: "We and you, and you and we." They brought greetings from home, even from the two hens, the only birds in the place, but Rudy never had anything to do with them.

As young as he was, he had traveled pretty far for such a little fellow. He had been born in the upper part of the canton of Valais[2] and carried here from over the mountains. Recently he had walked to the near-by *Staubbach*[3] that waves in the air like a silver ribbon in front of the snow-covered blinding white mountain, *The Jungfrau*.[4] And he had been on the big glacier at Grindelwald, but that was a sad story. His mother had died there, and there, said his grandfather, "little Rudy's childhood joy had been blown away." His mother had written that when the boy was less than a year old, he laughed more than he cried, "but after he came out of the ice crevice his disposition had entirely changed." Grandfather didn't talk much about it, but everyone on the mountain knew about it.

Rudy's father had been a postman, and the big dog in the living room had always followed him on the trip over the Simplon pass, down to Lake Geneva.[5] Rudy's relatives on his father's side still lived in the canton of Valais in the Rhone valley. Rudy's uncle was an excellent goat-antelope hunter and a well-known guide. Rudy was only a year old when he lost his father, and his mother wanted to return then with her little child to her family in Berner-Oberland. Her father lived a few hours from Grindelwald. He was a wood carver and earned enough from that to support himself. So in the month of June she walked, carrying her little child, homewards over the Gemmi pass towards Grindelwald in the company of two antelope hunters. They had almost finished their journey and had already gone through the high pass and reached the snow fields above her home town. They could see the familiar wooden houses spread out in the valley below, but they still had to cross the difficult upper part of one of the big glaciers. The snow had freshly fallen and hid a cleft that was deeper than a person's height, although it did not reach all the way to the bottom, where the water roared. All at once the young woman, carrying her child, slipped, sank, and disappeared without a cry or a sigh. But they heard the little child crying. It took over an hour for the two guides to get a rope and poles from the closest house to try to help. After tremendous difficulty, two apparent corpses were brought out from the ice cleft. They used all the means they could to resuscitate them and succeeded in saving the child, but not the mother. And so the old grandfather ended up with a grandson in the house instead of a daughter, the little one, who laughed more than he cried. But now he had been broken of that habit. The change had most likely happened while he was in the cleft, in that cold strange world of ice, where the souls of the condemned are locked until the day of judgment, as the dwellers in the Swiss mountains believe.

The glacier lies not unlike roaring water, frozen to ice and pressed into green blocks of glass, one huge piece of ice toppled on the other. In the depths below roars the furious stream of melted snow and ice. Deep caves and mighty clefts rise in there, making a wonderful ice palace, which the Ice Maiden, the queen of the glacier, has made her dwelling. Half child of the air and half mistress of the mighty rivers, she kills and crushes, and can rise with the spring of a goat-antelope to the highest peak of the mountains where the most daring mountain climbers have to chop footholds for themselves in the ice. She sails on the thinnest spruce twig down the rushing river and leaps from cliff to cliff surrounded by her long, snow-white hair, wearing her blue-green dress that glimmers like the water of the deep Swiss lakes.

"To crush, hold tight! Mine is the power!" she says. "They stole a lovely boy from me, a boy I had kissed, but not to death. He's amongst people again. He guards the goats on the mountain and climbs higher, always higher, away from the others, but not from me! He is mine and I shall fetch him."

And she asked *Vertigo* to tend to her errands. It was too muggy in the summertime for the Ice Maiden in the greenery where the mint thrives. And *Vertigo* rose and bowed. Here came one and then three more. *Vertigo* has many sisters, a whole flock of them, and the Ice Maiden chose the strongest of the many who ruled both indoors and out. They sit on stair banisters and on tower railings. They run like squirrels along the mountain edge, leap out treading air like swimmers treading water, and lure their victims out and down into the abyss. *Vertigo* and the Ice Maiden both grasp after people like the octopus grasps anything that moves around it. *Vertigo* was to seize Rudy.

"Seize him who can!" said *Vertigo*. "I'm not able to do it! The cat, that wretch, has taught him her tricks. The child has a power that pushes me away. I can't reach the little fellow when he hangs on the branches over the chasm where I'd like to tickle the soles of his feet, or give him a ducking in the air. I can't do it."

"We could do it!" said the Ice Maiden. "You or me! Me!"

"No, no!" A response came to them like a mountain echo of church bells, but it was a song and words in a fused chorus from other spirits of nature: the gentle, good and loving daughters of the sunbeams. They pitch camp each evening in a wreath around the mountain tops. They spread out their rosy wings that blush redder and redder as the sun sinks. The high Alps glow and people call it the *Alpenglow*. When the sun has set, they pull into the mountain tops, in the white snow and sleep there until the sun rises. Then they come out again. They especially love flowers, butterflies, and human beings, and among the human beings, they were particularly fond of Rudy.

"You won't catch him! You won't catch him!" they cried.

"I have caught and kept bigger and stronger people than him!" said the Ice Maiden.

Then the sun's daughters sang a song about the wanderer whom the whirlwind tore the cloak from and carried away in a mad rush. The wind took his covering, but not the man. "You children of nature's force can seize but not hold him. He is stronger. He is more spiritual even than we are. He can rise higher even than the sun, our mother. He knows the magic words to bind wind and water so that they must serve and obey him. You release the heavy oppressive weight, and he lifts himself higher!"

Such was the lovely song of the bell-like choir.

And every morning the rays of the sun shone through the only small window in Grandfather's house and fell on the quiet child. The sunshine's daughters kissed him. They wanted to thaw out, warm up, and destroy the ice kisses that the glacier's royal maiden had given him when he lay in the deep ice cleft in his dead mother's lap and was saved as if by a miracle.

2. Journey to a New Home

When Rudy was eight years old, his uncle in the Rhone valley, on the other side of the mountains, wanted to take the boy to live with him. He could be more easily educated there and would have more opportunities. Grandfather realized this too, and let him go.

Rudy was leaving. There were others besides Grandfather to whom he had to say good bye. First there was Ajola, the old dog.

"Your father was a postman, and I was a post dog," said Ajola. "We traveled both up and down, and I know the dogs and people on the other side of the mountains. It's never been my habit to talk much, but now that we won't be able to talk to each other much longer, I will say a little more than usual. I will tell you a story that I've always thought a lot about. I don't understand it, and you won't be able to either, but that doesn't matter because I have gotten this much out of it: things are not distributed quite the way they should be, either for dogs or for people in this world. Not everyone is created to sit on laps or drink milk. It's not something I've been used to, but I have seen a puppy ride on the postal coach sitting in a passenger seat. The woman who was his mistress, or perhaps he was the master, had brought a milk bottle with her that he drank from. He was given cake, but he couldn't be bothered to eat it. He just sniffed at it, and so she ate it herself. I was running in the mud beside the coach, as hungry as a dog. I chewed on my own thoughts. It wasn't right, but then again there is much that isn't. I hope you'll end up on a lap and in the coach, but it's not something you can do by yourself. I haven't been able to, either by yipping or yawning."

That was Ajola's speech, and Rudy put his arms around the dog's neck and kissed it right on its wet snout. Then he picked up the cat, but it squirmed.

"You have become too strong for me, and I don't want to use my claws! Climb over the mountains. I have taught you to climb, you know! Never think that you will fall, and you'll manage!" And then the cat ran away because it didn't want Rudy to see the sorrow in its eyes.

The hens were running around on the floor. The one had lost its tail. A tourist who wanted to be a hunter had shot the tail off because he thought the hen was a bird of prey.

"Rudy's going over the mountains," said one hen.

"He's always in a hurry," said the other, "and I don't like saying good-bye!" And both of them pattered off.

He also said good by to the goats, and they cried, "Nayhhh, nayhhh." They wanted to go along, and it was so sad.

There were two good guides in the district who were just then going over the mountains. They were going down the other side through the Gemmi pass. Rudy went with them, on foot. It was a rigorous hike for such a little fellow, but he had great strength and tireless courage.

The swallows flew with them for a distance. "We and you,

and you and we!" they sang. The route went over the rapid
Lutschine that gushes forth in many small streams from
Grindelwald glacier's black cleft. Loose tree limbs and boulders act as bridges here. Now they were high in the scrub alder
and started up the mountain, close to where the glacier sepa-
rates from the side of the mountain, and then they went out
on the glacier, over blocks of ice and around them. Sometimes
Rudy had to crawl, sometimes walk. His eyes shone with pure
pleasure, and he stepped firmly with his iron clad mountain
boots as if he wanted to mark where he had walked. The black
earth deposits on the glacier spawned by the mountain water
flow gave it the appearance of being calcified, but the blue-
green, glassy ice still shone through. They had to walk around
small pools that were damned up by the ice pack, and once
they came close to a big boulder that was rocking on the edge
of an ice fissure. The rock lost its equilibrium and fell rolling.
The echo came resounding from the glacier's deep hollow
caverns.

Upward, ever upward they walked. The glacier itself
stretched up in height like a river of wildly towering ice masses,
squeezed between sheer cliffs. For a moment Rudy thought
about what they had told him—that he had lain deep down in
one of these cold-breathing crevices with his mother, but soon
such thoughts were gone. It was to him like one of the many
similar stories he had heard. Now and then when the men
thought it was a little too hard for the boy to climb, they
reached out and gave him a hand, but he wasn't tired, and he
stood as surefooted as a goat-antelope on the ice. Then they
came out on the bare rock again, sometimes walking between
barren rocks, sometimes between dwarf spruces, then out on
grass-covered slopes. Always changing, always new. Around
them rose the snow-covered mountains, those that he, like
every child here, knew: *The Jungfrau, Munken,* and *Eiger.*

Rudy had never been so high before, never before been on
the outstretched ocean of snow, lying there with immovable
waves of snow that the wind blew a few flakes from, like it blows
foam from the ocean. The glaciers hold each other by the
hand, if you can say that about glaciers, and each is a glass

palace for the Ice Maiden whose power and will is to capture
and bury. The sun was shining warmly, and the snow was blinding and looked like it had been sown with sparkling whitish-
blue diamonds. Innumerable insects, especially butterflies and
bees, lay dead in masses on the snow. They had flown too high,
or the wind had carried them until they died in the cold.
Around *Wetterhorn* a threatening sky hung like a finely carded
wad of black wool. It sank down bulging with its hidden *Föhn*,
a violent force when it broke loose. The impressions of the entire journey became forever fixed in Rudy's memory: staying
overnight on the mountain, the path from there, and the deep
mountain ravines where the water had sawed through the
boulders for so long it made him dizzy to think of it.

An abandoned stone hut on the other side of the sea of
snow gave them shelter for the night. They found charcoal and
tree branches there, and a fire was soon lit. They prepared for
the night as best they could. The men sat around the fire,
smoked tobacco and drank the hot, spiced drink they had
made themselves. Rudy received his share, and then the men
talked about the mysterious creatures of the Alps and the
strange giant snakes in the deep lakes, about the folk of the
night, the legions of ghosts who carried the sleeper through
the air to the wonderful swimming city of Venice. They talked
about the wild herdsman who drove his black sheep across the
pastures. Even if they hadn't seen them, they had nevertheless
heard the sound of their bells, and heard the uncanny bleat-
ing of the herd. Rudy listened curiously, but without fear because he was never afraid. As he listened he thought he could
sense the ghostly, hollow bellow. It became more and more au-
dible. The men heard it too and stopped talking. They told
Rudy not to go to sleep.

It was the *Föhn* blowing. The violent stormy wind that flings
itself from the mountains down into the valley and cracks trees
in its fury as if they were reeds. It moves log houses from one
side of the river bank to the other as easily as one moves a
chess piece.

After an hour had passed they told Rudy that now the storm

was over and he could sleep. He slept as if on command, so tired was he from the trek.

They broke camp early in the morning. That day the sun shone for Rudy on new mountains, new glaciers and fields of snow. They had arrived in the canton of Valais and were on the other side of the mountain ridge you could see from Grindelwald, but still far from Rudy's new home. Other mountain ravines, other grassy pastures, forests and mountainous paths unfolded before them. They saw other houses and other people, but what people they were! Indeed, they were deformed, grim, fat with yellow-white faces. Their throats were heavy, ugly clumps of flesh hanging out like bags. They were cretins.[6] They dragged themselves sickly forward and looked with dumb eyes at the strangers. The women looked the worst. Were these the people of his new home?

3. RUDY'S UNCLE

At his uncle's house, when Rudy got there, the people, thank God, looked like the people Rudy was used to. There was only one cretin there, a poor foolish lad. One of those poor creatures who in their poverty and loneliness live by turns in families in canton Valais. They stay a few months in each house, and poor Saperli happened to be there when Rudy came.

Rudy's uncle was still a strong hunter, and in addition he was a barrel-maker. His wife was a lively little person with an almost birdlike face, eyes like an eagle, and a long and quite downy neck.

Everything was new to Rudy—the clothing, the customs, even the language, but his childish ear would soon learn to understand that. It was clear that they were better off here than at Grandfather's home. The rooms they lived in were bigger. The walls were covered with antelope antlers and highly polished guns. Over the door hung a picture of the Virgin Mary with fresh rhododendrons and a lamp burning in front of it.

Rudy's uncle, as mentioned, was one of the district's best goat-antelope hunters and was also the best and most experienced guide. Rudy would now become the darling of the house, although there was already one there. This was an old, blind, and deaf hunting dog who was no longer of any use, but who had been so. They remembered the animal's ability in earlier years, and he was now a member of the family who would live out his life in comfort. Rudy pet the dog, but it wouldn't have much to do with strangers, and of course Rudy was still a stranger. But not for long. He soon took root in the house and in their hearts.

"It's not so bad here in Valais canton," said Rudy's uncle. "We have goat-antelopes, and they won't soon die out like the mountain goats did. It's much better than in the old days no matter how much people talk about their glory. It's better now. There's a hole in the bag now, and fresh air has blown into our enclosed valley. Something better always comes forward when the old antiquated things fall away," he said. When Rudy's uncle became very talkative, he talked about his childhood years and about the years when his father was in his prime, when Valais was, as he put it, a closed bag with way too many sick people, the pitiful cretins. "But then the French soldiers came, and they were real doctors. They soon killed the illness, and the people too. The Frenchmen could fight all right, strike a blow in more ways than one, and the women could strike too!" and Rudy's uncle nodded to his French-born wife and laughed. "The French were able to strike the rocks so they'd give way. They built the Simplon[7] road out of the cliffs, built that road so that I could now tell a three-year-old child to go down to Italy. Just stay on the road, and the child will find Italy if he stays on the road." And then Rudy's uncle sang a French ballad and gave a cheer for Napoleon Bonaparte.

That was the first time Rudy had heard about France and about Lyon, the big city on the Rhone where his uncle had once been.

It wouldn't take many years for Rudy to become a good antelope hunter because he had an aptitude for it, said his uncle, and he taught him to hold a gun, take aim, and shoot. In the hunting season he took Rudy along up in the mountains and let him drink the warm antelope blood, which was supposed to keep dizziness from the hunter. He taught him to know what time avalanches would happen on the various mountain sides, whether at dinner time or in the evening, depending on how the sun beams worked the slopes. He taught him to observe the antelope and learn from them how to leap so that you could land on your feet and stand firmly, and if there wasn't footing in the mountain clefts, how you had to support yourself with your elbows, clinging fast with the muscles of your thighs and legs. You could even keep yourself in place with your neck if it was necessary. The goat-antelopes were smart and even posted a lookout, but the hunter had to be smarter, and get downwind from them. He could fool them by hanging his cloak and hat on his walking stick, and the antelope would mistake the cloak for the man. His uncle played this trick one day when he was hunting with Rudy.

The mountain path was narrow. It really wasn't a path at all, just a thin ledge, right by the dizzying abyss. The snow was lying half melted there; the stone crumbled when you walked on it. That's why Rudy's uncle laid down on his stomach, long as he was, and crept forward. Every stone that broke off fell, careened, and broke, skipped and rolled again, bounced from cliff to cliff before coming to rest in the black depths. Rudy stood on the outermost firm cliff crag a hundred steps behind his uncle. He saw an enormous vulture approaching in the air, swaying over his uncle. With one flap of its wings, the bird could throw the creeping worm into the abyss to turn it into carrion. His uncle had eyes only for the antelope that was visible with its kid on the other side of the cleft. Rudy kept his eye on the bird, understood what it wanted to do, and so he had his hand on the gun ready to shoot. Then the antelope leaped up, and Rudy's uncle fired. The animal was killed by the shot, but the kid ran as if it had practiced fleeing its whole life. The huge bird flew quickly away, frightened by the shot. Rudy's uncle didn't realize the danger until Rudy told him about it.

As they were on their way home in the best of spirits, Rudy's uncle whistling a tune from his childhood, they suddenly heard an odd sound from not far away. They looked to both sides, and then upward, and there on the heights, on the sloping mountain ledge, the snow cover was lifting. It was waving as when the wind sweeps under a spread-out sheet of linen. The tops of the waves snapped as if they were plates of marble cracking and breaking up and then released in a foaming, plunging stream, booming like the muffled roar of thunder. It was a rushing avalanche, not right on top of Rudy and his uncle, but close—too close.

"Hold on tight, Rudy!" his uncle cried. "Tightly, with all your might!"

And Rudy threw his arms around a nearby tree trunk, while his uncle clambered over him up into the tree's branches and held on tightly. Although the avalanche was rolling past many yards from them, all around them the air turbulence and gusts of wind cracked and broke trees and bushes as if they were but dry reeds and scattered them widely. Rudy lay pressed to the ground. The tree trunk he was holding was now a stump, and the crown of the tree was lying a long way off. Rudy's uncle lay there, amongst the broken branches. His head was crushed, and his hand was still warm, but his face was unrecognizable. Rudy stood there pale and trembling. This was the first fright of his life, the first time he had known horror.

He brought the tidings of death home in the late evening, a home that was now a house of grief. His uncle's wife reacted without words, without tears. Only when the corpse was brought home, did grief erupt. The poor cretin crawled into his bed. No one saw him the whole day, but towards evening he came to Rudy.

"Write a letter for me! Saperli can't write. Saperli will take the letter to the post office."

"A letter from you?" asked Rudy, "and to whom?"

"To the Lord Christ!"

"Who do you mean by that?"

And the half-wit, as they called the cretin, looked at Rudy with pleading eyes, folded his hands, and said so solemnly and piously: "*Jesus Christ!* Saperli wants to send him a letter and ask that Saperli may lie dead and not the master."

Rudy squeezed his hand. "That letter wouldn't reach him. That letter wouldn't bring him back to us."

It was hard for Rudy to explain how impossible this was.

"Now you're our sole support," said his foster mother, and that's what Rudy became.

4. BABETTE

Who's the best shot in Valais canton? Well, the goat-antelopes knew that. "Watch out for Rudy!" they would say. "Who's the best looking shot?" "Well, that's Rudy," said the girls, but they didn't say, "Watch out for Rudy!" Even their serious mothers didn't say that because he nodded just as cordially to them as to the young girls. He was so bright and happy. His cheeks were brown, his teeth fresh and white, and his eyes shone coal-black. He was a handsome fellow and only twenty years old. The icy water didn't bother him when he swam, and he could turn in the water like a fish. He could climb like no other and cling tight to the cliff walls like a snail. He had good muscles and sinews, and this was evident too in his jumps and leaps which he had first learned from the cat and later from the goat-antelopes. You couldn't entrust your life to a better guide, and Rudy could have amassed a fortune from that. He wasn't interested at all in barrel-making, which his uncle had also taught him. All his delight and longing was for shooting antelope, and that also brought in money. Rudy was a good match, as they said, as long as he didn't set his sights too high. At dances he was a dancer that the girls dreamed about, and one and another of them thought about him when they were awake too.

"He kissed me while we were dancing," Annette, the school teacher's daughter, told her dearest friend. But she shouldn't have said that, even to her best friend. It's not easy to keep quiet about such things. It's like sand that runs out of a bag with a hole in it. Soon everyone knew that Rudy, no matter how proper and good he was, kissed girls while dancing. And yet he had not kissed the one that he most wanted to.

"Watch him!" said an old hunter. "He kissed Annette. He's started with A and will most likely kiss through the whole alphabet."

A kiss while dancing was yet all that could be gossiped about Rudy, but he had kissed Annette, and she was not at all the flower of his heart.

Down by Bex, between the big walnut trees and right next to a little rushing mountain stream, there lived a rich miller. His house was a big one with three stories. It had small towers, covered with wooden shingles and fitted with pieces of tin that shone in the sun and moonlight. The tallest tower had a weather vane in the shape of an apple with a shiny arrow through it. It was supposed to represent Wilhelm Tell's arrow. The mill looked prosperous and neat, and could be both drawn and described, but the miller's daughter could neither be drawn nor described. At least that's what Rudy would say, and yet he had her picture in his heart. Her two shining eyes were burning there like a fire. It had flared up at once, like fire does, and the strangest thing about it was that the miller's daughter, the lovely Babette, had no idea about this. She and Rudy had never spoken so much as two words to each other.

The miller was rich, and that wealth meant that Babette occupied a high position, difficult to reach. But nothing sits so high that you can't reach it, Rudy said to himself. You have to climb, and you won't fall down if you believe you won't. He had learned that lesson at home.

And so it happened that Rudy had an errand in Bex. It was a long trip because at that time the railroad hadn't been built there yet. From the Rhone glacier, at the foothill of the Simplon mountain, and between many mountains of various heights, stretches the wide Valais valley with its great river, the Rhone. It often waxes and washes over fields and roads, destroying everything. Between the towns of Sion and St. Maurice there is a curve in the valley. It bends like an elbow, and below St. Maurice becomes so narrow that there is only room for the river bed and a narrow road. There is an old tower on the mountainside that stands like a sentry for the canton of Valais, which ends here. It overlooks the brick bridge that leads to the toll house on the other side. The canton of Vaud begins here, and not far away is Bex, the closest town. On this side, with every step you take, everything swells with abundance and fertility. It's like a garden of chestnut and walnut trees, and here and there cypress and pomegranate flowers peek out. It's as southerly warm as if you had come to Italy.

Rudy reached Bex, carried out his errand, and looked around. But he did not see a fellow from the mill, much less Babette. It wasn't supposed to be like this!

It was evening. The air was filled with the fragrance from the wild thyme and the flowering linden. A bright, airy blue veil seemed to lie on the forest-covered mountains. There was a pervasive silence, not of sleep nor of death, but it was as if all of nature were holding its breath, as if it felt silenced because it was going to be photographed against the backdrop of the blue sky. Here and there among the trees, and across the green fields, stood poles that carried the telegraph wires through the quiet valley. An object was leaning up against one of these, so still that you would think it must be a dead tree limb. But it was Rudy who stood as still as his surroundings, not sleeping and certainly not dead. But just as great world events or situations with great meaning for certain individuals often fly through the telegraph wires without a tremble or tone of indication in the wire, just in this way powerful, overwhelming thoughts—his happiness in life and from now on his *idée fixe*—flew through Rudy's mind. His eyes were fastened on a point between the foliage, a light in the miller's house, where Babette lived. So still was Rudy standing that you might think he was taking aim to shoot an antelope, but at this moment he was like the antelope himself, who can stand as if chiseled from stone for minutes, and then suddenly, when a rock rolls, leap up and run away. And that's exactly what Rudy did as a thought, like a rolling rock, came to him.

"Never give up!" he said. "Go to the mill. Say 'good evening' to the miller, 'good evening' to Babette. You can't fall if you think you can't. Babette has to see me some time, after all, if I'm to be her husband."

And Rudy laughed, and in good spirits he went to the mill. He knew what he wanted. He wanted Babette.

The river with its whitish yellow water was rushing along. Weeping willows and lindens overhung the swiftly flowing water. Rudy walked on the path, and as it says in the old children's ditty:

> "... and on to the mill,
> Where no one was home
> But a cat on the sill."

But the housecat was standing on the steps. He arched his back and said, "Miaow!" but Rudy didn't pay attention to this. He knocked on the door. But no one heard, and no one opened the door. "Miaow!" said the cat. If Rudy had been little, he would have understood animal language and would have heard the cat say, "No one's home here." But he had to go over to the mill to hear this. There he got the news that the master was on a trip, far away in the city of Interlaken. "*Inter Lacus*, between the lakes," as the school master, Annette's father, had explained in his teaching. The miller had taken that long trip, and Babette was with him. There was a big marksmanship competition, which would start the following day and last for a week. People from all the German-speaking cantons would be there.

Poor Rudy, you could say. It wasn't the best time for him to come to Bex. He could just as well turn back, and that's what he did. He took the road via St. Maurice and Sion, to his own valley and his own mountains, but he wasn't dispirited. His spirits, which had risen before the sun rose the next morning, had never been down.

"Babette is in Interlaken, many days' journey from here," he said to himself. "It's a long way if you take the road, but it's not so far if you go over the mountains, and that's the road for a hunter to take. I've gone that way before. That's my native soil, where I lived with grandfather when I was little. And they're having a shooting competition in Interlaken! I will take first place there and will also be first with Babette, when first I meet her in person!"

Rudy packed his Sunday clothes in his light backpack, took his rifle and hunting bag, and went up the mountain, the short way, which was still quite long. But the competition was just starting that day and would last a good week. He'd been told that the miller and Babette would be at their relatives in Interlaken the whole time. Rudy headed for the Gemmi pass.[8] He wanted to come down by Grindelwald.

Happy and healthy he set out, upwards in the fresh, light, invigorating mountain air. The valley sank deeper, the horizon became wider. First one and then another snow-topped mountain came into view, and then the whole shining chain of the Alps. Rudy knew every mountain. He headed towards *Schreckhorn*, which lifted its snow-powdered rocky finger high into the blue sky.

Finally he was across the high mountains. The grazing meadows sloped downward towards the valley of his childhood. The air was light, as was his mind. The mountains and valleys were filled with flowers and greenery. His heart was full of the thoughts of youth: I'll never get old, I'll never die. Live! Prevail! Enjoy! He was as free and light as a bird. And the swallows flew by and sang as they had in his childhood: "We and you, and you and we!" All was soaring and joyous.

Down below lay the velvet green meadow, studded with the brown wooden houses. The *Lütschine* river rushed and roared. He saw the glacier with its glass-green edges in the dirty snow and the deep clefts. He saw both the upper and lower glacier, and heard the bells ring in the church as if they were welcoming him home. His heart beat more strongly and filled with memories, so that Babette was forgotten there for a moment.

He walked again on that road where he had stood as a little fellow by the ditch with the other children selling carved wooden houses. Up there behind the fir trees grandfather's house was still standing, but strangers lived there. Children who wanted to sell things came running down the road. One of them gave him a rhododendron. Rudy took this as a good sign and thought about Babette. Soon he was down and over the bridge, where the two *Lütschine* rivers run together. The deciduous trees increased, and the walnut trees gave shade. Then he saw waving flags, the white cross on a red background, as both Switzerland and Denmark have. In front of him lay Interlaken.

It was really a splendid city, like no other, thought Rudy. A Swiss town in its Sunday best. It wasn't like other market cities—a crowd of big stone buildings, heavy, forbidding, and distinguished. No, here it looked like the wooden houses from the mountains had run down into the green valley by the clear, rapidly flowing river and had lined themselves up in rows, a little uneven, to make streets. The most magnificent of all the streets had appeared since Rudy had last been there as a boy. It was as if all the beautiful wooden houses grandfather had carved, and which the cabinet at home was full of, had positioned themselves here and grown up, like the old, the very oldest chestnut trees. Every house was a hotel, as they are called, with carved woodwork around the windows and balconies. They had projecting roofs, so neat and elegant, and there was a flower garden in front of each, all the way out to the paved road. The houses stood along the road, but just on one side. Otherwise they would have hidden the view of the fresh green meadow, where the cows grazed with bells that clang like they did in the high Alpine meadows. The meadow was surrounded by high mountains that seemed to step aside right in the middle so that you could clearly see the dazzling, snow-covered *Jungfrau*, the most beautifully shaped of all the Swiss mountains.

What a crowd of elegant gentleman and ladies from foreign countries! What a swarm of residents from the various cantons! The marksmen who were competing wore numbers on their hats. There was music and singing, barrel organs and wind instruments, shouting and noise. Houses and bridges were decorated with verses and emblems. Flags and banners were waving, and the guns fired shot after shot. This was the best music to Rudy's ears, and with all this he completely forgot Babette, for whose sake he had come in the first place.

The marksmen wanted target practice, and Rudy was soon among them. He was the best and the luckiest. He always hit the bulls-eye.

"Who is that stranger, the very young hunter?" people asked. "He speaks French like they do in Valais canton. He can also make himself well understood in our German," said some.

"It's said that he used to live in the district by Grindelwald as a child," one of them knew.

There was life in the young fellow! His eyes shone. His eye was sure, and his arm was steady. That's why he hit the mark. Success produces courage, and of course, Rudy had always had that. Soon he had a whole circle of friends around him. He was both acclaimed and applauded. Babette was nearly out of his thoughts. Then a heavy hand fell on his shoulder, and a gruff voice asked him in French, "Are you from canton Valais?"

Rudy turned around and saw a fat man with a happy red face. It was the rich miller from Bex. Hidden behind his wide body was dainty delicate Babette, who soon peered around him with her radiant dark eyes. The rich miller was flattered that it was a hunter from his canton who was the best shot and was being praised. Rudy certainly was good fortune's child! What he had wandered in search of, but had almost forgotten, had now sought him out.

When you meet someone from your home when you are far away, then you speak to each other like you know each other. Rudy was the best at the shooting competition, just as at home in Bex the miller was the best because of his money and his good mill. So the two men shook hands, which was something they had never done before. And Babette also took Rudy's hand so innocently. He pressed her hand in return and looked intensely at her so that she blushed.

The miller talked about the long way they had traveled to get there, and of the many big cities they had seen. It was a real journey. They had sailed on a steamship, taken the train, and also the mail coach.

"I went the shorter way," said Rudy. "I came over the mountains. No way is so high you can't take it."

"But you can also break your neck!" said the miller. "And you look like you'll break your neck one day, as daring as you are!"

"You won't fall if you don't think you will," said Rudy.

The miller's relatives in Interlaken, where the miller and Babette were visiting, asked Rudy to stop by to see them. After all, he was from the same canton as their relatives. That was a good invitation for Rudy. Luck was with him, as it always is for those who believe in themselves and remember that "God gives us the nuts, but he doesn't crack them open for us."

And Rudy sat like part of the family with the miller's relations, and a toast was proposed to the best shot. Babette toasted with him, and Rudy thanked them for the toast.

Towards evening they all went for a walk under the old walnut trees along the pretty street by the neat hotels. There were so many people, such crowds, that Rudy had to offer Babette his arm. He was so happy that he had met people from Vaud, he said. Vaud and Valais cantons were good neighbors. He expressed his joy so sincerely that Babette thought she should clasp his hand. They walked along almost like old friends, and she was so funny, the lovely little person! Rudy thought it so becoming the way she pointed out the comical and exaggerated in the foreign women's dress and manner of walking. And it wasn't to make fun of them because they could be very honest people, sweet and lovable, Babette knew that. She had a godmother who was a very distinguished English lady. Eighteen years ago, when Babette had been baptized, the godmother had been in Bex. She had given Babette the expensive brooch that she wore on her vest. Babette had gotten two letters from her godmother, and this year they were supposed to meet her here in Interlaken, along with her daughters. They were two old maids, almost thirty, said Babette. She herself was only eighteen.

The sweet little mouth didn't stop for a moment, and everything Babette said seemed to Rudy of the utmost importance. He, in turn, told her what he had to tell. He told her how often he had been in Bex, how well he knew the mill, and how often he had seen Babette, but that she very likely hadn't noticed him. The last time he had been there he had many thoughts he couldn't mention, but she and her father had gone, were far away, but not farther than that he could clamber over the wall that made the road long.

Yes, he said *that*, and he said so much more. He told her how much he thought of her, and that he had come there for her sake, not for the shooting competition.

Babette became silent. What he had confided to her was almost too much to bear.

While they walked, the sun sank behind the high mountain wall. *Jungfrau* stood in all its magnificence and glory, surrounded by a wreath of the nearer forest-clad mountains. All the people stopped quietly and looked at it, and Rudy and Babette looked at all the grandeur too.

"There is no place more beautiful than here," said Babette.

"No place!" said Rudy and looked at Babette.

"I have to leave tomorrow," said Rudy a little later.

"Visit us in Bex," whispered Babette. "That would please my father."

5. On the Way Home

Oh, how much Rudy had to carry, when he headed home the next day over the high mountains! He had three silver cups, two very good guns, and a silver coffeepot. That would be useful when he settled down. But those weren't the weightiest. He carried something much more important, more powerful, or perhaps it carried him home across the high mountains. But the weather was raw and grey, rainy and heavy. The clouds descended on the mountain heights like black mourning crepe and shrouded the snow-clad tops. From the forests rang the last blows of the axe, and down the mountainside rolled tree trunks that looked like flimsy sticks from that height, even though they were huge trees. The *Lütschine* river sounded its monotonous music. The wind sang, and the clouds sailed. Suddenly a young girl was walking right beside Rudy. He hadn't noticed her until she was right beside him. She was also going over the mountain. Her eyes had such power that you had to look into them. They were so strangely clear, like glass, deep and bottomless.

"Do you have a sweetheart?" asked Rudy. All his thoughts were filled with having a sweetheart.

"I don't have one!" she said and laughed, but it sounded like she wasn't telling the truth. "Let's not go the long way around," she said. "We have to go more to the left. It's shorter."

"Yes, if you want to fall into an ice crevice!" said Rudy. "How can you be the guide if you don't know the way better than that!"

"Oh, I know the way," she said. "And I have my wits about me. I guess yours are down in the valley. Up here you must think of the Ice Maiden. People say she's dangerous to human beings."

"I'm not afraid of her," said Rudy. "She had to let me slip when I was a child. I will surely give her the slip now that I'm older!"

It started to get dark. The rain fell and then snow. It brightened and blinded.

"Give me your hand, and I'll help you climb," said the girl and she touched him with ice-cold fingers.

"You help me?" said Rudy. "I don't yet need the help of women to climb!" And he picked up speed and moved away from her. The snowstorm wrapped around him like a curtain. The wind whistled, and behind him he heard the girl laughing and singing. It sounded so strange—must be a troll girl in service of the Ice Maiden. Rudy had heard about this when he had spent the night here as a boy on the journey over the mountains.

The snowfall decreased, for the clouds were under him. He looked back. There was no one in sight, but he heard laughter and yodeling, and it didn't sound like it came from a human being.

When Rudy finally reached the highest part of the mountain pass, where the path went down towards the Rhone valley, he saw two clear stars in a strip of clear blue sky in the direction of Chamouny. They twinkled brightly, and he thought about Babette and about himself and his happiness, and he warmed at the thought.

6. A Visit to the Mill

"You're bringing grand items home with you!" said Rudy's old foster mother, and her strange eagle eyes flashed. Her thin neck moved in odd gyrations even faster than usual. "Good fortune is with you, Rudy. I must kiss you, my sweet boy."

And Rudy submitted to the kiss, but you could see by his

face that he considered it one of those inconveniences that you have to put up with. "How handsome you are, Rudy!" said the old woman.

"Don't make me think that," said Rudy and laughed, but it pleased him.

"I'll say it again," said the old woman. "Luck is with you."

"There I agree with you," he said and thought about Babette.

He had never before longed for the deep valley like this. "They must be home by now!" he said to himself. "It's already two days past the time when they were to come. I must go to Bex."

And Rudy went to Bex, and the miller's family was home. He was well received, and the family in Interlaken had sent their regards. Babette didn't say much. She had become so silent, but her eyes spoke, and that was enough for Rudy. The miller, who normally liked to talk, and who was used to people laughing at his whims and word play—after all, he was the rich miller—acted like he'd rather listen to Rudy tell hunting stories. And Rudy told about the difficulties and dangers that the goat-antelope hunters endured on the high mountain cliffs, and how they had to crawl on precarious ledges of snow that the wind and weather plastered to the mountain rim—how he crawled on the dangerous bridges that snowstorms had formed over deep chasms. Rudy looked so brave, and his eyes shone while he told about the hunter's life, the antelope's shrewdness and daring leaps, the strong *Föhn*,[9] and the cascading avalanches. He noticed very well that with each new description he was winning over the miller, and that what the miller especially liked hearing about was the description of the vulture and the bold golden eagle.

Not far from there, in the canton of Valais, there was an eagle's nest built very ingeniously in under an overhanging mountain cliff. There was an eaglet there, but it couldn't be taken. Just a few days ago an Englishman had offered Rudy a whole fistful of gold to bring him the eaglet alive, "but there's a limit to everything," he said. "That eagle's nest is unreachable. It would be madness to undertake it."

The wine flowed, and talk flowed, but Rudy thought the evening was much too short, and yet it was past midnight when he ended his first visit to the mill.

The lights still shone for a short while through the window and through the green branches. Out from the open venting in the roof came the housecat, and along the gutter came the kitchen cat.

"Is there anything new at the mill?" asked the housecat. "We have a secret engagement in the house! Father doesn't know about it yet. Rudy and Babette stepped on each other's paws all evening under the table. They stepped on me twice, but I didn't miaow because it would have caused attention."

"Well, I would have miaowed!" said the kitchen cat.

"What's fitting in the kitchen isn't fitting in the parlor," said the housecat. "I just wish I knew what the miller will say when he finds out about the engagement."

What would the miller say? Rudy wanted to know that too, but he couldn't wait a long time to find out, and so a few days later, when the coach rolled over the Rhone bridge between Valais and Vaud, Rudy was sitting within, optimistic as usual. He was thinking good thoughts about being accepted that very evening.

And when evening came, and the coach drove the same way back, Rudy was sitting in it again, going back the same way, but at the mill the housecat ran around with news.

"Have you heard about it, kitchen cat? Now the miller knows everything. A fine ending, I'll say! Rudy got here towards evening, and he and Babette had a lot to whisper about. They were standing in the hallway right outside the miller's room. I lay by their feet, but they had no word or thought for me. 'I'm going straight in to your father,' said Rudy. 'It's an honorable matter.' 'Shall I go with you?' asked Babette. 'It will give you courage.' 'I have enough courage,' said Rudy, 'but if you come along, he must look kindly upon us, whether he wants to or not.'"

"So they went in. Rudy stepped hard on my tail! He's so clumsy. I miaowed, but neither he nor Babette had ears for me. They opened the door, and both went in. I went first, but jumped up on the back of a chair. I had no way of knowing what direction Rudy would kick next. But the miller is the one who kicked out! And it was a good kick. Out of the door, and up into the mountains to the antelope! Now Rudy can aim at them and not at our little Babette!"

"But what was said?" asked the kitchen cat.

"Said! Everything was said that people say when they're courting: 'I love her, and she loves me. And if there's enough milk in the pail for one, there's enough for two!' 'But she's too far above you,' said the miller, 'She's sitting on grain, golden grain, as you know. You can't reach her.' 'Nothing is so high that it can't be reached if you really want it,' Rudy said, because he's quick on the draw. 'But you said last time that you can't reach the eaglet! And Babette sits higher than that!' 'I'll take both of them,' said Rudy. 'I'll give her to you when you bring me the eaglet alive,' said the miller, and he laughed until he cried. 'Thanks for the visit, Rudy. If you come back tomorrow, there'll be no one home. Good bye, Rudy.' And Babette said good bye too, as pitifully as a little kitten who can't see its mother. 'A man's as good as his word,' Rudy said. 'Don't cry, Babette, I'll bring the eaglet.' 'I hope you'll break your neck,' said the miller, 'then we'll get out of seeing you here.' I call that kicking! Now Rudy's gone. Babette is crying, and the miller is singing in German. He learned that on his trip. I'm not going to cry over it. It doesn't help."

"But there are always appearances," said the kitchen cat.

7. The Eagle's Nest

On the mountain path the yodeling rang out merrily and loudly. It suggested good spirits and confident courage. It was Rudy on his way to see his friend, Vesinand.

"You have to help me! We'll get Ragli to come along. I must get the eaglet up on the cliff edge."

"Why don't you get the dark of the moon first? That would be just as easy," said Vesinand. "You're in a good mood."

"I'm thinking about getting married. But seriously now, I'll tell you what I've gotten myself into."

And soon Vesinand and Ragli knew what Rudy wanted.

"You're a foolhardy fellow!" they said. "It's impossible! You'll break your neck!"

"You won't fall if you don't think you will," said Rudy.

At midnight they started off with poles, ladders, and ropes. The path went through scrub and bushes, and over rocky slopes, always upwards, upwards in the dark night. The river was rushing down below. Water was trickling above them, and heavy rain clouds chased by in the air. The closer the hunters got to the steep mountain edge, the darker it became. The walls of the cliffs almost met, and only high up above through the narrow cleft did the sky lighten. Close by, under them, there was a deep abyss with the sound of roaring water. All three sat quietly waiting for dawn when the eagle would fly out. It had to be shot before the eaglet could attempt to be taken. Rudy squatted, as still as if he were a piece of the rock he sat on. He had his rifle in front of him, ready to shoot. His eyes never left the upper cleft where the eagle's nest was hidden under the overhanging cliff. The three hunters waited for a long time.

Then high above they heard a terribly loud rushing sound and a huge, hovering object darkened the sky. Two gun barrels aimed as the black eagle flew out of the nest. A shot rang out. For a moment the widespread wings moved, and then the bird slowly fell. It was as if its size and wing span would fill the entire cleft and pull the hunters down with it in its fall. But the eagle sank into the depths. They heard the creaking of tree branches and bushes that cracked from the bird's fall.

Then they got busy. Three of the longest ladders were tied together. They had to reach all the way up, but when they were placed on the outermost safe footing at the edge of the abyss, they didn't reach far enough. The side of the cliff was as smooth as a wall a considerable way further up, where the nest was hidden in the shelter of the uppermost overhanging cliff crag. After some deliberation they agreed that the best thing to do was to lower two ladders tied together into the cleft from above, and then connect these to the three that were already set up from below. With great difficulty two ladders were dragged furthest up and ropes attached. The ladders were lowered over the projecting cliff and hung swaying freely over the abyss. Rudy was already sitting on the lowest rung. It was an ice-cold morning. Clouds of fog drifted upward from the black crevice. Rudy sat there like a fly sitting on a tottering straw lost by a nest-building bird on the edge of a factory chimney. But the fly can fly when the straw breaks loose, and Rudy could only break his neck. The wind rushed around him, and down in the abyss roared the rushing water from the thawing glacier, the palace of the Ice Maiden.

He set the ladder in a swinging motion, like when a spider tries to grab hold from its long, swaying thread. And when Rudy touched the tip of the lower ladders the fourth time, he got hold of them. He tied them together with a sure and steady hand, but still they wobbled as if they had worn hinges.

The five long ladders that reached up towards the nest looked like a swaying reed as they leaned vertically towards the mountain wall. Now came the most dangerous part. He had to climb like a cat climbs, but Rudy could do that. The cat had taught him. He didn't sense *Vertigo*, who was treading air behind him, reaching her polyp-like arms towards him. He was standing on the ladder's top rung and realized that even here he couldn't reach high enough to see into the nest. He could only reach it with his hand. He tested how solid the thick, lower, intertwined branches that made up the lower part of the nest were, and when he was sure that he had a thick, unbreakable branch, he swung from the ladder up to the branch and got his head and chest above the nest. But he was met with the sickening stench of rotting meat. Rotted lambs, antelope, and birds lay there torn to pieces. *Vertigo*, who wasn't able to touch him, blew the poisonous reek into his face so that he would get dizzy, and down in the black, gaping depths on the rushing water sat the Ice Maiden herself with her long, white-green hair gazing with eyes deadly as gun barrels.

"Now I'll catch you!"

In a corner of the eagle's nest he saw the eaglet sitting, big and powerful. It couldn't fly yet. Rudy fastened his eyes on it, held on with all his might with one hand, and with his other hand threw a sling around the young eagle. It was captured alive, its leg in the tight cord. Rudy slung the sling with the bird over his shoulder, so the eagle dangled a good distance below him, and clung to a helpfully lowered rope until his toes again reached the top rung of the ladder.

"Hold on tight! Don't think you'll fall and you won't." It was the old mantra, and he followed it. He held on tight, crawled, was sure he wouldn't fall, and he didn't fall.

There was yodeling then, loud and happy. Rudy stood on the firm rocky ground with his eaglet.

8. The Housecat Has News

"Here's what you called for," said Rudy, who walked into the miller's house in Bex and set a big basket on the floor. He took the cloth off and two yellow, black-rimmed eyes glowed out, so flashing and wild that they looked like they could burn into and through anything. The strong, short beak was gaping to bite, and its neck was red and downy.

"The eaglet!" cried the miller. Babette shrieked and jumped aside, but couldn't take her eyes off Rudy or the eaglet.

"You don't scare easily!" said the miller.

"And you always keep your word," said Rudy. "We each have our distinguishing feature!"

"Why didn't you break your neck?" asked the miller.

"Because I held on," answered Rudy, "and I'm still doing it. I'm holding on to Babette!"

"Make sure you have her first," said the miller and laughed, and Babette knew that was a good sign.

"Let's get the eaglet out of the basket. Look how terribly he's glaring! How did you get a hold of him?"

And Rudy told the story while the miller's eyes grew bigger and bigger.

"With your courage and luck you could support three wives," said the miller.

"Thank you! Thank you!" cried Rudy.

"Well, you don't have Babette yet," said the miller, and slapped the young hunter on the shoulder in jest.

"Did you hear the latest from the mill?" The housecat asked the kitchen cat. "Rudy has brought us the eaglet and is taking

Babette in exchange. They kissed each other right in front of Father. They're as good as engaged. The old fellow didn't kick. He pulled in his claws, took a nap, and let the two sit there and fawn over each other. They have so much to say that they won't finish by Christmas."

And they didn't finish by Christmas. The wind whirled the brown leaves. The snow drifted in the valley as it did on the high peaks. The Ice Maiden sat in her proud palace that grew bigger when winter came. The cliff walls were glazed with ice, and there were yard-wide icicles as heavy as elephants in places where the mountain streams waved their veils in the summer. Garlands of fantastic ice crystals shone on the snow-dusted spruce trees. The Ice Maiden rode on the roaring wind over the deepest valleys, and the snow blanket reached all the way down to Bex. She could ride there and see Rudy indoors, more than he was used to being. He was sitting with Babette. The wedding would be in the summer. Their ears were often ringing, so much was the wedding discussed among their friends. There was sunshine, and the loveliest glowing rhododendron. There was the merry, laughing Babette, as lovely as the spring that came. Spring—that had all the birds singing about summer, and about the wedding day.

"How those two sit and hang on each other!" said the housecat. "I'm tired of that miaowing of theirs!"

9. THE ICE MAIDEN

Spring had unfolded its lush green garlands of walnut and chestnut trees that were especially luxuriant from the bridge by St. Maurice to Lake Geneva along the Rhone, which rushed with tremendous speed from its source under the green glacier, the ice palace where the Ice Maiden lives. She lets herself be carried on the piercing wind up onto the highest fields of snow and in the bright sunshine stretches out on the drifting pillows of snow. There she sat and looked with her far-sighted glance down in the deep valleys, where people busily moved about, like ants on a sunny rock.

"Powers of reason, as the children of the sun call you," said the Ice Maiden. "You're nothing but vermin. A single rolling snowball, and you and your houses and towns are crushed and obliterated!" And she lifted her proud head higher and looked around widely and deeply with her death-flashing eyes. But there was a rumbling sound from the valley, the blasting of rocks. This was the work of men—roads and tunnels for the railroad were being built.

"They're playing mole!" she said. "They're digging passages. That's why there's a sound like gunfire. If I were to move my palaces, there would be roaring louder than the boom of thunder!"

Smoke lifted up from the valley, moving forward like a fluttering veil, a waving plume from the locomotive that was pulling the train on the newly laid tracks. It was a winding snake whose joints were car after car. It shot forward swiftly as an arrow.

"They're playing God down there, those powers of reason!" said the Ice Maiden. "But the powers of nature are the rulers," and she laughed and sang so it resounded in the valley.

"Another avalanche," said the people down there.

But the children of the sun sang even louder about human ideas. Thought that rules. It has subjugated the sea, moved mountains, and filled valleys. The human mind is the master of the natural powers. Just at that moment a party of travelers came across the snowfield where the Ice Maiden was sitting. They had tied each other together with a rope to make a bigger body on the slippery ice, along the deep crevices.

"Vermin!" she said. "How can you be the masters of natural forces?" and she turned away from them and looked mockingly down in the deep valley, where the train went roaring by.

"There they sit, those *thinkers*! They're sitting in nature's power. I can see each of them. One is sitting alone as proudly as a king. Others are sitting in a bunch. Half of them are sleeping. And when the steam dragon stops, they climb out and go their way. Thoughts going out into the world!" And she laughed.

"There went another avalanche," they said down in the valley.

"It won't reach us," said two people in the steam dragon. "Two minds but with a single thought," as the saying goes. It was Rudy and Babette, and the miller was also along.

"As baggage," he said, "I'm along because I'm necessary."

"There those two sit," said the Ice Maiden. "I have crushed many a goat-antelope, and I have beat and broken millions of rhododendrons. Not even the roots remained. I wipe them out! Thoughts! People of reason!" And she laughed.

"Another avalanche!" they cried down in the valley.

10. GODMOTHER

In Montreux, one of the closest towns, that along with Clarens, Vernex and Crin form a garland around the northeastern part of Lake Geneva, Babette's godmother, the distinguished English lady, was staying with her daughters and a young relative. They had recently arrived, but the miller had already paid them a visit, announced Babette's engagement, told about Rudy and the eaglet, and the visit to Interlaken; in short, the whole story. This had pleased them to the highest degree and made them interested in Rudy and Babette, and the miller too. All three of them must come for a visit, and so they did! Babette was going to see her godmother, the godmother to see Babette.

By the little town of Villeneuve, at the end of Lake Geneva, lay the steamship that would reach Vernex, close to Montreux, after a half-hour trip. It's a coast sung about by poets. Here under the walnut trees by the deep, blue-green lake, Byron sat and wrote his melodic verse about the prisoner in the sinister mountain castle of Chillon. At Clarens, where the town is mirrored in the water with its weeping willows, Rousseau walked dreaming of Heloise. The Rhone river flows along under the high snow-covered mountains of Savoy. Not far from its mouth in the lake lies a small island. It's so small that from the coast it looks like a little boat out there. It's a skerry, and a hundred years ago a woman had it surrounded by rocks and filled with soil. She had three acacia trees planted there. Now they shade the entire island. Babette was transported with delight when she saw it. She thought it was the loveliest sight on the whole boat trip—they should land there—they must land there! She thought it would be so marvelous to be there. But the steamship went by and docked where it was supposed to, at Vernex.

The little party walked from there up through the white, sunlit walls that surround the vineyards around the little mountain village of Montreux. The farmers' houses are shaded by fig trees, and laurel and cypress trees grow in the gardens. Half way up was the bed and breakfast where Babette's godmother was staying.

They were very warmly received. Godmother was a big, friendly woman with a round, smiling face. As a child she must have had one of Raphael's cherub faces, but now she had an old angel's face, surrounded by abundant silver–white curls. Her daughters were neat and elegant, tall and thin. Their young cousin, who was with them, was dressed in white from tip to toe. He had golden hair and such big gilded sideburns that they could have been divided among three gentlemen. He immediately paid the utmost attention to little Babette.

Richly bound books, sheets of music, and drawings lay spread across the big table. The balcony door stood open to the lovely view of the wide lake that was so calm and still that the mountains of Savoy with towns, forests and snowcaps were reflected in it upside down.

Rudy, who usually was so cheerful, lively, and confident, felt like a fish out of water, as they say. He acted as if he was walking on peas spread on a slippery floor. How slowly time passed! It was like a treadmill. And now they were going for a walk! That went just as slowly. Rudy had to take two steps forwards and one back to be in step with the others. They went down to Chillon, the sinister old castle on the rocky island, to see the torture stakes and cells of death, and rusty chains in the rocky wall. They saw stone bunks for the condemned, and the trapdoors through which poor unfortunates were pushed to fall impaled onto iron spikes in the surf. And this is supposed to be a pleasure to see! It was a place of execution, lifted into the world of poetry by Byron's song. Rudy sensed the horror. He leaned against the big stone window ledge and looked down into the deep, blue-green water, and over to the lonely little island with the three acacia trees. He wished he were there, free of the whole prattling company, but Babette felt very happy. She had enjoyed herself tremendously, she said later. She thought the cousin was just perfect.

"Yes, a perfect fool," said Rudy, and that was the first time Rudy said something that she didn't like. The Englishman had given her a little book as a souvenir of Chillon. It was Byron's *The Prisoner of Chillon* in a French translation so that Babette could read it.[10]

"The book might be all right," said Rudy, "but that dandy who gave it to you didn't make a hit with me."

"He looked like a flour sack without flour in it," said the miller and laughed at his joke. Rudy laughed too and said that he had hit the nail on the head.

11. The Cousin

When Rudy visited the mill a few days later, he found the young Englishman there. Babette was just serving him poached trout, which she herself had garnished with parsley to dress it up. That was totally unnecessary. What did the Englishman want? What was he doing here, served and waited on by Babette? Rudy was jealous, and that amused Babette. It pleased her to see all sides of him, the strong and the weak. Love was still a game, and she played with Rudy's heart; and yet it must be said that he was her happiness, in all her thoughts, the best and most wonderful in the world. But the gloomier he looked, the more her eyes laughed. She would gladly have kissed the blond Englishman with the golden sideburns if it would have caused Rudy to run furiously away. That would have simply proved how much he loved her. It wasn't right, wasn't smart of little Babette, but she was only nineteen years old. She didn't think about it, and thought even less of how her behavior could be interpreted by the young Englishman as more frivolous and irresponsible than what was appropriate for the miller's modest, newly engaged daughter.

The road from Bex runs under the snow-covered mountain

tops called *Diablerets* in French, and the mill was not far from a rapid mountain stream that ran whitish grey like whipped soapy water. But this wasn't the stream that drove the mill. There was a smaller stream that rushed down from the cliffs on the other side of the river and through a stone culvert under the road where its power and speed lifted it into a wooden dam and then through a wide trough, over the larger river. This drove the mill wheel. The trough was so full of water that it flowed over, and so the rim presented a wet and slippery route for anyone who might think to use it as a short cut to the mill. This idea presented itself to the young Englishman. Dressed in white, like a mill worker, he climbed up there one evening, guided by the light in Babette's window. He hadn't learned how to climb and almost went head first in the stream, but he escaped with wet arms and splattered pants. Dripping wet and muddy, he came under Babette's window, where he climbed up into the old linden tree and imitated the hoot of an owl. He couldn't do any other bird calls. Babette heard it and peeked out through the thin curtains, but when she saw the man in white and realized who it was, her little heart beat with fright, but also with anger. She quickly put out the light, made sure that all the windows were hooked, and let him sit there howling and yowling.

It would be terrible if Rudy were at the mill now, but Rudy was not at the mill. No, it was much worse. He was right there below. She heard loud angry words. There was going to be a fight, maybe even a killing.

Babette opened the window in fright, called Rudy's name, and asked him to leave. She said she couldn't stand to have him stay.

"You can't stand that I stay!" he yelled, "So you've arranged this! You're expecting good friends, better than me! Shame on you, Babette!"

"You're detestable!" said Babette. "I hate you!" and she started crying. "Go! Go!"

"I didn't deserve this," he said and he went. His cheeks were on fire, and so was his heart.

Babette threw herself crying on the bed.

"As much as I love you, Rudy! How can you think so badly of me!"

She was angry, very angry and that was a good thing for her. Otherwise she would have been broken-hearted. But she could fall asleep and sleep the refreshing sleep of youth.

12. EVIL POWERS

Rudy left Bex and took the road home, up the mountains in the fresh cooling air, where the snow lay, where the Ice Maiden ruled. The leafy trees stood deep below, as if they were the tops of potato plants. The spruce and bushes grew smaller. The rhododendrons grew in the snow in patches like linen laid out to bleach. He saw a blue gentian, and crushed it with the butt of his gun.

Higher up he saw two antelope, and a glint came to his eyes, and his thoughts went in a different direction. But he wasn't close enough for a good shot. He climbed higher, where only a strip of grass grew between the boulders. The antelope were walking calmly on the snowfields. Eagerly he quickened his pace. Clouds of fog fell over him, and suddenly he was standing by the sheer cliff wall. Rain began to pour.

He felt a burning thirst, and his head was hot, but the rest of his body felt cold. He took out his flask, but it was empty. He hadn't thought about it as he stormed up the mountain. He had never been sick, but now he knew what it felt like. He was tired. He just wanted to lie down and sleep, but everything was soaked with water. He tried to pull himself together, but objects shimmered so strangely before his eyes. But then he saw what he had never seen here before—a low, newly built house, right up against the cliff. There was a young girl standing in the doorway, and he thought it was the schoolmaster's daughter Annette, whom he had once kissed while dancing. It wasn't Annette, but he'd seen her before—maybe close to Grindelwald, the evening he returned from the shooting match in Interlaken.

"How did you get here?" he asked.

"I'm home," she said. "I'm tending my herd."

"Your herd? Where is it grazing? There's only snow and rocks here."

"You sound like you know what you're talking about," she said and laughed. "Down behind here a ways there's good grazing. That's where my goats are. I take good care of them and never lose one. What's mine stays mine."

"You're pretty bold!" said Rudy.

"So are you!" she answered.

"If you have some milk, give me some because I'm so unbearably thirsty."

"I have something better than milk," she said. "And you shall have it! Some travelers came by here yesterday with their guide. They forgot half a bottle of wine, better than you've ever tasted. They won't come back for it, and I won't drink it. You can drink it!"

And she brought out the wine, poured it into a wooden bowl, and gave it to Rudy.

"It's good," he said. "I've never tasted a wine so warming and full of fire!" His eyes shone, and a life and fervor arose in him as if all his sorrows and burdens evaporated. Natural human feelings arose in him, fresh and lively

"But you're the schoolmaster's Annette!" he exclaimed. "Give me a kiss!"

"Well, give me that pretty ring you wear on your finger!"

"My engagement ring?"

"That's the one!" said the girl, poured wine in the bowl, and put it to his lips. He drank. The joy of living streamed through his blood. He felt like the whole world was his. Why worry? Everything is created to enjoy and make us happy! The current of life is a current of joy—be carried along by it—let yourself be carried by it! That is bliss. He looked at the young girl. It was Annette and yet not Annette, even less was she the phantom troll, as he had called her, whom he met by Grindelwald. The girl here on the mountain was as fresh as newly fallen snow, as lush as the rhododendron, and as light as a kid. But yet she was formed from Adam's rib, a human being like Rudy. And he threw his arms around her, looked into her strange clear eyes—only for a second—and how to explain in words what he saw? Was it the spirit of life or death that filled him? Was he lifted up, or sunk down into the deep, killing ice chasm, deeper, always deeper? He saw the walls of ice like blue-green glass. Bottomless crevices gaped all around him, and water dripped tinkling like a clock and as clear as pearls, lighting with blue-white flames. The Ice Maiden gave him a kiss that sent a chill through his spine into his forehead. He gave a cry of pain, tore himself loose, tumbled and fell. His eyes closed in darkness, but he opened them again. Evil powers had played their tricks.

The mountain girl was gone. The sheltering hut was gone. Water was streaming down the naked cliff wall. Snow was all around. Rudy was shaking with cold, wet to the skin, and his ring was gone. The engagement ring Babette had given him. His gun lay in the snow by his side. He picked it up and tried to shoot, but it didn't go off. Wet clouds lay like masses of snow in the crevices. *Vertigo* was sitting there watching for powerless prey, and under her in the deep cleft there was a sound as if a boulder fell, crushing and sweeping away anything breaking its fall.

But at the mill Babette sat crying. Rudy had not been there for six days. Rudy, who was in the wrong, and who should ask her for forgiveness since she loved him with all her heart.

13. In the Miller's House

"Talk about frightful nonsense with those people!" said the housecat to the kitchen cat. "Babette and Rudy have broken up again. She's crying, and he probably doesn't think about her anymore."

"I don't like that!" said the kitchen cat.

"Me neither," said the housecat, "but I'm not going to cry about it. Babette can just as well be sweethearts with the red sideburns. But he hasn't been here either since he tried to climb up on the roof."

Evil forces play their tricks, both outside and within us. Rudy had realized this and thought about it. What had happened around him and in him high up there on the mountain? Had he seen visions, or was it a feverish dream? He had never had a fever or been sick before. He had gained an insight into himself when he judged Babette. He thought about the wild chase in his heart, the hot *Föhn* that had blown there so lately. Could he confess everything to Babette? Every thought that in the moment of temptation could have become an action? He had lost her ring, and in that loss she had regained him. Would she confess to him? He felt like his heart would break to pieces when he thought about her. There were so many memories. He saw her large as life in front of him, laughing, a high-spirited child. Many a loving word that she had spoken in the fullness of her heart flew like a flash of sun into his breast, and soon there was nothing but sunshine there for Babette.

She must be able to confess to him, and she would!

He came to the mill. They confessed everything. It started with a kiss and ended with Rudy being the sinner. *His* big fault was that he had doubted Babette's faithfulness. That was really abominable of him. Such distrust and such impetuosity could have led them both to disaster. Most assuredly! And therefore Babette delivered a little sermon to him. She enjoyed it, and it was most becoming, although in one respect Rudy was right: godmother's relative was a fool. She would burn the book he had given her, and not keep anything that would remind her of him.

"Now it's over and done with," said the housecat. "Rudy is back. They understand each other, and they say that's the greatest happiness."

"Last night," said the kitchen cat, "I heard the rats say that the greatest happiness is to eat tallow candles and to have plenty of tainted bacon. Whom should we believe, the rats or the sweethearts?"

"Neither of them," said the housecat. "That's always the best bet."

The greatest happiness for Rudy and Babette still lay ahead. They still had the most beautiful day, as it's called, in front of them—their wedding day.

But the wedding wasn't going to be in the church in Bex, nor in the miller's house. Godmother wanted the wedding to be celebrated at the bed and breakfast, and have the ceremony take place in the lovely little church in Montreux. The miller backed this request. He alone knew what godmother had in mind for the newlyweds. They would get a wedding gift from her that was certainly worth such a small concession. The day was set. They were going to travel to Villeneuve the evening before and take the boat over to Montreux in the morning in time for godmother's daughters to dress the bride.

"I suppose they'll have another wedding celebration here the day after," said the housecat. "Otherwise, I don't give a miaow for the whole thing!"

"There's going to be a party," said the kitchen cat. "Ducks have been butchered, doves beheaded, and there's a whole deer hanging on the wall. It makes my mouth water to see it all. Tomorrow the trip begins!"

Yes, tomorrow! That evening Rudy and Babette sat at the mill for the last time as an engaged couple. Outside was the *Alpenglow*, the evening bells rang, and the daughters of the sunbeams sang, "What happens is always for the best."

14. VISIONS IN THE NIGHT

The sun had set, and the clouds settled into the Rhone valley between the high mountains. The wind blew from the south, an African wind, down over the high Alps, the *Föhn*. It tore the clouds into fragments, and when it was gone there was a moment of complete stillness. The fragmented clouds hung in fantastic forms between the forest-clad mountains above the swiftly flowing Rhone River. They looked like prehistoric sea animals, like hovering eagles of the sky, and like leaping frogs from the marsh. They descended to the raging river and sailed on it, and yet they sailed in the air. The current was carrying an uprooted fir tree, and in front of it the water formed whirling eddies. It was *Vertigo* and her sisters, who were spinning around on the turbulent torrent. The moon shone on the snow of the mountain tops, on the dark forests, on the strange white clouds—night visions, spirits of nature's powers. Mountain folk saw them through their windows. They sailed down there in flocks in front of the Ice Maiden. She came from her palace in the glacier, sitting on her flimsy ship, the uprooted fir. Water from the glacier carried her down the stream to the open lake.

"The wedding guests are coming," was sighed and sung in air and water.

Visions outside and visions inside. Babette had a strange dream.

She had been married to Rudy for many years. He was out antelope hunting, but she was at home, and there with her was the young Englishman with the gilded sideburns. His eyes were so warm, and his words had a magical power. He reached out his hand to her, and she had to follow him. They walked away from her home. Always downwards! And it felt to Babette that there lay a burden on her heart that became heavier and heavier. It was a sin against Rudy, a sin against God. Suddenly she was alone. Her clothes had been torn to pieces by thorns. Her hair was grey. She looked upward in pain, and on the mountain edge she saw Rudy. She stretched her arms out towards him, but dared neither to shout nor pray, and it wouldn't have helped because she soon saw that it wasn't Rudy at all, but just his hunting jacket and hat, hanging on a walking stick the way hunters do, to trick the antelope. And in unbounded pain she whimpered, "Oh, if I could have died on my wedding day! My happiest day! Lord, my God, it would have been a mercy, the good fortune of my life. That would have been the best that could have happened for Rudy and me. No one knows his future!" And in godless grief she threw herself into the deep ravine. A string snapped, a song of sorrow sounded.

Babette woke up. The dream was over and forgotten, but she knew she had dreamed something terrible and dreamed about the young Englishman, whom she hadn't seen or thought about for several months. Was he in Montreux? Would she see him at the wedding? A little shadow passed over her fine mouth, and she frowned. But soon she was smiling, and her eyes were sparkling again. The sun was shining so beautifully outside, and tomorrow was she and Rudy's wedding day.

He was already in the living room when she came down, and soon they were off for Villeneuve. They were both so happy, and so was the miller. He laughed and beamed with the greatest good humor. He was a good father and an honest soul.

"Now we're the masters of the house," said the housecat.

15. THE END

It was not yet evening when the three happy people reached Villeneuve and had dinner. The miller sat in an easy chair with his pipe and took a little nap. The young couple walked arm in arm out of the town, on the road under the cliffs covered with bushes, along the deep blue-green lake. The sinister Chillon with its grey walls and thick towers was reflected in the clear water. Even closer was the little island with the three acacia trees. It looked like a bouquet on the water.

"It must be lovely over there," said Babette. She once again had such a strong wish to visit the little island, and that wish could be fulfilled at once. There was a boat by the bank. The rope that held it was easy to loosen. They didn't see anyone to ask for permission, so they just took the boat. Rudy knew how to row.

The oars caught the yielding water like the fins of a fish. Water is so soft and yet so strong. It has a back to bear weight, and a mouth with which to swallow. Gently smiling, softness itself and yet a terror, with shattering strength. There was a foamy wake following the boat that reached the little island within a few minutes, and the two went ashore. There was only enough room for the two of them to dance.

Rudy swung Babette around two or three times, and then they sat down on the little bench under the overhanging acacia trees. They gazed into each other's eyes, held each other's hands, and everything around them shone in the splendor of the setting sun. The fir forests on the mountains had a violet cast that made them look like blooming heather, and the rocky stones above the tree line glowed as if the mountain were transparent. The clouds in the sky were lit up like red fire, and the whole lake was like a fresh, blooming rose petal. As the shadows rose higher and higher up the snow-capped Savoy mountains, these turned to dark blue, but the highest peaks shone like red lava. It was as if they repeated a moment from their creation, when these massive mountains rose up glowing from the earth's womb, still burning. It was an *Alpenglow* unlike any Rudy or Babette had ever seen. The snow-covered *Dent du Midi* shone like the disc of the full moon as it rises above the horizon.

"What beauty! What happiness!" they both said. "The world has nothing more to give me," said Rudy. "An evening like this is really a whole life. How often have I sensed my joy, as I sense it now and thought that if everything were to end, what a happy life I have had! How blessed this world is! And that day was over, but a new one began and I thought *that* one was even more beautiful! How good and great God is, Babette!"

"I am so happy," she said.

"The world has nothing more to give me," exclaimed Rudy.

And the evening bells rang from the mountains of Savoy, from the Swiss mountains. In golden glory the dark black Jura mountains rose up in the west.

"May God give you the most wonderful and best!" Babette exclaimed.

"He will!" said Rudy. "Tomorrow I'll have it. Tomorrow you'll be all mine. My own lovely little wife."

"The boat!" screamed Babette at the same time.

The boat that was to ferry them back had torn loose and was drifting away from the island.

"I'll get it," said Rudy. He cast off his jacket, tore off his boots, and ran into the lake, swimming swiftly towards the boat.

Cold and deep was the clear blue-green ice water from the mountain glaciers. Rudy looked down into it, only a single glance, and it was as if he saw a gold ring roll, gleam, and sparkle. He thought about his lost engagement ring, and the ring became bigger, and widened out into a glittering circle. Inside of it the clear glacier was shining. Infinitely deep crevices were gaping all around, and water dripped tinkling like a carillon, and shining with white-blue flames. He saw in an instant what we must describe in many long words. Young hunters and young girls, men and women—those who at one time had sunk in the glacier's crevasses—stood here alive with open eyes and smiling mouths. And deep under them sounded church bells from buried towns. The congregation kneeled under the church vault. The mountain stream played the organ, whose pipes were pieces of ice. The Ice Maiden sat on the clear, transparent floor. She rose up towards Rudy, kissed his feet, and an icy chill shot through his limbs—an electric shock—ice and fire! You can't tell the difference from a quick touch.

"Mine! Mine!" resounded around him and inside him. "I kissed you when you were little! Kissed you on the lips! Now I kiss your toes and heel. You are solely mine!"

And he was gone in the clear, blue water.

Everything was still. The church bells stopped ringing. The last tones disappeared with the radiance on the red clouds.

"You're mine!" resounded in the depths. "You're mine!" resounded in the heights, from the eternal.

It's lovely to fly from love to love, from the earth into heaven.

A string snapped. A song of sorrow sounded. The kiss of death conquered the perishable. The prologue ended so that the drama of life could begin. Disharmony dissolved in harmony.

Would you call this a sad story?

Poor Babette! For her it was a time of terror. The boat drifted further and further away. No one on land knew that the couple had gone to the little island. Evening came. The clouds descended, and it got dark. Alone and despairing she stood there moaning. There was a devilish storm brewing. Lighting flashed over the Jura mountains, over Switzerland, and over the Savoy. Flash after flash on all sides—thunder boom after boom, rolling into each other and lasting for several minutes. It was as bright as sunlight in the lightning flashes. You could see each individual grapevine as if at midday, and then the brooding black darkness returned. The lightning came in ribbons, rings, and zigzags, struck all around the lake, and flashed from all sides, while the thunder claps grew in echoing rumbles. On land people pulled boats up on the shore. Everything living sought shelter. And the rain came streaming down.

"Where in the world are Rudy and Babette in this terrible weather?" asked the miller.

Babette sat with folded hands, her head in her lap. Mute with grief and from her screams and sobs.

"In the deep water!" she said to herself, "Deep down, as if under the glacier, is where he is!"

She thought about what Rudy had told her about his mother's death, and his rescue, when he was pulled as a corpse from the cleft of the glacier. "The Ice Maiden has taken him again."

And there was a flash of lightning as blinding as the sun on white snow. Babette jumped up. The lake rose in that instant like a shining glacier. The Ice Maiden stood there—majestic, pale blue, shining—and at her feet lay Rudy's corpse. "Mine!" she said, and then there was pitch darkness again, and pouring water.

"It's horrible," whimpered Babette. "Why did he have to die just as our day of joy had come? God! Help me understand! Enlighten my heart! I don't understand your ways. I'm groping for your omnipotence and wisdom."

And God enlightened her heart. A flash of thought, a ray of mercy—her dream from last night, large as life—flew through her in a flash, and she remembered the words she had spoken: the wish for the best for Rudy and herself.

"Woe is me! Was the seed of sin in my heart? Was my dream my future, whose string had to be snapped for the sake of my salvation? Miserable me!"

She sat whimpering in the pitch dark night. In its deep stillness she thought Rudy's words still rang out—the last thing he said here: "The world has no more joy to give me." Words uttered in an abundance of happiness, repeated in a torrent of grief.

———

A few years have passed since then. The lake is smiling. The shores are smiling, and the grapevines are heavy with grapes. The steamship with its waving flags hurries by, and the pleasure boats with their two out-stretched sails fly like white butterflies across the mirror of the water. The railroad above Chillon is open and runs deep into the Rhone valley. Tourists get off at every station. They consult their little red bound travel guides to learn what attractions there are to see. They visit Chillon, see the little island with the three acacia trees out in the lake, and read about the engaged couple who rowed over there early one evening in 1856. They read about the bridegroom's death and how "only the next morning did those on shore hear the bride's screams of despair."

But the travel guide doesn't say anything about Babette's quiet life with her father. Not at the mill—strangers live there now—but in the pretty house by the railroad station from where she can still see on many evenings the snow-capped mountains above the chestnut trees where Rudy once played. In the evenings she sees the *Alpenglow*. The sunshine's children camp up there and repeat the song about the wanderer whom the whirlwind tore the cloak from and carried away. It took his covering but not the man.

There's a rosy radiance on the mountain snow, and a rosy radiance in every heart that believes that "God lets the best happen for us!" But it's not always as apparent to us as it was for Babette in her dream.

NOTES

1. Schreckhorn (13,379') and Wetterhorn (12,142') are mountains in the Bernese (Swiss) Alps.
2. Canton in southern Switzerland that is predominantly French speaking.
3. Waterfall in south-central Switzerland, near Interlaken.
4. Swiss mountain (13,642') not far from Grindelwald.
5. I have omitted "As we know" from this sentence. Andersen had given information about Rudy's father in an earlier version of the story. This "as we know" reference is evidently a remnant from an earlier version overlooked by Andersen in the final story.
6. Cretinism, mental and physical retardation caused by a lack of thyroid hormones, was more common in Switzerland than in other European countries because of an iodine deficiency in the water of the Swiss Alps. A survey carried out in 1810 in what is now the Swiss canton of Valais revealed 4,000 cretins among 70,000 inhabitants.
7. Mountain pass in the Alps in southern Switzerland.

8. Pass in the Bernese Alps connecting Bern and Valais cantons.
9. Warm dry wind that blows down the northern slopes of the Alps.
10. English Romantic poet George Gordon, Lord Byron (1788–1824), wrote *The Prisoner of Chillon* after visiting the castle with fellow poet Percy Bysshe Shelley in the summer of 1816. The castle, on Lake Geneva, was for the most part built by the counts of Savoy in the late twelfth and thirteenth centuries, although the site had been occupied for hundreds of years. During the sixteenth century the castle was used as a prison.

Evangelical and Religious Tales

THE SNOW QUEEN
AN ADVENTURE IN SEVEN STORIES

THE FIRST STORY
WHICH IS ABOUT THE MIRROR AND THE FRAGMENTS

ALL RIGHT! NOW WE'LL begin. When we're at the end of the story, we'll know more than we know now, for we'll know just how evil this troll was. He was one of the absolute worst. He was "the devil" himself! One day he was in a really good mood because he had made a mirror that caused everything good and beautiful it reflected to shrink to almost nothing, and anything that was worthless and ugly to stand out and look even worse. The most beautiful landscapes looked like cooked spinach in it, and the best people became nasty looking or stood on their heads without stomachs. Faces became so contorted that they were unrecognizable, and if you had a freckle, you could be sure that it would cover your nose and mouth. The devil said that it was great fun. If a person had a good, pious thought, a sneer would appear in the mirror, and the troll devil would laugh in glee at his clever invention. All those who attended the troll-school—you see, he conducted a troll-school—spread the word that a miracle had occurred. It was now possible to see, they said, what the world and people really looked like. They ran around with the mirror, and finally there wasn't a country or a person who hadn't been distorted in it. Then they wanted to fly up to heaven itself to make fun of the angels and the Lord. The higher they flew with the mirror, the more it sneered. They could hardly hold on to it. Higher and higher they flew, closer to God and the angels. Then the mirror shook so violently from sneering that it flew out of their hands and fell to the earth where it broke in hundreds of millions, billions, and even more pieces, bringing about even more unhappiness than before. This was because some of the pieces were no bigger than a grain of sand, and these flew about in the world, and when they got into people's eyes, they stayed there and people saw everything wrong, or only had an eye for what was wrong with a thing since every little piece of mirror retained the power of the whole. Some people also got a little piece of the mirror in their hearts, and it was quite dreadful. The heart became like a clump of ice. Some of the mirror pieces were so big that they were used for window panes, but you wouldn't want to look at your friends through those. Other pieces were used for glasses, and then it went badly when people put them on just to see and to see justly. The devil laughed so his sides split, and he was tickled pink! But in the air some pieces of mirror were still flying around. Now listen to what happened!

SECOND STORY
A LITTLE BOY AND A LITTLE GIRL

In the big city, where there are so many houses and people that there isn't enough space for all people to have a little garden, and where most people have to be contented with flowers in pots, there lived two poor children who had a garden slightly larger than a flowerpot. They weren't brother and sister, but they loved each other as if they were. Their parents lived right next to each other in two garret rooms, where the roof from one house leaned right up against its neighbor, and the gutters ran along the edges of the roof. From each house a little garret window opened, and you just had to stride over the gutters to get from one window to the next.

The parents each had a large wooden box outside their windows, and here they grew kitchen herbs that they used for cooking, and a little rose tree. There was one in each box, and they grew very nicely. Then the parents decided to place the boxes crosswise over the gutters so they almost reached from one window to the next, and it looked almost exactly like two flower beds. The peas hung down over the boxes, and the rose trees shot out long shoots that wound around the windows and turned towards each other so that it became almost a kind of arbor of greenery and flowers. Since the boxes were very high, the children knew that they couldn't climb on them, but they were often allowed to climb out to each other and sit on their small footstools under the roses. And they played there very nicely.

*All those who attended the troll-school spread
the word that a miracle had occurred.*

Of course in the winter, that pleasure was over. The windows were often covered with frost, but then they warmed copper pennies on the stove, laid them against the frosty panes, and made delightful peepholes that were perfectly round. Behind each peered a gentle and friendly eye, one from each window; it was the little boy and the little girl. His name was Kai and hers was Gerda. In the summer they could easily see each other with just a leap, but in the winter they had to go down many, many steps and then up many more steps, and outside the snow drifted around.

"The white bees are swarming," said the old grandmother.

"Do they have a queen bee too?" asked the little boy because he knew that the real bees had one.

"They do!" said grandmother. "She is flying where they are closest together. She is the biggest of them all, and she never rests on this earth. She flies up into the black clouds. Many winter nights she flies through the city's streets and peeks in the windows, and then they freeze so strangely, like flowers."

"Oh yes, I've seen that!" said both children, and then they knew it was true.

"Can the Snow Queen come inside here?" asked the little girl.

"Just let her come," said the boy, "and I'll set her on the warm stove so she'll melt."

But the grandmother smoothed his hair and told other stories.

That evening when little Kai was home and partly undressed, he crept up on his chair by the window and peered out of his little peephole. A couple of snowflakes fell outside, and one of these, the biggest, remained lying on the edge of one of the flower boxes. The snowflake grew and grew, finally it became a woman, dressed in the finest whitest gauze, as though she were made of millions of star-like specks. She was very beautiful and fine, but made of ice, the dazzling, gleaming ice—still she was alive. Her eyes stared like two clear stars, but there was no calm or quiet in them. She nodded at the window and waved her hand. The little boy became frightened and leaped down from the chair, and then it was as if a big bird flew by the window.

The next day there was clear frost—and then came spring. The sun shone, greenery sprouted, the swallows built nests, windows were opened, and the little children once again sat in their little garden high up in the gutters above all the stories of the house.

The roses bloomed so exceptionally that summer; the little girl had learned a hymn, and there were roses in it, and when she heard it, she thought of her own and sang it for the little boy, and he sang along:

> *"Roses in the valley grow*
> *And baby Jesus there we know"*[1]

And the little ones held hands, kissed the roses, and looked at God's clear sunshine and talked to it, as if the Christ child were there. What beautiful summer days they were! How blessed it was to be out by the fresh rose trees that never seemed to stop blooming!

Kai and Gerda sat looking at a picture book of animals and birds, it was then—the clock struck five on the big church tower—that Kai cried, "Ouch! Something stuck my heart! And I have something in my eye!"

The little girl took hold of his neck to look. He blinked his eyes—no, there was nothing to be seen.

"I think it's gone," he said, but it wasn't gone. It was one of those splinters that had come from the mirror, the troll mirror, the one that we surely remember: the nasty glass which made everything good and great reflected in it seem small and ugly, while the evil and worthless qualities stood out, so that every flaw in a thing was immediately noticed. Poor Kai had also gotten a piece right into his heart. It would soon become like a clump of ice. After a while it didn't hurt anymore, but it was there.

"Why are you crying?" he asked. "It makes you look ugly! There's nothing wrong with me! Yuck!" he cried out. "That rose there is worm eaten! And look how crooked that one is!

Those really are some ugly roses. They look like the boxes they're standing in," and he kicked hard with his foot against the box and tore the two roses off.

"Kai, what are you doing!" cried the little girl, and when he saw her alarm, he tore another rose off and ran through his window away from dear little Gerda.

When she came later with the picture book, he said it was for babies, and if Grandmother told stories, he always had a *but*—whenever he could he would walk behind her, put on glasses, and talk like her. It was a good imitation, and people laughed at him. Soon he was able to mimic the speech and walk of all the people in the street. Everything that was peculiar to them and unattractive, he was able to mimic, and people said, "That boy's got a good head on him," but it was because of the glass he had gotten in his eye, the glass that sat in his heart, and that was why he also made fun of little Gerda, who loved him with all her soul.

His games were now quite different than before. They were so rational. One winter day when the snowflakes were drifting around, he came with a big magnifying glass, held out the blue tail of his jacket and let the snowflakes fall on it.

"Look through the glass, Gerda," he said, and every snowflake looked much bigger and looked like a magnificent flower or a ten pointed star. It was lovely to see.

"Do you see how intricate they are?" Kai asked, "It's much more interesting than with real flowers! And they have no flaws at all. They're quite perfect, if they just don't melt."

A little later Kai came wearing big gloves with his sled on his back, and he yelled right into Gerda's ears: "I'm allowed to go sledding in the big square where the others play," and off he ran.

In the square the boldest boys often tied their sleds to the farmer's wagon and rode a good distance with it. It was the greatest fun. As they were playing, a big sleigh arrived. It was painted all white, and there was someone sitting in it wrapped in a wooly white fur and with a white wooly hat. The sleigh drove around the square twice, and Kai quickly got his little sled tied to it, and rode along. It went faster and faster, right into the next street. The one who was driving turned its head and nodded in such a friendly way to Kai; it was as if they knew each other. Every time Kai wanted to loosen his sled, the person nodded again, and so Kai stayed. They drove right out of the city gates. Then the snow started falling so hard that the little boy couldn't see his hand in front of his face, but he rushed along. He quickly dropped the rope to get loose from the big sleigh, but it didn't help; his little sled was stuck, and they rushed on as fast as the wind. He cried out loudly then, but no one heard him, and the snow drifted around, and the sleigh rushed on. Every now and then it gave a leap, and it was as if it rushed over furrows and fences. He was very scared and wanted to say the Lord's Prayer, but he could only remember the multiplication tables.

The snow flakes became bigger and bigger; finally they looked like big white hens. Then they fell to the side, the big sleigh stopped, and the person driving it stood up. The coat and hat were made of snow. It was a woman, so tall and dignified, so shining white—it was the Snow Queen.

"We're making good time," she said, "but you're freezing. Creep into my bearskin fur," and she placed him in the sleigh with her, put the fur around him, and it was as if he sank into a snowdrift.

"Are you still cold?" she asked and then she kissed him on the forehead. Oh, it was colder than ice. It went right into his heart, which of course was partly a clump of ice. He felt like he was going to die—but only for a moment, then it felt good, and he didn't notice the cold around him anymore.

"My sled! Don't forget my sled!" was the first thing he thought of, and it was tied to one of the white hens, that flew after them with the sled on its back. The Snow Queen kissed Kai one more time, and by then he had forgotten little Gerda and Grandmother and all of them at home.

"Now you can't have more kisses," she said, "otherwise I'd kiss you to death!"

Kai looked at her. She was so beautiful, a wiser more lovely face he couldn't imagine. She didn't seem to be ice, like the time she sat outside his window and waved at him. To his eyes

Kai and the Snow Queen.

she was perfect, and he didn't feel at all afraid. He told her that he could do math in his head, with fractions, knew the areas of countries, and how many inhabitants they had. She kept smiling at him, and then he felt that what he knew wasn't enough. He looked up into the great high sky and she flew with him, flew high up to the black cloud, and the storm whistled and whined as if it were singing centuries-old songs. They flew over forests and lakes, over oceans and land. Under them roared the cold wind, the wolves howled, and black screaming crows flew over the sparkling snow. But above them the huge moon shone brightly, and Kai watched it the whole long, long winter night. In the daytime he slept by the Snow Queen's feet.

THIRD STORY
THE FLOWER GARDEN OF THE WOMAN WHO KNEW MAGIC

But how was little Gerda getting along now that Kai wasn't there anymore? Where was he anyway?—No one knew, no one could tell. The boys could only tell that they had seen him tie his little sled to a magnificent big one that drove into the street and out the city gates. No one knew where he was. Many tears were shed, and little Gerda cried her eyes out. Then they said he was dead, drowned in the river that ran close by the city. Oh, what long dark winter days these were!

Then spring came with warmer sunshine.

"Kai is dead and gone," little Gerda said.

"I don't believe it," said the sunshine.

"He's dead and gone," she said to the swallows.

"I don't believe it," they answered, and finally little Gerda didn't believe it either.

"I'll put on my new red shoes," she said one morning, "the ones Kai has never seen, and go down to the river and ask about him."

It was early. She kissed her old Grandmother, who was sleeping, put on her red shoes, and went by herself out of the gate to the river.

"Is it true that you've taken my little playmate? I'll give you my red shoes if you'll give him back to me!"

And she thought the waves nodded so strangely, so she took

her red shoes, her most prized possession, and threw them out into the river, but they fell close by the bank, and the little waves brought them right back to her. It was as if the river didn't want to take the dearest thing she had since it didn't have little Kai. But she thought that she hadn't thrown them out far enough so she climbed into a boat that lay in the rushes. She went to the farthest end of the boat and threw the shoes, but the boat was not tied firmly, and the motion she made caused it to glide away from shore. She noticed it and hurried to get out, but before she could, the boat was over a yard away from land and was moving more quickly still.

Little Gerda became very frightened and started to cry, but no one heard her except the little grey sparrows, and they couldn't carry her to land. But they flew along the bank and sang as if to console her, "Here we are! Here we are!" The boat flowed with the current. Little Gerda sat quite still in her stocking feet. Her little red shoes were floating behind, but they couldn't reach the boat, which was moving faster.

It was lovely along the banks, with beautiful flowers, old trees and slopes with sheep and cows, but there was not a person to be seen.

"Maybe the river will carry me to little Kai," and that thought cheered her up. So Gerda stood up and looked for many hours at the lovely green banks. Then she came to a big cherry orchard where there was a little house with strange red and blue windows, a straw roof, and two wooden soldiers who saluted all who passed by.

Gerda called to them because she thought they were real, but of course they didn't answer. She came quite close to them for the river was pushing the boat towards shore. Gerda shouted even louder and then an old, old woman came out of the house. She was leaning on a crooked cane, and she wore a big sun hat decorated with the most beautiful flowers.

"You poor little child," said the old woman, "how did you get out there in that strong current, pulled along into the wide world?" and the old woman walked out into the water, hooked the boat with her cane, pulled it ashore, and lifted little Gerda out.

*"How did you get out there in that strong current,
pulled along into the wide world?"*

Gerda was glad to be on solid ground again, but a little bit afraid of the strange old woman.

"Come and tell me who you are, and how you got here," she said.

And Gerda told her everything, and the old one shook her head and said, "Hm, hm." When Gerda had told her everything, and asked her if she had seen little Kai, the woman said that he had not passed by, but he would surely come. Gerda shouldn't be sad, but taste her cherries and look at her flowers, they were more beautiful than any picture book; each of them could tell a whole story. Then she took Gerda by the hand, and they went into the little house, and the old woman locked the door.

The windows were very high up, and the glass was red, blue, and yellow. The day light shone in so strangely with all the colors, but on the table stood the most lovely cherries, and Gerda ate as many as she wanted because she wasn't afraid to do that. While she ate, the old woman combed her hair with a gold comb, and the hair curled and shone beautifully around the friendly little face that was so round and looked like a rose.

"I have really longed for such a sweet little girl," said the old woman. "You'll see, we'll get along nicely together." And as she was combing her hair, Gerda forgot more and more about her foster-brother Kai because the old woman could do magic, but she wasn't an evil troll at all. She just did a little magic for her own pleasure, and now she wanted to keep little Gerda. So she went out into the garden, stretched her crooked cane out towards all the rose trees, and with their lovely blooms they sank down into the black earth, and you couldn't see where they had been. The old woman was afraid that if Gerda saw the roses, she would think of her own roses, remember little Kai, and then run away.

She led Gerda out into the garden.—Oh, what scents and sights! All imaginable flowers, for every season, stood here in magnificent bloom. No picture book could be more colorful or beautiful. Gerda jumped with joy and played until the sun went down behind the big cherry trees. Then she was given a lovely bed with red silk comforters, filled with blue violets, and she slept and dreamed as beautifully as any queen on her wedding day.

The next day she played again with the flowers in the warm sunshine—and so passed many days. Gerda knew each flower, but despite how many there were, she seemed to feel that one was missing, but she didn't know which one. Then one day she sat and looked at the old woman's sun hat with the painted flowers, and the most beautiful one was a rose. The old woman had forgotten to remove it from the hat, when she conjured the others into the ground. But that's what it's like to be absent-minded! "What!" said Gerda, "There aren't any roses here!" and she ran through the flower beds, looked and looked, but there were none to be found. Then she sat down and cried, but her hot tears fell just where a rose tree had sunk, and when the warm tears watered the earth, the tree shot up at once, as full of blooms as when it sank, and Gerda embraced it, kissed the roses, and thought about the beautiful roses at home and with them of little Kai.

"Oh, I've been delayed too long!" said the little girl. "I was going to find Kai!—Don't you know where he is?" she asked the roses. "Do you think he's dead and gone?"

"Dead he's not," said the roses. "We've been in the earth where you can find the dead, and Kai wasn't there."

"Oh, thank you!" little Gerda said, and she went to the other flowers and looked into their cups and asked, "Don't you know where little Kai is?"

But every flower stood in the sunlight and dreamed its own adventure or story, and Gerda heard so many of them, but no one knew anything about Kai.

And what did the tiger lily say?

"Do you hear the drum: boom boom! There are only two tones, always boom boom! Hear the women's song of lament! Hear the priests' shouts!—In her long red coat the Hindu wife stands on the pyre. The flames shoot up around her and her dead husband, but the Hindu wife is thinking of the living within the circle: he, whose eyes burn hotter than flames, the fire in whose eyes touches her heart more than the flames that soon will burn her body to ashes. Can the flame of the heart die in the flames of the bonfire?"

"I don't understand that at all!" said little Gerda.
"That's my tale," said the tiger lily.
What does the morning glory say?

"Overhanging the narrow mountain road there's an old feudal castle. Thick vinca minor grows up the old red walls, leaf upon leaf, up to the balcony. There's a lovely girl standing there. She leans over the railing and looks down the road. No rose hangs more freshly from its branches than she does. No apple blossom, when the wind carries it from the tree, sways more lightly than she does. How the magnificent silk dress rustles. 'Isn't he coming?'"

"Do you mean Kai?" asked little Gerda.
"I am just talking about my own story, my dream," answered the morning glory.
What does the little snowdrop say?

"Between the trees on a rope hangs a wide board. It's a swing, and two lovely little girls—dresses as white as snow, long green silk ribbons waving from their hats—are swinging. Their brother, who's bigger than they are, stands up on the swing. He has his arm around the rope to hold on, but in one hand he has a little saucer, in the other a little clay pipe. He's blowing soap bubbles. The swing is swinging, and the bubbles fly with lovely changing colors—the last is still hanging at the pipe bowl and bends with the wind. The swing is swinging. The little black dog, as light as the bubbles, stands up on its hind legs and wants to get on the swing. It swings by. The dog falls, barks, and is angry. It's being teased, the bubbles burst—a swinging board, a leaping lathering picture is my song!"

It is possible that it's really lovely, what you're talking about, but you tell it so sadly and you don't mention Kai at all."
What do the hyacinths say?

"There were three lovely sisters, so transparent and delicate. One had a red dress, the second one's was blue, and the third's quite white. They danced hand in hand by a quiet lake in the clear moonlight. They weren't fairies; they were human beings. There was a wonderful sweet fragrance, and the girls disappeared into the woods. The scent grew stronger—three coffins, in which the lovely girls lay, glided out from the edge of the forest over the lake. Shining glowworms flew around like small wavering lights. Are the dancing girls sleeping or are they dead? The flower fragrance says they're corpses—the evening bell rings for the dead!"

"You make me really sad," said little Gerda. "Your scent is so strong that I have to think of dead girls! Oh, is little Kai really dead? The roses have been in the ground, and they say he's not!"

"Ding, dong," rang the hyacinth bells. "We aren't ringing for little Kai; we don't know him. We're just singing our song, the only one we know!"

So Gerda went to the buttercup, shining out from between glistening green leaves.

"You're a clear little sun!" Gerda said, "Tell me if you know where I can find my playmate?"

And the buttercup shone so beautifully and looked at Gerda again. What song could the buttercup sing? It wasn't about Kai either.

In a little yard God's sun shone so warmly the very first day of spring. The rays slid down the neighbor's white wall, close by grew the first yellow flowers, shining gold in the warm rays of the sun. Old grandmother was sitting out in her chair. Her granddaughter, a poor pretty servant girl, came home for a short visit; she kissed her grandmother. There was gold, the heart's gold, in the blessed kiss. Gold on the lips, gold on the ground, gold in the morning hours all around!

"See, that's my little story," said the buttercup.

"My poor old grandmother!" sighed Gerda. "I'm sure she's longing for me and is sad about me, like she was for little Kai. But I'll soon be home again, and I'll bring Kai with me. It's no use asking the flowers, they only know their own songs, and can't tell me anything." And then she tied up her little dress so she could run faster, but the narcissus hit her in the leg as she jumped over it so she stopped, looked at the tall yellow flower, and asked, "Do you perhaps know something?" She bent right down to the narcissus, and what did it say?

"I can see myself! I can see myself!" said the narcissus. "Oh, how I smell!—In the little garret room, partly dressed, is a little dancer. First she stands on one leg, then on two, she kicks at the whole world. She's only an optical illusion. She pours water from a teapot onto a piece of fabric that she's holding. It's her girdle—Cleanliness is next to Godliness! The white dress hangs on a hook. It's also washed in the teapot and dried on the roof. She puts it on; the saffron yellow scarf around her neck makes the dress shine whiter. One leg lifts! Look how she stands tall on one stem! I can see myself! I can see myself!"

"I don't care about that at all," said Gerda. "That's nothing to tell me!" And then she ran to the edge of the garden.

The door was closed, but she wiggled the rusty metal hook so it came loose, and the door flew open allowing little Gerda to run out into the wide world in her bare feet. She looked back three times, but no one was coming after her. After a while she couldn't run any more and sat down on a big rock, and when she looked around, the summer was over. It was late in the autumn. You couldn't notice that inside the beautiful garden, where there was always sunshine and the flowers of all seasons.

"God, I've wasted so much time!" said little Gerda. "It's autumn already! So I dare not rest!" And she got up to go.

Oh, how tender and tired her little feet were, and all around it looked so cold and damp. The long willow leaves were all yellow and fog dripped into the water from them, one leaf after another fell, only the blackthorn had fruit on it, firm and sour. Oh, how grey and dismal seemed the wide world!

FOURTH STORY
A PRINCE AND PRINCESS

Gerda had to rest again. Right above where she was sitting a big crow hopped on the snow. It had been sitting and watching her for a long time and turning its head. Now it said, "Crocay—goo day goo day." It couldn't say it any better but it meant well, and asked where she was going so all alone in the wide world. That word—alone—Gerda understood very well and felt the concern so she told the crow her whole life story and asked it if had seen Kai.

And the crow nodded quite thoughtfully and said, "Could be, could be."

"What? You think so?" cried the little girl and almost squeezed the crow to death from all the kisses she gave him.

"Take it easy, take it easy!" said the crow. "I think, I know— I think it could be little Kai, but I guess he's forgotten you for the princess!"

"Is he living with a princess?" asked Gerda.

"Yes, imagine," said the crow, "but it's so hard for me to speak your language. If you understand Crocawish, I can explain it better."

"No, I haven't learned that," said Gerda, "but my grandmother knew it, and she knew High Falutin too. If only I'd learned it!"

"It doesn't matter," said the crow. "I'll speak as well as I can, but it'll be awful anyway," and then he told her what he knew.

"In this kingdom, where we're sitting, there lives a princess who is immensely intelligent, but then she has also read all the newspapers in the world and forgotten them again, that's how smart she is. The other day she was sitting on her throne, and they say that isn't much fun. Then she started humming a little song, the one that goes: 'Why shouldn't I get married?' 'There's something in that,' she said, and then she wanted to get married, but she wanted a husband who could answer when you said something to him, not just one who stood around looking distinguished, because that's so boring. Then she had all the ladies in waiting drummed up, and when they heard what she wanted, they were very pleased. 'I like that,' they said, 'I thought about that the other day myself.' Every word I'm saying is true," said the crow. "I have a tame sweetheart who has complete access to the castle, and she tells me everything."

Naturally his sweetheart was also a crow, for birds of a feather flock together, and so crows pick crows.

"The newspapers came out right away with a border of hearts and the princess's signature. You could read that any young man who was attractive was welcome to come up to the castle and talk to the princess, and the one who talked well about what he knew, and spoke the best, would be the one the princess would marry!—Well, well," said the crow, "Believe you me, as sure as I'm sitting here, people came streaming to the castle. There was a rustling and bustling, but it was of no use, neither the first day nor the next. They could all speak well enough when they were out on the street, but when they entered the castle gates and saw the sentries in silver and lackeys in gold livery up the steps, and the big lighted rooms, they became disconcerted. And when they stood in front of the throne, where the princess sat, they couldn't say a thing except repeat what she had just said, and she didn't care to hear that again. It was as if people in there had eaten snuff and had fallen into a trance until they were out on the street where they could talk again. There was a row of them all the way from the city gates to the castle. I myself went in to have a look!" said the crow, "They were both hungry and thirsty, but they didn't even get a glass of lukewarm water from the castle. Some of the smarter ones had taken some sandwiches along, but they didn't share with their neighbors. They were thinking: 'Let him look hungry, then the princess won't pick him.'"

"But Kai? little Kai?" asked Gerda. "When did he come? Was he among the many?"

"Just wait, just wait. We'll get to him in a moment. It was on the third day, and a little person arrived without a horse or a wagon, quite confidently marching right up to the castle. His eyes shone like yours. He had lovely long hair, but his clothes were poor!"

"It was Kai!" rejoiced Gerda. "Oh, I have found him!" and she clapped her hands.

"He had a little knapsack on his back," said the crow.

"No, that must have been his sled," said Gerda, "because he went away with his sled."

"That could be," said the crow. "I didn't pay such close attention. But I have it from my tame sweetheart that when he came through the castle gates and saw the sentries in silver and the lackeys in gold up the steps, he wasn't the least bit dispirited. He nodded at them and said, 'It must be boring standing on the steps; I'll go inside.' Inside the rooms were shining with lights, and Privy Councilors and Excellencies walked in bare feet bearing gold platters—there was reason enough to feel solemn. His boots were creaking terribly loudly, but he still didn't become afraid!"

"It's certainly Kai," said Gerda. "I know he had new boots. I heard them creaking in grandmother's parlor."

"Well, they certainly creaked!" said the crow, "and he went dauntlessly in to present himself to the princess, who was sitting on a pearl as big as a spinning wheel. All the ladies-in-waiting with their maids and maids' maids and all the cavaliers with their servants and servants' servants, with their pages, were standing all around. And the closer they stood to the door, the prouder they were. The servants' servants' page, who always wears slippers, stood so proudly by the door that you almost couldn't look at him."

"That must be awful," said little Gerda, "but Kai actually got the princess?!"

"If I weren't a crow, I would have taken her, even though I am engaged. He is to have spoken as well as I do when I speak Crocawish, according to my tame sweetheart. He was confident and lovely. He had not come to propose, just to hear the wisdom of the princess, and he approved of it, and she approved of him too."

"Yes, of course it was Kai," said Gerda. "He's so smart he can

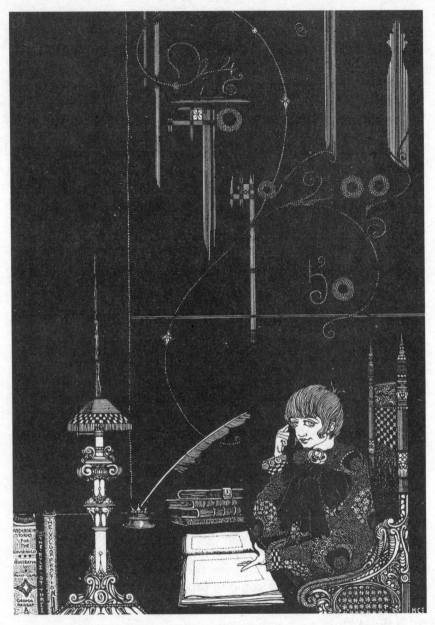

"He's so smart he can even do math with fractions in his head."

even do math with fractions in his head. Oh—won't you take me to the castle?"

"That's easier said than done," said the crow. "How would we do that? I'll talk to my tame sweetheart about it. She'll give us advice, but I must tell you that a little girl like you will never be allowed in there."

"Oh yes, I will," said Gerda. "When Kai hears I'm here, he'll come right out and get me."

"Wait for me by those steps over the fence," said the crow, who cocked his head and flew away.

Not until it was dark did the crow come back: "Caw caw," he said. "I bring many greetings from her, and here's a little bread for you. She took it from the kitchen. There's plenty there, and you must be hungry—it's not possible for you to enter the castle because you're barefoot. The sentries in silver and lackeys in gold would never allow it, but don't cry. You'll get up there anyway. My sweetheart knows a little back stairway that leads to the bedroom, and she knows where to take the key."

And they went into the garden, into a big avenue, where one leaf after another fell, and when the lights in the castle started going out, one after another, the crow led little Gerda to a back door that was standing ajar.

Oh, how Gerda's heart was pounding from fear and longing! She felt as if she were going to do something wicked, but she only wanted to know if it was little Kai. Oh yes, it had to be him! She could so vividly see his wise eyes, his long hair. She could really see how he smiled just like he had when they sat at home under the roses. He would surely be glad to see her and hear what a long way she had come for his sake, and know how sad they all were at home when he didn't come back. Oh, such fear and joy!

Then they were on the steps. There was a little lamp burning on a cupboard. In the middle of the floor stood the tame crow and cocked its head from side to side and observed Gerda, who curtsied as her grandmother had taught her.

"My fiancé has spoken very well of you, my little miss," said the tame crow. "Your *vita*, as it's called, is also very touching—

if you'll take the lamp, I'll lead the way. We'll go straight there. Then we won't meet anyone."

"I think there's someone coming behind us," said Gerda, and something roared past her. There were shadows on the walls, horses with flying manes and slender legs, hunters, and men and women riding.

"That's only the dreams," said the crow. "They come and take their Highnesses' thoughts along hunting. That's good because then you can see them better in bed. But be sure, if you get honor and favor, to show a thankful heart!"

"Well, that's nothing to talk about!" said the crow from the woods.

Then they entered the first room. There were pink satin walls with artificial flowers. Here the dreams were flying past them, but they went so fast that Gerda didn't see their Highnesses. One room was more magnificent than the next. You really could be stupefied! And then they were in the bedroom. The ceiling in there looked like a big palm with fronds of glass, expensive glass, and in the middle of the floor hung two beds on a thick stalk, and they looked like lilies. One was white, and in it lay the princess. The second was red, and that's where Gerda looked for little Kai. She bent one of the red leaves to the side and saw a brown neck.—Oh, it was Kai!—She called his name quite loudly, and held the lamp up to him—the dreams roared by on horses back to the hall again—he awoke, turned his head and—it was not little Kai.

The prince only resembled him in the neck, but he was young and handsome. And the princess peered out from the white lily bed and asked what was happening. Then little Gerda started crying and told her whole story, and everything that the crows had done for her.

"You poor little thing," said the prince and princess, and they praised the crows and said they weren't angry with them at all, but they shouldn't do it again. However, they would get a reward.

"Do you want to fly free?" asked the princess, "or do you want permanent positions as Court Crows with all the scraps in the kitchen?"

And both crows bowed and asked to have permanent positions because they were thinking of their old age and said, "It's better to have a bird in the hand than two in the bush," as they put it.

The prince got up from his bed and let Gerda sleep there, and he couldn't do more than that. She folded her small hands and thought, "How good people and animals are," and then she closed her eyes and slept so peacefully. All the dreams came flying in again, and they looked like God's angels, and they pulled a little sled, and Kai was sitting on it nodding; but it was all only dreams, and so it was all gone as soon as she awoke.

The next day she was dressed from top to toe in silk and velvet. She was invited to stay at the castle and have a good future, but she only asked for a little carriage with a horse and a pair of little boots. Then she would drive out in the wide world again to find Kai.

And she was given both boots and a muff. She was dressed beautifully, and when she was ready to leave, there was a new coach of pure gold waiting by the door. The prince and princess' coat of arms shone from it like a star. The coachman, servants, and outriders—for there were outriders too—were wearing gold crowns. The prince and princess helped her into the coach and wished her luck. The forest crow, who had gotten married, followed along the first three miles. He sat beside her because he couldn't stand driving backwards. The other crow stood at the gate and flapped her wings. She didn't come along because she suffered from a headache ever since she had gained a permanent position and too much to eat. Inside, the coach was lined with sugar pastries, and under the seats were fruits and peppernut cookies.

"Farewell, farewell," shouted the prince and princess, and little Gerda cried, and the crow cried—that's how the first miles went. Then the crow said good bye too, and that was the hardest parting. He flew up in a tree and flapped his black wings as long as he could see the coach, which shone like clear sunshine.

Fifth Story
The Little Robber Girl

They drove through the dark forest, but the coach shone like a flame, and it blinded the robbers so they couldn't stand it.

"It's gold! It's gold!" they yelled, rushed forward, seized the horses, killed the little outriders, the driver, and servants, and pulled little Gerda from the coach.

"She is plump. She is sweet. She's been fed on nut meats," said the old robber crone. She had a long, bristly beard and eyebrows that hung down over her eyes. "She's as good as a fat little lamb! Oh, she'll be tasty!" And then she pulled out her shiny knife that glittered so it was frightful.

"Ouch!" cried the crone just then. She had been bitten in the ear by her little daughter, who hung on her back, and who was so wild and naughty that it was a delight to watch her. "You loathsome brat!" said her mother, who didn't have time to butcher Gerda.

"She's going to play with me!" said the little robber girl. "She'll give me her muff and her lovely dress, and she'll sleep with me in my bed." And then she bit again so the robber woman jumped in the air and spun around, and all the robbers laughed and said, "See how she dances with her kid!"

"I want to get into the coach," said the little robber girl, and she must and would have her own way because she was so spoiled and stubborn. She and Gerda sat inside, and then they drove over stubble and thorns deeper into the forest. The little robber girl was as big as Gerda, but she was stronger, more broad-shouldered, and dark-skinned. Her eyes were quite black and looked almost sad. She put her arm around Gerda's waist and said, "They won't slaughter you as long as I don't get angry with you! I guess you're a princess?"

"No," said little Gerda, and told her everything she had experienced, and how much she cared about little Kai.

The robber girl looked quite seriously at her, nodded her head a little, and said, "They won't kill you, even if I get angry with you. I'll do it myself." Then she dried Gerda's eyes and

"She is plump. She is sweet. She's been fed on nut meats."

put both her hands into the beautiful muff that was so soft and warm.

The coach stopped. They were in the middle of the court-yard of a robber castle. It was cracked from top to bottom, and ravens and crows flew out of the open holes. Big vicious dogs that looked like they could each swallow a person leaped high in the air, but they didn't bark because that was forbidden.

In the big, old, sooty main room there was a great fire burn-ing in the middle of the stone floor. The smoke drifted up under the ceiling and had to find its own way out. Soup was boiling in a big kettle, and both hares and rabbits were on the spit.

"You'll sleep here with me tonight with all my little pets," said the robber girl. They had something to eat and drink and then went into a corner where straw and blankets were lying. Above them were almost a hundred pigeons, sitting on sticks and perches. They all seemed to be asleep, but they turned a bit when the little girls came.

"They're all mine!" said the little robber girl and quickly grabbed one of the closest birds. She held it by the legs and shook it so that it flapped its wings. "Kiss it!" she commanded and flapped it in Gerda's face. "These are the wood rascals," she continued and pointed behind a number of bars that were covering a hole high up on the wall. "They're wood rascals, those two. They fly right away if they aren't properly locked in. And here is my old sweetheart, Bae," and she pulled the horn of a reindeer. He had a shiny copper ring around his neck and was tied up. "We have to keep him tied up too, or he would run away from us. Every single evening I tickle his throat with my sharp knife. He's very afraid of it." And the little girl pulled a long knife from a crack in the wall, and let it glide across the reindeer's throat. The poor animal kicked his legs, and the robber girl laughed and pulled Gerda into the bed with her.

"You take the knife to bed with you?" asked Gerda and looked a bit anxiously at it.

"I always sleep with my knife," said the little robber girl. "You never know what might happen. But now, tell me again what you said before about little Kai, and why you went out into the wide world." And Gerda told the story from the beginning, and the wood pigeons cooed in their cage while the other pigeons slept. The little robber girl laid her arm across Gerda's neck, held the knife in her other hand, and slept so that you could hear it. But Gerda couldn't close her eyes at all. She didn't know whether she would live or die. The robbers sat around the fire singing and drinking, and the robber woman turned somersaults. Oh, it was just awful for the little girl to see!

Then the wood pigeons said, "Coo, coo! We've seen little Kai. A white hen was carrying his sled, and he was sitting in the Snow Queen's coach. It flew low over the forest as we were lying in our nest. She blew at us young ones, and all died except us two—coo, coo!"

"What's that you're saying up there?" called Gerda. "Where did the Snow Queen go? Do you know anything about that?"

"She probably went to Lapland because there's always snow and ice there. Ask the reindeer who's tied up with the rope."

"There's ice and snow there, and it's a good and blessed place," said the reindeer. "You can run freely around in the big bright valleys there. It's where the Snow Queen has her summer tent, but her permanent castle is up by the North Pole on the island called Spitsbergen."

"Oh Kai! Little Kai!" sighed Gerda.

"Lie quietly now," said the robber girl, "or you'll get the knife in your stomach!"

In the morning, Gerda told her everything the wood pigeons had said, and the little robber girl looked very serious, but nodded her head and said, "It doesn't matter. Never mind.—Do you know where Lapland is?" she asked the reindeer.

"Who would know better than me?" said the animal, and his eyes sparkled. "I was born and bred there, and I have run all over the snowy fields of Lapland."

"Listen," said the robber girl to Gerda, "you can see that all the men are gone. But mother is still here. She'll stay, but sometime during the morning she'll drink out of that big bottle and take a little nap. Then I'll do something for you." She jumped out of bed, threw her arms around her mother's neck, pulled at her beard, and said, "My own sweet billy goat, good morning!" And her mother pinched her nose so it turned red and blue, but all of it was done out of love.

When her mother had drunk from her bottle and was taking a little nap, the robber girl went to the reindeer and said, "It would give me the greatest pleasure to continue to tickle you many more times with my sharp knife because you're so much fun then, but it doesn't matter. I'm going to loosen your rope and help you outside so that you can run to Lapland, but don't let the grass grow under your feet. Take this little girl to the Snow Queen's castle where her playmate is. You've certainly heard what she told me because she spoke loudly enough, and you eavesdrop."

The reindeer leaped up in joy. The robber girl lifted Gerda onto the reindeer and took care to tie her fast, and even gave her a little pillow to sit on. "Never mind," she said, "here are your fleecy boots because it will be cold. But I'm keeping the muff. It's way too beautiful! But you won't freeze. Here are mother's big mittens. They'll reach all the way up to your elbows. Put them on!—Now your hands look just like my horrid mother's."

And Gerda wept for joy.

"I can't stand that wailing," said the little robber girl. "Now just be happy. And here are two breads and a ham for you, so you won't starve." Both of these were tied onto the reindeer's back. The little robber girl opened the door and coaxed the big dogs inside. Then she cut the rope with her knife and said to the reindeer, "Now run! But take good care of the little girl."

And Gerda stretched out her hands, with the big robber mittens on them, towards the robber girl and said good bye. The reindeer flew off over bushes and stubble through the big forest, over swamps and plains as fast as he could. The wolves howled, and the ravens shrieked. Sounds like "Soosh, Soosh" came from the sky as if it were sneezing redness.

"Those are my old northern lights," said the reindeer. "See how they shine!" He ran even faster, night and day. The breads were eaten—the ham too—and then they were in Lapland.

SIXTH STORY
THE SAMI WOMAN AND THE FINN WOMAN

They stopped at a little house. It was so pitiful. The roof reached down to the ground, and the door was so low that the family had to creep on their stomachs when they wanted to go in or out. There was no one home except an old Sami woman, who was frying fish over an oil lamp. The reindeer told Gerda's entire story, but first his own because he thought that was much more important, and Gerda was so frozen from cold that she couldn't talk.

"Oh, you poor things!" said the Sami woman. "You still have a long way to go. You'll have to go over a hundred miles into Finnmark because that's where the Snow Queen is now, and she burns northern lights every night. I'll write a few words on a dried cod—I don't have any paper—for you to take to the Finn woman up there. She can give you better information than I can."

And after Gerda had warmed up and had had something to eat and drink, the Sami woman wrote a few words on a dried cod and told Gerda to take good care of it. Then she tied Gerda firmly on the reindeer's back again, and off it sprang. "Soosh, soosh" came from the air, and all night the most beautiful blue northern lights shone. They came to Finnmark and knocked on the Finn woman's chimney because she didn't even have a door.

It was so hot in there that the Finn woman herself had almost no clothes on. She was little and had quite muddy skin. She loosened Gerda's clothing right away and took her mittens and boots off; otherwise she would have been too hot. She laid a piece of ice on the reindeer's head and then read what was written on the dried cod. She read it three times so she knew it by heart and then put the fish in the kettle, for it could certainly be eaten, and she never wasted anything.

The reindeer told his story first and then little Gerda's, and the Finn woman blinked with her wise eyes, but didn't say anything.

"You are so wise," said the reindeer, "I know you can tie the

winds of the world with a thread. When the captain unties the
first knot, he gets a good wind. When he unties the second, it
blows stiffly, and if he unties the third and fourth, it will storm
so trees blow down. Won't you give the little girl a drink so she
can gain the strength of twelve men and conquer the Snow
Queen?"[2]

"The strength of twelve men," said the Finn woman, "yes,
that should help!" She went to a shelf and took down a large
rolled-up hide and spread it out. There were remarkable letters written on it, and the Finn woman read so intently that
sweat poured from her forehead.

But the reindeer begged again for little Gerda, and Gerda
looked pleadingly at the Finn woman with her eyes full of tears
so that the woman started blinking her eyes again and drew
the reindeer into a corner. She whispered to him while he got
a fresh piece of ice on his head:

"Little Kai is with the Snow Queen and finds everything to
his liking. He thinks it's the best place in the world, but that's
because he has gotten a splinter in his heart and a little chip of
glass in his eye. They have to come out first, or he'll never become human again, and the Snow Queen will keep her power
over him."

"But can't you give little Gerda something to take so she can
gain power over all of it?"

"I can't give her greater power than she already has. Can't
you see how great it is? Don't you see how people and animals
must serve her, how she has come so far in the world, even
barefoot? We can't tell her of this power; it's in her heart. It's
because she is a sweet innocent child. If she can't reach the
Snow Queen by herself and get the glass splinters out of little
Kai, we can't help. The Snow Queen's garden starts two miles
from here. Carry the little girl in there and let her off by the
big bush with red berries standing in the snow. Don't waste
time gossiping, but hurry back here." And the Finn woman
lifted Gerda onto the reindeer, and he ran off as fast as he
could.

"Oh, I forgot my boots! I forgot my mittens!" called the little girl who noticed this in the biting cold. But the reindeer

didn't dare stop. It ran until it came to the bush with the red berries. There he let Gerda off and kissed her on the lips. Big bright tears ran down the animal's cheeks, and then it ran back as fast as it could. Poor Gerda was standing there without shoes, without gloves, in the middle of terrible ice-cold Finnmark.

She ran ahead as fast as she could. Then a whole regiment of snowflakes appeared. But these didn't fall from the sky, which was quite clear and shining with northern lights. The snowflakes ran along the ground, and the closer they came, the bigger they got. Gerda certainly remembered how big and odd they had looked the time she saw the snowflakes through the magnifying glass, but here they were certainly much bigger and more terrible. They were alive—they were the Snow Queen's sentries. They had the strangest shapes. Some looked like large nasty porcupines, others like big bunches of snakes with their heads sticking out, still others like small fat bears with their hair bristling. All of them were shining white, and all of them were living snowflakes.

Then little Gerda said the Lord's Prayer, and the cold was so intense that she could see her own breath. It came out of her mouth like smoke. It became more and more condensed and formed into small bright angels. They grew and grew when they touched the ground, and all of them had helmets on their heads and spears and shields in their hands. They became more and more numerous, and when Gerda had finished her prayer, she had a whole legion around her. They struck with their spears at the dreadful snowflakes so that they broke into a hundred pieces, and little Gerda walked safely and confidently forward. The angels patted her feet and hands so she didn't feel the cold as much, and she walked quickly towards the Snow Queen's castle.

But now we should see how Kai is doing. He certainly wasn't thinking about little Gerda, and least of all that she was standing outside the castle.

SEVENTH STORY
WHAT HAPPENED IN THE SNOW QUEEN'S CASTLE
AND WHAT HAPPENED LATER

The castle's walls were made of drifting snow, and the windows and doors of cutting winds. There were over a hundred rooms, depending on how the snow drifted. The largest stretched for many miles, and they were all illuminated by the northern lights. They were so vast, so empty, so icy cold, and so dazzling. There was never any gaiety here, not even so much as a little bear ball where the storm could blow, and the polar bears could walk on their hind legs and show their fine manners. Never a little party game with snout slapping and paw clapping. Never a little coffee klatch for the white fox maidens. The Snow Queen's rooms were empty, vast, and cold. The northern lights shone so regularly that you could calculate when they would be at their highest and when at their lowest. Right in the middle of the empty unending hall of snow was a frozen lake. It was cracked in a thousand pieces, but each piece was exactly alike so it was a work of art, and in the middle of this is where the Snow Queen sat when she was at home. And she said that she sat on the mirror of reason, and that it was the world's only and best one.

Little Kai was quite blue from cold, actually almost black, but he didn't notice it because the Snow Queen had kissed the icy shivers from him, and his heart was practically an ice clump. He was carrying around some sharp, flat pieces of ice which he positioned in all sorts of ways, trying to make something out of it. It's like when the rest of us use little wooden pieces and make figures from them. It's called a tangram. Kai was also making figures and very complicated ones. It was the game of Icy Reason. To his eyes the figures were quite excellent and of the very highest importance. That was because of the bit of glass in his eye! He made whole figures that composed a written word, but he could never write the one word that he wanted: eternity. The Snow Queen had told him, "If you can figure out that design for me, you'll be your own mas-

ter, and I'll give you the whole world and a new pair of skates."
But he couldn't do it.

"Now I'm off to the warm countries," said the Snow Queen.
"I want to go there and peek into the black pots!" She meant
the fire-sprouting volcanoes Etna and Vesuvius as we call them.
"I'm going to whiten them up a bit! They need it, and it looks
good on the lemons and grapes." And the Snow Queen flew
away, and Kai sat quite alone in the many-mile long empty ice
hall and looked at the ice pieces and thought and thought
until his brain creaked. He sat quite stiff and still. You would
think he had frozen to death.

And it was then that little Gerda walked into the castle
through the big portal that was filled with biting winds. But she
said an evening prayer, and the winds died down as though
they wanted to go to sleep. She walked into the vast, empty,
cold hall and saw Kai. She recognized him, and threw her arms
around his neck. She held him tight and called, "Kai! sweet little Kai! Now I've found you!"

But he sat completely still, stiff and cold. Little Gerda
started crying hot tears. They fell on Kai's chest and pressed
into his heart where they melted the clump of ice and consumed the little bit of mirror in there. He looked at her, and
she sang the hymn:

> *"Roses in the valley grow*
> *And baby Jesus there we know"*

Then Kai burst into tears. He cried so that the splinter of
glass washed out of his eye. He recognized her and cried joy-
fully, "Gerda! sweet little Gerda! Where have you been so long?
And where have I been?" He looked around. "How cold it is
here! How big and empty it is!" and he held Gerda tight. She
laughed and cried for joy. It was so wonderful that even the
pieces of ice danced with joy all around them, and when they
were tired and lay down, they lay precisely in those letters that
the Snow Queen had said he should find. So now he was his
own master, and she would give him the whole world and a
new pair of skates.

As Gerda kissed his cheeks, they flushed. She kissed his eyes, and they lit up like hers. She kissed his hands and feet, and he was hale and hearty. The Snow Queen could return. His release was written there in shining pieces of ice.

And they held hands and walked out of the big castle. They talked about Grandmother and about the roses up on the roof. And wherever they walked, the winds were still, and the sun came out, and when they reached the bush with the red berries, the reindeer was waiting. He had another young reindeer with him, whose udder was full and she gave the little ones her warm milk and kissed them on the lips. Then they carried Kai and Gerda first to the Finn woman, where they warmed up in the hot room and got information about the trip home, then to the Sami woman who had sewn new clothes for them and who had prepared her sleigh.

The reindeer and the young reindeer ran along side and followed them to the border of the country. There where the first green appeared on the ground they parted from the reindeer and the Sami woman. "Farewell," they all said. And the first little birds started chirping. There were green buds on the trees, and riding out of the trees came a magnificent horse that Gerda recognized, for it had pulled the gold coach, and on this horse was a young girl with a shining red cap on her head and pistols in front. It was the little robber girl, who was bored with being at home and wanted to travel first north and then to other quarters if she wasn't satisfied. She recognized Gerda right away, and Gerda recognized her. What a joy it was!

"You're a fine fellow for trudging about!" she said to little Kai. "I wonder if you deserve having someone run to the ends of the earth for your sake!"

But Gerda patted her on the cheek and asked about the prince and princess.

"They're traveling abroad," said the robber girl.

"And the crow?" asked little Gerda.

"Well, the crow is dead," she answered. "The tame sweetheart has become a widow and walks around with a piece of black yarn around her leg. She complains pathetically, but it's all nonsense! But tell me how it went and how you found him!"

So both Gerda and Kai told their stories.

"All's well that end's well," said the robber girl, took them both by the hand and promised that if she ever came by their city she would look them up, and then she rode off into the wide world. But Kai and Gerda walked hand in hand. They walked through a lovely springtime, and there were flowers, and it was green. The church bells rang, and they recognized the high towers of the big city. It was the one they lived in, and they entered it and went to Grandmother's door, up the stairs, into the living room, where everything was in the same place as before, and the clock said "tick, tock" as the hand turned. But as they went through the door, they noticed that they were grown up. The roses from the roof gutter were blooming inside the open windows, and there stood the small children's chairs. Kai and Gerda each sat down on theirs and held hands. They had forgotten like a heavy dream the cold empty magnificence of the Snow Queen's castle. Grandmother was sitting in God's clear sunshine reading aloud from the Bible: "Verily I say unto you, except ye become as little children, ye shall not enter the kingdom of heaven."

And Kai and Gerda looked into each other's eyes and understood at once the old hymn:

> *"Roses in the valley grow*
> *And baby Jesus there we know"*

And there they both sat, grown up and yet children—children in their hearts—and it was summer, the warm blessed summer.

NOTES

1. From the hymn "Den yndigste Rose er funden" (1732; "Now Found Is the Fairest of Roses"), by H. A. Brorson.
2. The Finns were thought to possess magic powers. Andersen took his information about the Sami from a book by B. M. Keilhau, *Reise i Øst- og Vest-Finnmarken samt til Beeren-Eiland og Spitsbergen i Aarene 1827 og 1828* (1831; *Travels in East and West Finnmark, Bear Island, and Spitsbergen in the years 1827 and 1828*). The Sami are the indigenous people of northern Scandinavia.

THE RED SHOES

ONCE THERE WAS A little girl who was so delicate and lovely, but in the summer she always went barefoot because she was poor. In the winter she wore big wooden shoes, and her little insteps turned so red that it was terrible.

In the middle of the village there lived an old shoemaker's widow. She sewed a pair of little shoes out of old, red strips of cloth as best she could. They were quite awkwardly made, but she meant well, and they were made for the little girl. The little girl's name was Karen.

The very day her mother was buried, she received the red shoes and wore them for the first time. They weren't exactly appropriate for mourning, but she didn't have any others, and so she walked behind the poor straw coffin in the red shoes without stockings.

Just then a large, old coach came by and in it sat a large, old woman. She looked at the little girl and felt sorry for her so she said to the parson, "Listen, let me take that little girl. I'll be good to her."

And Karen thought it was because of the red shoes, but the old woman said they were awful, and they were burned. Karen herself was dressed in neat, clean clothes. She had to learn to read and sew, and people said that she was pretty. But the mirror said, "You're much more than pretty—you're beautiful!"

One day the queen was traveling through the country, and she had her little daughter, the princess, with her. People streamed to the castle—Karen too—to see the little princess standing in lovely white clothes in a window being admired. She was wearing neither a train nor a gold crown, but had lovely red leather shoes on. Of course, they were altogether nicer than the shoes the old shoemaker had sewed for Karen. Yes, nothing in the world can compare to red shoes!

Now Karen was old enough to be confirmed. She had gotten new clothes, and she was also to have new shoes. The rich shoemaker in town measured her little foot. This was in his own house, where there were big glass cases full of elegant shoes and shiny boots. They were lovely, but the old woman couldn't see very well so she got no pleasure from them. Among the shoes was a pair of red ones, just like those the princess had worn. How splendid they were! The shoemaker said they had been made for a count's daughter, but had not fit.

"They must be patent leather," said the old woman, "they're shiny."

"Yes, they are shiny," said Karen, and they fit and were bought, but the old woman didn't know they were red. She would never have allowed Karen to wear red shoes for Confirmation, but that is what she did.

Everyone looked at her feet, and as she walked up the church aisle towards the chancel, it seemed to her that even the old pictures on the tombs, the portraits of ministers and their wives with stiff collars and long black garments, looked at her red shoes. When the minister laid his hand on her head and talked about holy baptism, the covenant with God, and that she was now to be a true Christian, all she thought about was the red shoes. The organ played so solemnly, beautiful children's voices sang, and the old cantor sang too, but Karen thought only about the red shoes.

By afternoon the old woman had been told by everyone that the shoes were red, and she said that that was indecent and improper. She told Karen that in the future she should always wear black shoes to church, even if they were old.

The next Sunday there was communion, and Karen looked at the black shoes and looked at the red ones—and then she looked at the red ones again and put them on.

It was a beautiful sunny day. Karen and the old woman took the path through the cornfield, and it was a little dusty. There was an old soldier with a crutch standing by the church door. He had a strange long beard that was more red than white, in fact it was red, and he bowed way down to the ground and asked the old woman if he could wipe off her shoes. And Karen also stretched out her little foot. "My, what lovely dancing shoes," said the soldier, "Stick tight when you dance!" and then he tapped the soles with his hand.

The old woman gave the soldier a coin, and then she and Karen went into the church.

And all the people there looked at Karen's red shoes, and all the pictures looked at them, and when Karen knelt at the altar and put the gold chalice to her lips, she thought only about the red shoes, and it was as if they were swimming in the chalice in front of her. She forgot to sing the hymns, and she forgot to say the Lord's Prayer.

Then all the people left the church, and the old woman climbed into her coach. Karen lifted her foot to follow behind her, but the old soldier, who was standing nearby, said, "What lovely dancing shoes!" And Karen couldn't help herself; she had to do a few dance steps, and once she started her legs kept dancing. It was as if the shoes had power over them. She danced around the corner of the church. She couldn't stop. The coachman had to run after her and grab her, and he lifted her into the coach, but her feet kept on dancing so that she kicked the good old woman horribly. Finally they got the shoes off, and her legs stopped moving.

At home the shoes were put away in a cupboard, but Karen couldn't help looking at them.

Then one day the old woman became ill. They said she wouldn't live long. She needed to be cared for and watched over, and no one was better suited to do this than Karen, but in town there was a great ball and Karen had been invited. She looked at the old woman, who couldn't live anyway, and she looked at the red shoes and there wasn't any harm in that. She put on the red shoes, and she certainly could do that too—but then she went to the dance and started dancing.

But when she wanted to go right, the shoes danced to the left, and when she wanted to dance up the floor, the shoes danced down—down the stairs and through the streets and out the gates of the town. Dance she did and dance she must, way out into the dark woods.

There was something shining up in the trees, and she thought it was the moon, because it was a face. But it was the old soldier with the red beard. He nodded and said, "What lovely dancing shoes!"

Then she got scared and wanted to throw the red shoes away, but they stuck fast, and she flung off her stockings but the shoes had grown onto her feet. Dance she did and dance she must, over fields and meadows, in rain and in sunshine, night and day, but it was worst at night.

She danced into the open churchyard, but the dead weren't dancing there. They had much better things to do than dance. She wanted to sit down on the grave of the poor where the bitter tansy grew, but there was neither rest nor repose for her, and when she danced towards the open church door, she saw an angel there with long white robes and wings that stretched from his shoulders to the ground. His face was stern and serious, and in his hand he held a sword, broad and shining.

"Dance you shall!" he said, "dance in your red shoes until you are pale and cold! Until your skin shrinks together like a skeleton. Dance you shall from door to door and wherever proud and vain children live, you are to knock at the door so that they hear you and fear you! Dance you shall, dance—!"

"Mercy!" cried Karen. But she didn't hear what the angel answered because the shoes carried her through the gate, out to the fields, over roads and paths, and she had no choice but to dance.

One morning she danced past a door she knew well. There was the sound of hymn singing from inside, and they carried out a coffin decorated with flowers. Then she knew that the old woman was dead, and she believed that now she was deserted by everyone and cursed by God's angel.

Dance she did and dance she must, dance in the dark night. The shoes carried her away over thorns and stubble that scratched her until she bled. She danced over the heath until she came to a lonely little cottage. She knew that the executioner lived there, and she tapped on the window with her fingers and said:

"Come out! Come out!—I can't come inside because I'm dancing."

And the executioner said, "Maybe you don't know who I am? I chop heads off evil people, and I notice that my axe is vibrating!"

"Don't chop my head off!" said Karen, "because then I can't repent my sin. But chop off my feet along with the red shoes."

And then she confessed all her sins, and the executioner chopped off her feet along with the red shoes, but the shoes with the small feet in them danced away over the meadow into the deep forest.

Then he whittled wooden legs and crutches for her, taught her a hymn that sinners always sing, and she kissed the hand that had guided the axe and went on across the heath.

"Now I have suffered enough for the red shoes," she said. "I'll go to the church so everyone can see me." And she walked quite quickly towards the church door, but when she got there, the red shoes were dancing in front of her, and she became terrified and turned around.

All week long she was sad and cried many heavy tears, but when Sunday came she said, "Surely now I have suffered and struggled enough. I should think that I am just as good as many of those who sit and hold their heads high in church." And she walked quite bravely, but she didn't get further than the gate when she saw the red shoes dancing in front of her. She was terrified, turned around, and regretted her sins with all her heart.

Then she went to the parsonage and asked if she could work there. She would be diligent and do everything she could. She didn't care about the salary, she just wanted a roof over her head and to be with good people. And the minister's wife felt sorry for her and gave her a job. And she was diligent and thoughtful. She sat still and listened in the evenings when the minister read aloud from the Bible. All of the little children liked her very much, but when they talked about finery and frills and about being as beautiful as a queen, she shook her head.

The following Sunday they all went to church, and they asked her if she wanted to go along, but with tears in her eyes she looked sadly at her crutches, and so the others went to hear God's word while she went alone into her little room. It was only big enough for a bed and a chair and she sat there with her hymnal, and as she read it with a pious spirit, the wind carried the organ music from the church to her, and she lifted her face with tears in her eyes and said, "Oh, God help me!"

Then the sun shone brightly and right in front of her stood God's angel in the white robes, the one she had seen that night in the church door. But now he wasn't holding the sharp sword, but rather a lovely green branch that was full of roses. He touched the ceiling with it, and it rose up so high and where he had touched there was a golden star shining. Then he touched the walls and they extended, and she saw the organ, which was playing. She saw the old pictures with ministers and their wives. The congregation was sitting in the decorated pews, singing in their hymnals. The church itself had come home to the poor girl in the narrow little room, or maybe she had come to the church. She sat in the pews with the others from the parsonage, and when they had finished the hymn and looked up, they nodded and said, "It's good you came, Karen!"

"It was grace," she said.

And the organ sounded, and the children's voices in the choir sang so softly and beautifully! The clear sunshine streamed so warmly through the window into the church pew where Karen sat. Her heart grew so full of sunshine, peace, and joy that it burst. Her soul flew on the sunshine up to God, and there was no one there who asked about the red shoes.

THE LITTLE MATCH GIRL

IT WAS SO AWFULLY cold. It was snowing, and it was beginning to get dark. And it was New Year's Eve, the last evening of the year. In this cold and darkness a poor little girl came walking down the street. She was both barefoot and bareheaded. She had been wearing slippers when she left home, but it hadn't helped. They were very big slippers, used last by her mother. They were so big that the little girl lost them when she hurried across the street as two coaches rushed swiftly by. She couldn't find the one slipper, and a boy ran off with the other.

He said that he could use it for a cradle when he had children of his own.

The little girl walked along on her naked little feet that were red and blue from cold. In an old apron she had a bundle of matches, and she was carrying a bunch in her hand. No one had bought any the whole day, and no one had given her so much as a shilling. She walked, hungry and frozen, and looked so dejected, poor little thing! Flakes of snow fell on her long yellow hair that curled so lovely around her neck, but she wasn't thinking about her appearance. Lights shone out from all the windows, and there was such a lovely smell of roasted goose in the street. It was New Year's Eve, after all, and that's what she was thinking about.

In a corner between two houses, one stuck out into the street a little further than the other, she sat down and huddled up. She had drawn her little legs up under herself, but she was still freezing more and more, and she didn't dare go home since she hadn't sold any matches, hadn't earned a single shilling. Her father would hit her, and it was also cold at home. They had only a roof over their heads, and the wind blew through, even though the biggest cracks were stuffed with straw and rags. Her small hands were almost dead with cold. Oh, a little match could do a lot of good! If she only dared pull one from the bundle, strike it against the wall, and warm her fingers. She pulled one out, "ritsch!" How it sparked! How it burned! It was a warm, clear flame, like a little candle when she held her hand around it. But it was a strange light! It seemed to the little girl that she sat in front of a big iron stove with shiny brass knobs and brass fixtures. The fire burned so blessedly, warmed so well. But what's this? The little one had already stretched her feet out to warm them too when the flame went out. The stove disappeared. She sat with a little stump of burned out match in her hand.

Another one was struck, it burned and sparkled, and where the light fell on the wall, the wall became transparent like a veil. She could look right into the living room where the table was set with a glossy white tablecloth, fine porcelain, and a splendid steaming roast goose, filled with prunes and apples!

It shone all around, and her old grandmother appeared in the glow.

And what was even more marvelous: the goose sprang from the platter, waddled across the floor with the fork and knife in its back, right over to the poor girl. Then the match went out, and she could only see the thick cold wall.

She lit another one. Then she was sitting under the most beautiful Christmas tree. It was even bigger and better decorated than the one she had seen through the glass door of the rich merchant this past Christmas. Thousands of candles burned on the green branches, and colorful pictures, like those that graced store windows, looked down at her. The little girl reached both arms into the air—then the match went out. The many Christmas candles rose higher and higher. She could see that now they were the clear stars. One of them fell and made a long streak of fire in the sky.

"Now someone is dying!" said the little girl because her old grandmother, who was the only person who had been good to her but was now dead, had told her that whenever a star falls, a soul rises to God.

She struck another match against the brick wall. It shone all around, and her old grandmother appeared in the glow, so clear, shining, so gentle and kind.

"Grandma!" shouted the little one. "Oh, take me with you! I know you'll be gone when the match goes out. Gone like the warm stove, the lovely roast goose, and the great splendid Christmas tree." And quickly she struck the whole bundle of matches that were left. She wanted to keep grandmother there. The matches shone with such splendor that it was lighter than bright daylight. Grandmother had never been so tall and beautiful before. She lifted the little girl into her arms, and they flew in joy and glory—so high, so high. There was no cold, no hunger, no fear—they were with God!

In the corner by the house in the cold morning light the little girl was sitting with red cheeks and a smile on her lips—dead, frozen to death on the last evening of the old year. New Year's Day dawned on the little corpse, sitting with her matches, almost all burned up. She had tried to warm herself, they said. No one knew the beauty she had seen, and in what radiance she with her old grandmother had gone into the joy of the New Year.

THE BOG KING'S DAUGHTER

THE STORKS TELL THEIR young so many fairy tales, all from the bog and the marsh. They usually adapt the stories to age and apprehension. The youngest ones are satisfied if they say, "cribble crabble paddle waddle," which they think is super. But the older ones want a deeper meaning, or at least something about the family. We all know one of the two oldest and longest stories that the storks have preserved—the one about Moses who was placed in the waters of the Nile by his mother. He was found by a princess, given a good upbringing, and became a great man even though we don't know where he's buried. That's a well-known story!

The other story is not well known, maybe because it's more a domestic story. This story has been passed from stork mother to stork mother for a thousand years, and each of them has told it better and better. And now we shall tell it best of all.

The first stork couple who experienced it and told about it had their summer home on a Viking log house by *Vildmosen* in *Vendsyssel.* That's a great bog in Hjørring County, close to Skagen in Jutland, if we are to give a precise description. It's still an enormously big bog. You can read about it in the Hjørring county description. It was once a sea bottom, but it heaved itself up. It stretches for miles in all directions, surrounded by damp meadows and ponds, peat bogs, cloudberry plants, and stunted trees. There's almost always a fog hovering over the bogs, and seventy years ago there were still wolves there. It really deserves its name, "Wild Bog," and you can imagine how wild it was, how much bog and water there were a thousand years ago! But for the most part, you saw the same things then that you see now. The reeds are the same height and had the same long leaves and purplish brown feathery flowers that they have now. The birch stood there with white bark and its fine airy leaves as it does now, and as far as living things that came there are concerned—well, the fly carried the same cut to his black funereal outfit as he does now, and the stork's colors were white with black and red stockings. In contrast, the people had a different cut to their clothes then than now, but it happened the same for all of them, peasant or hunter—everyone—who walked onto the quagmire a thousand years ago, as it does today. They fell through and sank down to the bog king, as they called him, who rules in the great bog kingdom. You could also call him the swamp king, but we think it's better to say bog king. And the storks called him that too. Very little is known about his reign, but that's probably for the best.

Close to the bog, right by the Lim fjord, lay the Viking's log house with a cellar of stone, a tower, and three floors of logs. The storks had built their nest at the top of the roof. The mother stork was lying on her eggs and was certain that all would go well.

One evening stork father was out later than usual, and when he came home, he looked ruffled and uneasy.

"I have something quite terrible to tell you," he said to mother stork.

"Don't do it!" she said. "Remember that I'm brooding. I could take injury from it, and that would affect the eggs."

"You have to know about it," he said. "The daughter of our host in Egypt has come up here. She dared to make the trip, and she has disappeared!"

"The one who's related to the fairies? Oh, tell me! You know that I can't stand being kept waiting when I'm brooding."

"You see, mother, she came to believe what the doctor said, like you told me. She believes that the white water lilies here might help her sick father, and she flew here in swan-skin with the two other swan-skin princesses, who fly up here every year to bathe and be rejuvenated. She came, and she is gone!"

"You're so long-winded," said stork mother. "The eggs can catch cold! I can't stand being kept in suspense!"

"I keep alert, you know," said stork father, "and this evening, as I was walking in the reeds where the swamp can support me, three swans came flying. There was something about the flying style that told me: pay attention—these are not really swans—

they are just swan-skins! You have a feeling about it, mother. Like me, you know what is real!"

"Of course," she said, "but tell me about the princess. I am tired of hearing about swan-skins."

"Well, here in the middle of the bog, you know, it's like a lake," said stork father. "You can see a little of it if you get up. By the reeds and the green quagmire there's a big alder stump. The three swans landed on that, flapped their wings, and looked around. One of them threw off her swan-shape, and I recognized the princess of our house in Egypt. She sat with no other cape than her long black hair. I heard her ask the other two to take good care of the swan-skin while she dove under the water to pick the flower she thought she saw. They nodded and then rose up and took along the empty swan-skin. 'I wonder what they are going to do with that,' I thought, and she must have asked them the same thing because she got an answer, right in front of her eyes. They flew up in the air with her swan-skin. 'Dive down,' they shouted, 'you'll never fly in swan-skin again, never see Egypt! Stay in the wild bog!' and then they tore her swan-skin in hundreds of pieces so that the feathers were flying everywhere like in a snow storm. And the two wretched princesses flew away."

"That's ghastly!" said stork mother. "I can't stand hearing about it—tell me what happened next!"

"The princess moaned and cried! The tears rolled down onto the alder stump, and then it moved—because it was the bog king himself! The one who lives in the bog. I saw how the stump turned, and then it wasn't a stump any longer. Two long mossy branches reached up, like arms. The poor child was frightened and ran away into the quivering quagmire, but the bog can't bear me, much less her, and so she sank right down. The alder trunk sank with her, for it was he who was pulling her down. Big black bubbles rose, and then there was no trace left. Now she is buried in the wild bog. She'll never bring the flower back to Egypt. Oh, you wouldn't have been able to stand the sight of this, mother!"

"You shouldn't tell me things like this at such a time! It can affect the eggs. The princess will take care of herself, I'm sure.

I suppose some one will help her. Now if it had been you or me, or one of ours, it would have been all over!"

"Well, I'll keep a close eye on it," said stork father, and he did.

And a long time passed.

Then one day he saw a green stalk shoot up deep from the bottom, and when it reached up to the surface of the water, a leaf grew out, wider and still wider. Close by there was a bud, and when the stork flew over it one morning, it opened in the strong rays of the sun, and right in the middle of it lay a lovely child, a little girl. She looked as if she had just gotten out of her bath. She resembled the princess from Egypt so much that at first the stork thought it was her, who had become little again. But when he thought about it, he realized it was more likely that she was the child of the princess and the bog king. That's why she was lying in a water lily.

"She can't remain lying there," thought the stork, "and there are already so many of us in my nest. But I have an idea! The Viking's wife doesn't have any children, but she wishes she had a little one. Since they say I bring the little ones, I might as well do it for once! I'll take the child to the Viking woman. That will make her happy."

And the stork took the little girl and flew to the log house. He pecked a hole with his beak in the pig bladder window, laid the child at the Viking woman's breast, and flew home to stork mother and told her about it. Indeed the children listened too, for they were old enough to hear it.

"You see, the princess isn't dead. She has sent the little one up here, and I've placed her."

"It's what I said from the beginning," said stork mother. "Now think a little bit about your own! It's almost time to travel. Every now and then I feel a tickle in my wings. The cuckoo and the nightingale have already left, and I heard the quails saying that we will soon have a good tail wind. Our kids will manage the maneuvers just fine, if I know them."

Well, how happy the Viking woman was when she woke up in the morning and found the lovely little child at her breast! She kissed and patted it, but the child cried terribly and flailed her arms and legs. She didn't seem at all happy. Finally she cried herself to sleep, and the sight of the sleeping child was the most beautiful thing you could imagine. The Viking woman was so happy and light-hearted, and it occurred to her that now perhaps her husband with all his men would return just as unexpectedly as the child had come. So she and the others got busy to have everything ready. They hung up the long, colored tapestries that the woman and her maids had woven themselves with the representations of their idols: Odin, Thor, and Freya. The slaves had to scrub the old shields that decorated the walls. Cushions were placed on the benches and dry firewood piled in the fireplace in the middle of the hall so the fire could quickly be lit. The Viking woman worked too so that in the evening she was very tired and slept well.

When she woke up towards morning, she was totally aghast because the little child was gone. She leapt up, lit a pine tar torch, and looked around. There, lying by her feet when she stretched them out in bed, lay not the little child, but a big hideous frog. She was disgusted, took a big pole, and was going to kill the frog, but it looked at her with such strange sad eyes that she couldn't do it. Once again she looked around. The frog uttered a faint, pitiful croak. The woman gave a start and sprang from the bed over to the shutter and opened it. The sun came out at the same time and cast its rays right into the bed onto the big frog, and all at once it was as if the beast's wide mouth pulled together and became little and red. The limbs stretched out and turned into small, lovely shapes. It was her own lovely little child lying there, and not an ugly frog.

"What's this?" she said. "Have I dreamed a bad dream? It's my own lovely fairy child lying there!" And she kissed it and pressed it to her breast, but it scratched and bit and acted like a wild kitten.

The Viking didn't come home that day or the next, although he was on his way. The wind was against him, and blew towards the south for the sake of the storks. A tail wind for one is head wind for another.

After a few days and nights it was clear to the Viking woman what was happening with her little child. The child was bewitched. During the day it was as lovely as a fairy but had an evil, wild disposition. At night, in contrast, it was an ugly frog, quiet and whimpering, with sorrowful eyes. There were two natures that shifted back and forth, both internally and externally. It was because the little girl that the stork had brought had her mother's exterior during the day combined with her father's disposition. At night she resembled her father in her bodily shape, but her mother's mind and heart were evident within. Who could break this black magic spell? The Viking woman was sad and worried about it, but she still loved the poor little creature, whose condition she didn't dare tell her husband about. Now that he would soon be home, he would undoubtedly, as the custom was, lay the child outside on the highway to be taken by whomever wanted it. The kind woman didn't want that to happen and decided that her husband should only see the child by daylight.

One morning the whistling of stork wings was heard over the roof. More than a hundred stork couples had rested there that night after the big maneuvers. Now they flew upwards to start heading south.

"Everyone ready!" came the shout. "Wives and children too!"

"I'm so light," said one of the young storks. "There's crawling and creeping way out in my legs as if they were full of living frogs. Oh, how lovely it is to be traveling abroad!"

"Stay with the flock," said father and mother, "and don't chatter too much, it saps your breathing."

And they flew off.

At the very same moment a horn was heard across the heath. The Viking had landed with all his men. They turned towards home with rich booty from the Gallic coast, where the people, like in Wales, prayed in their fright:

"From the fury of the Northmen, O Lord, deliver us!"[1]

Now what life and merriment there was in the Viking house by the wild bog! The mead vat was brought into the hall. The fire was lit, and horses were slaughtered. This was going to be

They turned towards home with rich booty from the Gallic coast.

a real feast! The sacrificial priest sprayed the horse blood on the slaves as a consecration. The fire crackled, the smoke drifted up to the ceiling, and soot dripped from the beams, but they were used to that. Guests were invited, and they received good gifts. Intrigues and deceitfulness were forgotten. They drank and threw gnawed bones in each other's faces—that was a sign of being in a good mood. The skald—he was a kind of musician who was also a warrior—had been with them and knew what he was singing about. He sang a ballad in which they heard all about their heroic deeds and remarkable events in battle. After each stanza he sang the same refrain:

> *"Cattle die, kinsmen die,*
> *one day you die yourself;*
> *I know one thing that never dies—*
> *the dead man's reputation."*[2]

And then they all pounded on their shields and hammered with their knives or bones on the table. They made a lot of noise.

The Viking woman sat on the cross-bench in the open banquet hall. She was wearing a silk dress and gold arm-rings and big amber beads. She was wearing her best clothes, and the skald also mentioned her in his song. He talked about the golden treasure she had brought her rich husband. And the Viking was truly fond of the lovely child. He had only seen it in daylight, but he liked her wild disposition. He said that she could become a formidable valkyrie who would conquer a warrior. Her eyes wouldn't blink when a practiced hand, in jest, cut off her eyebrows with a sharp sword.

The mead vat was emptied, and a new one brought in. They drank copiously. They were people who could hold their liquor. In those days the saying was: "The herds know when it's time to go home and give up grazing, but a foolish man will always forget the size of his stomach."[3] They knew that, all right, but do as I say, not as I do! They also knew that "love turns to loathing if you sit too long on someone else's bench,"[4] but still they stayed. Meat and mead are good things! They had a good time, and at night the slaves slept in the warm ashes, dipped their fingers in the greasy soot, and licked them. It was a glorious time!

The Viking went out on a raid again that year although the fall storms had started. He traveled with his men to the coast of Wales, which was just "over the pond," he said. And his wife remained at home with her little girl, and the fact was that she soon cared more for the poor frog with the gentle eyes and deep sighs than the lovely girl who scratched and bit her.

The raw, damp autumn fogs that gnaw leaves, which they called *mouthless*, spread over the forest and heath. *Featherless birds*, as they called the snowflakes, were flying one after the other. Winter was coming. The sparrows commandeered the storks' nest and commented in their way on the absent owners. And where was the stork couple with all their children now?

The storks were in Egypt, where the sun was shining warmly like a lovely summer day here. The tamarind and acacia trees were flowering everywhere. The crescent moon of Mohammed shone brightly from the domes of the temples, and there were many pairs of storks resting on the slender towers after their long trip. Big flocks of them had nests next to each other on the enormous columns and broken arches of temples and forgotten ruins. The date palm lifted its umbrella roof high up, as if it wanted to be a parasol. The greyish white pyramids stood like shady outlines against the clear sky towards the desert, where the ostrich knew it could use its legs, and the lion sat with big wise eyes and watched the marble sphinx that lay half buried in the sand. The waters of the Nile had receded, and the entire riverbed was crawling with frogs, and for the stork family this was the most beautiful view in the whole country. The young ones thought that it was an optical illusion, so incredible did they find everything.

"This is what it's like here, and it's always like this here in our warm land!" said stork mother, and the little ones' stomachs tingled.

"Is there more to see?" they asked, "are we going to travel further into the country?"

"There's nothing more to see!" said stork mother. "On the fertile side there's only trackless forest where the trees grow into each other and are entangled with prickly vines. Only the elephants with their thick legs can find their way through there. The snakes there are too big for us, and the lizards are too lively. And if you go into the desert, you'll get sand in your eyes at best, and at the worst you'll get into a sand storm. No, it's best here! There are frogs and grasshoppers! I'm staying here, and so are you!"

And they stayed. The old storks sat in their nests on the slender minarets and rested, but still were busy grooming their feathers and rubbing their red stockings with their beaks. Then they lifted their necks, greeted each other solemnly, and raised their heads with the high foreheads and their fine, smooth feathers. Their brown eyes shone so wisely. The little female storks walked solemnly through the succulent reeds, glanced at the other young storks, made acquaintances, and with every third step, swallowed a frog, or walked around with a little snake dangling from their bills. They thought it looked becoming, and the snakes were tasty. The young male storks quarreled with each other, flapped their wings at each other, pecked with their beaks, even drawing blood, and then one got engaged and another got engaged, the young females and the young males. This was what they lived for, after all. They built nests, and then came new quarreling, since in the hot countries everyone is so hot tempered. But it was all fun and brought great joy to the old storks. One's own children can do no wrong! The sun shone every day, and every day there was plenty of food. There was nothing to do but enjoy oneself. But inside the rich palace of the Egyptian landlord, as they called him, there was no enjoyment.

The rich, powerful master lay on a couch, all of his limbs stiff. He was stretched out like a mummy in the middle of the big hall with the colorfully painted walls. It looked like he was lying in a tulip. Relatives and servants stood around him. He wasn't dead, but it couldn't really be said that he was living either. The water lily flower from the northern land, the one that had to be sought and picked by the one who loved him best, the one that could bring deliverance, would never be brought. His beautiful young daughter, who had flown away over sea and shore in the shape of a swan, far towards the north, would never come back. "She is dead and gone," the two returning swan maidens had reported. They had constructed a whole story between the two of them, and it went like this:

"All three of us flew high up in the air. A hunter saw us and shot his arrow. It hit our young friend, and slowly she sank like a dying swan down into a forest lake, singing her last farewell. We buried her there on the bank under a fragrant weeping birch. But we have taken revenge. We tied smoldering tinder under the wing of a swallow that nested under the eave of the hunter's reed roof. It flared up. The house went up in flames, and he was burned to death. The flames lit up the lake all the way to the weeping birch, where she now lies, earth in earth. She'll never come back to Egypt."

They both cried, and when stork father heard the story, he chattered his beak so it rattled: "Lies and fabrication!" he cried. "I would like to stab them in the heart with my beak!"

"And break it off," said stork mother. "Then you'd look really attractive! Think about yourself and your family first. You should keep out of everything else."

"But I'll sit up on the edge of the open dome tomorrow when all the wise and learned men gather to talk about the sick man. Maybe then they'll come a little closer to the truth."

And the wise and learned men gathered and talked a lot, talked widely about things that the stork couldn't get anything out of—and nothing came out of it for the sick man either, or for his daughter in the bog. But we may as well listen a little bit, since there's so much to listen to anyway.

Indeed, the right thing is to hear and know what happened before this, so we can follow the story better. We should at least know as much about it as stork father does:

"Love brings forth life! The highest love brings forth the highest life! His life's salvation can only be won through love!"

is what was said, and it was exceptionally wise and well said, the learned ones assured each other.

"That's a lovely thought," stork father said right away.

"I don't quite understand it," said stork mother, "but that's not my fault. It's the idea's fault. But it doesn't make any difference because I have other things to think about."

And then the learned men had talked about love in one way and another, and the difference between the love between lovers and that between parents and children; between the light and growing things, how the sun kisses the mud and that causes sprouts to shoot forth—it was so long-winded and technically explained that it became impossible for stork father to follow along, much less repeat it. He became quite pensive about it, partly closed his eyes, and stood on one leg for a whole day afterwards. Scholarship was very difficult for him to bear.

But stork father had understood one thing. He had heard both the common people and the most distinguished speak from their hearts. It was a great misfortune for thousands of people, and for the whole country too, that that man had taken ill and wouldn't recover. It would be a joy and blessing if he could regain his health. "But where does the flower grow that can bring him back to health?" They had all asked that, searched in long articles, in the twinkling stars, in wind and weather, searched all the roundabout methods that could be found, and finally the learned and wise, as already mentioned, found the answer: "Love brings forth life, the life of the father," and in this they were saying more than they realized themselves. Then they repeated this and wrote it up as a prescription: "Love brings forth life," but how the whole thing was going to be worked out, they didn't know. Finally they agreed that the help must come through the princess—she who loved her father with all her heart and soul. They also finally figured out how it should be done. That was more than a year and a day ago now. At night when the new moon had set, she was to go to the marble sphinx by the desert, brush away the sand from the door in its foot, and go through the long hallway that led to the middle of one of the big pyramids. One of antiquity's great kings lay there as a mummy, surrounded by splendor and magnificence. She was to lean her head next to the king, and it would be revealed to her how she could revive and save her father.

She had done all of that, and learned in a dream that she had to bring home a lotus flower from the deep bog in Denmark, the first flower to touch her breast in the deep water. The place was described precisely, and this flower would save her father.

And that is why she flew in the swan-skin from Egypt to the wild bog. Stork father and stork mother knew all this, and now we know it more clearly than we did before. We know that the bog king pulled her down to himself and know that she is dead and gone for those at home. Only the wisest of all of them still said, like stork mother, "She will take care of herself," and they waited for that because they didn't know what else to do.

"I think I'll filch the swan-skins from those two wretched princesses!" stork father said. "Then they can't get back to the bog and do any more harm. I'll hide them up there until there's a use for them."

"Where will you hide them there?" asked stork mother.

"In our nest by the bog," he said. "I can carry them with our youngest children, and if they get too heavy for us, then there are enough places on the way where we can hide them until the next trip. One swan-skin was enough for her, but two are even better. It's a good thing to have lots of traveling clothes in the northern countries."

"No one will thank you for it," said stork mother, "but you're the boss. Nobody listens to me except in brooding season!"

In the Viking house by the wild bog, where the storks flew towards spring, the little girl had been named. They had called her Helga, but that name was much too sensitive for a nature such as the one the lovely girl had. That became clearer month after month, and as the years passed, and the storks made the same journey—in the fall towards the Nile, in spring toward the bog—the little girl became a big girl, and before you knew it, she was a lovely maiden of sixteen. She had a beautiful shell, but she was hard and rough to the core, and wilder than most in that hard, dark time.

It was a pleasure for her to spatter the steaming blood of the butchered sacrificial horse with her white hands, and with savagery she bit the head off the black hen that the priest was going to butcher. She told her foster father in complete seriousness:

"If your enemies came here and threw a rope over the beams of the roof and tore it off your bedroom while you slept, I wouldn't wake you if I could. I wouldn't hear it, that's how the blood is still rushing in that ear that you boxed years ago! I remember!"

But the Viking didn't believe her. He was, like the others, fooled by her beauty. He didn't know how Helga's soul and skin changed. She sat on her horse as if grown to it, without a saddle, as it galloped at full speed. She wouldn't jump off even if it started fighting with other angry horses. She often jumped out from the face of the cliff into the fjord with all her clothes on and swam in the swift currents out to meet the Viking as his ship sailed towards land. She cut the longest lock from her lovely, long hair and braided herself a bowstring. "Self made is well made," she said.

The Viking woman was strong in both will and spirit as women of those times and custom were, but she acted like a gentle, anxious woman towards her daughter. Of course she knew that it was black magic that swayed the dreadful child.

It was as if Helga, out of pure sadistic pleasure, would often sit on the edge of the well when her mother stood on the balcony or walked out in the yard. She would flail her arms and legs around and let herself fall into the narrow, deep hole. There, with her frog nature, she would plop under the water and crawl out again as if she were a cat. Then she would walk into the hall dripping water so that the green leaves that were spread on the floor turned over in the stream of water.

But there was one thing that held little Helga: the twilight. Then she became quiet and a little thoughtful. She would listen and obey. A kind of inner feeling drew her to her mother then, and when the sun sank and the transformation, outer and inner, followed, she sat there still and sad, crumpled together in her frog shape. The body was now much bigger than a normal frog, and just for that reason the more gruesome. She looked like a pitiful dwarf with a frog head and webbing between her fingers. There was something so sad about the eyes that looked out. She had no voice, just a hollow croak like a child who sobs in its dreams. Then the Viking woman would take her in her lap. She forgot the ugly appearance and only looked at the sad eyes and said more than once: "I could almost wish that you were always my mute frog child. You are more awful to look at when the beauty turns outward."

And she wrote runes against sorcery and sickness and cast them over the miserable child, but there was no improvement.

"You wouldn't think that she was once so small that she lay in a lily pad," said stork father. "Now she's a grown person and looks just like her Egyptian mother whom we never saw again! She didn't take care of herself, as you and the learned thought she would. I have flown for years now hither and yon across the bog, and there was never a sign of her. Well, I can tell you that in those years when I came up here a few days before you, to repair the nest and mend this and that, I have flown continually across the open water the whole night, as if I were an owl or a bat, but to no use. And we didn't have any use for the two swan-skins either. The children and I dragged them up here from the land of the Nile, and that was hard enough. It took us three trips. Now they have lain for many years in the bottom of the nest, and if there's ever a fire here, if the house burns, then they are lost!"

"And our good nest would be gone!" said stork mother. "You think less about that than you do about that feather-suit and your bog princess! You should just go down to her and stay in the mud! You are a poor father for your own children, as I've said from the first time I laid eggs. Just so we or the children don't get an arrow in our wings from that crazy Viking girl! She doesn't know what she's doing. She should realize that we have lived here longer than she has. We never forget our duty. We pay our rent every year: a feather, an egg and a young one, as is only right. Do you think I dare to go down there when she's outside, like I did in the old days, and like I do in Egypt, where I'm like a friend to them—without forgetting who I am—and even peek in the pots and pans? No, I sit up here and am irritated with her, that hussy—and I'm irritated with you too! You should have left her lying in the lily pad. Then she would be gone!"

"You are much more worthy of respect than one would think from your talk," said stork father. "I know you better than you know yourself."

And he made a jump, two heavy flaps of his wings, stretched his legs out behind him and flew, sailing away, without moving his wings. He was pretty far away when he gave a powerful wing flap. The sun shone on the white feathers, with the neck and head stretched out in front. He was flying fast and high.

"He is still the handsomest of them all!" said stork mother, "but I won't tell him that."

That fall the Viking came home early with his booty and captives. Among these was a young Christian priest, one of those men who persecuted the idols of the northern countries. There had been a lot of talk lately in the halls and among the women about the new religion that had already spread widely in the south, even reaching up to Hedeby by Slien[5] through the missionary Ansgar. Even young Helga had heard about the belief in the white Christ, who in love had given himself to save them. But for her it was, as they say, in one ear and out the other. She only seemed to have a sense of the word love when she sat in her shriveled frog shape in her closed-up room. But the Viking woman had listened and felt herself strangely affected by the stories and legends that were going around about the son of one true God.

The men who had come home from their raids told about the magnificent temples of costly chiseled stone that had been raised for the one whose message was love. They had brought home a pair of large, gilded vessels, artistically carved and of pure gold. Each of them had a peculiar spicy fragrance. They were censers that the Christian priests swung in front of the altar where blood never flowed, but wine and consecrated bread were transformed in *his* blood—He who had given himself for as yet unborn generations.

The young captured Christian priest was brought down into the deep, stony cellar of the log house with his feet and hands bound with ropes of hemp. He was handsome. "He looks like Balder,"[6] said the Viking woman, and she was touched by his suffering. But young Helga wanted them to pull a rope through his hamstrings and tie him to the heels of the wild oxen.

"Then I would let the dogs out. Whee! Away across the bogs and thickets to the heath! It would be fun to see, even more fun to follow him on the trip!"

The Viking did not want him to suffer that death, but since he had denied and persecuted the high gods, he would be offered to them tomorrow on the blood stone in the grove. It would be the first human sacrifice there.

Young Helga asked if she could be allowed to spatter the idols and the people with his blood. She sharpened her shiny knife, and when one of the big, ferocious dogs, of whom there were enough of there, ran by her feet, she stuck him in the side with the knife. "I wanted to test it," she said, and the Viking woman looked sadly at the wild, evil-natured girl. And when night came and the characters of beauty in body and soul shifted in her daughter, she spoke warmly and sincerely to her from deep in her sorrowing soul.

The ugly frog with the troll body stood in front of her, fastened the brown sorrowful eyes on her, listened, and seemed to understand with human thought.

"Never, even to my husband, have I spoken of how doubly I suffer because of you!" said the Viking woman. "There is more pity in my heart for you than I could have believed myself. A mother's love is great, but there was never love in your heart! Your heart is like a cold clump of mud. From where did you come to my house?"

Then the pathetic creature trembled strangely. It was as if the words touched an invisible bond between body and soul, and big tears appeared in its eyes.

"Hard times will come for you one day!" said the Viking woman. "And it will be terrible for me also! It would have been better if you had been set out on the highway and had the cold of night lull you to death." And the Viking woman cried bitter tears and went away angry and sad, behind the loose skin curtain that hung over the beam and divided the room.

The huddled-over frog sat alone in the corner. She was silent, but every once in a while from inside her came a partly stifled sigh. It was as if a life was being born in pain deep in her heart. She took a step forward, listened, then went another step and with her clumsy hands grasped the heavy bar that was shoved across the door. Slowly she moved it and quietly pulled the peg that was set in over the latch. She grasped the lit lamp that was standing in the room. It was as if a strong will gave her the strength. She drew the iron peg out of the closed trapdoor and sneaked down to the captive. He was sleeping. She touched him with her cold, clammy hand, and when he awoke and saw the hideous creature, he shivered as if at a dreadful vision. She drew her knife, cut the ropes that bound him, and motioned to him to follow her.

He spoke holy names, made the sign of the cross, and when the creature remained unchanged, he said these words from the Bible:

"'Blessed is he who considers the poor! The Lord delivers him in the day of trouble.' Who are you? Why this form of an animal and yet full of acts of compassion?"

The frog beckoned and led him through an empty hallway behind sheltering hides out to the stable and pointed at a horse. He swung himself onto the horse, and she also leaped up and sat in front holding onto the horse's mane. The captive understood her, and at a rapid pace they rode a path that he never would have found out to the open heath.

He forgot her awful shape and felt that the Lord's mercy and compassion were working through this monster. He recited pious prayers and sang hymns, and she trembled. Was it

the power of the prayer and the song that affected her, or was
it a shiver from the cold in the morning that would soon
come? What was it she felt? She lifted herself high in the air,
wanted to stop the horse and get off, but the Christian priest
held her as tightly as he could and sang a hymn loudly as if it
could loosen the spell that held her in the hideous frog shape.
The horse ran on, and the sky became red. The first ray of the
sun shone through the cloud and with the clear flood of light
came the transformation. She was again the beautiful young
girl with the demonic evil nature. He held the most beautiful
young woman in his arms and, terrified at this, he sprang from
the horse and stopped it. He thought he had met another
wicked wile of witchcraft. But with one jump young Helga was
also on the ground. The short child's dress she was wearing
reached only to her knees. She pulled the sharp knife from her
belt and rushed at the surprised priest.

"Just let me get you!" she screamed. "Let me get you, and my
knife will be in you! You are as pale as hay, you beardless slave!"

She lunged towards him. They wrestled in battle, but it was
as if an unseen power gave the Christian strength. He held her
tightly, and the old oak tree close by seemed to come to his aid
by ensnarling her feet in its roots that were partly loosened
from the ground when they slid under them. There was a
spring close by, and he splashed the fresh water over her breast
and face, prayed for the unclean spirits to leave her, and
blessed her as in Christian custom, but the water of baptism
does not have any power where there is no inner flood of faith.

But in faith too he was the strong one. More lay in his act
than man's strength against struggling evil power, and it was as
if it captivated her. She dropped her arms and looked with a
wondering gaze and paling cheeks at this man who seemed to
be a powerful wizard, strong in magic and the black arts. Those
were dark runes that he read, and he drew symbols in the air.
She would not have blinked if he had swung a gleaming axe or
a sharp knife towards her eyes, but she did so when he drew
the sign of the cross on her forehead and breast. Now she sat
like a tame bird with her head bent on her chest.

Then he spoke to her gently of the act of love she had

shown towards him in the night when she came to him in the shape of the ugly frog. She had cut his bonds and led him out to light and life. She was also tied, he said, tied with stronger bonds than had bound him, but she also would come to light and life with his help. He would take her to Hedeby, to the holy Ansgar. There, in that Christian place, the enchantment would be broken. But he didn't dare have her sit in front of him on the horse, even if she sat there willingly.

"You must sit behind me on the horse, not in front. Your magical beauty has a power that comes from evil. I fear it—and yet the victory will be mine in Christ!"

He bent his knee and prayed so piously and sincerely. It was as if the quiet forest was consecrated thereby to a holy church. The birds started singing as if they belonged to the new congregation. The wild curled mint wafted as if it wanted to substitute for the ambergris and incense. He preached aloud the words from Holy Scripture: "To give light to those who sit in darkness and in the shadow of death, to guide our feet into the way of peace."

And he spoke to her about "creation waiting with eager longing," and while he talked the horse, that had carried them at such a furious pace, stood still and pulled at the big blackberry vines so that the ripe juicy berries fell down in little Helga's hand, offering themselves for refreshment.

She patiently allowed herself to be lifted onto the horse's back, and sat there like a sleepwalker, who neither wakes nor wanders. The Christian man tied two branches together with a cord of fibers in the shape of a cross. He held it high in his hand, and they rode through the forest that became denser and denser. The road went deeper and deeper and finally disappeared altogether. The black-thorns stood like barriers, and they had to ride around them. The spring did not become a running stream, but rather a stagnant bog, and they had to ride around it. There was restoration and refreshment in the fresh forest air, and there lay no less power in the gentle words that resounded with faith and Christian love in the heartfelt desire to lead the possessed one to light and life.

They say that raindrops hollow out the hard rock. Over time

He bent his knee and prayed so piously and sincerely.

the waves of the sea polish the angular stones until they're round. The dew of grace that fell over little Helga hollowed out the hardness and rounded the sharpness. But she didn't recognize that, didn't know it herself. Does the seed in the earth, when it's dampened by life-giving moisture and the warm rays of the sun, know that it hides growth and a flower within itself?

Just as the mother's song roots itself unnoticed in the child's mind, and the child repeats the single words without understanding them until they become clearer with time, so was the word working here, with the power to create.

They rode out of the forest and over the heath and then again through trackless woods, and towards evening they met a band of robbers.

"Where did you steal that beautiful girl from?" they shouted. They stopped the horse and pulled the two riders off, for there were many of them. The priest had no other weapon than the knife he had taken from little Helga, and he thrust with it to all sides. One of the robbers swung his axe, but the young Christian luckily jumped aside, otherwise he would have been struck. The axe flew deeply into the neck of the horse so the blood flowed out, and the animal fell to the ground. Little Helga, who awoke from her long, deep trance, threw herself over the gasping horse. The Christian priest stood in front of her to defend her, but one of the robbers swung his heavy iron hammer against his forehead so that it smashed, and blood and brains sprayed all around. He fell to the ground dead.

The robbers grabbed little Helga around her white arm, but just then the sun set. The last ray of sunshine disappeared, and she was changed to a hideous frog. The whitish green mouth stretched across half her face. The arms became thin and slimy, and a wide hand with webbing stretched out like a fan. The robbers dropped her terrified. She stood as a hideous monster in their midst and in the manner of a frog, she jumped into the air, higher than her own height, and disappeared in the thicket. The robbers thought that this must be Loki's evil trick,[7] or secret black magic, and they hurried from that place terrified.

The full moon was already risen. It gave radiance and light, and out from the thicket crept little Helga, in the pitiful shape of the frog. She stopped by the corpse of the Christian priest and by her murdered steed. She looked at them with eyes that seemed to cry. The frog head gave a start as when a child bursts into tears. She threw herself over first one and then the other. She took water in those hands that grew larger and more hollow with the webbing and poured it over them. They were dead, and dead they would remain! She understood that. Soon the wild animals would come and eat their bodies. No! That must not happen! So she dug in the ground as deeply as she could. She would dig a grave for them, but she had only a hard tree branch and both her hands to dig with, and between her fingers the webbing soon ripped and blood flowed. She realized that she would not be able to do it. So she took water and washed the dead man's face, and covered it with fresh, green leaves. She brought big branches and laid them over him, shook leaves in between them, and took the largest stones she was able to lift and laid them over the dead limbs. Then she stuffed moss into any openings, and thought that the burial mound was strong and safe, but during this hard work the night passed. The sun came up and little Helga stood there in all her beauty, with bleeding hands and with tears on the rosy youthful cheeks for the first time.

During the transformation it was as if the two natures were fighting within her. She trembled and looked around as if she were waking from a troubling dream. She ran to a slender beech tree and held onto it for support, and then suddenly she climbed up like a cat to the tree top and clung to it. She sat there like an uneasy squirrel, sat there the entire long day in the deep forest loneliness, where everything is still and dead, as they say—dead? Well, there were a couple of butterflies fluttering around each other, in play or dismay. There were some ant hills close by, each with several hundred little creatures scurrying back and forth. Countless mosquitoes were dancing in the air, swarm after swarm. They chased past crowds of buzzing flies, ladybugs, dragon flies, and other little flying creatures. The earthworms crept out of the damp ground. The moles pushed up earth. Yes, as a matter of fact it was quiet, dead all around, as it's said and understood. No one paid any attention to little Helga except the jays that flew shrieking around the tree top where she sat. They hopped on the branches towards her with bold curiosity. A blink of her eyes was enough to chase them off again, but they didn't get any wiser to her, nor she to herself.

When evening was near, and the sun started to sink, the transformation summoned her to new action. She let herself slide down the tree, and as the last ray of light disappeared she stood there in the frog's crouched shape with her hands' torn webbed membranes, but the eyes now shone with a beauty that they didn't have before when she was in beauty's form. They were the mildest, gentlest eyes of a young girl that shone out from the frog's mask. They witnessed to the deep spirit and the human heart. The beautiful eyes burst into tears and cried the heart's heavy tears of release and relief.

The cross of branches, tied together with the fiber cord, and the last work of the priest who was now dead and gone, was lying beside the raised grave. Little Helga picked it up, and the thought came by itself—she planted it among the stones that covered him and the murdered horse. With the sad memory tears burst forth, and in this frame of mind she scratched the same sign into the earth around the grave, fenced around it so neatly—and as she formed the sign of the cross with both hands, the webbing fell off like a torn glove, and when she washed herself in the water of the spring, and wondered at her fine, white hands, she again made the sign of the cross in the air between herself and the dead man. Then her lips moved, and her tongue moved and that name that she most often had heard sung and spoken on the ride through the forest came audibly from her mouth. She said it: "Jesus Christ!"

Then the frog skin fell. She was the beautiful young girl, although her head bowed in fatigue. Her limbs needed rest, and she slept.

But her sleep was short. She was awakened at midnight. In front of her stood the dead horse, so radiant and full of life. Its

Then the frog skin fell. She was the beautiful young girl.

eyes were shining, and radiance shone out from its wounded neck. Right beside him was the murdered Christian priest. "More handsome than Balder!" the Viking woman would have said, but yet he appeared luminous.

There was a seriousness in the big, gentle eyes; a righteous judgment, such a penetrating glance that it seemed to illuminate into every corner of her heart. Little Helga trembled from it, and her memory was awakened with a power as if on the Day of Judgment. Every good done for her, every loving word spoken to her became as if living in her again. She understood that it was love that had sustained her in these days of trial, in which the offspring of soul and clay was fermenting and striving. She acknowledged that she had only followed feelings and impulses and not done anything for herself. Everything had been given to her. Everything had been guided somehow. She bowed her head, humble and humiliated, shameful in front of him who could read each fold of her heart, and in this moment she perceived the blaze of the Holy Spirit in a flash of purification's flame.

"You child of the bog," the Christian priest said. "From earth, from the soil you were taken—from the earth you will again be resurrected! The sunlight that is incarnate in you will return to its creator—not a ray from the sun, but from God! No soul will be lost, but temporal time is long. It is life's flight into eternity. I come from the land of the dead. One day you too will travel through the deep valley into the luminous mountainous country where mercy and perfection live. I can't lead you to Hedeby for a Christian baptism. First you must shatter the shield of water over the deep bog bottom and drag up the living root of your conception and cradle. You must fulfill this deed before you can be consecrated."

And he lifted her up on the horse and handed her a gilded censer like the one she had seen in the Viking house. There was a fragrance so sweet and strong coming from it. The open wound in his forehead shone like a radiant diadem. He took the cross from the grave and lifted it high in the air, and they flew away through the air, over the whispering forest, over the mounds where Viking kings were buried sitting on their horses. And the powerful figures rose up, rode out, and stopped on their mounds. The wide golden bands with gold clasps shone on their foreheads in the moonlight. Their capes whipped in the wind. The great snake—the lind-snake—that broods over treasure, lifted its head and looked after them. The dwarves peered out from mounds and furrows. They swarmed with red, blue and green lights. It looked like sparks in the ashes of burning paper.

Over the woods and heath, rivers and ponds they flew, up towards the great wild bog. They floated over it in a vast circle. The Christian priest lifted the cross high. It shone like gold, and from his lips came the chanting of the mass. Little Helga sang along as a child follows its mother's song. She swung the censer, and there was a fragrance of the altar so strong and miraculous that the reeds and rushes of the bog bloomed because of it. All sprouts shot up from the deep bottom. Everything living arose. A profusion of water lilies spread out as if it were a woven carpet of flowers, and lying on it was a sleeping woman, young and beautiful. Little Helga thought she was looking at herself, her mirror image in the still water, but it was her mother she saw, the bog king's wife, the princess from the land of the Nile.

The dead Christian priest commanded that the sleeping woman be lifted onto the horse, but it sank under the weight as if its body was only a shroud flying in the wind. But the sign of the cross strengthened the mirage, and all three rode to firm ground.

Then the rooster crowed in the Viking house, and the visions dissolved in fog and were carried away in the wind, but standing there facing each other were the mother and daughter.

"Is it myself I see in the deep water?" asked the mother.

"Is it myself I see in the shiny shield?" exclaimed the daughter and they moved closer to each other. Breast to breast, they embraced. The mother's heart beat strongest, and she understood why.

"My child! My own heart's flower! My lotus from the deep waters!"

And she clasped her child in her arms and cried. The tears were a new life and baptism of love for little Helga.

"In the shape of a swan I came here and then threw it off," said the mother. "I sank down through the swirling marsh mud, deep down in the morass of the bog where it was like a wall closing around me. But I soon perceived a fresher current, and I was drawn deeper and ever deeper by some power. I felt sleep pressing on my eyelids, and I fell asleep. I dreamed. It seemed that I was once again in Egypt's pyramid, but in front of me was the rocking alder stump that had startled me on the surface of the bog. I observed the cracks in the bark, and they lit up in colors and became hieroglyphics. I was looking at a mummy case. It burst, and from it stepped the thousand year old king, the mummy figure. He was black as pitch, glistening black like the forest snails or the greasy black mud. The bog king or the mummy of the pyramid? I didn't know which. He threw his arms around me, and I felt I had to die. I didn't perceive life again until I felt a warmth on my breast. There was a little bird sitting there flapping his wings, chirping and singing. It flew from my breast high up towards the heavy darkness above, but it was still tied to me by a long green ribbon. I heard and understood its notes of longing: Freedom! Sunshine! To the Father! Then I thought about my father in the sunlit land of home, my life and my love! And I loosened the ribbon and let it flutter away—home to father. Since that time I haven't dreamed. I slept a deep and heavy sleep, until this hour when the sounds and scents lifted and released me!"

The green ribbon tied from the mother's heart to the wings of the bird—where was it fluttering now? Where was it left lying? Only the stork had seen it. The ribbon was the green stalk, the bow the shining flower, cradle for the child who now had grown so beautiful, and who once again rested by her mother's heart.

And as they stood there with their arms around each other, stork father flew in circles above them and then flew to his nest, fetched the swan-skins that had been hidden there for years, and threw one to each of them. The skins folded around them, and they lifted from the earth as two white swans.

"Let's talk!" said stork father. "Now we understand each other's language, even if the beak of one is different from that of the other! It is the luckiest thing imaginable that you came tonight because tomorrow we would be off, mother, the children, and I. We're flying south. Well, look at me! I'm an old friend from Egypt, you know, and so is mother. But it's in her heart rather than her neb. She always thought that the princess would take care of herself. The children and I carried the swan-skins up here. Oh, how happy I am! And how fortunate it is that I'm still here. We'll be off at daybreak. A big flock of storks. We'll fly in front, you can follow us. Then you won't get lost. The children and I will also keep an eye on you!"

"And the lotus blossom I was to bring," said the Egyptian princess, "flies by my side in the shape of a swan. I have my heart's flower with me, and that's the solution! Homeward! Homeward!"

But Helga said that she couldn't leave Denmark before she saw her foster mother, the dear Viking woman, one more time. Helga thought of every good memory, every kind word, each tear, that her foster mother had cried. At that moment it was almost as if she loved that mother the best.

"Yes, we must go to the Viking house," said stork father. "Mother and the children are waiting there, you know. How their eyes will pop and how they will chatter! Well, mother doesn't say so much. She speaks briefly and to the point, but she means it all the more. Now I'll just rattle a bit with my beak so they'll know we're coming."

So stork father rattled with his beak, and he and the swans flew to the Viking hall.

Everyone there was still sleeping soundly. The Viking woman hadn't gone to sleep until late at night. She lay worrying about little Helga who had been missing for three days along with the Christian priest. She must have helped him escape. It was her horse that was missing from the stable, but by what power had this occurred? The Viking woman thought about all the miracles that were said to be connected to the white Christ, and with those who believed in him and followed him. Her shifting thoughts took form in a dream. It seemed to her that she still sat awake on her bed, thinking. Outside was a brooding darkness. A storm was coming. She heard the sea rolling in the west and east from the North Sea and the Kattegat. The monstrous serpent that encircled the world in the depths of the sea shook with spasms.[8] The night of the gods, *Ragnarok*, as the pagans called it, was approaching. The end of time when everything would perish, even the gods. The Gjallarhorn sounded, and the gods rode over the rainbow, clad in armor, to fight their last battle. Ahead of them flew the winged valkyries, and the procession ended with the figures of the dead warriors. The whole sky was lit around them like the northern lights, but darkness conquered there. It was a terrible time.

Next to the frightened Viking woman sat little Helga in her dreadful frog shape. She also was trembling and pressed herself up against her foster mother, who took her in her lap and held her tightly with love, no matter how dreadful the frog shape seemed. The air echoed with the sounds of clashing swords and clubs; whistling arrows like a storm of hail flew over them. The hour had come when earth and sky would break, the stars fall, and everything be destroyed in Surt's fire. But she knew that a new earth and sky would come. Wheat would wave where the sea now rolled over the barren sands. The unmentionable God would rule, and Balder rise up to him, the gentle, dear one, released from the realm of the dead. He came—the Viking woman saw him. She knew his face. It was the captured, Christian priest. "White Christ!" she called aloud, and as she did so she pressed a kiss on the forehead of her hideous frog-child. Then the frog skin fell, and little Helga stood there in all her beauty, gentle as never before and with radiant eyes. She kissed her foster mother's hands and blessed her for all the care and love she had granted her through the days of trials and troubles. She thanked her for the thoughts she had ingrained and awakened in her mind, thanked her for speaking the name she repeated: White Christ! And little Helga arose as a powerful swan, the wings spread wide with a whistling sound like a flock of birds flying away.

With this the Viking woman awoke. Outside she could hear the same strong flapping of wings. She knew it was the time when the storks departed. That was what she was hearing. She wanted to see them again before they flew, and tell them good bye! She got up and went out on the balcony, and she saw stork upon stork on the side roof and around the farm. Over the tall trees flocks were flying in great circles, but straight ahead of her, on the edge of the well, where little Helga had so often sat and frightened her with her savagery, two swans were now sitting. They looked at her with wise eyes, and she remembered her dream, and it still consumed her completely, as if it were reality. She thought about little Helga in the shape of a swan. She thought about the Christian priest, and all at once felt a great joy in her heart.

The swans flapped their wings and bowed their heads as if they also wanted to greet her, and the Viking woman stretched out her arms towards them, as if she understood that. She smiled through her tears and tumbling thoughts.

Then all the storks arose chattering with flapping wings for their trip south.

"We won't wait for the swans," said mother stork. "If they want to come along, they must come. We can't stay here until the plovers leave! There's something really lovely about traveling as a family, not like the chaffinches and sandpipers where the males fly by themselves and the females too. It's strictly speaking not decent! And what kind of formation are those swans making?"

"Everyone flies in his own way," said stork father. "The swans diagonally, the cranes triangularly and the plovers in curves like a snake."

"Don't mention snakes when we're flying," said stork mother. "It just gives the children inclinations that can't be satisfied!"

———————

"Are those mountains down there the ones I have heard about?" asked Helga in her swanskin.

"Those are thunderclouds drifting below us!" said her mother.

"What are those white clouds that are so high?" asked Helga.

"Those are the always snowcapped mountains you see," said her mother, and they flew over the Alps, and down towards the blue Mediterranean.

"Africa's land! Egypt's strand!" the daughter of the Nile in her swan-skin shouted with joy, as she saw her native soil from high in the air. It appeared as a whitish-yellow wavy stripe.

The birds saw it too and sped up their flight.

"I smell the Nile mud and the wet frogs!" said stork mother. "There's tickling in me! Now you'll taste something! And you'll see the African storks, ibis, and cranes. They all belong to our family, but are not as pretty as we are. They act distinguished, especially ibis, for the Egyptians have spoiled him. They mummify him, and stuff him up with spicy herbs. I'd rather be stuffed with living frogs and so would you! And you will be! Better to have something in your tummy when you're alive than be made a fuss of when you're dead! That's my opinion, and I'm always right!"

"Now the storks have come!" they said in the luxuriant house by the Nile, where the royal gentleman was stretched out in the open hall on soft leopard skin cushions. He lay not living but not dead, hoping for the lotus blossom from the deep bog in the north. Relatives and retainers stood around him.

And into the hall flew two magnificent white swans that had come with the storks. They threw off the dazzling feather covers, and there stood two beautiful women as alike as two drops of dew. They bent over the pale, shrunken old man, and threw back their long hair. And as little Helga leaned over her grandfather, his cheeks grew rosy, his eyes regained their luster, and life returned to the stiff limbs. The old man rose up healthy and rejuvenated. His daughter and granddaughter embraced him in their arms as if they were giving him a morning greeting after a long heavy dream.

There was joy in the entire court and in the stork nest too, but there it was mostly because of the good food. The place was teeming with frogs. And while the learned ones quickly wrote a hasty story of the two princesses and about the flower of health that was such a great occurrence and blessing for house and country, the stork parents told the story in their way and for their family. But not until everyone was full, because otherwise they would have other things to do than listen to stories.

"Now you'll become something!" whispered stork mother. "Nothing else is fair!"

"And what should I become?" said stork father, "and what have I done? Nothing!"

"You've done more than any of the others! Without you and the children the two princesses would never have seen Egypt again, or cured the old man. You'll become something! You'll definitely get a doctor's degree, and our children will inherit it and then their children and so on! And you already look like an Egyptian doctor—in my eyes!"

The learned and wise ones explained the basic idea, as they called it, that ran through the whole course of events: "Love brings forth life!" It could be explained in different ways. "The warm sunbeam was Egypt's princess who went down to the bog king and from their meeting the blossom sprang forth—"

"I can't repeat the words exactly," said stork father, who had listened from the roof and was telling about it in the nest. "What they said was so complicated, and it was so wise that right away they received high rank and gifts, even the cook got a big medal, but I think it was for the soup."

"And what did you get?" asked stork mother. "They certainly didn't forget the most important one, which is you? The learned men only talked about everything! But you will get your reward too, I'm sure."

Late at night when the peace of sleep was resting over the rich and happy house, there was one who was still awake, and it wasn't stork father, even though he stood up in the nest on one leg, sleeping watch. It was little Helga who was awake. She leaned out from the balcony and looked at the clear sky with the big shining stars, bigger and clearer in their radiance here than she had seen them in the north, but yet the same. She thought about the Viking woman by the great wild bog, about her foster mother's gentle eyes and the tears she had shed over the poor frog-child who was now standing in radiance and starry splendor in the lovely spring air by the waters of the Nile. She thought about the love in the pagan woman's heart, the love that she had shown a pathetic creature, who was an evil animal in human form and in animal form nasty to see and touch. She looked at the shining stars and remembered the radiance from the forehead of the dead, when they flew over the woods and swamps. Strains rang in her memory, words she had heard spoken when they rode away, and she had sat there as one possessed. Words about love's great source: the greatest love that encompassed all things.

Oh, how much had not been given, won, and gained! Little Helga's thoughts encompassed, day and night, her entire sum of happiness, and she looked at it like the child who turns quickly from the giver to the given—all the lovely gifts. She was completely absorbed in the increasing bliss that could come, would come. She had been brought to always greater joy and happiness through miracles, and one day she lost herself so completely in that that she didn't think about the giver any longer. It was her youthful daring spirit making its rapid spring, and her eyes were alight with it. But she was torn from her thoughts by a loud noise down in the courtyard below her. She saw two powerful ostriches running hurriedly in tight circles. She had never seen this animal before, such a large bird and so clumsy and heavy. The wings looked like they were clipped, and the bird itself looked like it had been injured. She asked what had happened to it, and for the first time she heard the legend that the Egyptians tell about the ostrich.

His kind had once been beautiful with large, strong wings. Then one evening the forest's other powerful birds had said to it, "Brother, should we fly down to the river tomorrow and drink, if God wills it?" And the ostrich answered, "I will it!" The next morning they flew away, first high up towards the sun, God's eye. They flew always higher and higher, with the ostrich way ahead of the others. He flew proudly towards the light. He trusted in his powers, not the giver of them. He did not say, "If God wills it." So a punishing angel drew the veil away from the flaming rays, and in that instant the ostrich's wings were burned, and it sank miserably to earth. He and his kind will never be able to rise up again. He runs in fright, rushes around in circles in a narrow space. This is a reminder for us humans in all our thoughts and with each act to say, "God willing!"

And Helga bent her head thankfully and looked at the chasing ostrich. She saw his fear and his foolish joy at the sight of his big shadow on the wide sunlit wall. And gravity sank its deep roots in her mind and thoughts. A life so rich, so full of blessings had been given and won—what would happen? What would still come? The best: "God willing!"

Early in the spring, when the storks headed north again, little Helga took her golden bracelet, carved her name inside it, and beckoned to stork father. She placed the bracelet around his neck and asked him to take it to the Viking woman. She would understand from it that her foster daughter was alive and happy and remembered her.

"It's heavy to carry," thought the stork, when it was placed around his neck, "but you can't throw gold and honor on the road. Now they'll know up there that the stork brings good fortune!"

"You lay gold, and I lay eggs!" said stork mother. "But you only lay once, while I do it every year! But neither of us gets any appreciation! That hurts!"

"*We* are aware of it, mother," said stork father.

"Well you can't decorate yourself with that," said stork mother. "It gives neither a fair wind nor a meal!"

And then they flew away.

The little nightingale who sang in the tamarind bush would soon fly north too. Little Helga had often heard it up there by the great bog. She would send a message with it. She knew the language of the birds which she learned when she flew in the swan-skin and had often talked to the stork and swallows since then. The nightingale would understand her, and she asked it to fly to the beech forest on the peninsula of Jutland where the grave of rock and branches was raised. She asked it to request all the small birds there to stand guard over the grave and sing a song and yet another.

And the nightingale flew away—and time flew too!

One autumn day an eagle on a pyramid saw a stately caravan of richly laden camels. There were expensively dressed, armed men on snorting Arabian horses, shining white like silver and with red, trembling nostrils, whose manes were big and thick and hung down between their delicate legs. Rich guests, a royal prince from Arabia, handsome as a prince should be, came to the proud house where the stork nest stood empty. Those who lived there were in a northern country, but they would soon be back. And it so happened that they returned that very day, when there was so much joy and happiness there. There was a wedding party, and little Helga was the bride, dressed in silk and jewels. The bridegroom was the young prince from Arabia. They sat at the head of the table between mother and grandfather.

But she didn't look at the bridegroom's brown, manly cheek, where a black beard curled. She didn't look at the ardent dark eyes that were fastened on her. She looked out and up at the twinkling, sparkling stars shining down from the sky.

Then came the rushing sound of strong wings in the air. The storks were coming back, and the old stork couple, no matter how tired they were from the trip, and how much they needed to rest, flew right down on the railing by the veranda. They knew what the celebration was for. They had already heard at the border that little Helga had had them depicted on the wall. They were part of her story.

"That was very thoughtful," said stork father.

"It's not much," said stork mother, "It was the least she could do!"

When Helga saw them, she got up and went out on the veranda to clap them on the back. The old stork couple curtsied with their necks, and the youngest children watched and felt honored.

And Helga looked up at a gleaming star that was shining more and more clearly, and between it and her a figure moved, clearer even than the air and therefore visible. It swayed quite close to her. It was the dead Christian priest. He too came on her day of celebration, came from heaven.

"The glory and splendor there surpasses anything known on earth," he said.

And little Helga asked so sweetly and sincerely, as she never had begged for anything before, if she could for just a single minute look in—just cast one glance into the heavenly kingdom, to the Father.

And he lifted her up in glory and splendor, in a stream of tones and thoughts. And there was light and sound not just outside of her, but inside too. Words cannot describe it.

"Now we must return. You are missed!" he said.

"Just a glance yet," she asked, "only a single short minute!"

"We must get back to earth. All the guests are leaving!"

"Only a glance—the last!"

And little Helga stood on the veranda again, but all the torches there had been put out, and all the lights in the banquet hall were out too. The storks were gone, and there were no guests to be seen, no bridegroom. Everything had vanished in three short minutes.

Then Helga felt afraid. She walked through the big empty hall, and into the next chamber. Foreign soldiers were sleeping there. She opened the side door that led to her room, but when she went in there, she was standing outside in the garden. It wasn't like this here before! The sky was glimmering red. It was almost dawn.

Only three minutes in heaven, and an entire earthly night was gone!

Then she saw the storks. She called to them, spoke their language, and stork father turned his head, listened and came closer.

"You speak our language!" he said. "What do you want? And why have you come here—a foreign woman?"

"But it's me! It's Helga! Don't you know me? Three minutes ago we were speaking together over there on the veranda."

"You're mistaken," said the stork. "You must have dreamed all of it."

"No, no!" she said and reminded him of the Viking log house and the great bog, and the trip down there!

Then stork father blinked his eyes. "That's an old story that I heard from my great, great, great grandmother's time! Of course, there was such a princess from Denmark here in Egypt, but she disappeared on her wedding night many hundreds of years ago and never came back. You can read it yourself on the monument in the garden. There are both swans and storks carved on it, and on top you're standing there yourself in white marble."

That's how it was. Little Helga saw it and understood and fell to her knees.

The sun shone forth, and as in days of old when the frog skin fell because of its rays, and the lovely creature came to light, so now by the baptism of light rose a beautiful figure clearer and purer than the air—like a beam of light—to the Father.

Her body fell to dust. A withered lotus flower lay where she had been standing.

"That was a new ending to the story," said stork father. "I hadn't expected that! But I liked it quite well."

"I wonder what the children will say about it?" asked stork mother.

"Well, that's the most important thing, of course," said stork father.

NOTES

1. Prayer attributed to Celtic monks of the eighth and ninth centuries, but unverifiable.
2. Stanza from *Sayings of the High One* (*Hávamál*); from *Poems of the Elder Edda*, translated by Patricia Terry, revised edition, Philadelphia: University of Pennsylvania Press, 1990.

3. From *Hávamál*, Terry translation.
4. From *Hávamál*, Terry translation.
5. Ansgar the missionary received permission to build a church in Hedeby by the Slien River in Schleswig in 850.
6. A god of Nordic mythology, Odin's son. At the instigation of the evil god Loki, the beautiful and good Balder was killed by a sprig of mistletoe, the only thing that could hurt him.
7. Loki is the trickster figure of Nordic mythology.
8. The Midgard serpent, which encircles the world and is destined to fight Thor at Ragnarök (the end of the world of gods and men).

THE GIRL WHO STEPPED ON BREAD

YOU MUST HAVE HEARD about the girl who stepped on bread to avoid dirtying her shoes, and how badly things turned out for her? It's been both written down and printed.

She was a poor child, proud and arrogant. There was a bad streak in her, as they say. As quite a young girl she used to enjoy catching flies and pulling their wings off to make crawlers out of them. She took June bugs and dung beetles and stuck pins in them. Then she would put a green leaf or a little scrap of paper up to their feet and the poor bugs would clasp onto it, turn and twist it, to try to get off the pin.

"Now the June bug's reading!" said little Inger. "Look how it's leafing the page!"

As she grew up, she became worse rather than better, but she was pretty, and that was her misfortune. Otherwise she probably would have been treated harsher than she was.

"Desperate diseases must have desperate remedies," said her own mother. "You often stepped on my apron as a child, and I'm afraid you'll step on my heart when you're older."

And she did too!

She went into service out in the country with some distinguished people. They treated her as if she were their own daughter, and dressed her like it too. She looked good, and her arrogance grew.

When she'd been there a year, her mistress said, "You should really visit your parents sometime, little Inger!"

She went, but it was to show off. She wanted them to see how fine she had become. But when she came to the edge of town, she saw girls and boys gossiping by the pond, and her mother was sitting there on a rock resting with a load of firewood that she had gathered in the woods. Inger turned around because she was ashamed that she, who was so finely dressed, should have a mother who was so ragged, and who gathered sticks. She didn't regret turning around; she was just irritated.

Half a year went by.

"You should go home one day and see your old parents, little Inger," said her mistress. "Here's a big loaf of white bread you can take along for them. They'll be glad to see you."

And Inger put on her best clothes and her new shoes, and she lifted her skirts and walked so carefully so that her feet would stay nice and clean, and one can't blame her for that. But when she got to where the path went over some marshy ground, and there was water and mud for a long stretch, she threw the bread into the mud so she could step on it and get across with dry shoes. But as she stood with one foot on the bread and lifted the other, the bread with her on it sank deeper and deeper. She completely disappeared and there was nothing to be seen but a black bubbling pool.

That's the story. Oh, you'd like to hear what happened to her?

Well, she came to the bog woman, who brews in the marsh. The bog woman is an aunt of the elf maidens. Everyone knows the elves. Ballads have been written about them, and they've been painted. But about the bog women people only know that, when there's mist on the meadows in the summer, it's the bog woman who's brewing. Well, Inger sank down to her brewery, and you can't stand it there for long. A cesspool is a light, magnificent apartment compared to the bog woman's brewery. Every vat stinks so badly that humans faint from it, and the vats are pressed against each other. If there's a little opening between them anywhere, where you could squeeze through, you can't anyway because of all the wet toads and fat snakes that are matted together there, where little Inger sank. All the nasty living mass was so icy cold that her body shivered through and through, and became more and more stiff from it. She was stuck to the bread, and it pulled her, like a clump of amber pulls in a little straw.

The bog woman was home. That day the brewery was being inspected by the devil and his great-grandmother. She is an old, very venomous woman, who's never idle. She never goes out without her needlework, and she had it here too. She was sewing trick insoles for people's shoes so they couldn't stop moving. She embroidered lies and crocheted thoughtless words that had fallen to the ground. Everything she did was for harm and depravity. Yes, that old great-grandmother could sew, embroider, and crochet.

She saw Inger, put her glasses on, and looked at her once again. "That's a girl with talent," she said. "I'd like to have her as a souvenir of my visit here. She would do for a pedestal in my great-grandson's anteroom!"

And she got her. That's how little Inger went to hell. People don't always go straight to hell, but they can get there the long way around, if they have talent.

There was an unending anteroom there. You would get dizzy looking forward and dizzy looking back, and there was a languishing crowd of people who were waiting for the doors of mercy to open, and they would wait for a long time. Big fat waddling spiders spun a thousand-years web over their feet, and this web tightened like screws in the foot and held them like copper chains. Added to this was the eternal anxiety in each soul, a painful anxiety. The miser had forgotten the key to his money chest, and he knew it was standing in the lock. Well, it would take too long to rattle off all of the torments and tortures that were felt there. Inger felt that it was gruesome to stand as a pedestal. It was as if she was clamped from below to the bread.

"That's what you get for wanting to keep your feet clean," little Inger said to herself. "Look how they're staring at me!" Yes, everyone was looking at her. Their evil desires shone from their eyes and spoke without sounds from the corners of their mouths. They were a terrible sight.

"It must be a pleasure to look at me," thought little Inger. "I have a pretty face and good clothes." She moved her eyes, her neck was too stiff to move. She hadn't thought of how dirty she had gotten in the bog woman's brewery! Her clothes were coated with a single big slimy blob. A snake had gotten tangled in her hair and was dangling on her neck, and from every fold of her dress a toad peered out and croaked like a wheezy pug. It was very unpleasant. "But everyone else down here looks terrible too," she consoled herself.

But worst of all was the dreadful hunger she felt. Couldn't she bend and break off a piece of the bread she was standing on? No, her back had stiffened; her arms and hands were stiff. Her whole body was like a stone statue. She could only move the eyes in her head. She could turn them completely around and see backwards, and it was an awful sight. And then the flies came. They crawled all over her eyes, back and forth. She blinked her eyes, but the flies didn't fly. They couldn't because their wings had been torn off. They had become crawlers. It was a torment, and then there was the hunger—at last she thought that her insides had eaten themselves up, and she was empty inside, so hideously empty.

"If this continues much longer I won't be able to stand it," she said, but she had to stand it, and it did continue.

Then a burning tear fell down on her head and rolled over her face and breast right down to the bread. Another tear fell, and many more. Who was crying over little Inger? Didn't she have a mother up on earth? Tears of sorrow that a mother cries for her child always reach the child, but they don't set it free— they only burn and make the torment greater. And then this unbearable hunger and not being able to reach the bread she stepped on with her foot! Finally she had the sensation that everything inside of her had eaten itself up. She was like a thin, empty pipe that pulled every sound into itself. She could hear clearly everything that concerned her up on earth, and everything she heard was bad and hard. Her mother was indeed crying deeply and sadly, but she said, "Pride goes before a fall! That was your misfortune, Inger! How you grieved your mother!"

Her mother and everyone up there knew about her sin, how she had stepped on the bread and sunk in the mud and disappeared. The cow herder had told them. He had himself seen it from the slope.

"How you have grieved your mother, Inger!" said her mother, "but this is what I thought would happen."

"I wish I'd never been born!" thought Inger at this. "It would have been much better for me. It doesn't help that my mother is crying now."

She heard how the master and mistress, those good-natured people who had been like parents to her, talked. "She was a sinful child," they said. "She didn't respect the Lord's gifts but trod them underfoot. The doors of mercy will be hard for her to open."

"They should have disciplined me better," thought Inger, "and cured me of that nonsense."

She heard that a ballad had been written about her: *The arrogant girl who stepped on the bread to have pretty shoes*, and it was sung all over the country.

"That I have to keep hearing about it! And suffer so much for it!" thought Inger. "The others should also suffer for their sins. There would be a lot to punish! Oh, how I'm tormented!"

And her mind became even harder than her shell.

"You certainly can't improve here in this company! And I don't want to be better. Look how they glare at me!" And her mind was angry and hateful to all people.

"Now they have something to talk about up there! Oh, how I am tormented!"

And she heard them tell her story to the children, and the little ones called her the ungodly Inger. "She was so horrid!" they said. "So awful, she deserves to be tormented."

The children spoke nothing but hard words against her.

But one day as indignation and hunger gnawed in her hollow shell, she heard her name mentioned and her story told for an innocent child, a little girl. Then she perceived that the little one burst into tears at the story of the arrogant, finery-loving Inger.

"But won't she ever come back up?" asked the little girl.

And the answer came:

"She'll never come back up."

"But if she asked for pardon and promised never to do it again?"

"But she won't ask for pardon," they said.

"I really wish she would," said the little girl. She was quite inconsolable. "I will give my dollhouse if she can come back up again. It's so horrible for poor Inger!"

And those words reached down into Inger's heart and seemed to do her some good. It was the first time that anyone had said "poor Inger," and not added the slightest mention of her mistake. A little innocent child cried and begged for her. It made her feel so strange. She would have liked to cry herself, but she couldn't cry, and that was also a torment.

As years passed up above, there was no change down there. She heard sounds from above less often. She was spoken of less and less. Then one day she perceived a sigh, "Inger, Inger how you grieved me! I thought you would." It was her mother, who was dying.

Sometimes she heard her name mentioned by her old master and mistress, and the mistress' words were the gentlest. "I wonder if I'll ever see you again, Inger. You never know where you will go."

But Inger understood that her fine old mistress would never come where she was.

More time passed, long and bitter.

Then again Inger heard her name mentioned and saw above her something like two bright stars shining. They were two gentle eyes that closed on the earth. So many years had passed from the time that the little girl had cried inconsolably over "poor Inger" that the child had become an old woman who was now being called to the Lord. And just in this moment when thoughts from her whole life raised up, did she also remember how she as a little child had cried so bitterly when she had heard the story about Inger. That time and that impression were so vivid to the old woman at her time of death that she exclaimed aloud, "Lord, my God, haven't I, like Inger, often stepped on your blessed gifts without thinking about it? Have not I also walked with arrogance in my heart? But in your mercy you have not let me sink, you have held me up! Don't desert me in my last hour!"

And the old woman's eyes closed, and the eyes of the soul

opened for what had been hidden, and since Inger was so vividly in her last thoughts, she saw her, saw how far she had sunk, and with that sight the good woman burst into tears. She stood in heaven and cried for Inger like a child. Those tears and prayers rang like an echo down to the hollow, empty husk that surrounded the imprisoned, tortured soul who was overwhelmed by the unimagined love from above. An angel of God was crying over her! Why was she granted that? The tortured soul remembered all the acts she had done on earth, and trembled with the tears that Inger had never been able to cry. She was filled with remorseful grief and realized that the gates of mercy could never open for her. And at the same time as she brokenheartedly admitted this, a beam shone down into the abyss. The beam shone with more power than the sunbeam that melts the snowman boys build in the yard. And then, faster than the snowflake that falls on a child's warm mouth melts to a drop of water, Inger's petrified figure dissolved, and a little bird flew in zigzag-like lightning up towards the human world. But it was afraid and shy of everything around it. It was ashamed of itself and all living creatures and quickly hid itself in a dark hole it found in a decayed wall. It sat there huddled over, trembling over its entire body. It couldn't give forth a sound. It had no voice. It sat there a long time before it calmed down enough to see and perceive all the glory out there. Oh, it was magnificent! The air was so fresh and mild. The moon shone so brightly. There were fragrances from the trees and bushes, and it was so pleasant sitting there in a fine clean coat of feathers. Oh, how all creation was brought about in love and splendor! The bird wanted to sing out all the thoughts that moved in its breast, but it wasn't able to do so. It would have liked to sing like the cuckoo and the nightingale sing in the spring. But God, who hears the worm's soundless hymn of thanksgiving, perceived the paean that arose in the chord of thought just as the psalm sang in David's breast before it had words or a melody.

For days and weeks these soundless songs grew and swelled. They would be expressed with the first wing beat of a good deed, and this had to be done.

Then came the holy celebration of Christmas. The farmers

raised a pole close by the wall and tied a sheaf of oats to it so that the birds should also have a happy Christmas and a good meal in this season of the Savior.

The sun rose on Christmas morning and shone on the oat sheaf and all the twittering birds that flew around the pole feeder. Then from the wall also was heard "peep peep." The swelling thought became a sound. The faint peep was an entire hymn of joy—a thought of a good deed had awakened, and the bird flew out from its hiding place. In heaven they knew who the bird was!

Then winter came with a vengeance. The lakes were deeply frozen, and the birds and animals in the forest had a hard time finding food. The little bird flew by the road and found a kernel of grain here and there in the tracks from the sleds. At the places where the travelers rested it found a couple of crumbs, but only ate one of them and summoned all the other starving sparrows so they could eat. It flew to the towns, scouted about, and where a friendly hand had thrown bread from the window for the birds, it ate a single crumb, and gave the rest to the others.

During the course of the winter the bird gathered and gave away so many bread crumbs that together they weighed as much as the bread that little Inger had stepped on to avoid dirtying her shoes, and when the last bread crumb was found and given away, the bird's grey wings turned white and grew larger.

"There's a sea swallow flying over the lake," said the children who saw the white bird. Sometimes it dived down into the water, and sometimes flew high in the clear sunshine. It shone in the sun so it was impossible to see what became of it. They said that it flew right into the sun.

THE BELL

WHEN THE SUN WENT down in the evening in the narrow streets of the big city, and the clouds shone like gold up between the chimneys, first one person and then another often heard a strange sound, like the chiming of a church bell. But it was only heard for a moment because there was such rumbling from the carriages and such shouting, and those noises would drown it out. "Now the evening bell is ringing," people said. "Now the sun is going down."

Those who went outside the city where the houses were farther apart and where there were gardens and small fields, could see the evening sky even better and hear the pealing of the bell much louder than in the city. It was as if the sound came from a church deep within the quiet, fragrant forest. People looked towards the forest and became quite solemn.

As time passed, people would ask each other, "I wonder if there's a church out there in the woods? That bell has such a lovely, strange sound. Why don't we go out and take a closer look at it?" So the rich people drove, and the poor people walked, but the road was so oddly long for them, and when they came to a grove of willow trees that grew by the edge of the forest, they sat down and looked up into the trees and thought they were really out in the woods. A baker from town went out there and put up his tent, and then another baker came and hung a bell over his tent, and it was a bell that was weather-proofed, but the clapper was missing. When people went home again, they said that it had been so romantic— quite different from a tea party.[1] Three people insisted that they had gone all the way through the forest, and they had heard the strange pealing all the time, but it seemed to them that it was coming from town. One wrote an entire poem about it and said that the bell rang like a mother's voice to a dear, bright child. No melody was lovelier than the peal of the bell.

The emperor of the country found out about it too and promised that whoever could determine where the sound was coming from would have the title *Bellringer of the World* even if a bell wasn't making the sound.

Many went to the woods for the sake of getting that appointment, but there was only one who came back with any kind of explanation. No one had gone deeply enough into the forest, and he hadn't either, but he said that the ringing sound came from an enormous owl in a hollow tree. It was an owl of wisdom that continually hit its head against the tree, but although he couldn't with certainty say if the sound came from the head or from the hollow trunk, he was made *Bellringer of the World.* Every year he wrote a little paper about the owl, but really no one was the wiser for that.

It was Confirmation day. The minister had preached so beautifully and fervently. The confirmands had been very moved by his sermon. It was an important day for them because they suddenly went from childhood to adulthood. The childish soul was now supposed to somehow pass over into a more reasonable person. The sun was shining brightly, and the young people who had been confirmed went out of the city. From the forest the big unknown bell was pealing remarkably loudly. Right away they had such a desire to find it, all except three of them. One was going home to try her dance dress because the dress and the dance were the reason she had been confirmed now; otherwise she wouldn't have done it. The second was a poor boy who had borrowed his confirmation suit and shoes from the landlord's son and had to bring them back at a certain time. The third said that he never went to a strange place unless his parents were along, and that he had always been a good boy and he would remain so, even if he was confirmed. And you shouldn't make fun of that, of course—but that's what they did!

So three of them didn't go along. The others set out. The sun was shining and the birds were singing, and the young people sang along and held hands because they didn't have jobs yet and were all confirmed before the Lord.

But pretty soon two of the smallest ones got tired and turned back to town. Two young girls sat down and braided wreaths, so they didn't go along either, and when the others got to the willow trees where the baker's tent was, they said, "Well, now we're out here, but the bell really doesn't exist. It's just something you imagine."

Just then the bell rang out sweetly and solemnly deep in the forest, so four or five of the young people decided to go further into the woods. It was so dense and full of leafy growth that it was really hard to move forward. Woodruff and anemones grew almost too high. Flowering bindweed and blackberry vines hung in long festoons from tree to tree where the nightingale sang, and the sunbeams played. Oh, it was so beautiful, but it was no place for the girls—their clothes would be torn. There were big boulders covered with moss of all colors, and the fresh spring water trickled up, making an odd "gluck gluck" sound.

"Could that be the bell?" one of the young people asked, and lay down on the ground to listen. "This really needs to be looked into!" so he stayed there and the others went on.

They came to a house of bark and branches. A big tree full of wild apples hung down over it, as if it wanted to shake its blessings over the roof, which was flowering with roses. The long branches were spread over the gable, and a small bell was hanging from it. Could that be the one they had heard? They all agreed that it was, except one boy who said that the bell was too little and fine to be heard so far away as it had been, and that the tones it would produce wouldn't stir the heart as the bell had. The one who spoke was a prince, and so the others said, "Someone like him is always such a know-it-all."

So they let him go on alone, and as he walked his breast became more and more filled with the loneliness of the woods, but still he heard the little bell that had satisfied the others, and sometimes when the wind was in the right direction, he heard them singing over tea at the baker's. But the deep pealing was stronger, and it was as if an organ were playing along. The sound came from the left, from the side where the heart is.

Suddenly there was a rustling in the bushes, and a little boy stood in front of the prince. He was wearing wooden shoes, and his jacket was so short that you could see what long wrists he had. They knew each other because the boy was the same one who couldn't come along because he had to go home and deliver the suit and shoes to the landlord's son. He had done that and now he was wearing the wooden shoes and his poor clothing. He had come into the woods alone because the bell pealed so loudly and deeply that he had to come.

"Well, then we can go together," said the prince. But the poor boy with the wooden shoes was quite shy. He tugged on his short sleeves, and said that he was afraid that he couldn't walk fast enough. And he also was convinced that the bell had to be sought to the right, since everything grand and magnificent lies on the right hand side.

"Well, then we won't meet again," said the prince and nodded to the poor boy, who went into the darkest and most dense part of the woods where the thorns ripped his worn-out clothes apart and bloodied his face, hands, and feet. The prince also got a few good scratches, but the sun shone on his path, and he's the one we'll follow because he was a bright lad.

"I must and will find the bell," he said, "if I have to walk to the ends of the earth!"

The nasty monkeys sat up in the trees, grinning and showing all their teeth. "Should we pelt him? Should we pelt him? He's a prince."

But he went steadily deeper and deeper into the forest where the most wonderful flowers grew. There were white paradise lilies with blood-red stamens, sky-blue tulips that sparkled in the wind, and apple trees whose apples looked exactly like big shining soap bubbles. Just imagine how those trees shone in the sunlight! Around the lovely green meadows where deer played in the grass magnificent oaks and beeches were growing, and where a tree had a crack in the bark, grass and long vines were sprouting in the crack. There were also large stretches of woods with quiet lakes where white swans swam and spread their wings. The prince often stood still and listened and thought that he heard the bell pealing from one of these deep lakes, but then he noticed that it didn't come from there, but was pealing from still deeper in the woods.

Then the sun went down, and the sky shone red like fire. It became very quiet, so quiet in the forest. And he sank to his knees, sang his evening hymn, and said, "I'll never find what I'm seeking! Now the sun's going down, and night is coming, the dark night. But maybe I can still see the round, red sun before it completely sinks behind the earth. I'll climb up on those rocks over there. They're as high as the tallest trees."

He grabbed hold of the vines and roots and climbed up the wet rocks where the water snakes twisted around and toads seemed to bark at him. But he reached the top before the sun had set. What grandeur could be seen from that height! The sea, the great magnificent sea, with its long waves rolling towards shore, lay stretched out before him. The sun stood like a large shining altar where sea and sky met, and everything melted together in glowing colors. The forest sang, and the sea sang, and his heart sang along with them. All of nature was a great holy church where trees and floating clouds were the pillars, the flowers and grass the woven velvet cloth, and the sky itself the great dome. The red colors went out up there as the sun disappeared, but millions of stars were lit, and then millions of diamond lamps were shining. The prince stretched his arms out to the sky, the sea, and the forest and, just then, from the right side came the poor boy with the short sleeves and the wooden shoes. He had gotten there at the same time, going his own way, and they ran towards each other and held each other's hands in Nature and Poetry's great church. And above them pealed the invisible holy bell, and blessed spirits swayed in a dance around it in a jubilant hallelujah!

NOTE

1. Satirical reference to the literary tea parties of the time, where literature that was new or as yet unpublished was read aloud.

THE THORNY PATH TO GLORY

THERE'S AN OLD FAIRY tale: "The thorny path to glory about a hunter named Bryde, who earned great honor and worth, but only after long and numerous tribulations and dangers in life." Many a one of us have probably heard this as a child, maybe read it later as an adult and thought about his own obscure thorny path and "numerous tribulations." The fairy tale and reality are not far apart, but the fairy tale has its harmonious conclusion here on earth, while reality often postpones it past earthly life into time and eternity.

The history of the world is a magic lantern that shows us in slides on the black background of their time how humanity's benefactors, the martyrs of science and art, wander the thorny path to glory.

From all times and from all countries these slides appear, each only for a moment, but encompassing a whole life—a lifetime with its struggles and triumphs. Let's look at, here and there, a few in this band of martyrs, one that won't end until the earth fades away.

We see a crowded amphitheater. Aristophanes' *The Clouds* sends streams of ridicule and merriment over the crowd. Athens' most remarkable man is being ridiculed in spirit and person from the stage. He who was the people's shield against the Thirty Tyrants: Socrates. He who saved Alcibiades and Xenophon in the din of battle.[1] He whose spirit rose above antiquity's Gods. He is present here himself. He has risen from the audience and displays himself so that the laughing Athenians can see if he and the caricature on the stage are similar. He's standing up there in front of them, lifted high over them all. The succulent, green, poisonous hemlock, not the olive tree, should be Athens' symbol.

Seven cities claim to be the birthplace of Homer. That is to say, *after he was dead*! Look at him while he lived—He walks through these places, reciting his verses to support himself. Thoughts about tomorrow have turned his hair grey. He, the greatest seer, is blind and lonely. The sharp thorn rips the poet-king's coat to pieces. His songs still live, and only through them live antiquity's gods and heroes.

Picture after picture billow out from the Orient and the Occident, so far from each other in time and place, and yet all on glory's thorny path, where the thistle doesn't set bloom until the grave is to be decorated.

Under the palm trees walk camels, richly laden with indigo and other precious treasures. They're being sent from the country's ruler to the one whose song is the joy of the people, and who is the glory of his country—He who fled his country because of envy and lies. They have found him. The caravan is approaching the little town where he found refuge. A poor corpse is brought out of the gates and stops the caravan. The dead man is just the one they seek: Firdusi[2]—his thorny path to glory is ended!

The African with his coarse features, the thick lips and black wooly hair, sits on the marble steps of the palace in Portugal's capital and begs—It's Camões'[3] faithful slave. Without him and the copper shillings that are thrown to him, his master, the singer of *The Lusiads* would starve to death. Now an expensive monument covers Camões' grave.

Yet another picture!

A deathly pale, straggly bearded man is seen behind the iron bars. "I have made a discovery, the greatest in centuries!" he shouts, "and they have imprisoned me here for more than twenty years!" "Who is he?" "A madman," says the guard. "What people can't think of! He believes that you can propel yourself with steam!" It's Salomon de Caus,[4] the discoverer of steam power, whose suspicious unclear words were misunderstood by Richelieu, and who dies, imprisoned in a madhouse.

Here stands Columbus! He who once was followed by street urchins and mocked because he wanted to discover a new world. He has discovered it. Enthusiasm's bells ring out at his triumphal return, but the bells of envy soon ring louder. The world explorer, he who lifted his golden America up from the ocean and gave it to his king, is rewarded with iron chains, the ones he wishes placed in his coffin. They bear witness to the world and to the values of his time.

Picture after picture—the thorny path to glory is rich with examples!

He is sitting here in pitch darkness—He who measured the mountains of the moon. He who pushed into space to the planets and stars. He, the great man who heard and saw the spirit in nature, and felt the world turn under him: Galileo. Blind and deaf he sits here in his old age, impaled on the thorn of suffering in the agony of repudiation, undoubtedly not strong enough to lift his foot, the one that once in the pain of his soul—when the word of truth was erased—stamped on the earth when he said "And yet it does move."

Here stands a woman with a child's mind, enthusiasm and faith—she carries the banner in front of the battling army, and she brings victory and salvation to her fatherland. Exultation rings—and the fire is lit: Joan of Arc, the witch, is burned. The following century spits on the white lily. Voltaire, the satyr of wit, sings of *La Pucelle*.

At the assembly in Viborg the Danish aristocracy burns the King's laws. They flame up and illuminate the times and the lawgiver, and throw the ray of a halo into the dark tower prison where he sits, grey-haired and bent, honing a furrow in the stone table with his finger—He who once was the ruler of three kingdoms. The prince of the people, friend of the citizens and farmers: Christian II. He had a harsh temperament for harsh times. Enemies wrote his story. We should remember the twenty-seven years of prison when we think about his guilt in bloodletting.

A ship is sailing from Denmark. Next to the tall mast stands a man who looks towards Hven[5] for the last time: Tycho Brahe, who lifted Denmark's name to the stars and was rewarded for it with insults and injury. He's traveling to a foreign country. "The sky is everywhere—what more do I need!" are his words as he sails away, our most famous man, honored and free in a foreign land!

"Oh, free! If only from the body's unbearable pains!" come the sighs down the ages to us. Whose picture? Griffenfeldt,[6] a Danish Prometheus, chained to the rocky island of Munkholm.

We're in America by one of the big rivers. A crowd has gathered. A ship is said to be able to sail against wind and weather, to be a power against the elements. Robert Fulton is the man who thinks he can do this. The ship begins its journey—suddenly it stops—the crowd laughs, hoots and whistles. His own father whines along: "Arrogance! Madness! It serves him right! The crazy guy should be locked up!" Then a little nail breaks that had stopped the machine for a moment, the wheels turn, the shovels scoop away the water's resistance. The ship is moving! The steam shuttle is changing the distance from hours to minutes between the countries of the world.

Humanity! Do you comprehend the bliss in such a minute of consciousness, the spirit's understanding of its mission? The moment in which all the scratches from glory's thorny path—even self inflicted—dissolve in knowledge, health, power, and clarity? The moment when disharmony becomes harmony, and people see the revelation of God's grace, revealed to one man and given by him to all?

The thorny path to glory is then revealed as a halo around the earth. Fortunate he who's chosen to wander here and, without his own merit, is placed among the bridge builders between humanity and God.

The spirit of history flies on powerful wings through time and shows—accompanying courage, confidence, and thought provoking gentleness—the thorny path to glory in shining pictures on a black background. A path that doesn't end as in the fairy tale with splendor and joy here on earth, but points past this world into time and eternity.

NOTES

1. Athenian statesman Alcibiades (c.450–404 B.C.) and Greek historian Xenophon (c.430–c.350 B.C.) were both influenced by Socrates.
2. Pseudonym of Persian poet Abu Ol-qasem Mansur (c.935–c.1020), author of the Persian national epic.
3. Luis de Camões (1524–1580), Portuguese poet and author of the epic poem *The Lusiads* (1572), which describes the opening of the sea route to India by Vasco da Gama.
4. French engineer and physicist (1576–1626) credited with the discovery of steam power. The statement that Richelieu had de Caus imprisoned is not true.
5. Small island in the sound between Denmark and Sweden, site of the observatory of Danish astronomer Tycho Brahe (1546–1601).
6. Danish statesman Peder Schumacher, count Griffenfeldt (1635–1699), was imprisoned in Copenhagen and at Munkholm in the Trondheim fjord.

THE JEWISH MAID

IN THE PAUPER'S SCHOOL there sat among the other little children a little Jewish girl, so attentive and good, the cleverest of them all. She couldn't participate in one of the subjects though—religion. She was in a Christian school, after all.

She was allowed to read in the geography book to herself, or she could finish her math assignment, but that was soon finished and the lesson done. There was a book lying open in front of her, but she didn't read it. She sat and listened, and soon the teacher noticed that she kept up with the lesson like few of the others.

"Read your book," he said gently and gravely, but she looked at him with her radiant black eyes, and when he asked her a question, she knew more than any of the others. She had listened, understood, and remembered.

Her father was a poor, honest man. He had stipulated when the child started school that she shouldn't be taught the Christian faith. To have her leave the room during the religion class would perhaps confuse the other little ones, raise suggestions and sentiments, so she remained there. But this couldn't continue any longer.

The teacher went to her father and told him that either he would have to remove his daughter from the school, or let her become a Christian. "I can't endure to see those burning eyes, the fervor and her soul thirsting after the word of the gospel," said the teacher.

And the father burst into tears. "I don't know much about our own religion myself, but her mother was a daughter of Israel, firm and strong in her faith. I promised her on her deathbed that the child would never become a baptized Christian. I must keep my promise because it's like a pact with God for me."

And the little Jewish girl was removed from the Christian school, and years passed.

In a humble, middle-class house in one of Jutland's smallest towns there was a poor maid of the Jewish community. It was Sara. Her hair was as black as ebony, her eyes as dark and yet full of brilliance and light as a daughter of the Orient. The expression of the fully grown girl was still the same as in the child when she sat on the school bench and listened with her thoughtful gaze.

Every Sunday the organ music and songs of the congregation could be heard through the street and into the house opposite where the Jewish maid was doing her work, diligent and dutiful in her vocation. *"Remember the Sabbath day, to keep it holy"* was her law, but the Sabbath for her was a Christian workday, and she could only keep it holy in her heart, which she didn't believe was enough. But what are the days and hours to God? That thought had awakened in her soul, and on the Christian Sunday the hour of devotion was less disturbed. When the sound of the organ and the hymns reached her in the kitchen by the sink, then even this place became holy and still. She read the Old Testament then, her people's treasure and property, but only this because what her father had told her and the teacher when she was taken out of the school was ingrained in her mind—the promise that was given her dying mother that Sara should not become Christian, not abandon the faith of her fathers. The New Testament was and would remain a closed book for her, and yet she knew so much about it. It shone in her childhood memories.

One evening she sat in a corner of the living room, listening to her master reading aloud, and she felt she could listen to that since it was not the gospels. He was reading from an old history book. She could surely listen to that. It was about a Hungarian knight who was captured by a Turkish Pasha, who had him tied with the oxen to the plow. He was whipped and suffered from unending mockery and thirst.

The knight's wife sold all her jewelry and mortgaged the castle and land. His friends gathered together the large sums, unbelievably large amounts, that were demanded for ransom, but they did it, and he was released from slavery and disgrace. Sick and suffering he arrived home. But soon there was a general call-to-arms against the enemies of Christianity. The sick man heard about it and could not rest until he was lifted onto his war horse again. The color came back to his cheeks, and he rode away to victory. The very Pasha who had hitched him to the plow, mocked and tormented him, became his captive and was brought home to his castle dungeon. But in the very first hour the knight came and asked his captive:

"What do you think will happen to you?"

"I know what will happen!" said the Turk. "Reprisal!"

"Yes, Christian reprisal," said the knight. "Christianity commands us to forgive our enemies and love our neighbors. God is love! Go in peace to your home and loved ones. Become gentle and good towards those who are suffering."

Then the prisoner burst into tears. "How could I have imagined that this would be possible? Since I was certain of pain and torture, I took a poison that will kill me within a few hours. I must die; there's no antidote. But before I die, preach to me the teachings that hold such love and mercy, for it is great and divine! Let me die in that faith, die as a Christian!" and his prayer was answered.

That was the legend; the story that was read. Everyone listened to it and followed along attentively, but none more intensely than she who was sitting in the corner, the servant girl Sara, the Jewish maid. It came alive for her. Large, heavy tears filled the shining, coal-black eyes. She sat there in her childhood innocence, as she had once sat on the school bench and felt the greatness of the Gospels. Tears rolled down her cheeks.

"Don't let my child become a Christian!" were her mother's last words on her deathbed. They rang through her soul and heart along with the words of the commandment: "*Honor thy Father and thy Mother.*"

"I am not a Christian! They call me the Jewish maid. The neighborhood boys called me that with derision last Sunday when I was standing outside the open church door looking at the altar candles that were burning, and the congregation was singing. From my school days I have felt a power in Christianity that is like sunshine, and even if I shut my eyes against its light, it still shines right into my heart. But, mother, I will not grieve you in your grave! I will not betray the promise that father gave you! I will not read the Christian Bible. I have the God of my fathers to lean on!"

—And years passed.

The master died, and the mistress was in poor circumstances. She would have to do without the maid, but Sara didn't leave. She was a friend in need and held everything together. She worked until late at night and supported them with the work of her hands. There were no close relatives to take care of the family, and every day the mistress became weaker and was sick in bed for months. Sara watched over her, nursed her, and worked, gentle and good, a blessing in the poverty-stricken house.

"The Bible is lying over there!" said the sick woman. "Read a little for me. It's a long evening, and I so deeply need to hear the word of God."

And Sara bowed her head. Her hands folded around the Bible, which she opened and read for the sick woman. She was often in tears, but her eyes became clearer, and clarity filled her soul: "Mother, your child will not take a Christian Baptism, not be counted within their society. You have demanded that, and I will keep that promise. We are united in that here on this earth, but beyond this world—there is a greater unity in God. '*He will be our guide forever!*' '*Thou visitest the earth and waterest it.*' I understand it! I don't know myself where it comes from—It is from Him, in Him: Christ!"

She trembled when she spoke His holy name and a baptism of fire shot through her body that was stronger than it could bear. She fell forward, weaker than the sick woman she kept watch over.

"Poor Sara!" they said. "She overexerted herself with work and care-giving."

She was taken to the infirmary for the poor, where she died. From there she was buried but not in the Christian cemetery. That was not the place for the Jewish maid. No, she was buried outside, up against the churchyard wall.

And God's sunshine, that shone over all the Christian graves, also shone over the Jewish maid's grave outside the wall, and the sound of hymns that were heard in the Christian cemetery reached her grave as well. The preaching reached there too: "There is resurrection in Christ!" He who said to his disciples, "*John baptized with water, but you shall be baptized with the Holy Spirit!*"

THE STORY OLD JOHANNA TOLD

THE WIND'S SIGHING THROUGH the old willow branches.

It's as if you heard a song. The wind is singing it, and the tree is telling the story. If you don't understand it, ask old Johanna in the poor house. She knows it. She was born here in the district.

Years ago, when the King's highway still passed by here, the tree was already big and conspicuous. It stood where it still stands, out from the tailor's white-washed half-timbered house right near the pond, which at that time was so big that the cattle were watered there, and where in the warm summer time, the farmers' small children ran around naked and splashed in the water. Right up under the tree a milestone of carved stone had been raised, but now it has fallen over, and brambles grow over it.

The new King's highway was laid right beside the rich farmer's land, and the old road became a track. The pond became a puddle, overgrown with duckweed. If a frog jumped in, the green separated, and you saw the black water. Cattails, bog beans, and yellow iris grew round about, and grow there still.

The tailor's house became old and crooked, and the roof became a hotbed for moss and houseleeks. The pigeon coop collapsed, and the starlings built their nests there. The swallows built nest upon nest along the gable of the house and under the roof, as if this were a lucky place to live.

And once it was. Now it had become lonely and quiet. But "poor Rasmus," as he was called, simple and weak-willed, lived there. He was born there and had played there as a child, running over meadows and jumping fences. He had splashed as a little boy in the open pond and climbed the old tree.

It lifted its big branches in magnificent beauty, as it still does, but storms had already twisted the trunk a little, and time had cracked it. Weather and wind had deposited dirt in the crack; grass and greenery were growing there, and even a little mountain ash tree had planted itself.

When the swallows came in the spring, they flew around among the trees and the roof—patching and repairing their old nests. Poor Rasmus let his nest stand or fall as it would. He neither patched nor propped it up. "What good does it do?" was his saying, as it had been his father's.

He remained in his home. The swallows flew away, but they came back, those faithful creatures. The starlings flew away, and they returned and whistled their songs. Once Rasmus had whistled in competition with them, but now he no longer whistled or sang.

The wind sighed through the old willow, and is still sighing. It's as if you heard a song. The wind is singing it, and the tree is telling the story. If you don't understand it, ask old Johanna in the poorhouse. She knows it. She knows a lot about old times. She's like a historical register, full of memoirs and old memories.

When the house was a good new one, the village tailor Ivar Ølse moved in there with his wife Maren. Both of them were hard-working, honest folks. Old Johanna was a child then, the daughter of a clog maker, one of the poorest men in the district. She got many a good sandwich from Maren, who didn't lack for food, and was on good terms with the mistress of the estate. She was always laughing and happy. She remained cheerful and used her mouth as well as her hands. She was as nimble with the needle as with her mouth and looked after her house and children. There were nearly a dozen of them, eleven to be exact—the twelfth failed to appear.

"Poor people always have a nest full of kids!" growled the squire. "If you could drown them like you do kittens and only keep one or two of the strongest, there would be less misery!"

"Good Lord!" said the tailor's wife. "Children are a blessing from God. They're the joy of the house. Every child is one more prayer to God. If things are tight, and there are many mouths to feed, then you work harder and find ways and honest means. The Lord doesn't let go, if we don't let go of him!"

The mistress of the manor agreed with her, nodded in a friendly way, and patted Maren on the cheek. She had done that many times and kissed her too, but that was when the mistress was a little child, and Maren was her nanny. They had always cared about each other, and they still did.

Every year at Christmas time winter supplies came from the manor to the tailor's house: a barrel of flour, a pig, two geese, a quarter barrel butter, cheese, and apples. That helped the pantry! Ivar Ølse looked pleased about it too, but soon expressed his old saying, "What good does it do?"

The house was neat and clean. There were curtains in the windows and flowers too, both pinks and impatiens. Hanging in a picture frame was a sampler with the family name, and close by hung an acrostic letter in rhyme that Maren Ølse had written herself. She knew how rhymes went. She was actually quite proud of the family name "Ølse" because it was the only word in Danish that rhymed with "pølse," sausage. "It's always something to have what no one else has!" she said and laughed. She always retained her good humor. She never said "What good does it do?" like her husband did. Her motto was "Have faith in yourself and the Lord." That's what she did, and that held everything together. The children thrived and grew from the nest, traveled far afield, and did well. Rasmus was the youngest. He was such a beautiful child that one of the great portrait painters from the city had borrowed him to use as a model, with him as naked as the day he was born. That painting hung now at the King's palace where the mistress of the manor had seen it and recognized little Rasmus, even without his clothes on.

But then came difficult times. The tailor got arthritis in both hands, and it left big knots in his hands. No doctor could help him, not even the wise woman Stine, who did some "doctoring."

"We mustn't get discouraged," said Maren. "It never helps to hang your head! Now that we no longer have father's hands to help, I must use mine more and better. Little Rasmus can also sew."

He was already at the table, whistling and singing. He was a happy boy. But he shouldn't sit there the whole day, his mother said. That would be a shame for a child. He should play and run around too.

The clogmaker's Johanna was his favorite playmate. She was even poorer than Rasmus. She was not pretty, and she went barefoot. Her clothes hung in tatters because she had no one to mend them, and it didn't occur to her to do it herself. But she was a child and as happy as a bird in the Lord's sunshine.

Rasmus and Johanna played by the stone milepost under the big willow tree.

He had big dreams. He wanted to become a fine tailor and

live in the city, where there were masters who had ten journeymen working for them. He had heard this from his father. He would be an apprentice there, and then he would become a master tailor. Later Johanna could come and visit him, and if she could cook, she would make food for all of them and have her own room.

Johanna didn't dare believe it, but Rasmus thought it would happen.

They sat under the old tree, and the wind sighed in the branches and leaves. It was as if the wind sang and the tree told the story.

In autumn every leaf fell from the tree, and rain dripped from the naked branches.

"They'll grow green again," said mother Ølse.

"What good does it do?" said her husband. "New year—new struggles to survive!"

"The pantry is full," said his wife. "Thanks to our kind mistress. I am healthy and strong. It's sinful of us to complain."

The gentry stayed in their manor in the country through Christmas, but the week after New Year they were going to the city, where they would spend the winter in pleasure and with entertainment. There would be dances, and they were even invited to a party at the Court.

The mistress had ordered two expensive dresses from France. They were of such a fine fabric, cut and assembly that Maren the tailor's wife had never seen anything so splendid before. She asked the mistress if she could bring her husband up to see the dresses. A village tailor would never see anything like that, she said.

He saw them, but didn't have a word to say until he got home, and what he said then was only what he always said, "What good does it do?" And this time his words proved to be true.

The gentry went up to town. The dances and partying had started, but in all that magnificence, the old gentleman died, and his wife never did wear the fancy clothes. She was grief-stricken and dressed from head to foot in closely woven, black mourning. There was not so much as a shred of white to be seen. All of the servants were in black, and even the best coach was draped with fine black cloth.

It was a cold frosty night. The snow was shining, and the stars twinkled. From the city the heavy hearse arrived with the body to the manor church, where it would be buried in the family vault. The farm manager and the district council official sat on horseback with torches at the gate to the churchyard. The church was alight, and the pastor stood in the open door of the church and received the body. The coffin was carried up into the chancel, and the entire congregation followed after it. The pastor spoke, and a hymn was sung. The widow was there in the church. She had been driven there in the black draped coach which was black both inside and out, and such a coach had never before been seen in the district.

People talked about the mourning pomp the entire winter. It really was a funeral for the Lord of a manor. "You can see what that man represented," the people of the district said. "He was nobly born and he was nobly buried."

"What good does it do?" asked the tailor. "Now he has neither life nor property. At least we have one of them."

"Don't talk like that!" said Maren. "He has eternal life in the kingdom of heaven."

"Who told you that, Maren?" said the tailor. "A dead man is good fertilizer. But this man here was evidently too distinguished to be a boon to the earth. He's to lie in a vault."

"Don't talk so irreverently!" said Maren. "I tell you again: He has eternal life!"

"Who told you that, Maren?" repeated the tailor.

And Maren threw her apron over little Rasmus. He mustn't hear such talk.

She carried him out to the woodshed and cried.

"Those words you heard over there, little Rasmus, were not your father's. It was the devil who walked through the room and took your father's voice. Say the Lord's Prayer. We'll both say it!" She folded the child's hands.

"Now I'm happy again," she said. "Have faith in yourself and the Lord."

The year of mourning was over. The widow bore half-mourning clothing, but only joy in her heart. It was rumored that she had a suitor and was already thinking of marriage. Maren knew a little about it, and the pastor knew a bit more.

On Palm Sunday, after the sermon, the banns were to be read for the widow and her fiancé. He was a wood carver or a stone carver. They didn't exactly know the name of his occupation because at that time Thorvaldsen[1] and his art weren't yet household words. The new lord of the manor was not noble, but still a very imposing man. He was someone who was something that no one understood. They said that he carved pictures, was good at his work, and he was young and handsome.

"What good does it do?" said tailor Ølse.

On Palm Sunday the marriage banns were announced from the pulpit, followed by hymn singing and Communion. The tailor, his wife, and little Rasmus were in church. The parents took Communion, but Rasmus stayed in the pew. He was not yet confirmed. Lately there had been a lack of clothing in the tailor's house. The old things they wore had been turned and turned again, sewed and patched. Now all three were wearing new clothes, but in black material as if for a funeral. They were dressed in the draping material from the funeral coach. The tailor had gotten a jacket and pants from it, Maren a high-necked dress, and Rasmus had an entire suit to grow into for Confirmation. Cloth from both the inside and outside of the coach had been used. No one needed to know what the cloth had been used for previously, but people soon found out anyway. The wise woman Stine and a couple of other wise women, who didn't support themselves by their wisdom, said that the clothes would draw disease and death to the house. "You can't dress in shrouding unless you're on your way to the grave."

The clogmaker's Johanna cried when she heard such talk, and when it now happened that after that day the tailor became more and more ill, it seemed apparent who the victim would be.

And it became apparent.

On the first Sunday after Trinity, tailor Ølse died. Now

Maren had to hold on to everything alone. And she held on, with her faith in herself and the Lord.

A year later Rasmus was confirmed, and he was going to the city to be apprenticed to a master tailor. Not one with twelve journeymen, but with one. Little Rasmus could be counted as a half. He was happy and looked pleased, but Johanna cried. She cared more about him than she herself knew. The tailor's widow remained in the old house and continued the business.

That was at the time when the new King's highway was opened. The old one that went by the willow tree and the tailor's became just a track. The pond grew over, and duckweed covered the puddle of water that was left. The milepost fell over. It had no reason to stay standing, but the tree stayed strong and beautiful. The wind sighed through its branches and leaves.

The swallows flew away, and the starlings flew away, but they returned in the spring; and when they returned for the fourth time, Rasmus also came home. He had finished his apprenticeship and was a handsome, if slender, fellow. Now he wanted to tie up his knapsack and travel to foreign countries. His mind was set on it. But his mother held him back. Home was best, after all! All the other children were widely dispersed. He was the youngest, and the house was to be his. He would have plenty of work if he would travel around the area. He could be a traveling tailor, sew for a few weeks at one farm and then at another. That was traveling too! And Rasmus took his mother's advice.

So he once again slept in the home of his childhood and sat again under the old willow tree and heard it sighing.

He was good looking and could whistle like a bird and sing both new and old ballads. He was welcomed at the big farms, especially at Klaus Hansen's, the second richest farmer in the district.

Hansen's daughter Else looked like the most beautiful flower and was always laughing. There were even people unkind enough to say that she laughed just to show off her lovely teeth. She was mirthful and always in the mood for jokes and pranks. Everything suited her.

She fell in love with Rasmus, and he fell in love with her, but neither of them said anything about it in so many words.

Rasmus became depressed. He had more of his father's disposition than his mother's, and was only in a good mood when he was with Else. Then they both laughed and joked and played pranks. But even though there was plenty of opportunity, he never said a single word of his love. "What good does it do?" was his thought. "Her parents will want prosperity for her, and I don't have that. It would be the smart thing to go away." But he wasn't able to leave because it was as if Else had him on a string. He was like a trained bird that sang and whistled for her pleasure at her command.

Johanna, the clogmaker's daughter, was a servant there on the farm, employed to do menial chores. She drove the milk wagon out in the field, where she milked the cows with the other maids. She also had to haul manure when needed. She never came up to the living room and saw little of Rasmus and Else, but she heard that the two of them were as good as engaged.

"Then Rasmus will be well-off," she said. "I'm pleased for him." And her eyes filled, but there was surely nothing to cry about!

It was market day, and Klaus Hansen drove to town. Rasmus went along and sat beside Else both coming and going. He was head over heels in love with her, but he didn't say a word.

"He has to say something to me about this!" the girl thought, and she was right about that. "If he won't speak, I'll have to scare him into it."

And soon there was talk around the farm that the richest farmer in the district had proposed to Else, and he had, but no one knew what she had answered. Rasmus' head was swimming.

One evening Else placed a gold ring on her finger and asked Rasmus what it meant.

"Engagement!" he said.

"And who with, do you think?" she asked.

"With the rich farmer," he answered.

"You hit it on the head," she said, nodded to him and slipped away.

But he slipped away too and came back agitated to his mother's house and packed up his knapsack. He was going away into the wide world, no matter how much his mother cried. He cut himself a walking stick from the old willow and whistled as if he were in a good mood. He was off to see the splendors of the world.

"This makes me very sad," said his mother. "But for you it's probably the right and best thing to get away, so I must bear it. Have faith in yourself and the Lord, and I will surely get you back again, happy and satisfied."

He set off on the new highway and saw Johanna coming with a load of manure. She hadn't seen him, and he didn't want her to see him. He sat down behind the hedge along the ditch. He was hidden there, and Johanna drove past.

Into the wide world he went. No one knew where. His mother thought he would return before the year was out. He would see new things and have new things to think about, and would fall into his old groove that couldn't be pressed out with any iron. "He has a little too much of his father's temperament. I would rather he had mine, poor child! But he'll surely come home. He can't let go of me and the house."

His mother would wait for ages. Else only waited for a month, and then she secretly visited the wise woman Stine Madsdatter, who did "doctoring," and could tell fortunes in cards and coffee grounds and knew more than the Lord's Prayer. And she knew where Rasmus was. She read it in the coffee grounds. He was in a foreign city, but she couldn't make out the name of it. There were soldiers and lovely young maidens in that city, and he was deciding whether to take up a musket or one of the girls.

Else couldn't stand hearing that. She would gladly use her savings to ransom him, but no one must know it was her.

And old Stine promised that he would come back. She knew a magic remedy, a dangerous one for the person concerned, but it was a last resort. She would set the pot to cooking for him, and then he would have to come. No matter where in the world he was, he would have to come home, home to where the pot was cooking and his sweetheart was waiting for him. It could take months for him to come, but come he must, if he was still alive.

Night and day without peace or rest he had to travel over sea and mountains, whether the weather was fair or foul, no matter how tired his feet were. He was going home. He had to go home.

The moon was in its first quarter, and that's how it had to be for the magic to work, said old Stine. The weather was stormy, so the old willow tree creaked. Stine cut off a branch, and tied it into a knot. This was going to help pull Rasmus home to his mother's house. Moss and house leeks were taken from the roof and placed into the pot that was put on the fire. Else had to tear a page from a hymnal, and as it happened she tore out the last one, the one with the printing errors. "It's all the same," said Stine and threw it into the pot.

Many things had to go into that porridge, and it had to boil and keep boiling until Rasmus came home. Old Stine's black rooster had to lose its red comb. It went in the pot. Else's thick golden ring went in, and Stine told her ahead of time that she'd never get it back. That Stine was so wise! Many things that we can't even name went into the pot. It stood on the fire continuously, or on glowing embers or hot ash. Only she and Else knew about it.

A new moon came and then waned. Every time Else came and asked, "Can you see him coming?"

"I know a great deal," said Stine, "and I see a great deal, but I can't see how long his road is. He's been over the first range of mountains. He's been on the sea in bad weather. His road is long through big forests. He has blisters on his feet, and fever in his body, but he must walk."

"No! No!" cried Else. "I'm so sorry for him!"

"He can't be stopped now. If we do that, he'll fall over dead on the road."

A long time passed. The moon was shining round and huge and the wind sighed in the old tree, and in the sky there was a rainbow in the moonlight.

"That is a sign of confirmation!" said Stine. "Now Rasmus is coming."

But still he didn't come.

"It's a long wait," said Stine.

"I'm tired of this," said Else. She came less often to Stine and didn't bring her any new presents.

She became happier, and one fine morning everyone in the district knew that she had accepted the rich farmer.

She went over there to look at the farm and fields, the cattle and the furniture. Everything was in good shape, and there was no reason to delay the wedding.

It was celebrated for three days with a huge party. There was dancing to the music of clarinets and violins. Everyone in the district was invited. Mother Ølse was there too, and when the festivities were over, and the hosts had said good bye to the guests, and the final fanfare was blown by the trumpets, she went home with leftovers from the feast.

She had only locked the door with a latch, and it was unhooked. The door stood open, and in the room sat Rasmus. He had come home, only just arrived. But dear God, what he looked like! He was just skin and bones, his skin pale and yellow.

"Rasmus!" said his mother. "Is it you? How seedy you look! But my soul is so happy to have you back."

And she gave him the good food she had brought home from the feast, a piece of roast, and a piece of the wedding cake.

He said that lately he had thought often of his mother, his home, and the old willow tree. It was odd how often in his dreams he had seen that tree and barefooted Johanna.

He didn't mention Else at all. He was sick and took to his bed. But we don't believe that the pot was at fault in this, or that it had had any power over him. Only old Stine and Else believed that, but they didn't talk about it.

Rasmus had a fever, and his illness was contagious. No one came to the tailor's house except Johanna, the clogmaker's daughter. She cried when she saw how miserable Rasmus was.

The doctor gave him a prescription, but he wouldn't take the medicine. "What good does it do?" he said.

"It will make you better," said his mother. "Have faith in yourself and the Lord. I would gladly give my life if I could see a little meat on your bones again, and hear you whistle and sing."

And Rasmus recovered from his illness, but his mother caught it. The Lord called her and not him.

It was lonely in the house, and it became a poorer place. "He's worn-out," they said in the district. "Poor Rasmus."

He had carried on a wild life in his travels, and it was that, and not the boiling black pot that had sucked the strength out of him and made him restless. His hair grew thin and grey, and he couldn't be bothered to engage in anything. "What good does it do?" he said. He was more often at the pub than in the pew.

One autumn evening he was walking with difficulty on the muddy road from the pub to his house, through rain and wind. His mother was long gone and buried. The swallows and starlings were gone too, those faithful creatures. But Johanna, the clogmaker's daughter, was not gone. She caught up with him on the road and walked along with him for a while.

"Pull yourself together, Rasmus!"

"What good does it do?" he said.

"That's a bad motto you have," she said. "Remember your mother's words: Have faith in yourself and the Lord! You aren't doing that, Rasmus, but you must and shall! Never say 'What good does it do?' because then you uproot all possible action."

She walked with him to his door, and then she left. He didn't go inside but headed for the old willow tree and sat down on a rock from the toppled milestone.

The wind sighed through the branches of the tree. It was like a song; it was like a story, and Rasmus answered. He spoke aloud, but no one heard except the tree and the sighing wind.

"Such a chill has come over me. It must be time to go to bed. Sleep! Sleep!"

And he went, not towards the house, but towards the pond

where he staggered and fell. The rain was pouring down, and the wind was icy cold, but he didn't notice. When the sun came up and the crows flew over the reeds in the pond, he woke up, half-dead. If he had laid his head where his feet were lying, he would never have gotten up. The green duckweed would have been his shroud.

During the day Johanna came to the tailor's house. She helped him and got him to the hospital.

"We have known each other since childhood," she said. "Your mother gave me both food and drink, and I can never pay her back. You'll get your health back and really live again."

And the Lord wanted him to live. But both his health and spirits had their ups and downs.

The swallows and starlings came and flew away and came again. Rasmus became old before his time. He sat alone in his house, which fell more and more into disrepair. He was poor, poorer than Johanna now.

"You don't have faith," she said, "and if we don't have the Lord, what do we have then? You should go take Communion," she said. "You probably haven't done that since you were confirmed."

"Yes, but what good does *it* do?" he said.

"If you say and believe that, then let it be. The Lord doesn't want to see unwilling guests at his table. But just think about your mother and your childhood years. You were a good and pious boy. May I read a hymn for you?"

"What good does it do?" he asked.

"It always comforts me," she answered.

"Johanna, I guess you've become a saint!" And he looked at her with dull, tired eyes.

And Johanna read the hymn, but not from a book. She didn't have one. She knew the hymn by heart.

"Those were beautiful words," he said, "but I couldn't quite follow it. My head is so heavy."

Rasmus became an old man, but Else, if we can mention her, wasn't young any longer either. Rasmus never talked about her. She was a grandmother, and had a little talkative grand-daughter who was playing with the other children in the village. Rasmus came and leaned on his cane and stood watching the children play. He smiled at them, and old times shone in his memory. Else's grandchild pointed at him—"Poor Rasmus!" she yelled. The other little girls followed her example and shouted, "Poor Rasmus!" They ran shouting after the old man.

It was a grey, oppressive day and more followed, but after grey and heavy days comes a day of sunshine.

It was a beautiful Whit Sunday. The church was decorated with green birch branches. It smelled like the forest in the church, and the sun shone over the pews. The big candles on the altar were lit, and there was communion. Johanna was among the kneeling, but Rasmus was not among them. Just that morning the Lord had called him, and with God he found mercy and compassion.

Many years have passed since then. The tailor's house is still standing there, but no one lives there now. It could collapse in the first storm in the night. The pond is overgrown with reeds and bog beans. The wind sighs in the old tree. It's as if you heard a song. The wind is singing it, and the tree is telling the story. If you don't understand it, ask old Johanna in the poor house.

She lives there and sings her hymn, the one she sang for Rasmus. She thinks about him and prays to the Lord for him, that faithful soul. She can tell about the times that are past, and the memories that sigh in the old tree.

NOTE

1. Danish neoclassical sculptor Bertel Thorvaldsen (1770–1844).

SHE WAS NO GOOD

THE MAYOR STOOD BY the open window. He was wearing a dress shirt with French cuffs, and a pin in the frilled neck piece. He was very well shaven, had done it himself, but he had nicked himself so that a little piece of newspaper was covering the cut.

"Say you!—Boy!" he shouted.

And the boy was none other than the washerwoman's son, who was passing by and respectfully took off his cap. The brim was bent so it could go in his pocket. The boy stood there respectfully, as if he were standing before the king, in his simple and clean but well-patched clothes and big wooden shoes.

"You're a good boy," said the mayor. "You're polite. I suppose your mother is washing clothes down by the river. That's where you're headed with what you have in your pocket. It's a sad thing about your mother. How much have you got there?"

"Half a pint," said the boy in a low, scared voice.

"And she had the same this morning," said the man.

"No, it was yesterday," the boy answered.

"Two halves make a whole! She's no good! It's a sad thing with that class of people. Tell your mother that she should be ashamed of herself! And don't you become a drunkard, but you probably will!—Poor child!—go on now!"

And the boy went on. He kept his cap in his hand, and the wind blew his blond hair so that it stuck out in long wisps. He walked down the street, into the alley and down to the river where his mother stood out in the water by her washing bench, beating the heavy linen with her paddle. There was a current in the water because the sluices were open from the mill. The sheets were pulled by the current and almost knocked the bench over. The washerwoman had to push against it.

"I almost went for a sail!" she said, "It's a good thing you came because I need a little something to build up my strength! It's cold out here in the water. I've been standing here for six hours now. Have you got something for me?"

The boy took out the bottle, and his mother set it to her lips and took a gulp.

"Oh, that does me good! How it warms me up! It's just as good as hot food, and not as expensive! Drink, my boy. You look so pale. You're freezing in those thin clothes. It's autumn, after all. Oh, the water is so cold. Just so I don't get sick. But I won't! Give me another swallow, and you drink too, but just a little bit. You mustn't get dependent on it, my poor, pitiful boy."

And she went over by the bridge where the boy was standing and climbed up on dry land. The water poured from the apron of rushes she had tied around her waist. Water was flowing from her skirts.

"I slave and toil and work my fingers to the bone, but it doesn't matter, as long as I can honestly raise you, my sweet child!"

Just then an older woman came. She was poorly dressed and looked badly too. She was lame in one leg and had an enormously large false curl covering one eye. The curl was supposed to hide her eye, but it only made the defect more noticeable. She was a friend of the washerwoman. The neighbors called her "Gimpy-Maren with the Curl."

"You poor thing, how you toil and slave standing in that cold water! You certainly need a little something to warm you up, but people begrudge you even the little drop you get!" And then the mayor's words to the boy were repeated to the washerwoman because Maren had heard all of it, and it had annoyed her that he talked that way to the child about his mother, and the little she drank, when the mayor himself was having a big dinner party with bottles of wine in abundance. "Fine wines and strong wines! Many will more than quench their thirst, but that's not drinking, oh no! And they're just fine, but you're no good!"

"So he's been talking to you, my boy?" said the washerwoman, and her lips quivered. "You have a mother who's no good! Maybe he's right, but he shouldn't say it to a child. I put up with a lot from those in that house."

"That's right, you worked there when the mayor's parents lived there, didn't you? It was many years ago. Many bushels of salt have been eaten since that time, so it's no wonder we're thirsty!" Maren laughed. "They're having a big dinner today at the mayor's. It should have been canceled, but it was too late because the food had been prepared. I heard about it from the yard boy. Just an hour ago a letter came with the news that the younger brother has died in Copenhagen."

"Dead!" exclaimed the washerwoman and turned deathly pale.

"Oh my!" said the other woman, "You're taking it rather to heart! Oh, you knew him, didn't you, when you worked there?"

"Is he dead? He was the best, the most wonderful person! God won't get many like him!" and the tears ran down her cheeks. "Oh, my God. I'm getting dizzy! It must be because I emptied the flask. It was too much for me. I feel so sick!" And she leaned against the wooden fence.

"Dear God, you're quite ill, dear!" said the woman. "Maybe it'll pass though—No, you really are bad off. I'd better get you home."

"But the clothes there—"

"I'll take care of it. Take my arm. The boy can stay here and watch things in the meantime, and I'll come back and wash the rest. There's just a little bit left."

And the washerwoman's legs buckled under her.

"I stood in the cold water too long, and I haven't had anything to eat or drink since this morning. I have a fever. Oh, dear Jesus, help me home! My poor child!" and she cried.

The boy cried too and was soon sitting alone on the bank close to the wet clothes. The two women walked slowly, the washerwoman wobbling, up the alley, down the street, past the mayor's house, and all at once she sank down on the cobblestones. People gathered around.

Gimpy-Maren ran into the house for help. The mayor and his guests looked out the windows.

"It's the washerwoman," he said. "She's had a drop too much. She's no good. It's a real shame for that good-looking boy she has. I really like the little fellow, but his mother's no good."

She regained consciousness and was led to her humble home, where she was put to bed. Good-hearted Maren made her a bowl of warm beer with butter and sugar. She thought that would be the best medicine. Then she went back to the river and did some well-meant but half-hearted rinsing. She really only pulled the wet clothes to the shore and put them in a box.

In the evening she sat with the washerwoman in her humble room. She had gotten a couple of roasted potatoes and a lovely fatty piece of ham from the mayor's cook for the sick woman. Maren and the boy enjoyed them. The sick woman was content with the smell. She said it was so nourishing.

The boy went to sleep in the same bed as his mother, but he had his spot crosswise at the foot of the bed. He had an old rug for a cover, sewn together from blue and red strips of cloth.

The washerwoman felt a little better. The warm beer had strengthened her, and the smell of the good food had helped.

"Thank you, you dear soul," she said to Maren. "I want to tell you everything when the boy falls asleep. I think he's already sleeping. Look how wonderful and sweet he looks with his eyes closed! He doesn't know what his mother is going through. May God never let him experience it.—I was working for the Councilman, the mayor's parents, and it happened that the youngest son came home, the student. I was young and wild in those days, but respectable, I swear to God," said the washerwoman. "The student was so cheerful and gay, so wonderful! Every drop of his blood was honest and good! A better person has never walked the earth. He was a son of the house, and I was a servant, but we became sweethearts, chastely and with honor. A kiss is not a sin, after all, when you really love each other. And he told his mother. She was like God on earth to him, and so wise and loving. He went away, but he placed his gold ring on my finger. When he was gone, my mistress called me in. She spoke to me seriously but gently, like the Lord might do. She explained to me in spirit and in truth the gap between him and me. 'Now he admires your beauty, but appearances will fade away! You haven't been educated like him, and you aren't on the same mental plane. That's the problem. I have respect for the poor,' she said. 'They will perhaps have a higher standing with God in heaven than many rich people, but here on earth you can't take the wrong road when you're driving or the carriage will topple over, and you two would topple over! I know that a good man—a tradesman—Erik, the glove maker, has proposed to you. He's a widower, has no children, and is well off. Think it over!' Each word she spoke was like a knife in my heart, but she was right! And it crushed me and weighed on me. I kissed her hand and cried salty tears, and even more tears when I got to my room and lay on my bed. That night was a bad night. The Lord knows how I suffered and struggled! Then on Sunday I went to Communion, for guidance. It was like an act of Providence: as I left the church, I met Erik, the glove maker. Then there was no longer any doubt in my mind. We belonged together in position and circumstances. And he was quite well-off. So I went right over to him, took his hand, and asked, 'Are you still thinking of me?' 'Yes, forever and always,' he said. 'Would you have a girl who respects and honors you, but doesn't love you, although that might come?' 'It will come!' he said, and we clasped hands. I went home to my mistress. I was carrying the gold ring that her son had given me against my bare breast. I couldn't wear it on my finger during the day, only at night when I lay in my bed. I kissed the ring until my lips bled, and then I gave it to my mistress and told her that the next week the engagement between me and the glove maker would be announced at church. Then my mistress took me in her arms and kissed me—She didn't say that I was no good, but in those days maybe I was better since I hadn't yet experienced many of the world's misfortunes. The wedding took place at Candlemas, and the first year went well. We had a journeyman and an apprentice, and you, Maren, worked for us."

"Oh you were a wonderful mistress!" said Maren. "I'll never forget how kind you and your husband were."

"You were with us in the good years! We didn't have children then. I never saw the student. Well, I saw him, but he didn't see me. He came home for his mother's funeral, and I saw him standing by the grave. He was chalk-white and so sad, but it was for his mother's sake. Later when his father died, he was abroad and didn't come home, and hasn't been back since. I know that he never got married. I guess he was a lawyer. He didn't remember me, and if he had seen me, I'm sure he wouldn't have recognized me since I've become so ugly. So that's for the best."

And she talked about the difficult days, how misfortune seemed to overwhelm them. They had five hundred dollars, and since there was a house for sale in their street for two hundred, they though it would pay to buy it and tear it down to build a new one. The house was bought. The masons and carpenters estimated that it would cost a thousand and twenty dollars more. Erik the glove maker had credit, and he got the money on loan from Copenhagen, but the captain who was bringing the money was lost in a shipwreck and the money with him.

"That's when I had my wonderful boy, who's sleeping here. His father fell ill with a terrible long-lasting illness. For nine months I had to dress and undress him. Things went from bad to worse for us. We borrowed and borrowed. We lost all our things, and then my husband died! I have toiled and worked, struggled and slaved for the sake of my child. I've washed floors, done laundry both fine and coarse. It's God's will that I don't do better, but he will surely let me go soon and then provide for my boy."

And then she slept.

Later in the morning she felt stronger and strong enough, she thought, to go back to work. She had just gone into the cold water when she was overcome by a shaking, a faint. Convulsively she reached out with her hand, took a step, and fell. Her head was lying on dry land, but her feet were in the river. Her wooden shoes that she had worn in the river—there was a bundle of straw in each of them—floated in the current. She was found by Maren, who came with coffee.

There had been a message from the mayor that she had to meet with him right away. He had something to tell her, but it was too late. A barber was fetched for blood-letting, but the washerwoman was dead.

"She drank herself to death!" said the mayor.

The letter that brought the news of his brother's death also contained the contents of the will. There was a bequest of six hundred dollars to the glove maker's widow, who had once served his parents. The money should be paid out to the woman and her child in larger or smaller amounts according to what was best.

"There were some dealings between my brother and her," said the mayor. "It's a good thing she's out of the way. The boy will get it all, and I'll place him with some good people. He could become a good tradesman." And God's blessing fell on those words.

The mayor summoned the boy and promised to provide for him, and told him what a good thing it was that his mother was dead. She was no good!

She was carried to the grave-yard, to the poor people's cemetery. Maren planted a little rose bush by the grave, and the boy stood beside it.

"My sweet mother!" he said and tears streamed down his face. "Is it true that she was no good?"

"No, she was good!" said the old maid and looked up towards heaven. "I know that from many years' experience and from her last night. I tell you, she *was* good. And God in heaven knows it too, no matter if the world says—'*She was no good!*'"

The Anthropomorphizing of Animals and Nature

THE UGLY DUCKLING

IT WAS SO LOVELY out in the country. It was summer. The wheat was yellow. The oats were green. The hay was up on haystacks down in the green meadows, and the stork walked there on his long red legs speaking Egyptian, a language he had learned from his mother. Around the fields and meadows there were big forests, and in the middle of the forests, deep lakes. Oh yes, it was really lovely there in the country. There was an old estate lying there in the bright sunshine. It had deep canals around it, and from the walls and down to the water big dock plants were growing, so tall that small children could stand upright under the largest of them. It was as overgrown in there as in the densest forest, and there was a duck there sitting on her nest. She was going to hatch her little ducklings, but she was getting tired of it because it took so long, and she rarely had company. The other ducks would rather swim in the canals than run up and sit under a dock leaf to yak and quack with her.

Finally one egg after another cracked. "Peep! Peep!" they said. All the egg yolks had become living and stuck their heads out.

"Quack! Quack! Quick!" she said, and they all quickly hurried the best they could and looked all around under the green leaves. Their mother let them look around as much as they wanted because green is good for the eyes.

"How big the world is!" all the ducklings said because they had quite a different amount of room now than when they were in the egg.

"Do you think this is the whole world?" asked their mother. "It stretches way down on the other side of the garden, right into the minister's field! But I've never been there. You're all here, aren't you?" And she got up. "No, I don't have all! The biggest egg is still lying there. How long is this going to take? I'm getting tired of this!" And she lay down again.

"How's it going?" asked an old duck who came to visit.

"The one egg is taking much too long," said the duck who

483

was lying there. "It won't hatch! But look at the others! They're the most beautiful ducklings I've seen. They all look like their father, that beast! He hasn't come to visit me."

"Let me see the egg that won't hatch," said the old duck. "You can be sure it's a turkey egg. I was fooled like that one time too, and I had a lot of trouble and care with those children because they're afraid of water, let me tell you. I couldn't get them in. I quacked and snapped, but it didn't help! Let me see the egg. Yes, it's a turkey egg. Just leave it lying there and go teach the others to swim."

"I'll just sit here a little bit longer," said the duck. "Since I've sat here this long, I can just as well sit a little longer."

"Suit yourself," said the old duck, and she left.

Finally the big egg cracked. "Peep, peep!" said the chick and tumbled out. He was so big and ugly. The duck looked at him. "That is one big duckling!" she said. "None of the others look like that. Can it be that it's a turkey chick? Well, we'll soon find out about that. He's going in the water if I have to kick him in myself!"

The next day the weather was lovely. The sun was shining on all the green burdock leaves. The mother duck with her whole family went down by the canal. Splash! She jumped into the water. "Quack, quack, quick" she said, and one duck after another plopped in. The water covered their heads, but they came up right away and floated very nicely. Their legs paddled instinctively, and they were all in the water, even the ugly gray chick was swimming along.

"No, that's no turkey," she said. "Look how nicely he uses his feet, how straight he holds himself. It's my own child! In reality he's really quite attractive when you look closely at him. Quack, quack, quick! Come with me, and I'll take you into the world and introduce you in the hen yard, but stay close to me so no one steps on you and watch out for the cats."

They went into the hen yard. It was terribly noisy there because there were two families fighting over an eel head, but in the end the cat got it.

"See, that's the way of the world," said the mother duck and licked her beak because she had also wanted the eel head.

"Now shake a leg," she said. "Hurry over and curtsey deeply to that old duck over there. She is the most distinguished of them all. She has Spanish blood. That's why she's so stout, and notice that she has a red cloth around her leg. That's extremely wonderful, and the greatest recognition a duck can have. It means so much. It means they'll never get rid of her, and she'll be recognized by animals and people—Hurry up!—Not pigeon-toed! A properly raised duckling places his feet far apart, like father and mother. All right, now duck from the neck and say 'Quack!'"

And so they did, but the other ducks around looked at them and said quite loudly, "So, now we'll have another set, as if there weren't enough of us already! And ugh, how ugly that one duckling is! We won't tolerate him!"—And right away a duck flew over to him and bit him in the neck.

"Leave him alone," his mother said. "He's not doing anything to anyone."

"No, but he's too big and too odd," said the duck who had bitten him. "So he has to be bullied."

"Those are lovely children mother has," said the old duck with the cloth around her leg. "All pretty, except that one, who isn't a success. I would wish she could make it over again."

"It can't be done, Your Highness," said the mother duck. "He isn't attractive, but he has a wonderful disposition and swims as beautifully as the others, maybe even better. I think he'll grow more attractive, or maybe with time he'll get a little smaller. He was in the egg too long, and so he didn't get the correct shape." Then she picked at his neck and smoothed him out. "And he's a drake after all," she said, "so it doesn't matter so much. I think he'll be strong and make a splash in the world."

"The other ducklings are lovely," said the old duck. "Make yourselves at home, and if you find an eel head, you may bring it to me!"

And they made themselves at home.

But the poor duckling who had been last out of the egg and who looked so dreadful was bitten, pushed, and made fun of, by both the ducks and the chickens. "He's too big," they all said, and the turkey rooster, who was born with spurs and thought he was an emperor, blew himself up like a clipper ship under full sail, went right up to him, gobbled at him, and turned red in the face. The poor duckling didn't know whether he was coming or going, and was very sad because he was so ugly. Indeed, he was the laughing stock of the entire hen yard.

That's how it went the first day, and later it became worse and worse. The poor duckling was chased by all of them. Even his siblings were mean to him and said continually, "if only the cat would take you, you nasty fright!" and his mother said, "I just wish you were far away." The ducks bit him, the chickens pecked him, and the girl who fed the animals kicked at him with her foot.

Then he ran and flew over the hedge. The small birds in the bushes flew up in the air in fright. "It's because I'm so ugly," thought the duckling and closed his eyes, but he ran off anyway and came out to the big marshes where the wild ducks lived. He lay there the whole night, tired and sorrowful.

In the morning the wild ducks flew up and looked at the new comrade. "What kind of a fellow are you?" they said, and the duckling turned from side to side and greeted everyone as best he could.

"You're remarkably ugly," said the wild ducks, "but it doesn't matter to us, as long as you don't marry into our family."— Poor thing! He wasn't thinking of getting married, only hoped he would be allowed to lie in the rushes and drink some of the marsh water.

He lay there for two whole days. Then two wild geese came, or rather two ganders, for they were both males, and they hadn't been out of the egg for long, and that's why they were so fresh.

"Hey fellow," they said. "You're so ugly that you're likable. Would you like to come along and migrate with us? Right near here in another bog are some sweet wild geese—all of them maidens who know how to quack, I tell you. You could get lucky, even as ugly as you are!"

Just then there was a "bang! bang!" up above, and both wild

geese fell dead into the rushes, and the water turned blood red. "Bang! bang!" sounded again, and whole flocks of wild geese flew up the rushes, and then there was more firing. It was a big hunt. The hunters were lying all around the marshes. Some were even sitting up in the tree branches that reached way out over the rushes. The blue smoke drifted like clouds in between the dark trees and hung far out over the water. Through the mud came the hunting dogs: splash, splash. Rushes and reeds swayed from side to side. It was frightful for the poor duckling who turned his head around to hide it under his wing, and just then a dreadfully big dog was right by him. The tongue was hanging out of its mouth, and the eyes were shining so terribly nastily. He brought his mouth right down to the duckling, showed his sharp teeth and—splash! splash! He was gone again without taking him.

"Oh, thank God," sighed the duckling. "I'm so ugly that even the dog can't be bothered to bite me."

And he lay perfectly still as the bullets whistled in the rushes, and shot after shot rang out.

Not until late in the day was it quiet, but the poor duckling didn't dare get up. He waited several more hours before he looked around, and then he hurried away from the marsh as fast as he could. He ran over fields and meadows. It was so windy that it was hard for him to keep going.

Towards evening he reached a humble little farmer's hut. It was so run down that it didn't know itself on which side to collapse so it remained standing. The wind was blowing so hard around the duckling that he had to sit on his tail to avoid blowing over, and it got worse and worse. Then he noticed that the door was hanging on one hinge and was hanging so crookedly that he could slip through the crack into the room, and that's what he did.

An old woman lived there with her cat and her hen, and the cat, whom she called Sonny, could arch his back and purr. He could even give off sparks if you petted him against the grain. The hen had quite small, low legs, and so she was called Cluckie-LittleLeg. She laid good eggs, and the woman was as fond of her as of her own child.

In the morning they noticed the foreign duckling at once, and the cat started to purr, and the hen to cluck.

"What's this?!" said the woman and looked all around, but she didn't see very well, and so she thought the duckling was a fat run-away duck. "This is a rare find," she said. "Now I can have duck eggs, as long as it's not a drake. We'll have to find out."

So the duckling was put on a three week trial, but no eggs appeared. The cat was the head of the household, and the hen was the mistress, and they said all the time, "*We* and the world" because they thought that they were half of it, and that the best half. The duckling thought there might be another opinion, but the hen wouldn't tolerate that.

"Can you lay eggs?" she asked.

"No."

"Well then, keep your mouth shut."

And the cat said, "Can you arch your back, purr, and give off sparks?"

"No."

"Well then you can't have an opinion when sensible people are talking."

And the duckling sat in the corner in a bad mood. He started thinking about the fresh air and sunshine and had such a great longing to float on the water. At last he couldn't help it, he had to tell the hen.

"What's the matter with you?" she asked. "You don't have anything to do, that's why you get these wild ideas. Lay eggs or purr, and it'll pass."

"But it's so lovely to float on the water," said the duckling. "So lovely to have it wash over your head and dive down to the bottom."

"Sure, that's a great pleasure," said the hen. "You've gone completely crazy! Just ask the cat—he's the wisest one I know—if he likes floating on the water or diving. I won't speak about myself. Ask our mistress, the old woman. No one in the world is wiser than she is. Do you think she wants to float and have water gush over her head?"

"You don't understand me!" said the duckling.

"Well, if we don't understand you, who would? You'll certainly never be wiser than the cat or the woman, not to mention me! Don't make a fuss, child! And thank your creator for all the good that's been done for you. Haven't you come to a warm house and companions you can learn from? But you're a fool, and it isn't fun to hang around with you. Believe me, it's for your own good that I tell you these unpleasant things, and it's how you can tell your true friends. Just take care to lay eggs, or learn to purr or give off sparks!"

"I believe I'll go into the wide world," said the duckling.

"Yes, you just do that," said the hen.

And so the duckling went. He floated on the water, and dove into it, but all the animals shunned him because of his ugliness.

Then autumn came. The leaves in the woods turned yellow and brown. The wind picked them up so they danced around, and the air looked cold. The clouds were heavy with hail and snowflakes, and on the fence the raven sat and cried, "Ow! Ow!" from the cold. You could really freeze if you thought about it, and the poor duckling truly was having a hard time.

One evening when there was a lovely sunset, a whole flock of beautiful big birds came out of the bushes. The duckling had never seen any more lovely. They were a quite shiny white with long supple necks. They were swans, and they uttered some really astonishing sounds, spread out their wide magnificent wings, and flew away from the cold climes to warmer lands, to open waters. They rose so high, so high, and the little ugly duckling became so strangely happy. He turned around in the water like a wheel, stretched his neck high up in the air towards them, and uttered a cry so loud and strange that it frightened him when he heard it. Oh, he couldn't forget the beautiful birds—the happy birds—and as soon as they were out of sight, he dove straight to the bottom. When he came up again, he was quite beside himself. He didn't know what the birds were called, nor where they were going, but still he loved them as he had never loved anyone. He didn't envy them. How could it occur to him to wish for such beauty? He would have been happy if only the ducks would have accepted him amongst them—the poor ugly animal!

And the winter was cold, so cold. The duckling had to swim around in the water to keep it from freezing solid, but every night the hole where he was swimming got smaller and smaller. The ice froze so it cracked. The duckling had to keep moving his legs to keep the ice from closing in. Finally he weakened, lay quite still, and froze into the ice.

Early in the morning a farmer came by, saw him, went out and kicked the ice in pieces with his wooden shoe, and carried him home to his wife where the duckling revived.

The children wanted to play with him, but the duckling thought they wanted to hurt him and flew in fright right up into the milk bowl so the milk splashed out into the room. The woman screamed and threw up her arms, and then he flew into the trough where the butter was and then down into the flour barrel and up again. What a sight he was! And the woman screamed and hit at him with the bellows, and the children ran here and there trying to catch the duckling, laughing and shrieking! Luckily the door stood open; out he flew through the bushes to the newly fallen snow, and there he lay in a swoon.

But it would be far too sad to tell all the suffering and misery he had to endure during that hard winter. When the sun started to warm up again, he was lying in the rushes between the reeds. The larks were singing, and it was spring, lovely springtime.

Then he lifted his wings all at once. They were stronger than before and carried him powerfully away, and before he knew it, he was in a big garden where apple trees were blooming, and where the lilacs smelled sweet and hung on long green branches right down towards the meandering canals. Oh, it was lovely there, so fresh and newly green, and right in front of him out of the thicket came three lovely white swans. They ruffled up their feathers and floated so lightly on the water. The duckling recognized the magnificent animals and was filled with a strange melancholy.

"I'll fly over to them, those regal animals, and they'll peck

"The newest one is the prettiest!"

me to death because I who am so ugly dare approach them. But it doesn't matter. Better to be killed by them than to be nipped by the ducks, pecked by the hens, kicked by the girl who watches the hen yard, and suffer in the winter." So he flew onto the water and swam towards the splendid swans. They saw him and plunged towards him with ruffled feathers. "Just kill me," said the poor bird, and he bent his head down towards the surface of the water and waited for death—but what did he see in the clear water? He saw his own reflection, and he was no longer a clumsy dark grey bird, ugly and nasty. He was himself a swan.

You see, it doesn't matter whether you're born in a duck yard as long as you've lain in a swan's egg!

He felt truly glad about all the distress and tribulations he had suffered. He understood his happiness now, and all the beauty that greeted him. And the big swans swam around him and stroked him with their beaks.

Some small children came into the garden. They threw bread and grain out into the water, and the smallest one cried: "There's a new one!"

And the other children chimed in, "yes, there's a new one!" They clapped their hands and danced around, ran after their father and mother, and bread and cakes were thrown in the water, and they all said, "The newest one is the prettiest! So young and so lovely." And the old swans bowed to him.

Then he felt quite bashful and stuck his head behind his wings. He didn't himself quite know why. He was too happy, but not at all proud because a good heart is never proud. He thought about how he had been pursued and persecuted and now heard everyone say that he was the most lovely of all the beautiful birds, and the lilacs bowed down their branches right down to the water to him, and the sun shone so warm and good. He ruffled his feathers, lifted his slender neck, and from his heart he rejoiced, "I never dreamed of this much happiness when I was the ugly duckling."

IN THE DUCKYARD

THERE WAS A DUCK who came from Portugal. Some said she came from Spain, but it doesn't matter because she was called the Portuguese. She laid eggs, was butchered and eaten—that was her life. All those who came from her eggs were called the Portuguese, and that really means something. Now there was only one remaining member of the family left in the duckyard, a yard where the hens also had access, and where the rooster strutted around with immense arrogance.

"He offends me with his violent crowing!" said the Portuguese. "But he is handsome—you can't deny that, notwithstanding that he's not a drake. He should learn to modulate himself, but modulation is an art. It shows higher culture, which the little songbirds in the neighbor's linden tree have. How delightfully they sing! There is something so touching in their song. I call it Portugal! If I had a little songbird like that, I would be such a good and loving mother to him. It's in my blood, my Portuguese blood."

Just as she was talking a little songbird fell headfirst from the roof. The cat was after it, but the bird escaped with a broken wing and fell into the duckyard.

"That's just like the cat, that scoundrel!" said the Portuguese. "I know him from when I had ducklings myself. That such a creature is allowed to live and walk around on roofs! I'm sure something like this would never be allowed in Portugal!"

And she felt sorry for the little songbird, and the other ducks, who weren't Portuguese, felt sorry for him too.

"Poor little thing!" they said, and one after another came. "It's true we don't sing ourselves," they said, "but we have some kind of inner sensitivity to it or something. We feel it even if we never talk about it."

"Well, I will talk about it!" said the Portuguese, "and I'm going to do something for the little thing, because that's one's duty." Then she went into the watering trough and splashed in the water so that she almost drowned the little

493

songbird with the drenching he received, but she meant well. "That was a good deed," she said. "The others can take an example from it."

"Peep!" said the little bird. Since his one wing was broken, it was hard for him to shake himself dry, but he understood very well that the shower was well meant. "You have a kind heart, m'am," he said, but did not ask for more.

"I have never given a thought to being kind-hearted," said the Portuguese, "but I do know that I love all my fellow creatures except the cat. But no one can expect me to love the cat. He has eaten two of my own. But make yourself at home here. I myself am from a foreign country, as you can probably tell by my bearing and my plumage. My drake is a native and doesn't have my bloodlines, but I'm not at all arrogant because of that. If anyone here can understand you, then I dare say it's me."

"She has porta-gall stones in her gullet!" said a little ordinary duckling, who was witty, and the other ordinary ducks thought the "porta-gall stones" were hilarious. It sounded like "Portugal." They nudged and quacked at each other. He was so extremely witty! And then they gathered in and started talking to the little songbird.

"The Portuguese is a gifted speaker," they said. "We don't use such great big words, though our sympathy for you is as great. But if we don't do anything for you, we'll be quiet about it. We find that the noblest."

"You have a lovely voice," said one of the oldest. "It must be wonderful to know that you bring joy to so many. I don't know anything about it at all, and so I keep my mouth shut. That's always better than saying something dumb, as so many others do."

"Don't pester him," said the Portuguese. "He needs rest and care. Shall I give you another shower, little songbird?"

"Oh no, let me stay dry," he begged.

"Hydrotherapy is the only thing that ever helps me," said the Portuguese. "But diversion is also good. Soon the neighbor hens will come visiting. There are two Chinese chickens that wear pantalettes. They are very cultured and were imported, which raises my respect for them."

And the hens came, and the rooster came too. Today he was very polite in that he wasn't as crude as usual.

"You are a real songbird," he said, "and you make the most of your little voice. But you have to have more power in your voice to be recognized as a member of the male sex."

The two Chinese hens went into raptures over the sight of the songbird. He looked so disheveled from the shower he had had that they thought he looked like a Chinese chick. "He's lovely!" they said, and started talking to him. They spoke in whispers and with the "P" sound of aristocratic Chinese.

"We are of your kind. The ducks, even the Portuguese, are web-footed, as I'm sure you've noticed. You don't know us yet, but who does know us, or has taken the trouble to? No one, even among the hens, although we were born to a higher perch than most of the others. But it doesn't matter. We mind our own business amongst the others, who don't have the same principles we have. But we always look for the good in everyone and talk about the good things, although it's hard to find where there isn't any. But with the exception of us two and the rooster, there is no one in the henhouse who is intelligent. But they are respectable. That's more than you can say for the residents of the duckyard. Here's a warning, little songbird. Don't trust the one over there with the short tail! She is treacherous. That speckled one there with the crooked wing pattern is crazy about debating and never lets anyone else get the last word, and she's always wrong. That fat duck talks ill of everyone, and that's contrary to our nature. If you can't say something nice, you shouldn't say anything at all. The Portuguese is the only one who has a little breeding, and with whom you can associate, but she's pretty passionate and talks too much about Portugal!"

"The two Chinese sure have a lot to whisper about," said a couple of the ducks. "But they bore me, so I've never talked to them."

Then the drake came over! He thought that the songbird was a grey sparrow. "Well, I can't tell the difference," he said, "and it's all the same to me. He's a musician, and if you've heard one, you've heard them all."

"Don't bother about what he says," whispered the Portuguese. "He's great in business matters, and that's all that matters to him. But now I'm going to take a little nap. I owe it to myself to be nice and fat when I'm embalmed with apples and prunes."

And she lay down in the sun and blinked with one eye. She was a good duck, and she lay well and slept well. The little songbird plucked at his broken wing and cuddled up close to his protector. The sun was shining so good and warm, and it was a good place to be.

The neighbor hens went about scratching the ground. They had actually only come over looking for food. The Chinese left first, and then the others. The witty duckling said of the Portuguese that the old thing would soon be in her second chickhood, and the other ducks roared with laughter, "Chickhood! Chickhood! How wonderfully witty he is!" and then they repeated the former joke, "porta-gall stones!" They had a lot of fun, and then they went to bed.

They had been resting for a while when suddenly someone threw some slop into the duckyard. It splashed so that all the sleeping ducks jumped up and flapped their wings. The Portuguese woke up too, shifted about, and squeezed the little songbird terribly.

"Peep!" it said. "You squeezed me so hard, m'am!"

"Why are you lying in the way?" she said. "You shouldn't be so touchy! I have nerves too, but you never hear me saying 'Peep'."

"Don't be mad at me," said the little bird. "That 'peep' just popped from my beak."

The Portuguese wasn't listening, but had run off to the slops and made a good meal out of it. When she had finished and lay down again, the little songbird wanted to be kind and sang:

> *"Tra ling-a-ling!*
> *Of your heart I'll sing.*
> *Oft and long*
> *I'll raise my song."*

"I have to rest after my meal," said the duck. "You have to learn the customs here. I'm going to sleep now."

The little songbird was quite taken aback, for he had hoped to please her. Later when the Portuguese woke up, he was standing in front of her with a little grain of wheat he had found. He laid it in front of her, but she hadn't slept well so naturally she was grumpy.

"You can give that to a chicken!" she said. "And don't hang over me all the time!"

"But you're mad at me," he said. "What did I do?"

"Du?"[1] said the Portuguese. "You can't speak to me like that!"

"Yesterday the sun was shining here," said the little bird. "Today it's dark and grey. I'm so terribly sad."

"You must not be able to tell time," said the Portuguese. "The day isn't over yet. Don't stand there and make a fool out of yourself."

"You're looking at me as angrily as those two bad eyes did when I fell down here into the yard."

"The impertinence!" said the Portuguese. "Comparing me with a cat—that carnivore! I who don't have a mean bone in my body! I've taken good care of you, and now I'm going to teach you a lesson."

And then she bit the head off the songbird, and he lay there dead.

"What's this?" she said, "Couldn't he take that? Well, then he really wasn't meant for this world. I know I've been like a mother to him. It's because of my good heart!"

The neighbor's rooster stuck his head into the duckyard and crowed powerfully.

"You'll be the death of someone with that crowing," said the duck. "It's all your fault. He lost his head, and I am close to losing mine."

"He doesn't look very impressive lying there," said the rooster.

"Speak of him with respect!" said the Portuguese. "He had a beautiful tone and song and was highly cultured. He was loving and sensitive, as is fitting for all animals as well as for so-called human beings."

And all the ducks gathered around the little dead songbird. Ducks have strong feelings, either with envy or with pity, and since they didn't envy the songbird, they pitied him. So did the two Chinese hens.

"There'll never be another songbird like him! He was almost Chinese," and they cried so they gurgled, and all the hens clucked, but the ducks had the reddest eyes.

"We have heart," they said. "Nobody can deny that."

"Heart!" said the Portuguese. "Indeed, we have! We have nearly as much as they have in Portugal!"

"Now let's think about getting something to eat," said the drake. "That's more important. If one musician's voice is stilled, there are still plenty more, after all."

NOTE

1. A wordplay on the Danish informal form of address that does not appear in the original. In Danish, "you" can be spoken or written either formally (using the word *de* in this case) or informally (*du*).

THE STORKS

ON THE LAST HOUSE in a little town there was a stork's nest. The stork mother sat in the nest with her four little children, who stuck their heads out with their little black beaks that hadn't turned red yet. A little distance away on the top of the roof, stork father was standing straight and stiff. He had pulled one leg up under him in order to take a few pains while he was standing sentry. You would think he was carved from wood, that's how still he stood. "It must look pretty impressive that my wife has a sentry by the nest," he thought. "They can't know I'm her husband. They probably think I've been commanded to stand here. It looks very impressive!" and he continued to stand on one leg.

Down on the street a whole gang of children were playing, and when they saw the storks, first the boldest boy and then

the others sang the old ditty about the storks, but they sang it
the way they remembered it:

> *"Fly Storky storky!*
> *Fly home to your door!*
> *Your wife's sitting there*
> *With baby storks four.*
> *One will be hanged,*
> *And the second be penned.*
> *The third will be burned,*
> *And the fourth turned on end!"*

"Listen to what the boys are singing," the little storks said.
"They say we'll be hanged and burned!"

"Don't pay any attention to that," said the stork mother.
"Just don't listen, and it won't matter."

But the boys kept singing, and they pointed at the storks.
Only one boy, whose name was Peter, said that it wasn't nice to
make fun of the animals and wouldn't have anything to do
with it. The stork mother consoled her children. "Don't worry
about it," she said, "Just see how calmly your father is standing
there and on one leg too!"

"We're so scared," said the little storks, and drew their heads
way down into the nest.

The next day when the children gathered again to play, they
saw the storks and started their song:

> *"The first will be hanged,*
> *The second be burned!"*

"Are we going to be hanged and burned?" asked the stork
babies.

"No, certainly not," their mother answered. "You're going to
learn to fly. I'll train you. Then we'll fly out to the meadow and
visit the frogs. They'll bow down to us in the water, and say
"croak, croak," and then we'll eat them up. It'll be lots of fun."

"And then what?" asked the little storks.

"Then all the storks in the country gather together, and we

The storks.

have fall maneuvers. You have to be able to fly well by then. It's very important because those who can't fly are stabbed to death by the General's beak. So be very sure to learn your lessons when the training starts!"

"So we'll be killed then anyway like the boys said, and listen: they're singing it again."

"Listen to me and not to them," stork mother said. "After the big maneuvers we'll fly to the warm countries. Oh far, far from here, over mountains and forests. We'll fly to Egypt where they have three-sided stone houses that end in a point up over the clouds. They are called pyramids and they are older than any stork can imagine. There's a river there that overflows so that the land becomes muddy. You walk in the mud and eat frogs."

"Oh!" all the children said.

"Yes, it's so lovely. You don't do anything but eat the whole day, and while we have it so good there, there's not a green leaf to be seen on the trees here. It's so cold here that the clouds freeze to pieces and fall down in little white patches." It was snow she meant, but she couldn't explain it any better.

"Do the naughty boys also freeze to pieces?" asked the stork babies.

"No, they don't freeze to pieces, but they aren't far from it, and they have to sit inside their dark houses and twiddle their thumbs. But you, on the other hand, will fly around in foreign lands where there are flowers and warm sunshine."

Time passed, and the young storks were so big that they could stand up in the nest and look all around, and stork father flew in every day with frogs, little grass snakes, and other tasty storky snacks that he found! Oh, it was fun to see the tricks he did for them! He lay his head way back on his tail, and he clattered his beak as if it were a little rattle, and then he told them stories from the marsh.

"All right, now you must learn to fly," said stork mother one day, and all four young storks had to go out on the ridge of the roof. Oh, how they tottered! They balanced with their wings but almost fell over!

"Watch me," mother said. "Hold your heads like this. Place

your legs like this. One, two! One, two! This is what'll get you moving up in life." Then she flew a little distance, and the children made a little clumsy hop and thud! There they lay because their bodies were too heavy.

"I don't want to fly," said one young stork, and climbed back into the nest. "I don't care about getting to the warm countries."

"Do you want to freeze to death here when winter comes? Shall the boys come and hang and burn and beat you? I'll call them."

"Oh no," said the young stork, and hopped out on the roof again with the others. By the third day they could actually fly a little, and they thought that they could sit and rest on the air too. They tried that, but thud! They took a tumble, and so they had to move their wings again. There came the boys down on the street, singing their song,

"Fly storky storky . . ."

"Shouldn't we fly down and peck their eyes out?" asked the young storks.

"No, forget about it," said their mother. "Just listen to me. That's much more important. One, two, three, fly to the right. One, two, three, now left around the chimney.—Oh, that was very good! That last stroke of the wings was so lovely and correct that you'll all be allowed to come to the swamp with me tomorrow. Several fine stork families will be coming there with their children. Let me see that mine are the prettiest, and be sure to hold your heads high. That looks good, and others will respect you."

"But won't we get revenge on the naughty boys?" asked the young storks.

"Let them cry whatever they want. You'll fly above the clouds, and come to the land of the pyramids, while they must freeze here without a green leaf or a sweet apple."

"But we'll get revenge," they whispered to each other, and then there were more maneuvers to do.

Of all the boys in the street none was worse at singing the

cruel ditty than the one who had begun it, and he was quite a small boy, not more than six years old. The young storks thought he was a hundred because he was quite a bit bigger than their mother and father, and what did they know about how old or big humans could be? They determined to be revenged on this one boy—he had started it, and he kept it up. The young storks were so irritated, and as they became bigger, they tolerated it even less. Their mother finally had to promise them that they would get revenge, but not until the last day they were to be in the country.

"First we have to see how you manage the big maneuvers. If you don't do well so that the General stabs his beak in your chests, then the boys would be right, at least in a way. Let's wait and see."

"And see you shall!" said the young ones, and they really took great pains. They practiced every day and flew so lovely and lightly that it was a pleasure to see them.

Then fall came, and all the storks started gathering to fly away to the warm countries while we have winter here. What a maneuver! They flew over the forests and towns just to see how well they could fly. There was a big trip lying ahead of them. The young storks did their flying so beautifully that they graduated frog and snake cum laude. That was the best possible mark, and they could eat the frog and snake, which they also did at once.

"Now our revenge!" they said.

"Yes indeed," said the stork mother. "I have thought of just the thing. I know where the pond is where all the little humans lie until the stork comes and brings them to their parents. The lovely little ones dream and sleep as beautifully as they never will again. All parents would gladly have such a little child, and all children want a brother or a sister. Now we'll fly to the pond and get a little child for each of those who didn't sing the naughty song and make fun of the storks, because those naughty children shouldn't get one!"

"But what about the one who started the song, the naughty, nasty boy," cried the young storks. "What'll we do to him?"

"In the pond there is a little dead child that has dreamed itself to death. We'll bring it to him, and then he must cry because we have brought him a dead little brother. But you haven't forgotten the good little boy have you? The one who said, 'It's a shame to make fun of the animals?' We'll bring him both a brother and a sister and since that boy was named Peter, you will all be called Peter too."

And it happened as she said, and all the storks were named Peter, and that is what they're called to this very day.

THE SPRUCE TREE

IN THE FOREST THERE was such a lovely spruce tree. It was well placed with sunlight and plenty of air, and all around it grew many bigger companions, both spruce and pine, but the little spruce tree was so eager to grow that it didn't think about the warm sun and the fresh air. It didn't care about the country children who chattered as they were out picking strawberries and raspberries. Often they came with a whole jar full, or had the strawberries strung on a straw. Then they sat by the little tree and said, "Oh, what a cute little tree," and the tree didn't like hearing that at all.

The next year it was a shoot bigger, and the next year even taller. Indeed, you can always tell how old a spruce tree is by how many shoots it has.

"Oh, if only I were a big tree like the others!" sighed the little tree. "Then I could spread my branches so far around and from the top see out into the wide world! The birds would build nests within my branches, and when the wind blows, I could nod as nobly as the others do."

It took no pleasure from the sunshine, or the birds, or the red clouds that sailed over it morning and evening. Often in the winter, when the snow lay glistening white all around, a rabbit would come hopping and jump right over the little tree—Oh, it was so irritating! But two winters passed, and by the third winter, the tree was so big that the rabbit had to go around it. Oh, to grow, to grow, to become big and old! That's the only beauty in this world, thought the tree.

In the autumn the wood cutters always came and chopped down some of the largest trees. It happened every year, and the young spruce tree, which was pretty well grown now, trembled because the big magnificent trees fell crashing and bashing to the ground. The branches were chopped off so they looked quite naked and long and narrow. They were almost unrecognizable, and then they were laid on wagons, and horses pulled them out of the forest.

Where were they going? What was going to happen to them?

In the spring, when the swallows and the stork came, the tree asked them: "Don't you know where they went? Didn't you see them?"

The swallows didn't know anything, but the stork looked thoughtful, nodded his head, and said, "Yes, I think so. Flying up from Egypt I met a lot of new ships, and on the ships were magnificent wooden masts. I dare say that that was them. They smelled like spruce, and I bring you greetings from them. They stood proudly, really spruced up."

"Oh, if only I were big enough to fly over the ocean! What is this ocean exactly, and what does it look like?"

"It takes too long to explain!" said the stork, and he left.

"Enjoy your youth!" said the sunbeams. "Enjoy your fresh growth, and the young life that's in you!"

And the wind kissed the tree, and the dew cried tears over it, but the spruce tree didn't understand.

When it was Christmas time some very young trees were felled—trees that weren't even as big or old as the spruce tree who had no peace and rest, but always wanted to be on its way. These young trees (and they were always the very prettiest) kept their branches. They were placed on the wagons, and horses pulled them out of the forest.

"Where were they going?" asked the spruce tree. "They aren't any bigger than me. There was even one a lot smaller. Why did they keep all their branches? Where did they go?"

"This-see-we! This-see-we!" chirped the grey sparrows. "We've peeked in the windows down in town. We know where they're going. Oh, they go to the greatest splendor and magnificence that can be imagined! We have looked through the windows and have seen how they're planted right in the middle of the warm living room and decorated with the most lovely things, such as gilded apples, honey cakes, toys, and many hundreds of candles!"

"And then—?" asked the spruce tree, trembling in all its branches. "And then? What happens then?"

"Well, we didn't see anything more. It was just splendid!"

"I wonder if I was born to go that shining way!?" rejoiced the tree. "That's even better than sailing on the ocean. Oh, how I suffer from longing! If only it were Christmas! Now I'm tall and stretched upward like the ones who were taken away last year!—Oh, if only I were already on the wagon! If only I were in the warm room with all the splendor and magnificence! And then—? Then something even better will happen, even more beautiful. Why else would they decorate me like that? Something even greater, even more splendid—But what? Oh, how I am suffering! I'm pining! I don't even know myself what's the matter with me!"

"Take pleasure in us," said the air and the sunshine. "Be happy in your fresh youth out in the open air!"

But the tree wasn't happy at all. It grew and grew. Both winter and summer it was green. Dark green it stood there, and people who saw it said, "that's a lovely tree," and at Christmas it was cut first. The ax cut deeply through the pith, and the tree fell with a sigh to the earth. It felt a pain and a powerlessness, and couldn't think of any joy. It felt saddened to be parted from its home, from the spot where it had grown up. It knew, of course, that it would never again see its dear companions, the small bushes and flowers all around, maybe not even the birds. The departure was not at all pleasant.

The tree came to itself in the yard, unpacked with the other trees, when it heard a man say, "That one's magnificent! We won't take any other!"

Then two servants in uniform came and bore the spruce tree into a big beautiful room. Portraits were hanging on the walls, and by the big porcelain stove there were Chinese vases with lions on the lids. There were rocking chairs, silk sofas, big tables full of coffee table books, and toys worth hundreds upon hundreds of dollars—at least that's what the children said. And the spruce tree was raised up in a big tub filled with sand, but no one could see that it was a tub because green material was wound around it, and it stood on a big embroidered rug. Oh, how the tree trembled! What was going to happen? Both servants and young ladies of the house decorated it. On one branch they hung small nets, cut from colored paper. Each net was filled with candies. Gilded apples and walnuts hung as if they had grown there, and over a hundred red, blue, and white candles were fastened to the branches. Dolls that looked as real as humans—the tree had never seen anything like them before—floated in the branches, and at the very top was placed a big gold tinsel star. It was magnificent, quite exceptionally magnificent.

"Tonight," they all said, "tonight it will be radiant!"

"Oh," thought the tree, "if only it were evening! If only the lights were lit soon! And I wonder what will happen then? I wonder if trees from the woods will come and look at me? Will the grey sparrows fly by the windows? I wonder if I'll grow permanently here and stand here decorated winter and summer?"

Well, that's what it knew about it! But it really had bark-ache from pure longing, and bark-ache is as painful for a tree as a headache is for the rest of us.

Then the lights were lit. What brilliance! What magnificence! All the branches of the tree trembled with it, so much so that one of the candles started a fire on a branch, and that really stung.

"God save us!" cried the ladies and put out the fire in a hurry.

Now the tree didn't dare tremble at all. Oh, it was terrible! It was so afraid of losing some of its finery. It was really quite bewildered by all the splendor—and then both folding doors were swung open, and a crowd of children rushed in as if they were going to tip over the whole tree. The older people followed composedly behind. The little ones stood quite silently—but only for a moment. Then they cheered again so it resounded in the room. They danced around the tree, and one gift after another was plucked off.

"What are they doing?" thought the tree. "What's going to happen?" And the candles burned right down to the branches, and as they burned down they were extinguished, and then the children were allowed to plunder the tree. Oh, how they rushed at it so that all the branches creaked! If it hadn't been fastened to the ceiling by the top and the gold star, it would have tipped over.

The children danced around with their splendid toys. No one looked at the tree except the old nanny, who was peering and peeking through the branches, but only to see if one more fig or an apple had been overlooked.

"A story! a story!" cried the children and pulled a little fat man over toward the tree. He sat down right by it, "for then we're out in nature," he said, "and it will be good for the tree to listen too. But I'll only tell one story. Do you want to hear the one about Dorky Porky or Clumpy Dumpy, who fell down the stairs and still gained the throne and got the princess."

"Dorky Porky," cried some. "Clumpy Dumpy," cried others. There was yelling and shouting, only the spruce tree was very quiet and thought, "Am I not part of this at all? Am I not going to do something?" Of course it had already done its part, what it was supposed to do.

And the man told about Clumpy Dumpy who fell down the stairs and still gained the throne and got the princess. And the children clapped their hands and shouted: "Tell more! Tell more!" They wanted to hear Dorky Porky too, but they were only told the one about Clumpy Dumpy. The spruce tree stood very quietly and thoughtfully. None of the birds in the woods had told stories like this. "Clumpy Dumpy fell down the steps and still got the princess! Well, well, that's how the world is," thought the spruce tree and believed the story was true since such a nice man told it. "Well, well, who can tell. Maybe I'll also fall down the steps and get a princess!" And it looked forward to the next day when it would be dressed with candles and toys, gold and fruit.

"Tomorrow I won't shake," he thought. "I'll enjoy myself in all my splendor. Tomorrow I'll hear the story about Clumpy

Dumpy again and maybe the one about Dorky Porky." And the tree stood quietly and thoughtfully the whole night.

In the morning the servants entered the room.

"Now the finery starts again," thought the tree, but they dragged it out of the living room, up the stairs, into the attic, and there, in a dark corner where there was no daylight, they left it. "What's the meaning of this?" thought the tree. "I wonder what I'm supposed to do here? I wonder what I'll hear here?" And it leaned up against the wall and thought and thought.—And it had plenty of time because days and nights passed. No one came up there, and when someone finally did come, it was to put some big crates in a corner. The tree stood quite out-of-sight. You would think that it had been completely forgotten.

"Now it's winter outside," thought the tree. "The earth is hard and covered with snow. The people couldn't plant me, so I'll stay sheltered here until spring! That's very smart! How good people are! If it just wasn't so dark and lonely here—not even a little rabbit. It was nice out in the woods with snow on the ground when the rabbit jumped by. Yes, even when it jumped right over me, but I didn't like it then. Still, up here it's really lonely."

"Squeak, squeak!" said a little mouse just then and popped out, and then another one came. They sniffed at the spruce tree and crept through the branches.

"It's awfully cold," the little mice said. "Otherwise it's nice being here. Isn't that right, you old spruce tree?"

"I'm not old at all," said the spruce tree. "There are many who are much older than I am."

"Where do you come from?" asked the mice, "and what do you know?" They were dreadfully curious. "Tell us about the most beautiful place on earth! Have you been there? Have you been in the kitchen where there's cheese lying on the shelves, and there are hams hanging from the ceiling? Where you dance on tallow candles and go in skinny and come out fat?"

"I don't know about that," said the tree, "but I know the woods, where the sun shines, and where the birds sing." And then he told all about his childhood, and the little mice had never before heard anything like that, and they listened carefully and said, "Oh, you have seen so much! How happy you have been!"

"Me?" said the spruce tree, and thought about what it had said. "Yes, they were actually pretty good times," and then it told about Christmas Eve, when it was decorated with cakes and candles.

"Oh," said the little mice, "how happy you have been, you old spruce tree!"

"I am not at all old," said the tree. "I just came from the forest this very winter. I'm in the prime of life. I'm just not growing right now!"

"You're a good storyteller," said the little mice, and the next night they brought four other little mice to hear the tree tell stories. The more it talked, the clearer it remembered everything, and it thought, "they really were fun times, but they can come again. They can come! Clumpy Dumpy fell down the stairs and still got the princess, maybe I can get a princess too." And then the spruce thought about such a lovely little birch tree that grew out in the forest—that was a truly lovely princess to the spruce tree.

"Who is Clumpy Dumpy?" asked the little mice. And then the spruce tree told the whole story. It remembered every single word, and the little mice almost climbed to the top of the tree in pure pleasure. The next night even more mice arrived, and on Sunday two rats, but they said that the story wasn't funny, and that saddened the little mice who then also thought less of it.

"Is that the only story you know?" asked the rats.

"The only one," the tree answered. "I heard it the happiest evening of my life, but at that time I didn't realize how happy I was."

"It's an extraordinarily bad story. Don't you know any about bacon and tallow candles? No pantry stories?"

"No," said the tree.

"Well, we'll say thanks anyway then," said the rats and went home to their own concerns.

Finally the little mice went away too, and the tree sighed. "It was also rather nice when those nimble little mice sat around me and listened to what I said. But now that is over too—but I will enjoy myself when I'm taken out of here again!"

But when would that happen? Well, there finally came a morning when people came up to the attic and puttered around. Boxes were moved, and the tree was pulled out; true, they threw it rather hard on the floor, but soon a man dragged it right towards the stairs, where there was daylight.

"Now life begins again," thought the tree. It felt the fresh air, the first sunbeam, and then it was out in the yard. Everything went so quickly; the tree completely forgot to look at itself, there was so much to see all around. The yard was right next to a garden, and everything was blooming there. The roses hung fresh and fragrantly over the little railing, the linden trees were blooming, and the swallows flew around and sang, "tweet sweet, my husband's come," but it wasn't the spruce tree they meant.

"Now I'll live!" it rejoiced, and spread out its branches. Oh, they were all withered and yellow, and now it was lying in a corner between weeds and nettles. The gold paper star was still sitting in the top and was shining in the clear sunlight.

In the yard a couple of the cheerful children, who had danced around the tree and been so happy with it, were playing. One of the smallest ran over and tore off the gold star.

"Look what's still sitting on the ugly old Christmas tree," he said and trampled on the branches so they cracked under his boots.

And the tree looked at all the flowers and freshness in the garden. It looked at itself, and it wished it had stayed in its dark corner in the attic. It thought about its fresh youth in the forest, the wonderful Christmas Eve, and the small mice, who had so happily listened to the story about Clumpy Dumpy.

"Over, all is over," said the poor tree. "If only I had been happy when I could have been. Over, all over."

And the servant came and chopped the tree into small pieces. A whole bundle lay there. It flamed up beautifully under the big boiler, and it sighed so deeply, each sigh was like a little shot. That's why the children who were playing ran in and sat in front of the fire, looked into it, and cried out, "Pop!" With every crack, that really was a deep sigh, the tree thought about a summer day in the forest, and a winter night out there when the stars were shining. It thought about Christmas Eve and Clumpy Dumpy, the only story it had heard and could tell—and then the tree burned out.

The boys played in the yard, and the smallest wore the gold star that the tree had worn on its happiest evening. Now it was over, and the tree was gone and the story too. Over, all over, as all stories are.

IT'S PERFECTLY TRUE!

"IT'S A TERRIBLE STORY!" said a hen over in the part of town where the event didn't happen. "A terrible story from a henhouse! I don't dare sleep alone tonight. It's a good thing there are so many of us on the roost." And then she told the story so the feathers stood on end on the other hens, and the rooster let his comb fall. It's perfectly true!

But we'll start at the beginning, and that was in a henhouse in another part of town. The sun went down, and the hens flew up. One of them—she had white feathers and short legs—laid her prescribed eggs and was, as a hen, respectable in every way. As she settled on the perch, she preened herself with her beak, and a little feather fell out.

"There went that one," she said. "The more I preen myself, the more beautiful I will surely become." And she said it in fun, because she was the cheerful soul among the hens and otherwise, as mentioned, very respectable. Then she fell asleep.

It was dark all around. One hen sat next to the other, and the one sitting next to her wasn't sleeping. She heard, and she didn't hear—as you must in this world to live in peace and quiet—so to her other neighbor she just had to say: "Did you hear what was said here? I'll mention no names, but there's a hen here who will pluck out her feathers for vanity's sake. If I were a rooster, I would despise her!"

Right above the hens the owl was sitting with her owl husband and little owly children. That family has sharp ears, and they heard every word that the neighbor hen uttered. They rolled their eyes, and mother owl fanned herself with her wings. "Just don't listen! But you did hear what was said, of course. I heard it with my own ears, and you have to hear a lot before your ears fall off. One of the hens has forgotten herself to the extent that she is plucking out all her feathers right in front of the rooster!"

"Little pitchers have big ears," said father owl. "This isn't fit for the children."

"I'll just tell the neighbor owl. She's such a respectable owl to whoop it up with." And away flew mother.

"Whoooo, whoooo" they both hooted, over to the neighbor's pigeon coop. "Have you heard? Have you heard? Whoooo? There's a hen who has plucked out all her feathers for the sake of a rooster. She's freezing to death, if she isn't dead already!"

"Where? where?" cooed the pigeons.

"In the yard across the street. I've as good as seen it myself. It's really almost unfit to tell, but it's perfectly true!"

"Truuuu, truuuu, every word," cooed the pigeons, and cooed down to its hen yard. "There's a hen—some say two— that plucked out all their feathers so they wouldn't look like the others and in order to attract the rooster. It's a daring game because you can catch cold and die of fever, and both of them are dead!"

"Wake up! wake up!" the rooster crowed and flew up on the board fence. He still had sleep in his eyes, but he crowed anyway. "Three hens have died from a broken heart because of a rooster! They plucked out all their feathers! It's a terrible story, and I don't want to keep it to myself—pass it on!"

"Pass it on!" peeped the bats, and the hens clucked, and the roosters crowed: "Pass it on! Pass it on!" and the story flew from henhouse to henhouse and finally back to the place where it had started.

"It's said that there were five hens who plucked all their feathers out to show who had gotten the thinnest for the love of a rooster, and they pecked at each other until they were bloody and fell dead, to the sorrow and shame of their families and a big loss for their owner!"

And the hen, who had lost the little feather, naturally didn't recognize her own story, and since she was a respectable hen, she said, "I despise those hens! But there are more of that type. Things like this shouldn't be hushed up, and I'll do my best to see that it gets into the papers so that everyone in the country will hear about it. Those hens deserve it and so do their families!"

And the story got into the papers and was printed, and it's perfectly true: one little feather really can become five hens!

THE DUNG BEETLE

THE EMPEROR'S HORSE HAD gold horseshoes. A golden shoe on each foot.

Why did he have golden shoes?

He was the most beautiful animal. He had delicate legs, wise eyes, and a mane that hung like a silk ribbon around his neck. He had carried his master through the fog of battle and rain of bullets, and heard the shots sizzle and sing. He had bitten, kicked and fought along when the enemy pressed forward. With his emperor on his back, he had jumped over the charging enemy's horse and saved his emperor's crown of red gold, saved his emperor's life, which was more than gold, and that's why the emperor's horse had gold shoes. A golden shoe on each foot.

And the dung beetle crept out.

"First the big ones, then the small," he said. "Although it's not size that matters." And he stretched out his thin legs.

"What do you want?" asked the blacksmith.

"Gold shoes!" answered the dung beetle.

"You must be out of your mind," said the smithy. "You want golden shoes too?"

"Gold shoes!" said the dung beetle. "Am I not just as good as the big beast that is waited on, curried, watched over, fed and watered? Don't I also belong to the emperor's stable?"

"But why did the horse get golden shoes?" asked the blacksmith. "Don't you understand that?"

"Understand? I understand that it's contempt for me," said the dung beetle. "It's an insult—and so now I will go out into the wide world."

"Bug off!" said the smithy.

"Coarse fellow," said the dung beetle, and then he went outside, flew a short distance, and came to a lovely little flower garden, where there was the smell of roses and lavender.

"Isn't it nice here?" asked one of the little ladybugs, who flew about with black dots on its red armor-plated wings. "How sweet it smells, and how pretty it is here."

"I am used to better!" said the dung beetle. "Do you call this pretty? There isn't even a dunghill here!"

He went on a bit further, into the shadow of a big stock plant. There was a caterpillar crawling on it.

"How lovely the world is!" said the caterpillar. "The sun is so warm! Everything is so pleasant. And when I shall one day fall asleep and die, as it's called, I'll wake up and be a butterfly!"

"Who do you think you are?" said the dung beetle. "Flying around like butterflies! I come from the emperor's stable, but no one there, not even the emperor's favorite horse, who wears my castoff golden shoes, has such imaginings! Get wings! Fly! Yes, now we're flying!" And the dung beetle flew. "I don't like getting annoyed, but I am annoyed anyway."

Then he plumped down on a large lawn where he lay for awhile and then fell asleep.

Gracious! What a cloud-burst! The dung beetle awoke from the splashing and wanted to crawl right into the ground, but he couldn't. He flipped over and swam on his stomach and his back. Flying was out of the question. He was sure he would not escape the lawn alive. He lay where he was and remained lying there.

When it let up a little, and the dung beetle had blinked the water from his eyes, he glimpsed something white. It was linen laid out to bleach. He crept over to it and crawled into a fold of the wet cloth. It certainly wasn't like lying in the warm dung in the stable, but there wasn't anything better here, and so he remained there a whole day and night while the rain continued. He crawled out the next morning, very annoyed at the climate.

There were two frogs sitting on the linen. Their clear eyes shone with pure pleasure. "What wonderful weather!" said one. "How refreshing it is! And the linen retains the water so well! My hind legs are tickling just as when I'm going to swim."

"I wonder," said the other, "if the swallow who flies so widely around has found a better climate than ours on its many trips abroad? Such rough weather and such rain. It's like lying in a wet ditch. If you don't like this, then you really don't love your country."

"You haven't ever been in the emperor's stable, have you?" asked the dung beetle. "The wetness there is both warm and spicy! I'm used to that. It's my climate, but you can't take it with you when you travel. Isn't there any hotbed here in the garden, where people of quality like me could go in and feel at home?"

But the frogs didn't understand him, or didn't want to understand him.

"I never ask a question more than once," said the dung beetle when he had asked three times without being answered.

He walked on until he came to a piece of broken pottery. It shouldn't have been there, but the way it was lying, it gave shelter. Several earwig families lived here. They don't need a lot of space, just lots of company and parties. The females are especially maternal, and so each of them thought her own children to be the prettiest and smartest.

"Our son has gotten engaged," said one mother. "The dear innocent! His greatest goal is to one day crawl into the ear of a minister. He's so lovably childish, and the engagement keeps him from excesses. It's such a joy for a mother!"

"Our son," said another mother, "was no sooner hatched than he was having a good time. He's so full of energy! He's sowing his wild oats. That's a great joy for a mother! Isn't that right, Mr. Dung Beetle?" They recognized the stranger by his shape.

"You're both right," said the dung beetle, and he was invited in, as far in as he was able to get under the pottery shard.

"You have to see my little earwig!" said a third, and then a fourth of the mothers. "He's the most lovable child and so much fun! They're only naughty when they have a tummy ache, but you get that easily at their age."

And every mother talked about her children, and the children talked too and used the little fork in their tails to pull at the dung beetle's whiskers.

"They think up all sorts of things, the little imps!" said the mothers, reeking of motherly love, but this bored the dung beetle, and so he asked if it was far to the hotbed.

"It's way out in the world, on the other side of the ditch," said the earwig, "I hope none of my children ever go so far, or it would kill me."

"I'm going to try to get that far though," said the dung beetle and left without saying good bye, which is the most elegant.

By the ditch he met several of his relations, all dung beetles.

"This is where we live," they said. "It's pretty cozy here. May we invite you down here where it's warm and wet? Your trip must have tired you."

"It certainly has!" said the dung beetle. I was lying on linen in the rain, and cleanliness especially takes a lot out of me. I've also gotten arthritis in a wing joint from standing in a draft under a pottery shard. It's really refreshing to be amongst my own kind again!"

"Maybe you came from the hotbed?" asked the oldest one.

"Higher up than that!" said the dung beetle. "I come from the emperor's stable, where I was born with golden shoes on my feet. I am traveling on a secret mission, and you can't ask me about it because I won't tell you."

Then the dung beetle settled down in the rich mud. Three young female dung beetles were sitting there. They giggled because they didn't know what to say.

"They're not engaged," said their mother, and then they giggled again, but from shyness.

"I haven't seen any more beautiful in the emperor's stable," said the traveling dung beetle.

"Now don't spoil my girls! And don't talk to them unless you have honorable intentions—but you do, and so I give you my blessing!"

"Hurrah!" all the others shouted, and the dung beetle was engaged. First the engagement and then the wedding. There was no reason to wait.

The next day went very well, the second jogged along fine, but on the third day one had to start thinking about supporting the wife and maybe children.

"I've let myself be taken by surprise," he said, "so I'd better surprise them too."

And he did. He was gone. Gone all day, gone all night—and his wife was a widow. The other dung beetles said that they had taken a real tramp into the family, and now had the burden of his wife.

"She can become a maiden again," said her mother. "Be my child again. Shame on that loathsome low-life who deserted her!"

In the meantime, he was on the move. He had sailed across the ditch on a cabbage leaf. In the morning two people came by. They saw the dung beetle, picked him up, and turned and twisted him this way and that. They were both very learned, especially the boy. "Allah sees the black beetle in the black rock on the black mountain. Isn't that what it says in the Koran?" he asked. Then he translated the dung beetle's name to Latin and explained its family and habits. The older scholar voted against taking him home since they already had equally good specimens there, he said. The dung beetle didn't think that was very polite, so he flew out of his hand. He flew a good way, and his wings had dried out. He reached the greenhouse and was able to fly in with the greatest of ease since a window was open. Then he burrowed down into the fresh manure.

"It's delicious here!" he said.

Soon he fell asleep and dreamed that the emperor's horse was dead and that Mr. Dung Beetle had gotten its golden shoes and the promise of two more. It was very pleasant, and when the dung beetle woke up, he crept out and looked around. It was magnificent here in the greenhouse! Big fan palms were spread out high above. They looked transparent when the sun shone through them, and below them an abundance of greenery streamed forth, and flowers were shining red as fire, yellow as amber, and as white as newly fallen snow.

"What a magnificent mass of plants! How marvelous it will taste when it rots!" said the dung beetle. "It's a luscious larder, and I'm sure I must have relatives here. I'll see if I can track down someone I can associate with. I'm proud and proud of it!" And he thought about his dream of the dead horse and the golden shoes he had gotten.

Suddenly a hand grabbed the dung beetle, and he was squeezed, turned, and twisted about.

The gardener's little son and his friend were in the greenhouse and had seen the dung beetle and were going to have some fun with it. He was wrapped in a grapevine leaf and put into a warm pants pocket. He crawled and crept around, but was squeezed by the hand of the boy, who went straight off to the big lake at the edge of the garden. Here the dung beetle was placed in an old cracked wooden shoe with a missing instep. A stick was tied on for a mast, and the dung beetle was tethered to it with a woolen thread. Now he was the captain and was going sailing!

It was a really big lake. It seemed like an ocean to the dung beetle, and he became so astonished that he fell over on his back and lay wriggling his legs.

The wooden shoe sailed, and there was a current in the water, but if the boat went out too far, then one of the boys pulled up his pant legs and waded out to get it. But when it was sailing again, someone called the boys—called them sternly—and they hurried off and let the wooden shoe be. It drifted further and further from land, always further out. It was dreadful for the dung beetle. He couldn't fly because he was tied to the mast.

He was visited by a fly.

"We're having wonderful weather," said the fly. "I can rest here and sunbathe too. You have it very comfortable here."

"You talk according to your lights! Don't you see that I'm tied up?"

"I'm not tied," said the fly and flew away.

"Now I know the world," the dung beetle said. "And it's a mean world. I'm the only honorable one in it! First they deny me gold shoes, then I have to lie on wet linen, stand in a draft, and finally they foist a wife on me! When I then take a quick step out into the world to see what it's like and how it will treat me, then a people-puppy comes along and sets me in a tether on the wild sea. And meanwhile the emperor's horse is walking around in gold shoes! That annoys me the most. But you can't expect sympathy in this world! My life is very interesting, but what good is that if no one knows about it? The world doesn't deserve to hear about it either, or it would have given me golden shoes in the emperor's stable when the favorite horse got them, and I reached out my legs. If I had gotten golden shoes I would have brought honor to the stable. Now it's lost me, and the world has lost me. Everything's over!"

But everything wasn't over yet because a boat sailed by with some young girls in it.

"There's a wooden shoe!" one of them said.

"There's a little animal tied up to it," said another.

They were right beside the wooden shoe and picked it up. One of the girls took a little scissors and cut the woolen thread without hurting the dung beetle, and when they got to land, she set it in the grass.

"Crawl, crawl! Fly, fly, if you can!" she said. "Freedom is a lovely thing."

And the dung beetle flew right through an open window in a big building and sank tiredly down in the fine, soft, long mane of the emperor's favorite horse who was standing in the stable where it and the dung beetle belonged. It clung to the mane and sat collecting its thoughts for awhile. "Here I am sitting on the emperor's favorite horse—sitting as a horseman. What's that I said? Well, now everything is clear to me! It's a good idea, and the right one. Why did the horse get golden shoes? He asked me about that, the blacksmith. Now I realize why! The horse got golden shoes for my sake!"

And that put the dung beetle in a good mood.

"You get clear-headed from travel," he said.

The sun shone in on him, shone very beautifully. "The world isn't so bad after all," said the dung beetle. "You just have to know how to take it." The world was lovely—the emperor's favorite horse had gotten golden shoes because the dung beetle was to be its rider.

"Now I'll just step down to the other beetles and tell them how much has been done for me. I'll tell about all the pleasures I enjoyed on my travel abroad, and I'll tell them that now I'll stay home until the horse has worn out his golden shoes."

THE BUTTERFLY

THE BUTTERFLY WANTED A sweetheart, and naturally he wanted one of the pretty little flowers. He looked at them. Each sat so quietly and steadily on her stalk, just like a maiden should sit when she's not yet engaged. But there were so many to choose among—it was too much trouble, and the butterfly couldn't be bothered, so he flew away to the daisy. The French call her *Margrethe*. They know that she can tell fortunes, which she does when people pick petal after petal, and with each one say, "She loves me—She loves me not—She loves me—She loves me not," or something like that. Everyone asks in his own language. The butterfly came to ask too, but he didn't pluck the petals off. Instead he kissed each one, believing that you catch more flies with honey than with vinegar.

"Sweet *Margrethe* Daisy," he said. "You're the wisest woman of all the flowers. You know how to tell fortunes. Tell me, will I have that one, or that one? Who will I get? When I know that, I'll fly right over and propose."

But *Margrethe* didn't answer at all. She didn't like being called a woman because she was an unmarried virgin and wasn't properly speaking a woman yet. He asked a second and then a third time. When he couldn't get a single word out of her, he couldn't be bothered to ask again, but flew directly away to propose.

It was early spring, and there were lots of snowdrops and crocuses. "They are very pretty," said the butterfly. "Sweet little

They were here today and gone tomorrow.

things who have just come out, but somewhat tasteless." Like all young men, he looked for older girls. So then he flew to the anemones, but they were a little too bitter for him, and the violets a bit too romantic. The tulips were too ostentatious, the narcissus too simple, and the lime blossoms were too small and had too many relations. The apple blossoms really did look like roses, but they were here today and gone tomorrow according to how the wind blew. He thought that would be too short a marriage! The sweet pea was the one who pleased him the most. She was red and white, pure and delicate. She was one of those domestic girls who look good and are also useful in the kitchen. He was just about to propose to her, but just then he saw a pea-pod with a withering flower on the end hanging close to her.

"Who's that?" he asked.

"That's my sister," said the sweet pea.

"Oh, so that's what you'll look like later!" That scared the butterfly, and he flew off.

The honeysuckle was hanging over the fence, full of those young ladies with long faces and sallow skin. He didn't care for that type. But what did he like? You've got to ask him yourself.

Spring passed, summer passed, and then it was autumn. But he got nowhere. And the flowers were wearing the most beautiful dresses, but that didn't help. They didn't have that fresh fragrance of youth. Fragrance is just what the heart needs with age, and there's not much of that in dahlias and hollyhocks. And so the butterfly flew down to the curled mint.

"She actually has no flower, but is a whole flower, fragrant from root to tip. She has fragrance in every leaf. I'll take her!"

And so he finally proposed.

But the curled mint stood stiff and silent, and at last she said, "Friendship—but nothing more! I am old, and you are old. We could certainly live for each other, but get married? No! Let's not make fools of ourselves in our old age."

So the butterfly got no one. He had searched too long, and one shouldn't do that. The butterfly became a bachelor.

It was late in the autumn, with rain and rough weather. The wind blew cold down the backs of the old willow trees so that they creaked. It was not the time to flit around in summer clothes—then you'd be in for it, as the saying goes. But the butterfly wasn't flying outside. He'd happened to get inside, where there was a fire in the stove. It was warm like summer. Here he could live, but "living is not enough," he said. "You must have sunshine, freedom, and a little flower!"

And he flew towards the window pane, was seen, admired, and mounted on a pin in a curio case. More couldn't be done for him.

"Now I'm sitting on a stalk just like the flowers," said the butterfly. "But it's certainly not perfectly comfortable. It must be like being married—you're pinned down then!" And he consoled himself with this thought.

"That's poor consolation," said the potted flowers in the living room.

"But you can't quite trust potted plants," thought the butterfly. "They associate too much with people!"

THE SNOWDROP[1]

IT WAS WINTERTIME. THE air was cold with a cutting wind, but inside it was cozy and warm. The flower lay inside. It lay in its bulb under earth and snow.

One day it rained. The raindrops sank down through the snow cover into the earth, touched the flower bulb, and told it about the world of light up above. Soon a delicate sunbeam bored its way through the snow, down to the bulb, and pricked at it.

"Come in!" said the flower.

"I can't!" said the sunbeam. "I'm not strong enough yet to open your door, but I will be in summer."

"When will summer come?" the flower asked and repeated it every time a new sun beam penetrated the earth. But it was a long time until summer. Snow was still lying on the ground, and the water froze on the ponds every single night.

"Oh, how long it's lasting, how long!" said the flower. "I feel crawling and creeping in me. I have to stretch, and I must stretch out. I have to open up and get out, and nod good morning to the summer! It will be a blissful time!"

And the flower stretched and stretched within the thin water-softened skin that the snow and earth had warmed, and the sunbeams had pricked against. It shot forth under the snow, with a light green bud on its green stalk and narrow thick leaves that seemed to want to protect it. The snow was cold, but shot through with light, and therefore easy to break through, and then came the sunbeams with greater strength than before.

"Welcome! Welcome!" each sunbeam sang and rang, and the flower rose over the snow into the world of light. The sunbeams caressed and kissed it so that it opened completely. It was white as the snow and adorned with green streaks. It bowed its head in joy and humility.

"Lovely flower!" the sunbeams sang. "How fresh and pure you are! You're the first, you're the only! You're our love! You ring in summer across the land and towns. All the snow will melt! The cold winds are chased away! We will rule! Everything will turn green. Then you'll have company—the lilacs, laburnum, and finally, roses. But you're the first, so delicate and pure!"

It was a great pleasure. The flower felt as if the air sang to it, and the rays of light pierced into its leaves and stalk. It stood there so delicate and easy to break, and yet so vigorous with young beauty. With its white tunic and green ribbons it praised summer. But summer was still far away. Clouds hid the sun, and sharp winds blew the flower.

"You've come a little too early," said the wind and weather. "We still have the power! You'll feel it and put up with it. You should have stayed inside and not run out in your finery. It's not time yet."

It was biting cold. The following days didn't bring a single sunbeam! It was the kind of weather such a little flower could freeze to death in. But it had more strength than it realized. It was strong in the joy and belief of the summer that had to come, the summer that was proclaimed with deep longing, and that was confirmed by the warm sunshine. So it stood with confidence in its white outfit in the white snow, bending its head when the snowflakes fell thick and heavily, and the icy winds blew over it.

"You're going to break!" they said. "Wither and freeze. Why did you come out? Why did you let yourself be lured? The sun has fooled you! It serves you right, you little snowdrop, summer fool!"

"Summer fool!" repeated the snowdrop in the cold morning hours.

"Summer fool!" shouted some children, who came into the garden. "There's one—so lovely and beautiful—the first and only one!"

These words did the flower a lot of good for they were words as warm as the sunbeams. In its joy, the flower didn't even notice that it was being picked. It lay in a child's hand and was kissed by a child's mouth. It was brought into the warm living room, looked at with gentle eyes, and put in water, strengthening and reviving. The flower thought that all at once it was summer.

There was a daughter in the house, a lovely young girl. She had just been confirmed, and she had a dear friend who was also confirmed. He was studying for his livelihood. "He shall be my summer fool," she said. She took the delicate flower and laid it in a piece of scented paper on which there were verses written. The verses started with summer fool and ended with summer fool, then "dear friend, be a winter fool!" She had teased him with summer. It was all in the poem, and it was sent as a letter. The flower was enclosed, and it was dark all around, as dark as when it lay inside the bulb. The flower went traveling, lay in a postbag, and was pressed and squeezed. It wasn't at all comfortable, but this too came to an end.

The trip was over. The letter was opened and read by the dear friend. He was very pleased. He kissed the flower, and along with the verses around it, it was put into a drawer where there were other lovely letters, but none with flowers. It was the first and the only, as the sunbeams had called it, and that was delightful to think about.

And the flower had a long time to think about it. It thought while summer passed, and the long winter, and when it was summer again, the flower was brought out. But now the young man was not at all happy. He grasped the papers roughly and threw the verses aside so that the flower fell on the floor. It had become flat and withered, but that was no reason to throw it on the floor! But still it was better than being in the fire, where the verses and letters were burning up. What had happened? What happens so often. The flower had fooled him—it was a joke. The girl had fooled him—that was no joke. She had chosen another friend in midsummer.

In the morning the sun shone on the little flat pressed snowdrop, which looked as if it was painted on the floor. The maid was sweeping and picked it up and laid it in one of the books on the table because she thought it had fallen out as she was putting the room in order. And once again the snowdrop was lying amidst verses, but these were printed ones. They are more distinguished than written ones, or at least more is spent on them.

Years passed, and the book stood on the shelf. Then one day it was taken out, opened and read. It was a good book—the poems and songs of the Danish poet Ambrosius Stub,[2] well worth knowing. And the man who was reading the book turned the page. "Why here's a flower!" he said. "A snowdrop, a summer fool! It surely means something that it's placed here. Poor Ambrosius Stub. He was a summer fool too, a poet fool! He was ahead of his time too, and because of that he felt sleet and sharp winds, lived by turns in the manor homes of Funen,[3] like a flower in a vase, flower in a rhymed letter! Summer fool, winter fool, jokes and pranks; and yet the first and only, still the fresh youthful Danish poet! Yes, be a bookmark in this book, little snowdrop. You were placed there for a reason."

And the snowdrop was placed in the book again, and felt both honored and pleased to know that it was a bookmark in that lovely songbook, and that he who first had sung and written about the snowdrop was a summer fool too and had been made a fool of in the winter. The flower understood it in his fashion, as we understand things in ours.

And that's the tale about the snowdrop!

NOTES

1. This story is often called untranslatable because its point and premise rest on the meaning in Danish of the flower name *sommergjæk*. The archaic verb *gjekke* means to hoax or tease. The *sommergjæk*, therefore, teases about the hope of summer because it blooms in the winter. There is also a Danish custom of sending the first snowdrop enclosed in an unsigned letter.
2. Danish poet (1705–1758).
3. Funen is the third-largest island of Denmark; its major city is Odense.

THE SUNSHINE'S STORIES

"NOW I'M GOING TO tell a story," said the wind.

"No, allow me, it's my turn," said the rain. "You've stood by the corner long enough and blown off everything you could."

"Is that the thanks I get," said the wind, "for turning all those umbrellas inside out, in your honor? Actually breaking them, when people haven't wanted to have anything to do with you?"

"*I* will tell a story," said the sunshine. "Be quiet!" It was said with brilliance and majesty, so the wind lay down flat, but the rain shook the wind and said, "And we have to tolerate this! She always breaks in, this Madame Sunshine. We don't want to listen! It's not worth the trouble to listen."

But the sunshine told this:

"A swan flew over the rolling sea. Its every feather shone like gold. One feather fell down on a big merchant ship that was gliding by at full sail. The feather fell into the curly hair of a young man, the supervisor of the wares. They called him 'Supercargo.' The feather from the bird of luck touched his forehead and became a pen in his hand. Soon he became a rich merchant who could buy spurs of gold and change gold plates to a noble's shield. I've actually reflected myself in it," said the sunshine.

"The swan flew further across a green meadow, where a little shepherd, a boy of seven, was lying in the shade of an old tree, the only one there. And in his flight the swan kissed one of the tree's leaves. It fell into the boy's hand, and the one leaf turned to three, then ten, and finally became a whole book. In it he read about the wonders of nature, about his mother tongue, and about faith and knowledge. At bedtime he lay the book under his head so that he wouldn't forget what he had read, and the book led him to school, to the table of knowledge. I have read his name amongst the scholars," said the sunshine.

"The swan flew into the lonely forest, and rested there on the quiet dark lakes where the water lilies and the wild forest apples grow, and where the cuckoo and wood pigeon live.

"A poor woman was gathering firewood of broken branches, and carried them on her back. She had her little child by her breast and was walking home. She saw the golden swan, the swan of good fortune, lift off from the reed-covered shore. What was that shining there? A golden egg. She held it to her breast, and it was warm. There must have been life in the egg. Yes, there was pecking inside the shell! She felt it and thought it was her own heart beating.

"At home in her poor hovel she took the golden egg out. 'Tick, tick!' it said, as if it were an expensive gold watch, but it was an egg with life inside. The egg cracked, and a little swan, with feathers as of purest gold, stuck its head out. It had four rings around its neck, and since the poor woman had four sons, three at home and the fourth that she had carried with her in the forest, she immediately realized that there was a ring for each child. As she grasped that—and them—the little golden bird flew away.

"She kissed each ring and had each child kiss one of the rings, and laid them by the children's hearts and then on their fingers.

"I saw it!" said the sunshine. "And I saw what happened afterwards.

"One boy sat in the clay pit, took a lump of clay in his hand, turned it with his fingers, and it became a statue of *Jason*,[1] who had taken the golden fleece.

"The second boy ran out in the meadow where the flowers were blooming in every imaginable color. He picked a handful and squeezed them so tightly that the nectar sprayed into his eyes and wet the ring. His hands and thoughts were itching with it, and some years later they were talking in the big city about the great painter.

"The third boy held the ring so tightly in his mouth that it sang out, an echo from the heart. Thoughts and feelings arose in strains, arose like singing swans, and dived like swans into the deep sea, the deep sea of thought. He became a master of music, and every land can now think, 'He belongs to me!'

"The fourth little one—well, he was an outcast. They said he was batty, had the 'pip.' He should be given pepper and whipped butter, like the sick chickens were. They said those words, 'pepper and whipped butter' with the stress on the whipped. And that's what he got, but from me he got a sunshine's kiss," said the sunshine. "He got ten kisses instead of one. He had a poetic nature and was both knocked about and kissed, but he had the lucky ring from good fortune's golden swan. His thoughts flew like golden butterflies, the symbol of immortality."

"That was really a long story," said the wind.

"And boring!" said the rain. "Blow on me, so I can freshen up."

The wind blew, and the sunshine said:

"The swan of good fortune flew over the deep bay, where the fishermen had cast their nets. The poorest of them was thinking of getting married, and he did get married.

"The swan brought him a piece of amber. Amber pulls things towards it, and this pulled hearts to it. Amber is the loveliest incense. There was a fragrance as of a church, a scent from God's nature. The two young people experienced the happiness of home life, contentment in straitened circumstances, and so their life was a whole sunshine story."

"Can't we break this off now?" said the wind. "Now the sunshine has talked long enough. I've been so bored."

"Me too," said the rain.

"And what do the rest of us who have heard the stories say?"

"We say: 'That's the end!'"

NOTE

1. In Greek mythology, the quest for the golden fleece is undertaken by Jason, who was the son of a Greek king, and the Argonauts, sailors in the ship *Argo*. Jason must obtain the fleece in order to reclaim his throne.

THE DROP OF WATER

I'M SURE YOU'RE FAMILIAR with a magnifying glass—one of those round lenses that makes everything look a hundred times bigger than it is? When you look through it at a drop of water from the pond, you see over a thousand strange animals that you otherwise wouldn't see in the water, but they're there and that's the truth. It almost looks like a whole plate full of shrimp sprawling around each other, and they are so ravenous that they tear arms and legs, ends and pieces out of each other, and yet they seem happy and satisfied in their way.

There was once an old man whom everyone called Creepy Crawley because that was his name. He always wanted to get the best out of everything, and when something didn't work, he used magic.

One day he was sitting and looking through his magnifying glass at a drop of water from a puddle in a ditch. My, how they were creeping and crawling in there! All of the thousands of little animals were hopping and jumping, pulling at each other and eating each other.

"Oh, but this is just disgusting!" said old Creepy Crawley. "Can't we get them to live in peace and quiet and mind their own business?" And he thought and thought about it, but couldn't come up with anything, so he had to use magic. "I'll give them color so they are more visible," he said, and he poured a little drop of what looked like red wine into the drop of water, but it was witch's blood of the very best quality that costs two shillings. So then all the strange animals turned pink all over their bodies. It looked like an entire town of naked savages.

"What have you got there," asked another old troll. He didn't have a name, and that was the best thing about him.

"Well, if you can guess what it is," said Creepy Crawley, "then I'll give it to you, but it's not easy to find out when you don't know."

And the troll who had no name looked through the magnifying glass. It really did look like an entire city, where all the people were running around without clothes! It was hideous, but even more hideous to see how they pulled and pushed against each other, how they nudged and nibbled, pinched and pounded at each other. What was on the bottom tried to get on top, and what was on top tried to get underneath. "Look, look—his leg is longer than mine! Snip! Away with it! There's one who has a little lump behind its ear, a little innocent lump, but it bothers him, and it will bother him more!" and they hit at it, and they hacked at him, and they ate him because of that little lump. One was like a little maiden, sitting quite still, and wanted just peace and quiet, but then she came forward, and they pulled at her and tugged at her, and they ate her too!

"This is really fun," said the troll.

"Well, but what do you think it is?" asked Creepy Crawley. "Can you figure it out?"

"That's easy to see," said the other, "It's obviously Copenhagen or another big city. They're all alike. A big city is what it is!"

"It's ditch water!" said Creepy Crawley.

THE FLEA AND THE PROFESSOR

ONCE THERE WAS A balloonist who came to grief. The balloon burst, and the man fell and was smashed to pieces. He had sent his boy down two minutes earlier in a parachute, which was lucky for the boy. He was unhurt and had great knowledge of being a balloonist, but he had no balloon nor any means to obtain one.

He had to live, and so he learned magic tricks and how to

talk with his stomach. That's called being a ventriloquist. He was young and good looking, and when he grew a moustache and wore good clothes, he could be mistaken for a noble youth. The ladies thought he was attractive, and one maiden was even so taken with his appearance and magic arts that she followed him to foreign towns and countries. There he called himself Professor. Nothing less would do.

His constant thought was to get a hold of a hot air balloon and go into the air with his little wife, but they still didn't have the means.

"It'll come!" he said.

"If only it would," she said.

"We are young people, you know, and now I'm a professor. Half a loaf is better than none."

She helped him faithfully and sat by the door selling tickets to the performances, and that was cold pleasure during the winter. She also helped him with one of the tricks. He put his wife in a table drawer—a big drawer—and then she crept into a back drawer and could not be seen in the front one. It was like an optical illusion.

But one evening when he pulled the drawer out, she had disappeared for him too. She was not in the front drawer, not in the back drawer, not in the whole house, not to be seen, not to be heard. That was her disappearing act. She never came back. She had gotten tired of it, and he was tired of it. He lost his good humor and couldn't laugh or make jokes anymore, and people stopped coming. His earnings were poor, and so were his clothes. Finally all he owned was a big flea, inherited from his wife, and so he was very fond of it. He dressed it up, taught it some magic tricks, and even how to present arms and shoot off a cannon, but a small one.

The professor was proud of the flea, and it was proud of itself. It had learned something, carried human blood in its veins, and had been in the largest cities. Princes and princesses had seen it perform, and it had won their highest approval. It was written about in newspapers and appeared on posters. It knew that it was a celebrity and could support a professor, even an entire family.

Proud it was and famous it was, and yet when it and the professor traveled, they traveled fourth class on the trains. You arrive just as quickly as first class passengers. They had a tacit agreement that they would never separate, never get married. The flea would become a bachelor, and the professor a widower. It's the same difference.

"Where you've had the greatest success, you mustn't go back," said the professor. He knew human nature, and that's also knowledge.

Finally they had traveled to all countries, except to the uncivilized ones, and so then he wanted to go there. They ate Christian people there, the professor knew, but he was not exactly a Christian, and the flea was not exactly a person so he thought they could travel there and make a good profit.

They traveled by steamship and by sail. The flea did his tricks, and so they traveled for free and then came to the land of the cannibals.

A little princess ruled there. She was only eight years old, but she was the ruler. She had taken power from her father and mother, for she had a strong will and was so exceptionally lovely and naughty.

Immediately when the flea presented arms and shot off the cannon, she was so completely entranced by him that she said, "Him or no one!" She was wild with love for him, and, of course, she was already wild from before.

"Dear sweet, sensible little child," said her own father. "If one could just make a human being out of him!"

"Leave that to me, old thing," she said, and that wasn't nicely said of a little princess talking to her father, but then she was wild.

She placed the flea on her little hand.

"Now you're a human being, and you'll rule with me. But you must do what I want, or I'll kill you and eat the professor."

The professor was given a large chamber to live in. The walls were of sugar cane, and he could lick them, but he didn't have a sweet tooth. He got a hammock to sleep in, and it was as if he were lying in the balloon which he had always wished for, and which was his constant thought.

The flea stayed with the princess, sat on her little hand and on her delicate neck. She had taken a hair from her head, and the professor had to tie it around the flea's leg. The other end she tied to the big piece of coral that she wore in her earlobe.

What a lovely time that was for the princess, and for the flea too, she thought. But the professor was not satisfied. He was a traveling man, and he liked moving from town to town, liked reading about his perseverance in the newspapers, and about his cleverness in teaching a flea human actions. He lay in the hammock day in and day out, lazy and eating good food— fresh bird eggs, elephant eyes, and roasted leg of giraffe. The cannibals didn't just live off of human flesh. That was a delicacy to them. "Shoulder of child with a pungent sauce," said the princess' mother, "is the most delicious."

The professor was bored and wanted to get away from the uncivilized country, but he had to have the flea with him. That was his wonder child and means of support. How could he catch and keep it? It wasn't so easy.

He exerted all his mental faculties, and then he said, "I've got it!"

"Father of the Princess, let me do something. May I drill the country's residents in presenting arms? That's what's considered culture in the world's greatest countries."

"And what can you teach me?" asked the princess' father.

"My greatest trick," said the professor, "that of firing a cannon so the whole earth moves, and all of the sky's most gorgeous birds fall cooked from the sky. There's some noise to that!"

"Bring the cannon!" said the princess' father.

But there was no cannon in the whole country except the one the flea had brought, and that one was too small.

"I'll make a bigger one," said the professor. "Just give me the means! I must have fine silk material, needle and thread, ropes and cords, and stomach drops for air balloonists—they blow it up so light and airy, and give the bang in the stomach of the cannon."

And he got everything he requested.

The whole country assembled to see the big cannon. The

professor didn't call them together until he had the balloon completely ready to fill and ascend.

The flea sat on the princess's hand and watched. The balloon was filled. It billowed and could hardly be held, it was so wild.

"I must have it up in the air to cool it down," said the professor and got into the basket that hung under it. "I can't steer it by myself. I have to have a knowledgeable companion along to help me. No one here can do it except the flea."

"I'll allow it but not willingly," said the princess and handed the flea to the professor who set it on his hand.

"Let go of the ropes and cords," he said. "Up goes the balloon!"

They thought he said, "Let's make a boom."

And the balloon rose higher and higher, up over the clouds, away from the uncivilized country.

The little princess, her mother and father, and all the people stood and waited. They are still waiting, and if you don't believe it, then travel to that uncivilized country. Every child there talks about the flea and the professor and believes that they will come again when the cannon has cooled off. But they won't come; they are home with us. They're in their native land, riding on the trains, first class, not fourth. They have good earnings and a big balloon, and no one asks how or where they got it. They are well-to-do folks, honorable folks— the flea and the professor.

THE SNOWMAN

"I'm creaking all over in this delightfully cold weather!" said the snowman. "The wind bites life into you, that's for sure. And how that glowing one is glowering!" He meant the sun that was just about to set. "She won't get me to blink. I know how to hang on to my bits and pieces!" These were two big triangular pieces of roof tile that he had for eyes. His mouth was a piece of an old rake, and so he had teeth. He had been born to the shouts of "hurrah" from the boys, and greeted by the ringing bells and cracking whips of the sleighs.

The sun went down, and the full moon came up, round and huge, clear and lovely in the blue sky.

"There she is again from a different direction," said the snowman. He thought it was the sun again. "I've broken her of glaring! Now she can just hang there and give some light so I can see myself. If I only knew how one goes about moving. I would so dearly like to move! If I could do that, I would go down and slide on the ice like I saw the boys doing. But I don't know how to run!"

"Be gone! Gone!" barked the old watchdog. He was a little hoarse and had been ever since he was a house dog and lay under the stove. "The sun will teach you how to run, I'm sure. I saw that with your predecessor last year and his predecessor too. Gone! Gone! And they're all gone."

"I don't understand you, buddy," said the snowman. "Shall *that* thing up there teach me how to run?" He meant the moon. "Well she ran before, it's true, when I stared at her. Now she's sneaking up from another direction."

"You don't know anything," said the watchdog, "but, of course, you've just been slapped up. The one you see there is called *the moon*. The one who went was *the sun*. She'll come back tomorrow and certainly teach you to run down to the moat. There'll soon be a change in the weather. I can tell by my left hind leg—it has a shooting pain in it. We'll have a weather change!"

"I don't understand him," said the snowman, "but I have the impression that he's saying something unpleasant. The one who glared and went away, the one he calls *the sun*—she's not my friend. I have a feeling about that!"

"Be gone! Gone!" barked the watchdog, turned around three times, and went into his kennel to sleep.

There actually was a change in the weather. A fog, thick and dank, lay over the whole neighborhood in the early hours, and at dawn a wind came up. The wind was so icy, and there was a heavy frost. But what a sight to see when the sun came up! All the trees and bushes were covered with hoar-frost. It was like an entire forest of white coral, as if all the branches were heaped with gleaming white flowers. Each and every one of the countless fine little branches that you couldn't see in the summer because of the leaves, now stood out. It looked like lace, and was so shiny white that it was as if every branch shone with a dazzling white radiance. The weeping birch stirred in the wind. There was life in it, as there is in the trees in summer. It was all incomparably beautiful. And when the sun shone, how everything sparkled as if it were powdered with diamond dust, and across the snow-cover big diamonds glittered, or you could have imagined that there were innumerable tiny little candles burning, whiter even than the white snow.

"What matchless beauty!" said a young girl, who stepped out into the garden with a young man. They stopped right by the snowman and looked at the brilliant trees. "There's no more beautiful sight in the summer," she said, her eyes shining.

"And you wouldn't find such a fellow as that either," said the young man, pointing at the snowman. "He's splendid."

The young girl laughed, nodded to the snowman, and danced with her friend across the snow, that crunched under their feet as if they were walking on starch.

"Who were those two?" the snowman asked the watchdog. "You've been here longer than I have. Do you know them?"

"Yes, I do," said the watchdog. "She has petted me, and he gave me a bone. I wouldn't bite them!"

"But what are they doing here?" asked the snowman.

"They're sweethearrrrrts," growled the watchdog. "They are going to move into a doghouse and gnaw bones together. Be gone! Gone!"

"Are those two as important as you and I?" asked the snowman.

"Well, they belong to the family," said the watchdog. "You sure don't know much when you're born yesterday! I can see that from you. I have age and wisdom and know everyone here! And I knew a time when I didn't stand here in the cold in chains. Gone! Gone!"

"The cold is lovely," said the snowman. "Tell me, tell me! But don't rattle your chain because it makes me queasy."

"Gone! Gone!" barked the watchdog. "I was a puppy once. Little and lovely, they said. At that time I lay in a velvet chair in the house, and in the lap of the master. I was kissed on the snout, and had my paws wiped with an embroidered handkerchief. I was called 'the loveliest' and 'little doggy-woggy,' but then I got too big for them! They gave me to the housekeeper, and I went down to the basement. You can see in there from where you're standing. You can see the room where I was the master because that's what I was at the housekeeper's. I guess it was a poorer home than upstairs, but it was more comfortable. I wasn't squeezed and carried around by the children like I was upstairs. The food was just as good as before, and there was more of it! I had my own pillow, and then there was the stove, which is the loveliest thing of all this time of year! I crawled way back under it, so I disappeared. Oh, I still dream about that stove! Gone! Gone!"

"Is a stove so lovely?" asked the snowman. "Does it look like me?"

"It's the very opposite of you! It's coal black. It has a long neck with a brass collar. It eats wood so flames come out of its mouth. You have to stay close to its side, very close, or under it. It's a boundless pleasure! You should be able to see it through the window from where you're standing."

And the snowman looked, and he really did see a black shiny polished object with a brass collar. The fire was shining out from below. The snowman felt so strange. He had a sensation that he couldn't himself account for. Unknown feelings came over him, but they were feelings that all human beings know, if they aren't snowmen.

"And why did you leave her?" asked the snowman. He felt that it must be a female being. "How could you leave such a place?"

"I couldn't help it," said the watchdog. "They threw me out and put me here on a chain. I bit the youngest boy in the shank because he took a shank-bone I was gnawing on. A shank for a shank, I thought. But they took it badly, and from that time on I've been chained here. I've lost my clear voice. Listen to how hoarse I am: Gone! Gone! That was the end of it."

The snowman wasn't listening any longer. He stared steadily into the housekeeper's basement, into the room where the stove stood on its four iron legs, about the same size as the snowman himself.

"There's such a strange creaking inside me," he said. "Will I never be able to get inside there? It's an innocent wish, and our innocent wishes surely must be granted. It's my greatest wish, my only wish, and it would really be injustice if it weren't fulfilled. I must get in there. I must lean up against her, even if I have to break the window!"

"You'll never get in there," said the watchdog. "And if you did get to the stove, you'd be a goner. Gone!"

"I'm as good as gone," said the snowman. "I think I'm breaking in two."

All day the snowman stood looking in the window. At dusk the room was even more inviting. There was such a soft glow coming from the stove, not like the light of the moon or the sun. No, like only a stove can glow when there's something in it. When someone opened the door, flames shot out of the stove, as was its habit. The snowman's white face turned red, and the red glow spread across his chest.

"I can't bear this," he said. "How it becomes her to stick out her tongue!"

The night was very long, but not for the snowman. He stood there with his own lovely thoughts that all froze creaking hard.

In the morning the basement windows were frosted over. They had the most beautiful ice flowers on them that any snowman could wish for, but they hid the stove. The panes wouldn't thaw out, and he couldn't see her. There was creaking and crunching, and it was just the kind of frosty weather that should please a snowman, but he was not pleased. He could and should have felt so happy, but he wasn't happy. He had Stuck-on-Stove Syndrome.

"That's a very dangerous illness for a snowman," said the watchdog. "I suffered from it myself, but I've recovered! Be gone! Gone! We're going to have a change in the weather."

And the weather did change. It changed to a thaw.

The thawing increased, and the snowman decreased. He didn't say anything, and he didn't complain, and that's a sure sign.

One morning he collapsed. There was something that looked like a broomstick standing in the air where he had been. The boys had built him around it.

"Now I understand his longing," said the watchdog. "The snowman had a stove poker inside him! That's what moved him so, but now it's over. Gone! Gone!"

And soon the winter was gone too.

"Be gone! Gone!" barked the watchdog. But the little girls sang in the yard:

> *"Sweet woodruff, fresh and proud, now sprout.*
> *And woolly willow, hang your mittens out.*
> *Come larks and cuckoos, sing so airy—*
> *Spring has sprung in February.*
> *'Cuckoo—tweet tweet'—I'll sing along.*
> *Come dear sun—shine soon and long!"*

And then no one thinks of the snowman.

The Humanization of
Toys and Objects

THE STEADFAST TIN SOLDIER

ONCE UPON A TIME there were twenty-five tin soldiers. They were all brothers because they were made from the same old tin spoon. They held rifles on their shoulders, and their faces looked straight ahead, above their lovely red and blue uniforms. The very first thing they heard in this world, when the lid was taken off the box, was "Tin Soldiers!" shouted by a little boy, clapping his hands. He had gotten them because it was his birthday, and he lined them up on the table. They all looked exactly alike, just one was a little different; he had only one leg, since he was made last, and there wasn't enough tin left. But he stood just as steadily on his one leg as the others did on two, and he's the one who turned out to be remarkable.

On the table where they were lined up, there were lots of other toys, but what really caught the eye was a beautiful paper castle. You could look right into the rooms through the little windows. There were small trees outside, around a little mirror that was supposed to be a lake. There were wax swans swimming there who were reflected in the glass. It was all just lovely, but the loveliest was a little maiden who stood in the middle of the castle door. She was cut out of paper too, but she had a skirt made of the clearest muslin and a narrow little blue ribbon over her shoulder like a scarf. There was a shining sequin right in the middle of it as large as her face. The little maiden had her arms stretched out because she was a dancer, and she had one leg lifted so high in the air that the tin soldier didn't see it, and so he thought that she had one leg just like he did.

"That's the wife for me!" he thought. "But she's quite aristocratic. She lives in a palace, and I only have a box, and twenty-five of us live there. That's no place for her. But I must meet her!" And he stretched out to his full length behind a snuffbox that was standing on the table. From there he could gaze at the fine little lady, who continued to stand on one leg without losing her balance.

Later in the evening, all the other tin soldiers were put into their box, and the people in the house went to bed. That's when the toys started to play. They played house, fought wars, and went to balls. The tin soldiers rattled in their box because they wanted to play too, but they couldn't get the lid off. The nutcracker turned somersaults, and the slate pencil wrote noisy pranks on the blackboard. There was so much noise that the canary woke up and started to sing along—and in rhyme at that. The only two who didn't move were the tin soldier and the little dancer. She held herself straight on tiptoe with both arms outstretched, and he was just as firm on his one leg. He didn't take his eyes off her for a second.

Then the clock struck twelve, and plunk! The lid flew off the snuffbox. But there was no tobacco in there. No, it was a little black troll. It was a jack-in-the-box.

"Tin soldier!" the troll said. "Keep your eyes to yourself!"

But the tin soldier pretended not to hear.

"Just wait until tomorrow!" the troll said.

When morning came and the children came in, the tin soldier was set on the windowsill. Now whether it was the troll or a draft, the window flew open right away, and the soldier fell out headfirst from the third floor. He fell terribly fast, his leg turned in the air, and he landed on his hat with his bayonet stuck in the cobblestones.

The maid and the little boy went down right away to look for the tin soldier, but, although they almost stepped on him, they didn't see him. If the tin soldier had shouted, "Here I am!" they surely would have found him, but he didn't think it was proper to shout when he was in uniform.

Then it started to rain, heavier and heavier, and it turned into a real downpour. When it was over, two street urchins came along.

"Look!" one said. "There's a tin soldier! He's going sailing."

And they made a boat out of paper, set the tin soldier right in the middle of it, and he went sailing down the gutter while both boys ran along side and clapped their hands. Good grief, what waves there were in that gutter, and what a current! Of course, it had been a downpour. The paper boat seesawed up and down, and in between it spun around so quickly that the soldier trembled, but he remained steadfast, didn't change his

"Tin soldier!" the troll said. *"Keep your eyes to yourself!"*

expression, looked straight ahead, and held his rifle on his shoulder.

Suddenly the boat sailed into a culvert. It was just as dark as it was in his box.

"I wonder where I'm going?" he thought. "Well, it's the troll's fault. If only the little maiden were sitting here in the boat, too, it could be twice as dark!"

Just then a big water rat that lived in the culvert came along.

"Do you have a passport?" asked the rat. "Give me your passport!"

But the tin soldier kept still and held his rifle even tighter. The boat kept moving with the rat following after. Ugh, how he ground his teeth and screamed to sticks and straw: "Stop him! Stop him! He hasn't paid his toll, and he didn't show his passport!"

The current became stronger and faster! The tin soldier could already see the light where the culvert ended, but he also heard a roaring sound that was enough to frighten a brave man. Just imagine, right past the culvert, the gutter flowed into a big canal. That would be just as dangerous for him as going over a high waterfall would be for us.

He was too close to it, and it was impossible to stop. The boat rushed out, and the poor tin soldier held himself as erect as possible. No one should be able to say that he so much as blinked. The boat whirled around three or four times and filled with water up to the rim so that it had to sink. The tin soldier was up to his neck in water, and the boat sank deeper and deeper while the paper dissolved more and more. Then the water went over the soldier's head, and he thought about the beautiful little dancer whom he would never see again, and he heard in his ears:

> *"Onward, Christian soldiers,*
> *Marching as to war . . ."*

Then the paper fell apart, and the tin soldier fell through, but right away he was swallowed by a big fish.

Oh, how dark it was in there! It was even worse than in the

culvert, and it was so cramped. But the tin soldier was steadfast and lay stretched out with his rifle on his shoulder.

The fish swam around and made the most horrendous movements. Finally the fish stopped moving, and then it was as if a bolt of lightning went through it. A light was shining brightly and a voice called out: "Tin soldier!" The fish had been caught, brought to market, and sold, and came into a kitchen, where the kitchen maid cut it open with a big knife. She took the tin soldier around the waist between two fingers and carried it into the living room, where everyone wanted to see the remarkable man who had traveled around in the stomach of a fish, but the tin soldier certainly wasn't proud of it. They set him up on the table and there—Well, will wonders never cease! The tin soldier was back in the very same living room where he'd been before. He saw the same children, and the toys were standing on the table. There was the lovely castle with the beautiful little dancer who was still standing on one leg and had the other high in the air. She was steadfast too. The tin soldier was so moved that he almost cried tears of tin, but that wouldn't be proper. He looked at her, and she looked at him, but they didn't say anything.

Then one of the little boys grabbed the tin soldier and threw it into the stove without any reason, but it was certainly the little troll in the snuffbox who was behind it.

The tin soldier stood there quite illuminated and felt a terrible heat, but whether it was from the actual fire, or from love, he didn't know. The colors on his uniform had faded completely away, whether from the trip or from sorrow, no one could say. He looked at the little maiden, and she looked at him, and he felt himself melting, but still he stood steadfastly with his rifle on his shoulder. Then a door was opened, the wind caught the little dancer, and she flew like a sylph into the oven to the tin soldier, flared up in flames, and was gone. Then the tin soldier melted into a blob, and the next day when the maid took out the ashes, she found him as a little tin heart, but the only thing left of the dancer was the sequin, and that was burned to a crisp.

THE SHEPHERDESS AND THE CHIMNEY SWEEP

HAVE YOU EVER SEEN a really old wooden cabinet, the kind that's dark with age and carved with scrolls and leaves? One just like this was standing in the living room. It had been inherited from Great Grandmother and carved with roses and tulips from top to bottom. It had the strangest flourishes, and in between them little stag heads with many antlers stuck out, but in the middle of the cabinet an entire man was carved. He was really funny to look at, and he made a funny face, but you couldn't call it a laugh. He had goat's legs, small horns on his forehead, and a long beard. The children in the house called him *GeneralBillyGoatlegs-OverandUnderWarSergeantCommander* because it was a hard name to say, and not many people have that title. To have carved him must have been hard too, but there he was now! He was always looking at the table under the mirror because there was a lovely little porcelain shepherdess standing there. Her shoes were gilded, and her dress was beautifully held up with a red rose. She had a golden hat and a shepherd's crook. She was beautiful. Right beside her stood a little chimney sweep, black as coal, but made of porcelain too. He was as clean and attractive as any one; the fact that he was a chimney sweep was just how he was cast, of course. The porcelain manufacturer could just as easily have cast him as a prince—it wouldn't have made any difference.

He stood there so nicely with his ladder and with a face as white and red as a girl, and that was actually a mistake because it could have been a little black. He stood quite close to the shepherdess. They had both been positioned where they were, and because of their positions they had gotten engaged. They were well suited for each other: they were young, they were of the same kind of porcelain, and they were both equally fragile.

Close by stood yet another figure who was three times as large. He was an old bobble-head Chinaman. He was also made of porcelain and said that he was the little shepherdess' grandfather, but although he couldn't prove it, he insisted that he had power over her, and therefore he had nodded his assent to *GeneralBillyGoatlegs-OverandUnderWarSergeantCommander*, when the general had proposed to the little shepherdess.

"There's a husband for you!" said the old Chinaman. "A husband who I think is made of mahogany. He will make you *Mrs. GeneralBillyGoatlegs-OverandUnderWarSergeantCommander.* He has a whole cabinet full of silver, not to mention what he has hidden away."

"I don't want to go into that dark cabinet!" said the little shepherdess. "I've heard that he has eleven porcelain wives in there!"

"Then you can be the twelfth!" said the Chinaman. "Tonight, as soon as the old cabinet creaks, there'll be a wedding, as sure as I'm a Chinaman." And then he nodded off to sleep.

But the little shepherdess cried and looked at her dearest sweetheart, the porcelain chimney sweep.

"I believe I'll ask you," she said, "to go with me out into the wide world, for we can't stay here."

"I'll do whatever you want," said the little chimney sweep. "Let's go right now. I am sure I can support you by my trade."

"If only we were safely off the table," she said. "I won't be happy until we're out in the wide world."

And he consoled her and showed her where to place her little foot in the carved corners and the gilded foliage of the table leg. He used his ladder too, and they made it down to the floor. But when they looked over at the old cabinet, what a commotion they saw! All the carved stags stuck their heads further out, raised their antlers, and twisted their heads. *General-BillyGoatlegs-OverandUnderWarSergeantCommander* leaped into the air and shouted to the old Chinaman, "They're running away! They're running away!"

That scared them, and they jumped quickly up into the drawer of the window niche.

Three or four incomplete decks of cards were in there, as well as a little toy theater that was put together as well as possible. There was a play going on, and all the queens—diamonds, hearts, clubs, and spades—sat in the front row and fanned themselves with their tulips. Behind them stood all the jacks and used their heads both at the top and the bottom, the way cards do. The play was about two star crossed lovers, and the shepherdess cried about that, because it was like her own story.

"I can't stand it!" she said, "I have to get out of this drawer!" But when they reached the floor and looked up at the table, they saw that the old Chinaman had woken up and was rocking his entire body back and forth because his body was one big clump, of course.

"Here comes the old Chinaman!" screamed the little shepherdess, and she fell right down on her porcelain knees; that's how miserable she was.

"I've got an idea," said the chimney sweep. "Let's crawl into that big potpourri jar in the corner. We can lie there on the roses and lavender and throw salt in his eyes when he comes."

"That won't work," she said. "Besides I know that the old Chinaman and the potpourri jar were engaged at one time, and there's always a little goodwill left over when you've been in such a relationship. No, we have no choice but to go out into the wide world."

"Do you really have the courage to go out into the wide world with me?" asked the chimney sweep. "Have you thought about how big it is, and that we can never come back here again?"

"Yes I have," she said.

And the chimney sweep looked steadily at her, and then he said, "My way goes through the chimney. Do you really have the courage to crawl with me through the stove and through the flue and pipes? We'll come into the chimney, and I know my way around there! We'll climb so high that they won't be able to reach us, and at the very top there's a hole out to the wide world."

And he led her over to the door of the wood-burning stove.

"It looks awfully dark in there," she said, but she went with him, both through the flue and the pipes, where it was pitch black night.

"Now we're in the chimney," he said "And look! Look up there—the most beautiful star is shining!"

*"Do you really have the courage to go out into the
wide world with me?" asked the chimney sweep.*

And it was a real star in the sky that shone right down to
them, as if it wanted to show them the way. And they crawled
and they crept—such a dreadful distance. Up, high up. But he
hoisted and helped her and made it easier. He held her and
showed her the best places to set her little porcelain feet, and
they reached the top of the chimney and sat down on the edge
because they were very tired and no wonder.

The sky with all its stars was above them and all the town
roofs below. They looked all around, way out into the world.
The poor shepherdess had not thought it would be like this.
She put her little head on her chimney sweep's shoulder and
cried and cried until the gold washed off her belt.

"It's just too much!" she said. "I can't stand it! The world is
much too big! I wish I were back on the little table under the
mirror. I'll never be happy until I'm back there again. Now I've
followed you out into the wide world—you can certainly follow
me home again, if you care about me at all!"

And the chimney sweep spoke reasonably to her, talked
about old Chinamen and about the *GeneralBillyGoatlegs-Overand-
UnderWarSergeantCommander*, but she sobbed so terribly and
kissed her little chimney sweep so he couldn't do other than
yield to her, even though he thought it was a mistake.

So then they crawled with great difficulty back down the
chimney, and they crept through the damper and the pipe. It
wasn't at all pleasant. And then they were standing in the dark
stove. They stood listening behind the door to hear what was
happening in the living room. It was completely quiet. They
peeked out—Oh! There in the middle of the floor lay the old
Chinaman. He had fallen off the table when he had tried to
chase them. He was broken into three pieces. His whole back
had fallen off in one clump, while his head had rolled into a
corner. *GeneralBillyGoatlegs-OverandUnderWarSergeantCommander*
was standing where he always did, thinking things over.

"This is terrible!" said the little shepherdess. "Old grandfather is broken to pieces, and it's our fault! I'll never survive
this!" and she wrung her tiny little hands.

"He can be mended," said the chimney sweep. "He can certainly be mended. Don't get so excited! After they glue his

back and give him a good rivet in his neck, he'll be as good as new and as unpleasant to us as ever."

"Do you think so?" she said, and then they crept up on the table again where they had stood before.

"So that's as far as we got," said the chimney sweep. "We could have saved ourselves all that trouble!"

"If only old grandfather were mended!" said the shepherdess. "Will it be very expensive?"

And he was mended. The family had his back glued, and he got a good rivet in his neck. He was as good as new, but he couldn't nod any longer.

"You have gotten stuck-up since you were smashed," said *GeneralBillyGoatlegs-OverandUnderWarSergeantCommander*. "But I don't think that is anything to be so proud of. Shall I have her or not?"

And the chimney sweep and the little shepherdess looked so pleadingly at the old Chinaman. They were so afraid he was going to nod, but he couldn't, and it was unpleasant for him to tell a stranger that he always had a rivet in his neck. So the porcelain couple remained together. They blessed grandfather's rivet and loved each other until they broke apart.

THE DARNING NEEDLE

ONCE UPON A TIME there was a darning needle that was so refined and stuck-up that she was under the illusion that she was a sewing needle.

"Just tend to what you are doing," said the darning needle to the fingers who picked it up. "Don't drop me! If I fall on the floor, I won't be found again because I'm so fine."

"Only moderately so," said the fingers and squeezed her around the waist.

"Do you see that I'm coming with my retinue?" said the darning needle, and she pulled a long thread behind her, but there wasn't a knot in it.

The fingers pointed the needle straight towards the cook's

slipper, where the leather upper had split and was now going to be sewed together again.

"This is lowly work!" said the darning needle. "I'll never make it through. I'll break! I'll break!" And then she broke. "I told you so!" said the darning needle. "I'm too fine."

Now she's not good for anything, the fingers thought, but they held on to her, and the cook dripped sealing wax on her and stuck her in the front of her scarf.

"See, now I'm a brooch!" said the darning needle. "I guess I knew that I would come into my own. When you are something, you always become something." And she laughed inwardly, because you can never tell from the outside that a darning needle is laughing. There she sat so proudly now as if she were riding in a coach and looking about in all directions.

"May I take the liberty of asking if you are made of gold?" she asked the pin who was stuck nearby. "You have a lovely appearance and your own head, even if it's a pinhead. You must try to grow it out a bit, since not everyone can be waxed on the end." And then the darning needle rose up so proudly in the air that she fell out of the scarf and into the wash, just as the cook was rinsing it out.

"Now we're traveling!" said the darning needle. "Just so I don't get lost," but that's what she did.

"I'm too fine for this world," she said as she sat in the gutter. "But I'm still good and sharp, and I can take pleasure in that." And the darning needle stayed straight as a pin and didn't lose her good humor.

All kind of things went sailing over her: sticks, straw, and pieces of newspaper. "Look how they're sailing!" said the darning needle. "They don't know what's stuck down here under them! I am sticking and I stick! See, there goes a twig. It doesn't think about anything in the world except 'twig' and that's what it is. There goes a straw floating by. Look how it's swaying and promenading. Don't think so much about yourself—you could bruise yourself on the cobblestones! There goes a newspaper! Everything written in it is forgotten and yet it spreads itself literally. I sit patiently and quietly. I know what I am and will continue to be."

One day something shone so beautifully close by the darning needle, and she thought it was a diamond. Actually it was a glass shard from a broken bottle, and when the darning needle saw it shining she spoke to it and introduced herself as a brooch. "I presume you are a diamond?" "Well yes, I am something of the sort." And they both believed that the other was very precious, and so they talked about how stuck up the world was.

"Well, I used to live in a box belonging to a young lady," said the darning needle, "and that young lady was a cook. She had five fingers on each hand, but anything more conceited than those fingers I have never known in my life. And yet they only existed to hold me, take me out of the box, and put me back again!"

"Was there any brilliance to them?" asked the bottle shard.

"Brilliance!" said the darning needle, "Oh no, they were so stuck-up! They were five brothers, all five of the "Finger" family. They all stuck proudly together, although they were of different sizes. At the end of the row was Tom Thumb. He was short and fat, and walked outside the ranks and only had one joint in his back. He could only bow once, but he said that if he was cut out of the ranks then the whole person would be spoiled for military service. Next to him was Slick-pot. He gets into everything, both sweet and sour, and points at the sun and the moon. It was he who squeezed whenever they wrote something. Then there was Middleman, who looked over the heads of the others. Ring Finger had a golden ring around his tummy, and the little guy on the end didn't do anything and was proud of it. Nothing but boasting and bragging all day long, so I went down the drain—washed up."

"And now we're sitting here sparkling," said the bottle shard. Just then more water flushed through the gutter. It ran over the edges and took the bottle shard along.

"Well, he has advanced!" said the darning needle, "I remain here. I am too fine, but that is my pride and worthy of respect," and she sat stiffly and continued thinking.

"I could almost believe that I'm born of a sunbeam, as fine as I am. It seems to me too that the sun is always searching me out under the water. Oh, I'm so fine that my own mother can't find me! If I had my old eye, the one that broke, I think I would cry! But I wouldn't do it anyway. Fine ladies don't cry!"

One day some street urchins were digging around in the gutters, where they found old nails, coins, and things like that. It was messy, but they enjoyed it.

"Ouch," said one. He had been pricked by the darning needle. "What kind of a fellow is this?"

"I'm not a fellow; I'm a young lady," said the darning needle, but no one heard her. The sealing wax had worn off, and she had turned black. But since black makes you look thinner, she thought she was even finer than before.

"There comes an egg shell floating," said the boys, and they stuck the darning needle into the shell.

"White walls and black myself," said the darning needle. "That's very becoming, and at least now I can be seen!—just so I don't get seasick because then I would throw up or get the bends and break. But she didn't get seasick, and she didn't get the bends and break.

"A good defense against seasickness is having an iron stomach, like me, and also always remembering that you are a little bit more than human! I'm feeling better. The finer you are, the more you can stand."

"Crunch!" said the eggshell. A wagon wheel rolled over it. "Oh, what pressure!" said the darning needle, "Now I'll get seasick after all! I've got the bends! I've got the bends and I'm breaking!" But she didn't break, even though a wagon wheel went over her. She was lying lengthwise—and there she can stay.

THE OLD HOUSE

UP THE STREET THERE was an old, old house. It was almost three hundred years old. You could read the year on the beam where it was carved, along with tulips and hop vines. There were whole verses spelled like in the old days, and over every window a grimacing face was carved in the beam. The upper story hung far out over the other one, and right under the roof was a lead gutter with a gargoyle on the end. Rain water was supposed to run out of its mouth, but it ran out of its stomach because there was a hole in the gutter.

All the other houses in the street were so new and neat looking, with wide windows and smooth walls. You could see that they didn't want to have anything to do with the old house. They were probably thinking: "How long is that old eyesore going to stand here as an object of ridicule? The bay window sticks out so far that nobody can see from our windows what is going on in that direction. The stairs are as wide as for a castle, and as high as a church steeple. Why the iron railings look like the door to an old burial vault, and there are brass knobs! It's totally tasteless!"

There were neat new houses right across the street too, and they thought the same as the others, but at one window sat a little boy with fresh, rosy cheeks and clear bright eyes. He certainly liked the old house best, both in sunshine and in moonlight. And when he looked over at the wall, where the plaster had come off, he could make out all kinds of odd pictures of how the street had looked before, with stairs, bay windows, and sharp gables. He could see soldiers with halberds and roof gutters that ran about as dragons and serpents. It was really a house to look at!

An old man lived there. He wore plush trousers, a coat with big brass buttons, and a wig that you could see was a real wig. Every morning an old fellow came by, and he cleaned up and ran errands. Otherwise, the old man in the plush trousers was all alone in the old house. Now and then he came to the window and looked out, and the little boy nodded to him, and the old man nodded back. In that way they became acquaintances and then friends, even though they had never talked to each other, but that didn't matter.

The little boy heard his parents say, "That old man over there is well-off, but he is so awfully alone."

The following Sunday the little boy wrapped something into a piece of paper, went down to the gate, and when the man who did errands came, the boy said to him, "Listen! Will you

take this to the old man over there for me? I have two tin soldiers. This is one of them. He's to have it because I know he's
so awfully alone."

The old fellow looked pretty pleased, nodded, and took the
tin soldier to the old house. Later a message came asking if the
little boy would like to come over himself for a visit. He was allowed to do so by his parents, and so he went over to the old
house.

The brass knobs on the iron railing were shining more
brightly than usual. You would think that they had been polished in honor of the visit, and it seemed as if the carved trumpeters—because there were trumpeters among the tulips on
the door—were blowing with all their might. Their cheeks
looked fuller than usual. They were playing "Tra-ter-ah-tra!
The little boy is coming, tra-ter-ah-tra!" and then the door
opened. The hallway was full of portraits, knights in armor and
women in silk gowns, and the armor rattled and the silk gowns
rustled. There was a stairway that went up a long way and then
down a little way again—and then you were on a balcony. It was
admittedly very rickety, with big holes and long cracks, but
grass and leaves grew up from all of them. The whole balcony
out there and the walls were so overgrown with green that it
looked like a garden even though it was only a balcony. There
were old herb pots standing there, with faces and donkey ears
on them. The flowers grew wherever they wanted. One pot was
over-flowing on all sides with carnations, that is to say, with the
green shoots, and seemed quite clearly to say, "The air has caressed me, and the sun has kissed me and promised me a little
flower on Sunday—a little flower on Sunday."

Then they went into a room where the walls were covered
with pigskin with stamped-on golden flowers.

> *"Gilding quickly dies*
> *But pigskin survives!"*

said the walls.

There were chairs there with such high backs and with carvings all over, and they had arms on both sides. "Sit down! sit

down!" they said. "Oh, how I'm creaking! I guess now I'm getting arthritis like the old cabinet! Arthritis in my back, oh!"

Then the little boy came into the room where the bay window was and where the old man was sitting.

"Thank you for the tin soldier, my little friend," said the old man. "And thank you for coming to visit me."

"Many thanks" or "creaks, cranks" came from all the furniture. There was so much of it that they nearly fell over each other in order to see the little boy.

There was a picture of a beautiful woman hanging in the middle of the wall. She was very young and happy, but dressed like they did in the old days, with powder in her hair and stiff skirts. She said neither "many thanks" nor "creaks, cranks" but looked at the little boy with her gentle eyes. He immediately asked the old man, "Where did you get her?"

"At the second-hand shop," said the old man. "There are so many pictures hanging there. No one knows or cares about them because they are all dead, but I knew her in the old days. She's been dead and gone for half a hundred years."

Under the picture a wilted bouquet of flowers was hanging under glass. They must have been half a hundred years old too, that's how old they looked. And the pendulum on the big clock swung back and forth, and the hands turned, and everything in the room became even older, but they didn't notice that.

"At home they say that you are so terribly alone," said the little boy.

"Oh," he said, "old memories, and everything they bring with them come to visit me, and now you came too!—I am doing just fine."

And then he took a picture book down from the shelf. There were long parades of people, the strangest coaches that you don't see nowadays, soldiers like the jack of clubs, and citizens carrying waving banners. The tailors' banner had scissors on it, held up by two lions, and the shoemakers' was an eagle with two heads, not a boot, since the shoemakers always have to have everything so they can say, "it's a pair." Yes, that was quite a picture book!

Then the old man went into the other room to get jam, apples, and nuts. Oh, what a treat it was to be in the old house!

"I can't stand it," said the tin soldier, who was standing on the chest of drawers. "It's so lonely and sad here. When you've lived in a family, you can't get used to this! I can't stand it! The days are so long, and the nights are even longer. It's not at all like it was at your house where your father and mother talked so pleasantly, and you and all the other children made such lovely noise. Oh, how lonely the old man is! Do you think anyone kisses him? Do you think anyone gives him a friendly look? Does he get a Christmas tree? He'll get nothing except a funeral!—No, I can't stand it!"

"Don't take it so hard," said the little boy. "I think it's really nice here, and all the old memories with everything they bring come to visit, you know."

"Well, I don't see them and I don't know them," said the tin soldier. "I can't stand it!"

"You must!" said the little boy.

And the old man came back with such a happy face and with the most lovely jam, apples, and nuts, so the little boy didn't think any more about the tin soldier.

The little boy went home happy and satisfied, and weeks and days went by with nods to and from the old house, and then the little boy went there again.

And the carved trumpets blared "Tra-ter-ah-tra!! There's the little boy. Tra-ter-ah-tra!" And the sword and armor in the knight's pictures rattled, and the silk dresses rustled, the pigskin talked and the old chairs had arthritis in their backs: "ouch!" It was just like the first time, because over there one day and hour were just like the next.

"I can't stand it!" said the tin soldier. "I have cried tears of tin. Everything is too sad here! Let me rather go to war and lose my arms or legs! That would be something different anyway. I can't stand it! Now I know what it's like to be visited by old memories, with everything they bring with them. I've been visited by mine, and believe me, there's no pleasure in it in the long run. I was about to jump down off the chest. I saw all of you over there in the house so clearly as if I really was there. It was that Sunday morning, you remember. All you children were standing by the table singing your hymns like you do every morning. You were standing there with folded hands, and your father and mother were just as solemn. Then the door opened, and your little sister Maria, who isn't even two years old yet, and always dances when she hears music or songs, no matter what kind they are, was let in—she shouldn't have been—and started dancing. But she couldn't get into the rhythm because the notes were so long. So first she stood on one leg and bent her head way forward, and then she stood on her other leg and bent her head way forward, but she couldn't get it. You were all very serious, although that must have been hard, but I laughed to myself and because of that I fell off the table and got a bump, which I still have, since it wasn't nice of me to laugh. But now it all comes back to me again, and everything similar I have experienced, and that must be the old memories with everything they bring. Tell me, do you still sing on Sundays? Tell me something about little Maria. And how is my comrade, the other tin soldier? He's happy, I'm sure of that. I can't stand it!"

"You've been given away," said the little boy. "You have to stay here. Can't you see that?"

The old man came in with a drawer in which there was much to see, both pencil, coin, and perfume boxes and old cards that were so big and gilded that you don't see anything like them today. Then other drawers were opened, and the piano was opened too. It had a landscape painted inside the lid, and it sounded so hoarse when the old man played it and hummed a tune. "She could sing that one," he said and nodded at the portrait he'd bought second-hand, and the old man's eyes shone so brightly.

"I want to go to war! I want to go to war!" shouted the tin soldier as loudly as he could and threw himself right down on the floor.

What happened to him? The old man searched for him, and the little boy searched for him, but the tin soldier was gone, and gone he remained. "I'm sure I'll find him," said the old man, but he never did find him. The floor was cracked and had holes in it. The tin soldier had fallen through a crack and lay there as if in an open grave.

And that day passed by, and the little boy went home. The week passed and several more weeks went by. The windows were frosted over. The little boy had to breathe on them to get a little peep-hole where he could look over to the old house, and there the snow had drifted into all the scrolls and inscriptions. It covered up the steps as if there was no one at home, and there wasn't anyone at home. The old man was dead!

A carriage stopped there in the evening, and they carried him out to it in his coffin. He was going to be buried out in the country, and the carriage drove away, but no one followed along. All of his friends were dead, you see. The little boy blew kisses to the coffin as it was driven away.

A few days later there was an auction at the old house, and the little boy watched from his window as things were carried away: the old knights and the old women, the herb pots with the long ears, the old chairs and the old cabinets. Some went to one place, some to another. The portrait of the woman that was found at the second-hand shop was returned there again, and there it would always hang, since no one knew her any longer. No one cared about the old picture.

In the spring the house itself was torn down, because people said it was a monstrosity. You could look right into the room with the pigskin wallpaper, which was tattered and torn. All the greenery around the balcony hung randomly on the fallen beams. And then it was cleaned up.

"That helped," said the neighbor houses.

A beautiful house was built there with wide windows and smooth white walls. But in front, right where the old house had stood, they planted a little garden and wild grapevines grew up the neighbor's walls. In front of the garden a big iron fence with an iron gate was built. It looked magnificent. People stood outside and peeked in. And scores of sparrows hung on the vines and chirped all at once as best they could, but they weren't chattering about the old house because they couldn't remember that. So many years had passed, and the little boy had grown up to be a good and capable man whom his

"Let me see him," said the young man.

parents were proud of. He had gotten married and with his young wife, had moved into the house where the garden was. He was there with her one day when she planted a wild flower that she thought was so lovely. She planted it with her little hand and patted the earth into place with her fingers. Oh! What was that? Something pricked her. Something sharp was sticking out of the soft soil.

It was—just think! It was the tin soldier, the one who had disappeared in the old man's house, and who had been rumbled and tumbled about between beams and gravel and then finally had been lying for many years in the ground.

The young wife cleaned off the soldier, first with a green leaf and then with her fine handkerchief that had such a lovely fragrance! And for the tin soldier, it was as if he woke up from a trance.

"Let me see him," said the young man, and he laughed and shook his head. "Well, it couldn't be him, but he reminds me of a story about a tin soldier I once had when I was a little boy." And then he told his wife about the old house, the old man, and the tin soldier he had sent over to him because he was so terribly alone. He told the story exactly as it had happened so that his young wife got tears in her eyes hearing about the old house and the old man.

"It's possible that it's the same tin soldier," she said. "I'm going to save it and remember everything you've told me, but you have to show me the old man's grave."

"I don't know where it is," he said. "No one knows! All his friends were dead. No one looked after it, and I was just a little boy."

"How terribly alone he must have been," she said.

"Terribly alone," said the tin soldier, "but it's lovely not being forgotten!"

"Lovely," shouted something near by, but no one but the tin soldier saw that it was a piece of the pigskin wallpaper. All the gold was gone, and it looked like wet earth, but it had an opinion and gave it:

> *"Gilding quickly dies*
> *But pigskin survives!"*

However the tin soldier didn't believe it.

THE RAGS

OUTSIDE THE FACTORY THERE were bundles of rags piled up in big stacks, gathered up from far and wide. Each rag had its story—each had a tale to tell, but we can't listen to all of them. Some of the rags were domestic, and others came from foreign countries. There was a Danish rag lying right beside a Norwegian rag. The one was Danish through and through, and the other was utterly Norwegian, and that was the entertaining thing about them, as every sensible Norwegian or Dane would agree.

They recognized each other by their speech, although the Norwegian said that their languages were as different from each other as French from Hebrew. "We go to the mountains to fetch our language raw and original, and the Dane makes his sugar-coated mushy gibberish."[1]

The rags continued to talk, and a rag is a rag in every country. They only count for something when they're in a rag pile.

"I am Norwegian!" said the Norwegian rag. "And when I say that I'm Norwegian, that's all I need to say! I'm as firm in my fibers as the primordial mountains of old Norway, a country that has a constitution just like free America! It tickles my threads to think of what I am and to let my thoughts clink like ore in words of granite!"

"But we have literature!" said the Danish rag. "Do you understand what that is?"

"Understand!" repeated the Norwegian. "You flat land liver!—I should lift you into the mountains and let the Northern lights enlighten you, rag that you are! When the ice thaws in the Norwegian sun, then old Danish tubs sail up to us with butter and cheese, actually edible wares, but Danish literature follows along as ballast! We don't need it! Where fresh water bubbles, you can dispense with stale beer, and in Norway there is a well that hasn't been drilled, that the newspapers haven't spread around and made known all over Europe, and that hasn't been disseminated through camaraderie and through author's travelogues to foreign lands. I speak my mind freely, and you Danes must get used to these free sounds. You will do that because you have a Scandinavian attachment to our proud mountainous land, the world's primeval mountains!"

"A Danish rag would never talk like that," said the Danish rag. "It's not our nature. I know myself, and I'm like all our rags. We are so good natured and modest. We think too little of ourselves, and that doesn't gain you anything, it's true. But I like it. I think it's completely charming. But, by the way, I can assure you that I very well know my own true worth. I just don't talk about it. No one can accuse me of that failing. I'm soft and flexible, tolerate everything. I don't envy anyone, and speak well of everyone. Except that there isn't much good to be said for most others, but let them worry about it. I just make fun of it all because I'm very gifted myself."

"Don't speak to me in that soft gooey language of your flat country—it makes me sick!" said the Norwegian rag, and was able to get free from his bundle with help of the wind and move to a different pile.

Both rags were made into paper, and as chance would have it, the Norwegian rag became stationery on which a Norwegian wrote a faithful love letter to a Danish girl, and the Danish rag became a manuscript for a Danish ode in praise of Norway's vigor and splendor.

So something good can come from rags, when they get away from their rag pile and are changed to truth and beauty. Then they shine with mutual understanding, and there's a blessing in that.

That's the story. It's quite amusing and won't offend anyone at all, except—the rags.

NOTE

1. Possibly a wordplay in the original since the Danish *aas* (mountain ridge) is similar to the name of Ivar Aasen (1813-1896), the Norwegian who created *nynorsk* (New Norwegian), one of the two official languages of Norway. The other official language is *bokmål* (book language), which is derived from Dano-Norwegian, the written language of Denmark/Norway for hundreds of years.

LEGENDS

HOLGER THE DANE

THERE'S AN OLD CASTLE in Denmark called Kronborg. It lies right out by Øresund where every day big ships by the hundreds sail by—English, Russian, and Prussian. They greet the old castle with their cannons: "boom!" and the castle answers with cannons: "boom!" because that's how cannons say "good day" and "many thanks." No ships sail in winter when ice covers everything clear over to Sweden, but it's really like a country road. Danish and Swedish flags wave, and Danes and Swedes say "good day" and "many thanks" to each other, but not with cannons. No, rather with friendly handshakes, and they get bread and pastries from each other because foreign food tastes best.

But the showpiece of it all is still old Kronborg castle. And under Kronborg in the deep dark cellar where no one goes sits Holger the Dane, dressed in iron and steel and resting his head on his strong arms. His long beard spreads out over the marble table, where it's grown fast. He's sleeping and dreaming, but in his dreams he sees everything that happens in Denmark. Every Christmas Eve an angel of God visits him and tells him that what he's dreamed is true, and that he can sleep on because Denmark is not yet in any real danger. But if that were to happen, well, then old Holger the Dane would rise up so the table would crack when he pulled his beard towards him. Then he would come out swinging so you could hear it all over the world.

This story about Holger the Dane was being told to a little grandson by an old grandfather. The little boy knew that whatever his grandfather said was true. While the old man told his story, he was whittling a big wooden figure that was to represent Holger the Dane as a figurehead on a ship. The old man was a wood carver who carved figureheads for ships according to the ship's name, and now he had carved Holger the Dane. He stood so straight and proudly with his long beard, and in one hand he held a big broad sword, and his other hand was leaning on the Danish coat-of-arms.

571

The old grandfather talked so much about remarkable Danish men and women that the little grandson at last thought that he knew just as much as Holger the Dane did, who could only dream about it, after all. And when the little boy went to bed he thought so much about it that he pressed his chin tightly into his comforter and felt that he had a long beard that had grown fast to it.

But the old grandfather continued his work and carved the last part, the Danish coat-of-arms, and then he was finished. He looked at his work and thought about everything that he had read and heard, and about what he had told the little boy that evening, and he nodded, wiped his glasses, put them on again, and said, "Well, Holger the Dane probably won't come in my time, but that boy in the bed there may get to see him and be there when it really counts." Then the old grandfather nodded, and the more he looked at his Holger the Dane, the clearer it became to him that he had made a really fine image. He thought it seemed to have color, and that the armor shone like iron and steel. The hearts in the Danish coat-of-arms became redder and redder, and the lions leaped with golden crowns on.

"That is really the most beautiful coat-of-arms in the world," said the old man. "The lions are strength, and the hearts are gentleness and love." He looked at the topmost lion and thought about King Canute,[1] who added mighty England to Denmark's realm. He looked at the second one and thought about Valdemar I,[2] who unified Denmark and subdued the Slavic Wends. He looked at the third lion and thought about Margrethe I[3] who united Denmark, Sweden, and Norway, but as he looked at the red hearts they shone even brighter than before and became flames that moved, and his thoughts followed each of them.

The first flame led him into a narrow, dark prison. A prisoner was sitting there, a beautiful woman. It was Christian IV's daughter, Leonora Christina Ulfeldt.[4] The flame sat as a rose on her breast and flowered together with her heart. She was the noblest and best of all Danish women.

"Yes, that's one heart in Denmark's coat-of-arms," said the old grandfather.

And his thoughts followed the flame that led him out onto the ocean where the cannons boomed, and ships were lying shrouded in smoke. The flames attached themselves like a royal ribbon on Huitfeldt's[5] chest as he saved the fleet by blowing up himself and his ship.

And the third flame led him to the miserable huts of Greenland where the pastor Hans Egede[6] worked with love in word and deed. The flame was a star on his chest, a heart in the Danish coat-of-arms.

The old grandfather's thoughts flew ahead of the flickering flame because his mind knew where the flame was going. In a peasant woman's simple main room Frederick VI[7] was writing his name with chalk on a beam. The flame moved on his chest and moved in his heart. His heart became a heart in Denmark's coat-of-arms in the home of the poor farmer. And the old grandfather dried his eyes because he had known and lived for King Frederick with his silver white hair and the honest blue eyes. He folded his hands and stared silently into space. Then the old grandfather's daughter-in-law came to tell him that it was late. It was time to rest, and supper was ready.

"But what a great job you have done, Grandfather!" she said. "Holger the Dane and our whole old Danish coat-of-arms! I think I've seen that face before!"

"No, I don't think you have," said the old grandfather. "But I've seen it, and I've striven to carve it into the wood as I remember it. It was at the time of the Battle of Copenhagen on April 2, 1801 when we learned that we were like the Danes of old! I was on the *Danmark* in Steen Bille's[8] fleet, and there was a man by my side. It seemed as if the cannon balls were afraid of him! He sang old songs cheerfully and shot and fought as if he were super-human. I still remember his face, but where he came from and where he went afterwards, I don't know. No one knows. I've often thought that maybe it was old Holger the Dane himself who had swum down from Kronborg to help us in our time of danger. That was my thought, and there is his image!"

The figure cast its huge shadow way up the wall, even onto the ceiling. It looked as if it were the real Holger the Dane himself standing back there because the shadow moved, but that could also be because the candle flame wasn't burning steadily. His daughter-in-law kissed the old grandfather and led him into the big chair by the table. She and her husband, who was the old grandfather's son and the father of the little boy in the bed, ate their supper, and the old grandfather talked about the Danish lions and hearts—about strength and gentleness, and he quite clearly explained that there was a strength other than that which lay in the sword. He pointed to the shelf where old books were lying, among them all of Holberg's plays. They were often read because they were so entertaining, and you really felt that you knew all the characters from the old days in them.

"See, he knew how to carve too," said the old grandfather. "He cut the wrong and rough stuff off of people the best he could." And old grandfather nodded over at the mirror, where the calendar was hanging with a picture of the Round Tower, and then he said, "Tycho Brahe[9] was another one who used the sword, not to cut flesh and bone, but to hew a clearer way through the stars in the sky. And then *he* whose father was of my trade, the old wood carver's son, whom we ourselves have seen with his white hair and the strong shoulders, who's known all over the world! Yes, he could carve. I only whittle. Holger the Dane can appear in many ways so that the whole world hears of Denmark's strength. Let's drink a toast to Bertel!"[10]

But the little boy in the bed clearly saw old Kronborg by the Øresund, and the real Holger the Dane, who sat deep down there with his beard grown fast to the marble table and dreamed about everything that happens up here. Holger the Dane also dreamed about the poor little room where the wood carver sat. He heard everything that was said and nodded in his dreams and said, "Just remember me, Danes! Keep me in your thoughts! I will come in your hour of need!"

And out at Kronborg it was a clear, sunny day, and the wind carried the sounds of the hunting horns from neighboring Sweden. The ships sailed by with their greeting "boom!

boom!" and from Kronborg came the reply "boom! boom!" But Holger the Dane didn't wake up no matter how loudly they shot since they were just saying "good day" and "many thanks." It will take a different kind of shooting to wake him up, but he will do so, for there is plenty of courage and strength in Holger the Dane.

NOTES

1. The Danish prince Canute I became undisputed king of England in 1016, as he did of Denmark in 1016 and Norway in 1028.
2. King of Denmark from 1157 to 1182.
3. Queen of Denmark, Norway, and Sweden who lived from 1353 to 1412.
4. Daughter of King Christian IV (1621–1698); for many years she was imprisoned, for suspected treason, in the blue tower at the castle in Copenhagen. Her *Jammersminde (Memory of Woe)* is considered a classic of Danish autobiography.
5. Native Norwegian Ivar Huitfeldt (1665–1710) was a Danish naval hero; he sacrificed himself and his ship *Dannebrog* in a battle on October 4, 1710, to prevent the Swedish advance into Køge Bay.
6. Norwegian missionary to Greenland (1686–1758).
7. King of Denmark (1808–1839) and of Norway (1808–1814).
8. Danish naval officer (1751–1833).
9. Danish astronomer Tycho Brahe (1546–1601) built an observatory on the island of Hven.
10. Danish neoclassical sculptor Bertel Thorvaldsen (1770–1844).

BIRD PHOENIX

IN THE GARDEN OF Eden, under the Tree of Knowledge, stood a hedge of roses. Inside the first rose that bloomed, a bird was born. Its flight was like light, glorious its colors and splendid its song.

But when Eve picked the fruit of the Tree of Knowledge, and she and Adam were chased from the Garden of Eden, a spark fell from the avenging angel's sword of flame into the nest and ignited it. The bird died in the flames, but from the red egg a new bird arose—the only—the always only—bird Phoenix. Legend tells that it nests in Arabia and that every hundred years it burns itself up in its nest, and from the red egg a new Phoenix flies, the only one in the world.

The bird flutters around us, swift as light, glorious in color and splendid in song. When the mother sits by her child's cradle, it's by the pillow and sweeps a halo around the child's head with its wings. It flies through the rooms of frugality and brings sunshine there, where the simple cupboards waft with the scent of violets.

But bird Phoenix isn't just Arabia's bird. It flutters in the glow of the northern lights over the icy fields of Lapland. It leaps amongst the yellow flowers in Greenland's short summer. Under the copper mines of Fahlun[1] and in England's coal mines, it flies like a moth with dust on its wings over the song book in the pious worker's hand. It sails on the lotus leaf by the holy waters of the Ganges, and the eyes of the Hindu girl light up when she sees it.

Bird Phoenix! Don't you know him? The bird of paradise, the sacred swan of song. It sat on the Thespian cart as a gossiping raven and flapped with its soiled black wings. With a swan's red sonorous beak it glided over Iceland's bards. It rested on Shakespeare's shoulder as one of Odin's ravens,[2] and whispered in his ear: Immortality. It flew with the song festival through the great hall of Wartburg.[3]

Bird Phoenix! Don't you know him? He sang the *Marseillaise* for you, and you kissed the feathers that fell from his wings. He came in the glory of paradise, and perhaps you turned away to the sparrow with gilded wings.

Bird of paradise! Renewed each century, born in flames and dying in flames. Your picture framed in gold hangs in the galleries of the rich, while you yourself often fly wildly and alone—a legend only: *Bird Phoenix* of Arabia.

In the Garden of Eden when you were born under the tree of knowledge, in the first blooming rose, God kissed you and gave you your right name—*Poetry*.

NOTES

1. Copper-mining town northwest of Stockholm.
2. In Nordic mythology, Odin has two ravens, Hugin and Munin, who

fly around the world every day and then whisper everything they see and hear in Odin's ear.

3. According to legend, Wartburg castle was the site of a minstrels' contest in 1207 ordered by Count Herman of Thüringen.

THE FAMILY OF HEN-GRETHE

HEN-GRETHE WAS THE only resident human being in the handsome new house that was built for the hens and the ducks at the manor. It stood where the old knight's castle had stood, with its tower, corbie-gabled roof, moat, and a drawbridge. Close by were overgrown trees and bushes. This was where the garden had been, which had stretched all the way down to a big lake that was now a swamp. Rooks, crows, and jackdaws flew screaming over the old trees—teeming flocks of birds. Shooting at them didn't decrease their number at all, in fact, they seemed to increase. You could hear them from inside the henhouse, where Hen-Grethe sat with ducklings running across the toes of her wooden shoes. She knew every hen and every duck from the time it hatched. She was proud of her hens and ducks and proud of the fine house that had been built for them. Her little room was clean and neat. This was insisted upon by the lady of the manor to whom the henhouse belonged. She often brought fashionable and distinguished guests to show them "the barracks of the hens and ducks," as she called it.

There was both a clothes closet and an easy chair. There was a chest of drawers, and on top of it was a shiny polished brass plate, engraved with the word "Grubbe." That was the name of the old noble family that had lived in the castle. The brass plate had been found during the construction there, and the schoolteacher had said that it had no other value than as an old keepsake. The schoolteacher knew a lot about the place and about old times. He had knowledge from books, and there were so many things he had written up in his desk drawers. He had great knowledge of olden days. Maybe the oldest crow knew more about it and shouted it in his language, but that was Crocawish and the schoolmaster didn't understand that, no matter how wise he was.

After a warm summer day a fog would rise from the swamp so that it looked like a whole lake lay out behind the old trees where the rooks, crows, and jackdaws flew. That's how it had looked when the knight, Grubbe, had lived there and the old castle stood with its thick red brick walls. At that time the watchdog's chain reached past the gate, and you came through the tower into the stone paved hallway that led to the rooms. The windows were narrow with small panes, even in the big hall where dances were held. By the time of the last Grubbe no one could remember the last dance, and yet there was still an old kettledrum lying there, that had been used for music making. There had been an elaborately carved cabinet in which rare flower bulbs were kept because Mrs. Grubbe had been fond of planting and cultivating trees and herbs. Her husband preferred riding out to shoot wolves and wild boar, and his little daughter Marie always accompanied him. At the age of five she sat proudly on her horse and looked around bravely with big black eyes. She enjoyed cracking the whip amongst the hunting dogs, but her father would rather she had cracked it at the peasant boys who came to watch the gentry.

The farmer in the earthen house close by had a son, Søren, the same age as the little noble maiden. He was good at climbing and always had to climb up in the trees to get bird nests for her. The birds screamed as loudly as they could, and one of the largest of them pecked him right over the eye so the blood streamed out. They thought the eye was lost at first, but it had not been injured. Marie Grubbe called him *my Søren*. That was a great favor, and it paid off for his father, poor Jon. One day he had done something wrong and was to be punished—he had to ride the wooden horse. It stood in the courtyard with four stakes for legs, and only one narrow plank for a back. Here Jon had to sit astraddle with some heavy bricks tied to his legs so he wouldn't sit too lightly. He grimaced in pain, and Søren cried and begged little Marie for help. She immediately ordered that Søren's father be let down, and when they didn't obey her, she stamped her feet on the stone bridge and pulled at her father's sleeve so it ripped. She wanted what she wanted, and she got her way. Søren's father was allowed to get down.

Mrs. Grubbe had come up, stroked her little daughter across her hair and looked at her with gentle eyes, but Marie didn't understand why.

She wanted to go with the hunting dogs, and not with her mother, who went into the garden and down towards the lake where white and yellow water lilies were in bloom, and cat tails and flowering rushes waved amongst the reeds. "How lovely," she said as she looked at the lush freshness. In the garden stood a tree that she had planted herself, a rare one at that time. It was a copper beech, and with its dark brown leaves, it stood like a kind of negro among the other trees. It needed strong sunlight, otherwise in constant shade it would turn green like the other trees and thereby lose its distinctiveness. There were many bird nests in the tall chestnuts and also in the bushes and grass. It was as if the birds knew that they were safe there where no one dared shoot off a gun.

Little Marie came into the garden with Søren one day. We know he could climb, and he collected both eggs and downy baby birds. The birds flew in fear and terror, small and big alike! The plovers in the meadow, and rooks, crows, and jack-daws from the treetops shrieked and shrieked. It's a cry that they have to this day.

"What are you children doing?!" shouted the gentle mistress. "These are ungodly acts!"

Søren was down-hearted, and the little noble maiden also looked away a little, but then said shortly and sullenly, "I have permission from father."

"Away! Away!" cried the big black birds and flew, but they came back the next day for that was their home.

But the quiet, gentle mistress wasn't at home there for long. Our Lord called her to him, and there she was also more at home than at the manor. Stately church bells rang out as her body was driven to the church. Many poor men's eyes were misty because she had been good to them.

When she was gone, no one took care of her plants, and the garden fell into decay.

It was said that Master Grubbe was a hard man, but his daughter, young as she was, could cope with him. He had to laugh, and she got her way. She was twelve years old now, big and strong, and her black eyes pierced right through people. She rode her horse like a man, and shot her gun like an experienced hunter.

One day a great and most distinguished company came to that part of the country. It was the young king and his friend and half-brother, Ulrik Frederik Gyldenløve. They were hunting wild boar and would stay at Sir Grubbe's castle for the day and night.

Gyldenløve sat beside Marie Grubbe at the table. He turned her head and gave her a kiss, as if they were relatives, but she slapped him and said that she couldn't stand him. Everyone laughed a lot at that, as if it were very entertaining.

And perhaps it was at that because five years later, when Marie had turned seventeen, a messenger brought a letter. Mr. Gyldenløve asked for the noble maiden's hand. That was something!

"He is the most distinguished and courteous man in the kingdom," said the squire. "This can't be rejected."

"I don't care much for him," said Marie Grubbe, but she didn't reject the country's most distinguished man, who sat by the side of the king.

Silver, woolens, and linens were sent by ship to Copenhagen. She made the journey by land in ten days. The trousseau met head winds or no wind, and four months passed before it arrived. When it did, Mrs. Glydenløve was gone.

"I'd rather lie on coarse canvas than in his silk bed!" she said. "I'd rather walk barefoot than drive with him in the coach!"

Late one evening in November two women came riding into Aarhus. It was Glydenløve's wife, Marie Grubbe, and her maid. They had come from Veile, where they had arrived by ship from Copenhagen. They rode up to Sir Grubbe's brick walled villa. He was not happy about this visit and had angry words for her, but he gave her a chamber in which to sleep. In the morning she got sweet porridge but not sweet words. She was not used to having her father's evil temper turned towards her, but since she didn't have a mild temperament, she gave as good as she got. She talked back to him and spoke with bitterness and hatred about her husband. She didn't want to live with him— She was too decent and respectable for that.

A year passed, and it did not pass pleasantly. Harsh words were exchanged between father and daughter, and that should never happen. Harsh words bear harsh fruit. How would this end?

"We two can't remain under one roof," her father said one day. "Move out to our old castle, but bite your tongue off before you start spreading lies!"

So the two parted. She moved with her maid out to the old castle where she had been born and grown up, and where her quiet pious mother lay in the burial chamber of the church. An old cattle herder lived on the property, but he was the only servant. There were cobwebs hanging in the rooms, black and heavy with dust. The garden was growing wild. Hops vines and bindweed twisted nets between trees and bushes, and hemlock and nettles grew bigger and spread. The copper beech was overgrown and standing in shade. Its leaves were now as green as the other ordinary trees, and its days of splendor were past. Teeming flocks of rooks, crows, and jackdaws flew over the tall chestnut trees. There was screaming and shrieking as if they really had news to tell each other. Now she was back, the little one who, with her friend, had stolen their eggs and young ones. The thief himself, who had done the stealing, had become a sailor. He sat on the high mast and received a flogging when he didn't behave himself.

All of this was told by the schoolmaster in our own time. He had collected and gathered it together from books and notes. It all lay hidden away in the drawer with many other writings.

"Rise and fall is the way of the world," he said. "It's a strange story." And we do want to hear what happened to Marie Grubbe, but we mustn't forget Hen-Grethe. She's sitting in her fine henhouse in our own time. Marie Grubbe sat here in her time, but with a different disposition than old Hen-Grethe's.

The winter passed, spring and summer too, and then the

blustery autumn came again with clammy, cold fogs from the sea. It was a lonely life, a boring life there in the castle.

Marie Grubbe took her gun and went out on the heath. She shot hares and foxes and whatever birds she could hit. More than once she met the nobleman Palle Dyre from Nørrebœk, who was also out with his gun and dogs. He was big and strong, and he boasted about that when they spoke together. He could have measured up to the deceased Mr. Brockenhuus from Egeskov in Fyn, whose strength was legendary. Palle Dyre had followed his example and had had an iron chain fastened to the top of his entrance portal. It had a hunting horn attached to it, and when he rode home through the gate, he grabbed the chain and lifted himself and his horse off the ground and blew the horn.

"Come see for yourself, Mrs. Marie," he said. "There's fresh air at Nørrebæk!"

It's not recorded when she moved to his manor, but engravings on the candlesticks in Nørrebœk church say they were gifts of Palle Dyre and Marie Grubbe of Nørrebœk.

Palle Dyre had a big body and brute strength. He drank like a sponge and was like a barrel that could never be filled. He snored like a whole pen full of pigs and was red and puffy looking.

"He's cunning and mischievous!" said Mrs. Palle Dyre, Grubbe's daughter. She was soon bored with that life, but that didn't help.

One day the table was set, and the food was getting cold. Palle Dyre was out hunting fox, and his wife was nowhere to be found. Palle Dyre came home about midnight, but Mrs. Dyre came neither at midnight nor in the morning. She had turned her back on Nørrebæk and had ridden away without so much as a word.

The weather was grey and wet. A cold wind was blowing, and a flock of black screaming birds flew over her, but they were not as homeless as she was. First she rode south, to the German border. She sold a pair of gold rings with precious stones and then headed towards the east. Then she turned and went west again. She had no goal, and was angry with everyone, even gracious God, so miserable was her spirit. Soon her body became so as well, and she could hardly lift her foot. The plover flew up from its tuft when she stumbled over it, and cried as it always cries: "Raah-ber raah-ber." She had never stolen anything, but she had had eggs and young birds brought to her from tuft and tree when she was a little girl. She thought about that now.

From where she lay she could see the sand dunes. Fishermen lived over there on the shore, but she was too sick to reach them. The big white seagulls came flying over her and cried like the rooks, crows, and jackdaws cried over the garden at home. The birds flew quite close to her, and at last it seemed to her that they appeared coal black, but then everything went black for her.

When she opened her eyes again, she was being lifted and carried. A big, strong fellow had her in his arms. She looked right into his bearded face, and saw that he had a scar over his eye so that it looked like his eyebrow was divided into two parts. He carried her, as miserable as she was, to the ship, where he got angry words from the captain for his actions.

The next day the ship sailed. Marie Grubbe had not come ashore. Indeed, she was taken along. But did she come back? Well, when and where?

The schoolmaster knew about this too, but it was not a story he had put together himself. He knew the whole strange course of events from a credible old book, one that we could take out and read ourselves. The Danish storyteller Ludvig Holberg,[1] who has written so many books worth reading and those funny comedies in which we recognize his time and its people, tells about Marie Grubbe in his letters, and about where and how he met her. It's worth hearing, but we certainly won't forget Hen-Grethe, who is sitting happy and satisfied in the magnificent henhouse.

The ship sailed off with Marie Grubbe. That's where we left off.

Years and years passed.

It was 1711, and the plague was raging in Copenhagen. The queen of Denmark went to her home town in Germany. The king left the capital, and everyone who could manage it hurried away from the city. Students, even if they had free room and board, left town. One of them, the last one left in the so-called Borch residence, right by the residence close to the Round Tower, was now leaving too. It was two o'clock in the morning. He had his knapsack with him which had more books and written materials in it than clothing. There was a wet, clammy fog hanging over the city, and not a person was to be seen on the street where he walked. Crosses had been posted on doors and gates round about, which meant that there was plague inside or that the people had died. There weren't any people to be seen on the wider, curving Kjød-manger street, as it was called, either—the street that goes from the Round Tower down to the King's castle. Then a big hearse went rumbling by. The driver was cracking his whip, and the horses galloped. The wagon was full of bodies. The young student held his hand to his face and smelled the strong alcohol that he carried on a sponge in a little brass box. From a pub in one of the alleys came raucous singing and cheerless laughter from people who were drinking the night away in order to forget that the plague was at their door and wanted to add them to the hearse with the other dead. The student headed towards the bridge by the castle where there were a couple of small boats. One was just pulling away to escape the infested city.

"If God allows us to live, and we have a good wind, we're headed to Grønsund by Falster," said the captain and asked the student, who wanted to go along, for his name.

"Ludvig Holberg," said the student, and the name sounded like any other name. Now it resounds as one of the proudest names in Denmark, but then he was just a young, unknown student.

The ship sailed past the castle. It wasn't quite light yet when it came into the open sea. A light breeze blew and the sail swelled. The young student sat with his face to the fresh wind and fell asleep, which wasn't really advisable.

By the third morning the ship was already lying off Falster.

"Do you know a place I can stay here that's not too expensive?" Holberg asked the captain.

"I think you could do well with the ferryman's wife at Bor-rehuset," he answered. "If you want to be especially courteous, her name is Mother Søren Sørensen Møller. But she might get angry if you are too high-class with her. Her husband was arrested for some misdeed, so she drives the ferry herself. She certainly has the fists for it!"

The student took his knapsack and walked to the ferry house. The living room door was not locked, the latch opened, and he walked into a paved room where a sleeping bench with a huge pelt comforter was the most noticeable thing. A white hen with chicks was tied to the bench and had tipped over the water dish so water was spilled all over the floor. There was no one in this room, or the little chamber next to it except a baby in a cradle. The ferry was on its way back, and there was only one person in it. It wasn't easy to say if it was a man or a woman. The person had a big cloak wrapped around itself and a man's hat with ear flaps, but tied under the chin like a woman's hat. The boat docked.

It was a woman who came into the room. She looked pretty big when she straightened up and had two proud eyes under black eyebrows. It was mother Søren, the ferryman's wife. Rooks, crows, and jackdaws would call her by another name that we would know better.

She looked sullen and didn't seem to like to talk, but this much was said and decided—the student bargained for room and board for an undetermined time—while things were so bad in Copenhagen.

One or another pair of decent citizens from the nearby town were in the habit of frequenting the ferry house. Frands the knife-maker and Sivert the sack-peeper[2] were two of them. They drank a pint of beer in the ferry house and talked with the young student. He was a competent young man, who understood practical things, as they called it. He also read Greek and Latin and knew about learned things.

"The less you know, the less you're burdened," said Mother Søren.

"You have a hard life," said Holberg one day, when she was

washing her clothes in warm soapy lye water, and had to chop wood stumps into firewood herself.

"Leave me to it," she answered.

"Have you had to work so hard from childhood on?"

"I guess you can read that in my hands," she said and held out two quite small but hard, strong hands with bitten nails. "You are so learned, you can read these."

Christmas time brought a strong snowstorm. It became very cold, and the wind blew as if it were washing people in the face with nitric acid. Mother Søren didn't let it affect her. She threw her cloak around her and pulled the hat down over her head. It became dark in the house early in the afternoon. She laid wood and peat in the fire and sat down to darn her stockings. There was no one else to do it. Towards evening she spoke more to the student than she was in the habit of doing. She talked about her husband.

"He accidentally killed a man, a captain from Dragør, and has to work in irons for three years on Holmen. He's just a common sailor, so the law must take its course."

"The law also applies to the higher classes," said Holberg.

"Do you think so?" said Mother Søren and looked into the fire. But then she started talking again. "Have you heard about Kai Lykke who ordered one of his churches to be torn down? And when Pastor Mads thundered about it from the pulpit, Lykke had him thrown in irons, and sentenced him to lose his head, and lose it he did. That was not accidental, and yet Kai Lykke walked free as air!"

"He was in the right according to the views of that time," said Holberg. "But that time is past now."

"You can make fools believe that," Mother Søren said. She got up and went into the chamber where "Lassy," the little baby, lay. She picked her up, and laid her down again. Then she made up the bed on the bench for the student. He got the pelt comforter because he was more sensitive to cold than she was, even though he was born in Norway.

New Year's Day was a clear sunny day. There had been a heavy frost so cold that the snow was frozen solid so you could walk on it. The church bells were ringing for services, and student Holberg wrapped his woolen cloak around him and went to town.

Rooks, crows, and jackdaws flew over the ferry house with cries and shrieks. You couldn't hear the church bells over the squalling. Mother Søren was outside filing a brass kettle with snow to melt over the fire for drinking water. She looked up towards the flocks of birds, and thought her own thoughts.

Student Holberg went to church. On the way there and coming back he went by Sivert the sack-peeper's house at the gate and was invited in for a mug of warm beer with syrup and ginger. The talk fell to Mother Søren, but the sack-peeper didn't know much about her. Nobody did. She wasn't from Falster, he said. She had evidently had a little money once. Her husband was an ordinary sailor with a hot temper. He had beat a captain from Dragør to death. "He whips his old lady too, and yet she defends him."

"I wouldn't tolerate such treatment!" said the sack-peeper's wife. "But I come from a better class. My father was a royal stocking weaver."

"And therefore you also married a royal civil servant," said Holberg and made a deep bow to her and the sack-peeper.

It was Twelfth Night Eve.[3] Mother Søren lit for Holberg a Twelfth Night light, that is to say, three tallow candles she had dipped herself.

"One candle for each man!" said Holberg.

"Each man?" said the woman and stared hard at him.

"Each of the wise men from the east," said Holberg.

"Oh, them," she said and was quiet for a long time. But in that Twelfth Night he learned more about her than he had known before.

"You care about the man you're married to," said Holberg, "but people say that he mistreats you."

"That only concerns me," she answered. "Those blows could have done me some good as a child. I guess I get them now because of my sins, but I know what good he has done for me." She stood up. "When I lay on the open heath, and no one cared about me, except maybe the rooks and crows who wanted to peck at me, he carried me in his arms and received only angry words for bringing me to the ship. I wasn't made for illness. So I got well. Everyone has his own way, and Søren has his. You can't judge the horse by the halter. I have lived more happily with him than with the one they call the most courteous and distinguished of all the king's subjects. I was married to Governor Gyldenløve, the king's half-brother. Later I married Palle Dyre. It makes no difference. Each has his own way, and I have mine. That was a long talk, but now you know it!" And she left the room.

It was Marie Grubbe! How strange were her changes of fortune! She didn't live many more Twelfth Nights. Holberg wrote that she died in June of 1716, but what he didn't write, because he didn't know, was that when Mother Søren, as she was called, lay in her coffin in the ferry house, a flock of big black birds flew over. They didn't shriek, as if they knew that silence belongs to funerals. As soon as she was buried, the birds were no longer seen, but the same evening enormous flocks of rooks, crows, and jackdaws were sighted in Jutland, by the old castle. Each screamed louder than the next, as if they had something to tell. Maybe it was about him who as a little boy had taken their eggs and downy chicks, the farmer's son, who ended up in irons on the king's island; and about the noble maiden, who ended up a ferryman's wife at Grønsund. "Bra! Bra!"[4] they cried.

And their relatives cried "Bra, bra!" when the old castle was torn down. "They are crying it yet, and there's nothing left to cry over," said the schoolteacher as he related it. "The family has died out. The castle was torn down, and where it stood now stands the stately henhouse with the gilded weathervane, and with old Hen-Grethe inside. She is so happy to have her lovely house, and if she hadn't come here, she'd be in the poorhouse."

The doves cooed above her. The turkeys gobbled round about, and the ducks quacked. "No one knew her," they said. "She has no family. It's an act of mercy that she's here. She has neither a drake father nor a hen mother, and no offspring."

But she did have a family. She didn't know it, nor did the schoolmaster, no matter how much material he had in his table drawer. But one of the old crows knew and told about it. From its mother and grandmother it had heard about Hen-Grethe's mother and grandmother, whom we know too, from the time she rode as a child over the drawbridge and looked around proudly as if the whole world and all its bird nests were hers. We saw her on the heath by the sand dunes, and finally at the ferry house. Her grandchild, the last of the family, had come home again where the old castle had stood and the wild black birds had screamed. But she sat amongst tame birds, known to them and knowing them. Hen-Grethe had nothing more to wish for. She was happy to die, and old enough to die.

"Grave! Grave!" croaked the crows.

And Hen-Grethe got a good resting place, but no one knows where, except the old crow, unless she's dead too.

And now we know the story about the old castle, the old kinships, and all of Hen-Grethe's family.

NOTES

1. Often called the father of Danish and Norwegian literature, Ludwig Holberg (1684–1754) was the most important intellectual and writer in eighteenth-century Denmark and Norway; he wrote drama, comedies, history, and essays on a wide variety of topics.
2. Reference to a nickname for tollgate attendants who collected tax on products at town gates. The name comes from Ludvig Holberg's play *Den politiske Kandestøber (The Political Tinker)*.
3. The twelfth day after Christmas is called Epiphany. The evening before (sometimes the evening of) this day is called Twelfth Night.
4. In Danish *bra* means "good" or "fine." Andersen is very fond of onomatopoeia.

EVERYTHING IN ITS PROPER PLACE

IT WAS OVER A hundred years ago.

Back in the forest beside the big lake there was an old manor house, and around it there was a deep moat full of rushes and reeds. Right by the bridge to the entrance gate stood an old weeping willow, whose branches leaned over the reeds.

From the high banked road she heard horns and the tramping of horses so the little goose girl hurried to get her geese off the bridge before the hunting party came galloping over. They came so fast that she quickly had to jump up on one of the high stones by the bridge to avoid being run down. She was still half a child, thin and delicate, but with a blessed expression on her face and two pretty clear eyes, but the lord of the manor didn't look at that. At the great pace he was traveling, he turned his whip in his hand and in coarse merriment, he poked her with the shaft right in the chest so she fell over backwards.

"Everything in its proper place!" he yelled, "into the dirt you go!" and then he laughed. It was supposed to be so funny, and the others laughed too. The whole party was yelling and screeching, and the hunting dogs were barking. It really was "rich birds come a'whistling," but God knows how rich he still was then.

The poor goose girl reached out as she fell and grasped one of the over-hanging willow branches. She was able to hold herself up from the mud, and as soon as the hunting party and the dogs were well inside the gate, she struggled to pull herself up. But the branch broke off at the top, and the goose girl fell heavily backwards in the reeds just as a strong hand from above grabbed her. It was an itinerant peddler who had seen what had happened from a distance and had hurried to help her.

"Everything in its proper place," he said in jest, mimicking her master, and pulled her up on dry land. He put the broken branch back in the place where it had broken off, but "in its proper place" doesn't always work! So then he stuck the branch down in the soft earth—"grow if you can and may a flute cut from you make that master pay the piper!" He thought that the master and his friends deserved a whipping. Then the peddler went up to the manor, but not to the main hall—he wasn't good enough for that. He went to the folks in the servants' quarters, and they looked at his wares and bargained with him. But from the banquet hall came yells and bawling. It was supposed to be singing, but they weren't good at it. There was laughter and barking of dogs, gorging and boozing. Wine and old beer foamed in the glasses and mugs, and the pet dogs feasted too. The young noblemen kissed first one and then another of them, after they first wiped the dogs' snouts with their long ears. The peddler was called up to show his wares, but only so they could make fun of him. When the wine goes in, the wit goes out. They poured beer into a stocking for him so he could drink with them, but quickly! It was all so very clever and witty! And whole herds of cattle and farms with farmers too were bet and lost on just one card.

"Everything in its proper place," said the peddler when he was well away from "Sodom and Gomorra," as he called it. "The open road is my proper place. I was really out of place up there." The little goose girl nodded to him from the fence.

And days went by and weeks passed, and it turned out that the broken willow branch that the peddler had stuck down in the moat stayed fresh and green. It even put out new shoots. The little goose girl realized that it must have taken root, and she was very happy about it. It seemed to her that it was her tree.

Well, the tree thrived, but nothing else on the estate did, with the guzzling and the gambling that went on. Those are two stilts that aren't easy to stand on.

It wasn't even six years before the lord of the manor wandered away from the estate with a sack and a staff as a poor man. The manor was bought by a rich peddler, the very same man who had been the object of ridicule and offered beer in a stocking. But honesty and hard work bring prosperity, and now the peddler was lord of the manor. From that day forward, no card playing was allowed there. "Cards are poor reading," he said. "And that's because, when the devil first saw the Bible, he wanted to make one like it, and he invented card playing."

The new master took a wife, and who do you think it was? It was the little goose girl, who had always been good-natured, gentle, and kind. And in her new clothes she was so fine and beautiful as if she had been born an aristocratic lady. How did all this happen? Well, it's too long a story for our busy times, but it happened, and the most important part comes later.

Now there was happiness and prosperity on the old estate.

Mother was in charge of the house, and father the farm. Blessings poured down upon them, and money makes money. The old buildings were renovated and painted. The moats were cleaned out, and fruit trees were planted. Everything looked so pleasant and nice. The living room floor was as shiny as a bread board. In the winter evenings the mistress sat with her maids in the big hall spinning wool and linen. Every Sunday evening the Bible was read aloud, and that by the councilman himself. Yes, the peddler became a councilman—but not until he was quite old. The children grew—there were children— and they were all well educated, but they didn't have equal brains of course, just as in every family.

And the willow branch out there had become a fine, large tree that stood free and untrimmed. "That's our family tree," the old folks said, and they told their children, even the less bright ones, that the tree was to be respected and honored.

And a hundred years went by.

Now it was our own time. The lake had become a bog, and it was as if the old manor house had been erased. There was an oblong puddle of water with some stone circles on the side. Those were the remains of the deep moat, and there was still a grand old tree standing there with stooped branches. It was the family tree. It showed how beautiful a weeping willow can be when it is allowed to get along on its own. True, the trunk had split, right from the root up to the crown. Storms had twisted it a little, but it was standing, and grass and flowers were growing from all the cracks and crevices where wind and weather had deposited humus. It was like an entire little hanging garden with raspberries and chickweed, especially at the top, where the big branches divided. Even a tiny little rowanberry tree had rooted there and stood so slender and delicate right up in the middle of the old willow tree. The tree was mirrored in the black water when the wind drove the duckweed to the other corner of the pond. A little path over the meadows went right by the tree.

High on a hill by the forest, with a wonderful view, lay the new manor house, large and splendid, with windows so clear that you would think there was no glass in them. The big stairs by the door looked like they were wearing an arbor of roses and large-leafed plants. The lawn was so perfectly green that it looked as if each blade was tended both morning and night. Expensive paintings hung in the hall inside, and there were silk and velvet chairs and couches that could almost walk on their own legs. There were tables with shiny marble tops and books of fine leather with gilt edges. Rich people lived here, distinguished people—the baron and his family.

And one matched the other. "Everything in its proper place!" they also said, and because of that all the pictures that had once been the pride and joy of the old manor house were now hanging in the servants' wing. They were real junk, especially two old portraits, one of a man in a rosy-red coat and a wig, and the other of a lady with powdered hair piled high on her head and a red rose in her hand. Both were surrounded by big wreaths of willow branches. There were lots of holes in the old portraits because the baron's little children always shot their bow and arrows at the two old folks. It was the Councilman and his wife, from whom the family descended.

"But they aren't really part of our family," one of the small barons said. "He was a peddler, and she was a goose girl. They weren't like Pappa and Mamma!"

The pictures were just poor rubbish, and when "everything in its proper place" was applied, great grandfather and great grandmother ended up in the servants' quarters.

The minister's son was the live-in tutor on the estate. He was out walking one day with the little boys and their elder sister, who had just been confirmed. They walked on the path down towards the old willow tree, and while they walked she bundled up a bouquet of wild flowers with "everything in its proper place," and it made a beautiful whole. At the same time she listened carefully to everything that was said, and it pleased her so much to hear the minister's son talk about the powers of nature and of history's great men and women. She had a good, healthy disposition, noble in soul and thought, and with a heart that could embrace all of God's creation.

They stopped by the old weeping willow. The smallest boy wanted a willow whistle made from the tree. He had had them whittled before from other willows. The minister's son broke off a branch.

"Oh, don't do that!" said the young baroness, but it was too late. "That's our famous old tree, and I'm so very fond of it! They all laugh at me about it at home, but that doesn't matter. There's a legend about that tree—"

And she told everything that she had heard about the tree, about the old manor, about the goose girl and the peddler who met there, and became the ancestors of the distinguished family and the young baroness herself.

"They wouldn't accept a title, the decent old folks," she said. "They had a saying, 'Everything in its proper place' and they didn't think they would be in the proper place if they were elevated to the nobility because of their money. It was their son, my grandfather, who would become a baron. It's said that he had great knowledge and was highly regarded and thought of by princes and princesses, always invited to their parties. Everyone else in the family thinks the most of him, but—I don't really know why—there's something about the old couple that draws my heart to them. It must have been so pleasant and patriarchal in those times in the manor, when the mistress sat spinning with all her maids, and the old gentleman read aloud from the Bible."

"They were pious, sensible people," said the minister's son, and then they started talking about nobility and the middle class, and it was almost as if the minister's son didn't belong to the middle class, the way he talked about the nobility.

"It's a good thing to belong to a family that has distinguished itself—to have an incentive in your blood, in a way, to continue doing good things! It's wonderful to bear a family name that opens all doors to you. Nobility means noble. It's the gold coin that has been stamped with what it's truly worth. It's a fashion of our times, and many poets share the view, that everything that is aristocratic is false and foolish, and that the lower in society you go, the more true nobility shines. But that's not my opinion. I think that's wrong, completely wrong. You can find many moving noble incidents in the upper classes. My mother told me one, and I could give others. She

was visiting at a distinguished family in town. I think my grandmother had nursed the noble mistress. My mother was standing in the living room with the aristocratic old husband when
he saw an old woman coming along the courtyard on crutches.
She came every Sunday and was given a few shillings. 'There's
the poor old thing,' the man said. 'It's so hard for her to walk.'
And before my mother knew it, he was out the door and down
the steps. The seventy-year-old Excellency went down to the
old woman himself to save her the arduous trip up the steps
for the money she came for. Of course, that's just one poor little example, but just like the 'widow's mite' it comes from the
heart, from human decency. Poets should be pointing out, especially now in our time, things which inspire good, things
that mitigate and reconcile. But when a human being throws
his weight around in the street just because he has noble blood
and a family tree like an Arabian horse, or says, 'It smells like
the street in here' when a common person has been in the
room, then nobility has rotted, become a mask as in Thespis,[1]
and then we laugh at such a person and satirize them."

That was what the minister's son said. It was somewhat long,
but in the meantime the whistle had been whittled.

They were having a big party at the manor. Many guests had
come from the surrounding area and from the capital. Some
women were dressed tastefully, and others without taste. The
big hall was full of people. The local ministers were standing
respectfully in a group in a corner. It looked a little like a funeral, but it was entertainment, although it hadn't really
started yet.

There was going to be a big concert, and that's why the little baron brought his willow flute along, but he couldn't get a
peep out of it. His pappa couldn't either, so it wasn't any good.

There was music and singing of the kind that is most fun for
those who perform it, but lovely, by the way.

"You're a virtuoso," said a young cavalier, who was like his
parents, to the young tutor. "You play the flute, even carve it
yourself. Genius is certainly ruling here—sitting on the right
hand side—God bless us! I keep up with the times, you have to
do that. Won't you please us all by playing your little instru-

ment?" and he handed him the little willow flute that was carved from the willow tree down by the moat. Loudly and clearly he announced that the tutor was going to play a flute solo.

It was easy to see that he was making fun of the tutor, who didn't want to play although he certainly could, but they insisted and pressed him, and so he took the flute and set it to his lips.

It was a strange flute! They heard a tone that was as persevering as what you hear from a steam locomotive, but even louder. It could be heard all over the estate, the garden, and the woods and for miles around the countryside, and with the sound came a stormy wind that roared, "Everything in its proper place." And then Pappa, the Baron, was carried by the wind out of the manor house and right down into the cottage where the man lived who tended the cows. And the cattleman flew up—not to the great hall, he didn't belong there—but up to the servants' quarters among the finest servants who wore silk stockings. And those proud fellows were struck numb to think that such an inferior person dared sit at the table with them.

But in the great hall the young Baroness flew up to the head of the main table, where her place was, and the minister's son sat beside her. They sat there together as if they were a bridal couple. An old count who belonged to one of the oldest families in the land remained in his place of honor because the flute played fair, as one should. The witty cavalier who was responsible for the flute playing, and who was like his parents, flew head-first into the henhouse, but he was not alone.

The flute could be heard for miles, and odd things happened. A rich merchant and his family, driving in a four-horse carriage, were blown completely out of the carriage and couldn't even find a place on the back. Two rich farmers, who recently had grown too big for their own cornfields, were blown down into a muddy ditch. It was a dangerous flute. Fortunately it cracked with the first tone, and that was a good thing. It went back in the young man's pocket: "Everything in its proper place!"

The next day nobody talked about what had happened, and that's why we have a saying—"Stick a pipe in it." Everything was once again where it was before except for the two old portraits of the peddler and the goose girl. They had been blown up to the wall in the great hall, and when someone who was an art expert said that they were painted by a master, they were repaired and remained hanging there. No one knew before that they were any good, and how would you know that? Now they hung in a place of honor. "Everything in its proper place" and eventually that's where everything ends up. Eternity is long— longer than this story.

NOTES

1. In Greek tradition, the sixth-century inventor of tragedy; little is known of his life and work.

Commentaries on the Tales

❧

The dates given below are those of first publication. Andersen first published several of his tales in periodicals, then collected them in book form, sometimes a year or more after they had originally appeared.

THE ARTIST AND SOCIETY

THE NIGHTINGALE (NATTERGALEN, 1844)

As a young boy, Andersen had a sweet voice and was called "the little nightingale of Fyn," a reference to the island on which Odense was located. Clearly, in his story Andersen identified with the nightingale, which is depicted as his ideal model of the artist, who must determine his "authentic" role within a system of patronage. Andersen also associated the little bird with Swedish singer Jenny Lind, famous because of her exquisite voice and known as the "Swedish Nightingale." Andersen first heard Jenny Lind sing in the fall of 1844 and fell in love with her.

In European folklore and literary tradition the nightingale, a tiny bird, has been related to Philomela, a figure in Greek mythology; after her brother-in-law raped her and then cut out her tongue, the gods turned Philomela into a nightingale. In medieval literature the nightingale is depicted as a fearful creature, afraid of snakes, that presses a thorn against her breast to keep herself awake at night and therefore utters a mournful song. Andersen's nightingale is a not a female and is not mournful. His bird is more like a bird of spring that rejuvenates the emperor.

Andersen had been fascinated by China since his childhood and was also interested in mechanical inventions. In the Tivoli Gardens, which opened on August 15, 1843, in Copenhagen, several "Chinese" edifices reflected popular interest in the Orient. Andersen's visit to Tivoli soon after it was opened may have influenced him to write what he called his "Chinese fairy tale."

THE GARDENER AND THE GENTRY
(GARTNEREN OG HERSKABET, 1872)

Written at the end of Andersen's life, this tale reflects his disappointment about the reception of his works by the Danish aristocracy, despite his fame. The artist as a magnificent gardener is an apt metaphor for Andersen's conception of himself as an innovative cultivator of Danish folklore. The tale was immediately translated into English as "The Gardener and the Noble Family" and published in *Scribner's Monthly* (August 1872).

THE FLYING TRUNK (DEN FLYVENDE KUFFERT, 1839)

The source for this tale is "Malek and Princess Schirina," in French Orientalist Petis de la Croix's *Mille et un jours* (*The Thousand and One Days*, 1710), a collection of tales allegedly based on a Persian original called *Hazar Yek Ruz*. Very popular in the eighteenth and nineteenth centuries, *Mille et un jours* was translated from French into English and German, and into Danish in 1759. In Andersen's tale Malek is the son of a rich merchant who buys a mechanical coffer that flies through the air. After he wastes away his inheritance, he flies off to a foreign realm called Gazna, ruled by King Bahaman, and, pretending to be the Prophet Mahomet, marries the Princess Schirina. At one point Malek even protects the realm of Gazna from invasion by a neighboring king. However, his flying coffer catches fire; once it is destroyed, Malek leaves Gazna and becomes a weaver in Cairo, thus fulfilling a prophecy that the princess would one day be betrayed by a man.

To a certain extent, Andersen's story is similar to many Oriental tales featuring flying carpets or horses. The traditional tale begins with a son of a rich merchant spending his inheritance foolishly and being abandoned by his friends, then stumbling upon some lucky charm. In Andersen's tale, the trunk (which in the Arabic tales can be a carpet, lamp, horse, or some other helper) enables him to regain his former social status and enjoy a brief period of pleasure. However, since he does not take care of his lucky object, he fails to attain complete happiness in the end. Andersen introduced the motif of the hero as storyteller who must tell a moral, refined, and amusing tale. Ironically, the tale parallels the fortune of the merchant's son and exposes his major foible: pride. Embedded in Andersen's story is a notion that good tales can expose even the storyteller.

THE WILL-O'-THE-WISPS ARE IN TOWN
(LYGTEMÆNDENE EER I BYEN, SAGDE MOSEKONEN, 1865)

For this story, written a year after Denmark had fought a bitter war with Prussia and lost the region of Schleswig-Holstein, Andersen had to overcome a writer's block. The tale reflects his dark mood during this period in his life. The search for the fairy tale parallels his own search for a means to overcome his depression. Ultimately, the story ends on an optimistic note, evidence of the power of the fairy tale to provide hope.

THE PIXIE AND THE GARDENER'S WIFE
(NISSEN OG MADAMEN, 1868)

This tale, first published in *Folkekalender for Danmark*, was based on a Danish folk tale about a pixie that teases a chained dog. Andersen transformed this tale into a more significant commentary on the pretentiousness of minor writers, flattery, and the fickleness of audiences.

THE PUPPETEER (MARIONETSPILLEREN, 1851)

Andersen published a version of this tale in his travel book *In Sweden* (1851). The tale reflects his concerns about controlling characters in his plays or stories. What happens to the theater manager when his puppets come to life is a dilemma for the writer or author, who must know how to handle his characters. E. T. A. Hoffmann's tale "Seltsame Leiden eines Theater-Direktors" ("Strange Sufferings of a Theater Director," 1819), which deals with the difficulties of a director, may have influenced Andersen in his writing of this tale.

"SOMETHING" (NOGET, 1858)

Andersen stated that this legendary tale was based on a real incident in Schleswig, where an old woman burned her house to warn people out on nearby ice that a spring flood was coming. He also employed motifs from the folk tradition in which five brothers are sent out into the world to acquire skills that bring them fortune. A major element of this tale is Andersen's parody of critics. In particular, Andersen drew a caricature of Danish critic Christian Molbech, who often attacked Andersen's plays and writings. Molbech died in 1857.

WHAT ONE CAN THINK UP
(HVAD MAN KAN HITTE PAA, 1869)

Originally published in English as "What One Can Invent" in *The Riverside Magazine for Young People*, the tale was published several months later in the book *Tre Nye Eventyr og Historier* (*Three New Fairy Tales and Stories*). Andersen detested any sort of criticism of his works, and in this tale he gets his revenge by depicting critics as writers who lack imagination. At the same time, he also voiced his optimism about the progress of technology.

THE MOST INCREDIBLE THING (DET UTROLIGSTE, 1870)

This story first appeared in English in *The Riverside Magazine for Young People* under the title "The Most Extraordinary Thing" and was published in Danish the same year in *Nyt Dansk Maanedsskrift* (*New Danish Monthly Magazine*). Although Andersen was not political, he was disturbed by the looming threat of the Franco-Prussian War (1870–1871), just as he had been upset by earlier wars between Denmark and Prussia. Since he admired Prussia but regarded himself as a loyal Danish patriot, despite his feelings of alienation it was difficult for him to accept the Prussian aggression. Although the tale was written before the eruption of the war, there are clear references to the dispute. But the tale is more than a political commentary. It is a manifesto about the power of art and poetry, which will always triumph over brutality and violence. For Andersen, especially in his old age, it was important to proclaim the integrity and immortality of art.

AUNTIE TOOTHACHE (TANTE TANDPINE, 1872)

Though Andersen had begun this story in June 1870, he did not finish it until July 1872, and it is generally considered to be among the last tales he wrote. It is thus perhaps no surprise that it is a cynical commentary on the role of writing. Andersen wondered toward the end of his life whether all the pains he took to write would be worth the effort, and he worried about his stature as a writer. It seemed to him that his works might end up in a waste barrel. Some scholars consider the character Aunt Mille to be based on Andersen's friend Henriette Wulff, who greatly admired his works.

THE CRIPPLE (KRØBLINGEN, 1872)

Written between July 12 and July 18, this tale, along with "The Story Old Johanna Told," was dedicated to the Melchior family in gratitude for the care and hospitality they had given the author. He was inspired to write this tale, which reflects Andersen's belief in the healing power of fairy tales, after thinking about the old tale "The Woodchopper and His Wife." When he sent it to Horace Scudder, the American editor of his works, in New York, it had the title "The Fairy Tale Book." The plot is based on an anecdote that J. T. Kragh told Andersen: A poor couple had a mentally handicapped son who told them a story about a king who could regain his health only if he found the shirt of the happiest man on earth.

FOLK TALES

THE TINDERBOX (FYRTØJET, 1835)

"The Tinderbox" has deep roots in the Oriental and European oral traditions. There are clear similarities to the medieval Arabic tale "Aladdin and the Magic Lamp," which was part of the Antoine Galland's French collection of *The Thousand and One Nights*, translated into Danish in 1757 and 1758. Andersen is said to have heard this story as a child. In addition, the Brothers Grimm published "The Blue Light" (1812) in the first edition of their *Children's and Household Tales*, and Andersen may have been familiar with this tale, which is very close to Andersen's narrative. Finally, Bengt Holbek, the great Danish scholar, points out that Andersen may have known the Danish folk tale "The Spirit of the Candle," of which there are many variants, as well as Adam Oehlenschläger's play *Aladdin* (1805). The tale may have had a personal significance for Andersen because his father had served as a common soldier during the Napoleonic Wars and returned to Odense a broken man in 1814; he died two years later.

LITTLE CLAUS AND BIG CLAUS
(LILLE CLAUS OG STORE CLAUS, 1835)

This type of tale, generally referred to in German as a *Schwank* (a farcical tale or comic anecdote), was widespread throughout the medieval period. A Latin poem, "Versus de Unibove," which was published in the Netherlands in the eleventh century, describes how a farmer, mocked by his neighbors, makes fools out of them, a plot that became common in Italian and French stories of the Renaissance. Elements of the tale can be found in the fourteenth-century Latin collection of tales and anecdotes entitled *Gesta Romanorum* (*Deeds of the Romans*) as well as in Giovanni Boccaccio's the *Decameron* (1348–1353) and Poggio Bracciolini's *Liber facetiarum* (*The Fracetiae*, 1438–1452), a collection of jests and anecdotes. The theme of the clever swindler who does not respect the norms of society is related to many other ancient tales that depict a small clever hero who uses his wits to outsmart a giant, ogre, or monster, or a group of threatening people. These tales, which tend to be realistic portrayals of peasant life, convey a social critique of the injustices suffered by poor peasants. In these farcical tales, the peasants are portrayed for the most part carrying out menial tasks, such as chopping or gathering wood, spinning, weaving, or tending herds of sheep, goats, or geese. The exaggeration of their circumstances serves to highlight their desperate plight; the ending is often a wish-fulfillment in which the clever peasant has plenty of money and plenty to eat. In the early 1550s

Giovan Francesco Straparola published a hilarious Italian version "The Priest Scarpacifico," and in 1812 the Brothers Grimm included in their *Children's and Household Tales* the story "The Little Farmer," which is similar to Andersen's tale. There were also earlier Danish versions of the tale.

THE PRINCESS ON THE PEA
(PRINSESSEN PAA ÆRTEN, 1835)

Andersen probably became acquainted with this tale as a young man; it was very popular in Sweden. Known as the bed test or test of sensitivity, it has deep and ancient roots in the oral traditions of Asia, the Middle East, and Europe. Generally speaking, the princess who is being tested has an animal adviser who tells her to complain about something that prevents her from having a good night's sleep. In many stories the objects placed in her bed are beans, pins, stones, and knitting needles. It was—and still is—commonly assumed that aristocratic people were more sensitive than common people, and that the only way to determine whether a princess was truly of noble heritage was to place a small object under many mattresses and see whether she felt it. One of the oldest versions of the tale can be found in *Katha Sarit Sagara* (*The Ocean of Story* or *Ocean of Streams of Story*, a collection of Indian tales written in Sanskrit about 1070 by the poet Somadeva. The Brothers Grimm printed a version in 1845 but retracted it after they discovered that Andersen had already published his tale.

THE TRAVELING COMPANION (REISEKAMMERATEN, 1835)

Throughout Europe the commonly known tale type of the "grateful dead" depicts a young man who has set out into the world and comes upon men who are mistreating a corpse and refusing to bury it. The protagonist either pays the dead man's debts or gives him a decent burial, then proceeds on his journey. Shortly thereafter the dead man appears—sometimes in human form, sometimes in the shape of an animal, such as a fox or a horse—in order to help him. After enabling the protagonist to acquire a fortune or marry a princess, the dead man reveals his true identity to the young hero and often disappears. Andersen adapted a Fyn folk tale, "The Dead Man's Help," and published it as "The Ghost: A Fairy Tale from Fyn" in 1829. When he rewrote it in 1835 for his second pamphlet of fairy tales, he transformed it into a Christian tale that spells out his religious beliefs and that reveals his misogynist traits, which also appear in other tales, including "The Little Mermaid" and "The Red Shoes." The folk tale was very well known in the European tradition, as Bent Holbek points out in his essay "Hans Christian Andersen's Use of Folktales" (see "For Further Reading"). The Brothers Grimm also published a variant, "The Grateful Dead Man and the Princess Rescued from Slavery," in their annotations of 1856; they had received a dialect version from the Haxthausen family some time between 1814 and 1816. The motif concerning the Princess Turandot, who would marry only the man who could guess her thoughts, has its origins in *The Thousand and One Nights*; it served as the basis for eighteenth-century plays about Turandot by Carlo Gozzi and Friedrich Schiller. Simon Meisling, Andersen's headmaster, translated the Gozzi play in 1825, and Andersen undoubtedly knew his version.

THE WILD SWANS (DE VILDE SVANER, 1838)

One of the most popular motifs in the European oral and literary tradition is the innocent sister who seeks to become acquainted with and/or rescue her brothers, who were banished from her family upon her birth. Andersen probably knew a Danish folk variant and may have known one of the Grimms' versions. The Grimms were familiar with the Italian Giambattista Basile's "The Seven Doves" (1634) and published three tales in *Children's and Household Tales* that dealt with this theme—"The Six Swans," "The Twelve Brothers," and "The Seven Ravens"; they retained the pattern of Basile's tale and a German oral tale they heard while preparing their collection. Wilhelm Grimm's reworking of the narrative emphasizes two elements: the dedication of the sister and brothers to one another, and the establishment of a common, orderly household in the forest, where they live peacefully together. It is not clear whether Andersen knew the different German versions. He may have been more familiar with Mathias Winther's "The Eleven Swans," published in *Danske Folkeventyr* (*Danish Folk Tales*, 1823). After Andersen and the Brothers Grimm made this tale popular, the well-known German writer Ludwig Bechstein included versions of "The Seven Ravens" and "The Seven Swans" in his *German Fairy Tale Book* (1845).

The underlying social issue in these tales concerns the legacy of a family and the right of succession and inheritance. If such rights were based on ultimogeniture (inheritance by the youngest) rather than primogeniture (inheritance by the oldest child), the older children might be sent away so that the youngest could inherit the family property. It is also possible that the tale arose in societies that were based on matrilineal rites.

THE SWINEHERD (SVINEDRENGEN, 1842)

The taming of a proud princess or aristocratic woman who thinks she is too good to marry any man—especially one who is or appears to be beneath her in social rank, such as a gardener, a fool, a lower-class man, or a prince disguised as a beggar or peasant—became an important didactic motif in the medieval oral and literary tradition. In a thirteenth-century erotic tale written in middle high German verse, "Diu halbe Bir" or "Die halbe Birne" ("Half a Pear"), a mighty king offers his daughter in marriage to a knight who shows his valor and wins a tournament. When a knight named Arnold wins the tournament, he is invited to a feast where pears are served, one for every two people. He cuts a pear in half without peeling it. After he eats his half, he offers the princess the other half, and she is so insulted because he has not peeled it for her that she berates him before all the guests. Enraged, Arnold departs, swearing revenge. He returns later as a court jester and is allowed to enter the salon of the princess to entertain her and her ladies. She becomes so aroused by his antics that she yields to his amorous advances. When Arnold leaves and returns to the court as a knight, the princess begins to mock him as the one who had offered her half a pear. He responds with a retort that makes her aware that he was the one she had been with the night before. Consequently, he compels her to become his wife.

A similar version can be found in the fourteenth-century Icelandic saga "Clárus," attributed to Jón Halldórsson. Shakespeare used the motif in *The Taming of the Shrew* (early 1590s), and Luigi Allemanni's novella *Bianca, Daughter of the Count of Tolouse* (1531) had a direct influence on Giambattista Basile's "Pride Punished" (1634) and the Grimms' "King Thrushbeard" (1812). The popularity of literary tales had a strong influence on the oral tradition, and the development of different versions led to Andersen's "The Swineherd" (1842) and Ludwig Bechstein's "Vom Zornbraten" ("About the Angry Roast," 1857). For the most part, tales about so-called shrews represented a patriarchal viewpoint of how women, particularly courtly women, were to order their lives according to the dictates and demands of their fathers or husbands. In addition, the women fulfill the wish-dreams of men's imaginations. The sadism of such tales is often concealed by the humorous manner in which a haughty woman learns "humility."

MOTHER ELDERBERRY (HYLDEMOER, 1844)

Andersen based this tale on Danish folklore. According to folk belief, there was an "elder woman" who made her home in the elder tree, and if anyone harmed the tree she would take revenge. Andersen heard a tale about a man who chopped down an elder tree and died soon after the event; it was probably based on a legend that appeared in volume 2 of Just Mathias Thiele's *Danmarks Folkesagen II* (*Danish Legends II*, 1818–1823). Andersen's version was first published in the magazine *Gaea*.

THE HILL OF THE ELVES (ELVERHØI, 1845)

This tale is based on an old Danish folk tale. Like many writers of his time, including J. L. Heiberg, Andersen had a strong interest in elves; in 1830 he had written a poem that dealt with them. He was also influenced by the poet Just Mathias Thiele (see the note directly above).

CLOD HANS (KLODS-HANS, 1855)

The naive and innocent hero who competes with his two older brothers for the hand of a princess is a common character in European folklore, and this tale type was widespread in the late Middle Ages. Andersen's humorous version is intended to poke fun at the marriage rituals of the upper classes.

WHAT FATHER DOES IS ALWAYS RIGHT
(HVAD FATTER GØR, DET ER ALTID DET RIGTIGE, 1861)

Andersen heard a folk version of this tale as a child. The story of two peasants who manage to make their way through life despite their stupidity was a common tale type in European folklore. The characters are appealing because they are so good-natured, and because of their good hearts, fortune inevitably shines on them.

ORIGINAL FAIRY TALES

THE SHADOW (SKYGGEN, 1847)

The major source for this tale is Adelbert Chamisso's fairy-tale novella *Peter Schlemihl* (1813), about a young man who sells his shadow to the devil and wanders the world in search of salvation. E. T. A. Hoffmann also dealt with the *Doppelgänger* motif in his remarkable stories "Die Abenteuer der Sylvester Nacht" ("The New Year's Adventure," 1819) and "Die Doppeltgänger" ("The Doubles," 1821). Andersen was familiar with these stories; he even makes reference to Chamisso's story at the beginning of his tale, which he wrote in Naples in June 1846. Perhaps one of Andersen's most personal and most profound psychological tales, it is a symbolic representation of his relationship with Edvard Collin, the son of his patron, whom he admired and loved most of his life. Andersen was frustrated because Collin never allowed the two to become intimate. Collin never even permitted Andersen to use the informal word for "you" (*du* in Danish) in addressing him; instead, Andersen had to use the formal you (*de*, which translates as "thou"). This situation disturbed Andersen, who felt humiliated by it. The more famous he became, the more he wished Collin would recognize him and speak and write to him on equal terms. "The Shadow" can thus be regarded as a tale of bitter revenge. However, more than just a personal vendetta, it can also be viewed as a psychological exploration of the master/slave relationship and a philosophical exposition on the nature of identity. It is also related to Andersen's works about art, for a learned man who produces works of art can wind up being obfuscated by the shadow they cast.

THE LITTLE MERMAID (DEN LILLE HAVFRUE, 1837)

Andersen first wrote a version of this tale in his play *Agnete and the Merman* (1833), which incorporated his tender feelings for Edvard Collin; indeed, the play and the tale "The Little Mermaid" have often been interpreted as a representation of Andersen's unrequited love for Collin. However, the motif of a water nymph who desires a human soul has deep roots in medieval folklore about mermaids, water nixies (water sprites), sirens, and sylphs. This tale is clearly related to Friedrich de la Motte Fouqué's fairy-tale novella *Undine* (1811), in which a sprightly water nymph seeks a human soul through marriage with a young knight. Set in the Middle Ages, this tragic story shows how Undine wins the love of a handsome aristocrat and is transformed into a devout and pious Christian. However, when her husband betrays her, she is compelled to revert to her pagan condition and to kill him. E. T. A. Hoffmann, a good friend of Fouqué, used the tale as the basis for his opera *Undine* (1816), and other operas, such as Antonin Dvořák's *Rusalka* (1900), have been based on the plot.

Andersen recast the water nymph as a mermaid who redeems herself by refusing to take revenge on an innocent prince. Instead, she sacrifices herself, and Andersen makes it clear she will gain some kind of salvation because of her good deeds.

Andersen's version served as the basis for numerous films in the latter part of the twentieth century. The Walt Disney Company made two important animated films based on Andersen's "The Little Mermaid," and Russian, British, Czech, and Danish filmmakers also have adapted the story for the cinema.

THE EMPEROR'S NEW CLOTHES
(KEJSERENS NYE KLÆDER, 1837)

This tale can be traced to the fourteenth-century *Libro de Patronio* (*Patronio's Fifty Stories*), by Prince Juan Manuel, who collected Arab and Jewish stories and published them in Spanish. In the Spanish tale, the weavers declare that only men who are truly the sons of their fathers can see the clothes they make; otherwise, the clothes are invisible. In the oral and literary traditions of Europe, the exposure of the emperor occurs in a variety of ways; the tricksters—con men, weavers, or tailors—use various tests to expose the gullibility and pomposity of rulers. Andersen apparently added the child in his narrative at the last moment in order to associate innocence with truth.

THUMBELINA (TOMMELISE, 1835)

Andersen's tale—his unusual version with a female Tom Thumb—owes a great debt to oral tradition and literary versions that also can be traced to "Little Tom Thumb" (1697), written by Charles Perrault, and to "Thumbling" (1815) and "Thumbling's Travels" (1815), published by the Brothers Grimm. Folk stories about Tom Thumb began appearing in English chapbooks in the seventeenth century. According to Arthurian Legend, the magician Merlin grants a childless couple a child who is no bigger than a thumb. Named Tom Thumb, the little creature, assisted by fairies, faces numerous dangers because of his diminutive size. Many of the situations are comic, and Tom must learn how to use his wits to survive. The plots of similar tales found in Japanese, Indian, and European lore vary, but they all begin with a separation of Tom from his parents that sets off a chain of episodes as he tries to find his way home. Andersen's contribution is the invention of a female protagonist and her conventional marriage with a prince.

THE NAUGHTY BOY (DEN UARTIGE DRENG, 1835)

This tale is based on a work by Greek lyric poet Anacreon (c.582–c.485 B.C.), who wrote short poems called monodies (lyrical verses for a single voice) that celebrated love and wine. Andersen was probably influenced by Christian Pram's translation of the Anacreon poem. In contrast to Anacreon, Andersen provides an ironic view of the power of love in this story.

THE GALOSHES OF FORTUNE
(LYKKENS KALOSKER, 1838)

This story can be considered one of the first science-fiction tales in European literature. It consists of time-travel episodes in which people come upon "lucky" galoshes that transport them in time and compel them to consider their real situations. The galoshes are somewhat related to the folk motif of seven-league boots that enable people to travel great distances in a matter of seconds. However, seven-league boots are rarely used to carry a protagonist to the past or the future, as the galoshes do in Andersen's tale.

THE GARDEN OF EDEN (PARADISETS HAVE, 1839)

Andersen may have first heard this tale as a child, but it is more probable that he read or heard about Madame d'Aulnoy's fairy tale "Île de la Félicité" ("The Island of Happiness"), which was incorporated in her novel *Histoire d'Hypolite, comte de Duglas* (1690), translated into Danish in 1787. In this tale the prince of Russia is transported by Zephyr, the west wind, to a paradise and spends centuries there. He loses his love and his life when he tries to return to Russia and forgets the warning of the princess of paradise never to descend from his horse, otherwise Death would capture him.

THE BRONZE PIG (METALSVINET, 1842)

Andersen conceived this tale in 1833 and 1834 while visiting Florence, where he saw the statue of the bronze boar on the Via Porta Rossa. The tale concerns the miraculous development of a poor, oppressed boy into an artist, a motif that appears in several of Andersen's tales. It was first published in his travel book *A Poet's Bazaar* (1842). He may have based the story on the life of Danish painter Wilhelm Bendz, who was born in 1804 in Odense and died in Italy in 1832.

THE ROSE ELF (ROSEN-ALFEN, 1839)

This tale, whose title is sometimes translated as "The Rose Fairy," was based on a story taken from Boccaccio's *Decameron*.

THE PIXIE AT THE GROCER'S
(NISSEN HOS SPEKHØKEREN, 1852)

Andersen was often concerned with the conflict between materialism and art that is mirrored in the pixie's existential dilemma. Pixies—intermediaries between the natural and the supernatural worlds—are important characters in Danish folklore. They appear in Andersen's "The Traveling Companion" and "The Hill of the Elves," among other works.

IB AND LITTLE CHRISTINE
(IB OG LILLE CHRISTINE, 1855)

Andersen wrote this tale during a period of depression. It is a sentimental and moralistic picture of a poor young man who is dedicated to the simple, pure life in the country, while his childhood sweetheart, Christine, is corrupted by the materialism of the big city.

THE ICE MAIDEN (IISJOMFRUEN, 1862)

This tale, written while Andersen was visiting Switzerland, bears a strong resemblance to Johann Peter Hebel's "Unverhofftes Wiedersehen" ("Unexpected Reunion," 1811) and E. T. A. Hoffmann's "Die Bergwerke zu Falun" ("The Mines at Falun," 1819), in which a young miner is captured by a dangerous queen of an underground realm on his wedding day. His petrified body is found many years later by his former bride, now an old woman.

The allure of an erotic, mysterious woman, a common motif in romantic fairy tales, was often set in opposition to a safe, bourgeois life. Andersen's tale is less about this dichotomy and more about the tragedy of a young man whose rise in society is undermined by immoral forces. Even though Rudy is a good and talented person who trusts in God, he does not succeed. As Andersen comments, "God gives us the nuts, but he doesn't crack them open for us." The episode about the eagle's nest,

Rudy's marital test, was an actual story told to Andersen by the Bavarian poet Koppel. Andersen was originally going to write just the episode about the eagle's nest but changed his mind after reading a travel book about Switzerland, in which he came across the incident concerning the bridal couple.

EVANGELICAL AND RELIGIOUS TALES

THE SNOW QUEEN (SNEEDRONNINGEN, 1845)

Although Andersen had already introduced the Christian quest tale in "The Traveling Companion," published in his second collection of tales, it was not until "The Snow Queen" that he fully developed this motif; in this tale he uses children as his main characters. The prologue, which concerns the origins of evil in the world, prepares the reader for the conflict between the good-hearted children, Kai and Gerda, and the demonic Snow Queen. It is only because of Gerda's purity of soul and the help of angels that she is able to rescue Kai. The tale's moral message is that only those who have faith in God can triumph over the most difficult obstacles in life. This evangelical message was generally omitted or glossed over in late-twentieth-century adaptations, especially cinematic ones; instead the spiritual theme was transformed into a secular one about the power of love. Andersen combined pagan beliefs with an unusual interpretation of Christianity in this tale, but the tone and style overwhelmingly emphasize the theme of Christian salvation.

THE RED SHOES (DE RØDE SKO, 1845)

In his autobiography of 1847 Andersen relates that an incident from his childhood influenced the writing of this tale. On the occasion of his confirmation he was given a new pair of boots that squeaked when he walked on the church floor. The squeaking drew the attention of the congregation, and Andersen was pleased that everyone would notice that he was wearing his first pair of new boots. At the same time, he was ashamed because his thoughts were turned away from God. It is not clear whether Andersen specifically referenced this childhood incident in "The Red Shoes," but the stark Christian message is clear. Karen's alleged vanity is punished so mercilessly in the name of the Lord that the story has often been criticized for its misogynism.

THE LITTLE MATCH GIRL
(DEN LILLE PIGE MED SVOVLSTIKKERNE, 1845)

Andersen wrote this tale as a commission from the magazine *Dansk Folkekalender*. While traveling outside Copenhagen, he received a letter from the publisher, asking him to address one of three pictures that he enclosed. Andersen chose a drawing by Danish painter J. T. Lundbye that portrays a poor little girl with a bunch of matches. As in many of his tales about poor children, there is divine salvation at the end. Andersen may have been recalling an incident in his mother's childhood when she was sent out to beg; when she returned, she was reprimanded for not obtaining any money.

THE BOG KING'S DAUGHTER
(DYND-KONGENS DATTER, 1858)

Part of this complex tale, whose title is sometimes translated as "The Marsh King's Daughter," was first told to one of Andersen's friends, who related it to Andersen. After he wrote it down, he made several drafts and added new elements before he was satisfied with it. Though Andersen uses pagan motifs from animal fables as well as Scandinavian folklore and legend, he creates a religious story about the taming of the wild spirit in Helga, who becomes humble and merciful through her encounter with the priest.

THE GIRL WHO STEPPED ON BREAD
(PIGEN, SOME TRAADTE PAA BRØDET, 1859)

The title of this narrative is also translated as "The Girl Who Trod on the Loaf." It is based in a tale Andersen heard in his childhood. He transformed it into a moral tale of salvation, similar to "The Red Shoes" and with the same misogynistic tendencies. The girl is punished for her sinful actions and is transformed into a bird only after she learns the lesson of Christian humility. The motif of bread turning to stone originated in medieval oral tales and may have belonged to traditional legends of Odense.

THE BELL (KLOKKEN, 1845)

This tale, published in *Maanedsskrift for Børn* (*Monthly Journal for Children*) and supposedly Andersen's own invention, celebrates the divine and mysterious qualities of nature that can be attributed only to God. The motif of the bell also can be found in the poems of German writers Friedrich Schiller and J. L. Heiberg.

THE THORNY PATH TO GLORY (ÆRENS TORNEVEI, 1856)

This tale was first published in *Folkekalender for Danmark*. All the great protagonists depicted in the narrative have attributes similar to those of Jesus Christ. Their lives parallel the lives of many of Andersen's protagonists, who must endure great suffering before becoming famous.

THE JEWISH MAID (JØDEPIGEN, 1856)

Based on a Hungarian legend, this tale was first published in *Folkekalender for Danmark*. The story's notion of Christian redemption is striking. Although Sara does not convert to Christianity because of the vow she has made to her mother, she is redeemed by Christianity. Several scholars believe that the story is based on Andersen's childhood memories of a Jewish girl named Sara Heimann.

THE STORY OLD JOHANNA TOLD (HVAD GAMLE JOHANNE FORTALTE, 1872)

Composed between September 16 and September 24, this fairy tale was the last Andersen ever wrote. The first English translation, with the title "The Story Old Joan Told," appeared in *Aunt Judy's Christmas Volume, 1873*. It was based on a tale that Andersen had heard during his youth from an old woman. Andersen had been struck by the appearance of an old withered man, and the old woman told him the tale about the boiling pot with a special brew that a wise woman could use to bring a young man back from foreign lands to his sweetheart, no matter how far he had traveled. The only difficulty was that the brew often caused the young man to become decrepit. In Andersen's version of the story he transforms the young tailor, who is a man without faith in God, and it is this lack of faith that brings about his downfall.

SHE WAS NO GOOD (HUN DUGDE IKKE, 1853)

This tale was Andersen's endeavor to portray his mother, who was an alcoholic, in a positive light and to transform her story into a parable of religious salvation. Andersen's relationship with his mother was fraught with contradictions. He barely mentions her in his diaries and was evidently filled with shame because of her low social status and her drinking.

THE ANTHROPOMORPHIZING OF ANIMALS AND NATURE

THE UGLY DUCKLING (DEN GRIMME ÆLLING, 1844)

One of Andersen's most successful tales, "The Ugly Duckling" is not only a clear autobiographical narrative of his rise from rags to riches and a wish-fulfillment story that captures the deepest psychological wishes of powerless children; it is also a remarkable example of the animal fable with a clear moral. In Andersen's narrative the path to survival and success is ironically tied to Darwin's notion of the survival of the fittest. Though Andersen was opposed to Darwin's theories, his tale demonstrates that there are species in the animal world that are more adapted to survival and more beautiful than others. Andersen implies that faith in one's true self will lead to happiness and thus aligns himself with the philosophy of essentialism. His essential identity was noble, and his nobility was a nobility of the soul and the true artist. Once this tale became famous, Andersen often identified himself as the ugly duckling.

Originally this tale was to be called "The Swan Chick," but Andersen changed the title so there would be an element of surprise when the so-called duckling changes into a swan.

IN THE DUCKYARD (I ANDEGAARDEN, 1861)

This grim tale uses the proud and haughty Portuguese hen to comment on snobbery and the survival of the fittest. It can be regarded as a counter-tale to "The Ugly Ducking." The story also is apparently a tale of revenge. Andersen often used animals to satirize people he knew. In this case, the rooster and the Portuguese hen clearly represent people he detested, but scholars have not been able to identify them.

THE STORKS (STORKENDE, 1839)

In this tale, based on the superstitious belief that storks bring babies, Andersen provides an ironic moral twist to criticize the cruelty of children. Several of Andersen's stories include the stork, his favorite bird.

THE SPRUCE TREE (GRANTRÆET, 1845)

This powerful parable, which deals with the vain pursuit of fame, may reflect some of Andersen's personal concerns as he desperately tried to become famous. More than that, the tale is a perfect allegory about misguided notions of celebrity, and its initial light tone turns cynical in the end. In addition to attempting to expose the artificiality and superficiality of the upper classes, Andersen tried to show how gullible people might be caught up in the false glow of fame.

IT'S PERFECTLY TRUE! (DET ER GANSKE VIST! 1852)

This ironic tale is a delightful comic commentary on how rumors spread and return to haunt the people who start them.

THE DUNG BEETLE (SKARNBASSEN, 1861)

This tale was inspired by a statement Charles Dickens published in his magazine *Household Words*: "When the Emperor's horse got his golden shoes, the beetle also stretched his leg out." Dickens recommended that Andersen write a story based on this Arabian proverb, and this satirical tale about a pompous beetle was the result. Andersen thought that Dickens had written the passage. However, it was part of a series of proverbs compiled by Dickens's co-editor Richard H. Horne.

THE BUTTERFLY (SOMMERFUGLEN, 1861)

This tale, first published in *Folkekalender for Danmark*, was conceived in Switzerland during a trip Andersen made in August 1860 and was completed in Slagelse, Denmark, while he was staying at Basnaes Manor, in November. There is a good deal of self-irony in this story, in which a choosy butterfly ends up as a lonely bachelor.

THE SNOWDROP (SOMMERGÆKKEN, 1863)

This tale was first published in *Folkekalender for Danmark* and was written in response to a request by Andersen's friend Adolph Drewsen, who complained about how traditional names were constantly being changed. Drewsen pointed out that "sommergæk" (summer fool) had been changed to "wintergæk" (winter fool) and that the name of the flower had thus lost its significance. As a response, Andersen wrote a tale about teasing and flirting.

THE SUNSHINE'S STORIES (SOLSKINS-HISTORIER, 1869)

This tale, a light parody of optimistic stories, was first published in English in *The Riverside Magazine for Young People* (1869); it was published later the same year in the book *Fra Nordiske Digtere* (*From Nordic Poets*). Andersen wrote the tale after he heard Mozart's *Die Zauberflöte* (*The Magic Flute*, 1791). The motif of the fortunate gift at birth is one Andersen used in several of his tales.

THE DROP OF WATER (VANDDRAABEN, 1847)

This terse and bitter tale—dedicated to the famous Danish physicist and chemist Hans Christian Ørsted, who wrote the book *The Spirit in Nature* (1850)—is an ironic commentary on the way humans in a large city behave like animals. The tale, part of *A Christmas Greeting to My English Friends*, appeared in English before it was published in Danish. Andersen had first viewed microscopic creatures when he visited botanist Niels Hofman-Bang in 1830. He also may have been influenced by reading a description of creatures present in a drop of water in Edward Bulwer-Lytton's *Night and Morning* (1841).

THE FLEA AND THE PROFESSOR
(LOPPEN OG PROFESSOREN, 1873)

This comic tale was published in *Folkekalender for Danmark* and
in *Scribner's Monthly* (April 1873). The influence of Jules Verne,
French author of *Cinq semaines en ballon* (*Five Weeks in a Balloon*,
1863) whom Andersen admired, is clear in this tale in the reference to hot-air balloons. He was also inspired by French
politician Léon Gambetta, who during the Franco-Prussian
War escaped besieged Paris in a balloon and fled to Tours. Andersen often developed real incidents into fantastic stories that
are related to science fiction.

THE SNOWMAN (SNEEMANDEN, 1861)

Andersen wrote this tale during the Christmas holidays in 1860
on a visit to Basnaes Manor near Slagelse, where he often
stayed; the setting is based on that locale. The story, which con-
tains a good deal of self-irony, reflects Andersen's concern
about the transient nature of all living things.

THE HUMANIZATION OF TOYS AND OBJECTS

THE STEADFAST TIN SOLDIER
(DEN STANDHAFTIGE TINSOLDAT, 1838)

Andersen was a great admirer of E. T. A. Hoffmann and was familiar with his "Nussknacker und Mausekönig" (The Nutcracker and the Mouse King," 1816). Though there is no
direct parallel with Hoffmann's tale, it is apparent that Hoffman's transformation of the toys and the battle to win the affection of a young girl played a role in Andersen's writing of
"The Steadfast Tin Soldier" and other tales that feature talking
inanimate objects. Hoffmann was among the first writers of
fairy tales to set a story in the nursery room of a middle-class
home, and Andersen followed him in doing this. Once he became famous he would tell tales in the nursery rooms of his
friends.

THE SHEPHERDESS AND THE CHIMNEY SWEEP
(HYRDINDEN OG SKORSTEENSFEIEREN, 1845)

As with "The Steadfast Tin Soldier," this tale shows the influence of E. T. A. Hoffmann's work, especially "The Nutcracker and the Mouse King" (1816). Andersen's story served as the basis for one of the most brilliant animated films in the twentieth century, Paul Grimault's *La Bergère et le ramoneur* (*The Curious Adventures of Mr. Wonderbird*, 1959), which was revised and reproduced in 1979 as *Le Roi et l'oiseau* (*The King and the Bird*).

THE DARNING NEEDLE (STOPPENAALEN, 1845)

Andersen was probably inspired by the Danish sculptor Bertel Thorvaldsen to write this tale, which was first published in the magazine *Gaea*.

THE OLD HOUSE (DET GAMLE HUUS, 1847)

Andersen based this tale on his memories of visits to homes of his friends in Germany and Denmark. He was given a tin soldier by the son of German poet Julius Mosen in 1847. The two-year-old daughter of Danish composer Johan Hartmann, who danced to the singing of her brothers and sisters, served as the model for the laughing child.

THE RAGS (LASERNE, 1869)

Andersen wrote this tale, composed some eight or ten years before its publication in *Folkekalender*, as a satire on young Norwegian writers who were criticizing better-established Danish writers. It was originally based on his observations at a paper factory, where he saw large piles of rags that were eventually made into paper. As Norwegian writers gained a higher profile, Andersen thought that the satire no longer held true. Nevertheless, the comic situation retained its appeal. Andersen had earlier used the contrast between Norwegians and Danes in "The Hill of the Elves."

LEGENDS

HOLGER THE DANE (HOLGER DANSKE, 1845)

This tale, based on a piece of Danish folklore about a legendary king who will rise to save Denmark, is similar to the German legend of the twelfth-century German king and Holy Roman Empire Fredrick Barbarossa, who is said to be buried in Kyffhauser Mountain and will return one day to bring glory to Germany. Andersen based the old man in this tale on his grandfather and on the father of Danish sculptor Bertel Thorvaldsen, who were both wood carvers. During the nineteenth century there were numerous adaptations of Christian Pedersen's adaptation of a French medieval romance, *Ogier le Danois*, which was related to the legend. While Andersen knew the legend from his school days, a new edition of Pedersen's work was published in 1842. Andersen also would have known Just Mathias Thiele's poem about Holger the Dane (1830).

BIRD PHOENIX (FUGL PHØNIX, 1850)

This symbolical tale about the rise of poetry was first published in *Den Nye Børneven*, an illustrated magazine for children. Beginning in the medieval period, in European literature the phoenix was a common figure representing resurrection and immortality. The origin of the myth is considered to be Oriental and Egyptian. The Egyptians believed that the bird lived about 500 years and toward the end of its life built a nest of spice branches and set it on fire, dying in the flames. From the ashes, a new phoenix would arise and fly to the city of the sun.

THE FAMILY OF HEN-GRETHE
(HØNSE-GRETHES FAMILIE, 1869)

This tale was first published in English in *The Riverside Magazine for Young People*. Andersen based the story on a newspaper article about Marie Grubbe, a young aristocrat, who had been married three times, first to the half-brother of Christian V, Ulrich Frederick Gyldenløve, then to a nobleman from Jutland, and later to a seaman. Andersen uses the history of a castle as his frame for telling a fascinating legend about Marie Grubbe; he transforms her into a proud and willful woman, and has the famous Danish writer Ludvig Holberg meet her while he was escaping a plague that had spread to Copenhagen.

EVERYTHING IN ITS PROPER PLACE
(ALT PAA SIN RETTE, 1853)

This inventive tale by Andersen demonstrates his ability to create his own "original" legends. Inspired by the poet Just Mathias Thiele, it is a satirical representation of class conflict in Denmark. A common motif in European folklore, the magical flute is generally used to expose lies and hypocrisy.

Inspired by Andersen's Fairy Tales

LITERATURE

Hans Christian Andersen is a unique figure in the history of the fairy tale. As a young boy, he was influenced by the wondrous tales of the Brothers Grimm, E. T. A. Hoffmann, and other German Romantic writers, as well as by Danish folklore, and his tales cannot be fully appreciated without understanding his interest in these works. But Andersen went his own way: He was the first European writer to appeal both to children and to adults with stunning and provocative tales. Indeed, he developed an inimitable style and tone that transformed fairy tales into passionate and ironic stories that recorded the bitter struggles of artists and marginalized people to discover a modicum of joy in their lives. Throughout his life Andersen experimented with idiomatic language and popular art forms, endowing the fairy tale with novel motifs and characters that anticipated modernism. Andersen was always on a quest for something new. He traveled widely in Europe and based his tales on his personal experiences and encounters with the leading European artists of his time.

In his extensive travels Andersen made the acquaintance of many eminent writers, including Ludwig Tieck, Friedrich de la Motte Fouqué, the Brothers Grimm, Honoré de Balzac, Alexandre Dumas, Victor Hugo, Henry James, Heinrich Heine, and Charles Dickens (to whom Andersen dedicated *A Poet's Day Dreams*, 1853). Andersen was also a close friend of poets Robert and Elizabeth Barrett Browning. Once, when visiting the Brownings in Rome, he read aloud "The Ugly Duckling" as Robert Browning clownishly acted it out for a group of children. Elizabeth Browning dedicated her final poem—

"North and South"—to Andersen; in it "North" refers to Andersen's native Denmark, while the city of Rome, a popular vacation spot, is the "South." The poem's final stanza reads:

> *The North sent therefore a man of men*
> *As a grace to the South;*
> *And thus to Rome came Andersen.*
> *—"Alas, but must you take him again?"*
> *Said the South to the North.*

Andersen influenced and was influenced by numerous writers during his lifetime, but it was after his death that his works became significant referential points for many European and American writers of fairy tales, short stories, and novels. In England, the fairy tales of Oscar Wilde and Andrew Lang were marked by Andersen. At the beginning of the twentieth century Franz Kafka and Thomas Mann noted that they were influenced by Andersen's tales when they were young. Indeed, throughout the twentieth century, writers of fairy tales around the world, along with illustrators, demonstrated time and again in their works that the fairy tale as a genre had to reckon with Andersen's presence.

FILM

Between the 1930s and the 1950s the Walt Disney Company distinguished itself as the most enterprising animation studio and produced a string of critically acclaimed feature-length cartoons, including *Snow White* (1937) and *Bambi* (1942). But as the cost of producing animation rose, Disney's commitment to major animation efforts waned, and after releasing *Sleeping Beauty* (1959), the company failed to produce a remarkable animated picture for nearly thirty years. In 1989 *The Little Mermaid*, based on Andersen's fairy tale, put Disney back on the map. Written and directed by John Musker and Ron Clements, *The Little Mermaid* showcases bright, fluid animation in a palette based on the sea—coral colors like fuchsia and butter yellow alongside shades of aquamarine. The film is buoyed by the witty songwriting of Howard Ashman and Alan Menken (*Little Shop of Horrors*).

What makes *The Little Mermaid* a classic equal to the movies of Disney's golden age is the clever, rebellious, and winsome character Ariel. The crux of the story is Ariel's defiance of her father, King Triton, ruler of the sea, who forbids her from venturing above water into the human realm. But when she falls in love with a handsome prince and swaps her trademark voice (supplied by Jodi Benson) for a pair of human legs with the help of Ursula, a cunning sea-witch octopus, Ariel must rely on her friends Flounder and Sebastian, a calypso crab. Together the three wend their way toward romantic happiness and a state of harmony among creatures of the land and sea—in a departure from Andersen's original, in which the main character is transmuted into sea-foam.

The trend of using computer-generated imagery to supplement animation began, albeit to a limited degree, with *The Little Mermaid.* The Oscar category Best Animated Picture was not instituted until the 2001 Academy Awards, well into the age of CGI animation. Nonetheless, *The Little Mermaid* held its own at the 1990 Oscars. Menken and Ashman were nominated for their song "Kiss the Girl," which was beat out by another, even catchier number from the film: Sebastian's "Under the Sea." Alan Menken earned an award for his score.

After regaining its status as an animator with a spate of releases during the 1990s, Disney again turned to Andersen as source material for *The Emperor's New Groove* (2000). Written by David Reynolds and directed by Mark Dindal, the film takes Andersen's "The Emperor's New Clothes" as a loose premise and plays upon it most creatively. The result is a fun-filled romp, with the Peruvian emperor Kuzco, played with sarcastic relish by David Spade, changed into a llama by his embittered adviser Yzma (Eartha Kitt). *The Emperor's New Groove* is an episodic journey filled with gags and spectacle, plus musical offerings such as the occasional buddy song sung by Kuzco and John Goodman's Pacha (a peasant whom Kuzco had earlier threatened to banish) and Tom Jones's crooning contribution, "Perfect World." *The Emperor's New Groove* earned an Academy

Award nomination for Best Song, for "My Funny Friend and Me," composed by Sting and David Hartley, and performed by Sting.

Disney is not the only film studio to have produced remarkable films based on Andersen's fairy tales. Paul Grimault and Jacques Prévert produced one of the finest animation films, *Le Roi et l'Osieau* (*The King and the Bird*, 1979), based on "The Shepherdess and the Chimney Sweep." In addition, film studios in Russia, the United Kingdom, Denmark, Czechoslovakia, Germany, and Canada have produced more than thirty films based on such popular tales as "The Princess on the Pea," "The Emperor's New Clothes," and "The Little Mermaid."

MUSIC

It is fitting that many composers have paid tribute to Andersen with their music, as his remarkable singing voice inspired the childhood nickname "Nightingale" and he later became an accomplished librettist. He counted among his friends composers Robert Schumann, Felix Mendelssohn, Richard Wagner, Franz Liszt, and many others.

Charting Andersen's influence in Scandinavia alone, Danish author Gustav Hetsch, in *H. C. Andersen and Music* (1930), listed twenty-nine Nordic composers who had set music to Andersen's tales and poems or who had written music inspired by Andersen's life. Christoph Weyse, a Danish composer who was known mainly for his sacred music and songs, and in 1819 was appointed court composer, became Andersen's first benefactor. Along with Danish poet and dramatist Adam Oehlenschläger, Andersen wrote five cantatas (*singspiels*) and one light opera for Weyse. And Andersen wrote operatic libretti to two works by Sir Walter Scott, both produced in 1832: Weyse's *Kenilworth* and I. Bredal's *The Bride of Lammermoor*. Andersen's close friend Schumann based his "Five Songs" (1840) on five pieces from Andersen's oeuvre of more than a thousand poems. For another collaborator, J. P. E. Hartmann, Andersen wrote the libretto to *Little Kirsten* (1846), which remains one of the most popular Danish operas.

By this time, Andersen was seen as a literary giant and a national hero. At the relatively young age of forty-five, he completed an epic homage to his homeland, *In Denmark I Was Born*, that was rendered into music by Henrik Rung (1850); in 1926 Poul Schierbeck premiered his own version, which pays tribute to Andersen and Rung. In 1865 Andersen met Norway's preeminent composer, Edvard Grieg, in Copenhagen. Their resulting friendship led to Grieg's collection "The Heart's Melodies," which features songs inspired by Andersen, including two for piano and soprano: the teasing, playful "Two Brown Eyes" and "I Love You," which sounds like a cross between a jazz ballad and a Danish show tune.

After Andersen's death, musical compositions inspired by his writings multiplied and today show no sign of abating. A list of these, by no means comprehensive, includes Johan Bartoldy's operetta *The Swineherd* (1886); Igor Stravinsky's brief opera *The Nightingale* (1914); Finn Høffding's *It's Perfectly True* (1943); Frank Loesser's musical film *Hans Christian Andersen* (1952); the symphonic works *The Most Incredible Thing* (1997), by Sven Erik Werner, and *The Woman with the Eggs* (1998), by the Danish composer known only as Fuzzy; and Svend Hvidtfelt Nielsen's chamber opera *The Little Mermaid* (1999–2000).

Comments & Questions

In this section, we aim to provide the reader with an array of perspectives on the texts, as well as questions that challenge those perspectives. The commentary has been culled from sources as diverse as reviews contemporaneous with the works, letters written by the author, literary criticism of later generations, and appreciations written throughout the works' history. Following the commentary, a series of questions seeks to filter Hans Christian Andersen's Fairy Tales *through a variety of points of view and bring about a richer understanding of these enduring works.*

COMMENTS

Søren Kierkegaard
[H. C. Andersen] cannot separate the poetic from himself, because, so to speak, he cannot get rid of it, but as soon as a poetic mood has acquired freedom to act, this is immediately overwhelmed, with or without his will, by the prosaic—precisely therefore it is impossible to obtain a total impression. . . . Andersen totally lacks a life-view.
>   —as translated by Howard V. Hong and Edna H. Hong,
>   from *From the Papers of One Still Living:
>   Published Against His Will* (1838)

Charles Dickens
Whatever you do, do not stop writing, because we cannot bear to lose a single one of your thoughts. They are too true and simply beautiful to be kept safe only in your own head.
>   —from an undated letter (most likely 1847)

L. Frank Baum
The winged fairies of Grimm and Andersen have brought more happiness to childish hearts than all other human creations.
>   —from his introduction to *The Wonderful Wizard of Oz* (1900)

Hilaire Belloc

What a great thing it is in this perplexed, confused, and, if not unhappy at least unrestful time, to come across a thing which is cleanly itself! What a pleasure it is amid our entwining controversies to find straightness, and among our confused noises a chord. Hans Christian Andersen is a good type of that simplicity; and his own generation recognised him at once; now, when those contemporaries who knew him best are for the most part dead, their recognition is justified. Of men for whom so much and more is said by their contemporaries, how many can stand the test which his good work now stands, and stands with a sort of sober triumph? Contemporary praise has a way of gathering dross. We all know why. There is the fear of this, the respect for that; there is the genuine unconscious attachment to a hundred unworthy and ephemeral things; there is the chance philosophy of the moment overweighing the praise-giver. In a word, perhaps not half a dozen of the great men who wrote in the generation before our own would properly stand this test of a neat and unfringed tradition. . . .

Andersen could not only tell the truth but tell it in twenty different ways, and of a hundred different things. Now this character has been much exaggerated among literary men in importance, because literary men, perceiving it to be the differentiation which marks out the great writer from the little, think it to be the main criterion of letters. It is not the main criterion; but it is a permanent necessity in great writing. There is no great writing without this multiplicity, which is sometimes called imagination, sometimes experience, and sometimes judgment, but which is in its essence a proper survey of the innumerable world. This quality it is which makes the great writers create what are called "characters"; and whether we recognise those "characters" as portraits drawn from the real world (they are such in Balzac), or as figments (they are such in Dickens), or as heroines and heroes (they are such in Shakespeare and in Homer, if you will excuse me), yet that they exist and live in the pages of the writer means that he had in him that quality of contemplation

which corresponds in our limited human nature to the creative power.

—from *On Anything* (1910)

William Dean Howells
Never has a beautiful talent needed an introduction less than
Hans Christian Andersen from the sort of glibness which is
asked to officiate in that way at lectures and public meetings
and in the forefront of books. Every one knows who this gentle
Dane was, and almost every one knows what he did. . . . I suppose there never were stories with so little harm in them, so
much good. Each of them has a moral, but so neatly tucked
away that it does not stick out at the end as morals usually do,
particularly in stories meant for children, but [it] is mostly im-
parted with the sort of gay wisdom which a friendly grown-up
uses with the children when they do not know whether he is
funning or not. The great beauty of them is the homely ten-
derness which they are full of, the kind of hospitality which wel-
comes all sorts and conditions of children to the same intimacy.
They are of a simplicity always so refined that there is no touch
of coarseness in them; with their perfect naturalness they are of
a delicate artistry which will take the young children unaware of
its perfection, and will only steal into their consciousness perhaps when they are very old children. Some may never live to
feel the art, but they will feel the naturalness at once.

How wholesome, how good, how true, how lovely! That is
what I think, when I think of any of Andersen's stories, but perhaps I think it most when I read "The Ugly Ducking," which is
the allegory of his own life, finding its way to fame and honor
through many kinds of difficulty and discouragement from others and from the consequences of his own defects and foibles.
Nobody could have written those benignant fables, those loving
parables, who had not suffered from impatience and misun-
derstanding such as Andersen exaggerates in his autobiography
and travesties in that story; and his rise to good will above the
snubs and hurts which he somewhat too plaintively records is as
touching a thing as I know in literary history. His sole revenge
takes in that sweet satire, and it is no great excess after owning

himself an ugly duckling if he comes at last to see himself a swan. He was indeed a swan as compared with most ducklings that grow up to ordinary proportions of ducks from their humble origin, but I do not care if in his own nature and evolution he did not always get beyond a goose. There are many ducklings who do not get as far as being geese, and I mean what I say for high praise of our poet. Swans are magnificent birds, and as long as they keep in the water or the sky they are superbly graceful, with necks that curve beyond anything, but they are of no more use in the world than eagles; they have very bad tempers, and they bite abominably, and strike with their wings with force to break a man's bones, so that I would have ugly ducklings mostly stop short of becoming swans.

But here I am, trying to put a moral in the poet's mouth, not reflecting that a moral is the last thing he means in his fairy tales and wonder stories. They are of a witchery far beyond sermoning, in that quaint humor, that subtle suggestion, that fidelity to what we know of ourselves, of our small passions and vanities and follies as young children and our full-sized faults as old ones. You might go through them all with no more sense of instruction, if you pleased, than you would feel in walking out in a pleasant country, with here and there a friendly homestead, flocks grazing, and boys and girls playing. But perhaps such a scene, such a mild experience, makes one think as well as a direct appeal to one's reason or conscience. The children, however, need not be afraid. I think I could safely assure the worst of them (and how much better the worst of them are than the best of us!) that they can get back to themselves from this book, for the present at least, with no more trouble of spirit, if they choose, than if they had been reading the Arabian Nights. Long afterward it may be that, when they have forgotten many Arabian Nights, something will come to them out of a dim memory of these fairy tales and wonder stories, and they will realize that our dear Hans Christian Andersen meant so and so for their souls' good when he seemed to be merely amusing them. I hope so.

—from his Introduction to
Hans Andersen's Fairy Tales and Wonder Stories (1914)

W. H. Auden

Hans Andersen, so far as I know, was the first man to take the fairy tale as a literary form and invent new ones deliberately. Some of his stories are, like those of Perrault, a reworking of folk material—"The Wild Swans," for example, is based on two stories in the Grimm collection, "The Six Swans," and "The Twelve Brothers"—but his best tales, like "The Snow Queen," or "The Hardy Tin Soldier," or "The Ice Maiden" are not only new in material but as unmistakeably Andersen's as if they were modern novels.

—from his introduction to *Tales of Grimm and Andersen* (1952)

Alison Lurie

Mutual romantic love is very rare in Andersen's tales. Again and again, his protagonists are rejected by those they court— and in this they share the unhappy experience of their author. All his life, Andersen continually fell in love with upper-class or titled persons, both male and female. Though he made many acquaintances, he had almost no romantic success: these people liked having him come to their houses, tell stories to their children, and sign books, but their attitude always remained one of friendly, slightly distant patronage.

—from *Boys and Girls Forever: Children's Classics from Cinderella to Harry Potter* (2003)

QUESTIONS

1. Is there a philosophy, theory, thesis, morality, or conception of human life that holds these tales together?
2. What do these tales reveal to us about Andersen's understanding or feeling about the relations between the sexes?
3. Money certainly holds a prominent place in Andersen's tales. Can you think of anything in the tales that has greater value?
4. If you were told you had to invent a tale of the sort Andersen wrote, what, in brief, would it be about? Compose a paragraph-length synopsis of your plot.

For Further Reading

❧❧❧

TRANSLATIONS OF ANDERSEN'S WORKS IN ENGLISH

Andersen, H. C. *Author's Edition* [Andersen's Works]. 10 vols. Boston: Houghton Mifflin, 1869–1908.

The Andersen-Scudder Letters. Edited and translated by Waldemar Westergaard; introduction by Jean Hersholt; interpretative essay by Helge Topsøe-Jensen. Berkeley: University of California Press, 1949. Andersen's correspondence with American editor, publisher, and writer Horace Elisha Scudder.

Brothers, Very Far Away and Other Poems. Edited by Sven Rossel. Seattle, WA: Mermaid Press, 1991.

The Diaries of Hans Christian Andersen. Edited and translated by Patricia Conroy and Sven Rossel. Seattle: University of Washington Press, 1990.

The Fairy Tale of My Life. Translated by W. Glyn Jones. New York: British Book Centre, 1954.

The Fairy Tale of My Life. Translated by Horace Scudder. New York: Hurd and Houghton, 1871.

Hans Christian Andersen's Correspondence with the Late Grand Duke of Saxe-Weimar, Charles Dickens, etc. etc. Edited by Frederick Crawford. London: Dean and Son, 1891.

The Improvisatore; or, Life in Italy. Translated by Mary Howitt. 2 vols. London: Richard Bentley, 1845.

In Spain. Translated by Mrs. Bushby. London: Richard Bentley, 1864.

In Spain, and A Visit to Portugal. New York: Hurd and Houghton, 1870.

Lucky Peer. Translated by Horace E. Scudder. *Scribner's Monthly* (January, February, March, and April 1871).

Only a Fiddler! and O.T.; or, Life in Denmark. 3 vols. Translated by Mary Howitt. London: Richard Bentley, 1845.

Pictures of Sweden. Translated by I. Svering. London: Richard Bentley, 1851.

Pictures of Travel in Sweden, among the Hartz Mountains, and in Switzerland, with a Visit at Charles Dickens's House, etc. New York: Hurd and Houghton, 1871.

A Poet's Bazaar. 3 vols. Translated by Charles Beckwith Lohmeyer. London: Richard Bentley, 1846.

Rambles in the Romantic Regions of the Hartz Mountains. Translated by Charles Beckwith Lohmeyer. London: Richard Bentley, 1848.

Seven Poems—Syv digte. Translated by R. P. Keigwin. Odense: Hans Christian Andersen's House, 1955.

The Story of My Life. Translated by Horace E. Scudder. Boston: Houghton Mifflin, 1871.

To Be, or Not to Be? Translated by Mrs. Bushby. London: Richard Bentley, 1857.

The True Story of My Life. Translated by Mary Howitt. London: Longman, Brown, Green, and Longmans, 1847.

The Two Baronesses. 2 vols. Translated by Charles Beckwith Lohmeyer. London: Richard Bentley, 1848.

A Visit to Portugal 1866. Translated and edited by Grace Thornton. London: Peter Owen, 1972.

A Visit to Spain and North Africa. Translated and edited by Grace Thornton. London: Peter Owen, 1975.

CRITICAL WORKS

Andersen, Jens. *Hans Christian Andersen: A New Life.* Translated by Tiina Nunnally. Woodstock: Overlook Press, 2006.

Atkins, A. M. "The Triumph of Criticism: Levels of Meaning in Hans Christian Andersen's *The Steadfast Tin Soldier.*" *Scholia Satyrica* 1 (1975), pp. 25–28.

Bain, R. Nisbet. *Hans Christian Andersen: A Biography.* New York: Dodd, Mead, 1895.

Bell, Elizabeth, Lynda Haas, and Laura Sells, eds. *From Mouse to Mermaid: The Politics of Film, Gender, and Culture.* Bloomington: Indiana University Press, 1995.

Böök, Fredrik. *Hans Christian Andersen: A Biography.* Translated by G. Schoolfield. Norman: University of Oklahoma Press, 1962.

Born, Ann. "Hans Christian Andersen: An Infectious Genius." *Anderseniana* 2 (1976), pp. 248–260.

Brandes, Georg. "Hans Christian Andersen." In *Eminent Authors of the Nineteenth Century.* Translated by R. B. Anderson. New York: Crowell, 1886.

Braude, L. Y. "Hans Christian Andersen and Russia." *Scandinavica* 14 (1975), pp. 1–15.

Bredsdorff, Elias. *Hans Andersen and Charles Dickens: A Friendship and Its Dissolution.* Copenhagen: Rosenkilde and Bagger, 1956.

———. *Hans Christian Andersen: The Story of His Life and Work, 1805–75.* London: Phaidon, 1975.

Bredsforff, Thomas. *Deconstructing Hans Christian Andersen: Some of His Fairy Tales in the Light of Literary Theory—and Vice Versa.* Minneapolis: Center for Nordic Studies, University of Minnesota, 1993.

Browning, George. *A Few Personal Recollections of Hans Christian Andersen.* London: Unwin, 1875.

Burnett, Constance B. *The Shoemaker's Son: The Life of Hans Christian Andersen.* New York: Random House, 1941.

Dahlerup, Pil. "Splash! Six Views of "The Little Mermaid." *Scandinavian Studies* 63:2 (1991), pp. 141–163.

Dal, Erik. "Hans Christian Andersen's Tales and America." *Scandinavian Studies* 40 (1968), pp. 1–25.

Duffy, Maureen. "The Brothers Grimm and Sister Andersen." In *The Erotic World of Faery.* London: Hodder and Stoughton, 1972, pp. 263–284.

Frank, Diane Crone, and Jeffrey Frank. "A Melancholy Dane." *The New Yorker* (January 8, 2001), pp. 78–84.

———. "The Real Hans Christian Andersen." In *The Stories of Hans Christian Andersen,* translated by Diane Crone Frank and Jeffrey Frank. Boston: Houghton Mifflin, 2003, pp. 1–36.

Godden, Rumer. *Hans Christian Andersen: A Great Life in Brief.* New York: Alfred A. Knopf, 1954.

Grønbech, Bo. *Hans Christian Andersen.* Boston: Twayne, 1980.

Haugaard, Erik C. "Hans Christian Andersen: A Twentieth-Century View." *Scandinavian Review* 14 (1975), pp. 1–15.

Hees, Annelies van. "The Little Mermaid." In *H. C. Andersen: Old Problems and New Readings*, edited by Steven Sondrup. Provo, UT: Brigham Young University, 2004, pp. 259–270.

Heltoft, Kjeld. *Hans Christian Andersen as an Artist*. Translated by Reginald Spink. Copenhagen: Royal Danish Ministry of Foreign Affairs, 1977.

Holbek, Bengt. "Hans Christian Andersen's Use of Folktales." In *A Companion to the Fairy Tale*, edited by Hilda Ellis Davidson and Anna Chaudri. Cambridge: D. S. Brewer, 2003, pp. 149–158.

Houe, Poul. "Going Places: Hans Christian Andersen, the Great European Traveler." In *Hans Christian Andersen: Danish Writer and Citizen of the World*, edited by Sven Rossel. Amsterdam: Rodopi, 1996, pp. 123–175.

———. "Andersen in Time and Place—Time and Place in Andersen." In *Hans Christian Andersen: A Poet in Time*, edited by Johan de Mylius, Aage Jørgensen, and Viggo Hjørnager Pedersen. Odense: Odense University Press, 1999, pp. 87–108.

Johnson, Spencer. *The Value of Fantasy: The Story of Hans Christian Andersen*. La Jolla, CA: Value Communications, 1979.

Jones, W. Glyn. *Denmark*. New York: Praeger, 1970.

———. "Andersen and Those of Other Faiths." In *Hans Christian Andersen: A Poet in Time*, edited by Johan de Mylius, Aage Jørgensen, and Viggo Hjørnager Pedersen. Odense: Odense University Press, 1999, pp. 259–270.

Jørgensen, Aage. *Hans Christian Andersen Through the European Looking Glass*. Odense: Odense University Press, 1998.

Koelb, Clayton. "The Rhetoric of Ethical Engagement." In his *Inventions of Reading: Rhetoric and the Literary Imagination*. Ithaca, NY: Cornell University Press, 1988, pp. 202–219.

Kofoed, Niels. "Hans Christian Andersen and the European Literary Tradition." In *Hans Christian Andersen: Danish Writer and Citizen of the World*, edited by Sven Rossel. Amsterdam: Rodopi, 1996, pp. 209–356.

Lederer, Wolfgang. *The Kiss of the Snow Queen: Hans Christian*

Andersen and Man's Redemption by Women. Berkeley: University of California Press, 1986.

Manning-Sanders, Ruth. *Swan of Denmark: The Story of Hans Christian Andersen.* London: Heinemann, 1949.

Marker, Frederick. *Hans Christian Andersen and the Romantic Theatre: A Study of Stage Practices in the Prenaturalistic Scandinavian Theatre.* Toronto: University of Toronto Press, 1971.

Massengale, James. "The Miracle and A Miracle in the Life of a Mermaid." In *Hans Christian Andersen: A Poet in Time,* edited by Johan de Mylius, Aage Jørgensen, and Viggo Hjørager Pedersen. Odense: Odense University Press, 1999, pp. 555–576.

Meynell, Esther. *The Story of Hans Andersen.* New York: Henry Schuman, 1950.

Mishler, William, "H. C. Andersen's 'Tin Soldier' in a Freudian Perspective." *Scandinavian Studies* 50 (1978), pp. 389–395.

Mitchell, P. M. *A History of Danish Literature.* Copenhagen: Gyldendal, 1957, pp. 150–160.

Mortensen, Finn Hauberg. *A Tale of Tales: Hans Christian Andersen and Danish Children's Literature.* Four parts in 2 vols. Minneapolis: Center for Nordic Studies, University of Minnesota, 1989.

Mouritsen, Flemming. "Children's Literature." In *A History of Danish Literature,* edited by Sven Rossel. Lincoln: University of Nebraska Press, 1992, pp. 609–631.

Mudrick, Marvin. "The Ugly Duck." *Scandinavian Review* 68 (1980), pp. 34–48.

Mylius, Johan de. *The Voice of Nature in Hans Christian Andersen's Fairy Tales.* Odense: Odense University Press, 1989.

———. "Hans Christian Andersen and the Music World." In *Hans Christian Andersen: Danish Writer and Citizen of the World,* edited by Sven Rossel. Amsterdam: Rodopi, 1996, pp. 176–208.

Mylius, Johan de, Aage Jørgensen, and Viggo Hjørnager Pedersen, eds. *Hans Christian Andersen: A Poet in Time.* Odense: Odense University Press, 1999.

Nielsen, Erling. *Hans Christian Andersen (1805–1875): The*

Writer Everybody Reads and Loves, and Nobody Knows. Copenhagen: Royal Danish Ministry of Foreign Affairs, 1983.

Pedersen, Viggo Hjørnager. *Ugly Ducklings? Studies in the English Translations of Hans Christian Andersen's Tales and Stories.* Odense: University Press of Southern Denmark, 2004.

Prince, Alison. *Hans Christian Andersen: The Fan Dancer.* London: Allison and Busby, 1998.

Reumert, Elith. *Hans Christian Andersen the Man.* Translated by Jessie Bröchner. London: Methuen, 1927.

Robb, N. A. "Hans Christian Andersen." In *Four in Exile.* 1948. Port Washington, NY: Kennikat Press, 1968, pp. 120–151.

Rossel, Sven, ed. *A History of Danish Literature.* Lincoln: University of Nebraska Press, 1992.

———, ed. *Hans Christian Andersen: Danish Writer and Citizen of the World.* Amsterdam: Rodopi, 1996.

Rubow, Paul V. "Idea and Form in Hans Christian Andersen's Fairy Tales." In *A Book on the Danish Writer Hans Christian Andersen: His Life and Work.* Copenhagen: Committee for Danish Cultural Activities Abroad, 1955, pp. 97–135.

Sells, Laura. "'Where Do the Mermaids Stand?' Voice and Body in *The Little Mermaid.*" In *From Mouse to Mermaid: The Politics of Film, Gender, and Culture,* edited by Elizabeth Bell, Lynda Haas, and Laura Sells. Bloomington: Indiana University Press, 1995, pp. 175–192.

Sondrup, Steven, ed. *H. C. Andersen: Old Problems and New Readings.* Provo, UT: Brigham Young University Press, 2004.

Spink, Reginald. *Hans Christian Andersen and His World.* London: Thames and Hudson, 1972.

Stirling, Monica. *The Wild Swan: The Life and Times of Hans Christian Andersen.* London: Collins, 1965.

Toksvig, Signe. *The Life of Hans Christian Andersen.* London: Macmillan, 1933.

Trites, Roberta. "Disney's Sub/version of *The Little Mermaid.*" *Journal of Popular Television and Film* 18 (1990/1991), pp. 145–159.

Wullschläger, Jackie. *Hans Christian Andersen: The Life of a Storyteller.* London: Allen Lane, 2000.

Zipes, Jack. *Fairy Tales and the Art of Subversion: The Classical Genre for Children and the Process of Civilization.* London: Heinemann, 1983.

———. *Hans Christian Andersen: The Misunderstood Storyteller.* New York: Routledge, 2005.

Alphabetical Index of the Tales